BELONGING TO

CIVITAS NOMINA

BOOKS BY D. M. CORNISH

Foundling
Lamplighter
Factotum

PART THREE

Factotum

D.M. CORNISH

with illustrations by the author

FIREBIRD

AN IMPRINT OF PENGUIN GROUP (USA) INC.

Title page illustration: One of the many bloodmarks scrawled on Madam Lux

FIREBIRD
Published by the Penguin Group
Penguin Group (USA) Inc., 345 Hudson Street, New York, New York 10014, U.S.A.
Penguin Group (Canada), 90 Eglinton Avenue East, Suite 700, Toronto, Ontario, Canada M4P 2Y3
(a division of Pearson Penguin Canada Inc.)
Penguin Books Ltd, 80 Strand, London WC2R 0RL, England
Penguin Ireland, 25 St Stephen's Green, Dublin 2, Ireland (a division of Penguin Books Ltd)
Penguin Group (Australia), 250 Camberwell Road, Camberwell, Victoria 3124, Australia
(a division of Pearson Australia Group Pty Ltd)
Penguin Books India Pvt Ltd, 11 Community Centre, Panchsheel Park, New Delhi – 110 017, India
Penguin Group (NZ), 67 Apollo Drive, Rosedale, Auckland 0632, New Zealand
(a division of Pearson New Zealand Ltd.)
Penguin Books (South Africa) (Pty) Ltd, 24 Sturdee Avenue, Rosebank, Johannesburg 2196, South Africa

Registered Offices: Penguin Books Ltd, 80 Strand, London WC2R 0RL, England

First published in the United States of America by G. P. Putnam's Sons,
a division of Penguin Young Readers Group, 2010
Published by Firebird, an imprint of Penguin Group (USA) Inc., 2011

3 5 7 9 10 8 6 4 2

LIBRARY OF CONGRESS CATALOGING-IN-PUBLICATION DATA IS AVAILABLE

ISBN 978-0-14-241944-1

Design by Tony Sahara
Set in Perpetua

Printed in the United States of America

For Dyan,
without whom this would never exist

CONTENTS

LIST OF PLATES

ACKNOWLEDGMENTS

TO OUR ASTONISHING GOD, for doing everything so aptly; to
Dyan, for steering the ship; to Celia, for steadiness and better words;
to Tim, for bravery under fire; to my parents, for their prayers; to
my delight, Tiffy, who climbs the mountain with me, every misstep and skun knee; to those teachers who gave to me a wonder for
what is true and best: Stuart Gluth, Margie Hooper, Judith Bruton,
Mary Smith, David Robson, Mark Treloar, Stuart and Mary Leggett,
and Bob Philips; to Louis Decrevel, for doing this too; to Will and
Mandii, faithful travelers daring (still!) the journey with me; to my
cousin, Joshua Lock, for the word paphron; to Sue Ellen, Jacey,
Andrew and Sarah Currie, and Peter, for reading words unfit for
human consumption; to Aidan Coleman, for courage, for beauty,
for loving words and people; to Jason Lethcoe (Ilex Mile is for
you). Also to Alyosha, Monday, ENR, Anna Martinsen, (the other)
Anna, Carlita, Pizza, Portals, Ms. Ventress, Ryan K., Tenya S. Vågen,
Ryan Kjolberg, Ellorneo, Sara Charlotta Johansson, Noelle, Ben
Bryddia, me, Sam Hranac, Winter, Bill Bittner, Zakk, Aphrodine,
Curiousmouth, Lawrence Mikkelsen, and all the rest of you who stop
by at the Blog or the Cult, MySpace, or sent me an e-mail—I thank
you so much for keeping me inspired; to Patrick Brooks, for running
the Monster Blood Cult, and to JackofSpade444, for running the
Forum; to Hays Enoch, for letting me know that muskets push rather
than kick; to Erin Montemurro, for the sewing, the love, and the
astonishing results; to Evan Blanton, fellow originiere; to Lisa Perry
at Ophelia's Books, shop on! To Rita Faye and to Jay—I hope you are
well; and to all those who deserve a mention but have not received
one. And, finally, to Kierah Siegel of NYC—you may take this book,
m'lady, as a personal favor!

This is a map of the southern and central portions of the Half-Continent.
The area within the small rectangle is shown in detail on the following page.

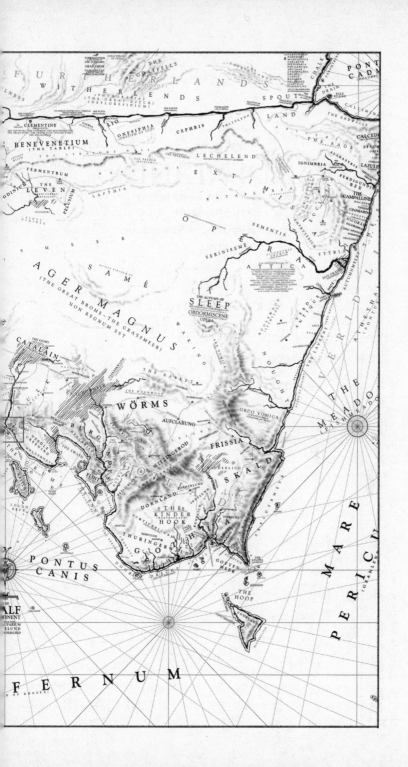

 THE

BRANDENLANDS
BEING THE TRACTS SURROUNDING THE GREAT CITY OF
BRANDENBRASS
INCLUDING THE NORTHERN COASTS AND WATERS OF
THE GRUME

◎   MAJOR TOWN OR SMALL CITY

◦   MINOR SETTLEMENT

▫   LONE STRONGHOLD

▭   RIVERGATE

   ROAD

   SWAMPLAND

1

ACROSS THE GRUME

packet ram any class of ram that has been radicaled; that is, had part of its lower decks cleared of guns and at least one of its masts unstepped (lowered or removed, making the vessel "short-masted") to allow for the taking on of cargo and/or passengers. Such vessels are usually privately owned, the tariffs for loading and unloading and the fares being their owners' income. Neither fighting vessel nor true cargo, nevertheless what a packet ram loses in carrying capacity it makes up for in firepower and—in the case of a converted frigate—speed.

At a mere four hours, the passage from High Vesting to Brandenbrass was, as water-faring journeys go, rather brief. Though certainly not the busiest sea lane on the vinegar seas, it was nevertheless plied every day—and sometimes into the night too—by all manner of vessels. The most common of these were the packet rams, old naval frigates rescued from breaking and put into civil service, taking people and goods back and forth ceaselessly. Yet for Rossamünd, who sat at the tossing prow of the small packet ram *Widgeon* plowing stoutly through the milky gray-green swell and holding tightly to his newest hat lest it be blown off his crown, the crossing could not be quick enough.

Since their departure from the Imperial Lamplighters' fortress of Winstermill and throughout the entire journey to High Vesting and aboard the *Widgeon,* the two retired vinegaroons, Fransitart and Craumpalin, had been tight-lipped and unyieldingly alert—as taut as Rossamünd had ever known them. Only now, treading across the Grume and many miles distant from the deadly allegations of the Master-of-Clerks and his ambitious surgeon, Grotius Honorius Ludius Swill, did they seem to unbend a little.

Embarked early that morning on what was his very first proper seagoing voyage, Rossamünd was aware that at some other time he might have thrilled to the rough passage of the *Widgeon;* that with each mile he might have savored the bitter sting of the spindrift sprayed by the clash of ram with wave, and his soul soared with the cries of the sooty terns, the mollyhawks and the whimbrel-gulls that teemed in the pale sky above.

Yet he did not.

Two days' journey from that ordeal, Rossamünd found himself pinned between sweet relief and restless, anxious dismay. He was free, yes, saved once again by Europa of Naimes, fulgar teratologist and Duchess-in-waiting, but *what* was he? Though he had escaped the grip of his accusers, he could not escape their accusations turning endlessly in his head. At first indicting him for sedonition, the surgeon, Swill, had stood to claim on evidence that Rossamünd was not just a simple sedorner—a monster-lover—but a monster in and of himself. *A rossamünderling,* or so Swill had called him—"little pink lips," a monster that looks like an everyman. His proofs? The startling effect Rossamünd had upon dogs, his monster-slaying strength, even his own name. The man had gone as far as to take some of Rossamünd's own blood to mark Fransitart with a proving cruorpunxis. It was then—with a puncting only just begun on the ex–dormitory master's arm—that Europe had intervened. Yet the worst of it was that his old masters, who had known him longest and best, had looked burdened during the inquest, and this was horribly suggestive that the surgeon's wild claims might very well be true.

Can they really have carried such a bizarre secret with them for so long? Why not tell me sooner? Could I really be such a preposterous thing? Rossamünd tried not to think of his emerging strength, or of his clear affinity with monsters. He strove to ignore the feeling, but the thoughts persisted. *Why else would Craumpalin have me splash myself with Exstinker every day?*

What of the calendar, Threnody, the daughter of the Lady Vey and the first girl lighter? Irascible and inscrutable, she had nevertheless become a faithful friend, only to be tricked into betraying him by the shrewd phrasings of Laudibus Pile, the Master-of-Clerks' falseman, and the unavoidable evidence of Rossamünd's own peculiarity. They had barely said goodbye before she was hurried off by her high-handed mother. Rossamünd looked through masts and rigging toward the low, steadily retreating hills of High Vesting, imagining Threnody in the sequestury of Herbroulesse far beyond and quarreling even now with the Lady Vey.

He let out a long, melancholy sigh.

Of one role he was happy to be certain. He was factotum

to Europe—heiress of Naimes, monster-slaying teratologist and once again his savior—now standing by the *Widgeon*'s master at the helm as an honored guest. Rossamünd glanced back to find her regarding him impassively, thin strands of her flyaway fringe dancing on the contrary winds blowing up from the south, one hand gripping a thick cable of mast rigging as the teak deck heaved. Clad in a thick cloak of deep red, she had wrapped her mouth and nose in an olive green vent, a silken cloth soaked in neutralizing potives against the sting and acrid stink of the sea. She regarded him briefly, her gaze determined, even hard, though to Rossamünd there was something unusually pensive lurking in those hazel depths.

Little had thus far been said between the four of them upon the miscarried inquest at Winstermill and its remark-able conclusion. Though clearly grateful to the fulgar for her intervention, Fransitart and Craumpalin seemed unsure of her still, reluctant to speak until their harbor was sure. Now, aboard a ram—even one reduced for civic service—his two old foundlingery masters had quickly occupied themselves with shipboard tasks. Craumpalin was below, dispensing stomach-easing draughts for passengers suffering the queam—or seasickness; Fransitart was mere yards away by the mainmast, helping the first mate run up the bunting and colored burges that communicated with shore and other vessels and keeping a weather eye out for Rossamünd under the watch of his new mistress.

A flight of oystercatchers caught the new factotum's at-tention, the heavy-billed birds calling to each other *kleep,*

kleep on the wing, dashing across the path of the packet ram in patent haste.

There before the *Widgeon* was the wide bay of the Brandenmeer and the safer waters of the Branden Roads where long oblong cargoes trod, a great line of them disappearing to the south, waiting to be piloted into harbor, every vessel filled to its load line. Beyond, Rossamünd could make out the low pale mass of Brandenbrass itself, the greatest naval and mercantile city of the Soutlands, indeed, of the world—if the boasts of its inhabitants were to be believed. Domes and square towers, peaked tenement roofs and many, many foundry stacks poked high above its already high sea walls. To left and right the coast was tamed by brick and stone, bound fast by generation upon generation of accumulating architecture, a spreading blockish scab grown for miles along the western shore of the Grume. As he watched, a great belching of distant steam rose from some southern district, the venting of some ceaseless foundry or shipyard.

Between the *Widgeon* and these safer waters lay the threatening line of the arx maria—five squat, near-impregnable sea forts Rossamünd well knew from his lessons at the foundlingery: round towers of concrete and granite founded on the very bed of the sea, rising up from the water, each a mile apart from the next. The broad upper works were painted in giant checks of sable and leuc—black and white—and above each flew a great spandarion of the same, the flag of the Sovereign State of Brandenbrass. Pocked with many small slit windows and loopholes, the walls of the upper works sloped inward slightly, their crowns bristling with great-guns, lambasts and tormentums, chimneys, flag posts and weathercocks.

"Lo and lively, pipsqueak!" one salty jack returning from breakfast below barked to Rossamünd as he hustled past, his bowlegged steps strangely soft and muffled by dainty black deck-slippers. "Ye better pull yer legs inboard! We'd rather ye not go baiting the hags by offering easy morsels!"

Remarkably, even as the man spoke, some waxen-skinned thing with an arching, steggled back breached gracefully beneath Rossamünd's feet and slipped along beside the rostrum of the *Widgeon*'s ram, pushed along by the vessel's rapid progress. With a start Rossamünd pulled his absently dangling legs aboard. *A grindewhal!* He recognized the creature from a plate in his peregrinat, lost in the destruction of Wormstool. The slimy water-beast let out a soft puff from some unseen orifice and disappeared with a wet slap into the opaque waters.

Suddenly, far to the left, a brilliant orange glare shot into the sky. The pulsating light was speeding in a steep arc; a thin and high keening shrilled above the clash of water and hull, wailing up then down the scale. It was a sibaline flare. Another whistling light quickly joined it, fired from the deck of a distant vessel—long yet oddly blocky—struggling out in the roads, burges flying their urgent message on its single mast.

"A distressed bastler!" cried Fransitart, pointing to the low lumbering vessel with its blunt prow. "They're towing some heavy catch: look how the unhandy butterbox lies in the water. Must've enticed a prowling ambusher by accident. It is a brave beastie to come in this close."

6

"A thalasmachë!" came the general cry.

Rossamünd's innards gripped. *A thalasmachë! A battle of nadderer and ram!* Gripping a stay and leaning forward to see, he was able to make out a great churning in the swell not far abaft the harried craft. With a great whoosh and spray of milky waters a black thing leaped, throwing itself at the vessel. At such a distant vantage the nature of the nadderer was still clear: blunt calipaced head, great disc-eyes and snapping, armored jaws. Somewhere between delight and horror, Rossamünd blinked in astonishment: *here* was a kraulschwimmen, one of the terrors of the deeps.

"Stays of bone!" came the exclamations of the crew. "What a beauty."

"A right ugly article!"

"Enough to stretch yer eyes!"

Well away to their right, a dark drag-mauler was racing from the north, coming between two arx maria, all bunting flying, signaling that it knew of the bastler's distress, its powerful over-large ram throwing up a broad bow wave as it rushed on. But even with its great speed it was too far away to be of any immediate help to the stricken vessel.

Seeing that he was in a better position to offer more immediate aid, the master of the *Widgeon* bellowed in fine navy fashion, "All hands to quarters!" adding to his first mate, "Run up the red Jack, Mister Sage; let them know we're coming!" declaring most emphatically with this order of his intention to intervene. He deferred with a nod of a bow to Europe. "If that be all right with ye, great lady?"

"Carry on, Master Right," the heiress of Naimes returned,

nodding politely, a slight and amused arch to her spoored brow.

There was no beating of drums to call the crew to action—the *Widgeon* was no longer a navy-run vessel—and shouts were enough to get the crew's obedience.

"Ladeboard watch, ahead all limbers to the screw!" came the master's cries, echoed by his first mate to the deck and his third down an ox-horn speaking cornet to the decks below. "Gather as she goes! Strike the nasty hag full abeam!"

With a shiver right through its frame and the planks of its teak deck, the great silent muscles of the gastrines in the organ deck below turned harder. The *Widgeon* gathered speed, and its sharp bow came about several points to steerboard to make directly for the bastler and its monstrous harasser. Once a properly commissioned frigate in naval service, the vessel put on a fair pace, and Rossamünd was astonished at the great lathers of vinegar that began to spume from the proud and deadly ram.

"Steerboard watch to quarters!" rang the commands. "Spring the lambasts! Run out the guns!"

"Come on, Rosey me lad," Fransitart called, catching himself expertly as the vessel smashed over a rolling wave. "We'll be better service on the gun deck."

Below in the low width of the gun deck—painted a pleasant duck-egg blue rather than an efficient, gore-hiding red—Rossamünd and his old foundlingery master offered their service. Undergunned to better serve her more mundane role, the *Widgeon* had barely a dozen long twelve-pounders on either broadside. Even then, at only seventy-odd crew, she did not have enough hands to work her gastrines and man her armaments too, and every soul available and willing was called from among the dozen passengers sharing the ride to serve a gun.

As boys ran between them bearing prefashioned cartidges carried in pails from the powder room to their assigned gun crews, the flustered second mate directed Rossamünd to join these scurrying lads.

"I'd rather 'e fought with me, if ye don't mind, matey," Fransitart offered with the knowing look of a fellow seafarer.

At first the mate seemed fit to argue, but knowing Fransitart to have once been a gunner—the seniormost gunnery officer aboard proper naval rams—he agreed and promptly gave the ex–dormitory master charge over number three gun, *Leaping Ladie* scrawled by some eager crew member on its truck.

Fransitart easily took on the role as gun captain, organizing the brave yet clearly ignorant passengers whom need had pressed into service with an eagerness Rossamünd had never seen in him before. "Cast loose yer gun!" the old salt cried, the command echoed by other gun captains up and down the deck. "Take out yer tampion—aye, the *plug* at the *front*. Now, grasp them handspikes, gents—aye, them long posts there—and lift the breech—aye, the barrel; we need to get it depressed so's to have good shot at the slug . . ."

Joined by two rather refined-looking gentleman passengers, cheeks flushed with excitement, and three crew members, Rossamünd did all that was asked, careful not to put too much weight into his actions and therefore reveal himself as an aberration.

"Shot and wad 'er!"

A cloth cartridge of powder, a heavy iron shot and finally a wad of junk—old cut-up rope—were rammed home.

"Run 'em out! Heave on the rope there, ye happy gents, *heave!*"

In all it was clumsy work, yet there were enough seasoned seamen among them to get the task done.

"Steady, now," Fransitart warned when *Leaping Ladie* was loaded, run out and fixed with a couple of turns of the breeching rope about the cascable of the twelve-pounder, "an' wait fer the word to fire."

"Look at 'er!" someone farther down the vessel cried in fright. "The whole sea is alive with the terrors!"

Bending to peer through the open port, Rossamünd caught tossing glimpses of the beleaguered fishing vessel coming closer and closer. Smaller creatures were assailing it, leaping from the water, trying to snatch fishermen down into the caustic brey.

"It's pro'bly blighted wee lagimopes," one of Rossamünd's own gun crew muttered. "They like ta follow and feed at any sheddin' o' blood."

"*Steady . . . ,*" Fransitart growled with grim authority, immediately calming not only his gun crew but those on either side.

Another muffled command from above decks and the *Widgeon* shuddered again, a deep noiseless quake, gaining yet greater speed like a colt let free from its winter stall

10

at last, sending spray even past the midship gun ports.

"Brace yeself tight, gents!" barked Fransitart, planting his feet wide and grasping an overhead deck beam. "We're goin' to strike hard!"

There was a yawning moment of horrid, expectant silence, then the *crash!* of a great shock that rang like thunder in the closeness of the deck, flinging Rossamünd forward then quickly back again, sending his senses spinning. Several men fell, yet the young factotum kept his feet. Something massive and glistening black heaved and thrashed in the milky waters directly ahead, and Rossamünd was shocked to feel the recoiling shudder of living flesh scraping under the blade of the ram, quaking along the entire length of the *Widgeon*. Rossamünd could see, running out abeam from the vessel, a great coil of scaled back heaving out of the water. By the power of ancient muscles of incomprehensible pith, the front of the vessel was lifted, toppling many crew.

"Fend off!" was the master's anxious shout between the loud metallic *twang!* of lambasts above loosing their venom-tipped barbs. "Back pull to the screw!"

With a great trembling like a groan, the packet ram changed screws and began to wind its way ponderously backward, its bow dropping sharply into the vinegar with an astounding thump. A fellow by number two gun began to scream all murder; something slick and greenish gray was reaching in from the gun port to drag the man a-sea. Number four gun detonated with a mighty sound, right into the sallow face of a bold pout-faced sea-monster seeking to clamber aboard.

Abruptly, Rossamünd was seized on the thigh by a cold, merciless clutching, something slithering and gray. Completely surprised, he was already half out the port before he could catch a better grasp on the breech rope. In a flash, something took hold of his coat and Rossamünd was hauled backward, head over end, left hand still clenching the rope. Upside down and hanging against the iron-plated side of the *Widgeon*, he had the briefest glimpse of the water boiling all about the packet ram as the smaller sea-nickers sought now to take out their rage on this new foe. Immediately below, cold black eyes beheld him hungrily, and wide pouting mouths slavered as the nadderers twisted in frustration at the unwilling strength resisting them. Powerful were the grips that had him, yet glaring down at the vile sea-nickers Rossamünd held fast to the cable and would not let go. In a moment of shocked recognition the beasts yielded a little, as if they realized something peculiar in the nature of their prey. In that hesitation, Rossamünd heaved against them, even as Europe thrust through the port, face distorted with fury, striking down savagely with a metal worm and a flash of arcing into the dial of one of the beasts. The ravenous clenching slackened, and Rossamünd drew himself inward with a prodigious jerk, to land face-first and panting in fright on the deck.

"Watch your step, little man," the fulgar insisted mildly. "I do not want you knocked on the head before we have properly begun."

"Almost lost ye," Fransitart murmured. The ex–dormitory master helped Rossamünd to stand.

The thumping of guns could be heard now, getting closer, coming from some other vessel. Through the ports Rossamünd saw a larger ram, a drag-mauler perhaps, cutting across the retreating bow of the *Widgeon*, the blade of the newcomer's overlarge rostrum forcing a deadly course through the waters teeming with sea-monsters. Beyond, he caught sight of the bastler freed from the sea-monsters' attentions and beating a limping retreat.

A confused din of frenetic footsteps thudded overhead, as if the crew there were dancing a wild jig. From fore to aft of the gun deck, crew and passengers alike contended with a great invasion of lagimopes—slippery creatures, small yet powerful, their backs vaned with tall fishlike fins. By the puffs of bothersalts farther back on the gun deck, Rossamünd could spy Craumpalin proving his place in the fight, appearing to be creating a barrier of foul stinging fume to keep the sea-nickers away from weaker passengers. Caught in the thick, Fransitart lay about himself with a handspike like a younger man while Europe struck left and right almost perfunctorily with the bottom of her balled fist, bright arcs blinking, dropping a lagimope dead with every blow.

Rossamünd took up the closest weapon to hand—a rope-handled pail—and swinging it in sweeping loops sought to drive any lagis before him from the deck and back out the gun ports whence they had come. At first the creatures proved unwilling to confront Rossamünd directly, as if unsure upon whose side the young factotum fought. Yet, as he smote one after another, the remaining lagimopes soon settled him as an adversary and began to pay him especial attention. The more madly he swiped with the pail, the more madly did his foes beset him. Finally, the pail was stripped from his grasp and Rossamünd fought with hands alone, wrestling back and forth across the deck, punching with fist and elbow, picking one little sea-nicker up bodily, grasping it hard through its slime to hurl it from a port. Strong, oddly jointed hands pawed and tore at him, tried to pin him down and pull away his sturdy proofing, but every time the young factotum found a way free.

In it all Europe was an indomitable force of scarlet and sparks. The lagimopes tried to drag her down from behind, but she would have none of this, and, twisting sharply, snatched the offending nadderers by their heads and filled them with death-dealing levin. Faced with the wrath of a fulgar at the height of her powers and a crew determined to resist, the shrunken swarm of fishy monsters quickly gave up and slithered back into the sea to disappear to wherever such creatures skulked.

Sooty with the dust of expelled potives, Craumpalin pushed through the passengers and crew silent in the shock of victory, the aging dispenser grinning to see his companions alive and well enough. "How good it does me to see thee lay about thyself so manful," he declared, grasping Rossamünd enthusiastically by the shoulder.

Europe dusted a smudge from her sleeve. "Well, I cannot say I see why the navy prefers wits over we fulgars in such straits," she observed. "As my first sea-fight, that was not *too* troublesome at all."

"Aye, I suppose not," Fransitart grudgingly concurred,

A LAGIMOPE

throwing the fulgar a dark look. "As thalasmachës can go . . ."

Stained and smeared in lagi oil, feeling badly bruised and half strangled, Rossamünd gathered his hat—amazingly not cast a-sea in the fight—from the deck and simply leaned against the truck of a gun to catch his breath.

More rams arrived, chase guns thudding as they hounded the nadderers away south into deeper waters. The butcher's bill at nine wounded—the fellow seized overboard already retrieved, only slightly sizzled from the caustic waters—Master Right declared Europe the heldin of the hour. In a fit of gratitude he wrote up a recommendation promising to have his agents refund her the crossing fee for herself and her three worthy servants.

"Not all forces of the Empire are against us, it seems," Europe murmured to Rossamünd as they stood at the helm watching the heavy drag-maulers speeding to the south as they chased the kraulschwimmen off.

A little shaky as she resumed her original course, the aged packet ram *Widgeon* trod her way to Brandenbrass.

THE HOUSE OF
THE BRANDEN ROSE

cabinet pictures among those of disposable means and dark tastes there is a fashion for depictions of the foulest violence and horror, showing the spoiling of monsters by despicable acts. There is a vigorous clandestine trade in such images, and those who produce them are greatly esteemed by graphnolagnian connoisseurs and make good money from the trade. Many struggling fabulists have been forced by poverty to try their hand at such depravity, and though never signing such pieces, some who have gone on to more legitimate fame have an anonymous catalog of cabinet pictures ready to bring them to ruin.

T HE residence of Europe, the Branden Rose, fulgar teratologist and the Duchess-in-waiting of Naimes, was situated in the very midst of the great city of Brandenbrass. Cloche Arde it was called, its address—as Rossamünd heard given to the takeny driver—Footling Inch, the Harrow Road, in the suburb of Ilex Mile. A pilot boat had brought the four travelers to the pier at the Fine Lady's Steps, where they had disembarked and passed, as they must by law, through the crowded files of the Arrivals and Admissions House. Europe's fame and station affording them a smoother passage among the long lines of newcomers and the frenzy of clerical rigor, they were soon in a hired takeny-coach progressing down long streets alive with a bustling mass Rossamünd could scarce comprehend. It was a fair trot before they entered quiet, opulent suburbs where, set in their parklike gardens, each residence seemed like a thin vertical palace.

"Home once more . . . ," Europe declared softly, peering from the carriage's window as they crossed carefully now over a steep bridge that leaped the gap of a broad drain known as the Midwetter to a small artificial island.

Craning to see, leaning out from the glassless carriage window, Rossamünd beheld the grandest house yet towering from behind an iron-spined wall of darkened stone. Founded on the very rock of an island, it stood isolated amid the graceful terraces and their well-groomed gardens, rising as high as all the noble roofs about. Six lofty stories of grim, dusken granite and stately staring windows; a solitary spire set against the flat, late-morning gray. However grand a structure it might be, Rossamünd thought it somehow strange to consider the great adventuring Branden Rose as possessing something so domestic as a home.

The lentum turned abruptly through high wrought gates already opened in answer to the message Europe had sent ahead by scopp—a fast-running messenger child—of her arrival. In the gaunt space beyond lined with scant trees, the carriageway of white gravel quickly terminated in a large oval turnabout with a single thin cypress in its midst, a pivot about which carriages could circle. Arranged in near-martial order upon the front steps of the house like lighters and auxiliaries at a pageant-of-arms, a small quarto of

CLOCHE ARDE
THE HOUSE OF THE BRANDEN ROSE

senior staff was already waiting, turned out in black frock coats and stomacher-skirts with flashes or facings of red and magenta. One slender person was conspicuous among them in kitchen-white. Rossamünd sat back bashfully, suddenly nervous.

The door to the carriage was opened by a wan-looking man with iron-gray hair who handed Europe stiffly from the cabin. "Welcome, gracious lady," he said with a solemn smile, his voice a sour-humored rasp.

"Hello, Mister Kitchen," Europe declared to her hander, continuing with a wry turn in her mouth. "Raise the flag—your mistress has returned."

Mister Kitchen responded with the ghost of a smirk, as if some small jest had been exchanged.

Senses reeling from the crossing upon the *Widgeon,* clothes still bearing the stains of the thalasmachë, Rossamünd clambered clumsily from his seat, rocking the takeny-coach as he dismounted.

"This young fellow"—the fulgar's slight smile became a little more sincere as she gestured fluently to him—"is now my factotum. His name is Rossamünd Bookchild. Lodge him in the factotum's set and accord him all the usual privileges. Rossamünd, this is Mister Kitchen, my steward—the rest of my staff you shall discover later." She took in her humbly waiting servants in a glance.

In their turn, the senior staff eyed Rossamünd evenly while footmen and the takeny driver tackled luggage.

Rossamünd gave them all a short and awkward bow.

If any had thoughts upon his unfortunate name, his youth

or the grime of battle on his clothes, these serving folk did not betray them.

"Mistress Clossette," Europe continued as Fransitart and Craumpalin alighted, speaking to a black-haired servant woman with a severe face. "We shall have a late meal in the solar, and these old salts—Messrs Fransitart and Craumpalin—shall be eating with us."

Barely exited from the takeny, Rossamünd's old masters nodded first to Europe and then her servants.

"Thank ye, miss," Fransitart muttered.

Mister Kitchen, Mistress Clossette and the knot of staff eyed them somberly in return. Some strange new boy as a factotum was one thing, but tired, scabrous and aged vinegaroons was clearly another.

"As you wish it, gracious lady," responded Clossette flatly.

Guiding Rossamünd before her, the Branden Rose strode into the house, staff in tow, Fransitart and Craumpalin following after.

Through a narrow black door was a cold obverse of marble in a green so dark it was almost black, whorled with pallid coils, the night's fumes made solid. Complete with stoppered loopholes, it existed more by tradition than need, a lingering feature from isolated high-houses built out in threwdish wilds. Through this Europe led them into a grand vestibule hall of equally somber marble, where in a line on either side, the junior staff awaited their mistress.

The heels of Europe's sturdy equiteer boots clapped clear upon the slick floor of checkered black basalt and green serpentine as she strode to the stair.

"This, Rossamünd," she said, pivoting arms out, palms up, "will be your home whenever we are in this infamous city."

Framed by white fluted pilasters and broad lintels, white doors stood stark in the dark walls on either hand. High above, the ceiling was a blatant sanguineous red, its wide moldings and cornice-works of glistening gold. There was no furniture here, just this empty, ponderous space. Dominating the opposite end of the hall was a broad stair of the same swarthy stone with a carpet intricately woven in reds and fawns and golds running up its center.

Astounded, Rossamünd thought himself inside the great hall of one of the historied Attic queens and their fabled black palaces where moments of history played. He drew in a breath, filling his senses with the faint yet distinct savor of Europe's perfume, her essence lingering like some watchful presence.

Sending her staff scurrying to draw baths for her and for Fransitart and Craumpalin too— "to soak out the sea-stink before eating"—Europe summoned Rossamünd to follow.

Exchanging parting glances with his old masters, wide-eyed at this gauntly palatial setting, Rossamünd let himself be hustled upstairs, his mistress ahead, Kitchen coming after. The next floor was little more than a landing before a rather heavy door set back in an alcove painted a rich mossy green and figured with golden flowers. The panels of this door were intricate with snarling, leering bogles gamboling amid leaves and budding blossoms.

"Through here is my file," Europe declared, standing before this astonishing portal, "and beyond, my boudoir. You may not enter here unless I have summoned you or you come bearing my treacle. However, the front rooms of the next floor are for you," she declared, nodding to the next flight of stairs. "They are *your* quarters, the factotum's set. No other servant may enter unless on established routine or at your bidding. As for you, Rossamünd, you answer to me only; not even Mister Kitchen has say over your affairs."

Uncomfortable in the authority of such a position, Rossamünd nevertheless nodded gravely. He looked sidelong at Mister Kitchen but could discern nothing in the solemn steward's blank face.

Her hand on the green-copper handle of the door, Europe fixed Rossamünd with an appraising eye. "You will reconcile yourself to your new lot quickly enough, little man," she offered with smooth irony. "Now up you go and organize yourself, then you and your masters may join me for a proper meal to make up for the thin fare they called *food* aboard the *Widgeon*." With that she retreated through the carven door.

Kitchen gestured to him to climb once more.

On the next floor he was shown right down a moss green passage almost as long as the house was wide. At its end Rossamünd was ushered into a vast room with ceilings easily as high as those in the Master-of-Clerks' file at Winstermill.

"The factotum's set, sir," Kitchen intoned.

The *set* was as pristine as every other part of Cloche Arde Rossamünd had so far seen, yet there was a gloom here, something ineffably oppressive. Its walls were wood panels so stained they appeared black, hung with tiny thick-framed images too small to read from where he stood. Three tall windows dominated the opposite wall, admitting a panorama of a field of roofs hunkered beneath the gray day, yet their generous light did little to dispel the murkiness of the room.

For furniture there was a cupboard, sideboard, side table, writing desk, tandem and coat stand. Each piece was lacquered in glistening black just like the fulgar's treacle box, some finished with gilt edges and fine swirling patterns of a foreign design. Yet all this profusion of furnishings seemed little more than minor detail in the inky expanse of the room. The one relief of color was a broad yet delicate screen erected in the farthest corner. Made of five panels, it was painted with some elaborate scene in a disturbing yet refined, imported style. Rossamünd could not make it out clearly; the general impression was of a woman about to be beset by some kind of slavering nicker.

"Is—was this Licurius' room before?" He frowned at the memory of Europe's former factotum, his cruel grip, his hissing voice muffled by the sthenicon he never took off.

"Yes . . . it was," Kitchen replied evenly. Though the steward's voice was flat, Rossamünd sensed deeper meaning: *What is this to you?* "And now, sir, it is yours."

Rossamünd frowned, uncomfortable at occupying the chamber of a dead man, of sleeping in the place of someone who had actually tried to kill him. It was then that he realized there was no bed. "Mister Kitchen, where do I sleep?" he asked, hoping very much that his bunk might be in another room.

"In here, sir—I shall have a cot moved in for you before the day does come to its end."

"Ah, aye . . ." Rossamünd's soul sank a little. "Thank you."

The steward left him to establish himself with the aid of the young, weasel-faced servant girl who had followed—the alice-'bout-house, Pallette, a young lass not more than two, maybe three, years his senior. Dressed in typical maid's garments—very much like those that dear Verline wore—this girl stood in dutiful stillness by the door and stared straight ahead as Rossamünd sat on the silk-upholstered tandem. Laying his hat aside, he heaved a heavy sigh, seeking to exhale the unhappy knot that had set itself like a splinter in the very pit of his chest. One moment he was a lowly lamplighter and nigh a prisoner of the Master-of-Clerks in Winstermill's unwelcome stalls, the next he was a peer's companion established in a grand, tomblike boudoir of his own.

"M-Master Licurius used to sit right where you do now, sir, and . . . and take his nod sat upright," a meek voice said uneasily, interrupting his reverie. It was Pallette. There was fear in her tone and a glimmer of suspicion in her eyes.

"I beg your pardon, miss?"

"That tandem were once dear Master Licurius' bed," the alice-'bout-house repeated. "He would sit to sleep in the end. His box made it hard for him to lay his head like other folk do. He was a great help to our lady, sir," she added quickly, as if in doubt of Rossamünd's own capacity.

Rossamünd promptly stood, uneasy at being in contact with the spot where that blighted laggard had reclined.

25

"I don't reckon I'll be needing it," he said, unsure how to react to someone who described Europe's old murderous, malevolent leer as *dear*. Indeed, it struck him that all these folk serving busily in Cloche Arde knew Licurius, maybe intimately. *What kind of home is this that looks kindly on such a fellow?* "Maybe we can have it taken out."

There was only the merest hesitation before Pallette said, "Yes, sir . . . If you have any other needs, you call for assistance by a pull of this handle," she added, gently touching a brass lever in the shape of a claw sticking from the wall by the door, "and me or another will come."

It was perplexing to have a stranger offer her obedience to him so readily.

"But if our lady wants you, sir," Pallette continued, "this bell just by it will sound, and then you are to go to her right away—you know the way?"

"Aye, thank you."

"Certainly, sir."

"My name is Rossamünd."

"Yes, sir."

His meager count of dunnage—most of his belongings lost in the destruction of Wormstool—arrived and was deposited on waiting stands by a pair of huffing, puffing footmen. With only the slightest reticence these fellows obeyed as Pallette repeated Rossamünd's instruction to remove Licurius' tandem.

"Maybe a simpler chair will do," Rossamünd added awkwardly. "Or maybe just a stool."

"As you would have it, sir."

With the footmen lifting out the furniture, Pallette began sorting his belongings. Shirts and drawers and trews and all were carefully laid, each in its appropriate spot within cupboards and drawers. *Who are you,* her action seemed to be saying, *to try to replace our dear dead Licurius? Look how small you are!*

Rossamünd took closer inspection of the small, broad-framed pictures hanging upon the walls. They were little more than a thumb-length high and the same wide. Admiring the profound skill that must have been required to paint so lifelike a finish at such a scale, he realized with an involuntary jolt what he was looking at. Each image was of some kind of wicked and depraved violence twixt men and monsters—foul tortures and cruel injuries. He caught only a glimpse, but that was all he needed.

Cabinet pictures!

Such an innocent name for such vile objects. Rossamünd knew ever so vaguely of them; that among those of disposable means and dark tastes there was a barely legal fashion for depictions of the foulest violence and horror. This was the art of monster-haters, high fashion for coarse-minded invidists so twisted, it looked to Rossamünd—even with the brief eyeful he received—to be almost a distorted kind of outramour. *This* was the heart of Licurius laid bare.

The young factotum backed away from the images. "And you . . . you may take these down from the walls too," he said to the departing footmen with a shaky voice and a sterner tone than he intended.

They and Pallette swapped quick, uneasy looks.

27

"Y-yes, sir," the alice-'bout-house answered very softly, blinking at him in discomfort. "As you would wish."

And to his astonishment, the servants said nothing and began lifting the pictures from the wall.

For luncheon—although so soon departed from the lamplighters he could not help but still think of it as middens—Rossamünd was shown to a modest-sized chamber. The *solar,* Europe had called it. The room was not grimly dark; rather it was a soft, deep red, its high ceiling entirely gold. In its midst, before many tall windows, was an oval table of glistening scarlet, thinly etched with strangely formed flowers in golden filigree. About it were arranged high-backed chairs upholstered in the softest silk woven with curling golden stems and dyed with the shapes of petals in shades of ruby and crimson.

Sitting upon two of these at the far end waited Fransitart and Craumpalin, looking ill at ease but refreshed, like drab stains in the clean, gleaming ruddiness.

"Well, hullo, me boy," Craumpalin declared, making an easy showing but possessing a distinct air of a man interrupted. "What does thee make of thy new berth? Not much in the way of a cheerfully homey place, is it?" He lifted his eyes archly to include the room and the entire house with it. "She has treated thee with such expense and magnificence we cannot help but be grateful . . ."

Rossamünd gave a halfhearted smile.

"Aye," Fransitart concurred. "Her generosity is as deep as her pockets."

"Aye to that, Frans," Craumpalin continued, looking up.

28

"She can afford to keep her sconces a-glowin' all day."

Above, on golden rope, was suspended a great light, a cluster of thin red crystalline flutes bent at their bases like lips, sleek bright-limns luminous even in the day with a subtle rose glow.

In the far corner stood a screen of very similar style to the one in Rossamünd's new billet. On it some bizarre heldin flourished a hammerlike weapon over a beaten nicker that looked much like a round-faced, round-eyed dog, while two more hound-monsters ran off with a strangely demure maiden. Stepping close to get a better view of each panel, he frowned at the image, not certain who to feel for the most: the fallen monster, the maiden or the heldin-man. *Am I one of those?* he fretted, peering at the goggle-eyed bogles abducting the woman to a presumably foul end. *Am I some half-done monster born from the muds, as Swill has said?*

On the journey away from Winstermill, Rossamünd had held his questions, his pressing self-doubts. Now, safely harbored in the high-walled bosom of Cloche Arde, the time had come for all troubles to be answered, all long-kept secrets to be revealed.

"Whatever are you at, little man?" Europe demanded mildly, her voice attended by the thump of an opening door.

Rossamünd turned about quickly.

Standing in the entrance, the Branden Rose was out of her fighting harness and now wrapped in a flowing house-cloak of stiff satin of such dusky red that it seemed in its folds to be black. Her chestnut hair was down in a left-hand plait hung over her shoulder, reaching to her waist.

"I—I was just wondering at all your remarkable things, Miss Europe . . . especially this screen here."

"Yes, yes, very pretty." The fulgar took a place at the end of the table. "I am told they are called a bom e'do or some such. This and the one in your room are part of a whole set given to me by some besotted Occidental princeling from Sippon. He thought they might buy my affections." She paused. "They did not. . . . Apparently one alone costs more than an average man is worth a year."

"Thirty sous each?" Rossamünd exclaimed after some brief internal arithmetic as he took the seat shown him at the opposite end of the table.

"Oh, no, little man, not quite *that* average," Europe replied with a slight smile.

Shrinking within, the young factotum was spared his blushes with the arrival of food.

Dished at Kitchen's direction on to fine Gomroon, with genuine shimmering silverware arranged beside, was food such as Rossamünd had never known: tepid pyet ponce— or magpie stew—and seethed eagle wings accompanied by pickled winkles in butter-boiled cabbage on the side.

"Look thee at this fancy fare, Frans." Rossamünd heard Craumpalin's faint mutter across the table to Fransitart. "Smells as if it'll go down hearty."

"Why, thank you, Mister Craumpalin," Europe said with an amused look to the old dispensurist.

"Thank'ee in ye turn, miss," Fransitart replied evenly. "Ye keep a handsome table."

The cook snorted reproachfully as she served a healthy

spooning of cabbage onto the ex–dormitory master's fine white plate. "Of course it is . . . ," Rossamünd heard her mutter. "Handsome table, indeed!"

With slow grace, Kitchen poured tots of fine claret into the biggest, most delicate-looking glasses Rossamünd had ever beheld—half water for him. When all was served and the other servants disappeared again to their manifold labors in other parts of the stately home, the steward went to stand faithfully in the corner near Europe's right hand.

She, however, half raised a hand and said, "You may leave us to talk, man."

After a pause, the steward obeyed.

"I will brook no disturbance," his mistress added as Kitchen quietly closed the servants' port at the back of the room, leaving them alone with their meal and the great quandary of Rossamünd's true nature.

Yet, now it had come to it, Rossamünd did not know how to broach the questions he had held back for the last two days, and poked at his fancy meal in a dilemma of possible starts. From the edge of his sight he could sense Europe observing her guests silently, watching over the rim of her ample claret glass while the old vinegaroons did indeed eat hearty. Knotting his courage, Rossamünd tried to speak again the question still unanswered at their exit from the lamplighters' mighty fortress. *Who am I? What am I?*

"Sirs," Europe said suddenly, "I might not have a falseman's *knack,* but it was obvious that *you,* Master Vinegar," she said to Fransitart, "and *you,* Master Salt," to Craumpalin, "were heartily discomfited by things said during that farcical inquiry. From such a show I would dare to say there is truth in the pratings of that surgeon. If you have a deeper inkling into Rossamünd's history, now is the time to be out with it."

The ex–dormitory master became still, fork poised between plate and mouth, its load slipping sloppily back to the dish. He looked wearily to Craumpalin. It was the merest glance, yet laden with deep, long-lived understandings.

The expression on Craumpalin's face in reply was clear. "I reckon the lad's ears are ready to hear, Frans."

Slowly, gravely, Rossamünd drew in a breath and held it.

Folding his hands against the edge of the glossy red tabletop, Fransitart looked at them for a moment. "This is something we . . . *I* might 'ave told ye a long stretch of years ago," he began with cracking voice. "I have pondered long an' often about how to steer me words—a truth half spoke is worse than none—but I'll not let that quill-licking basket Swill have th' last say on th' matter." He took a toss of claret and a breath. "Th' tale of it starts when I first took to me station at th' foundlingery . . . Whether th' deed were intended as a mercy or a mischief I can't rightly say, but . . . but th' very day I bore up at Madam Opera's"—he lifted his glass to the late marine society proprietress burned up in the foundlingery fire—"I spied a little bogle fumblin' with a parcel on th' Madam's very doorstep. An odd boggler it was, with the head of an oversized sparrow and all dressed in fine clothes like some midget Domesday struttin' fluff. I hailed th' mite with some angry remonstration, makin' to scare it off. Th' basket just looked at me cool as sit-on-yer-tail an' did not budge."

Cinnamon! Rossamünd could hardly credit it. "I have seen such a fellow myself!" he exclaimed. "Freckle said he has been watching out for me . . ."

"Freckle?" Europe arched her diamond-spoored brow. "The bogle I saw skulking about Bleak Lynche after Wormstool fell . . . The bogle *you* had me free from the *Hogshead* . . ." Her voice trailed off in displeasure.

"Ah—aye . . ."

Fransitart looked at them a moment before he went on. "Well, that Freckle bogle sounds blithely enough—ye ought not to judge a bugaboo too quick, as I knew well enough even then."

Europe shifted in her seat yet said nothing.

"Be that as it is," the ex–dormitory master pressed on, "I was determined to fright it away; a city is no place for a nicker, nor a nicker—blithely or otherwise—th' right one for a city. So I lay alongside this sparrowling, me cudgel in hand to make me point more clear"—the old dormitory master raised his hands in demonstration—"an' I hailed it, 'Avast, Master Sparrow! What's yer mischief with that bundle? Clear off if ye value yer crown. Worse folks than me p'rambulate these streets!'—or some such I said. Yet far from affrighted, th' basket stood an' faced me though it was not more than half a fathom tall. Looking me a-loft an' a-low with its big blinking peepers, it spoke an' tells me, 'Ye take good care of this 'un'—I can't do its voice right, Rossamünd, all twittery and tuneful and wi'out me salty glot—but 'Take care of this 'un', it says. 'This one'll be eaten by worse than me if I let 'im stay out in th' good-lands, so to th' world o' wicked men an' kind he must come.' That's when I realized just what manner of parcel it was in its clutches."

Rossamünd's throat constricted and tasted unpleasantly sharp. Somehow, he already knew what his old master was going to reveal.

"That parcel, Rossamünd—," said Fransitart, looking to him. "That parcel were ye, lad . . ."

Rossamünd's mouth went dry. He forced down a mouthful of watery claret.

"This sparrow-thing puts ye all tiny an' quiet in me arms," Fransitart continued, "an' it says, 'His name is what he is.' An' it points to that hatbox bit with th' scrawl of yer forename on it, Rossamünd. Yet afore I can ask any more, open springs the foundlingery door an' there is th' Madam—rest her—arms akimbo an' glarin' like she did. Afore she could fathom its true nature, Master Sparrow harefoots it down th' Vlinderstrat an' was gone. But th' Madam? She only had eyes for ye, lad, an' takes ye, name-card an' all, an' writes ye up in her book, *Rossamünd Bookchild*. She weren't nothin' if not efficient." He respectfully raised a glass again, Craumpalin doing so with him.

Blinking, Rossamünd stared at the old men, astounded at the long years Fransitart had lived enduring such a secret.

Europe leaned back in her seat, owlish gaze calculating.

Such a frank confession left them utterly vulnerable to her mercurial mercies.

"So that's the short of it," Fransitart went on. "Ye were hauled off to the cribs an' me to watch o'er ye and all the others with ye as a master. I kept the matter to meself, dwelt on it, stored it up in me soul until some time on, Master Pin fetched up to work at the Madam's—under me sage advice. Soon as he arrived an' I had th' chance, I found the bit of card an' took it into him an' told him just what this sparrow-fellow had spake: 'His name is what he is . . .' Never one to be spooked by oddities, ye thought an' ye thought on it, di'n't ye, Pin? Sent away to his soup-makin', tome-thumbin' friends on it . . ."

Head bowed, Craumpalin gave a single nod.

"An' he found such as we never hoped he would—prob-ably in the same line of cryptic book as that dastard butcher claims to have investigated," Fransitart growled. "It said much as Swill claimed, that rossamünderlings were an an-cient monster's name for bogles that look like everymen. We knew of such too, though by other names, that blighted Biargë lass being th' most famous among vinegars—"

"Such is the trouble that comes of talking to bogles," Craumpalin muttered, speaking for the first time.

"Why not call me something else?" Rossamünd insisted.

"Because Madam O wrote thee up right quick." Craum-palin looked squarely at Rossamünd. "Once thy name were in the Madam's book, it was a matter of ineffaceable public record. There was no renaming thee after that, and no fuss could be made without lookin' mightily suspicious. So we had to luff up and let the matter be. I comforted Frans and meself it was such an obscure word, I reckoned on none that thee might meet ever knowing of it . . . other than the name of a lass mistakenly given to a lad, that is."

35

"Unfortunate in itself, I would have thought," Europe added quietly.

Fransitart gave her an unhappy look. "We never reckoned on such dangersome waters as ye finding yerself thrust into service with a book-eatin' massacar like Swill," he said bitterly.

"They do seem to be everywhere," the Duchess-in-waiting returned dryly.

The ex–dormitory master scowled again. "Once it came time to take yer place in the world, lad, Pin an' I were at full stretch to know what to do with ye. Let ye go an' risk some kind of discovery . . ."

"Which was what I was vouching for," Craumpalin inserted. "Holding that risk to be small—"

"Aye, or go my way of it an' keep ye back where we could know ye were safest—"

"Aye," Craumpalin interrupted again. "Inviting suspicions and dooming the lad to some half-lived life."

Old troubles flashed in Fransitart's dark eyes. "So ye said then, Pin, an' I followed yer lead an' 'ere we are now—"

"We would be in this or some other strait by either heading, Frans." The aging dispensurist looked wounded. "It has always been a matter of time's passing. The stone and the sty if ever a siteeation was . . ."

The ex–dormitory master looked instantly regretful. "Aye, Pin, aye . . ."

"That is why you had me wrapped in nullodour," Rossamünd interjected. Critchitichiello the hedgeman had said Master Craumpalin's Exstinker would never foil a monster's senses. "The noses you were keeping me safe from weren't monsters but dogs and—and men." This it had most certainly done. If it had not been for the Exstinker, Rossamünd knew full well that in his native monster's stink he would have been slain out-of-hand by Licurius while he still hid in the boxthorn growing in the pastures of Sulk End or set dogs howling after his blood well before he was near them.

"Aye," Craumpalin answered softly. "We wanted to give thee every chance at success."

"Perchance locking him in a chest and hiding it in the buttery might have served better," Europe murmured.

"But why did you not tell me before, Master Fransitart?" Rossamünd persisted, heedless of his mistress' ironies. "Surely I could have avoided dangers better if I had known who—what—who I really am."

"Hear, hear," murmured Europe, attending them in perfect stillness. "Why not indeed . . ."

For a beat there was a painful silence.

Fransitart beheld his former charge, regret clear in his eyes. "We . . . ," he croaked. "What would we tell ye, my boy? *How* do we tell ye? Of what dare we say? 'Why, Rossamünd, did ye know ye was handed up to us by a bogle who claimed ye to be monstrous-born?' Would ye believe me? Who would? The less spoke on it, the less folks to know, and the less heavy going we make of it."

"You—," Rossamünd started, but what could he say? Who *would* believe such outrageous stuff? He looked at his hand, to see that it was still real, that he was still *he,* and found that it was shaking uncontrollably.

"Thee has to fathom, Rossamünd," Craumpalin said, coming to his old mate's aid, "that if we ever spoke on it, such a calumn'ous revelation would only have thee ever worrying to thy back to see who might discover thy terrible secret."

Swill's witness he could discount: that his arrival in this world had never put a woman abed, that instead he had emerged fully knit from the boggy sump of some threwdish haunt, the mud-born replica of a poor bewildered and long-fallen child . . . *This* he could dismiss, but not the evidence of his dear masters. Suddenly Freckle's words, spoken so long ago in the putrid hold of the listing *Hogshead*, rose unbidden . . . *The time might come for knowing things,* the glamgorn had said, *and when the need of knowing's nigh, you'll know then what I do now* . . . "I fathom it, Master Pin," Rossamünd murmured. "I fathom it . . ."

Europe's penetrating hazel gaze lingered on Rossamünd. "It seems remarkable to me that some diminutive bogle made it right into the heart of your city," she said at last, "managing such a feat of utter invisibility to get over walls and elude every dog and gate ward."

"Size ain't no reckoning of potency, ma'am." It was Craumpalin who answered. "The antiquarians have it that such feats are not beyond the mighty ones and that some of the leastly baskets in stature can be mightiest of them all."

"You run it close to a sedorner's prating, Master Salt," the fulgar said warningly. "I can see from where you inherited your dangerous notions, little man." She peered now at Rossamünd, her expression guarded, her thoughts opaque.

He held her gaze, wanting to say something about truth

and knowing and doing right, yet nothing sensible formulated rapidly enough to speak.

The fulgar let out a long tired breath. "It might be said that worm-riddled texts with notions as crumbling as their spines and superstitious navy-men long past their prime do not make for trusty sources any more than a book-learned butcher with a grudge to grind. Let me, however, for Rossamünd's sake, presume this is possible," she said with a sidelong look to the ex–dormitory master. "I would think such fantastic claims required tangible proofs."

"If that is how ye will have it," Fransitart countered with sailorly bluntness, his jaw jutting and firm-set, looking first to Europe, then to Rossamünd, "there will be proof a-plenty in nigh on a seven-night paired. *This* mark here will show itself as cruorpunxis or braggart's scab and end all argumentations!" He gripped at where the bandaged puncting had been made: that terrible experiment he and Rossamünd had submitted to at the hands of the surgeon Swill.

"A seven-night paired, indeed, man," Europe said, raising a brow. "Such delightful argot: I gather you mean a fortnight?"

"Aye, madam. In a twin o' weeks *all* wranglings will end."

Rossamünd slouched in his seat as grim certainty established itself.

Europe might require such *tangible proofs,* yet he already fathomed which way the mark—made from his very own blood—would turn: that in two weeks less two days the puncting made with his own blood on Fransitart's arm would show as a cruorpunxis, a monster-blood tattoo.

ON BEING A FACTOTUM

man-of-business one who acts partly as lawyer, computer, counterman, broker, manager, representative, secretary and clerk. They are either hired in their hundreds by the great mercantile firms or work individually for select, well-paying clientele, those with kinder souls representing the less shrewd in the maddening world of bureaucracy. In practice these fellows can range from the most sedentary quill-licks to the keenest, most ruthless minds of the day.

I N somber silence the meal was soon concluded. After a sip of claret, Europe stood and declared, "Time for parting ways, Rossamünd. You have tasks to attend."

Confusedly, he gave an affirming bob. But . . . he wanted to say, what of all this! *I'm likely a monster yet you still keep me? Why not have me dead and another cross puncted on your arm?* "They—they are not staying here?" was what actually came out of his mouth.

"Thank'ee, m'lady," Fransitart inserted quickly, Craumpalin joining him in a bow. "We had thought to shift for ourselves. We have a longtime mate to look in on an' need not be a trouble to ye. We'd best get to it before the day is out . . ."

"Good for you, sirs," Europe returned evenly. "Shift as

you will." Then, instructing Rossamünd to join her in her file, she left the three to their goodbyes.

"Where will you go?" Rossamünd suddenly did not want to be parted from these best of men.

"We'll lay along to the Dogget & Block," Fransitart answered, a kindly light in his soulful eyes. "It's an alehouse an' hostelry some ways from here, just off Little Five Points on the Tailor's Wigh. The proprietor once served with us aboard the *Hammerer*."

"Ahh, Casimir Fauchs—fine fellow," Craumpalin seemed to say to himself. "Our cloud's silvery trimming. Come and visit us when thee is able, Rossamünd."

Despite the ponderous import of their revelations, relieved of their burden at last the two fellows were clearly lighter of soul.

"We'll send ye word when we are settled ourselves," Fransitart offered. "An' ye must send for us whene'er ye need. I can't think yer mistress will keep ye cooped in this . . . place all of yer days." He looked sidelong at the ponderously opulent room. "Watch how ye come on; no need giving away suspicions with carelessness."

"And keep to dousing in me Exstinker for now," Craumpalin added intently. "I shall make thee something new to better hide thee."

With that they departed, out into the clearing afternoon.

"Hold fast, Rossamünd," Fransitart called gruffly from the window of Europe's own day coach. "We'll see ye through yet."

Waving farewell, Rossamünd watched them out of the

gates and across the bridge. He remained until the sound of them was lost in the drone of city life, alone on the steps of the house of the Branden Rose.

For the rest of the afternoon he was introduced to his tasks as factotum: the making of Cathar's Treacle—of course—and other necessary draughts, and with this the continual inventory and replenishing of all parts and scripts; the oiling and storage of the fulgaris—fuse and stage; the finding of knaving work; and fetch, carry and all other singular labors urgent or petty to which his mistress turned her mind. He was presented formally to the two divisions of servants: her retainers, with Mister Kitchen as their chief and of whom Rossamünd was in principle a part, and the house staff under the grave, squinting authority of Mistress Clossette.

Feeling overstretched and strangely blank, he nevertheless attended to this orientation as Europe showed him from bottom to top the towering extents of his new home.

First was the flashy hiatus, opposite the solar, where guests were to wait in awed comfort. Filled with plush seats, it had red walls like the solar, but a ceiling of black, molded with gilt cornice work. The somber wood of the floor was covered with a great carpet of red and magenta checks edged in clean white, while a leering mask of some Occidental face glowered from above a basalt fireplace. At the rear of the hiatus, dark nadderer-figured doors led to a state hall reserved for grand dinners. Here, beneath the elaborately molded ceiling of gold and red, ran a broad frieze of leaping battling figures—man and monster, the most frequent being a woman in red whom Rossamünd quickly fathomed was Europe herself. All four friezes on all four walls were filled, the fabulist run out of space. Tall south-looking windows stared out from the golden walls upon the green flow of the Midwetter swimming with brilliant orange fish and the neighbors' lofty roofs on the farther bank.

Opposite Rossamünd's own set was a surprisingly well-stocked library and attached billiard, its vast table laid with red felt. There were various parlors and guest chambers, drawing rooms and meeting rooms on the floors above, spaces of green and gold, white and red, each furnished in ubiquitous black lacquer.

The highest proper story was given over almost entirely to what Europe named the ludion, a long space of dark empty floorboards and unclear use, plainly lit by a great line of windows, the light doubled by the equally expansive row of mirrors that made the opposite wall. By a deft touch, one of the mirrors sprang open, and Europe led him by a curling stair into the attics. Here were arranged a series of small trophy rooms displaying the various prizes, weapons and oddities of an extended and highly successful monster-destroying career. Turning to leave, the young factotum got a mighty shock, for rearing by the main door was a squa-mous, almost froglike nicker thrice his height. Arching up, its glassy, fishy eyes were staring horribly; its webbed claws were lifted and ready to tear, the broad mouth of tiny dag-ger teeth gaping hungrily. Yet it was a dead thing, stuffed and mounted on display.

"A display of gratitude," Europe explained, the ghost of a

smile crossing her dial. "The watery beast was making home of a local pond and I relieved my neighbors of its unpleasant charms, *so* they in turn gave me this as a grateful token. They were no longer as troubled to have one of my ilk in their districts after that."

At the end of it all, he was taken through to the narrower, plainer servants' walks at the rear of the stately house and finally down to the kitchens. As pristine as the rest of the great house and as white as everywhere else was not, these were a-bustle with preparations for mains. Maids, under-cooks, turnspits and a brace of scullions: so many people for just one woman, all working with steady, dignified indus-try. There was no heft and hurry as in Winstermill's kitchen under Mother Snooks, nor the makeshift one-man chaos of Wormstool's mess. The staff eyed him uncertainly, the turn-spits and scullions clearly uneasy to have their mistress step-ping into their own domain; yet all bobbed politely, pausing in their work and waiting.

Only vaguely aware of them, Europe wound boldly through it all. "One more nook for you to see, little man," she declared over her shoulder.

In an alcove between scullery and pantry was a black door with a tongue-poking face of a saucy bogle carved into the thick paneling. This opened onto a stone stepway that spiraled down into Cloche Arde's foundations, terminating in a small hexagonal chamber dedicated to the brewing of Europe's draughts.

The saumery.

By the clear light of fresh bright-limns, Rossamünd

could see that every wall was fashioned from marble of lustrous and oddly swarthy green, each corner crowded with pilasters of the same. The floor was arranged in an intricate fretwork of emerald and crimson tiles, with a sizeable test-cupboard standing at the far end. Lacquered black, the cupboard had brass feet cast in the shape of grinning mustachioed serpents, corners molded in the appearance of entwined flower-maidens, and many handles gripped in gaping brass mouths. It was permanently set here, its chimney flue disappearing into the dusken green ceiling. Arranged in nooks in the stonework at either side were parts-cabinets, tall cylinders of glossy red. Upon each semicircular drawer were cunningly fashioned brass slots that held neatly marked labels: Sugar of Nnun, bezoariac, xthylistic curd and so much more—many well beyond Rossamünd's ken. A small duodecimo of obscure title lay still open atop one of the drawers, as if put down in the midst of reading.

"I shall leave you to make this your own," said Europe, turning to depart. "All you need is here. Mister Kitchen will help you if it isn't. I shall have my treacle in my file in one hour."

Momentarily lost, Rossamünd revolved slowly, hands on hips, trying to get a bearing in this dim test. He discovered four more cabinet pictures hanging two-a-side on the angling back walls of the saumery and, stuffing them promptly into a recess of the test cupboard, spent the next hour learning the place of everything, rearranging as he saw fit, wondering at this command he had over an entire and well-stocked room. With the stove plate already hot and all pots, gradients and parts ready handy, when it came time to brew, the making was easy and the task quickly completed.

"You take it to her by your own hand, young sir," was Kitchen's firm instruction once Rossamünd was done. "'Tis the only fashion she will have it. I shall show you there."

Standing on the first floor before Europe's file door, Rossamünd hesitated in unconscious fascination at the forms of tiny figures in the panels of the door, showing all attitudes of arching, dancing, sneering bogles of tribes he did not know existed.

Behind him, Kitchen made a small, polite cough.

Rossamünd rapped at an elliptical plate of worn brass high in the midst of the graven revelry.

The door opened.

There was little light within—curtains must have been drawn and no bright-limns turned. Out of the murk the Branden Rose loomed, giving Rossamünd a shock. "A timely testing, little man. Perhaps I'll not regret you after all."

Rossamünd's heart fumbled a beat. *Regret my service?*

"Thank you, Kitchen, for your bony wing," Europe continued. "I am sure you guided him with your usual warm and fatherly care. That will be all."

The steward gave a bland smile and departed obediently.

Rossamünd lingered, looking back to be certain that Kitchen had truly gone. "Miss Europe?" he said just as her file door was closing.

The blank gap between door and jamb hovered, a mere sliver, a test of patience.

A long-suffering sigh.

MISTER KITCHEN

The gap widened.

"Uh . . . Thank you for rescuing me."

"Tish tosh," the fulgar dismissed from ill-lit space. "That wretch Whympre and his lapdog Swill were acting up a show for their secretarial friend and I could no longer let them mishandle you, so here you are." She leaned into the light and beheld Rossamünd closely. "Know, Rossamünd, that some will think me puzzle-headed for taking on a child as my second. You bore your duty with the lamplighters admirably, but my *load* is heavier still. Yet under my hand I believe you will quickly learn to acquit yourself as a man. So watch your way; a factotum does more than make treacle and cover my back in a stouche. You are my chief representative; what you say *I* have said, what you do *I* have done. You are chief of this household, and though Kitchen and Clossette will tend to its running quite happily, you may intervene on any of their transactions as you see fit."

"No—ah, yes, Miss Europe." Swallowing, Rossamünd tried to let what he supposed was a manly calm spread through his members.

"Welcome to a life of violence, little man," she said portentously in parting and slowly closed the file door.

Returning to his new room—his *set*—Rossamünd found that a bed had been delivered in his absence. A great four-poster now butted against the wall. Covered with an enormous scarf of immaculate black silk run through with dyed flowers of red and blue and warm yellow, its white linen was stark in the inky room and it looked about as comfortable as a bed could look.

After six months with the lighters he was well used to having every point of his time organized for him, and was now at a bit of a loss. He fossicked through cupboards and drawers Pallette had dutifully organized to locate the meager count of his worldly goods. How he regretted the loss of his peregrinat in the conflagration of Wormstool; it would have been a comfort to read.

Fed a light supper of nine-cheese melted on sour bread in his room, Rossamünd lay upon the bed at last, almost swallowed by its downy coverlets. Through the lofty third-story windows he could easily see the eastern sky behind the silhouette of treetops and ridge-caps, a sea of sloping homogenous slate and chimney pots. The heaven-haze was a delicate pink of staggering beauty, darkening into a deep violet as it rose. Picked out low against this were tiny, tightly fluffy clouds of glowing russet and pallid carnation. In awe, Rossamünd just looked, silent, barely breathing till the view darkened and then vanished in encroaching night, and daysounds gave over to sparse cricket song.

To the thin tune of early spring insects, he stared at the dark ceiling, fingers pressing absently into the stiff facings of his quabard. He half expected to hear the muffled cry, "Douse lanterns!" that rang every night to proclaim bedtime in the prentices' cell row at Winstermill. He wanted sleep, yet anxious, tumbling contemplations kept him in tossing-and-turning wakefulness until the dead of night—*Who am I? What am I?*—and it was only exhaustion and the lingering rocking of the Grume crossing that finally pressed him to sleep.

The new day was clear and cool. Still clothed, Rossamünd was woken by Pallette bearing a great jug of water for washing, accompanied by a young step-servant called Pardolot, arms full of wood and kindle to light a new fire. "You had not risen timely, sir, so I thought it best to wake you before the morning got on too much," she explained nervously.

"Thank you, thank you . . . ," Rossamünd repeated blearily.

He hurried through the kitchen, blinking unsteadily in the stark morning light made brighter by the flawless pallor of the walls, the servants assiduously avoiding his eye.

"In!" Europe declared when Rossamünd arrived at the file door with her steaming treacle. She was dressed today in the wonderful scarlet coat he knew so well, though her hair was still down in a plait.

Obediently he stepped across the threshold and into the fulgar's sanctum.

It was long and large, the long venal red wall opposite perforated by many thin windows hung with velvet drapes pulled aside now to let in the bright daybreak. There were silk paintings of vile-looking nickers and a floor-to-ceiling mirror in between. An enormous exotic carpet occupied a large part of the dark wood floors, and at the center of this sat a desk of mahogany, its uncluttered top inlaid with a vast blotter of the black hide of some unnameable creature.

Telling Rossamünd to remain, Europe took her morning dose, and—as he dutifully stood by and waited—continued to look through a great book spread over a large portion of her desk. It was a garland, filled with tinted plates of mild-faced people wearing coats and weskits and cloaks, similar to volumes Rossamünd had once seen in Madam Opera's boudoir.

A light thunk of an opening door and Claudine, the tiring maid, appeared from behind a bom e'do screen in the corner of the file, coming from what presumably was Europe's own bedchamber. At Europe's instruction she began to take Rossamünd's dimensions for what the fulgar called *more appropriate attire*. "Your other quabard is entirely the wrong hue," his mistress explained, speaking of his lamplighter's harness with its Imperial mottle of rouge and or—red and cadmium.

Gently prompted to turn about with such slow and nervous care that he hardly felt a prod or poke, the young factotum could see an enormous obsidian fireplace at the far end of the room, the warm, energetic firelight catching the glint of fine white flecks in the dark green stone. Above the dark mantel was a vast painting of a young girl, maybe four or five years older than him, with a trefoiled heart figured in white above her left shoulder. In the shadows at the girl's feet lay some slain, fearsome nicker while other deformed shades lurked and cowered behind. The girl's daubed expression was one Rossamünd knew all too well: sardonic self-satisfaction. At first, for the briefest instant, and rather stupidly, he thought it was a rendering of Threnody: the same taut insolence and a deeper sorrow too. With a small shock he realized he was gaping at a portrait of a young

Europe. Dumbfounded, he looked from the image to the real woman and back. The former was radiant with the blooming beauty of youth; plumper, she was dressed like a boy in a skirted coat of magenta with a high dramatic collar, her face pristine of spoors or the thinness of the lahzarine ravage. The whole manner of her pose was defiant, full of energy, even of hope. The latter sat in living flesh, intent on her medicinal drink and her fashion book, her beauty stretched, almost gaunt, yet undiminished.

"Today you will be meeting my man-of-business," the fulgar said suddenly, marking a page and closing the garland. "He is a bright fellow, a man of many parts, with clear ambitions in the magnate line. I do not begrudge him his plans for improvement—many have them, I suppose—and he completes his labors for me admirably." Finally, she looked at her new arrival properly. "This came for you," the fulgar stated blandly, holding out a folded paper.

It was a simple note from Fransitart.

> Rossamünd,
>
> We are safely harbored at the Dogget & Block, in the district of Fishguard. Any takenyman will know its bearings, as might your Branden Rose. Will look in on you in the middle of the afternoon watch if we do not have report from you first.
>
> With respect,

There was a knock.

With an absent "In!" from Europe between gulps of trea-cle, a portly, thoroughly starched, clerical-looking gentle-man entered the file. Dressed in a glossy blue-gray frock coat with darker collar and cuffs and sensibly restrained hems, he wore his own sandy hair above an extremely broad face; the slicked locks, parted evenly and jutting over either ear, were gathered in a small black bow at the back. About him hung a distinctly mercenary air.

"Ah, Mister Carp. Here you are, my man-of-business, even as we speak of you," declared the fulgar.

"Your return is happy and welcome, gracious lady," this Carp fellow offered—as starchily as his appearance prom-ised—bowing low and long and taking no notice of Ros-samünd. "I came from my offices directly I got your word." Behind him came two equally stiff lackeys in glossy gray, each bringing an armful of folios and bow-tied papers.

Europe gave a brittle laugh. "Nonsense, man! I am fully aware my return is of great inconvenience to you all. Gone are comfortable days in my pay done at your usual rhythm."

"Ah, your grace," said Carp, smiling tautly, "you are any-thing but inconvenient—"

"Tish tosh," the Branden Rose returned evenly. "Now! *This* is Rossamünd Bookchild, come here as my new factotum."

"Yes, yes. Kitchen explained as much upon my arrival," Carp said gravely with a look of cautious regard to Ros-samünd. *And* who *are* you? his pale eyes seemed to say. "We were all most distressed when we received news of noble Licurius' gallant fall."

Europe looked owlishly at the man. "I am sure you were," she said quietly. She stared at her man-of-business for a moment and then said, "Here, Rossamünd, is the silver-tongued Pragmathës Carp."

Mastering a faint animosity toward this fellow, Rossamünd bowed and did his best with gentlemanly civility. "Pardon me, Mister Carp, sir, but do you have a relative living up in Boschenberg?" he asked cheerfully enough, thinking that there might be a connection between the person before him and Madam Opera's manservant.

The man-of-business just blinked at him and remained silent.

Rossamünd stared out of the file window and hoped neither Europe nor the uncivil Carp noticed his burning cheeks.

"Mister Carp," Europe declared, as the man-of-business directed his aides to deposit their loads and depart, "today you are to show Rossamünd to the coursing house so he might tell them that I am arrived and am available for work." She glanced to Rossamünd. "There is no benefit in sitting idly about giving needless scope to all manner of dour maunderings. You are to aid him fully, sir, in learning these clerical particulars." She leaned back in her seat.

Carp inclined his head. "Most certainly, good lady."

Daunted, Rossamünd only nodded; he had no notion how to be both monster and monster-hunter at once. He could only hope that he might somehow steer his mistress' choices or drive the bogles away before she could get to them, just as Threnody said Dolours did with the unfortunate Herdebog Trought.

Europe sat up and produced a folio from a wide drawer in her elaborate desk. It was a sheafbook; a flight of pale golden egrets figured on the ebony cover, and it was filled with the ribbon-bound leaves of many different papers. "This is my vaingloria—well, the most recent of them. It is a testament to my aptitude and proof of your representation of me." She looked at Rossamünd steadily. "Take this, present it to the underwriters at the knavery and inform them that I am here. That is my task for you today; a simple beginning. Mister Carp will put you aright if needed, will you not, man?"

"Most certainly, good lady."

The fulgar drew forth a key from some secret place upon her. "You must fit yourself appropriately for going forth on the knave with me." A hint of kinder feelings played about the corners of the fulgar's eyes and mouth. "What arts do you think will suit you in the stouche?"

Puckering his mouth, Rossamünd frowned. "Potives work best, I reckon," he said with an emphatic nod. "They do for many more foes than one blow of a stock or one shot of a firelock can."

"Truly . . . A ledgermain, are we?" Europe replied with a twinkle in her eye. "Mister Carp will write you out a folding note to twenty sous"—at this the man-of-business shifted his weight just a little—"for you to take to Perseverance Finest Parts on Foul Soap Lane after your excursion to the knavery. Set yourself up with whatever you deem necessary to meet the need, Any change you may keep for future expenses."

Rossamünd could hardly credit what his ears were hearing.

Twenty sous!

"May I bring Master Craumpalin with me?" he asked breathlessly. "He knows all there is to know about the properties of scripts."

"If it will help you to spend, then, yes, you may."

What a turn! To be let free at a dispensary with a learned dispensurist and almost as much money as Rossamünd could earn in a year of lamplighting.

At Europe's instruction, Carp went to a heavy bureau in the corner behind her and there drew up a bill of folding money. Passing the new-minted note to Rossamünd, the man-of-business could not help the warning, "Disperse this wisely, young fellow—we will want receipts."

The young factotum goggled at Carp's fine pen work on the bill, at the import of the words the man had inscribed there.

PLENIPOTENTIS EX IMPERIA

THROUGH THE LETS & PROSCRIPTIONS OF THE BUREAU IMPERIAL OF THE PURSE, I.M.I.R
WITH THE CONCOMITANT & NECESSARY CONSENTS OF THE BUREAU IMPERIAL OF EXCISE, I.M.I.E
THIS CERTIFICATE GRANTS THE BEARER A SUM IN EQUIVALENT OF

Twenty sous

OF THE COIN OF THE REALMS & EXTENTS OF THE RIGHTFUL

HAACOBIN EMPIRE~

ALL SUBJECTS OF THE IMPERIAL WILL SHALL RECEIVE & REDEEM THIS BILL TO THE VALUE STATED
SO GRANTED BY THE LAWFUL PROVISION & MANUUS OF HIS MOST BENIFICIENT EMPEROR'S SERVANT
OR THEIR PROPER REPRESENTATIVE & BY THE SOVEREIGN MARQUE OF THE SAME

Pragmathës Carp Notary, Clerk-Fiduciary

lgt. Her Grace Europa, Duxe In Exspectae Naimes,
Marchessa Nenne

PLENIPOTENTIS EX IMPERIA

Europe folded her arms in an easy manner. "Now go!" she proclaimed, with a light and easy twirl of her fingers. "See! Do! Spend! And if you are able, find me a new driver for my landaulet."

Before he left, he wrote a note to his old masters at his own writing desk in his new room, with stylus and a ream of fine, thick parchment. He sought to frame a grandly formal missive with capitals and all, just as an agent of a mighty peeress ought.

> Dear, dear Masters Fransitart & Craumpalin,
>
> Please do me the Honor of meeting with me at your Chosen Establishment, the Dogget & Block, on this very day at the Second Bell of the Afternoon Watch, and from there to join me in the Purchase of Many Scripts and Many Parts from Perseverance Finest Parts, Foul Soap Lane.
>
> Your Servant
> Most Faithfully,

. . . Here he steadied himself and marked his name, refashioning it after his memory of Sebastipole's own fine manu propa:

4

TO BRANDENTOWN

elephantine(s) named for their great corpulence, these folk are the highest rank of magnate in central Soutland society. Much of the Half-Continent pivots on the idea that certain folk are better than others, that some are worthy and most of all should lead and succeed, whereas others are not worthy and ought to suffer at their betters' expense. This is very much the stated position of the peers, lords and princes—an inherited notion fundamental to their understanding of themselves and their place in relation to other lesser folk, the wellspring of their callousness and arrogance abetted by all levels of society and the source of their social power. Though dukes, marches, counts and barons may in their heart of hearts look down upon the elephantines, vulgarines and other magnates, the raw power that money affords induces the former to concede and treat them as equal.

OUT in the wood-smoky morning, aboard a dyphr driven by Mister Carp, Rossamünd ventured into the city at last, glad to have business to keep his cares at bay. His money stowed securely in his wallet and his trunk freshly doused in Exstinker, Rossamünd was ready to explore.

Riding down wide avenues of fine city manors in a dyphr was quite different from riding in a lentum or takeny, a more lively bobbing motion putting wind in his ears and lifting his soul. Out in the spring-warming hush, over the creak of the springs and harness and the clash of wheels on flagstone, he discerned an all-surrounding hum of activity, a sustained buzz of energy and momentum such as he had never known before, not even in the civilian mass of Boschenberg. *How big is this city?* he marveled, clutching his thrice-high determinedly to his head.

"So you are to be Licurius' substitute." The man-of-business broke his silence with an ironic smile as he coaxed his gray mare left. He was wearing his copstain—or stovepipe hat—at a jaunty angle on his head and a merry flush on his cheeks. "Where do you hail from?"

"I was raised in Boschenberg . . ."

"As I can see from your cingulum," Carp interjected, meaning Rossamünd's black-and-brown checkered baldric.

"But lately I have come from Winstermill."

"Never heard of it," Carp declared with a dismissive wave of his hand.

Rossamünd was incredulous. "The great fortress of the lamplighters at the beginnings of the Idlewild?"

The man-of-business twisted his mouth in contemplation. "Perhaps I may have heard it spoke of in passing, but certainly nothing memorable. Of the Idlewild I am somewhat informed—an eminent client of mine has a small interest in a going concern at Gathercoal; but of this Winstermill, nothing. Is it newly raised?"

Rossamünd could scarce contain an indignant splutter. "It was built long ago, right on the foundations of old Winstreslewe! Has never once been breached."

"I do not doubt you, young fellow." Carp made a noncommittal gesture. "But it is not Brandenbrass, is it? As *they* say, the world *is* Brandenbrass and Brandenbrass *is* the world, the very center of the cosmos—or did *you* not know that? *Everything* comes here and *everything* goes out again—and clever souls position themselves somewhere in between to skim the gleanings."

"Oh" was all the deflated young factotum could think to say. Brandenbrass shared most of Boschenberg's trading lanes and was her greatest rival.

The man-of-business peered at him, an impertinent glimmer in his eye. "I wonder how old Boxface would find it, superseded by a child—it's almost comical." He actually laughed, a sound of honest flabby delight in his thick throat.

Near speechless, Rossamünd kept his gaze fixed down the route of high, pale gray buildings. "I beg your pardon, sir?" he forced as politely as he might through gritted teeth.

"No, no, mistake me not, m'boy," Carp quickly asserted. "It is truly rather fitting. The Branden Rose was never one to tread convention's path. Why would she not as soon employ a boy-factotum over some wizened old bleak-souled sensurist like Licurius, stolen from her mother's employ?" The man was growing loquacious the farther they went from his patroness' scrutiny. "You seem a much cheerier fellow than that laggard. I declare, he was getting grimmer by the day, last I knew him. Did you ever see those ghastly images he paints—or painted, rather? A regular graphnolagnian."

"Aye." Rossamünd stared at the man-of-business fully in his shock; yet it fitted well that those wretched daubs he had banished from set and saumery were the work of so cruel a fellow.

PRAGMATHËS CARP

"He was quite famous among certain circles, so I hear, veritably hailed for the deftness of his marks and his attention to detail." Carp clucked in his cheek, and the young factotum liked him just a little for that. "A dubious honor if ever there was."

Nodding, not knowing what else to say, Rossamünd inadvertently caught the eye of a filthy onion-seller toiling along the walk, bowed under a pole strung thickly with a great weight of onions. The seller glared at him, then stepped forward as if to offer a sale. The young factotum quickly looked away.

"How did you come by such a fancy name?" asked Carp as the dyphr passed on, turning down a broad way brimming with market crowds.

Closing his eyes, Rossamünd groaned inwardly. "It was written on a card that came with me when I was found on the doorstep of my foundlingery," he sighed.

"I see," the man-of-business uttered, as if for him this explained all he wished to know. "And have you, perchance, come to Brandenbrass afore?"

Rossamünd said he had not.

The farther Carp took them from Cloche Arde, the busier the streets became, and tighter too, long direct roads dissecting the city into small sections run through with alleys and lanes. Turning right off the Harrow Road as it bent west, mucky smokestacks, thin and very tall, began to show above the high rooftops blotched with lichen, leaking strange smokes into the morning smog.

"Ahh, old Brandentown," the starchy fellow waxed encyclopedically, "historied beauty of the Grume—of the whole Sundergird no less!—whose long-gone metropolitans sought to transact business with the Tutin invader rather than resist him, thus preserving much of the autonomy we still enjoy today. Such a superb mercantile tradition is the shrewd and potent praxis—the great egalitarian system—upon which even one as small and ignoble as I can rise to heights unattainable by any other man in other lands. Employ your money wisely here, Rossamünd Bookchild, and you will surely find yourself elevated to a patron of the peers themselves . . ."

With a flick of reins, Mister Carp took the dyphr quickly about a crossway, a circuit where the road they were on met several other streets at oddly obtuse angles. A fat memorial pillar was raised at its center; flower sellers gathered at its base, and every corner was crowded with many-storied shop fronts. Bustling through, they clattered straight down a street signed simply *The Dove* and Rossamünd suddenly found that they were running right by a stone-and-iron wall that enclosed a rather wild-looking park. From the elevation of his bobbing seat Rossamünd could see a broad common beyond, its darkling trees shaggy with yellowing lichens and pallid trailing mosses, its grasses left to grow thick and wild. It seemed still and empty yet strangely pensive too, affording no glimpse of a street or buildings on the other side, just dim, brooding shadows. Any strolling folk kept to the farther side of the road.

"We call it the Moldwood Park," Carp explained. "Good for kindling, bird's nests, a million rabbit holes and not much else. It is said that its middle is a proper woodland—all that

is left of the forest that grew natively here before our Burgundian ancestors arrived—not that I would know this for
myself, having never ventured in."

"It's threwdish!" Rossamünd exclaimed reflexively. It was
a subtle, suppressed feeling of watchfulness, a warning caution constrained on every side by human habitation. *In the
heart of an everyman's city: how can this be?*

The man-of-business gave him a quick, curious look. "It is
an uneasy place, I grant you. People are daunted by antique
stories of terrible consequences for those who have tried to
clear it, though I am told thorough surveys have turned up
nothing unpleasant. The place is a cleveland, protected by
an ancient permanare per proscripta—a legal ban—and so
it has been left, as you see, generally ignored by all but the
very needy, the very cold or the very hungry."

"The hungry? Hungry for what?"

"Why, the rabbits, sir! Rabbits—scrawny, barely eat-able
rabbits—burrowed in walls, hiding in parks and forgotten
nooks, but most of all in the Moldwood here. There is a reason, Master Bookchild, that such a beast is the sigil on our
stately flag, for the city is veritably plagued with 'em—and
their droppings, into the bargain! So much so that rats have
a hard time establishing themselves. A good thing, mayhap,
for our indigent and hungry masses—bunny daube is ate
most nights of the week in downtrod districts. The city is
famous for the dish." Carp took a pinch of spice aura from a
tiny silver vinaigrette as ward against the stink of this down-
at-heel neighborhood, then offered some to his passenger.

Rossamünd declined—such flash manners were not for

him. Feeling eyes upon him, he peered up at the sagging tenements on the opposite side, their stained sills hung with washing. A nursing mother in over-laundered gray stared down at him sullenly from a high window.

"People live willingly next to it?" he marveled.

"Those who cannot afford the higher rents elsewhere, yes."

"Are they not *bothered* by the . . . by being so close?"

Carp made a puzzled frown. "I should think none has ever asked them—they should be thankful for a roof at all. It is as *some* say, young fellow: the starveling has no fancy . . ."

At the dyphr's hectic rate they were soon past this peculiar park, going through the high arch of a bastion—the Cripplegate—its heavy iron-studded doors open wide to the ceaseless human flow. Gate wardens leaned on muskets and watched all with complacent scorn, their fine spit-and-polish making many of the amblers look squalid. Passing along a congested thoroughfare of narrow-fronted counting-houses, Carp worked with frowning application to avoid the dolly-mops in bright versions of maid's clobber and low-grade clerical gents laughing and chatting and careless of horse or carriage. Finally the relentless momentum thrust them onto a vast rectangular circuit rushing with impatient traffic. Magnificently tall buildings rose even higher on every side, casting their long shadows in the thin morning light. Imposing like a bench of magistrates, most were fronted with soaring colonnades topped with rain-streaked friezes of stone that depicted portentous moments of great matter.

"The Spokes," the man-of-business explained as they

launched into the mayhem of traffic that swarmed here. "That august building upon our right," he continued, pointing to a great square structure of dirty gray stone topped with a green-copper roof bright lit by the rising sun, "is where we need to be today. The Letter and Coursing House, postal office and knavery in one."

Post-lentums, town coaches, takeny-carriages and jaunty dyphrs barely avoided each other as drivers dodged balking horses, slow-moving planquin-chairs or white-suited scopps. These tireless children dashed to and from every cardinal with their precious messages, leaping headlong from the walkways without ever a look for rushing carriages. Several times Carp was forced to pull up sharply, his horses snorting in dismay. From the sumptuously furnished window of a park drag next to them, one gigantically corpulent fellow impatiently hollered, jowls wobbling, spittle flying as he blindly harangued the delays and glared at Rossamünd as if *he* were the cause of not just the current impediments but of all the world's ills too.

Standing bravely at strategic places among the anxious commotion were grim-looking fellows dressed in long coats of black and doing their utmost to make order of the chaos. *Duffers,* Mister Carp called them, the strict constabulary of Brandenbrass. Their waists wrapped about with checks of sable and leuc and wearing black mitres like a haubardier's, they raised and dropped lamps as signal; when one lifted a clear light, humanity flowed left but ceased to go right; when a blue light was high, the reverse occurred.

Gripping the sideboard, Rossamünd did all he could to

hang on, his knuckles white, as the dyphr hastily circumvented a wide pond right in the center of the grand circuit. A great many ibis waded in its reedy soup and used a weather-grimed statue of old bronze and stone—some neglected commemoration of ancient victories—in its middle as a perch. A faint wakefulness seemed to hover over the water, though no one else appeared to heed it.

"That brackish bog has a proper name," Carp cried over the racket—Rossamünd wishing the man would keep his eyes better fixed upon their progress—"but none of we goodly locals calls it by anything else but the Leak."

Rossamünd saw a line of shackled folks, their heads and hands jammed in flat wooden casques and ranked in full and shaming view upon a stone stage at the edge of the pond. Passing people hissed and waved white kerchiefs at them.

"What did they do?" he asked, twisting in his seat to see, yet too far to read the bill of fault nailed to each casque.

"Oh," the man-of-business answered complacently, "you'll find them to be loan defaulters, pinch-dough bakers, fraudulent mendicants, suspected grabcleats, hat-snatchers and thimble-rig sharpers; contrarified malcontents and cheap-souled tricksters all—folk not worth your anxious looks."

Slowing easy among the clutter of other carriages waiting beneath the beetling loom of the Letter and Coursing House, Mister Carp deposited his dyphr to the care of the bridle-minders, scruffy fellows disguised by fine coats. Round-eyed, mind spinning at all this novelty, Rossamünd followed the man-of-business closely as they joined the pedestrian throng. Pushing through a line of water caddies, shooing aside pleading crossing-sweeps and nosegay sellers, Carp negotiated his young charge about a rather noisome pile of various excretions of dung—including a great many rabbit pellets—but was brought up short by a quarto of serious gents. Robustly harnessed and bearing pistols and cudgels, they were moving through the crowd as a single mass, making a way for a singularly enormous fellow shambling with them, the very one who had bawled at him from the pack drag. Between the cleats of a tentlike soutaine, Rossamünd spied a wheeled frame extending down from the overlarge man's waist—a lard-barrow—the device straining to hold up the pendulous massing of the man's satin-wrapped flesh. Here was one of the infamous elephantines of the Grumid states, the wealthiest, most powerful magnates who boasted their great affluence and influence by the equal extremity of their girth.

Mister Carp blessed the bloated fellow with a solemn bow.

Tiny porcine eyes coldly calculating, the sweating elephantine sneered at the man-of-business, said nothing, and the humorless assembly moved on.

"That was His Most Elephantine Pendulous Ib," Carp breathed with disturbing admiration, shepherding Rossamünd before him to climb the broad steps of the coursing house. Between massive trunk-thick columns were two doors, the right-hand admitting and releasing a steady rush of scopps and postmen in their distinctive Imperial mottle hauling great bags of letters.

"Right for post! Left for knaves!" the man-of-business

said, pausing only briefly at the left-hand portal to wait gallantly for an ebony-skinned skold in white conice, fitch and cloak with startling white spoor-stripes down either side of her dark face. A scion of lands well to the north, far away N'go or somesuch, this skolding woman nodded gratefully to Carp and dazzled Rossamünd with her brilliant smile as she led a long line of servants from the knavery.

The interior of the Letter and Coursing House was a wide space divided down its middle by a massive wooden structure that reached up to the carbuncles of small, ever-glowing gretchen-globes hanging from a lofty dome punctured with a constellation of portholes. At the very back of the hall was a pair of huge arched windows, their central panes orbs of fiery scarlet encircled with rays glazed alternately deep transparent brown or translucent white. An arcade of pillars ran left along the wall, each post painted from base to capital with murals of teratologically violent scenes. Gazing up to the balconies, Rossamünd saw bureaucratical folk leaning on the balustrades taking their ease and looking down smugly over the variety of adventuring sorts gathered beneath them.

A whole collection of teratologists and attached staff were milling in the echoing expanse, even more fabulous than the sell-swords who had paraded through Winstermill. Here were wits, fulgars, skolds, pistoleers, sagaars, ledgermains, leers and startling combinations of the same in one soul. Most sat easy in the arcade beneath the balconies, waiting for their servants to sort the finer points. Less gaudy, threadbare pugnators waited in line themselves, queuing with the ordinary factoti and agents before the lattice-windows of the knaving-clerks. It was an entire room of monster-slayers.

What was Europe thinking to send me here? Swallowing hard, Rossamünd was heartily glad he had fresh splashings of Exstinker wrapped about his middle.

"Longest line shrinks quickest," Carp proclaimed, and went straight to the end of a lengthier queue. "Though not that line," he continued quietly, indicating the largest collection of people farther on, most carrying some fashion of stained or heavy-looking bag. "They are waiting to claim their prizes."

Well reckoning what grisly trophies these contained, Rossamünd did not dwell on them long.

Carp peered askance at the motley teratologists lined before him. "Goose-a-score incompetents," came his snide mutter. "A knave cannot be much chop if he has to represent *himself* to an underwriter." He breathed a know-it-all sigh. "It is easy enough to buckle on proofing, sling an arm at your side and pretend to yourself and others that you are thew, but only a scant few are what you would call true teratologists."

Bothered as he was by the man-of-business' superior tones, Rossamünd had to agree it would have been entirely *unseemly* for Europe to stand there like some common agent, meekly waiting her turn. Even he, in his weathered blue frock coat, looked finer than many of the dowdy bravoes ahead of him. With so many teratologists about, he could well imagine why some might struggle to make enough to even keep themselves "in biscuits"—as Master

70

Fransitart might say. Staring at this collection of gaudily dressed destroyers, he suddenly felt acutely anxious for monster-kind. How could they survive such a horde, incompetent or not?

"What is laughable," Carp continued, low-voiced, "is that there are many places in the Empire that would be fortunate indeed to see even *one* such inferior sort in half-a-dozen months, let alone a pugnator of proper capability. Such as these might make themselves a vizer's hoard from work in lonely habitations if they dared to forsake city comforts."

Rossamünd thought of Wormstool sacked and Bleak Lynche in terror of the monsters marauding out in the Frugelle, isolated folks at the mercy of carnivorous nickers. Yet these honest folk were there to take the land for themselves by force, subtle or overt.

"Still," Carp rattled on in his dry, supercilious tone, "there is always work here if they wish to spurn themselves to the magnates and lords."

A slight, hungry-looking skold in front frowned vaguely over her shoulder, her eyes sunken and haunted. Mister Carp smiled a self-satisfied smile at her. As she was called forward, a leer—obvious with a sthenicon strapped to his face—walked near, clad in a haubardine of woodland hues. The fellow seemed to pause as he passed. Rossamünd instinctively shied, pushing before Mister Carp, seeking to hide behind the man-of-business.

"My word! Steady on, young fellow," Carp exclaimed.

Yet in a hall filled with all manner of residual monstrous smells the leer did not pay him especial heed and moved on.

71

"Well-a-day, child, how might I aid you?" came a bored voice through the lattice in front of them.

Mister Carp gave a cough and cocked a brow toward the speaker.

"Oh." Rossamünd stepped forward hastily, peering at the barely discernible figure—a knaving underwriter. He held up Europe's vaingloria and announced steadily, "I am the factotum of Europa, Duchess-in-waiting of Naimes, the Branden Rose."

"Are you now?" was the amused response. "You are certainly of lesser proportions to her usual man. Is he poorly?"

"Aye, I am, and no, he is not poorly. He died in the Brindleshaws not six months ago."

"This is all true and correct," Carp confirmed, leaning into the view of the lattice.

There was a moment's silence. "Oh" was the eventual response. "Well-a-day, Pragmathës Carp . . . I—I take it her ladyship will be expecting advertisements of work to be sent to her as is usual?"

"Aye," Rossamünd replied, and then repeated the formula Europe had given him. "The Branden Rose wishes it to be known that she is at her usual seat and awaiting coursing work, either writ or singular."

"If you but pay the clerking fee, sir," the clerk stated with breathy efficiency, "two sous to register your mistress' intent and ten sequins for the clerk-at-foot to bring the advertisements to you. We shall fill an intent for you and send all writs and singulars to your mistress as soon as we might." There was a pause accompanied by the sound of pages turning behind the screen. "Cross your hands over your soul," the clerk eventually added.

With a quick blink, Rossamünd obediently put one hand over the other, right where his ribs met his stomach, feeling the folds of the nullodoured bandage hidden beneath.

"Now answer me this if you would, sir," the underwriter declared with a slightly more officious tone. "Do you, upon your solemn, continuing and mortal affirmation, declare that you are the true and foremost representative of Europa of Naimes, astrapecrith and teratologist; that you accept all culpability should the aforesaid prove to be false whether by intent or ignorance; and that you accept that I, Dandillus Pym, Coursing Underwriter, inquisit this by general and representative authority in the name of His Most Serene Highness, the Emperor Haacobin, and of His Rightful Pleni-potentiary, the Duke of the Sovereign State of Brandenbrass, and his Cabinet: how say you?"

"Ah—aye," Rossamünd answered, understanding the in-tent of the question, if not the actual words. With that said, and monies paid from his own purse so as not to break the newly writ twenty-sou bill, he was back out on the steps of the grand knavery above the clatter and bustle, feeling not a little relieved that his first clerical duty as factotum was completed.

By the light of the westering sun, Rossamünd returned via takeny-coach to Brandenbrass' substantial suburbs, restored at last to the starkly glorious bosom of Cloche Arde after a long day in town.

73

Many hours earlier he had been deposited by Carp at the Dogget & Block alehouse, where, over a lunch of griddled scringings and tots of ol' touchy, Craumpalin had insisted he knew a better supplier of parts than Perseverance Finest.

"So artful is he," the old dispenser had waxed, "I fathom even this confectioner of whom thy mistress is so fond gets their finer properties from him."

This vaunted fellow proved to be a humble script-grinder by the name of Pauper Chïves, found on Sink Street right by the pungent chalky waters of Middle Harbor. Yet the sheer size, excellence and completeness of his proporium—his salt-store—filled floor to ceiling with drawer upon drawer of parts and complete scripts—bore out Craumpalin's high estimation, and the saumiere's keen understanding and wise affability only elevated him in Rossamünd's own esteem.

Now, finally returning home and in an acme of satisfaction, the young factotum clutched the most prized of his myriad purchases. First was a thick compleat—a listbook of scripts—its crisp wasp-paper pages bound in sturdy black ox-buff and tied shut with a ribbon of deep green velvet.

"Wasp paper," Pauper Chïves had explained, "will get wet but not puff and wrinkle like the common kind, and the gauld-leather cover makes excellent protection . . . May it never be required."

The second was an exquisite pair of digitals that Craumpalin had insisted—with dogged generosity—upon buying for him They were compact devices of black enamel and silver—much smaller and more convenient to carry than stoups. "These are as fine as I have seen afore." The old fellow had smiled in satisfaction, pressing at the clasps of each of the six slots to prove their mechanism. "Wear them on thy belt or satchel-strap. They'll keep yer potives dry should thee get it in thy intellectuals to leap into another river."

Rossamünd grinned to himself, fondly turning one of his sleek new devices over and over, admiring the compact knots of silverwork perfectly set in the glistening black enamel.

Alighting by Cloche Arde's shut-fast gate, Rossamünd overpaid the takenyman—"Well, a *goodly* night to thee, good sir!"—and hefted his purchases from the cabin and the back-step trunks and wondered how he might gain entry. Beyond the dark, lonely shadow of Europe's abode, pale violet-gray clouds roiled, massive rising structures edged in radiant yellow light making the sky a glory of splayed sunbeams.

After a quick observation he discovered a blackened chain hung in a groove at the side of the right-hand gate post. Pulling this in assumption that it would summon a gate ward or yardsman, Rossamünd stood back to wait.

A flurry above him.

A sparrow perched upon the petrified snarl of the bulging-eyed, blunt-snouted dog statue that capped the right-hand post, observing him frankly.

He peered at it narrowly. Was it *that* sparrow, the sparrow-spy of the Duke of Sparrows that had dogged him all the way from Winstermill to Wormstool, come here to watch and bring more mischief? His first reaction was to cry at it to *leave him be!* and drive the bold and beady-eyed mite away. Yet a curious, almost threwdish, inkling made him change his plan. "Hello, my shadow," he said softly to the tiny bird.

It blinked at him in a familiar and forward way, but remained silent.

Buoyed by the delights of the day, Rossamünd carried on as if in amiable conversation. "Does the sparrow-king fare well?"

This time the creature did respond, a single chirrup that sounded ever so disturbingly like "Yes!"

At the report of footsteps approaching behind the garden wall, the sparrow took wing with an irritable squeak.

"Until again," Rossamünd murmured.

"Did you speak, sir?" A sour voice startled him. It was Nectarius, the sleek nightlocksman. He was bearing a truncated double-barreled fowling piece and a vigilant expression.

"Ah—just to myself, Mister Nectarius," Rossamünd stammered.

"Forgot our key, did we?"

"I was not given one in the first," the young factotum answered unconcernedly.

Let in the gate, Rossamünd hefted the several small yet cumbersome chests of his parts-shopping booty thoughtlessly under either arm—much to Nectarius' bemusement. Making some shuffling excuse that they were "really not that heavy . . ." he proceeded hurriedly to the saumery to make treacle.

With a happy flourish he opened his compleat to the thaumacra for Cathar's Treacle and, feeling like a proper skold, gleefully—though needlessly—followed its cues for the making. If he had known how, he would have whistled while he worked, yet instead took up a joyously tuneless humming.

The treacle brewed to perfection, he went—potive, papers and all—to the fulgar's file. Here he found Europe, legs perched carelessly upon desktop, looking as if she had remained in that attitude since their morning's meeting. She downed the plaudamentum and gave a satisfied lip-smack. "Your excursion was a success, then?"

"Aye."

"Do you have a driver for the landaulet?"

"Not specifically . . ."

"However do you mean, *specifically*? Have you found a driver or no?"

"Not a proper lenterman, no . . ."

"Well, *who* then?"

"I thought . . . I thought Master Fransitart could do it, with Master Craumpalin to help him."

Europe's expression contracted skeptically. "Truly? You *thought*, did you?"

"They are far less expensive than hired lentermen," he explained quickly, "and aren't afraid to face dangers when they come." He paused, casting about for something more sellable. "Besides which, Master Craumpalin is a brilliant dispensurist."

The fulgar closed her hazel eyes. "As you like, little man," she said softly, stroking the diamond-shaped spoor on her left brow.

"I have my receipts from buying potives too."

Europe took the papers, cursorily at first but then, looking more closely at the chits, hesitated. "Shall such displays of free will be a feature of your service to me, Rossamünd?"

she said, with a return of familiar wintriness.

He blinked at her uncomprehendingly.

"*Who* is this Pauper *Chives?*" she demanded, mispronouncing the name to sound like the herb.

"Oh, Master Craumpalin holds Mister *Chives*"—Rossamünd pointedly pronounced the "ee" of Chïves—"to be the best saliere in all the city!"

"And your dear master would know, would he?"

"Aye, Miss Europe," Rossamünd declared firmly, "he surely would."

The fulgar raised a wry brow. "Look at your precious loyalty flaring," she said coolly. "I would hope you defend me with the same solemn vigor when others speak ill of me."

"Aye, I would, Miss Europe."

She regarded him for many long breaths. "What, pray, is *that?*" The fulgar indicated a curl of pamphlets thrust up under Rossamünd's left arm. In a fit of enthusiasm he had bought them from a wandering paper-seller as he left Pauper Chïves. The most obvious had its title clear: *Defamière*.

"That is not a scandal, is it?" she demanded. "I thought you more discerning in your reading tastes than to peruse such gossip-mongering poison."

"I got it as a handful with these other pamphlets. They were sold as a lot for five guise by the pamphleteer down on the Sink Street, some still warm straight from the pressing."

"Scandals are the vomit of famigorators and the sputum of pox-riddled gossips, fit only for weathercocks and flimsymen," she said, her mild voice contradicting the spirited words. "I myself have been the subject of more than one barbed article within their pages . . . and most of all in *that* particular paper you grasp there. Almost none of it is true and even less of it maintained with proof. If you are to insist on plunging into the sordid sheaves of the sewer press, then at least read something with some pretension to wit—*Quack!* or the *Mordant Mercer* might suit you better. Otherwise I would stick to the more sensible readers you have there." She nodded to the next pamphlet—*Military & Nautical Stores*—in Rossamünd's slipping grip. "Now! Dine with me, and then your day is done."

Released from duty at meal's ending—parched flake in seethed winkle sauce washed down with a fresh grass-wine that Europe hailed absently as an excellent accompaniment—Rossamünd stared out from the set window as night grew at the green and yellow window lights on either bank of the Midwetter, glad to be lifted away from the claustrophobic city.

Changing out of harness, he snuggled into the unfamiliar downiness of bed in that pitch-colored room and took out his compleat and the pamphlets, ready to lose himself in their delights. Morbid curiosity guided his hand to the large magnum folio of the *Defamière*. A dark thrill thrumming in his innards, he flicked over the first pages, but was soon slowed by the manner of titles he read: cruel jibes and asinine gossip that by comparison made his usual pamphlets lofty works of literature. Little wonder Europe despised it so.

One self-righteously horrified heading line stopped him flat:

Our Lady Squander of Naimes
BECOME
Sedorner?

as related by one Contumelius Stinque ~

The "bee's buzz" – as the vulgar cant goes,

It was accompanied by a crude cartoon of a rather fictional Europe, shooting lightning from one hand and hugging a monster with the opposite, while the trefoiled heart of Naimes hovered in the air beside them. *About all the blighted fabulist has got right is her crow's-claw hair tine,* he thought angrily, barely able to credit what he saw.

The article was brief; written by a certain Contumelius Stinque, it said:

> The "bee's buzz"—as the vulgar cant goes, and come to me this very day from the bumpkin lands

of the Sulk End—is that the Branden Rose is rumoured to have wielded QGU in the defence and release of a suspected yet unproven sedorner. With firm reputation for Erratic Conduct, the particulars of the terrible astrapecrith's newest and most appalling deviancy remain obscure. A Private Voice for the Lady-Rose told of the loss of a most Valued Servant, and it can only be guessed that this may well be a cause of this latest aberration. The identity of the sedorner (accused) remains undisclosed.

The printing and distribution of pamphlets within a city was typically quick—a matter of days. The calculation of the movement of information about the Empire was, however, measured in weeks; for this shocking report to have found its way already into such a gazette was surely a feat of deliberate and malicious alacrity.

The Master-of-Clerks must have sent an agent riding through day and *night for passage on a fast boat to Brandenbrass to get this here already!*

Rossamünd was not free of his accusers yet.

With one angry action he twisted the pamphlet into a tight ball and threw it clear across the room. In distress he turned the bright-limn and lay in the waning light, staring through an open window at Phoebë, three-quarter-faced and rising amid thin inky strands of silver-lined cloud.

The night was old by the time sleep overtook him.

5

OF WRITS AND SINGULARS

Singular Contract, a ~ also known as a personal assignment or simply a singular; an offer of employment made by a private citizen or organization seeking a teratologist to hunt and claim the prize-money for killing a troublesome nicker. Singulars are the private counterpart of the bureaucratic Writs of the Course; that is, official, governmental commissions to slay teratoids. Both can be obtained at a knavery, though singulars, often offering less prize-money, are surprisingly preferred, as typically they are more promptly paid.

IN the clarity of a new morning, Rossamünd rescued the ruined pamphlet from the far corner of his chamber. Flattening it out as best he could, he removed the vile cartoon with its slander of Europe, folded the tearing and stowed it in his wallet. Yet as he supped on breakfast with her in the solar—the finest milling of porridge Rossamünd had ever broken his fast upon—he kept the offending article to himself. *"I told you, little man,"* is all she'll say. *"Tilly fally, it's all spit and dribble! Why did you insist on reading it?"* Instead he asked, "Miss Europe, what would happen if the Master-of-Clerks tried to get at us?"

"He would be a very foolish fellow!" The Branden Rose scowled at him as if *he* were the offending subject. She was at queenly ease in a soft robe of darkest green streaked with curling waves in cloth-of-gold. Two embroidered orange crawdods reached up from either hem, their great spiny feelers curling up to the collar and out over either shoulder. Her hair was held up by a rounded comb of dappled jade, thrust straight down into the mass of locks. Since he had known her, Rossamünd had not once seen her looking ruffled in the morning. Even ailing from spasmed organs and grinnling bites at the Harefoot Dig she had kept an air of fathomless repose. "I do not doubt the blaggardly little fly will seek yet to buzz in my face. Let him go to his buzzing and discover how heavy a blow a peeress of the Empire can bring. As for now, I shall not be bothered by him or any other—the lords of Naimes are not so easily troubled."

Were it not so far from one end of the dining table to the other, Rossamünd might have leaped up and given the fulgar a hug.

The Branden Rose, however, did not notice such lifts of fine sentiment. Rather, as she ate, she picked through a hefty stack of letters and calling cards, reading some, tossing others aside with an impatient sniff. "One might think that after so many refusals these dreary people would tire of inviting me to their dreary routs. Yet no . . ." She lifted an unfurled fathom of glittering card dripping with seals and crimped ties. "I am scarcely arrived and . . ." She made as if reading the card. "To her most irritable Duchess-in-waiting, Europa of Naimes; please come and stuff yourself piglike on twelve dozen courses at my interminably dull fête as our most honored patron and garnish to dessert. With all respect and starved felicitations, et cetera, Lady Tish Tosh of Beanpaste."

Unsure if she was angry or making fun, Rossamünd stifled a laugh in his juice-of-orange.

The heiress of Naimes dropped the offending favor to the floor. "All these fat magnateers and low-order peerlets want me to give their tawdry turnouts legitimacy. I will not be made the ornament of some upstart's public posturing."

Having never been to even a humble country fête, Rossamünd would not have minded one jot to be an ornament at a rout, however small or tawdry. He wisely kept this to himself.

Europe picked up another card. This was smaller, a sedate gray with scant decoration beyond finely formed writing. "Fortunately," she said after a quick reading, "*some* are worthy of an answer . . ."

From out in the yard came the grinding of feet on the gravel. After a gentle knock and a murmur of greetings in the vestibule hall beyond the solar door, Mister Kitchen eased himself in to interrupt their breakfast.

"Lord Finance, m'lady," he offered in the tone of an apology.

"Of course it is." Europe sighed heavily, waving her hand like a capitulation and allowing in a well-fed, smartly dressed man of later middling years in the almost feminine curls of a natural wig of pale blond and a frock coat of magenta silk.

"My lady! My lady!" he declared with all the vigor of a cheery spring day. Possessing a particularly long and narrow nose, rouge-rosied cheeks and wide, sparkling, cheerful eyes of the thinnest blue, he was the very picture of the perfect grandsire.

Europe regarded the man with curiously candid fondness. "Finance, dear fox, you come to me so soon, sir," she said. "Are there not more pressing wants of state to occupy you?"

"No need of our state is more pressing than the well-being of its next duchess, noble lady," Mister Finance returned with unfazed and frank affection. "And slander's wings are swift!"

The heiress of Naimes peered down her shapely nose at him.

"I am beginning to apprehend the most peculiar reports of you, gracious lady, of sedonition, QGU and the taking of a child in replacement of dear departed Licurius . . . And here I find that at least one portion is true and now wonder upon the rest." He looked askance at Rossamünd and then abruptly bent to him half a bow. "Hello to you, sir. I must say, your arrival brings complexity."

With a clatter of chair legs the young factotum stood and simply said, "Good morning, sir."

"Rossamünd Bookchild," Europe made introduction. "Here is Lord Idias Finance, the Baron of Sainte, Captain-Secretary and Chief Emissary of my mother's diplomatic mission here in Brandenbrass."

"A society child." The Baron of Sainte seemed to beam, yet regarded Rossamünd narrowly. "Delighted. You must possess *remarkable* parts for my lady to take you on, sir . . ."

"I—uh . . ."

Europe intervened, a wily glimmer in her eye. "He is everything I require, Baron."

The man smiled warmly. "Of course, of course." He became quickly grave. "The Duchess has expressed most pointedly her regrets at Licurius' passing—"

"I am sure she has," the fulgar said heavily. "Enough with your subtleties, fox! Out with it now; why have you come to me so promptly?"

The Baron dipped his head obediently. "I have come so that I might give your mother, the Duchess Magentine, a better report of your wielding of quo gratia than the worrisome distortions that bruit and rumor will bring."

Europe blinked slowly at him. "You may *tell* my mother that its use was just and apt and done in the defense of the defenseless."

"It is said, gracious duchess-daughter, that this *defense* was done for a . . . a sedorner . . ." The barron's voice dropped ever so slightly.

Sitting once more, Rossamünd felt the man's regard turn to him and kept his attention on his porridge.

"A flimsy pretext devised by dastardly men of creeping ambition," the fulgar declaimed, "seeking only to magnify themselves at others' cost and so cover their own scheming."

"Ahh, the fall of Dido writ small," Finance murmured, his bright, unconvinced eyes belying his smiling mien.

"Indeed." The fulgar's tone was frosty, yet her own gaze glimmered with amusement.

"That is all, gracious lady?"

"That is enough . . ."

The Baron drew a highback out close to Europe and sat. "You must know that unkind eyes are upon you, that your application of QGU weakens you, especially under such . . . *confused* circumstances."

Weakens? Rossamünd repeated inwardly, innards sinking in dismay. *What trouble have I brought?*

"I know it, sir." Europe's hazel eyes became genuinely hard.

Standing, the Chief Emissary conceded with a gracefully extended bow.

An inordinately loud pounding at the front door was soon followed by the reappearance of Mister Kitchen bearing offers of coursing work delivered directly by scopp from the knaving house. Come as a parcel, the offers were covered in black leather and bound with black ribbon.

"And timely too!" Europe pronounced, and immediately sent summons for Mister Carp. "You must excuse us, my Lord Finance. I have work of my own, as I am sure you do too."

"Absolutely, m'lady!" Finance proclaimed, and stooped once more.

Rossamünd smiled to himself. *He certainly likes a good bow.*

"My role is ever a restless one and I must be away." The Chief Emissary bent in the middle one final time. "Good day to you . . . and to *you,* Mister Bookchild," he said with a last skeptical glance to Rossamünd, and left the way he had come.

Climbing after his mistress as she proceeded to her file, Rossamünd peered uncertainly at the offers, seltzer-light gleaming dully on the binding ribbons.

Taking a seat by the fresh-stoked fire under the painted

gaze of her child self, Europe undid all the ribbons and wrappings and drew out a card paper coverfold fat with individual handwritten sheets.

Sitting meekly upon a low soft turkoman beside her, Rossamünd watched intently as the Branden Rose read through each document and placed it either on a low table before her or—the smaller pile—on the seat beside her. Soothed by the hearth's warmth, Rossamünd began to read.

"The only Imperial Forms offered are those seeking aid for your old masters at Winstermill," the Duchess-in-waiting said finally with slow distraction and abruptly reviving him. "They are very much the same as the one I responded to some months ago when I met you there."

Rossamünd nodded glumly. Whatever ruin the despicable wiles of the Master-of-Clerks had achieved, the young factotum still held a deep connection to the beleaguered lamplighters of Winstermill themselves.

"As for singulars . . . ," Europe continued, "they have sent a goodly many—the Idlewild is not alone in its troubles—but most are too far or pay too little. I think one or more of *these* will answer . . ." From the small collection beside her she placed three writs on the floor before Rossamünd.

A curiously grim excitement knotting in his gizzards, Rossamünd bent over them to see.

The first read:

Only for the fittest and most thewsome teratologist ~ A necrophagous seltling by reputation
named as the Swarty Hobnag is pestering the par-

ish tombs about Spelter Innings in the Polder Nil. This vile blight on the innocent lives of men has already slain two boundary wardens and keeps all peltrymen, gentry spurns and labouring hands frighted away. The mayors and notables of the parish offer two sous for each day's journey there, twenty sous for driving the thing off and a further twenty for proof of its destruction.

"Excuse me, but a necrafugous who?" Rossamünd quizzed.

"A necrophagous seltling—a corpse-eating nicker." The fulgar sounded jaded. "A monster that eats the dead."

"Oh."

The second went:

A pastoralist of substance and situation with vasty properties in the north-o-west meadows of the Hollymidden between Broom Holm and Holly-midden, and along with his neighbours, men of the same noble stripe, seeks assistance to rid his flocks and fields of a tenacious tribe of murder-ous blightlings. He has exhausted all personal and local solutions and seeks for a doughty city knave to clear his lands of threat. All billet and board will be provided at his own expense and a single generous prize of one hundred sous is guaranteed for evidence conclusive of the plaguing beasts' destruction.

The objects of both these jobs sounded foul enough; though it was a higher prize for the second contract, each could be any kind of hungry bogle simply seeking sustenance and not necessarily a true wretcher.

The final singular was the highest paying:

> A chance for extraordinary renown in the green beauty of Coddlingtine Dell and Pour Clair! The Gathephär, a locally famous nicker long thought destroyed by the region's ancient forebears, has arisen and will not be shifted. Families devoured hand and foot, remote high-houses found smashed and bereft of their dwellers, hams and villages starving for lack of regular supply—the complete tale of a most thorough haunting. An opportunity for memorial deeds no mighty catagist worth their fame should pass over. Eight sous a day alone for time spent traveling there and fro, a return of fifty sous simply for taking the work and making the journey, plus collected prizes from a gathering of interested parties to the total of two hundred sous. Arriving enquiry can be directed to the masters of either municipality.

Two hundred sous! A lamplighter would take a decade to earn as much. More than forty sous, one hundred sous, *two hundred* sous! With such vast amounts offered for a single job it was little wonder people risked wind and limb to turn teratologist.

Attached to the final singular was a covering notion, evidently added by a third party. It read:

OFFER OF CORPORATE GLORY ~ A pistoleer, a skold and a laggard have entered pact together to rid the world of this historied beast, the Gathephär. In such capacity they now require a fourth member in their undertaking to ensure its complete success. Expenses and Energies will be shared. REWARDS will be divided equally at the anticipated triumphant completion of the accompanying singular work-bill. Panegyrists and pens also welcome for a set fee. All enquiring parties to refer aforementioned work-bill to the underwriters at the Letter and Coursing House, the Spokes, else seek Aristarchus Budge, Gntlmn & Lockstrait, at the Laughing Spectioneer hostelry, Saltenbrink Street, Pawnhall.

"If this is such a chance for *extraordinary renown* and *corporate glory*—and pays so well," Rossamünd wondered aloud, "why is this Mister Aristarchus Budge fellow looking for help? Why has no one else taken it before?"

"In part I would surmise for its location," Europe said matter-of-factly. "Some would have it that the marches of Coddlingtine Dell and Pour Clair are too near the Pendle Hill—a place where people are held to be a touch, shall I say, *insular*: backwoodsmen—all cousins and next of kin and wonderfully cross-eyed. False-gods are said to be worshipped there by folk hidden away so deviously my cousin duke's most cunning servants rarely reach them, and if they do, seldom return alive."

False-god worshippers? The young factotum could bare reckon it. *Fictlers,* they were properly called—bloodthirsting souls who gathered together for perverse reasons not clearly fathomed, seeking to summon up their chosen falsegod, thus bringing the destruction of all land-born creatures, whether everyman or ünterman. Despite such dark repute, most city folk held fictlers to be nothing more than a puzzle-headed nuisance.

"More the likely though," the fulgar continued, "is that the beast itself is too much for most. This Gathephär is of notorious antiquity, and the greater the prize, the greater the chance of an untimely conclusion to your days. Yet, what other hands avoid, I seize . . . Besides which," she finished with a wry look, "this singular offers the kind of traveling I desire."

"Would you join with this Gentleman Budge fellow and his *pact,* Miss Europe?"

She looked up at him sharp and quick, a mild frown rumpling her forehead, holding his gaze for a moment before returning her attention to the remaining documents in her hand. "No, I would not," she said.

With a disconcerted blink, Rossamünd read the job-bill again. *The Gathephär . . .* He felt as if he might have read of it once in some obscure pamphlet footnote. It certainly sounded terrible enough: a creature emerged straight from the rumors of history.

"Tell me, little man, which would you take?"

He stared at the three papers, willing one of them to give him the right response. *I don t want men to die, but neither do I want nickers needlessly ended . . .*

Europe shifted in her seat.

"The third job," the young factotum declared without certainty. "That Gathephär basket sounds nastiest, the people the most needful if their prize is anything to go by, and . . . and nothing can stop the Branden Rose," he finished a little lamely.

"Hear, hear," Europe concurred with bland irony.

In truth Rossamünd had no notion which nicker was worst; he would simply have to make the best of the course once it had begun.

The fulgar peered at him. "I think that we shall actually take all three."

Rossamünd's innards sank.

This was going to be harder than he thought.

"The path they make will lead us in a circle of sorts out of Brandenbrass and back again," Europe continued, "if we take them in the order you have read them. A fine spell of coursing. It will keep us out for a fortnight or even a month, which shall be timely given the current fuss." She paused, almost pointedly. "So, Rossamünd, you will need to take our selections to the knavery—and return these," she said, indicating the pile of unwanted writs. "Tomorrow you will set to work with Mister Kitchen to ready the landaulet and its stores. This coming Domesday you may have as a proper rest—I am not so severe as to deny you a chance to take your ease—yet I will have us on the road by Solemnday."

93

Upon returning with Mister Carp to the Letter and Coursing House knavery, Rossamünd was dismayed to discover
that the Singular Contract for the corpse-eater at Spelter
Innings had been filled that very afternoon by—on Carp's
inquiry—a certain wit by the name of Fläbius Flinch. The
man-of-business quietly recommended that the other two
jobs would do, and Rossamünd followed his advice. So, to
the clerical music of turning pages, of paper shuffled, of
quills licked, the knavery count was marked, two repre-
sentations were made, a pair of bills of attainment were
filled, the attainment-money was paid—the mighty sum
of fifty sous!—and a single certificate of recompense was
franked.

An obstruction of wagons on the Dove slowed them on
their way back to Cloche Arde, forcing them to go one
leisurely clop upon another beside the city-bound woodlands of Moldwood Park, brooding, quiet and impossibly
threwdish.

*How can such land stay like this in a city as old as Branden-
brass?* Rossamünd marveled. Continuing the thought aloud,
he said, "Don't powerful people want to build tenements
and mills and foundries on it?"

Carp blinked at him. "Build tenements and foundries on
what?"

"On the Moldwood."

"Oh." Carp smiled stiffly. "Spoken like a true Brandenard," he said dryly. "A permanare per proscripta is a powerful thing, Master Bookchild. Besides such, we greatly
esteem our broad garden spaces here; it is a mighty city

indeed that can waste ground in such a pretty fashion."

Indistinctly from somewhere within the trees, Rossamünd was certain he could hear distant music. Volume ever shifting, it seemed a peculiar, twanging, crashing tune, wild and rolling, the vague hints stirring his soul at turns with grim earthy excitements or foreign, sorrowful longings. "What is that music?" he asked, leaning out of the dyphr to hear more.

To this the man-of-business gazed absently for a breath at the slow passing park and simply shrugged. "Brandenbrass is a puzzling place for those not acquainted with her," he concluded unsatisfactorily, and flicked his horse to pick up its pace.

Reentering the gate of his new home, Rossamünd passed a lank-haired fellow exiting the grim town house wearing a cingulum of black edged with white and a look of scarce-contained dismay. By the calibrator in one hand and the thick book in the other, the young factotum recognized the man as a variety of concometrist. As Carp passed him without the merest acknowledgment, the fellow gave Rossamünd a brief and mournful glance, a worldly weight heavy in his gaze and a hungry hint of envy too.

"Hallo, sir," Rossamünd greeted him, wondering how it was that a person of such noble profession should look so careworn.

"Well-a-day," the concometrist replied without conviction, going on and out of the gate.

"Oh, he was a simple illustrator" was Europe's explanation of the stranger, when Rossamünd returned to her file. "One of the many mendicant freelancers who seek me out for my patronage. The fleas take scant time to infest the new-washed dog. This fellow was the second imagineer to come in as many days, asking if I had need of a fabulist to prepare etchings of my travels. Our course will be crowded enough without some inky booby slowing me up to scribble all *and* sundry too."

Carp sniggered.

"He looked sorely hipped, Miss Europe," Rossamünd uttered before thinking. "You might have let him draw you something for a fee. Concometrists are noble fellows," he concluded.

The fulgar, who had been scribing in her ledger, looked up at her factotum slowly, fixing him with a steely inspection. For a long moment she held him so. Then, eventually looking down to her book again, she said, by way of shifting subject, "What of my submissions to the knavery? They proceeded simply?"

"Aye, Miss Europe, though the . . . the singular for the corpse-eater was taken."

"Who took the contract?" she asked

"It was Fläbius Flinch," Mister Carp interjected, his tone weighty with meaning. "Filled at one of the parish knaveries."

"Hmm," Europe murmured, with a slight curl of lip and a contemptuous cluck of tongue. "That oily toad still lives, does he . . ." She picked at some spot on her coat hem. "Too bad for you, little man: it was my intention to let you receive the entirety of the prize for that writ, but now I guess you must forgo the forty sous."

"I guess I must, Miss Europe," he replied in honest indifference. "It does not worry me."

"Truly . . ." The Branden Rose looked long at him again with feline calculation. "An easy boast for you, Rossamünd, when it is another who puts the food on your table and a roof above your sleeping head."

Stung and painfully aware of the man-of-business standing only a pace to his right, Rossamünd could conjure no answer. Instead he looked determinedly at a silk painting immediately behind his mistress—a twisted, strangely posed heldin aboard a flimsy curricle spearing a sea-nicker through the cranium—and kept black thoughts at bay.

"So we are off to remote adventures again, little man!" Europe spoke into the uncomfortable moment with a sudden and strange lightness that Rossamünd did not recognize.

Keeping check of his soured temper, he placed all the knavery documentation and the fifty-sou folding note in her expectant palm.

"Before I forget it, Mister Carp!" The fulgar shifted subject as rapidly as she took the papers. "Write up a presage exemption for our young extravagant here—I do not want the best treacle-tester this side of the Marrow to be suddenly bundled away into naval service by some uppity press gang or a short-listed arming contractor."

In a moment she had taken Rossamünd to the depths of shame and then lifted him to a bliss of gratification. *The best treacle-tester this side of the Marrow . . .* , he repeated to himself glowingly as Mister Carp obeyed, rummaging the lock-safe bureau at the near corner with silent efficiency.

A knock at the door brought with it the arrival of Kitchen at the head of another guest: a moderately tall man in long black soutaine, his short, equally inky hair slicked and sleeked back over the dome of his slightly flattened skull. Europe rose and stepped out from behind her marvelous desk, greeting the somber fellow and introducing him to Rossamünd as Mister Oberon, Companion of the White, eminent surgeon and examining transmogrifer. "He has come to make sure my innards have stayed in their proper trim after my excursion to Sinster."

The serious transmogrifer gave a gracious nod to all three. "*Ut prosim*—that I might be useful."

Rossamünd returned a gracious bow of his own.

A real and living transmogrifer!

"Allow me to name my factotum, Mister Rossamünd Bookchild." The fulgar completed introductions, to which Mister Oberon let slip only the mildest surprise before returning to a fixed, opaque expression. "Mister Bookchild," he intoned with an oddly deep voice, gray eyes searching the young factotum's face, as if seeking to know him entirely by sight alone.

"I thought it was illegal to transmogrificate in the Empire, sir?" Rossamünd asked a little carelessly, to distract this untoward inspection.

Europe gave a laugh of open delight.

"That it is, sir," the transmogrifer conceded, "though a discreet exam of an existing mimetic construction is not."

"You must forbear with my factotum, Mister Oberon,"

MISTER OBERON

the fulgar said almost indulgently. "He is diligently after my welfare."

Rossamünd did not know whether she sought to mock him or encourage him.

"As all good employees should be, I am sure," the transmogrifer said flatly, with a nodding bow.

Midafternoon saw the advent of a thin, superciliously smiling gentleman in dark and deeply fashionable gold-striped purple, with volumes of white ruffles gathered at neck and cuff. After many ingratiating bows he introduced himself. "Brugel, Master Gaulder and Armouriere, presenting himself for your eminentical service, sir."

He soon had Rossamünd pinned in rough cuts of sumptuous cloth intended for his new harness. For well beyond an hour the young factotum stood arms in, arms out, legs apart, legs together, in constant worry of being pricked by pin or needle. All the while Master Brugel paced about him, squinting, tapping his lips with his forefinger and calling numbers and obscure instructions to his dogged grayhaired assistant.

"I shall make you the most splendorous man of your trade," the armouriere enthused melodiously.

Trying to keep his neck twisted away from tickling threads, Rossamünd was not sure such promised splendor was worth it.

Evening came, Brugel left in his fancy-carriage and, the examination of Europe complete, Oberon departed too. Having delivered up her nightly dosing and taken his seat at the farther end of the solar, Rossamünd asked after her health.

"Most excellent," she declared, her eyes twinkling with self-contained triumph. "My repairers in Sinster exceeded themselves. Mister Oberon pronounced me better knit than I have ever been: I am in my fighting prime, it would seem. A happy reversal of my . . . *distress* in the Brindleshaws, would you not say, little man? Your valiant rescue was not in vain."

Rossamünd smiled, ducked his head and nodded.

Indeed, the fulgar was in such high spirits that she allowed him to remain with her in her file that evening, sitting by the fire in the crackling, ticking quiet under the defiant gaze of Europe's childhood portrait. While the Branden Rose perused the pages of massive garlands—half a person's size and delivered to her that very afternoon by Master Brugel—Rossamünd sat at a low table to organize the castes and salperts purchased the day before. There was the Frazzard's powder from his days with the lighters, and the less flammable beedlebane too. Loathly lady and botch powder were prescribed to frighten a foe and knock a soul unconscious. In place of evander, Pauper Chïves had provided levenseep, claiming it to be the superior restorative. By these Rossamünd laid out cylindrical wooden thennelevers of glister—dust to stun and daze—and beside them he placed with utmost care what looked very much like large geese eggs dyed a glaring red with waxen crowns of emerald green at both ends. A lepsis, so Pauper Chïves had named it, holding a powerful script known as greenflash, ". . . Bursts with a mighty flash of levin-fire like some thermistoring fulgar," the script-grinder had explained. "Handle it with grace," was the added warning. "You must throw it at least ten yards, else suffer its fury."

Safe and snug in a padded silt-cad were three dozen castes of hard glossy black glass, each holding a dose of what the saumiere called asper, and which Craumpalin held in awe as being "one of the nastiest repellents thy can use this side of scourging."

The young factotum stared in wonder at these and yet more all laid before him.

"So this is where my money went," Europe said, looking up from her perusing. "One would think you a true skold. But *who* will you hunt, I wonder . . ."

Rossamünd gave a bemused grin and then carefully found a place for each script in the digitals, assembling the more healing and helpful potives in his stoups. When all was arranged, then rearranged according to what he reckoned he would need most or least, he set himself to write letters on paper borrowed straight from the fulgar's great desk.

The first was a brief missive to Sebastipole, the lamplighters' agent, serving the Lamplighter-Marshal against wrongful accusation down in the Cousidine.

After this he scribbled three simple lines to Doctor Crispus languishing still in Winstermill, leaving off any distinguishing detail but his name for fear of the prying suspicions of the Master-of-Clerks and his mindless staff of loyal cogs.

His thoughts turned to Threnody, cornered by cunning questioning into betraying him at the inquest. She had looked in great distress when her betrayal was fully played, and he wanted to tell her that he understood, that he bore her no grudge, that he was in a far better situation now. However, Rossamünd well knew that Threnody was fractious and changeable, and he could not be certain she truly cared to receive such a communication. They had fought together, shed blood together, survived together, but still he did not know if his words would be welcome.

Ahh!

After a long time simply staring at the blank letter sheaf in a spin of indecision, he gave up on the notion and instead set about penning something to Verline. Yet even *here* he could not think of what to say. It was impossible for him to write to the beloved parlor maid and keep the full truth of events from her, yet how could he compose the unspeakable? He tried one line on a fresh sheaf:

> We are all waiting for the monster-blood tattoo
> made of my own blood in Master Fransitart's arm
> to show and prove that I am in truth a monster . . .

but with a low, frustrated growl that caused Europe to look up in mild and short-lived curiosity, he crushed the paper with its damning confession and threw it into the fire. He wanted to tell everything and so could not tell anything. Oh! How he wished most desperately that the terrible troublesome truth of those words might be consumed as easily as the paper by the flames and leave him free to live a quiet, simple life. In the end all he wrote was this:

Dear, dear Miss Verline,

I am no longer working for the lamplighters but
have entered the employ of the Duchess-in-waiting
of Naimes as her factotum. I am safe with her, well
fed and well paid.

I hope your nephew is doing well.

Forever your

Rossamünd

6

A DAY AT THE SEASIDE

weed-bunts small flat-bowed, sharp-prowed wooden sailers used by kelpmen to cut through and gather kelp, matted algaes and other seaweeds for either disposal or use, keeping common lanes clear of screw-fouling growths. A ubiquitous sight in any harbor, their operators labor in the hope that they might find some chance treasure churned up from the deeps by storms or the titanic struggles between the great beasts that dwell in the crushing dark.

T HE entirety of the next day was spent making preparations for the knave. In the morning Rossamünd worked in the rear parts of Cloche Arde guided by the ever-humorless Mister Kitchen and hindered by the territorial Mistress Clossette, directing the staff bustling to collect all the necessaries.

In the afternoon he went out to the stalls across the Harrow Road, and there, with Latissimus, the gentleman-of-the-stables, attached a laborium—one of the marvels bought from Pauper Chïves, a cooking-box that abolished the need to make fires for testing—to the back step of the landaulet. Spent but satisfied after a day of such busyness, at mains he ate hungrily.

"So, what are your plans for your Domesday vigil?"

Europe asked over her glass of claret. "Will you lie abed all day? Have a jaunt to the seaside?"

"Maybe a jaunt to the seaside," Rossamünd declared cheerfully. "I might ask Fransitart and Craumpalin to join me."

The fulgar beheld him with twinkling eyes. "Perhaps you could take Master Right's letter of refund to his agents and redeem our crossing fee," she posited. "A small errand. You may keep the proceeds as payment for your effort."

Rossamünd finished his meal with the hunger of the diligent and the rapidity of the excited and retired early.

After a profound sleep, he woke excitedly to a brilliant Domesday morning that glowed with the promise of a day of leisure ahead. Rising with a loud, stretching yawn, Rossamünd stared through open windows out over the mysterious roofs to the pink dawning sky.

Nine days until Fransitart's mark will show. The dark thought intruded, and he frowned at its unwelcome gloominess.

Peering down into the long sparse yard below, he could see a modest flock of sparrows sitting atop the yard wall, scooting and diving and playing chase-a-tail in threes and fours among the runners of a glory vine that spread across its face. Others were darting and disappearing in the compact branches of the cypress, and there Rossamünd discovered one all-too-familiar brother of their kind sitting on his own upon a high branch, attention fixed on him.

Good morning, little spy.

Chattering excitedly, a pair of female sparrows swooped up to land on either side of this lone watcher. In turn the bird puffed his feathers with a distinct air of grave self-importance and made a show of ignoring them utterly. Clearly expecting a different reaction, the female birds flapped about their brother for a moment and made to squabble and fret as sparrows normally do, yet the little fellow would have none of it. He gave a single loud and a rather angry *Chirrup!* that stopped the girl-sparrows still. They seemed to give each other a quick look that—to Rossamünd—appeared to say, *Well, if that is how you want to be!* and darted away, leaving this pompous sparrow-spy to his lonely spying.

Rossamünd smiled at their antics and drew in a deep, bracing breath. Just for one day he refused to be troubled by the insoluble complexities of his life and rumor's wicked work. He washed, applied what Craumpalin now called his *Abstinker*—an improvement on Exstinker reformulated by the old dispensurist in a letter sent from the Dogget & Block—hurried on his old longshanks, weskit and blue frock coat, tested Europe's treacle, ate breakfast promptly with little more than a "Good morning, Miss Europe!" took Master Right's letter of refund and set forth in the landaulet.

It was the strangest sensation to be at such liberty, largely unhindered to pursue his own plans, driven about by Latissimus like some young lord on important business. A feeling of expansion, of being capable of besting all useless doubts and hindering fears spread like dawning warmth through him, and it seemed almost that his soul might stretch out to fill every circuit of the wind. His first port was his old masters' hostelry to ask if they cared to join him while he secured the refund, and after that he would let the day do as it would.

The gentleman-of-the-stables took him slowly by roads he had not yet been, joining all the Domesday strollers and sunshine soakers in their vigil ease. Yet even now under the fancy dress, the parasols, the smiles and friendly greetings, the city hummed with irrepressible haste and industry.

As he stared and marveled, he found that the sparrow-spy was following, the bird making darting, stop-start loops from branch to wall-top, roof-spout to red-painted lantern, keeping pace with the landaulet, trailing them all the way to the Dogget & Block. Glowering his disapproval at this more penurious end of town and the lane just broad enough to admit the carriage, Latissimus let Rossamünd alight at the very front of the alehouse.

"Hold tightly to hat and wallet here, m'boy," the gentleman-of-the-stables warned, and, with a dour look up at the beetling salt-stained tenements, set back for Cloche Arde.

Barely avoiding a trip over a pole festooned with dead rats and mice tied on by their tails and rabbits tied by their ears, Rossamünd entered the pleasing world of timber pillars, hammer beams, high wattle-and-daub walls, eon-smudged wood benches and a crackling fire for a cool spring day. He nodded good morning to a sweet-smelling, remarkably clean scarper sat taking a tipple near the door, a rest between patrons—it must have been his rat-pole leaning against the door outside.

Rossamünd's inquiry of the horribly scarred and one-eyed Casimir Fauchs after his masters was met with the information that Fransitart and Craumpalin were not in—rather they had gone out to find a former-time sweetheart of one of them or some such thing, that it was unknown where they had gone to or when they might be back.

Assiduously avoiding the eye of the collection of musty-looking patrons, Rossamünd sat in a dim corner stall facing the door and, with a jug of pale duke to sip and a crust of bread to gnaw, waited for his onetime masters to come in. Toward the rear of the establishment was a gang of ticket-of-leave men—shore-going vinegaroons living large. These merrymakers, already sodden by the day's middle, banged out a gusty chant:

Twofold, threefold, fourfold, five,

Once I caught a nick alive!

When I tried to wring its hide,

It knocked me down upon me side.

As I went to stand up straight,

It put its jaws about me pate.

Happy then to quit the scene,

I tore the basket tooth from spleen.

Now its head hangs on the high,

Its mark a-puncted on me thigh . . .

Clashing mugs and whole demijohns together, they looked for all the here and vere just how Rossamünd thought landed limey Jack tar sea-dogs should.

An old, rudimentary horologue mounted sideways on

the wall above the small tapery to prove the excellence of its workings quietly tapped away the count of life. Through the magnifying dome of the glass face of the clock he watched the hands wind off half an hour . . . yet no show from his masters. *I'll wait five minutes more,* he told himself several times until forty-five minutes were gone, still without the advent of either aged vinegaroon. After yet another false hope—some shuffling white-haired street seller stepping in for a tot still wearing his cumbersome tray—Rossamünd paid for his beer and walked to the rush and commerce of Tight Penny Circle. There, among the strange red-bricked, blue-roofed market halls, he found several scarlet-doored takenys. Their drivers, sitting high at the rear of the conveyances and dressed in weskits of horizontal red-and-white stripes under coats of blue or bottle green, were simple to mark in the flurry.

"Phlynders & Pugh Commutation Agents, please, mister takenyman," he declared firmly, reading the address given on the master of the *Widgeon*'s recommendation. "It's on the Mill Strand, Subtle Bench—"

"I fully reckon where it is, Master Squidgereen!" the takenyman scolded, and whipped off with a tumbling lurch.

Through all fashions and repair of architecture Rossamünd was taken southeast, passing under no fewer than *three* bastion gates on the way. By one stood the famed Old Gate Sanguinarium with its axiomatic pensioners, the destination of most over-prime vinegaroons. *Stiff as an Old Gate pensioner* went the expression, even north in Boschenberg. Peering up through the takeny's window at the moldering stonework and blank windows, he did not like the idea one mite of Fransitart or Craumpalin ending up here to wait out their last days shut away.

Emerging from between the high buttresses of the mill works and imposing cartel buildings, the takeny found the sea, turning right down the crowded waterside way of Mill Strand. Instead of being protected by a sea wall, the entire district was raised well over twenty feet from the lapping harbor on a great man-made tableland of masonry. Rossamünd stared in wonder at edifice upon edifice of enormous smoke-belching mills and famous mercantile concerns. Plain-gulls and mollyhawks spun and circled in vast flocks above it all, riding on the updrafts of vented steams, adding their squawking discord to the clanging thunder and human bustle of modern industry. Rossamünd thought he could almost feel the great hammering of the gastrine-driven hammers pounding out all manner of metal and stone. He wrinkled his nose at the piquant confusion of stenches: the vinegar sea, foundry fumes, creosote, animal sweat and animal dung, and traces of a more chemical nature straight from a skold's testtle.

"Phlynders & Pugh, Mill Strand!" the takenyman cried, and abruptly halted, letting Rossamünd alight after a fare of a quarter and two cobs—nine guise—before a row of tall and rather similar mercantile clericies.

Alone in the chaos of load-bearing laborers, ponderous ox wagons and mule teams, clerk-carrying dyphrs or flash private lentums, and ubiquitous hurrying scopps, it took Rossamünd a moment to properly figure his destination from among the constellation of small signs arranged on every door up and down the street. His quest was not aided by the presence of many large bills pinned or pasted to the broad door posts, the newest declaring:

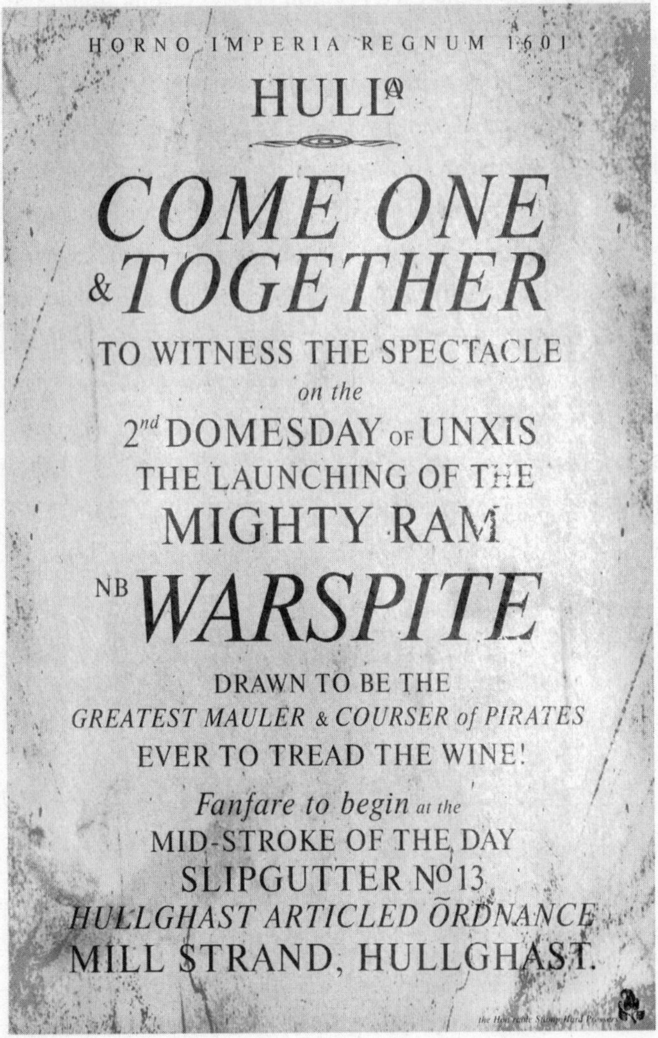

HORNO IMPERIA REGNUM 1601

HULL℠

COME ONE
& TOGETHER

TO WITNESS THE SPECTACLE

on the

2nd DOMESDAY OF UNXIS

THE LAUNCHING OF THE

MIGHTY RAM

NB **WARSPITE**

DRAWN TO BE THE
GREATEST MAULER & COURSER of PIRATES
EVER TO TREAD THE WINE!

Fanfare to begin at the
MID-STROKE OF THE DAY
SLIPGUTTER N°13
HULLGHAST ARTICLED ÕRDNANCE
MILL STRAND, HULLGHAST.

the Hon, and, Slipgutter Company

Finally finding his goal, he climbed the steps and entered a crowded and poorly lit file of pale green where, after a fair wait in line with folk buying tickets to all points of the compass, he was met with a latticed screen of wood similar to those in the Letter and Coursing House. Despite the affable "Good morning, sir," of the clerk behind it, Rossamünd handed across the letter in reluctant expectation of the more common clerical surliness. To his great gratitude he found that the commutation clerk had indeed already heard of the exploits of the Branden Rose and her excellent retainers aboard the *Widgeon* and was delighted to render a return of the crossing fee.

"I hear that you spared us much greater losses, sir," the clerk declared, his yellowed toothy grin obvious through the lattice as he beamed at Rossamünd.

The young factotum dipped his head under such approbation. "Well . . . We had little choice but to fight," he mumbled awkwardly. The refund made—two sous eight—Rossamünd inquired after the location of Hullghast Articled Ordnance.

"You think to attend the launching of the *Warspite*?" the cheerful commutation clerk replied. "Capital notion, sir! It is a good stiff walk south just down the way from here a little. You will make it out easily as you get near."

Taking the fellow's directions down the drab clerical street and out onto the fortified rim of the high seaside suburb, Rossamünd heard his destination well before he arrived: a profound throbbing as if of mighty gastrines rumbled in his innards, and with it a mute yet growing discord of clashing mill hammers and rattling traffic, the din of heavy industry never ceasing, not even for a Domesday. With every stride closer was slowly added a merrier note of happy voices, and soon enough Rossamünd found a mass of people gathering on the seaward side of a great heap of domed and turreted works. Most were squeezed against a tall iron fence that stood on the high seaward edge of the great foundation, kept from spilling onto the road by a platoon of implacable duffers stalking the fringe of the crowd. Cordoned in their midst, safe behind links of velvet rope, many quality folk were stood upon a temporary podium that gave them better view over the hefty railings: the silkened men in periwigs and wide satin-edged tricorns standing gravely as they waited, the fine ladies wrestling with the mild ocean winds that threatened to ruffle their dainty parasols and their dignity.

"Is this the launching of the *Warspite?*" he asked a portly chap in cheap finery.

The man just scowled at him—his expression clear, *What else would it be!*—and pulled away suspiciously as if Rossamünd were some kind of grabcleat pulling a trick.

Dodging the severe gaze of an approaching duffer, Rossamünd squeezed among the assembled to stare down through the bars of the fence. Tall as houses, great gates in the foundation wall had been slid aside, and from them protruded a slipway—a heavy frame of wooden rails slanting well out into the milky brey of the harborage of Mill Pond. Festooned with flags and ribbons and other bunting, it held the mastless hulk of a near-completed ram, leaning down to the water in a suspense of cables and balks, ready to slip into its native element. From the size and shape of her ram,

114

Rossamünd could well see that it was a drag-mauler. By her dimensions he reckoned her likely to be one of the largest of her rating afloat. From fo'c'sle to poop, carpenters, iron-working sheeters and vinegaroons made busy upon its uniformly flat main apron; posts, chasers and all the standard deck furniture were yet to be added.

Below this was the dark sand of the actual shore. Here was the genuine fringe of the Grume, the natural beach—or what was left of it. A myriad of pipes poked from the wall face, dribbling all manner of effluents down the foundation's bleached slabs. Piles of dun green kelp were washed up in rotting thickets right along the sand, making dams of the seeping city filth. Flies of several tribes swarmed about the decaying matter while combers picked through the putrescent sea-mat for flotsam, discarded treasure and rare biological matter, perhaps to sell to parts-sellers or other more ambiguous buyers. Catching a whiff of the rot, Rossamünd marveled at the olfactory resilience of the weed-picking combers.

Immediately below, other humbler people in white smocks labored to pretty the sand about the slipway's footings, employing wide rakes to push and pull the kelp into great piles that the combers happily foraged.

In this cleared space many of the lectry folk—the middle classes—unable to fit on the walk above were descending a narrow stair cut in the stone of the sea wall and daring to collect on the scant beach below, enduring the stink to get a better view of the launching. Seeing some of the younger folk cackling and squealing as they let themselves be chased by the corrosive ripples that lapped at the black sand, Rossamünd decided to join them. Pushing as politely as he could, he managed to find the heavy gate of the stair, and with an inward leap of delight hastened down the steep steps, amazed that he might be able to actually walk on sand, *on a real beach!* Now cheerfully ignoring the weedy stink, he was at once struck by the novel sensation of his boot soles sinking into the soft silt as he twisted through the thinner gathering on the shore and drew near the towering slipway.

Above them all sat the long, mastless bulk of the nascent ram, silent, waiting, fat-bellied, its tumblehome lines pronounced, where they hung high and fully exposed out of water.

Warspite!—Rossamünd mouthed the name, awed by the enormous screw of bright polished silverine alloy taller than two tall men. He started to count the bent heads of the pins that held the iron to the hull but, still on the first strake, lost his place somewhere just past two hundred.

With a great commotion of cheers, of fife and drum, the solemn, wonderful spectacle made of the launching of yet another ram began. One by one, the balks were removed by enterprising men with great hammers and lifted away by sheers, until the pristine, glossy rust brown vessel was held back from its final release by only a single massive cable.

Two-thirds of the way up the dribble-stained foundation by the slipway jutted a balcony of blackened iron beribboned in black and white and emerald green. Upon this three enormous men now appeared: elephantines, the presumed owners of Hullghast Articled Ordnance. Each took his turn to speak, bellowing through wide copper trumpets held up for them by lesser men, addressing the people both above and below with jowly movements of their flabby jaws. Crowded in the scant space behind them, their staff—a gaggle of the usual bureaucrats and secretaries—listened and nodded their approbation in fixed and glassy-eyed rapture. Among them Rossamünd identified three lean spurns—one a wit, and two fascin-wrapped scourges—standing taut and ready, and with them two falsemen reviewing the crowd critically. Automatically, the young factotum shrank from their gaze.

With a final flourish of music, and a "Hurrah!" from the throng and a splash of sour wine on its sharp ram, the ironclad man-of-war slid stern first with surprisingly little noise into the Grume, the workers on its deck riding the motion with practiced ease. A great swirl of milky green waves and the half-done vessel was free, all the pent potential of its gastrines in their element at last, the shackled beast set free. Soon they would be turning, taking the weight of the screw and the vast bulk of wood and iron for the first time.

The former longing to serve a'sea beat a weak memorial in Rossamünd's bosom, making time with the drumming. Yet his enthusiasm for a life in the Senior Service was surprisingly diminished, a memory of hope. Bidding mute farewell to this old dream, he watched sheer-drudges come to tow the new-launched ram to a watery berth where masts, cannon and all the appurtenances of a fighting vessel would be added.

The elephantines were wheeled away through doors in the stone at the back of the balcony, the band packed instruments in carriages and trundled away, and the multitude dispersed until Rossamünd was one of the few still watching on the sand. Wishing to hear the soft lapping of the vinegar removed from the pounding of industry, he decided to take an amble south, away from the slipways and the piers and the sheer mill-side walls. With great expectation he took off his boots and, for the first time ever, walked unshod upon an ocean shore. He squeezed the swarthy sand with his toes in delight, grinning unselfconsciously at the cool air puffing against his cheeks. Insensible in his glee to the filth and kelp-rot, he walked about the many slight curves and bays in the seaside and through the high leg-frames holding aloft the cable housings of tidal millwheels. He jumped over the faucetlike openings of creeks and drains, stopping to examine the ooze and the rippling filament algae in their effluent while swallows darted overhead, dashing to and from modest nests poked into rotten stonework cavities and under eaves, soft clicks in the sky as they snapped at near-invisible bugs.

Farther yet he went until the throb of gastrine enginry became muted to something almost tuneful. In quiet joy he watched the stocky red crabs that diddled jaunty sideways dances, waving cheerfully at him with their singular large claws. With a twist of iron he found half entombed in the silt he prodded at the kelp, washed from the coastal deeps where great forests of the weed grew and made the inshore waters less caustic. A hiss of flight caused him to look up and see a blue heron, neck bent back on itself, swoop in to harry a crab. With a mighty whoop, Rossamünd danced down the strand, waving his hat and driving the bird off before it could make a meal of the pitiable critter. He laughed for pure delight as the heron flapped a quick retreat, winging past him with a single croak and a glare of wounded dignity. *This,* he decided, would have to be the best Domesday vigil of his brief span in the world.

With a hungry lurch in his innards, Rossamünd chewed an insubstantial morsel—a crust end from the Dogget & Block—and pressed on south. Enjoying the lack of urgency beyond his own empty innards, he watched a row of weed-bunts and their diligent kelp-gathering crews draw about the sagging frame of a disused cofferdam and pass a wallowing prison hulk, ugly, black and rusting. He could not help but imagine the poor souls—deserving and undeserving together—mouldering in its dark holds: souls like those miserable shackled people he had seen in the spokes.

A mute fluttering dart and a *Tweet!* above him drew Rossamünd's attention. He looked up to find his little sparrow-spy hopping along the stone arch of the gateway to another flight of steps. It peered down at him in turn, beadily unafraid. In a kindly, thoughtless gesture, the young factotum offered his last morsel of crust to nibble. To his amazement the diminutive bird landed boldly in a bluster of nervous wings on the knuckle of his thumb and pecked with remarkable strength at the morsel, black defiant eyes regarding him closely.

Marveling at this plucky bird, Rossamünd suddenly declared, "You need a name!"

The sparrow blinked at him.

Nothing clever came to mind.

He is brown, I suppose . . . , the young factotum observed rather obviously. *And he dashes and darts about,* he pondered a little lamely, *sooo . . . Darter . . . Brown?*

"Darter Brown." He spoke it out.

It was an odd name, yet the self-important little creature chirruped brightly as if in approval. With something akin to excitement it leaped up to perch on Rossamünd's hat brim, causing the thrice-high to list over his eyes.

Rossamünd drew his coat collar about his neck and continued his little seaside adventure. Back on the sand he walked farther south, following the meager convex strand, Darter Brown flitting along before him, chasing fat, lazy maritime flies. Going about an outward kink in the shore, they came across a boneyard of vessels left rib-exposed in the tidal muds, stripped of iron, masts and cordage. Their chines protruded corpselike from the silt, skeleton wrecks wallowing unwanted to rot in the shallows, sheltering wading flocks of dappled sandpipers and red-legged stilts.

Maybe a hundred yards away on the inward bend of the kink, a group of well-dressed gentlemen were loitering on the sand, looking powerfully out of place in their urban finery. Something oddly furtive in their manner gave the young factotum pause, and one striking fellow caught his particular attention. Standing maybe forty yards apart from the main group, this gent was resplendent in a long frock coat of slick carmine with black longshanks and high bright-blacked

boots; his hair—tied in a whip-stock—was of the most surprising milk-white. Though he knew of white-blond hair,
Rossamünd had never seen such a thing, and its singular-
ity was magnified by the peculiar location in which it was
discovered. Words he did not catch were traded between
this white-tressed gallant and the group. A second individual
stepped from their midst, his baton-tailed hair a more ordinary brown but his attire of iridescent forest green no
less splendid. There was a shout and the group stood away,
scaling the begrimed sea wall by a long, jointed ladder that
they must have brought themselves, leaving White-hair and
Brown alone on the black strip. Another call and the two
were suddenly flourishing pistols, one in each hand, brought
out quick like true pistoleroes testing their speed. The qua-
druple *hiss-CRACK!* of their discharge came as a single stut-
tering report, their flashes of smoke whipped away by the
rising winds.

At the sound Rossamünd naturally ducked as if a mere
bundle of drying kelp could protect him, hands fumbling for
his potives in their unfamiliarly new digitals.

Darter Brown took wing and vanished over the wall.

Both had shot, yet only White-hair went down, folding
in on himself like the closing of a well-made test-barrow.
With a kick of sand in his foe's direction, Brown-hair sprang
laughing up the ladder, his chums peering down from above
sharing the joke. Once he was safely at the top, the ladder
was hauled away and the white-haired duelist left writhing
on the shore alone.

The cold, tingling touch of the encroaching tide on his

121

toes brought Rossamünd to sense. Running as quickly as only partly firm sand will permit, the young factotum approached the man, calling as he got close, "Ahoy, sir! Are you well? Ahoy!" Skidding as he stopped a few cautious feet from the double-bent fellow, Rossamünd bent down himself. "Are you badly done in, sir? Where are you shot?"

"I'm not shot," came the muffled reply, filled as much with impatience as pain.

"Pardon?" The young factotum craned further, trying to see the fellow's face, still buried in the huddle of his arms.

White-hair suddenly sat back and in a fright Rossamünd did the same.

"I am *not* shot!" the fellow insisted in tetchy embarrassment, lean face frightfully wan, hazel eyes streaming. "It was sack."

"Sack?"

"Yes, we load our irons with sack."

"Irons?"

"Yes! Irons! Dags! These!" The white-haired fellow lifted a beautiful black and silver pistola and waggled it irritably. "Firing-irons . . . Pistols . . ."

What kind of person is this? Rossamünd nodded his comprehension. "Do you need help, sir?"

Wincing, White-hair sucked deep, deep breaths before answering. "No . . . no, I shall . . . shall soon . . . soon walk again . . ." Another even deeper and ruttling gasp. "That pursemouse simply hit me in . . . in the bullet-bag—a lucky shot he won't ever repeat . . . but it will teach me for not wearing a likesome . . . *Always* wear a likesome," he said again, in the tone of repeating an instruction.

Likesome? This was a proofed covered frame of stiffed leather some in the fighterly line liked to wear over their groin. Suddenly the nature of the man's discomfort became clear to the young factotum, and, clearing his throat awkwardly, he reached into his stoup. "Might I at least offer you this," he said, producing a vial of levenseep from his skolding collection, "and help you to a stairway?"

White-hair peered at the bottle and then looked a little doubtfully to Rossamünd. "Leven-water, is it? I've not had that since Aunty saw me through the consumptive palsies of eighty-five. Well, thank you, my man." He took the vial and a healthy swig—more than necessary for a single dose—and smacked his lips as he gave the draught back. "There's the business!" he declared more cheerfully, with a couple of rapid, revivified blinks.

Peering about, Rossamünd helped him to his feet, taking the weight as White-hair pressed heftily on him to rise.

"My word, you're a stout fellow," the young man declared in open surprise, shaking sandy grains from his sumptuous coat hems. Picking up his pistols, he examined them intensely for a moment with a deeply unhappy expression. "Sand in the workings," he muttered glumly, shaking his head.

"They look like fine pieces, sir," Rossamünd observed conversationally.

"And well they are, sir!" the white-haired fellow exclaimed. "If you value your life over your purse, you will not spare even double money to buy a good dag: better an empty pocket than a cooling corpse, I say . . ." He blew hard over the locks and flints, cheeks bulging with the effort. With a quick glance to the sea, he returned them to the bright-black holsters hanging at either hip. "I believe it's time to depart. I suggest we go that way." He nodded back north, from where Rossamünd had already come. "The closest grece is there."

The young factotum readily submitted to what he presumed was the man's superior local reckoning. He had felt the sting of the acrid Grume before and had no wish to soak in it again. The fellow shook off his discomfort, and his pace, though at first slow, soon picked up. They walked in silence, the young factotum pondering black beach and white sea, until the white-haired fellow piped, "What do they call you?"

"Uh . . . Rossamünd . . . Rossamünd Bookchild."

"Is that so?"

Rossamünd could not tell whether the catch in his companion's voice was hesitation or the simple taking of a breath.

"How do ye do, Rossamünd Bookchild. I am Rookwood—Rookwood Saakrahenemus Fyfe."

For all his mature airs, this Rookwood fellow was actually rather young—certainly a lot younger than, say, Fouracres or Mister Sebastipole. In light of the fellow's recent humiliation, there was something smilingly winsome and altogether pleasant in his expression, and Rossamünd decided he liked him.

"Who was that other gentleman?" he asked.

"Oh." Rookwood became sheepish. "Uh—a *friend* . . . with a pretty wife . . . a strange turn of humor . . . and an overly

ROOKWOOD

fortuitous aim. Come! Let us be off before we are drowned."

With only a foot of treadable sand left between water and wall, they found a stairway off the beach.

"Here we are, still dry in cheery Pebble Knife," Rookwood said with a wry look to the lowering afternoon sky, the neglected seaside façades and the dour expressions and faded apparel of the few passing people. "This is no place to strut alone . . . Perhaps we can walk each other out of here as we look for a takeny each and then go upon our ways?" he finished, with a look left and right.

They walked north along the shorefront for a time, going by blunt bastion-towers on the right and once-bright paint and once-gaudy awnings now moldy and frayed on the left. Down alleys and blindways Rossamünd caught sight of twinkling pebbly eyes and tall twitching ears, quickly followed—when he tried to look closer—by the hasty bobbing flash of retreating cotton tails.

Rabbits!

In their own progress, Rookwood drew some dark looks himself from lowlier souls. He did not seem to mind them. Rather, walking with less of a limp now, he chatted merrily enough about airy things, and mostly about himself. "Being a Bookchild would make you orphaned, yes? As am I, sir, as am I. My mother perished of the fevers . . ." He paused, reflective, for a breath. "And my father was sunk at sea at the Battle of Maundersea."

"Your father is *Rear Admiral Fyfe?*" Rossamünd asked in astonishment, easily connecting this celebrated name from pamphlet tales and oft-taught lessons of naval matter; his admiration and wonder at this fellow were increasing with every moment.

"Indeed he was!" Rookwood frowned. "The great man himself, who died even as he won himself immortal fame defeating the Lombardy picaroons and so leaving me to the capricious generosity of my aunt Saakrahenemus—my mother's sister and of the main branch of family line," he added in rapid parenthesis. "Under her stringent care I have had a scant living paid at the start of each month that is— *Ah-hah!*" he exclaimed abruptly, interrupting himself. "The Lots grin on us! A moll potny!" He pointed to a lamppost corner where an olive-skinned girl in maid's smock and bonnet stood by a deep black pot sat atop a portable cast-iron stove. "Are you hungry, Master Bookchild?"

Rossamünd most certainly was, and eagerly admitted it.

This moll potny was selling the reputedly famous bunny daube, the dish proving to be a surprisingly meaty stew livened up with scringings and "extras"—as she called them. For a gosling—a half-guise piece—she dished the dark brown mass from the pot into simple wooden pannikins bought for another gosling. Indeed, even rudimentary turnery was for sale.

"With enough money a fellow might never need to own his own kitchen!" Rookwood grinned.

Eating as they walked—Rossamünd working hard to keep the sloppy daube from slipping down his coat front— they found a better quality of street that took them inland.

"If I may, how did you come by your hair?" Rossamünd asked.

"Oh . . ." The fellow made a wry face. "I am told it is evidence of a Turkeman skeleton in our esteemed familial closet, some shameful connection—upon my father's side, of course—with one of our Empire's northern rivals hidden in the shades of antiquity. My aunt will not suffer it to be spoken on, yet here I am as a constant reminder of her shame." He grinned.

"I think too many folk are far too troubled by others' wherefores," Rossamünd said seriously despite his own answering smile.

Rookwood peered at him wonderingly. "Just as I say, sir, just as I say . . . Isn't it always the way of it!" he complained suddenly. "When you are in need of a takeny, they are never there, and when you don't, they are all about you pestering for a fare! There should be a stand of them about that next corner."

Indeed there was, five in a row on Tomwither Walk, a thin curving street of limners and upholsterers and low-fashion perruquiers.

"Harkee, I thank you, young Rossamünd, for your assistance," the white-haired fellow declared with all the manner of one set on departing. "I have places to be this evening and must be away."

"As have I, sir," the young factotum concurred. "And treacle to brew when I get there," he added with an anxious glance to the glow of the latening sun, hiding now behind steep roofs and making cryptic shadows of chimneys and spouts.

"Treacle, is it?" Rookwood seemed suddenly more attentive. "As in plaudamentum?"

"The same, sir."

"I take it then that you are a factotum?" The young man's interest was definitely piqued.

"That I am, sir." Rossamünd doffed his thrice-high and gave a slight yet gentlemanly bow. "Factotum to the Branden Rose," he said proudly, then immediately regretted it as needless showing away. With another bow to cover his error he made to leave.

However, the effect of this revelation on his companion was marked.

"Come, come, fine fellow," Rookwood declared with a new animation, halting Rossamünd with a light touch on his upper arm. "I was so eager to honor my appointments I have done you discredit! You have helped me at my lowest and not left me in my embarrassment. The least I can return is some quisquillian deed as thank-you."

"Oh—uh—really, it is not—," Rossamünd tried to say, wondering just what a *quisquillian deed* might be.

"Please, please! I insist you join me this evening—my appointment can become yours as well; I am diaried to join good friends at a rather well-acclaimed panto-show, *The Munkler's Court*—hilariously cackleworthy, or so I am told. Have you seen it?"

"Ah . . . no, sir, I have not." Rossamünd did not know how to proceed. He had barely met the fellow, yet . . . what a grand finish it would be to step out with this flash son of the celebrated Rear Admiral Fyfe—a hero of both the pamphlets and real matter. On either hand, he had to get back to test the treacle, and said as much to Rookwood.

For a moment the young gent pressed a knuckle to musingly pursed lips. "I propose a plan that shall have you doing both," and even as he said this, he hailed a takeny-coach with an economic wave and a streetwise wink to the driver. "I shall accompany you to wherever you need to be to make your plaudamentum and, that done, you can don your gladdest threads and we shall make directly for the Hobby Horse, where the panto is playing."

Rossamünd hesitated in an agony of indecision. Curious and cautious in one, he agreed, and in the very next breath was aboard the takeny. "I've never seen a panto before," he admitted as they rattled along the darkening lanes back to Cloche Arde.

"Ah, Mister Factotum, then you will be in for a spectacle," Rookwood enthused. "Memories of my first show are still my most vivid. They are like an ever-giving gift; I have to but recall it and I return to bliss. I hope it turns the same for you, sir!"

In the waxing gloom Rossamünd could see scruffy black-coated streetlimners in stovepipe hats emerging to wind the shorter, distinctive red-posted seltzer lamps with their flimsy hooks—slight devices, nothing like the heavy martial fodicars employed by the Imperial Lighters of the Emperor's Highroads.

Keen to have Europe's plaudamentum made and be swiftly away again, the young factotum sprang enthusiastically from the takeny as it drew to a halt in the yard of Cloche Arde, leaving the young white-haired gent to keep the hired lentum waiting. "I might be some time," Rossamünd called behind him, before dashing through the front door of his new home.

"Take all the revolutions of the clock you require, sir!" Rookwood proclaimed munificently through the carriage window, ogling Cloche Arde with untoward fascination. "We have the time, and my friends will happily accept my excuses when they find who it is I have brought with me."

At mains on her own in the solar, Europe cocked Rossamünd a quizzical look as he bustled in to her with her late-made treacle and breathy apologies.

"And here was I, worried you'd chosen naval life after all . . . ," she said mildly, a droll glimmer in her eye. "Ugh! Step away, little man," she said curtly with a flick of her hand. "You stink of the Grume! Clearly your day was spent at the seaside . . ." Her draught drunk, she had no objections to his request to go out again. "I am not your mother, little man, to tell you how best to spend your free hours. I myself shall be elsewhere this evening, visiting with the Lady Madigan, Marchess of the Pike—one of the few folk in this city worth the time—and would have invited you with me . . . But no matter. Go, see, enjoy."

Now that he knew of this option, Rossamünd was mightily curious to accompany Europe and see the manner of person she might call friend. Yet having first accepted Rookwood's gesture, he stayed to his original course.

"Incidentally," the fulgar continued as Rossamünd turned to go, "your masters passed through this afternoon, rather keen to see you. Evidently you did not meet with them today, so I informed them that I have decided they will drive for me. They shall return tomorrow for a proper interview." About to turn back to her meal, she added, "Oh, and there is something waiting for you in your chamber."

Hurrying to his set, Rossamünd found a harness case open on the chest at the end of his bed. Inside was laid the most costly and truly *splendorous* set of fresh-gaulded proofing—evidently Brugelle labored on a Domesday. Foremost was a broad-frocked coat in the richest midnight soe curling with bracken-frond brocade, stitched in cloth-of-silver along its hems and cuffs and pockets. With it came a quabard half rouge, half viole—scarlet and pale magenta—and a sash checkered with the same colors. *The mottle of Naimes.* With the help of Pallette it took the long side of a quarter-hour to have it all properly adjusted. Next, he hung the two digitals—already charged with repellents and fulminants—from beneath his sash at either hip. When all was finally fitted, Rossamünd admired the delicate shimmer of the swarthy silk, the gleam of the silver fancywork, the sheen of the black enamel, feeling like the fine-dressed prince of some sumptuous court. After a quick redistribution of valuables from old coat to magnificently new, he returned, all breathless thanks, downstairs.

Shooing aside his gratitude, Europe had him turn about thrice to show the fine cut, inquiring as he slowly spun, "Tell me, Rossamünd, what play will you see?"

"Oh, *The Munkler's Court*, I believe," he answered with rapid gusto, peering from the front hall through the door into the solar. "At the Hobby Horse."

"Truly?" The fulgar raised a knowing brow. "An interesting choice . . . ," she said slowly and gave Rossamünd a pointed glance he did not understand. "Have a care, little man" was all she said in parting.

"I shall," he said eagerly as he turned to go, yet as he stepped out to the waiting takeny, her warning repeated inwardly like a twist in his conscience.

7

A NIGHT IN THE TOWN

Droid second-brightest star in the Signal of Lots, the constellation presiding over choices and chances; it is the superlative (Signal Star) most sought when testing fate and taking knowing risks, its position in the heavens relative to other lights telling on your future, should you care to heed such stuff—though such scrying is said to be the province of scoundrels, mendicants, and the weak-headed.

Slotted on Paneglot Street in the playwrights' suburb of Pantomime Lane between drab three-story tenements, the Hobby Horse was a brilliant, blatant red, with a domed roof of stark cobalt blue. The apex of the crimson façade was topped with a curling escutcheon in white bearing the head and legs of a laughing horse.

Beneath it, set in hollows, were two pallid statues, the ancient patrons of the stage: the immortal blank-masked clown Ratio in comic pose on the right, and on the left the ageless tragedian Stillicho, wrapped in heavy drapes and reaching down imploringly to high-minded theatasts and common vigil-night revelers alike.

Scarcely missing some limnlass lighting the way of a grog-swaying couple along the street, the takenyman depos-

134

ited the two passengers on the very edge of the panto-going
night steppers. Censured by other takeny-drivers for daring
to halt in their way, and in his own hurry to be off again with
another fare, the takenyman demanded his fee with a snarl.

"If you get this'un, Mister Bookchild," Rookwood said as
he reached for his wallet, "I'll go in for the entry."

The wait at Cloche Arde made the price steep, yet Rossamünd had sufficient change from the original twenty sous
folding money and the refund of the crossing fee and was
happy to cover his share of the night. Intent on some destination well within the blue-and-yellow foyer of the Hobby
Horse, Rookwood took him by the cuff and wheedled them
through the squeeze. Close with a confusion of perfumes,
rumspice and the breath of a hundred souls, the panto house
bubbled with every variety of accent: familiar Bosch, Brandenard with its flatter vowels, near-incomprehensible Gott,
the Patricine lilt, the rolling passion of Sedian voices—these
and more, all raised in animated and amiable clamor. Beg-
garly gleedupes moved through it all, deep trays full of folios

the reason you are so late?"

"Mister Bookchild," Rookwood said, smiling reassuringly, "my chums." With open palm he gestured to the leftmost, a short girl, poorly pale and wrapped neck-to-toe warm in a cloak of peacock blue with a collar of fur in a similar hue. "First may I name Frangipanni of Wörms, come to study skolding at the Saumachutra, dear confidante and rent-sharer."

About her head and neck Frangipanni wore a blue wimple topped by a shaggy hispinster of the same cerulean pelt; across her mouth was a deep prüs spoor—a thick band reaching from ear to ear and darkening her top lip, the mark of a skold . . . With the narrow, tilted eyes of her race she regarded Rossamünd stonily, yet acknowledged him with a curtailed bow.

Rossamünd lifted his hat politely.

"Here, with her excellent questions," Rookwood continued, indicating the middle girl, her face spoored with thin black spikes coming down from either eye to her jaw and wearing a small thrice-high fixed to her black hair with tines, "is Eustacia Brick—"

Glowering at Rossamünd as if to shrivel the very contents of his soul, the girl cleared her throat very loudly and pointedly.

"I mean," Rookwood corrected, "Miss Avaïce—raised on the Brandentown high streets just as I."

Composing herself, the one who named herself Avaïce blinked at him languidly. "Good evening," she murmured.

With a name like Eustacia Brick, Rossamünd could hardly blame her for the change. He doffed his thrice-high to her as well.

"Lastly—yet equally"—Rookwood directed attention to the final girl, most notable in that she wore a high crown of mauve wax-paper—"is Madamielle Trudgette, sent up from the south by her parents much exercised by her *frolics* at home and saving coin for Sinster."

Madamielle Trudgette loured at her presenter, her pale eyes made fierce by the curling black spoors figured completely about them. Wrapped tight in winds of fine, almost gossamer cloth of richly delicate pink, she clutched a thin staff to her side, much like a fuse in dimensions but with a five-pointed star at the top.

Saving coin for Sinster . . . Rossamünd had a sudden flash of Europe as she was in the portrait in her file—youthful, hopeful, resolute on' becoming an astrapecrith. Feeling a strange connection with this Trudgette, Rossamünd graced the pink-swathed yearnling-girl with a slightly deeper beck.

Attention fixed on her friend, Trudgette ignored him completely. "I am only doing as Epitomë Bile or ze Casque Rogine or Violette Lune or even ze Branden Rose 'ave done," she said defensively. "Free from Mama and Papa, I am set for ze life of adventure."

"Well, happy day for you, m'dear." Rookwood beamed. "For my new friend," he said, patting Rossamünd warmly on the back, "is none other than the factotum of the very *same* Branden Rose you so enthusiastically emulate! Is that not so, sir?"

"It is——"The young factotum was stopped in the face of their flowering amazement as each girl stared at him as if he were the Emperor himself.

"Truly!" Avarïce breathed, suddenly sociable.

"'Ow did ze come by such an *admirable* appointment?" Trudgette asked, wide-eyed and now not looking nearly as fierce.

Unbalanced by such rare and open admiration, Rossamünd could not help but boast, "I—I make the best treacle she has ever had."

"I thought her script-fellow was supposed to be an authentic full-formed man who came with a box on his face." Avarïce's delight was soured with a slight yet sudden skepticism. "What is his name . . ."

bright
blue

FRANGIPANNI

"Licurius," Trudgette answered quickly, her accent giving the foul fellow's name a lyrical lift it did not deserve. "But 'e was nicker-killed zis six months passing."

"How did you know?" Rossamünd was a little thrown that utter strangers might have tell of this.

"Because . . . ," Rookwood answered, pulling a folded bundle of paper from his pocket, "we like to know all the doings of the lahzarines and other orgulars." He tapped the top sheet.

The Wasp, it read in gaudy print. It was a scandal.

A small knot clutching in his innards, Rossamünd hoped that the *Defamière* was on this fellow's reading list. Clearly, these four excited young souls were obsequines, ardent devotees of monster-hunters and especially lahzars. Rossamünd peered at them guardedly.

"There, we are all met!" Rookwood declared happily. At the shimmering *hoom* of a gong he added, "Shall we go in?" He grasped Rossamünd's arm. "Come along, the show is about to begin!"

Letting himself be carried along in this bluster of jovial enthusiasm, the young factotum, with his new companions, was shown by a footman through a door to a balcony stall. These were *very* good seats—close to the small stage and looking right over the boards.

Though dim, ready for the imminent performance, the heaven-blue theater was far taller and deeper than it appeared possible from its small front upon the street. Every edge and skirting and corner was gilt-rimmed, the long ceiling painted to look like a bank of fluffy moon-shone clouds warm-lit beneath as if illuminated by the radiance of the stage itself.

140

Every balcony stall was filling with periwigs, gleaming silk, feathery frills and peering lorgnettes, the benches all but taken by scratch-bobs, straw bonnets and tricorns.

Rookwood waved to some associate down in the inferior benches. Rossamünd saw the briefest glimpse of a thin fellow with round spectacles beckoning in return before all useful light was extinguished.

Only the soft glow from the musicians' pit to the left of the open stage remained.

The young factotum's chest thumped in anticipation.

To the swell of reedy nasal piping and clashing tambourine, the stage light flared and the panto began. Before a backdrop of wide idealized wildlands, tableau pines and elegant poplars dotting low and aesthetically pleasing hills, a man emerged from the side shadows. Dressed in an elaborate silver frock coat and silver-gray wig, the fancy's face was paste-white, his cheeks garishly rouged. For all his finery he held an ax that he flourished like some overly eager woodsman. "Lards, ladles and gentlespoons!" he cried with high-speaking elocution and many a *rrr*rolling "r" that reminded Rossamünd of poor Master Pinsum, burned up in the fire of the marine society. "Our opening offe*rrr*ing we b*rrr*ing before you is sure to titivate your humours with its happy hijinke*rrr*y. Here now the Buffoon Courteous Players playing *the Thrrree Brrrothers Hob!*"

The auditorium near burst with boisterous, hallooing applause.

Flushed with enchantment and glad to have been invited, Rossamünd chortled and clapped with the rest as the players pranced a-stage. They wore grotesque wide-mouthed masks with crooked horns and protuberant ears—the classic lampoon of a nicker. Pronking about the boards, they waggled their back-ends at the cackling crowd and cried out with extreme and comic gravity. One farce steadily gave way to the next, and the entire panto unfolded as a bitter invective against monsters, the age-old anger submerged in cheap laughter and rowdy and hissing fun. Rossamünd's delight diminished with each shoddy insult until he was sitting hunched in his seat. Yet beside him Rookwood laughed with such unabashed glee—rocking and hooting his approval at each new and authentically comical novelty—that the young factotum could not help smiles of his own.

Finally the show was run, and in an acme of relief, Rossamünd was bustled by Rookwood and friends onto the cool street at last. Barreling aboard a takeny and on to the next venue without a pause, they were joined by the bespectacled friend seen waving from the benches: Eusebus *Something* . . . Rossamünd did not catch his family name. Tall and thin, with strangely cropped hair, Eusebus was an initiate at the city's sole athenaeum and proved only mildly impressed at the young factotum's credentials.

"How-now, Mister Bookchild." Rookwood grinned as the driver slowly extracted them from the near-riotous profusion of carriages and carelessly cheerful pedestrians. "You did not seem to smile much as the show went on. I trust it was a tickle to your fancybone?"

"Not planning on becoming a ridiculous eeker, are you?" Eusebus offered wryly.

"Well, I . . . ah——," the young factotum began, but was happily overborne by the sickly Frangipanni.

"For the *true* teratologist *and* her devoted servant the contest with the monster is too serious to be so lightly treated," she declared imperiously in Rossamünd's defense, a faint Gottish lift in her accent.

"You would surely know, Franny," Avarïce responded. "I have never seen a more serious teratologist than you, and you *never* laugh at the pantos."

The young skold stared at her coldly, coughed feebly and said nothing.

Unable to goad her, Avarïce turned to the young factotum. "So tell us, Master Factotum," she demanded happily. "Tell us of the Branden Rose."

So began an assault of questions.

"What is she like to work for? Is she overly harsh?"

"Well, she is not overly taut," Rossamünd tried.

"Does she pay well?" This from Eusebus.

To this Rossamünd just frowned, yet their eagerness was undiminished.

"Is she as careless of men as ze pamphlets say?"

Dumbfounded, all he could think to say was, "She is a private woman . . ."

"What first stance does she prefer? Procede sinister or procede dexter? Or does she do away with such formality and adopt perto adversus?"

"I——"

"I knew it! Perto adversus! Like any fighter with a proper, modern mind ought."

"How many *effreins*—nickers—has she killed?"

At this he shrugged. "A lot, certainly . . ."

"I heard she marks her arms with little crosses; is that true?" Avarïce pressed, and went straight on without an answer. "I shall do just the same upon my first kill—none of these vulgar so-called *noble marks* more *common* fighters get."

"Does she add anything . . . well, *additional* to her treacle?" Rookwood inquired knowingly.

Rossamünd could not think of what *additional* part might be so infamously *added* to treacle, beyond sweet-lass.

"Ah yes!" Avarïce added. "Some of Sinster's children like to have sang egregia or extract of goat weed put in their plaudamentum," she said with all the authority of a genuine factotum, "or replace xthylistic curd with lard of Nmis."

"Oh . . ." Rossamünd scowled, recognizing these parts as those that, though they went to make a person brave and strong, were dangerously habit-forming and spoiled a person's soul. "No, nothing beyond the proper list."

"Were you zere when zis Licurius fell?" Trudgette asked, her voice low and shaking with scarce-contained enthusiasm.

Not at all willing to explore such a memory publicly, Rossamünd simply stared at her.

Rookwood intervened. "Come! Let us not swamp the fine fellow with our zeal!"

That very moment, on a street of narrow-fronted countinghouses and clerical suppliers, the takeny overtook a gaggle of dolly-mops on their way to night-working mills and spinning halls, working even through a Domesday. Each was dressed in bright versions of maid's clobber, laughing and chatting and accosting any awkward fellow unfortunate enough to be in their path. Leaning far out from the window, Eusebus tipped his hat to them and sang loud and clear:

Dance with a dolly with a hole in her stocking,
a hole in her stocking, a hole in her stocking . . .

To this the laboring-girls shrieked friendly taunts.

"Come down here, my sweet, and we'll dance ye!"

"Ahh, modern girls." Eusebus beamed, at which his friends laughed heartily, and they passed on.

Though Rossamünd could have with fair accuracy found north, after only fifteen minutes of the carriage's mazing progress in the dark and the increasing fog down rows of storehouses and shipping clericies, he had little notion of where they arrived. Now that the carriage was still, saturnine tollings of floating hazard bells could be heard lolling on the waves—some near, some far, speaking of his proximity to the sea. Indeed, the sweet vinegar stink and the pocked precipice of the Stunt Veil sea wall confirmed it. Across the gloomy street stood a lonely house, four stories tall and built on the harbor's edge right into the sea wall. A green bright-limn hung above its cherry-red painted front door, one of the few lights visible in the miry night.

"What is this?" Rossamünd asked skeptically as they huddled from the damp beneath its eaves.

"The Broken Doll, my fine fellow!" Rookwood proclaimed cheerfully.

"The merry end of the night," Eusebus added, peering

through water-splashed lenses. "Vittles, vino and gaming vices. You'd better hope Droid is smiling down upon you."

Droid? Rossamünd frowned. He instinctively looked up to locate this heavenly light and was foiled by the obstructing cloud, a cloying roof on the night.

"How could Droid *not* smile on such an illustrious young man?" Rookwood returned, grinning at him grandly.

A correct answer from Eusebus to the rough challenge through an iron lattice at the top of the crimson portal had the six admitted by sleek-looking door wards in deep green soutaines. Led down a long obverse as red as the front door, Rossamünd felt shrewd observation from the row of grilled loophole slits on either hand. Through double doors of dark green they were brought into a suddenly swelling din. Here was a wide room of gilt furnishings, confidentially lit by large paper lanterns of white and vermilion, both walls and floor blood-red much as the gun deck of a ram, as if wild and splattering violence was expected. Folk of all stations gathered about oval tables to play each other at cards, lots and calling games. Coins sat in unequal count by each player—golden sous, oscadril billions, grassus from the Gottlands, silvery sequins, larger carlins, Hergott doubles, strange foreign counters of unusual shapes—and with them wads of folding money. Thick and uncomfortably tepid, the atmosphere was heavy with suppressed anger and naked greed.

Chanceries—gambling houses—were illegal in Boschenberg; surely it was the same in Brandenbrass?

Gaggles of admiring spectators collected wherever aristocratic clients played, oohing and ahhing at the twists and tricks, calling encouragements and commiserations as they sought to ingratiate themselves with their chosen sponsor. In his brief review, Rossamünd spotted a wit dressed in an unremarkable gray soutaine, his entire face spoored with a thick blue arrow; a sagaar wrapped in tight hide, wearing the mask of a white horse and gently rocking from foot to foot in the restless motion of the perpetual dance; and several pistoleers with their telltale curling mustachios. While he watched, there came a confused roar of dismay and delight. Cards were thrown down in disgust while one happy fellow in a high periwig gathered his winnings.

Ear bent to Rookwood's brief instruction, a footman in deep verdigris took the six on through the clamor and up broad red stairs to a smaller, quieter room arranged with a trio of gaming tables. One green wall was almost entirely formed of tall grated windows that peered north out on the rain-washed spectacle of Middle Ground at night. Harbor lights glowed dully, clustered in terrestrial constellations of blue and white and the occasional red. In one corner a high-wigged quartet of string-fiddlers sat playing gentle music for the quieter collection of clientele gathered about each table.

"Ahh," Frangipanni declared with a thin, rare smile of pleasure at the sweet melody.

"Hmm, yes, always like a snip of Stumphelhose," Rookwood added, naming the supposed composer and smug in his cultural enlightenment.

"It is Greenleaf Whit, actually . . . ," Frangipanni corrected with a derisive sniff and a slight unhealthy wheeze while the other three laughed.

"Ah . . ." The white-haired gent's face twisted to collect itself against embarrassment.

"Don't worry, my man," Eusebus smirked, patting Rookwood on the shoulder. "It is easy enough to confuse the two; one is a disciple of the other, after all."

"Certainly," the other returned tightly, then quickly went to sit at the available table standing by a massive white hearth taller than a man. "I'm always ardently fond of the fire here . . . Perfectly distinct and excellently warm!"

"You are not playing?" Avarïce inquired of Rossamünd, noticing him hanging back by the door as she took her seat.

"No, miss, I will just watch," he answered, recalling with a twinge of melancholy the friendly games of pirouette and lesquin he joined with Threnody and the lighters of Wormstool, where winners and losers traded only chores. "I might sit a hand for favors but not for money."

"Whoever heard of such a thing!" Avarïce returned.

"Perhaps he is shrewd enough to know that Droid is not in a smiling way for him," Eusebus interjected with a sardonic smirk and an understanding wink to Rossamünd.

The observation held some merit, for Rossamünd had never won a single hand with the Wormstool lighters. "I am not very good at cards," he concurred.

"Sit with us anyway, Master Rossamünd," Rookwood murmured in his ear. "*We* shall teach you proper carding."

"We surely will, my man," Eusebus declared winsomely to the young factotum. "Droid and I are poor friends when I sit the table, so we can lose together, you and I."

At such an invitation, Rossamünd consented, and while

food was ordered—pullet and ramsin broth, slices of warmed vinegar pie and bottles of zin—he watched the fall of cards.

The game they preferred was called flout, where—from what Rossamünd could fathom by the incomplete instruction he received—low cards were high and a player had to bluff his or her way to success. When he finally joined, he kept his face as blank as possible, betting small and losing small and wishing he had a falseman's eyes. Rookwood and Trudgette seemed best at the bluff, winning almost as much as each other, and despite himself, Rossamünd was drawn into the play, sipping his never-empty glass of vin with excitedly careless frequency. By the fourth round, the pot in the middle growing and growing until it was up to nigh on thirty sous, only Rookwood and Trudgette had stayed in too, their own hands spread before them, the want-to-be fulgar already triumphant with red hag and both crocidoles.

Gaze vibrating and unfocused, Rossamünd looked at his hand: red selt, black selt and a black hag—it could not get any lower. Nervously, he laid down his ask—his bet—small as always. Then, rather unceremoniously, he slapped his cards down on the black velvet tabletop to a collective gasp.

Astounded faces blinked in turn at him and at his play.

He had won!

"Ah-hah!" Rookwood exclaimed, clapping him heartily on the back. "Well done, that fellow! Droid smiles on you after all!"

Astonished, Rossamünd beheld the pile of silver and golden and crisp papery loot.

Smiling through their teeth, Rookwood's friends tried to appear as enthusiastic as their white-haired friend over Rossamünd's astounding win.

Perceiving this, the young factotum summoned a footman and asked for more drinks and a dish of the best taffies and glairs for them all.

"Perhaps our new friend might better like the entertainments below . . . ," Avarice offered, only somewhat mollified at his largesse, her voice heavy with suggestion.

"Um . . . yes, certainly." Rookwood rose. "Collect your *earnings*, Master Bookchild; allow me to show you the other delights here."

"I shall come with you," Eusebus declared. "I always do better at dogging than the table, anyway . . ."

Gathering his winnings by shaking handfuls into the ample pockets of his gorgeous new coat, Rossamünd followed the two young men out. Going by stairs to the floor below, his two hosts led him along a broad passage and down a double flight right into the foundations of the Broken Doll.

"If my sire had sent me to the abacus to learn counting as I had wished for, rather than the athenaeum," Eusebus whispered drolly to Rossamünd on the way, "I would do better at the table, I am sure."

"Certainly, Master Euse," came Rookwood's quiet rejoinder. "Yet if you were a mathematician they would never let you within sight of a table."

"So the Lots have spoken, then!" his lanky friend retorted. "Like my nanny-pander used to sing me:

Multiplication is vexation,
Division is as bad
The Rule of Three doth puzzle me
And practice drives me mad!

Alas, I am a student of nature now. Better dogging for
me, brother!"

The pair of young swells laughed as they halted two
floors lower before a pair of heavyset footmen standing
guard over an ironbound door. One footman was holding
the portal open for a couple emerging from the dark beyond, the woman in her tentlike finery clearly upset, hiding her blotched cheeks behind a frilled kerchief. "Why did
you bring me here?" she was demanding, voice tremulous.
"Why did you bring me here? I'll never be able to forget that
poor—" A sob rendered the next few words unintelligible.
"I'll be telling *Mother*—make no mistake, sir!"

Her partner in neat velvet frock coat was bent about her,
muttering rapid apologies. "I thought it might be a lark,
a variation on the usual salons . . . The Archduke himself is rumored to come here on occasion—even *owns* a
share here! And you so often complain of the tedium of
our usual settings . . . Don't tell your mother—we shall go
to Sachette's next vigil's eve and you shall order whatever
you will from the vin-compte . . ." He gave Rossamünd
a brief, almost imploring look, as if the young factotum

might somehow relieve him of his distress.

"The night was already started?" Eusebus enquired of the doorman when the troubled pair had moved on.

"It's yer happy ev'ning," one footman replied, looking them up then down. "The first bout's already begun and we was about to lock the doors and keep everyone safely shut in. But for such select young gents we'll make an exception." He smirked, with a touch to his forelock. "You'd best gallop along, sirs, if you want to make it for the next bout. Hope you like long stays, 'cause we won't be letting you out ag'in till half the bouts are done—can't have folks strolling in and out all night as they please," he concluded. Then, with narrow and meaningful scrutiny to Rookwood's fine pistols, he added, "Them irons better be filled with sack."

Rookwood made a face as if to say, *Since when are they not?* and passed the fellow a flashing silver coin.

Ogling the fine cut of Rossamünd's clobber, the other footman let him by with a wink.

Rossamünd gave a puzzled nod and hurried through.

Immediately beyond they found a tight descending stair— almost a furtigrade—leading to another equally black door. Rookwood pulled noisily on the door's brazen knocker. With a subdued thump the door opened and a young thin-faced doorman stepped out, all polite smiles and expectation. He raised a hand. "I am afraid you must wait, sir."

Through the doorway behind him was a dark blank like the throat of some ravenous sea-nicker. A tingle of sorrow shivered down Rossamünd's backbone—an almost *threwdish* kind of distress. *Here?*

A tiny bell made its tiny silvery tinkle, and they were let onward down a closely spiraling stair of stone, its walls covered with black leather dimpled and glistening. Smelling strongly of subterranean chalkiness and animal hide, the air here grew decidedly colder with every curve down. Rossamünd could hear the bubble of water through the leather and rock, and he imagined the immemorial currents pressing against eroded brickwork without. Were they under the harbor itself?

"Have you been dogging before, Rossamünd?" Rookwood asked chattily.

"Ah, no, sir, I have not . . . ," he answered, beginning to feel out of place. "What is it?"

"Ahh, you shall see. The night ends on a high note for you, sir!"

Achieving the bottom, they passed along a long brick passage lit with oil-burning cressets whose heat made the lime-painted walls sweat. Heavy-proofed men regarded them searchingly as the tunnel took them toward cheering: angry, almost hungry and unwontedly wild. With every yard the threwdish grief waxed, becoming a great weight of confusion and distress and frustrated rage. What manner of event could produce such a terrible cacophony of soul and sound?

"Come along, Mister Bookchild." Rookwood grinned. "By that ovation the first fight must be ending. This is a spectacle one of your caliber and trade will surely relish."

The other end stepped onto a wooden boardwalk that made a circuit behind a whole edifice of stall-boxes, very similar to those at the Hobby Horse. A great array of people were sitting in them: high and low, rich and poor, teratologist and naivine, thrust rudely together, all hollering at whatever was occurring below them with singular fascination. As Rossamünd observed, the whole mass erupted into a great whooping cheer, hands flung up, little tabs of paper flying and falling like the rare snows of deep Hergott winters.

"The cubes bet in a frenzy and the pigeons watch in high spirits!" Eusebus cried, looking happily to the celebrating crowd of said *cubes*—the true gamblers—and *pigeons*—the mere spectators. "Excellent evidence for an excellent night!"

A woman in thick face paint and a too-tight stomacher-dress greeted the older two with a saucy curtsy as if she knew them well and passed small white-daubed paddles to them. Rookwood shouted something in her ear, and she thrust a paddle into Rossamünd's grasp, crying, "Goodly evening, little lordling. Wave your pug to pose your stake! Chance your gooses wisely!"

Bemused, the young factotum took the pug and inched forward in the wake of Rookwood's and Eusebus' passage through the throng until they came to a high balustrade.

"The dogs!" Rookwood held out a presenting hand, eyes twinkling with excitement, while Eusebus pushed along the front row of the stalls to find seats.

Full of bawling, exuberant souls, some clapping each other on the back and others with face in hands, the stalls ran about the entire circumference of a large quadrangle, going up *and* down for several more stories. Below them all was a square pit cleft in halves by what appeared to be a brown iron gutter; new blood was soaking into the hard-packed floor. A proud-looking fellow strutted about its circumference, heavy chain gripped in fist, leading an enormous brindle tykehound, its gagged muzzle dripping gore, its still heaving flanks rucked and bleeding. Flowers and coins and paper rained on the brute stupid beast—half dead from whatever ordeal it had just faced—and its beaming owner. A servant came out to grovel for the spoils, and the man and his dog exited through a heavy iron door in the far corner to the farewell of one final hurrah.

The noise of the audience settled to a pent hubble-bubble.

With a sinking feeling, Rossamünd beheld the remains of what must have been a grisly desperate clash. He had little love for dogs, but to watch them tear each other apart was not his notion of entertainment. Steeling himself for an unpleasant spectacle ahead, he looked glumly about the crowd.

Far across on the opposite side were a set of canopied boxes hung with leaf-hued taffeta. In them sat a congregation clad almost uniformly in dark green and black. Mostly secretaries and spurns, they were gathered about a fellow proud in peacock silks and curly periwig of spotless white.

"Pater Pontiflex Maupin," Rookwood said in Rossamünd's ear. "He is the owner of the Broken Doll and has major interest in *this* place," he said, rolling his eyes at the pit, the stalls and all the ruckus with them.

Sitting on the right of this man was a young dandidawdler in a vibrant harness of blue-green stripe with pink, his throat thickly enfolded in a tortue, a high neckerchief of

155

white cotton. Most remarkable was his silver wig, its fringe twisted up into a pair of horns, its tail long and thick like that of a horse and held by greasy black ribbon. The wig twinkled under the cosmos of bright-limns hanging by hook or chain from the convoluted scaffold of heavy beams that held up the weight of the city far above.

Upon the other side sat a singular woman swathed in black with a flaring collar of black feathers making an unhallowed aura about her pale bald head. Her face was cold, her gaze unkind; a great spoor of a diamond and an arrow combined jutted above her right eye. She was a dexter—a wit and fulgar in one. Instinctively, Rossamünd began making a tally of the costly regimen of chemistry she would need to keep her collection of foreign and contrary organs from rebelling within and destroying her.

"Ah, *that* is Anaesthesia Myrrh," Rookwood explained. "She prefers spurning work to teratology. As much as I admire the lahzarine set, *she* truly frightens me . . ." Some distraction away to his left took his attention. "Euse has achieved only one other seat," he said after a moment's cryptic waving of fingers. "Do you want it, young sir, or . . ."

The dexter looked sharply at Rossamünd looking at her.

A hot flush in his cheeks and cold thrill of fright in his innards, the young factotum hastily turned his attention to his companion's question. "No, no . . . ," he said quickly, not relishing being pinned in among all these fervid spectators.

"Well, how about you remain here," Rookwood advised. "We shall sit out the first half." He shrugged. "Then we shall meet here again to call it even, yes?"

Left to stand at the balcony, Rossamünd crouched on his haunches and stared uneasily down through the posts at the blood-puddle becoming just one of the many stains in the swept earth of the pit, a rising apprehension pressing on his soul. The grieving threwd was so strong in that awful pit, it was almost audible. *Can the people not feel it?*

A clang of metal and a heavy man in a thick buff apron of bright blue stepped through the iron portal, raising a hand to the audience's renewed raptures. With him came two tractors leading a Greater Derehund of exceptional size. Its watery eyes full of death and hopelessness, the mighty dog snarled at the folk of the lowest stalls. The man in blue stopped before the canopied boxes and did honor to his patrons. At this Pater Maupin stood and, beholding the crowd, twirled a lace handkerchief in acknowledgment of their applause. He sat, and a fellow behind him in clerical black called down to the tractor, "Scion of the Geiterwand; which champion do you bring before us to do goodly battle?"

"I bring befer ye Skarfithin, the Blackheart of Dere!" the thickset handler cried in his best in-public voice. "Scion of the Geiterwand; winner o' thirteen full stouches and sixteen halves and as sure a wager as ever prowled the pit!"

More cheers.

"As you say, sir!" the clerical gent returned; then, twisting his attention to the stalls, he cried, "Who dares bid unseen against this mighty friend of men? Do I have any takers? You, sir!" He pointed to some invisible soul well above Rossamünd's vantage. "You appear the all-a'glory kind; will you dare a posit *against* this fearsome specimen?" He swept his

157

hand down to indicate the panting Derehund, Skarfithin.

A muffled, unintelligible cry from on high brought shouts of approbation and jeers of playful derision from many.

"Bravo to you, sir!" the clerk cried, and sat again.

Rossamünd could see several similar clerical fellows moving among the stalls, listening intently to the wagering calls of the chancers, scribbling upon tiny folds of paper and exchanging monies.

Rossamünd craned to see down over the lip of the balustrade to the access that he could just make out below, curious despite himself to see what tribe of dog the contender would be.

With a clunk and a sustained whining rumble the iron gutter now shifted. Rising out of the floor, it slowly became a metal curtain dividing the pit in two. The tractor released his anxious hound and quickly retreated, the beast ravening suddenly, chasing the fellow from the pit and giving Rossamünd a sharp start, though much of the crowd seemed well used to such shocks.

Left on its own, Skarfithin paced before the iron fence, its dripping tongue lolling hungrily, sniffing at the small holes that stippled the iron sheet.

Rossamünd held his breath. He looked up into the stalls to find Rookwood, but the fellow was intent on the beasts in the pit below and laughing and talking with great animation to Eusebus.

A thump and another *clang!* warned that the near door below him was opening.

With a collective gasp the entire audience went quiet.

158

What manner of tykehound was it that caused such corporate dismay?

Rossamünd pressed his forehead against the struts of the balustrade till it hurt, to get a glimpse of the competing dog. When the beast stalked into view, right there, right below him, the young factotum's innards went frigid. It was not another dog Skarfithin was to fight. It was . . . *a monster*.

Out stalked a nicker of the most weird appearance, walking upright with strange angular flexings of ropy, footless legs. Instead of a head it had a long writhing tentacle, with a similar appendage at its posterior end too, its arms of exactly the same form as its legs. Its warty skin was an ashen green, with vivid rings of purple mottling the darker hide of its back, its limbs and tentacles.

This was *worse* than a dogfight. It was a hob-rousing set between selthounds and bogles. *Here* was the cause of the anguished threwd!

Rossamünd's soul revolted. *What have I found!*

8

IN THE PIT

sabrine adept(s) also called percerdieres, lehrechtlers or spathidrils; said to be the cousins of the sagaars, originating long ago in some foreign northern land. Revering swordplay as the sagaars revere the dance, some go so far as to almost worship their swords, ancient therimoirs of forgotten make, though they have no time for devotion to constant motion as the sagaars do. The best of them, those warranted to teach, are known as sabrine magists or master sword-players, and will gather about them a loose association of adepts, serving together for a common ideal.

"GOODLY peoples," the rouse-clerk cried into the stunned hush from his safe seat in the lowest stalls, "I give you the Handsome Grackle!" He flung a dramatic gesture at the frighteningly alien and ungainly creature that awaited its doom in the rousing-pit. "What be your stakes?"

At this the watchers burst with the dispute of wagers, numbered white pugs waving as results were speculated and amounts offered. In the din it was still clear: most seemed convinced of the Derehund's victory.

Fixing his attention on the creature dubbed the Handsome Grackle, Rossamünd could well understand why, for the creature staggered in palsied jerks into the middle of the pit. Staying back from the perforated fence, it turned quickly from side to side, both tentacles reaching out and up, rippling as if they were testing the very air. Feeling a delicate flutter in his head like the gentlest sending of a talented wit, Rossamünd knew the thing was *looking*, searching by means unknown to find an escape. There was something about its parched, knobbled skin and bizarre physiology that spoke more of the vinegary deeps than of the bosky dells or forsaken pastures. As the beast twisted, the young factotum could see in the center of its torso a weird, vertical mouth quivering, making great "O's" as if it were gasping for breath.

Transfixed, Rossamünd swallowed at the clench in his throat, his hand already grasping for a potive.

A shriek of clashing metal silenced the crowd.

With a penetrating *boom!* the iron curtain dropped and the foes were immediately confronted. In an instant Skarfithin was all hackles and maddened, shuddering growls. Saliva drooled from its gnashing fangs; its small red-shot maniac eyes rolled. Without a face the Handsome Grackle seemed little affected: its only reaction was to bend its tentacles and wave them slightly at its canine foe.

Without a backward crouch the selthound sprang, leaping the entire gap between it and the Grackle. There was a frightful crunching like the chewing of a fresh apple as the dog bit deep into the startled monster's left arm, the momentum of the leap bringing both crashing to the hardened dirt. The Grackle did not make a sound as it fell, no cry of agony or shout of fear. Even if it had, none would have heard it as the willing audience let out a roar of delight at its fall. Gripping alien flesh in its mighty maw, Skarfithin shook its head violently until the whole form of the Grackle rocked. Finally some piece of it tore free, leaving a deep purple gash in its arm. The Derehund was not intent on morsels, and struck again and then again. With every chunk of seltling flesh ripped away, the dog's assaults grew more frenzied, not allowing the mauled and flailing Grackle time to right itself.

"Come on, ye mighty daggy, rend the mucky salamander!" were the shouts from the lower stalls.

"Huzzahrah! Mother and the boys'll be supping hearty a'morrow!"

"I declare, bravo! Smash the brute to flinders! My entire purse is on your head!"

"*Bravo!*" came the cries from the high stalls; even Rookwood was calling out with babbling gusto.

Rossamünd could scarce stand it. Without looking, he began counting through the slots of his digitals.

Suddenly the Grackle made a huffing, almost keening cry as, with a great thrust of its limbs, it threw Skarfithin back and sent the dog tumbling to the floor. Before Rossamünd's eyes and all the wagerers' with him, the monster's ghastly purple wounds began to ripple, the flesh bubble and the wounds close.

It's mending itself! Rossamünd stilled his face to contain his delight.

"It heals!" some observant soul across the way echoed, and a hush momentarily dampened the throng.

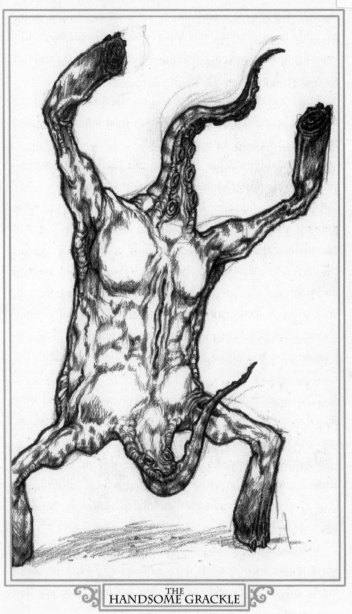

THE
HANDSOME GRACKLE

Undaunted, the Derehund pounced straight back as the Grackle tried to stand, the dog's great teeth clashing loudly on vacant air. Swinging its club-fisted arms, the nadderer managed to bay the Derehund.

Someone shouted, "Ten oscars on the sea-selt!" and the flurry of bets and jeers and mindless exclamations exploded again.

At this mighty noise Skarfithin got teeth into meat and pulled the nadderer's left arm, threatening to topple it again. Yet the Handsome Grackle was not so easily done for. With another austerating hiss it lifted its arm, hauling its foe, still clamped to the meat of its arm, clear off the floor. Writhing like a line-caught fish, Skarfithin growled and seethed and would not let go. The Grackle raised its other arm and, with a quick, powerful punch, sent the Derehund reeling, its mouth still full of monster-flesh, to smack with an unpleasant wet sound on the far wall and slide heaplike to the hard-packed dirt.

Dismayed at last, Skarfithin labored to stand and now paced more warily before its foe, head down, gaze murderous, calculating, its ribs heaving like a bellows.

Surrounded by puddles of its own gore, but its wounds almost entirely gone, the Grackle remained motionless; only the tips of its tentacles undulated minutely, bending toward the battered dog.

Snarling, the tykehound leaped once more, rushing the sea-monster from the left with astounding fortitude, seeking to catch the Grackle exposed as it twisted to face this new assault.

Worried now as much for dog as for monster, Rossamünd could barely watch, and half closed his eyes as the Derehund bit terrible hold of the nadderer's lower tentacle. Tugging powerfully left then right then left then right, Skarfithin tried to overset the Grackle and bring it down. The monster tottered perilously and toppled sideways. Yet it did not collapse; rather, one of its arms now became a leg, a stumped foot became a clubbed hand and the perversely vertical mouth was now more properly horizontal. Still the maddened dog tore and tugged, its jaw locked on soft tentacle flesh, until Rossamünd was sure it would tear the entire limb from the poor Grackle's trunk. With a hiss the nadderer rolled completely onto its other end. Weirdly deft acrobatics had it standing upside down, both arms now legs, both legs now arms, and Skarfithin was lifted high as the lower tentacle became the head.

Still the Derehund would not let go. Dangling, its growls like small thunder heaving in its throat, legs scrabbling and twitching impotently, it kept its hold.

The disconcerting maw of the Grackle gaped wide, its sphincterlike lips quivering, revealing row on row of rasping ridges. *Its teeth!* With a shrug it flexed its surprisingly powerful head-tentacle—dog and all—and swung the tenacious Skarfithin right into its open mouth. The rippling lips closed about its middle with a wet slap and a collision of bones.

The crowd was stunned silent.

The Handsome Grackle had bit Skarfithin, the Blackheart of Dere, clean in two . . .

In the quiet Rossamünd could hear a faint, breathy wailing coming from the victor as it flicked the dog's now lifeless head and shoulders splatteringly down.

Skarfithin had lost—and with it almost every soul in the room; though by the count of the losers, Pater Maupin and any other associate of the pit had done well. Mute shock quickly became a murmur of malcontent.

Clearly unsatisfied at the outcome, a brave soul leaped from the stalls down into the pit. He was a strangely dressed fellow in an odd, folded hat of red cloth, gathered over itself and tilting over one ear. For proofing he wore a short-sleeved frock coat of buff dyed dull olive, undershirt puffed over his elbows, thick black vambrins protecting forearm and hand, a red sash about his waist. The fellow wore no protecting boots, rather soled hose, one leg white, the other bright yellow and patterned with the figures of twisted black laurel-fronds. This was a sabrine adept; skilled at swordplay, they were said to taint their swords with venal pastes. Instead of the telltale black, however, this adept clutched a thin blade of glaucous translucent white, handle down. Its curved cutting edge reared behind his back.

A spathidril, Rossamünd realized in horror, the most deadly of all blades.

The adept betrayed no urgency, but stared almost in abstraction at the Grackle, approaching it one halting dance-like step at a time.

Neither pit-bobs nor the rouse-master tried to stop the adept, and the people began to mutter approvingly, eager for him to go to his deadly work and avenge their losses.

166

Bloody-mouthed and so terribly alone among all this hatred, the Grackle seemed to sense something truly dangerous about its new foe. Shuffling backward to the tunnel from which it had come, the nadderer's tentacles rippled in clear agitation, thrusting in the adept's direction, then retracting sharply as if they tasted something foul.

With an awed gasp from the chancers, the adept suddenly whipped forward, sword a wan blur betwixt man and monster, and sprang back to stand tall once more, noble, supercilious.

What just happened?

The Handsome Grackle seemed unaffected, yet the swordist had all the swagger of the victor.

Rossamünd looked more closely at the nadderer. Its tentacles were tight now, their ends blurring with a stunned vibration. As he watched, a terrible incision began to open from the left shoulder of the beast and down deep into its trunk. The Grackle wheezed gore and collapsed to the hard floor.

Its shocking wound did not heal.

It did not rise again.

Cheers!

Rapturous, delighted ovation!

Smiling with what seemed to Rossamünd feigned satisfaction, Pater Maupin stood again in his proud peacock silks and white periwig and bent down to shake the hand of the adept. Torn gambling chits fell like celebratory rain as every throat cried its approval of the swordsman—every throat but one.

The stark blank inside Rossamünd had no accompanying voice. Yet if it had, he could not speak such a thing in this invidical place. *I should have intervened . . .* He ached inwardly, doubling his fist about the caste of botch powder he had half consciously selected from his digital.

With tumblings of bolts and locks, the farther pit door was opened and the stricken tractor in blue buff collected what little was left of his once-mighty fighting hound. The adept was helped back up into the stalls by many reaching, congratulatory hands. The heavy corpse of the slaughtered Grackle was dragged away by a quarto of pit-bobs. The gory floor was quickly scrubbed by laboring lads, the ticket tearings swept away and the pit readied for the next bout.

What other undeserving creatures languished beneath the gambling house? *How can I leave them all there?* The young factotum was in torment. Yet how could he hope to ever set them all free?

Another dog was brought, this time a white-and-gray stafirhund led by a tractor in an orange-and-white apron.

"Patient souls!" came the rouse-clerk's cry as he swept an arm to point dramatically to the jowly, slobbering dog, "I give you our own darling—Truncheon, the Bogle-biting Bitch-queen of the Batch!"

Applause and catcalls from the stalls.

Up went the iron divide, Splitting the pit into two once more. *Thunk!* went the opening of the bogle-admitting door.

In full expectation of some great slavering wretchling, Rossamünd was utterly unprepared for what emerged.

FRECKLE!

His mouth went dry, his forehead fever-damp. Yet with an unpleasantly dark elation, he quickly discovered it was not in fact his little bogle friend but some other similar creature. Its wizened little face was broader, hairier, more lopsided, and its body longer. Dread writ clear on its squinty broad-nosed face, it was so much slighter than the dog baying and leaping at the divide; this was a mismatched bout to appease the crowd, reinvigorate their interest and keep them at wagering.

"Lords, ladies, all gentlefolk," the rouse-clerk cried. "This one calls itself *Gingerrice!*"

People hoomed and hissed.

"It names itself, upstart wretcher!"

"Filthy basket, how dare it!"

"Do not be fooled by its stuntedness," the clerk bawled, raising his volume theatrically. "It is sturdy enough to contest our darling Bogle-biter. What will be your wagers?"

In the clamor to make an easy gain, the patrons near toppled over each other to have their calls heard, pay their wagers and get their tickets.

Perversely inspired by the dashing display of the sabrine adept, Rossamünd knew what he would do; consequences come as they will, he was not going to watch the end of such an innocent.

At the shrieking drop of metal, Rossamünd lifted himself as if to join the upsurging cries of his fellow watchers waving paddles, shaking fists, but with a surreptitious yet powerful flick sent the botch powder hurtling at the dog. Innocuously small, the caste of botch powder struck the stocky stafirhund square on its crown and popped with a pleasing purple-and-yellow puff before the beast had even reacted to the revelation of the shrinking glamgorn. The dog gave a puzzled yelp and, taking several waddling steps rearward, looked about the pit stupidly. Then, head lolling, the Bogle-biting Bitch-queen of the Batch simply lay down as if it were taking a well-earned nap and moved no more.

Not one person about him seemed to realize it was Rossamünd who had caused such a dramatic intervention in the bout. The dog-door opened but a crack to admit the head and shoulders of a patently confused pit-bob. This small opportunity was all little Gingerrice needed. With a gleeful squeal it pounced straight for the door, throwing the pit-bob aside as with surprising strength it shoved the port open farther and shot through and away before anyone could think to intervene.

The rouse-clerk stood and bellowed, "STOP THAT BEASTIE!" but it was too late.

Shouts of anger and dismay rang out from the dark spaces beyond the door, joined by the ravenous baying of many hounds.

With a growing ruckus, people began to cast about for the upstart who had dared defend a monster and bring them further losses.

"Who was it?"

"Wait till I hook the treacherous basket—me babbies won't eat for a week now!"

And the worst—angry claims of "SEDORNER!" "SELT-KISSER!" "OUTRAMORINE!"

In the stalls to the left a riot began as disgruntled patrons of high and low class weary of the night's extraordinary vicissitudes and unafraid to use their fists and worse escalated their demands to the ticket writers. Officials in the lowest stalls called useless instructions lost in the furor.

Careful not to draw attention to himself, Rossamünd eased away from the balustrade, searching faces to see if he was seen, eyes rapidly ranging the increasing madness. Above him and to the right, Rookwood and Eusebus stood together, observing the anarchy with expressions of amused wonder. Across the pit Pater Maupin was bundled away, the feather-collared dexter, Anaesthesia Myrrh, flinging out her hands left and right, clearing a path before them through the angry press. Each time she threw out a hand, there was a pallid flash—not bright like a fulgar's arcs, but some bizarre combination of witting and arcing that tossed uppity customers left and right without the dexter laying an actual hand upon them.

A frightful crashing came from the rousing-pit below. More intent on departure, Rossamünd caught a peek of tentacles flailing and men flung high. There came a high hissing and with it another portentous smashing of wood and metal. *The Handsome Grackle!* Somehow, though the foul gash in its shoulder still gaped, the poor beast had survived after all and, on the loose, was smashing its way into the pit. Shrieking and chattering, other little bogles were rushing in behind it—released perhaps by the Grackle's raging—springing upon the tractors and the pit-bobs who charged in from the opposite portal with pistol and cudgel to stop them. Outnumbered, the foolhardy fellows were quickly thrown aside.

But escape would not be so easily won, for the sabrine adept who had sliced the Grackle before dropped again into the roust, drawing his mystic blade to finish the job. Bogles sprang wide about him and through the still open dog-door, following after Gingerrice.

The Handsome Grackle, however, was oddly sluggish to respond.

Dexters, swordist and all, the young factotum would not see it cut again. Taking out a thennelever of glister dust, Rossamünd gave it a powerful flick, tossing a dose of dazzling gray powder to shower down over the swordsman passing close below, catching several poor retreating spectators in the stunning dust too. Even as Rossamünd pushed through spluttering gagging folk and scrambled up the steps to flee, he caught the narrow scrutiny of the young dandidawdler with the glittering wig fixed upon him from across the pit. Instantly the fancy fellow put hand to temple. *He is a wit!* The patrons only just recovered from the dexter's antics thought they were to suffer a wit's puissance too. Oversetting each other in their desire to get out of the way, they toppled as a mass, tumbling the fancy fellow in their fall.

Reprieved, Rossamünd moved folk aside with heedless ease as he made a path down the sweating-walled tunnel, round and round up the spiral stair, bursting through door wards and footmen already struggling to control the untimely and panicked exit of other patrons. Somehow he managed to find his way to the main saloon, threading a way hastily between the chancers still largely ignorant of the trouble below. A sudden shout behind, "GRABCLEAT! SNEAK THIEF! BLAGGARD!" roused every attention, and pale round-eyed faces cast about in shock. Walking at the doubled double, Rossamünd dodged the grasp of a quick-headed patron and sprang for the green exit. To cries of alarm from the loopholes, he sprinted the crimson obverse, flinging more glister in the dials of the door wards bristling to stop him, driving them back gurgling and gasping. Eyes closed and breath clenched, he lunged for the red door, thrusting it wide to rush free from that abominable chancery and into the night's bitter fog.

Several yards down the road was a stationary line of takenys waiting in the weak glow of a street-lamp for the reveling set to seek their wending home, their horses ruminating noisily in nosebags. Uniformly red-and-white-striped vests showing under heavy cloaks, the muffled drivers stood in a group staring down the seaside road in Rossamünd's direction, clearly engaging in some animated discussion.

"Escaping yer comeuppance, hey, lad?" one quipped as the young factotum drew near.

"Cloche Arde, the Harrow Road, Ilex Mile!" was all Rossamünd gave in answer, springing into the cabin of the frontmost takeny.

"Wo-ho, little lord, what's with the hasty so late in the evening?" its rotund owner chided as the harnessed horse whickered angrily at the shaking of the coach on Rossamünd's hurried boarding. "I thinks we've found our culprit, boy-os," the plump takenyman called in aside to his fellows;

173

then to Rossamünd, "Fleeing yer creditors, are ye, young sir?"

"No, no. I just need Cloche Arde, the Harrow Road, Ilex Mile, and quick!" Rossamünd repeated in rising distress. *I never should have come out tonight. What was I thinking?*

"A'right, a'right, me masters! Not so speedy!" The takenyman wrangled. "It'll cost ye double for double speed!"

"I'll give you triple!" Rossamünd responded without hesitation and rattled coin in his pocket—part of his night's winnings—as proof of good intention.

The takenyman paused for an agonizing moment. "A'right then, off we go," he said, nimbly clambering to his high seat despite his girth. "Onward we hasty go." With a philosophical mutter and shake of his head, he added, "Another night in Brandentown . . ."

"Stay clear o' the duffers!" one of his fellows shouted as the horse was flicked to start, going the very way he had just come.

"The other way! The other way!" Rossamünd cried, but to no avail.

Passing the Broken Doll, the young factotum could see through the window grille unhappy patrons beginning to spill out from the chancery's scarlet door. At their lead among a gang of angry roughs was the distinct figure of the dandidawdling wit. In agonies that the takeny-driver was not proceeding nearly fast enough, Rossamünd knelt on the cabin seat, staring through the narrow slot of a back window.

The carriage had gone barely a quarter mile inland, down claustrophobic lanes with little traffic, when the wildly bobbing night-lantern of a pursuing carriage hove into view.

Pulling down the side sash, Rossamünd cried to the driver. "You need to go faster, sir!"

"A chase is it, 'ey? Well, I am going as quick as I dare to about these streets!" was the angry retort. "Another night at the Broken Doll . . . ," the fellow growled. "Ye do the sitting and I'll do the whipping!" As emphasis the driver gave his already tiring nag a clip of his long switch.

The takeny lurched and Rossamünd was tumbled to the footwell. Struggling to right himself, he clutched the door sill.

The takenyman made a tight right, putting the outward projections of town-house walls between them and the pursuit, and pulled his horse up short. For a dread moment Rossamünd thought he was going to be ousted from the cabin and left to his fate, yet the goodly driver actually took a close left turn into a cramped lane not intended for horse-drawn conveyances. With as much hurry as the benighted confines allowed—not more than a quick walk—the coach rattled on. The driver eased past scuttlebutts, handcarts and a startled night-soil man, ducking night-drying clothes strung like naval bunting on a line at angles across the meager gap. An irate cry from on high could be heard through the clatter of their transit.

Rossamünd peered through the back slot and thought he spied the bulk of the chasing carriage sprint by the lane yet not stop.

"Just as long as the other fellow don't smoke my ruse we'll get about nicely," he heard the takenyman call in explanation. "This improptatory path'll deposit us on South Arm and put ye a good sight nearer yer destination."

A much smaller shadow flitted up the lane and landed on the sill. It was Darter Brown, looking decidedly ruffled and beating his wings in agitation. The sparrow gave a loud *tweet!*

Even in the ferment of the chase, Rossamünd was grateful for this tiny ally.

Like the whir of butterfly wings in the core of his skull, he finally felt the edge of the wit's sending. It was more artful and precise than Threnody's clumsy fishing and, feeling desperately vulnerable under its all-finding cognizance, Rossamünd found himself wishing the girl lighter was at his side in this new crisis.

"Heh, felt that one." The takenyman sucked in a cautionary breath and dragged back on his horse to stop. "Wo-ho! Wo-ho!"

Darter Brown took to wing and disappeared into the dark.

Peering again through the rear window of the cab, Rossamünd could not see any trailing coach.

"Out with ye!" The takenyman had reached down with his blunt hookpole and opened the cabin door. "Runnin' from usual folks is a reasonable kind o' trot, but not a wit, my good son. *Out!*"

Rossamünd peered behind again, expecting pursuit at any beat. "I'll pay you four times!" Hands shaking, he withdrew a whole golden sou from the folds of his pockets. "More even! Up front!"

The sending pulsed for a second time, stronger now,

enough indeed to cause the takeny horse to stumble slightly and spoil the glittering promise of Rossamünd's plea.

The takenyman cooed to his faithful cob, then glared down at his young passenger. "OUT!" he yelled. With a cunning flick of reins he made his horse step forward a single jaunty step, causing the cab to lurch.

Rossamünd was thrown to the floor, half rolling out of the doorway.

"OUT, YE ILL-BRINGIN' SNIPE!" the takenyman cried again, an edge of panic in his voice, prodding at Rossamünd with his hook.

With the dandy wit getting closer, Rossamünd had little choice. He sprang clumsily from the takeny, alighting on hands and haunches amid the mucky debris of the lane.

His customer barely exited, the driver whipped wildly at his nag, omitting to collect the fare in his hurry, and quit the scene as fast as horse legs and cartwheels could take him.

Left on foot in the alley, Rossamünd ran, chasing the trail of the takeny, watching its swiftly receding splasher lamp disappear about a corner. Pushing harder on legs that seemed too slow, he skidded on moist cobbles, leaping back and forth over the dribbling gutter. Finally reaching the end of the lane, he found a proper street once more, a broad road of faded half-houses and, across the way, trees kept behind a wall of railing and stone.

Another subtle sending swept over and exposed him; then, like a blow, the full weight of proper scathing frission.

Rossamünd saw stars and stumbled, to sit in the gutter of the laneway. Through the haze of the scathing, he heard to his horror the distant clatter of hoof and wheel: the pursuing takeny was drawing swiftly near. Working his jaw like yawning and shaking his head to clarity, Rossamünd peered about the wall to see a carriage dashing toward him from the far end of the South Arm.

Cry for help?

But who would hear? Who would care?

Hide?

But how do you hide from a wit?

Stand to fight?

Even if he achieved the same feats of strength he had used to defeat the pig-eared gudgeon or the nickers of Wormstool, what use was this or a few potives against a neuroti-crith who could tell wherever he was and crush him from afar?

Thirty strides away across the street stood a tiny high-roofed cottage built into the wall that hemmed the trees. Beside it was an ironbound gate with a bright-limn glowing yellow above it.

Flee!

Springing forward, he sprinted the exposed span of flagstone footpath, head back, eyes wide and fixed on the goal of the light, running across the path of the swiftly advancing coach. Rather than stopping, the carriage kept clattering by, the driver flailing in distraction, swiping at the air as something small and feisty flapped and harried about his head.

Darter Brown!

Rossamünd did not slow to ponder, but dashed to the cast-iron gate. *Locked!* Of course it was at this time of night—public locksmen living in the cottage next door would have seen to that.

A frightened, whinnying shriek well down the street spoke of the driver finally pulling hard on the reins.

Abandoning soft notions of asking for the gate to be opened, Rossamünd seized two vertical bars of the gate and hauled, the metalwork in its hinges making a loud, startling clash as he bodily threw himself over the top. He dropped squarely on both feet and leaped forward, dashing down what little he could see of a raked path curving into the occult park.

Shouts came from behind, quickly followed by a wit's sending—invisible, airborne flexing, shuddering forth then back.

Rossamünd ducked as if avoiding a strike and changed direction sharply, off the wan hint of the path and into the pitch murk of the trees, hoping to foil the wit's preternatural senses. Sure enough, the frission came, yet though it drove the young factotum to his knees, skidding in the dew-damp clover, it was vague, unfocused.

Slithering on muddied hands and boot-toes, he got back to his feet, glancing at where he had come. He could just make out the distinctive figure of the wit and three rougher men standing in the dim lamplight on the opposite side of the gate, apparently thwarted and staring in through its bars. It seemed to Rossamünd that despite the impenetrable dark the richly dressed fellow was peering straight at him. With a sault of fright in his gizzards, Rossamünd sped among the trees on a wild zig-then-zagging course, blundering over

179

roots and rocks, seeking to put as much reach between his pursuers and himself as he could.

A piercing, iron ringing told him that the gate had in some way been forced, that the dandidawdling wit was through, and free to hunt him down. A powerful sending washed through the woodland park—detection and attack as one, its febrile fringe arresting Rossamünd enough to trip him again and send him flailing face-first into the fresh wet turf in a spray of chance-won coins. The wit must have possessed perverse determination to be employing his antics with such frequent potency.

What can I do against such a foe?

A little blur above him and Rossamünd caught the soft *cheep!* of Darter Brown alighting momentarily on a low perch in the dark. He could barely make out the little fellow eyeing him, turning its head to then fro. A tight thrum of wings and the sparrow was gone. After a moment a determined piping echoed out of the dark only a short span ahead. Rossamünd sprinted to the noise and Darter Brown dashed on yet farther to tweet again from the night. They kept at this until Rossamünd's breath began to rasp in his windpipes and he longed to drop and vomit. He slowed to a hurried, hip-arching walk, realizing that it had been some little time since he had felt the wit's frission.

He became still—just for a breath—to listen.

No footfall sounded in the soft sprays of clover and soursobs, just the creak of gentle shifting in the trees, of branches softly clacking against one another up in the dark, squeaking at their knotty joints. With it hummed the drone of the city in its small-hour motions, already so muffled from within the park that it seemed far off, and not just a bend in the path away. In the ringing quiet, he became aware of threwdishness about him, a quiet yet intent wakefulness. *I'm in the Moldwood,* he realized with a start.

There comes a point in concealing darkness that, even when one is desperate not to be seen, the need to see is far greater, and so possessed, Rossamünd hurriedly dug Mister Numps' limulight from the pocket of his frock coat and slid back the lid. Its gentle, blanched-blue effulgence picked out trunks and leaves and round-fronded grass. It took but a moment to get sight of a clear path, and, snapping the lid closed, the young factotum ran again, hampered by the increasingly uneven ground. In the meager light reflected off low clouds he could just make out a mass before him and felt the earth tilt and rise up the flank of a small hill.

Pulling on roots and weeds, even thick nettles—whatever he might to help his climb—he scaled the modest mound and upon achieving its summit was struck with the most profoundly piercing scathing he had yet felt. So strong was this witting attack that lights burst in his vision, joined by an inner blaze of woe and torment. The world truly did tilt now; Rossamünd toppled down the lee side of the hillock, only vaguely aware of the heavy fall as he came to a jarring stop at what he could only presume was the bottom. He lay, senses tumbling, vision popping with disorienting flickers, and felt a gentler sending from the wit. The previous had been pure violence, but now, supine and struggling, he was being pointedly sought. With a savage growl he forced clarity into his head, got to his knees and, leaning on a sapling, stood.

A clear footfall.

His innards froze. Breath held in dread, his ears keened with a pulsating, shimmering whine.

Coney in their covets,
Bunnies in their holes,
But who shall ferret my meal?

... came a doggerel song, a tuneful taunt from the shadows above. The dandidawdling wit appeared at the crown of the hillock, his skin soft-lit by luminous fungi sprouting in nook and bole, a revealing pallor in the bosky black. He slid down the bank with easy grace; with such power the pernicious servant of the rousing-pit had nothing to fear—*he* was the supreme monster here.

Rossamünd quickly pressed out a caste from his digital and flung it, the blue fire of loomblaze flaring as it ruptured against the pastel trunk of a sycamore where, but a blink before, the wit had been.

"O-ho, little rabbit, with your ledgermain tricks!" came a voice in the flickering dark. His relentless attacker seized Rossamünd in another unseen inward grip. "I do not know what pox-riddled alehouse you thought you had found tonight, little rabbit, but ours is not a place to fling stinks. Nor are we so easily swindled by a fast pair of legs. There shall be no getting away as easy as you please; my masters will have your soft *coney* flesh . . ."

The young factotum fell again, retching into the dripping grass and faintly luminescent toadstools, heartily exasperated with so much groveling. Cringing and trapped on his wet mud-mucked knees, he suddenly felt a great threwd approaching, pressing through the frission. It brought with it a glimpse of clarity, and Rossamünd was master of himself enough to look up. Something was coming from deeper in the park, something ineffably old and potent stepping from the darkling trees.

Surely just a desperate phantom . . .

Yet the dandily dressed wit must have seen this tall and horned beast too, for he touched hand to temple and reached a hand toward it as it loomed on the other side of the dell.

Even where he knelt crumpled, Rossamünd caught the nauseating peripheries of strong, focused witting. Expecting the great bestial thing to stumble and fall, he croaked in awe as it simply came on, bounding on all fours right over him.

The wit scathed again—a careless demonstration of puissance that caught Rossamünd too—but in a half-dozen awkwardly loping steps the horned thing was upon him. The witting reached its excruciating climax and the nicker—far taller than any man—reared, seizing the wit by his face and lifting him high. Before the fellow could do anything to extricate himself, he was shaken brutally like nothing more than a doll throttled by a tantrumming child. The wit's limbs flailed as he was swung violently back and forth by his neck. Loud meaty cracking broke the strange, shocked silence, a dreadfully flat sound among the bending trees. The wit's voluminous neckerchief unraveled and slipped to the mold, and the spangled silver wig fell from the telltale calvous head. With one last, ruinous *snap!* the monster flung the utterly broken wit aside, the body crashing lifelessly into a low olive bush.

There came a peculiar clicking noise from the horned thing's mouth. "Souls should choose better than to sing of ferreting conies and bunnies in *my* wood," it declared extravagantly with rasping yet resonant voice.

In the weak blue fungal glow Rossamünd could see it turn, head lowered, back arched, glaring directly at him through its steeply arching brows. Brain-bruised and sorely used, the young factotum scooted backward on his rapidly saturating end, boot-heels slipping unhelpfully on slick lawn. With a mere handful of wide-stepping strides the creature sprang toward him, halting abruptly to bend and peer right into the young factotum's eyes.

"Why have you disturbed me, manikin?" it demanded, its blunt mouth terrible with curved, overlong rabbitlike incisors. Threwd seeped from every follicle, every fiber, a mighty and terrible threwd that was masterfully and powerfully restrained. The air became heavy with a sickly sweet fragrance, a merging of animal-stink and spring-blossom perfume. "Why have you brought our foes to my serene courts and made my night so busy?"

"I-I," Rossamünd tried, astonished by the creature now clear before him. What he thought were horns were in fact ears—elongated rabbitlike ears; its blunt bestial snout ended in a soft, twitching rabbit's nose. "You—you are a rabbit . . . !" the young factotum breathed reflexively.

The rabbit-beast stood back and straightened, looming

high over him. "That I am, ouranin." It drew close again. "Haraman, the wild Piltmen called me; out in the parishes where I seldom visit any more I am Rabbit o'Blighty; in the east they speak of me in dread as the Kaminchin; and in writings of the quidnuncs I am regularly named Cunobillin, or at times the Great Lagornis. Many more names everymen have given me through history, but in these current times I am the Lapinduce—the Duke of Rabbits, true master of this festering city!"

Rossamünd was struck mum.

Here, regally upright before him, was an urchin, a monster-lord, an ancient ruler of the nickers and bogles.

Before Rossamünd could say or think or do any more, the Lapinduce reached down and gripped the young facto-tum by the back of his collars, hoisting him from the soggy ground. The front of his weskit, frock coat, solitaire and un-dershirt all rucked to cut into his gourmand's cork. Kicking and twisting in the irresistible grip of this lord of monsters, Rossamünd clutched his strangling collars away from his windpipe, yet his own well of strength did not avail him.

The Lapinduce, Duke of Rabbits, held him fast.

Giddiness surged through his intellectuals, the inner wounds of the dead wit's onslaught setting his eyes aching. The young factotum ceased his flailing and swung in dizzy dismay, each rocking stride of this mighty urchin carrying him farther into haunted sanctums of the threwdish park.

"Now for dreams," the Lapinduce proclaimed softly.

Bundling Rossamünd under arm like some package of new-fullered clothes, it stooped to pluck something from

185

the ground—a small fungus weakly glowing yellow green. It held this before the young factotum's face and crushed it. With an unexpected *pop!* a cloying gust of pollen and damp filled the young factotum's nostrils and coated his mouth.

He gagged and spat and writhed again in the prison of the monster's grip as he fought to clear his senses.

Stay awake! a sensible inward cry demanded. At the very depths of himself he wanted to stay, to obey; yet at the top of himself, in his head, in his throat, he was succumbing, and there was nothing he could do to stop it. His eyes drooped heavy; he lost the idea of his legs, then his arms, even his trunk, until only the tiny impotent spin of his determination remained.

Then nothing.

9

THE COURTS OF THE RABBIT

petchinin(s) monster-lords most concerned in their own immediate needs and their own schemes, neither attacking nor defending everymen except as circumstances might dictate or if said everymen are encroaching upon a petchinin's patch or plans. As such they are scorned—or at the very least, mistrusted—by both urchins and wretchins.

ROSSAMÜND roused ears-first to the sound of wild spinet music resonating as if down a tunnel, the notes clear—almost close—astringent at one turn, melancholy the next. It was a version of the melody he was sure he had encountered before but could not summon where . . . *Huh,* he said to himself with sluggish complaisance, wrapped in a cozying peace, *I did not know Miss Europe played the spinet . . .* He sighed sleepily. *Rouse out, sleepyhead, time to make treacle.*

Creeping eyes open against the drowsy crust congealed in their corners, Rossamünd was puzzled to find the ceiling a spotted roof of roots and compacted brown earth. In the soft light of glowing slimes and many thin, sunny beams of morning emitted through ingenious gaps in wood and soil, Rossamünd could see that some openings were windowed with alabaster marble so fine as to be translucent, the delicate effulgence carved into figures of hopping, dancing hares.

This was not Cloche Arde at all!

Recollection crashed like the dropping of a full-laden barrel. He had been taken by the Lapinduce and kept the night on a downy bed of moss in the den of that murderous monster-lord, trapped alone with no notion of any path or method of escape in some sunken warren. For a breath, terrible stories of weak souls carried away to a nicker's den to be feasted on slowly came unhelpfully to mind. Yet wherever *here* was, in the threwd that waxed and waned with the pulse of the music, there was no threat, no lurking promise of violence. All Rossamünd could collect was calm and self-sufficiency and the merest notion of more subdued affections.

He sat up, clouting his head upon the curve of the earthen wall into which his mossy cot was cut. A pile of what he first disgustedly thought was forest sweepings fell off him. He quickly realized it was a jumble of leaves in autumn shades, still supple, cunningly woven together to make a remarkably soft coverlet.

Curling fingers, flexing toes, Rossamünd felt no pains but the fresh bump upon his head. By all evidence the Lapinduce had not harmed him. Quite the contrary; even the dandi-dressed wit's dastardly work seemed cured. Rossamünd felt as hale and clear-headed as he ever had.

He looked about, blinking. At his left an entrance gaped in the white-daubed wall, a tall misshapen oval opening through roots. He sat listening; no movement beyond the

188

opening, just the spinet-song and beneath it the strangely compressed quiet of the underground . . . and tingling, self-possessed threwd.

Untwisting himself from the rucked constriction of his sleep-knotted frock coat, the young factotum stood slowly to discover that his feet were bootless and—after a needless pat on his crown—that his head was hatless.

He rolled his eyes and cast about for these items. A lingering, subterranean mist hung thinly mere inches above the smooth cold ground—tiled in a fine mosaic fashioned in the image of frolicking rabbits in fields of lush grasses and bending trees—but no boots and no thrice-high.

Even through his harness he could feel a gnawing cold, a marrow chill of buried places. Wrapping the leafy blanket about him, he stepped gingerly from the cell to find a high arching tunnel heeling away on either hand. Lit by effulgent fungus, its walls were densely entwined with every girth of root, permitting no sight of the dirt behind. Little drifts of blossom and old leaves gathered in nooks between burrow wall and tessellated floor.

A glissando of sharp spinet notes rang down the passage from the lighter end. Creeping toward the melody, Rossamünd recognized it as a close variation on that which he had heard only three days before, driving past the Moldwood with Mister Carp on the way to the knavery. As he stole forward, small skitterings whispered from the twilight behind. He became utterly still, but the florid playing only waxed louder, drowning any creeping noises. Rossamünd hurried from the dark and about a curve spied a line of three hand-carved archways a dozen yards ahead. Feet clad in soft trews, the young factotum noiselessly approached the first arch and squeezed a peek past its inward pilaster.

Beyond he found the deep cleared cellar of a completely floorless high-house, a square shell of a tower open to the heavens, lighter bands of brickwork among the gray stone and thin, many-mullioned windows evidence of missing stories. Rossamünd squinted up into the roofless height dappled with layered leaves and pastel morning sky. A venerable walnut tree grew bent and broad in its midst, much of its trunk and lower branches wound with creeping glory vine. There was no rubble or ruin about it; rather it grew from a paved square of black-and-white marble laid around the walnut's wide-spreading roots. And here, under its shade, sat the Lapinduce astride a stool fashioned of branches writhen together, playing at a spinet of lustrous caffene-colored wood. Clothed now in a heavy high-collared frock coat of shimmering midnight purple stitched with playful rabbits, the mighty beast's back was turned to Rossamünd as it hammered away in impassioned throes. Shuddering under this artful assault, the spinet glistened in the variegated light, every panel and plane of the instrument inlaid with traceries of ivory and gold.

The metallic fugue unraveled to a pounding, beautiful acme when, one note short of the final satisfaction, the Lapinduce hesitated, blunt-clawed hands hovering taut with potential by its great rabbit ears. Thus the monster-lord remained, motionless, head turned. Rossamünd stared in dread wonderment at the trace of its severe sky-gray eye, heedless of him, of the elderly tree, of the gutted shell of its musical well, of its playing. The young factotum could see subtle movements in the creature's mouth, a voiceless monologue as it stared into the air, into the fathomless sinks of history and memory beyond human record.

All *sensible* people held that such a creature was an impossibility, a dreadful rumor, a beautiful fiction. Yet here the impossible dwelt, in the very heart of a powerful city filled to its outer curtains with vigilantly invidical folk.

Without the music a great threwdish hush dwelt here; not even the baritone grumble of Brandentown's daily routine carried on the woody, bug-buzzing breath of the day's start. Kindly breezes whispered in the green above, branches barely squeaking as a gentle rain of blossoms and seedling puffs settled like clumsy snow. High to his left, water was dribbling from a circular grate a few feet up the sunken wall, its bubbling caught in a mossy runnel muttering down a marble drain by the arches where Rossamünd hid. A puff of forenoon breeze dropped from the cerulean gap above, bringing on its breath the smell of the great creature—an oily, spicy, bestial stink touched with rich spring blossom. Something wheedling within this scent worked to put the young factotum at ease.

In a tiny looping dash, Darter Brown flew down the chute of the gutted building to alight on a walnut branch reaching toward Rossamünd over the runnel.

Crouching, the young factotum smiled up furtively at his sparrow friend.

The bird, swallowing some twitching bug it had caught on

the wing, twisted his petite black-hooded head to one side and then the other and voiced a brief twitter of greeting.

"So, rossamünderling," the Lapinduce declared suddenly into the hush, its back still turned, "you wish still to be an everyman?"

Nearly toppling back, Rossamünd grabbed at the frame of the arch, righting himself. Feeling suddenly nude among the shadows he cast about wildly, looking to flee—but to where?

"Come out from the shadows, little ouranin," the urchin-lord persisted, relaxing his dramatic pose, "and let me greet you a'right."

Reluctantly Rossamünd stepped into the mottled light of the open arch, halting cautiously on the bank of the runnel. "Uh-h . . . Hello, sir . . . ," he stammered. "H-how . . ."

The mighty urchin pivoted upon its stool, arching about to fix him directly. Black fur bristling, head hunched low between tall collars, its great ears laid flat behind its head and out along its back, the Lapinduce barked, "*How?* How do I *know?* Know that you are *there* or know that you are a *rossamünderling?* An ouranin? A manikin? A hinderling? A pink-lips? A fake-foe?"

"Uh . . . b-both, sir," the young factotum squeaked.

In the elucidating light of day the creature's visage was clear: a dark, triangular face covered in a lustrous pelt like rich black velvet, with pale fur ringed about equally pallid eyes; shadowy stripes ran from beneath each lower lid, down and across each high cheek.

Its gaze narrowed.

Alarmed as he was, Rossamünd was awed by something eccentrically and inexpressibly handsome in this imposing monster-lord, its face appearing less like a rabbit to him now, more like that of some hunting cat such as he had read about in the scant count of natural philosophy books at Madam Opera's.

The damp black rabbit's nose—oddly endearing and bestial beneath such a humanly astute and judicious regard—twitched, testing the air. "I *know* because I was there, little ouranin," the urchin murmured, voice still carrying. "I was there when the fresh land sang with threwd so sweet and new as to reach an accord with the pure ringing of the very stars themselves."

A frown darkened its brow.

"I was there when the alosudnë, perfidious and haughty—those whom men now call the false-gods—rose up from the waters in their conceit to drive the gentle naeroë away as they sought to seize all three of the middling grounds as their own. I was there when my landling frair and I joined to beat the false-hearted alosudnë back to the utter deeps to slumber uselessly evermore."

The Lapinduce became quieter now, speaking rapidly in its passion. "I was there to watch men arrive—born of mud as we—to flourish and, finally, full of the pride of life, set to building tiny empires of their own, whelming and shackling each other, snatching at things once freely given as if they were their own. I was there when they sought to wrest the living sod from us and slew their first urchin by deeds of great and corporate treachery."

Sitting tall and manlike, the beast paused, smoothed its coat hems and continued in a more even tone. "I was there when one whole third of the theriphim declared their hatred of men and compacted to ever thwart them." It stood, reaching thick-sleeved arms out and up, pressing its over-long hands against a heavy walnut bough. At the crown of its swarthy head it would have exceeded eight feet; with its ears it gained another yard of height. Yet, in the lucidity of day's glow it did not appear quite as massive, and its coat lent the monster-lord a regal, almost human, aspect. "Long years have I ruled here till every particle about me has become my own, yet never once have I been greatly troubled by the too-brief souls about me." It took a breath. "*All* of this, little rossamünderling, is how I *know*."

Rossamünd waited, and though bursting with a swarm of questions provoked by this riddling sermon, he did not speak.

The pause stretched into a weighty silence.

Rossamünd blinked.

"Will you give me answer, ouranin?" insisted the monster-lord, breaking the stifling hush. It stepped toward him, a jaunting tip-of-toe stride, its legs elongated like a rabbit's. Unlike the close-cut claws of its hands, the claws on its large coney feet, clicking on the paving, were wicked long and wicked sharp.

Stoutly Rossamünd opened his mouth once, twice, but even on the third no more than an astounded gurgle came out of him.

Chirruping urgently, Darter Brown danced winging

THE LAPINDUCE

loops about the Duke of Rabbits' ears.

Ears drooping slightly, the Lapinduce shot a strangely chastened look to the agitated sparrow. "Be not afraid, little wing-ed merrythought," it murmured, addressing the bird directly. "I am no cacophrin nor simple sunderhallow to set on your friend and eat him! You may tell Lord Strouthion— my word to his ear—that though I might decline to bind myself to seek everymen's welfare, yet I am not so lost that I would devour our own." Ears once more erect, the Lapinduce stared down upon Rossamünd with its large limpid eyes, elbow in hand, stroking its hairy chin beneath enormous, protruding teeth in a very human manner. It gazed at him so searchingly the young factotum began to itch. "You are alive, now speak . . . What do they call you by?"

Rossamünd fumbled, not knowing how to address this primeval creature. "My . . . my name is Rossamünd Bookchild." He went to doff his hat diffidently and was reminded by empty, questing grasp that it was missing.

The monster-lord laughed, a coughing, oddly person-ish noise. "Of course it is! Who was it, to bestow you such an uninspired nomination?"

"I—uh—I suppose it was Madam Opera . . . ," the young factotum answered a little tightly, "though I reckon it was Cinnamon who gave it to me first."

"Cinnamon, you say?" The Lapinduce twitched its nose and flicked its ears. "Surely modest Cannelle would not be so dim?"

"Cannelle, sir?"

The creature looked at him as if he were simple. "Cannelle is the one you name as Cinnamon. He has always been curious beyond his place, wandering far and farther through the eons, outside his rightful range . . . though I reckoned him sharper-soiled than to give an ouranin such a simple name—"

Tweet! went Darter Brown touchily.

"I think it was more a label . . . ," Rossamünd elaborated.

The Lapinduce cast a shrewd look at both boy and bird. "He sought perhaps to play a tease upon the everymen?"

"Play a tease?"

"Most certainly—jest with them! Put a theriphim so thoroughly disguised among them and fool them all, yet leave the morsel of a hint to unravel the ruse and reveal the jest." Another coughing laugh.

Standing still on the opposite bank of the runnel, the young factotum could not help his frown. If his arrival on the foundlingery steps was a jest, it was a very poor one.

"Will you tell me, puzzled ouranin," the Lapinduce crooned, "why you remain in their realms? Why have you not joined us and kept yourself away from needless troubles?"

"I-I have not known of what I am supposed to be until only a fortnight gone. My master got a mark of my blood upon his arm to prove it, but it is yet to show."

"Oh, now." The urchin-lord's alien eyes went a little round. "Here you need no such gruesome proofs—I have told it is so; all doubts are ended."

His soul set so fixedly on the confirmation of Fransitart's cruorpunxis, Rossamünd did not know what to do with so blunt a revelation. "But can I truly have come from the mud?

Am I really the remaking of some lost everyman fallen dead in the wilds?"

The Lapinduce regarded him with glittering eyes.

"Whoever told you so told it true," it said simply.

Rossamünd gasped a steadying breath. "But am I an everyman or a monster?"

"Ahh." The Duke of Rabbits clacked its front teeth together impatiently. "Thus did Radica and Dudica, the darlings and saviors of the Brandenfolk, worry. 'Are we mannish monsters or monsterish men?' was ever their quest." The monster-lord became contemplative and so completely still, the young factotum thought he had been forgotten. Finally the creature stirred. "The answer is as it was for them: you are both at once, neither more one nor less the other, an everyman and euriphim congruently and indivisibly, unable to be separated into parts. No marks on arms nor hiding behind unsmells will make you more or less than what you already are and have always been, oh manikin."

Despite all the evidence, Fransitart's recounting and Rossamünd's own knowing, a self-denying blank reached out from Rossamünd's milt, prickling at his scalp and setting a disconcerting buzz ringing in his ears.

The Lapinduce gave a disgusted snort. "Look at these pullings of long faces! How does knowing what you are make you any different? You have been *you* all this time; you will remain *you* for the long stretch of your life regardless of the reckonings in your thinking soils. The only alteration you have undergone is to simply have information to remedy your self-doubtings. Cease these snivels!" Again it clacked its terrible front teeth together, a loud, disapproving sound.

The rabbit-duke turned, took up a fine glass goblet that had sat upon the wooden-keyed spinet and sipped heartily at the wriggling froth it held, chewing on a mouthful. "I welcome you, ouranin, to my warren in this miniature remnant wood of mine." The Lapinduce bowed to him. It spread its arms like an invitation. "Come, let us walk in the cool of the morning so I might show it to you."

With a slow watchful stride over the tiny watercourse, Rossamünd approached the urchin-lord under its ancient tree.

Another quaff of its frog-froth and the monster-lord coughed unexpectedly, two loud, clear hacks that bore the suggestion of language.

As if in response, two large buck-rabbits, brown with black faces and brooding jet eyes, hopped from a hole in the flagstones between a tight bole of walnut roots. Each rabbit bore one of Rossamünd's boots, carried somewhat uncomfortably in its teeth by the heel-loop.

The young factotum gave an involuntary chuckle of delight.

"This is Ogh." Clearly pleased at the young factotum's reaction, the rabbit-lord indicated the buck carrying his right shoe with an uncurling of its great hands. "And this"—it did the same for the rabbit holding the left boot—"is Urgh; if they had not held them for you, the littler ones might have carried your shoes away for keeping."

The two creatures dropped Rossamünd's boots carefully at his feet, and as he wrestled his footwear on, one pulled the leafy blanket from his shoulders and dragged it to its master. The other hopped in lazy lopes to disappear again beneath the walnut. As large as they were, there was nothing especially threwdish about them; they were just rabbits.

As if detecting its guest's inklings, the rabbit-duke declared, "They are of a long line of Oghs and Urghs who have served me ear and nose, keeping watchful eye while I ponder and I play to remember the sweet piping of the cosmic firstenings." The monster-lord reached down to fondle the ears of the one at its feet.

The other reemerged bearing Rossamünd's slightly soiled hat in its gentle mouth.

The young factotum laughed again as he took it gratefully.

Eyes glittering, the Lapinduce turned and beckoned him to follow, taking the young factotum through the arches upon the other side of the cellar. By winding root-paneled passages full of half-heard whispers, Rossamünd let himself be led upward, holding back cautiously as around and around they went, ever higher. Stooping through a veil of bracken and root fronds—the Duke of Rabbits almost bent to its oddly working knees—they emerged between the roots of an enormous olive onto a bright hillside glade.

Dazzled and blinking, Rossamünd perceived a host of rabbits grazing and loping about the thickly flowering grass hemmed by great thickets of thorny trees. To the east over the treetops, where the morning sun was well lifted into the wan blue, he thought he saw the gray misted curve of the city's entire harborage brimming with masts. Founded a dozen yards behind him on the summit dense with pungent sage like some fortalice, the hollow building of the Lapinduce's court rose for four stories. Its banks were grown around with massive ancient trees of many kinds—walnut, sycamore, olive, turpentine—obscuring much of the skeletal tower. A powerful slumbering peace dwelt here, giving no hint that they were indeed in the middle of a vast and hostile city. Alighting with a whir in the branches above, Darter Brown played with little wrens and woodland robins.

Closing his eyes, Rossamünd drew in a sweet cleansing breath.

Striding down the embankment, the Lapinduce was quickly gathered about by a milling, frolicking drove of coneys and hares. The monster-lord cooed for a moment to them, then held out its long arms and turned slowly about.

"When far-seeing Idaho was still on pap, this wood covered every dune and vale," it spoke with chanting tone, "from Lillian of the Faye to the People of the Dogs and far into the Piltmen's kingdoms. The Harholt, the Harleywood, Cacolagia, Nemus Cunicula . . . It has gone by many names, but each one gives it *my* name. Whether brave sires or cowardly heirs, wide-visioned conquerors or money-hearted goosesgrabbers, all souls have lived in it and about it by my consent."

"You let them cut your trees?" Rossamünd asked carelessly, more intent on keeping from crushing a rabbit as he stepped down to the grass.

"Trees do not concern me as long as I am let alone. The ambits of this park are enough; I seek only to be untroubled by man or monster, and I let all these little naughtbringers flurrying about me flourish. I am not bound to be kind to everymen; however, it pleases me to watch their self-important antics. Ahh, everymen, one brief span you get!" the rabbit-duke cried into the sky, its tiny charges crowding about its slender feet untroubled by the monster's passion. "You are like the twigs on a plum tree; in spring you blossom, in summer bear fruit, in autumn you drop your leaves and in winter fall and then are gathered up to be thrown as kindling on the fire . . . How I delight in watching you all scurry and toil so seriously only to depart too soon. I stop for but a movement of thought, then rouse, my nails grown again, to find that a once-familiar generation have all departed and their children have become grandsires. Think what troubles you could wreak, oh, busy, busy everymen, if your span of years were but doubled! What terrible momentum you might gather. It is well you fight with each other as much as with us and waste time making wagers over the fate of the weakling tykes in their pits."

The monster-lord returned its shrewd attention to its guest.

"Are you pecked?" it inquired with a peculiarly light tone, holding out its now near-drained goblet of wriggling froth.

Eyeing the offering with barely contained repulsion, Rossamünd declined while his stomach turned traitor and gave an audible burble.

"No? Maybe some thrisdina?" It walked over to an anciently knotted olive, reached up and pulled several strands of the diaphanous weed that hung limply from a lower branch.

The young factotum peered at the serving, a dull wan

green frond wet with dew and unappetizingly coiled on the Lapinduce's pale palm. Feeling obliged after his first refusal, Rossamünd opened his own hand to receive his morning repast and felt a soulful surprise of threwd shiver through his very marrow as the urchin's truncated claws brushed his bare palm.

The rabbit-duke did not appear to notice this contact, but explained with a strange and disarming chattiness, "You will find this growing almost anywhere with enough dampness in the air, and every variety is good for eating—whether for everyman or euriphim."

Rossamünd sniffed the mossy tendrils. They smelt of grass, of hidden forest glades, of dirt. He tried a nibble. It was like a mild variation on mushrooms, bland enough to be edible. "How do people not fathom you are here?" he asked, still chewing.

The Lapinduce tapped its long-whiskered upper lip ruminatively with a crooked finger, a voluminous cuff dropping to reveal its bony wrist. "Because I do not wish it. Though some do . . . " came the patient answer. "My steadfast ones . . . Oftentimes the short-lived dukes will know of me too and reckon well to keep mum."

Rossamünd could barely credit it. "They do not send in battalions of teratologists?"

The monster-lord peered at him as if this were a ridiculous notion. "I would fill this city full of terror and empty it, make it barren for generation upon generation to become a nest for sunderhallows and darkness . . . Though your concern for me is commendable, ouranin," it added dryly. "The last duke with whom I had to deal—and *all* those before him—have proved shrewd enough to keep such discernment to themselves. How-be-it, I do not know if the current fellow is the same fellow as before. Too quickly does each generation come and live and go again."

"Do other . . . *monsters*"—Rossamünd hesitated, wanting a better word—"dwell here with you?"

"I seldom seek the company of my frair. Too often they are spoiling to harm or help the everymen, pulling at me to do the same. I prefer stillness and memory."

Looking up, Rossamünd beheld eoned memories that shifted in the depths of the Lapinduce's inhuman gaze. Was this the fashion of the Duke of Sparrows' rule as well, to watch and wait and remember sweeter times? "Are you and the Duke of Sparrows kin, sir?"

It regarded him with what the young factotum could only read as amusement. "Ahh, the Sparrowlengis. As such things are reckoned, indeed we are—though you will find *him* less willing to admit the kinship. But we theraphim—you and I and the sparrow-king too—are frair all to each other *and* to the groaning earth too."

Rossamünd peered at the monster-lord in wonder. *Could I possibly be kin to such creatures?* "But what of the hob-rousing?" he dared to ask. "Does it not stir you to anger to have it in your land?"

The monster-lord's ears went flat again. "Am *I* to be the soul to solve the endless enmity twixt theriphim and naughtbringer?" it hissed, taking several large strides toward him and thrusting its visage into Rossamünd's own, the young factotum retreating a small step.

A sinister threwdishness—an angry surge that made the world go strangely dim—swirled about him. With a gasp of dismay, Rossamünd raised an arm as if to defend himself, vaguely aware of Darter Brown's own anxious twittering above him.

"I happen to know that Gingerrice won free!" the Lapinduce declaimed with low and sibilant ferocity. "As has that daftling Grackle; oft has he passed through the guts of kraulschwimmen and other terrible salamanders and always survived barely hurt! Did not I myself save you from that fluffed and perfumed neuroticrith looking to snatch you away? What more do you wish for, squidgereen! Do you seek to provoke me in my own city and question my mercies?" it snorted.

Its warm, scented breath—like flowers and new-turned earth—was strong in Rossamünd's nostrils. "No, sir, I do not," he said in a small voice, recalling all too lucidly that this mighty creature had slain a wit in his defense as thoughtlessly as a pantry maid might strangle a chicken for a meal.

"I—" continued the urchin-lord self-importantly, "*I* have never prevented the many shifting tribes of people from coming to dwell in my domain nor prevented them from conquering the previous tribe to establish themselves. I gave my consent when the two sisters Radica and Dudica—rossamünderlings just as you are and now long departed—defended this youngling city against an onrush of wretchling theraphim kin. I parleyed with the seventh duke—blind and deaf—of this current dynasty, for with me alone could

205

he commune, and in doing thus proved his crafty advisers mendacious and insincere. And yet, I let the schwimmenbeasts take from the harbors their share of iron boats with their toothsome marrows of muscle, and leave marauding *nickers* to take their fill of souls in the parish lands. Complexities within complexities . . . As it has ever been." It opened its mouth and clacked the long front teeth of top and bottom jaw together. "You might do well too to ask the sparrow-king—so righteous in his forest nest—why it is he lets revers be made in the hinter of his own autumn—his own realm!" It straightened to look down its long nose at him. "If you are of such wisdom and thew, frail ouranin, why do you not do better than me and go and bring out all the skulking, simple-souled sprosslings from those loathsome dog-fighting dens?"

"I-I am but one . . . boy . . . I could barely help one," he countered. "You are a great lord of the monsters!"

"A *boy,* forsooth! Is that how you see it, oh wise one? Have clean now! You are much more than a mere *boy!* That is ichor in your innards and there is cruor on your hands. You have felled our frair and used your great vigor in the defense of the everyman foe. How would *you* answer *me* if I were to call you to account and pronounce judgment, as is my long privilege?"

Rossamünd opened his mouth in response yet could offer none. He ducked his head, strange passion thrumming under his ribs.

The Lapinduce gave a grim smile, a disconcerting expression in such an animal face. "You are right, however, when you say that I am great. I am grandfather to the hills and elder brother to the vinegar's boundaries, but restrictions there are to my reach, margins that I have placed on myself and limits laid down upon me." It lapsed and its sight became inward as it began to walk about the woodland hollow, touching flower and branch, leaf and stalk, humming a muted variation to the tune it played so stridently on the spinet.

The glade was quiet but for this mellifluous purring. The soft caw of a high-passing ibis and the subdued whisper of wind-shifting trees only joined the sympathetic melody.

Rossamünd found himself swaying in accord with the monster-lord's throaty music, the very core of him vibrating with ponderous complex regret for the discord between monster and man; with anger confounded by a peculiarly happy melancholy that folded back to anger again; with great longing for an ease and joy once known so well so long ago. With a shock of clarity he realized that he must be feeling what the Lapinduce felt. He smudged away a lonely tear that had squeezed unheeded to tickle down his cheek.

"Ahh . . . this has been a most excellent deliberation," the Lapinduce abruptly declared, breaking the chant of its throaty music. "You are most certainly an unwitting yet faithful student of the Sparrowlengis, your watchful sparrow-duke. He too thinks better of men than they deserve and defends them in obedience to the ancient treaties." It eyed Rossamünd cannily, and he felt his very soul shudder. "Yet for me the blackest of all the blackest things I have seen is an everyman's evilness to a fellow everyman——"

"Or everymen—enemies only because they do not know better—flayed and splashed to the eight winds by a nicker's claws!" was the young factotum's own reflexive retort.

"Ahh." The monster-lord smiled narrowly. "Yet is their thoughtlessness an excuse?" It raised a blunt bony claw. "Who is responsible for one's thoughtlessness if not a soul itself? Enough evidence there is of *our* good support to change an everyman's opinion a score of times over should any care to look better, but they will not. The kingdoms of everymen stand much through the protection of our blithely frair, yet still they course and kill them."

"But there are those everymen who have thought better," Rossamünd countered stoutly. "I have seen monster-slayers show kindness . . ."

"Little doubt you speak with your mistress in mind—the Brambly Rose, who has taken you into her care."

The young factotum's eyes went round with amazement. "How—"

"*How* again, is it?" The Lapinduce's blank expression held the shadow of a bestial smirk. "*How* is it I know that you serve Europa of Naimes, Duchess-in-waiting, the Brambly Rose? How is it I know that—as I have done—she saved you from the grasp of selfish souls knitting abominations in their high stone hall on the edge of Master Sparrow's autumn?" It arched a brow. "Why, Lentigo has told me . . ."

"Lentigo, sir?"

"The one you know as Freckle, who goes huc illuc to all points and serves none but Providence."

To this Darter Brown puffed himself and gave an affirming kind of chirp.

"He is here?" Rossamünd looked about rapidly, thinking the plucky glamgorn might emerge from the shadows.

"Most certainly, quizzing ouranin! Lentigo has been and is now gone. Very anxious he is after your weal in the custody of one so infamous as is this orguline, the Rose of Brandentown. Ahh, a hindrance and blight to all euriphim is she . . . I would like to meet her before she all too soon perishes. She suspects, I think, that I am here. Many times has her square-faced servant-man stood under my trees to sniff me out . . . He failed, of course."

Suddenly the young factotum realized he had forgotten . . . *Europe's treacle!*

Anxious now to get back to Cloche Arde and attend his testtelating duties, Rossamünd opened his mouth to ask his leave of this perplexing creature. Yet before he could press his plea, the Lapinduce spoke.

"An ouranin as manservant to an orguline . . ." the Lapinduce's bestial eye twinkled with a cold mirth. "Complexity, I see, follows you like flies do a dung cart. Ever it is like this for an ouranin; never fitting, always searching on and on through generations and on into history . . . Come, let me show you a fine trick."

Immediately the monster-lord stalked out of the dell, ears back, finding a path that wended deviously among the thickets.

Keen not to get lost in the hedging woods, Rossamünd had to run to keep pace while Darter Brown dashed low before him. A goodly way into the park, breath rasping in windpipe, he found the Lapinduce had halted atop a size-able mound. Ears tall, standing alert in the thick shadow of a geriatric pine, the monster-lord peered down with keen intent on something below. Creeping on soft clover to hunker by the creature's side, Rossamünd could see through crooked branches a figure prowling down in the parkland gloom maybe only a half-a-hundred yards away, a heavyset fellow in a deep green soutaine and a black tricorn pulled over his white wig.

The young factotum's innards went still.

It was one of the Broken Doll's door wards.

Rossamünd clenched every muscle, ready to leap into hand strokes.

"They have trespassed deep indeed in search for their lost chum . . . and for you too, I think," the rabbit-duke breathed. "They will not seek for long. Watch. . . "

The intruding fellow was scowling at the darksome nooks and threatening crannies, patently uneasy at his task. Calls came through the trees—other searchers on the prowl. Shouting his own reply over his shoulder, the door ward approached the base of the hillock where the Lapinduce and Rossamünd were hid.

The Lapinduce closed its eyes and let out a slow hissing breath.

All around the threwd *thickened,* a settling dismal chill.

The young factotum shivered.

The door ward hesitated and stared anxiously about. There came another cry to the left, its unintelligible words possessing a warning. The intruder began to withdraw, the calls retreating with him until the woodland hush relaxed and the threwd eased to its usual gentle watchfulness.

"Come, ouranin," said the Lapinduce, "let us return to my court."

"So what of you, oh ill-named one!" Stepping to its spinet stool and sitting, the Lapinduce peered at Rossamünd keenly. "I did not save you to pass you back to bloodthirsting everymen." For a moment it sounded angry. "You ought depart from here to live in proper seclusion with the sparrow-duke and Cinnamon, so interested in your progress; let this generation and all its selfish single-mindedness pass into matter. I can grant you easy passage to your sparrow-lord to dwell in peace till all things are restored. Yet it is for *you* alone to choose your progress."

Rossamünd breathed long and deep. How simple it might be to take up the Lapinduce's offer, to retreat and live safe, and make forays out into the cities to overturn every rousing-pit or massacar he could find. For just a moment Rossamünd's soul soared with the idea. Yet, as quickly as it swelled, this hope sank again. "Europe has risked too much for me to desert her now," he breathed, swallowing back on the knot griping in his throat. "Fransitart and Craumpalin too . . ."

A melancholy shadow passed through the Lapinduce's ancient gaze. "An answer at last to my original question . . . ," it murmured heavily. "Brutish and short are the lives of every men; do not expect your own with them to be different."

211

Rossamünd looked to his hands—a man's hands, a monster's hands.

Born out of the mud from some other soul's parts . . .

"It is time for you to return to your chosen mistress," the rabbit-duke commanded abruptly. It coughed to summon Ogh and Urgh. "Follow them close and do not mind their bold divagations; they shall show you by their own route to familiar paths that will take you home again."

Rossamünd hesitated. He glanced anxiously to the sliver of forenoon sun peeking over the towering eastern wall—so much higher from this sunken vantage. *How did it get so high?* Surely they had talked only for some moments.

Flicking its coat hems to sit properly on its stool, the Lapinduce lifted long hands to play. "I will likely not see you again, ouranin," it said without looking to him. Flourishing a blunt-clawed hand, it gave the spinet voice once more, a wild tune that had the urchin-lord's arms and deft fingers running along every octave. It closed its eyes and was lost in the music.

Reeling, Rossamünd slowly heeded a gentle tugging at his right shin. Ogh—or was it Urgh—was pulling at his stocking with its teeth, while its twin was slowly hopping to the farthest of the three arches and out of the court. With a final, heavy-hearted glance at the furious playing of the Lapinduce, the young factotum followed, leaving the glorious monster-lord in its hidden musical court.

10

A BAD EXCUSE IS
BETTER THAN NONE

crimp(s) privately operating impress contractor, that is, a group or individual licensed to press people into naval or military service. They are usually given a quota by a ram's captain or a regimental colonel and with this authority trawl the streets of less well-heeled districts, seizing anyone appearing at that moment not to be engaged in gainful activity, regardless of the poor soul's true employment status.

I N dour fungal light the twin rabbits Ogh and Urgh took Rossamünd down the bending root-walled course, loping at an easy pace yet keeping out of his reach. He tried once to stride forward and pat one, and in an instant they shot ahead into the twilight of the tunnel that led away from the Lapinduce.

"Wait! Wait!" he called, finding them sitting in gloom in the middle of the passage floor, eyes glittering, noses twitching rapidly.

Guided by the flash of their bobbing sallow tails, he was shown through many dim intersections and lighted burrows, the flanks of the warren becoming coarser, more uneven. Tessellated floor gave over to cool earth and cold puddles, the walls to rough earth, then quickly to the brick and stone of the city's deep-sunk foundations. Finally even radiant fungus ceased, the threwd shrinking to little more than a sleepy suggestion, the merest hint for those who might care to notice.

Moldy twilight gave over to a strengthening warmer glow. Just about a bend he discovered Ogh and Urgh stopped, sitting silhouettes before a ragged window of umber and blue; the end of the hole.

"Thank you, good sirs," he said to the rabbits, bowing to each in turn, wishing they might respond with words of their own and divulge primeval secrets.

Mute, they regarded him blankly, noses ever *twitch twitch twitch*.

With a sigh, the young factotum pushed through the shrouding fringe of unchecked vegetation, and, blinking near-blinded in the bright afternoon sun, almost slid down the steeply slanted side of the brick-paved drain. Gripping the edge of the hole, he saw that he had emerged into the *usual* world from between the weedy roots of an old turpentine growing far beyond the bounds of the Moldwood in some tiny neglected common.

By its green trickle and orange carp he easily identified this channel. *The Midwetter!*—the very one flowing by Cloche Arde.

Darter Brown appeared over the top of the high roofs— somehow reckoning Rossamünd's path despite his hidden progress. With a *tweet!* the little fellow alighted on a spear-pointed post of the fence that lined the height of the drain.

Rossamünd straightened, set his thrice-high firmly on his head and went on by way of the channel, back to service and contradictions. Walking carefully along the slope, he had the disorienting sensation of rousing from a deep and convincing dream—some mystic abyss—to finally gasp mundane and sensible air. By the time he clambered up the side of the bridge to Footling Inch, his time with the Lapinduce was a small disquieting memory and his thoughts were more concerned with how he might explain his absence to his mistress.

Kitchen greeted him in the cold black vestibule. "Glad to see you have elected to return to us, Master Bookchild," the steward began, a little dryly. "You are *expected* in our gracious lady's file."

With a quiet knock at the carven door, Rossamünd waited for the usual "In." When it did not occur, he rapped a little louder, at which the portal opened, revealing not Europe in some splendid gown but Fransitart, his worn, worried-looking eyes going wide with sharp relief.

"Rossamünd!" he barked, grasping him by the shoulder as if never to let him go.

"Master Frans?" Rossamünd said. "Where is Miss Europe?" Part stepping, part pulled into the file, he found Craumpalin there too, rising quickly from an easy chair before the fire, looking at him like one returned from the grave.

"Pullets and cockerels! We thought ye pinched by the crimps, lad, and forced to serve upon a cargo!" Fransitart chided sharply, guiding him to the comfortable chairs.

"Oh, no, not the crimps, Master Frans." The young facto-tum frowned abstractedly as he took a seat by Craumpalin.

"Aye, or carried off by some ill-informed mercator!" the old dispensurist added gruffly.

"Where were ye at, Rossamünd?" Fransitart demanded, staring him hard in the eye. A penetrating, almost suspicious concern dawned in his eyes. "What troubles ye? What did ye see?"

At that point Europe chose to enter, looking flushed and puffing as if she had been running many miles. She was wearing a long-hemmed seclude of diagonal pink, red and dark magenta stripes clinched about her waist with broad black satin, its hems, collar and turned-up cuffs white em-broidered with thread-of-gold.

"Is this to be your mode from here on, little man?" she asked with cool irony by way of salutation. "Are you think-ing, now that I have released you from the straits of military life, to begin a career of adolescent revelry?"

"No . . . no, Miss Europe," he answered, a little surprised by his own directness. "Not intentionally, anyway."

"Well, out with it! A bad excuse is better than none. Where have you been?" Her gaze narrowed as she dabbed with a plush towel at the damp glow upon her forehead.

Rossamünd had no notion of how to proceed.

"I—"

He had assumed he would tell them everything. Now it had come to it, he was powerfully disinclined to reveal much at all of the Lapinduce. The monster-lord had demanded no such fidelity, yet it was surely a betrayal to reveal its presence. Regardless, a man had died in pursuit of him. Surely Europe needed to know of this!

"They—uh . . ." He gathered himself. "After the play, Rookwood and his obsequine friends took me to a chancery that was connected to a rousing-pit, where I—"

Fransitart sucked in sharply. "Avast ye, lad! What point o' compass did ye find such a place?"

"By tunnels under the Broken Doll . . ."

His old masters shifted unhappily in their places.

"There's an ill-hearted den." Craumpalin whistled in consternation.

Europe showed no such dismay. "And you did *what* there?" she pursued, shrewd suspicion dawning in her gaze.

"I-I botched a dog. One of the nickers got free, so I . . . I threw glister in the face of a swordist trying to slay it."

There was a beat of stunned silence.

"Why di'n't ye simply weigh and depart at th' outset, lad, when ye first knew what manner of people ye was with and what place ye was at?" Fransitart questioned.

"They had locked us in. Besides, I could not leave"—*my frair*, Rossamünd almost said—"the little fellow undefended in that foul hole!"

Europe closed her eyes long-sufferingly. "You do not always have to heed your conscience, Rossamünd. I find it is a troublesome guide to action, bringing all breeds of inconvenience. Was your *intervention* seen?"

Rossamünd felt his cheeks flush guiltily. "A spurn of one of the pit's patrons saw me. A wit . . ." His words caught in his throat. "He chased me from there."

"And my point is proven," the fulgar said bitterly. She sat carefully upon a tandem before the fire. "So tell me, little man, how did you manage to escape a wit?"

"I took a takeny from the Broken Doll, but once the driver realized a wit was on us, he put me out near the Moldwood and I ran into it. I hid far inside the park and stayed hidden all night. Th-then at day I came by the drain to get home."

Though he kept his words grave and even, a great wrench of compunction gripped his innards, the manifest tearing of loyalties. Firm, however, in his conviction to keep the Lapinduce hid, he held to his tale, fixing his gaze upon the fire lest they all see the evasion in his eyes.

Fransitart scrutinized him sharply, disappointment clear in his face.

Pulling at his beard, Craumpalin stared at the fine Turkic hearth rug.

Yet, astonishingly, they said nothing.

Europe regarded Rossamünd narrowly. "I wonder," she queried with subtle scorn, "if the patrons of the pit know they have hired the services of so *unskilled* a strivener as a fellow who loses another soul so *easily* in the limitations of a well-fenced park."

Resisting the urge to duck his head, Rossamünd kept his attention upon the consuming flames and said nothing.

An unpleasant quiet ruled.

Rossamünd's humours pounded like an accusation at his temples.

Europe flicked at some smidgen upon her thigh. "I see

you preserved your hat at least, little man. Bravo."

"Aye, Miss Europe."

"Since you have been awake hiding the entire night," his mistress went on, "perhaps you ought to go and rest now?"

His soul burned. "I . . . I am well enough, ma'am."

She stared at him searchingly. "It is good then that we are shortly to go on the knave," she said flatly.

"How might that aid us, m'lady?" Fransitart pressed. "Trouble keeps for safe returns."

Europe bent her spoored brow. "To go out and come back with my bag full of prizes and new-pricked marks upon my arm shall amply prove all bad wind and ill rumor unfounded." Closing her eyes, the fulgar smoothed her thin eyebrows with thumb and forefinger. "This has all been very diverting, but we have our own course to prepare. Banish fruitless recollections, Rossamünd; you have much to do to make ready. As for you, Masters Vinegar and Salt," she added to the old vinegaroons, "seek out Latissimus in the coach-house across the road for your duties. I was to have us away today but . . ."

"Delays change ways," Craumpalin muttered.

"Indeed, Master Salt." Europe blinked at him. "We shall spend what is left to us of today to make ready."

Caffene arrived in an elaborate steaming multivalved pot, and with it the information that Master Learned, stouching tutor, was awaiting their gracious mistress in the ludion, and they were dismissed.

"Oh, and should you be wondering, Rossamünd . . . I did my treacle myself this morning." She flicked her hand

219

in mild irritation at Rossamünd's chastened expression. "It was correct enough for the purpose, though I dare to admit my palate is happy you are returned." The fulgar gazed at him for a moment. "Please do not make me drink my own makings again."

For the rest of the day, Rossamünd attended to the preparations. Every store to be taken was gathered in the stowing room at the rear of the stately home. The landaulet was brought down the narrow drive between the flank of the house and the outer wall, and the whole collection steadily stowed in its holdfasts and panniers. Into a plethora of lacquered boxes and lidded hampers went all manner of fine foods that had once amazed Rossamünd on his first jaunt with the Branden Rose through the Brindleshaws. These included a profusion of whortleberries, of course, and, at Rossamünd's request, fortified sack-cheese. To his delight, there was also juice-of-orange. From the saumery came black-lacquered parts-boxes with ample quantities of all the salts needed for Europe's treacle. Largest of all was a great trunk for the coats and various other parts of harness for the Branden Rose, and lesser ones for her underclothes and for her shoes, the smallest her traveling fiasco. Each coat was numbered to a system he did not rightly understand, for to him every garment looked of comparably excellent make. Her Number 8, for example, was the richly furred magenta coat Europe had worn at the inquiry; her Number 2 was a magnificently embroidered black campaign coat similar to that which had been made for Rossamünd by Master Brugelle; and her Number 3 was the very scarlet frock coat his mistress had worn at his first sight of her from under the boxthorn on the Vestiweg. Her Number 1—of shifting carmine, its sleeves a mist of finest organza, its collar sprayed with delicately dyed feathers—did not come. From the armory in the foundations of Cloche Arde, Nectarius reverently brought the fulgaris—stage and fuse—cleaned and glistening with preserving oils.

Among all these items came a small box of silver and ivory. Daring a look within, Rossamünd found Europe's sprither, laid in padded plush of deep red. Used to draw the cruor— the dead blood—from a slain monster to be used to make monster-blood tattoos, it was the one tool common to every teratologist. Probably in vain, Rossamünd hoped he would never need to employ it on the knave. Worse, he contemplated with horror, was the thought of being the one Europe would expect to mark another little "x" of victory and add to those that already stood in ranks upon his mistress' arms. *She will employ a punctographist, surely* . . . he offered to himself as a comfort, and his thoughts instantly skipped to the marking upon Fransitart's arm that Rossamünd knew now *would* show as a cruorpunxis. It was a small comfort that they were to be out on the knave when it revealed itself.

Established as Europe's driver and navigator, Fransitart and Craumpalin went out to the Dogget & Block to retrieve their meager chattels and returned as the full reach of heaven was gilt by the slanting day. Rossamünd could not look them in the eye as they deposited their belongings to be packed. In their turn, the two old vinegaroons seemed all a-sea for words, and it was a great relief when Kitchen brought summons for them to repair inside to further discuss the terms of their service with Europe.

When the stowing was near completion, there came a commotion at the front of the house. Joined by Wenzel, one of Europe's footmen, Rossamünd walked up the short drive to see. Three glossy coaches driven by heavy-harnessed lentermen rattled to a halt in the narrow, shadowed coach yard. Doors were flung wide as each conveyance disgorged its plush belly of passengers. Most numerous were the more than half a dozen serious men in the sleek green harness of the Broken Doll, all firelocks and bludgeons and bristling hostility as they made a cordon about the carriages. With them came legal gents in their frilly legal solitaires, wads of paper firmly under arm.

Rossamünd's soul sank to knock in his knees. So soon had last night's consequences caught up with him.

"Bother me!" Wenzel cursed, and immediately scurried back down the side way.

From the press of manly green strode Pater Maupin, proprietor of the Broken Doll, stakeholder in the rousing-pit. Still handsome despite gaining age, he was an elegant man with oddly sallow papery skin, dressed in a long-frocked coat of shimmering purple, ruffles of silk spraying out about his throat and over his hands. Beneath his curling periwig he had a genial face with kindly eyes, yet Rossamünd thought he glimpsed cold steel in the soul that schemed behind them.

PATER MAUPIN

A strange burbling twitter in its throat, Darter Brown emerged from the pencil pine in the middle of the yard to land staunchly on Rossamünd's hatless head.

Coming as protector at Maupin's side was the very sabrine adept who had hacked at the Handsome Grackle, clad in his eccentric harness, his eyes yet raw from the glister thrown in his face. At the proprietor's other flank sashayed the deadly dexter woman, Anaesthesia Myrrh, dour-faced and festooned in black, thrusting before her the most startling arrival of them all. For there in her cruel grip, still dressed in his carmine coat and black longshanks, was Rookwood, downcast, defeated and utterly ashamed.

"Is *this* the little selt-kisser, then?" Pater Maupin demanded coldly of his white-haired hostage, his voice smooth like cream, his sneer like a blow. "Was this your worrisome guest of yesternight?"

Rookwood's harried glance flicked over Rossamünd.

Becoming glassy-eyed, submerging any guilt, the young factotum simply blinked at him.

Rookwood shrugged, and at a signaling flick of Maupin's silk-shrouded and violently jolted, contracting in on himself under the dexter's brief *encouragement*. Sagging in the woman's grasp, Rockwood nodded. "Yes . . . yes, it is . . ."

The old proprietor's eyes slitted in silent, vengeful fury.

Ears ringing, Rossamünd tautened, ready for desperate deeds.

"Pitter-Patter Maupin, Needle of the Dogs," Europe's voice purred from behind.

224

Rossamünd's shoulder tingled at the firm touch of her hand.

"What remarkable occasion has provoked you to shift from your seamy couch to belabor me at my own door?" Europe's feigned sociability was the barest mask. "I see you have brought your full menagerie," she continued. Wholly ignoring the swordist, she regarded Rookwood fleetingly, then cocked a dismissive brow to the dexter and said, "Anaesthesia," dipping her alabaster brow in mock courtesy to the black-clad lahzar.

Jerking the forlorn white-haired fellow aside, the dexter peered at the fulgar steadily, eyeing her as an untested rival. About her and her master the sturdy fellows closed, inflating their brave bosoms and glowering meaningfully. Watching Rossamünd closely, the swordist fondled the broad strapping of a bautis—the heavy wooden cylinder that held the deadly therimoir—hanging across his back.

The young factotum shivered at the thought of the virulent white blade.

"Well-a-day, Lady Bramble," Pater Maupin answered smoothly. "Is that the fashion in which one greets an old compatriot in the ancient struggle? I have come only to recoup grave *losses*," he said, lingering darkly on the word, "incurred through no provocation of my own—or that of my associates—by a member of your own staff, namely that stunted mewling there." He flicked a ruffled gesture Rossamünd's way.

"Truly . . ." Europe's word dripped sugary malevolence. "And how, pray, has that to do with me?"

225

Maupin smiled with his own cunning. "Perhaps you did not know the full and base character of such a fresh-appointed *employé*," he said sidlingly. "I know only too well that one cannot reckon every facet in a person before engaging them, and as such I—we—do not care to hold you personally indemnified . . ."

"How kind," Europe murmured, and regarded him languidly, a deadly kind of smirk fluttering at the sharp edges of her ruddy lips. "Yet I *know* the full character of this one *full* well, sir. If you have found exception with it, the fault can only lie with you."

The owner of the Broken Doll possessed himself enough to refrain from choking on her words. "If this were simply damage and depletion, I might accept such unkind expressions so ungraciously given and move on." Though he kept his voice even, a heavy passion lurked under it. "Yet it also involves the vanishment of a much valued deputy who had, this night gone, set out to fetch yon brat"—a glare for Rossamünd—"and present him to proper justice."

"Vanished, is it?" The fulgar's gaze flicked for the briefest inquiring glance to her young factotum. "How careless of you, Pitter-Patter, to lose dear people so . . ."

The proprietor's mien darkened. "It is more than this, sparking hag. My deputy is, I suspect, undone. Not slot nor drag nor particle of him can be found."

Rossamünd swallowed.

"Even less will you discover here, *sir*," the Branden Rose said coolly.

"I little doubt it." Lifting his chin, Maupin peered down

his cheeks at her, his expression plainly telling that he believed *her* the reason for the dandi-dressed wit's end.

The tingling in Rossamünd's shoulder where his mistress' hand rested became a needling.

"Surely you have more useful pastimes," she said, "than to impugn me and my staff upon the witness of confessions swingeingly extracted from some tetter-faced obsequine. You waste both our days, sir!"

Forgotten and slinking slowly to the fringe of the threatening host, Rookwood cringed at his mention and, with a bitter glance through the gang of roughs to Rossamünd, slunk yet farther from the epicenter of conflicting wills.

"Waste makes for want." Maupin smiled dangerously. "And I—and my associates—*want* fair due. Let this one"— he sneered once more to the young factotum, who balled his fists and scowled in return—"sit beneath a telltale's gaze. If he is condemned by his own words, I shall, as I said, not charge you as responsible. You can hire yourself another runt—there are plenty to be had."

"I happen to like this particular *runt*," Europe returned with utmost calm. "He shall stay with me."

Maupin's two spurns stepped forward, the swordist with bautis-box open, the dexter Anaesthesia smirking, her dark lace and black frills prickling with static.

The Branden Rose did not shift, yet her own menace seemed to magnify.

Staying his ground, Rossamünd wished he had more than his clenched fists for weapons and a simple weskit for proofing.

227

Here Maupin chose to raise his hand, the slightest sign for his own staff to yield. "No need for such vulgar behavior, I think," he said calmly.

The genteel clearing of a throat sounded from on high.

The young factotum—and everyone with him—looked above to find the windows on several floors of Cloche Arde thrown open, the slender barrels of several firelocks protruding from them with menace of their own. Among the various house staff Rossamünd spied Fransitart at the window of his set, a particularly heavy musketoon raised to his shoulder, and at the very next casement found Craumpalin, potives clearly in hand. The dispenser threw him a wink. Even Pallette was there, glowering down as if this were weapon enough. Below them, in Europe's file, stood Mister Kitchen, blunderbuss firmly under arm and trained squarely upon the proprietor of the Broken Doll.

"Might I humbly suggest m'lord choose more fulfilling activities for himself today," the steward offered steadily.

Pater Maupin's brows rose slightly, his eyes passionless as they took in the situation. He smiled an empty reptilian smile. "The quality of your help has sadly deteriorated, madam," he said, and with that he turned and walked through his servants, the roughs parting before him like the vinegar before the blade of a ram. The whole tribe of pugilists gathered themselves back into their coaches, the dexter Anaesthesia ever keeping her cold regard on Europe, staring at her still from the carriage window as the company went on their way.

Turning her back on it all, the heiress of Naimes fixed

Rossamünd with an inquisiting eye. "It seems the events of your excursion went a little more *eventfully,* little man."

Watching the glimpse of the last carriage retreat south down the Harrow Road, Rossamünd would not look to her. "They would not have fought, would they?" he asked solemnly.

"Maupin was certainly in earnest," the fulgar answered slowly. "How much further he might go, I cannot say." With a meaningful look and no further questions, she peered up at the jumble of staff still at Cloche Arde's windows. "Thank you, Mister Kitchen," she called. "Inform Condamine that it will be roast hart's tongue and a glass of vinothe for all tonight."

"As you will, m'lady." The steward becked, his eyes glittering with pleasure.

The yard empty of clattering racket, Rookwood was found, bruised and left behind, hobbling for the gate. Finding himself discovered, the young fellow halted and bobbed obsequiously.

"Are you well, sir?" Rossamünd inquired, hurrying to help the fellow.

"I'm sorry, my man," Rookwood breathed in apology. "They were just too . . . persuasive."

Summoning him over, Europe inspected her battered white-haired guest silently. "Mooning after lahzarines is simple stuff from a safe vantage," she said finally, "but commerce with Cathar's children will only bring you grief."

Clearly overwrought, Rookwood paled and quivered, bending low and uttering fumbling words of contrition. "They . . . they saw me with Rossamünd last night . . .

They sought me out . . . No harm on my part in any fashion intended . . . Threatened such grievous harms upon my aunt . . . I had no part in . . . in . . ."

The fulgar finally interjected. "Enough, sir! You have been tangled in more than your share. Sit in my hiatus until a carriage is brought."

"This is more than I deserve," Rookwood said, face contorting into an ugly imitation of a humiliated grin.

"Yes," said Europe coolly, "it is . . . ," and she left him to Rossamünd's uneasy care.

As their guest settled in the waiting room, rubbing his face with a wet cloth, some warming saloop was brought.

Eager to have a task to punctuate the awkwardness, the young factotum sought upstairs for his stoups and a measure of levenseep to mix with the beverage. "Are you hurt this time?" he asked upon his return, knowing full well what it was like to suffer a fulgar's puissance.

"More in honor than in limb, sad to say," Rookwood replied, ducking his head. "That's twice you've picked me off the ground in as many days, sir—I am in your debt." Shamefaced as he might have appeared, he was sipping saloop heartily enough. "So tell me, Mister Bookchild, did you *truly* throw stinging powders about the pit?"

"Aye—"

"Wo-ho!" The fancy fellow chuckled, his vigor clearly returning. "And I thought *I* had pluck . . . I don't know what made you do it, but you caused a genuine uprising, people running and crying out." He peered at Rossamünd admiringly. "I tell you, Pitter-patter More-Pins is terribly upset, as he kept telling me. Most of the pit's collection got free. Folks'll have to go to the Pin & Needle now for their pit-side thrills."

With a bemused smile, Rossamünd shrugged as if it were all a matter of course, keeping his satisfaction at such news to himself.

Perhaps mistaking this as something less happy, Rook-wood lifted a placating hand. "Never fear, my man, we have all done a fool's part in early life. I'll not begrudge you your eccentricities if you'll pardon my part in today's adventure." The fellow beamed at him as if doing him a great favor.

Relieved soon enough of Rookwood's company—the white-haired fellow leaving in good spirits with a promise that they should try such an adventure again presently—Rossamünd retreated to the peace of the saumery.

Steps rang on the stairs as Europe entered without a knock.

"I see you have been quick to refurbish," she observed lightly, eyes passing over the blanks where the cabinet pic-tures had once been. They came to rest on a copy of the "Notice to the People" from Winstermill, retrieved by Pal-lette from his old frock-coat pocket and fixed to the wall with court-plaster.

"Aye," Rossamünd answered a little cautiously.

Europe stood for a moment while he made show of fos-sicking through a parts drawer. "I thought it necessary to show you the making of the traces and lesser draughts I require," she said suddenly. "Yet first I must know that I can trust the one to

231

whom I show such learning." She paused pointedly, apparently absorbed in some mark on a parts drawer.

"I—" Rossamünd hung his head. "Aye, you can . . ."

"Do you think me simple, little man?" his mistress purred, turning her keen gaze on him.

A dark thrill of compunction rippled through his soul. "I—uh—n-no . . ."

"Do you truly think I would believe even the least wit could lose you as easily as you have told to me?"

Rossamünd had no response for this.

Europe took a seat on the sole highback in the room. "Pater Maupin is too well served for such a valued and missing servant to remain unfound . . . And you and I together know that *you* could not have ended your pursuer."

"No . . ." His voice was the merest breath of air.

Even this small admission was a profound relief.

The fulgar beheld him.

Glance by reluctant glance, Rossamünd lifted his attention to look at her squarely and found in her canny hazel regard that she understood much yet held her words . . . Rossamünd was grateful she did not press for more.

Abruptly, she produced a thin tome from her coat, handbound in scuffed and reddened reptilian hide. "*This* is an expurgatory, a lahzar's list—"

Rossamünd sucked in a breath.

"I see you know of them." Europe's smile was thin. "You must never be found with it—suspicion is one thing but proof another. Stow it the same with cunning you are employing to keep last night's secrets . . ."

Rossamünd stared at the small volume in awe as it was handed to him. Within was a collection of disparate papers, marked mostly in two hands: one he did not recognize and the other he instantly identified as Licurius' graceful script. The thaumacra were in order of incidence of use rather than letter-fall: saltegrade, unbordated felibrium, levinfuse, syntony, sangfaire and several more. Among the recipes were esoteric hints to sources of the best parts, impossible properties like falseman's ichor or kraulschwimmen gall, and their nearest alternatives, quotes of ancient lore and even scrawled obscenities against the ünterman.

"Saltegrade is for before every fight," Europe explained. "Levinfuse is for the biggest stouches, felibrium I have to take at the start of each week and am currently running low . . ." She went through them all.

A little lighter in his heart, Rossamünd stared at the script for saltegrade as if to press it into his mind, repeating the parts over and over under his breath, "Three parts Spice of Zichre . . . one part salt-in-gloom . . ." He looked up. "Miss Europe, I apologize for . . . for trying to save the Grackle . . . and provoking that Maupin fellow."

Pursing her lips, Europe considered him, her eyes clouded, her intent unclear.

"One might think," she said at last, "that with an Imperial Secretary, a military clerk and a massacar of minor talent as enemies, our tale had its count of antagonists without adding more."

Rossamünd looked at her shamefacedly, but she did not

233

notice, nodding rather to the black stink rising from the testing pan behind him.

"I think you will need to brew again, little man," the fulgar said mildly, "unless char is to be your latest *innovation* on my treacle."

11

A STATELY INVITATION

nuntio(s) official messengers of the Emperor and his regents, and, when required, bearing the authority of the one who sent them. Their private counterparts—used by magnates and peers—are the sillards (sing. silas). Both are distinct from scopps and mercers in that they are especially engaged by individuals for their exclusive service, rather than being available for general hire.

THE new day—the knaving day—was an insubstantial gleam when Rossamünd roused, washed, dressed, breakfasted and turned out in the coach yard with all the military haste of a pageant-of-arms at Winstermill.

"An unripe start for young and old, is it not, sir?" Latissimus muttered affably as he and the stablery hands heaved the tarpaulin-covered landaulet out into the yard proper, ready for hitching horses.

Rossamünd smiled and breathed into his cupped hands, staring up at the icily clear sky. To the south the element was souring, as spring was wont to do in these lower climes— a poor promise for a day of travel. The clitterty-clatterty jink and rough panting of horses sounded on the Harrow

Road, bringing his attention earthward. To his astonishment two taut fellows rode into the yard, each astride a horse of the richest velvet black harnessed in shortened petrailles. In his first shock, Rossamünd thought them agents of Pater Maupin and the roust sponsors returning to reassert their demand for satisfaction, yet he quickly fathomed by the cut and mottle of their harness that these two were of a more official sort.

One rider in a black long coat and mitre was clearly a duffer. His companion, a man in courtly splendor, equally sable-clad but with fine lacings of pristine white and wearing a thick periwig of black, peered up at the house with veiled apprehension as he let one of the stablery hands take his horse by its bridle.

"Well-a-day, good sirs," Rossamünd greeted them firmly, even as Mister Kitchen emerged from the house, Wenzel the footman in tow to do the same.

"Nuntio Malapropus," the splendid periwigged fellow enunciated, looming over them on his well-harnessed steed, attention turning back and forth between Rossamünd and Kitchen, unsure of whom to address. "I am sent by his pleni-potentiary graciousness, the Archduke, with a dispatch for the Lady Rose, Heiress of Naimes."

A nuntio! The young factotum marveled. Such as these were only ever sent from important folk to other important folk upon important occasions. Instructing Kitchen to usher the ducal messenger to the hiatus, Rossamünd hurried to Europe's file two or three steps at a time.

"The Branden Duke has dispatched a nuntio," the fulgar

observed coldly, issuing only half harnessed from the obscure door that led to her boudoir. "How sweet." Patently unhappy at the interruption, she peered down into the yard. "I wonder what can have moved him to send to such *humble* folks as we," she concluded frostily.

Taking her time to dress in partial harness, Europe finally stalked from her file, Rossamünd scuttling after. Down in the vestibule, the Branden Rose thrust open its glossy black doors with a flourish.

"Gracious lady," cried the sartorially splendid nuntio with stilted enthusiasm, turning with a hasty jerk from his candid inspection of a great painted screen of a bogle hunt stretching across one whole wall. Bowing long and low, the man swept his white-edged tricorn before him in a complex movement, ending with it wedged firmly under his left armpit. Draped across his black wide-hemmed frock coat with its white trimmings was a silken sash of sky blue that matched the vibrant stockings and fancy mules he wore instead of boots. High upon his back he bore a satchel of buff, cowhide naturally blotched black and white in the mottle of Brandenbrass. The nuntio straightened and stood tall, impressively dignified.

"I am come to stand for his grace, the Archduke of our most beloved city, and, upon his behalf and the behalf of his loyal Parliament, offer you a worthy invitation."

"An invitation, indeed," Europe returned, utterly unimpressed. "Have I been good or have I been bad, to warrant such a gesture?"

The nuntio said nothing but simply produced a black

237

hide envelope from his satchel and handed it to her.

Looking down at it with one brow arched, Europe took the communication between thumb and forefinger as if it were an unsavory item. "You shall have my answer presently, man."

The messenger hesitated, ashen-faced. Clearly he expected an immediate response. "I should not wish to burden you, my lady, with any insistence, but—"

"Then don't," Europe said with the finality of a firmly closed door, pulling a bell-rope. "You may remain in my yard—it is a fine day to be out. One of my servants shall bring a reply when there is one to bring. Mister Kitchen!" She tilted her head, raising her voice ever so slightly. "Please see Master Nuntio to the door, thank you."

The nuntio remained for a moment longer, weighing his response. Finally, with another grand sweep of hat and arm, he declared, "I shall await your answer outside." Bidding them good day in a cold, stately voice, he left, shepherded out by Europe's steward.

Europe left the hiatus to go to her file, black buff envelope in hand, still unopened. "Are you coming, little man?"

He hurried after.

In her file, the fulgar finally opened the communication, producing from it a fine-looking fold of high-quality paper edged in equispaced squares formed of some dark metallic substance. At the top was a sigil device in black of a rabbit in rampant pose above the letters *PDetC*.

"It is indeed an invitation," Europe affirmed, clearly reading far ahead of Rossamünd's own wondering, sluggish pace.

"The dear," she growled—by which Rossamünd could only assume she meant the Archduke of Brandenbrass—"wants this very day to meet with me!"

"Why?" Rossamünd said in fright. "Does it say?"

But she did not answer him, pronouncing instead, "Go, Rossamünd. Put on your new harness. Our knave is suspended again." She almost spat this last. "Today we meet instead with the ruler of this terrible city."

Kitchen was called, her reply given and the nuntio departed.

To the clatter of retreating hooves, Rossamünd went directly to his set to ready himself.

"A meeting with the duke hisself," Pallette breathed in awe as she bustled in bearing a new jug of water for washing.

Deeply impressed, Rossamünd washed for a second time that morning, scrubbing back of neck and behind ears; he pared his nails and Pallette waxed his hair so flat and stiff that it sat like an arming-cap upon his head. When all was done, he felt so clean it stung.

For such a meeting the Branden Rose went dressed in a long-hemmed weskit of scarlet soe with intricate black piping down its front and a high buttoned collar in black. Despite the cool spring day, her arms were thinly covered in bag-sleeves of white gossamer gathered tight over her forearm with short black vambrins. With this she wore a wide skirt of sleek deep magenta with glorious twirls and lacings of thread-of-silver along its pleats and hem, and her usual bright-black equiteer boots. Most of her hair she wore down, with her rebellious fringe pinned under a compact variation on a tricorn fixed somehow to her crown by a glossy black comb and two simple hair tines. Finished with a light dusting of cosmetic unctions, she looked almost girl-like, winsome even, someone you might want to protect.

Sitting next to her, Rossamünd tried not to blush.

"Whatever troubles you?" the fulgar asked him, her gaze at once challenging and amused. "Have you never seen a woman before?"

They set out aboard the covered town coach pulled by a pair of glossy black geldings. These were superb-looking creatures, different from the drab nag Rossamünd remembered taking them across the Brindleshaws all those months ago.

Barely across the Midwetter bridge, the coach was intercepted by a gaunt, plain-harnessed gentleman running before a planquin-chair borne by four wiry men liveried in rouge and deep carmine—the mottle of Naimes. Possessing an air of solemn, predatory confidence, the gaunt fellow looked into the cabin and regarded them with all the shrewd patience of a hunter.

"Mister Slitt, is it not?" Europe spoke first, crooking a brow at the man.

"Aye, m'lady, Elecrobus Slitt, appendant to the Legation of Naimes," the fellow answered, half bowing and touching a knuckle to his grizzled and balding pate. "And I pray thy pardon for the interruption, duchess-daughter, but my Lord Sainte wishes to speak with you."

Out from the comfortable box climbed Lord Finance, Baron of Sainte, Captain-Secretary and Chief Emissary of the Naimes diplomatic mission, his smile warmer than the weak morning sun. "I hear you are off to the Archduke's court," he observed lightly as he clutched the door frame and sprang boldly to the long step. "May I join your diurnal jaunt, gracious daughter of Naimes?"

Rossamünd looked sidelong at the man. *He already knows?*

Europe regarded Finance subtly. "I shall not hinder you, sir."

The Baron's smile broadened—if such a thing were possible. "Thank you, Mister Slitt," he called behind to the gaunt man standing guard close behind. "You may return to Highstile Hall."

Regarding his master with uncomplaining—Rossamünd thought almost sad—eyes, Mister Slitt gave a curt bow and led the dogged planquin-carriers back down the Harrow Road.

With unexpected nimbleness, the Baron leaned out, opened the carriage door and swung in to sit a little heavily beside Rossamünd. He let out a contented sigh. "I come to furnish you with *intriguing* intelligence regarding your ducal summons."

"Do you now, Baron?" Europe remained cool.

A pause.

The fulgar would not be drawn.

"You must have figured for yourself, duchess-daughter," the Baron continued, "that after his excursion from his seldom-left den to accost you yesterday, Pater Maupin went immediately to complain to the Archduke of you and, once again, of your servant brooding here beside me. You are quite the busy fellow, are you not, Mister Bookchild?"

Feeling his cheeks redden, Rossamünd maintained his inspection of the passing city. Was there *anything* this fellow did not know?

"He certainly tests an exceptional treacle," Europe added drolly, giving her young factotum a satirical look.

The Baron's expression was tight now. "I am sure, gracious heir, he does. But you must know too—as one of Brandenbrass' worst-kept secrets—that the duke himself has a stake in the pit your factotum is supposed to have spoiled *and* that the missing wit—one Syncratis Pater—is . . . or rather *was* a nephew of Maupin's."

Rossamünd held back a groan of regret. *I should have come home sooner!* He began to chide himself, then stopped. If he had done so, the Grackle would be dead now *and* Gingerrice, and a good many other undeserving frair with them. As hard as the way was becoming, it was still the better path.

"The servants of Maupin ought to think better than to come after my own," the Duchess-in-waiting proclaimed. "Do you truly conceive my small-framed factotum could have undone this Syncratis fellow?"

"Surely not, m'lady," the Baron conceded. "Yet which version do you figure the Archduke will prefer? He was, dare I confess, *pleased* to have such witness against you. I overheard him quip that the Rose was falling at last on her own thorns." He lingered on this last phrase pointedly.

"Tell me something novel, sir," Europe growled. "His resentment of my residence in his state is common stuff."

Touching his knuckle to his lips, Finance made a small coughing sound. "I have to own, gracious lady, that no stately

IDIAS FINANCE
BARON OF SAINTE

lord *would* desire the heir of a rival living within his curtains. As much as anything, he fears war with your mother should any ill befall you whilst in his *care* . . .

"So you side with the Archduke, Lord Sainte?"

Finance's genial manner finally slipped. "We have argued this at many turns, m'lady," he said gravely, "and you *know* my side is ever with you, limb and blood."

A pause lingered pregnantly.

The Baron pressed knuckle to lip again. "I might dare to offer that you consider leaving this city before we suffer more of Mister Bookchild's *adventures*."

Obstinacy flashed briefly in the fulgar's veiled thoughts, but her voice remained even. "We would be on the knave this very morning but for my cousin duke's beckoning."

Finance's mien brightened again, and he dipped his head in approval. "A politic endeavor, m'lady, its success working entirely in your favor and, I venture," he said with a pointed smile, "a better use of your servant's proclivity for mayhem . . ."

Rossamünd could not determine whether he liked or loathed this fellow.

Smirk subsiding, the Baron went on. "An Imperial Secretary arrived not two days gone via Vesting High—one Scrupulus Sicus—come directly from the obscure fortress, Winstreslewe, to complain boldly to this city's senior lord of none other than *yourself,* dear duchess-daughter, verifying all the rumor of you with compelling clarity."

Rossamünd fixed his attention on the passing streets, fully expecting some irate soul to step from the civic press, point and cry, "OUTRAGE! INFAMY! HERE IS THE BEASTLY BASKETLY BOY-MONSTER!"

"The Archduke was much moved to hear Secretary Sicus' report," Finance continued. "But he was most animated by the expositions brought by the Secretary's *protégé*: a surgeon and archivist by the ridiculously quadrupled appellations of Honorius Ludius Grotius Swill."

Innards clenching, ears ringing, Rossamünd stopped breathing.

Europe preserved her silence.

"This Swill fellow tells an uncommonly absorbing tale too, as simple as it is fabulous . . ." The Chief Emissary lingered pointedly, seeking a reaction. When it was not forthcoming, he pressed on. "He made claim to the nature of your young servant here . . . that he is not as he seems but is in truth the rarest tribe of creature, a monster in the form of a man, blaming the theroscades I hear are plaguing that region on this very allegation. He uttered his gruesome contentions with such credible passion—authenticated no less by Secretary Sicus himself—that he almost had me convinced . . ." Smiling, he inspected Rossamünd briefly.

The young factotum swallowed against the constriction clutching at his gourmand's cork. That very moment they passed by the Moldwood Park, dark, pensive, a reminder and an accusation.

Europe blinked slowly at Finance, her jaw working as if chewing upon a morsel. "And *are* you . . ."

"Should I be, dear lady?" The Baron of Sainte's eyes narrowed.

"Of course not, man!"

His cheerful façade remained, but the subtleties in his expression told that he believed the duchess-daughter by choice rather than conviction.

"It is Swill and the temporary Marshal Whympre with him who are exciting the local nickers with their traffic in revermen," Europe continued. "To this my factotum can openly *attest*."

"Truly?" Finance looked fully at the young factotum, wonder hid behind the bright regard of his pearl-gray eyes.

Rossamünd stiffened. "Yes, sir. I fought one of their gudgeons in the lower cellars of Winstermill."

"On your own?"

Rossamünd flashed a look to Europe. "Aye, sir."

Gaze twinkling, the Baron Sainte continued to regard him sagely. "Shall I set my amphigorers to start contrary rumor of our own, gracious lady?"

"Your offer is well intentioned, sir, but must be refused," the heiress of Naimes returned. "This is my private embroilment, and despite my mother's tireless desire to intervene in my affairs, I am sure you have better things to do with your agents."

The baron gave another of his winningly warm smiles. "When it is to do with you, marvelous lady, nothing is purely private . . ."

Europe considered him with a calculating look. "Indeed."

They traveled in silence for a time, passing the grandiose architecture of the governing district, its towering, many-columned structures replete with statues and whorled and knotted pediments and capitals. On some other, brighter day Rossamünd might have wondered at them, but now they and all the grandiose folk that walked so elegantly beneath them went by unheeded.

"If I may, benevolent duchess-daughter," Baron Finance eventually said, in continued gravity, "your graciousness takes our state down a strange and difficult path."

Rossamünd could see the man's gaze momentarily flick to him.

Passion flared in the deeps of Europe's eyes. "You can be assured, sir, that whatever path I take is the best to follow—and if it threatens otherwise, I will make sure that it becomes so."

The Chief Emissary bowed in his seat. "My lady will make a dread duchess," he said, and declared it an *anno praeposter*—an upside-down year.

The fulgar sighed a delicate laugh. "We all, dear Baron, are but murmurs in this tragical panto . . ."

12

THE ARBORLUSTRA

wigbold(s) wit who prefers complete anonymity, refusing to make any signifying spoors or other marks and covering his or her telltale hair loss with all manner of wig—hence the name. Some wear pieces so outlandish they are a signifier in themselves, yet other wigbolds dress as normally as is fashionable, deadly lahzars walking about unheeded by the unsuspecting.

THE seat of the historied city's government, the Brandendirk, was found well beyond the rush of the Spokes, among the many tall towers and halls of dark stone and red brick of a major bureaucratic district known as the Marchant. Scattering a crowd of ibis gathered on flagstones, the town coach ceased its journey in a wide square, the Florescende. Its faded paving, arranged in the forms of near-on every manner of blooming flower, was ceaselessly traversed by carriages and planquins careless of the beauty hurrying beneath hoof, foot and wheel. Low fortresslike façades of pale basalt stood about three sides of the Florescende, spiked and spired, perforated with a multitude of high, thin windows. This was the Parvis Main, the public courts of the Archduke of Brandenbrass. Towering over them at the farther end rose a lofty fortress, heavy and impregnable, the ancient stones of the Low Brassard visible from almost any high building in the city, the original keep about which through centuries the palace, the benches of government and bureaucracy, and indeed the city had grown.

"If I may, m'lady," Finance said, "I shall remain in your fit and return in it to Highstile Hall."

"Certainly, dear Baron," Europe agreed, then called through the front grille to Latissimus in the box seat above, "Deposit the Baron to Highstile and that done, return to wait here."

The Chief Emissary inclined his head in gratitude.

Rossamünd alighted to hand Europe out after him. "I should remain too," he offered.

"Tish tosh, little man!" she retorted softly. "Your absence would be as good as an admission. Come along."

Rossamünd kept close as she marched over a short drawbridge flanked by a platoon of figures cast of dark bronze. Massive double doors of dark, carven wood as tall as the building itself rose before them. The rightmost stood ajar to allow the steady ingress of human traffic to the darkness beyond. As they approached, a white-suited scopp-boy dashed out, bearing dispatches in his light satchel strapped soldier-style across his back, soon followed by another. Through this opening—broad enough to allow a pair of men to walk side by side—they discovered a long and high-arched obverse of dark slate, lined with a platoon of haubardier guardsmen proofed in black and white with a flash of heaven's blue. Past these grim wardens was another duo of enormous doors set with lesser, more human-sized portals in their lower halves. Here all incoming folk were met by severe gentlemen offering glowers for the lowly, stiff formality for the middling and bows for the lofty. Passing him a red velvet tab in exchange, one of the officious fellows took charge of the young factotum's digitals, "to be retrieved again upon departure."

The fulgar and her young factotum were then admitted to a shadowy hall paneled entirely in swarthy wood, its wide space made into aisles by row upon row of square wooden pillars. Above, the high ceiling of interlocking beams was pierced with numerous diamond skylights admitting the noonday in wanly luminous bands.

This public hall was filled with all manner of folk: people of humble station and even humbler clothes, and those of elevated degree in periwigs of glossy chestnut or lustrous silver, many wearing low wide tricorns with curled brims of a style Rossamünd had never seen before. Each kept with his or her kind, each class equally exclusive and dismissive of the rest. The mercantile set seemed most represented, men-of-business with thick folios of papers under arm and anxious, hawklike expressions on their faces, muttering one to the other. Yet whatever the social situation, every waiting soul was possessed by an impatient expectation till the room near vibrated with it, the collective murmur joining into a mumbling echo that muttered from every corner and made the air of the chamber fuggy, almost stifling.

Against this fervor, haubardiers stood fast about a series of clerical stages—three tiers of wooden platforms raised several feet off the main floor in the center of the space. Here a gaggle of secretaries and assisting clerks sat, lifted above the mass so that they could look down imperiously at the next poor citizen seeking their attention.

Among them all hurried scopps, distinct in their white coats and soft hats as they boldly approached the secretarial benches unbidden before sprinting off to some part of the mysterious palace or out of the enormous entrance.

Confronted with this scene, Europe did not hesitate but strode on with loud claps of her boot-steps on the flag-stones, the throng parting like butter from a hot knife as she moved through. Her expression a detached blank, she barely acknowledged the awkward *Beggin' ye pardon, miss*, the gallant *How do you do?* and near-salacious simpers that went wavelike before her. Rossamünd scampered in the brief gap left behind, stretching his stride to keep up with the confident pace of his mistress. To him she indeed looked like a rose—a radiant flower proud and glorious and untouchable among all these needy and ambitious men.

There were others here, however—hearers perhaps of foul gossip—who loured and sneered at her. From the thick someone dared in histrionic whisper, "Lady Squander, thorn among the roses . . ."

Loyalty flaring, Rossamünd searched for its dastardly origin but could not tell who or where it came from, which was perhaps just as well.

Ignoring it all, Europe aimed straight at a stage where a single secretary watched her approach with polite, almost conceited expectancy. Three paces to go she halted and stood aside for Rossamünd to pass, which he did, with only the briefest hesitation, handing the invitation to the secretary and saying the formula with as much resolution as he possessed, "Europa, Duchess-in-waiting of Naimes, the Branden Rose"—it felt very fine to reel off such a credential—"come upon the stated invitation of His . . . His Gracious Sufficiency the Archduke of Brandenbrass."

The secretary took the document, gave it the most cursory look and, without once acknowledging Rossamünd, looked to his mistress instead and said with an artificial smile, "M'lady, you are most welcome." With a wave of his hand crowds parted and a curator, fine-dressed in standard black and white, appeared. The invitation thrust unceremoniously back into his grasp, Rossamünd hurried to follow as Europe was taken to a door at the rear of the hall where the haubardier guards parted and they were let through.

Led by the curator, they traversed a vast hall; its extremities were lost in the murky shadows made by the pale sunlight, so defying any reckoning of its size. The Arborlustra, their guide proudly called it—the Illustrious Wood—and Rossamünd quickly discovered why. Arranged, indeed growing, in several rows down either hand through gaps in the very marble of the floor, were tall trees, sycamore and turpentine in sequence, one trunk pale, the next dark, forming a great natural colonnade of living columns, black then white, black then white all the way down.

Little lights of the softest blue shone from trunk and branch. About their roots and down the full length of the hall were arranged broad Dhaghi carpets figured with rabbits frolicking in black and white and gold woven into the sumptuous scarlet, worn almost to thread in places by un-counted years of footfalls. Up in the high vaulted spaces between the roof beams branches spread, obscuring the coffered roof lights, reaching right across the vacancy of each row to overlap and intertwine with the limbs of their fellow trees. The fitful tweeting of hidden birds sounded from this elevated, knotted green. Just below the canopy an ingenious awning of fine mist-nets caught leaves, nuts and bird-leavings, while black-aproned servants hovered in the dimness, ready to broom the spillings.

"Close your mouth, little man," Europe said dryly.

Standing between each trunk were several of the ducal lifeguards. These were the much celebrated Grognards—troubardiers whose members included modern heldins writ of in pamphlets—impressively harnessed in proof-steel lo-rica, checkered in black and bright metal, the long black hems of their frock coats flaring out from underneath. Upon their heads they wore black, brimless caps and upon their legs stockings of the most striking blue. They gripped cruel martels, long-handled hammers as tall as a man, with oc-tagonal heads and thorny barbs down their tangs.

Walking in the weird internal twilight, Rossamünd marked tiny movements in the shadows about the trunks. Looking closely, he saw rabbits great and small loping care-lessly over their carpet-woven cousins.

"Historic decree set the first troupe of coneys in our il-lustrious hall long before the Tutins came," their curator ex-plained, noticing Rossamünd's fascination. "Caretakers have ever since been put over them and, so established, a whole tribe has flourished in here since. Such was the reputation of these beasts that ancient folk once called our mighty city Largopolis. You may well still see it named thus among its official distinctions . . ."

Rossamünd nodded politely, yet he did not reckon the city's ancient name had to do with these little short-lived brothers and sisters of the great rabbit-lord ruling unfathomed from the heart of Brandenbrass. Feeling a cool attention upon him, he made a furtive search left and right to discover a figure pacing silently in the shadows on either side of them, well harnessed and neuroticrith-bald. His heart skipped beats. *Is Europe such a threat?*

Through a heavy wooden wall their path led them to a hubbub of many conversations coming through the trees ahead. In the midst of this disquieting imitation of nature, the twilight of the Arborlustra proper gave way to a high treeless space bright lit from above. Every recess of the coffered ceiling was perforated to allow light to stream in, the pallid folds of masonry reflecting it again and again until the roof seemed to glow of itself. "The Glade of Court," their curator announced. The wide red carpet they had walked now became a narrow path leading across the bizarre clearing of checkered black-and-white marble surrounded on every side by trees. Hung from cables at the back of the "glade" was an enormous spandarion, half sable, half leuc, sky blue framed with a rampant rabbit stitched in silver upon it.

Rossamünd stared in awe, glorying in his secret knowledge. Did these people have even an inkling for *whom* their rabbit sigil properly stood, or from *whom* their city took its ancient name?

Collected here were a whole assembly of circumstantial folk, gathered like often with like, each clearly ensconced in earnest, even strident conversation. There were local peers with their secretaries; enormous elephantines and vulgarines with their less rotund, more agile representatives; ducal marshals and lesquin captains in their parti-hued harness and campaign wigs, their chests and waists bedecked with all manner of garlands of merit and ribands of status; ambassadors and nuntios of other states and kingdoms; obscure lobbyists, skulking on the fringes with their books of legal precedents waiting for a moment to catch an important attention; singular teratologists of singular renown and eccentric harness who eyed Europe with especial enmity; and many other pompous souls able to govern the doom of lesser folk with a word or a stroke of pen.

Rossamünd swallowed hard. *Is Swill among these fellows?*

With operatic gusto the curator announced Europe's entrance.

The chatter was instantly stilled.

Sweating as if it were the height of a Turkic summer, a morbidly rotund magnate nearby raised an eyebrow first at the Branden Rose and then turned a little to do the same to Rossamünd, a small squeak of wheels coming from beneath the sweeping hem of the fellow's pavilionlike soutaine.

In consternation Rossamünd recognized Imperial Secretary Sicus with him, the young factotum's alarm rising as he saw his foe talking closely with none other than Pater

Maupin. Anaesthesia Myrrh stood to one side, watching the gathered aristocracy with scarce-veiled disdain. Seeing Europe, the dexter sneered then gave a nod to her master.

Maupin turned and, beholding Europe coolly, sauntered over to her. "My, my, Lady Bramble. We have this very moment been speaking of you!" he said with feigned affability. "What has drawn you to this illustrious court?"

"Certainly not because I wish it, sir," the Branden Rose returned dismissively, to Secretary Sicus' open disapproval.

Maupin smiled stiffly. "I have been engrossed with this worthy." He gestured to Sicus. "He and his man have such uncommonly interesting things to say of your more recent endeavors. It appears the loss of your trusty Licurius has made you a touch . . . *eccentric*. I was *especially* interested in what they offered regarding your troublesome runt." He shot a dark look at Rossamünd.

The young factotum bristled.

Europe betrayed nothing, but inspected the gathering as if that were vastly more interesting.

Between Sicus and Maupin, Rossamünd suddenly discovered the intent weasely mien of his chief accuser, the surgeon, Grotius Swill, staring in perverse fixation at Rossamünd, wearing a slight yet gloating smile very much like the smirk of a child who has tattled to the dormitory master and now expects retribution full and swift.

Rossamünd tried to shrink and disappear where he stood as Swill sidled about the Imperial Secretary and approached Europe.

"You may feign your innocence here, oh great lady," the

surgeon sneered softly to Europe, "but what will you do when the *mark* shows?" Though he addressed the Duchess-in-waiting, he never ceased his sour scrutiny of Rossamünd.

Bridling slightly, Europe eyed the impertinent fellow with brief and singularly feline contempt.

"Yes, yes, Master Swill," Maupin interjected. "Time and place, man, time and place." Looking again at Europe, he went on, "You ought to know that the Archduke has been most attentive in his concern over the distress your servant has done me. You see, a harm to me is a harm to the Archduke . . ."

"Away with you and your thin threats, man," Europe finally said, her tone entirely dismissive.

"I do not threaten, Lady Bramble, I *do*."

"Then please, *do* somewhere else, sir . . ."

"Oh, I sha—"

"Lo! It is the Rose of the Fulgars!" came the amiable call, almost like a rescue, from the midst of the courtly, hostile crowd. There, walking through a respectful channel made quickly amid the gathered, strode a moderately tall man in a gorgeous black and white and sky blue frock coat, head hatless, his dark, shining, long-groomed hair tied back in a blue riband whose ends hung well down his back.

The Archduke of Brandenbrass!

Keen and critical intelligence dwelt in the stately lord's dark eyes, and the evidence of a sardonic wit twitched at the corner of his mouth. His fine mustachios were curled and combed, as was his beard, a fashion he himself had made famous. Dressed very similarly to his Grognard guards, he stopped a polite distance from Europe and bent graciously low, a fine show of welcome glowing in his countenance—or was it gloating?

At his approach Maupin and Sicus and Swill bowed deeply and retreated.

"Here you are, m'dear," the Archduke crooned, "returned not a bare week from your coursing in the east, having slain a glorious count of dastardly nickers! Thank you for condescending to attend my spring court. I thank you too—as I always do—for your defense of the rightful place of everymen and our tenuous grip on the fringes of land allowed us by the murderous therian. What a joy it must be to put the wicked monster to flight and bring liberty to all the goodly people of this, our mighty Empire."

The assembled throng murmured in affected approbation. Some even began an awkward applause that, for want of general support, quickly sputtered and ceased.

The Duchess-in-waiting was openly unimpressed; even from Rossamünd's obscure view of the side of her face, the fulgar's distaste was obvious.

"How is my cousin Naimes?"

"Civil greeting to you, cousin Brandenate." Europe gracefully bobbed her head, eyes fixed boldly on this lofty man, arms extending elegantly, a fluid gesture of one equal to another. "I am well."

"Here, you have brought your faithful factotum." The Archduke peered directly at Rossamünd. "He has shrunk some since last I remember him. Did you leave him in a coat pocket for the fuller-lady to wash in too-hot water by

THE ARCHDUKE OF
BRANDENBRASS

accident?" He barely fluttered an eyelid at the approving laughter of his court.

Feeling tiny and utterly ignorant, Rossamünd stood behind his mistress, hands at sides, silent, as he had been schooled to do.

Europe herself showed the hint of a smile, the kind that spoke of death and danger. "I must confess you at an advantage, cousin Brandenate," she said with a nod. "I cannot speak on a fuller's labors and must defer to your obvious expertise in the lowly matter of laundry."

This elicited a spontaneous murmur of approbation from the court—far less in volume but greater in genuine mirth—that, with many coughs and shuffling feet, was quickly transmuted to a tart and uncharitable hubble-bubble.

The Archduke's self-approving grin tightened into a fixed grimace. "Dear sister Rose," he returned, his voice sickly kind, "how I miss your attendance at my court." He bowed to hide this patent lie. "I understand how diverting it must be to cast your long shadow upon the churls and bumpkins clamoring for your aid. As for myself," he went on before the Duchess-in-waiting could react, "I am preparing for this season's campaigning. The Emperor, as usual, wants me to join his grand Imperial armies against the sedorner kings of the west." He made a slight motion to the marshals and captains stood together, watching Europe with what Rossamünd could only think to call *hungry* eyes. "Care to accompany us?"

The Duchess-in-waiting simply tilted her head in refusal.

To this the Archduke smiled, a wolfish grin in expectation of such a response. "Here, let us walk together." He motioned toward a wider shadow between the trees. With that action half a dozen servants waiting on left and right braced up, their eyes fixed on their master, ready to obey.

"You will forgive me, my goodly honored guests. I shall return presently," he proclaimed to the gathered. "The Duchess-daughter of Naimes and I must talk of stately things." Gesturing to the fulgar to follow, the Archduke strode to one of many gaps in the trunks on the right, drawing a tail of staff after him.

None of the throng looked pleased, and several glared Europe down and up, envious of her clearly undeserved favor.

Disregarding all, she went along with her cousin peer, indicating by subtle signal for Rossamünd to come too.

Taking one last glance about the crowd of fawning political souls, Rossamünd saw Swill peering gloatingly at him, the butcher's regard never leaving him for a moment. Following the example of his mistress, Rossamünd returned the stare with as impassive an expression as he could muster and gratefully exited the Glade of Court.

The stately master of Brandenbrass took Europe for a stroll back into the gloom of the indoor forest, down an artificial avenue. Walking with the ducal attendants—several servants in tow of an intense clerical-looking fellow all flanked by a quarto of Grognards—the young factotum kept a handful of paces behind, head ducked respectfully, watching the two mighty folk through his brows. Materializing from the gloom, two conspicuously bald-headed lifeguards followed again beside them in the adjacent avenue.

Hands behind back, the lord of Brandenbrass set a leisurely pace.

"I hear your new factotum was *expensive* to obtain," he began.

Rossamünd concentrated on keeping step.

"His salary is no greater than any other aide's," the Branden Rose answered evenly.

"For truth?" The Archduke smiled a serpent's smile. "You do not think quo gratia a *high* price?"

The fulgar sniffed an odd, dismissive kind of laugh.

Unfazed in his turn, the mighty man's smile remained. "The use of our ancient right for such a purpose—as you can well imagine, my dear," he returned in fatherly tones, despite his near-equivalent age, "would do great dishonor to us all"—by which Rossamünd could only assume he meant the rulers and heirs of state—"and greatest of all to the one so misusing it . . . Though . . ." He gestured easy with his hand. "I need not tell you that, of course."

Half a smirk fluttering on her rouged lips, Europe simply looked at him. "You are direct indeed, cousin duke"—her words were heavy with irony—"and sound much like my mother."

Rossamünd's nape prickled with fright.

Here they were before one of the few souls in the Empire second only to the Emperor in power—who commanded armies and navies and could call for your death without any recourse—yet Europe bantered and cogged with him as if he were a senior member of her staff or some haggling high-street shopkeeper.

Yet the Archduke did not take umbrage but kept a steady, careful tone. "Even a beautiful untameable heir of state must explain herself once-of-a-while . . ."

"Such an untameable heiress might have much better uses for her time, sir."

"It might appear needless, I grant, but I hear such disconcerting *reports* about the *novelty* of your new factotum's origin." He glanced over his shoulder to give Rossamünd a sidelong inspection.

"What, pray, is *novel* about a marine society child from Boschenberg?" Europe countered in easy tones.

"Why nothing, little cousin Naimes. But a child that is actually a monster in a child's form? Now that is an *innovation!*"

A great lurching like guilt twisted in Rossamünd's gut, making his brow clammy. He judiciously scrutinized the sentinel wits from the corner of his sight; the severe fellows seemed solely intent on Europe.

The Archduke of Brandenbrass cocked his head congenially at her. "You were ever the vanguard of fashion, my dear."

"I wonder at you, cousin," the fulgar declared with quiet poise, "for putting so uncommon a trust in such dangerous and idling twitter. Such stuff I would expect to be believed by those in possession only of ears with little else than mouths between."

Now it was the Archduke's turn to chortle. "An Imperial Secretary is no simple ruffian come to complain about pigs in his 'taters; nor, my dear, is his power some overreliance on the pleading claims of ancient blood."

Rossamünd knew enough to recognize this as a slight

against his mistress, and an angry heat surged around his neck and scalp.

"It might serve you, cousin"—Europe's tone was didactic, as if scolding a simpleton—"to make a more *thorough* inquiry of the virtue of those bringing such accusations, and their *associates*. Investigation of the deeper cellars of their bastion might turn over good reason to discredit these ambitious colleagues of yours."

"You speak of course of the sanguine cause of the obscure and previous marshal of Winstermill," the lord of Brandenbrass purred ever so smoothly. "Sad, so sad . . ."

Rossamünd bridled silently at this slur upon the noble Lamplighter-Marshal.

"From what I know, he too has made such a claim," the Archduke was saying. "Yet extensive searches made by the current marshal have yielded nothing . . ."

"Possibly a proof in itself, I would have thought . . ." Europe smiled in queenly repose. "It strikes me, cousin, that if you have such damning testimony, such witnesses, such potent friends, you do not summon your lifeguards and your clerks to prosecute me and my *novel* staff here and now and bring satisfaction to all your complaints."

Half in expectation that this might indeed occur, Rossamünd reflexively reached for absent digitals.

Yet no one moved. No order came.

"Ha ha, my match is met!" the Archduke suddenly exclaimed with perfectly pitched mirth, his laughter strangely flat in this weird faux-forest. Yet his gaze was glittering as he stopped and turned to his guest, a conflict of choices wrestling in his twitching gaze. "Regardless of how you dodge and hide, sister, it must be said that if these proofs bear out, it would be a perverse turn, even for you, m'dear." He smirked. "I recall only last year at one of your rare appearances at an evening conversational with the Marchess of Pike, where I heard you say to Lady Madigan and the Reive of Lo that . . . What was it again?" He hesitated, relishing the moment as he leaned toward one of his secretaries as if they might remind him. "Oh, yes . . . that monsters were only good for sport or slaughter . . ." He watched her as if to observe the fall of a well-aimed shot.

Unmoved, the fulgar's diamond-spoored brow rose slightly. "And here was I, thinking you were too interested in the Baroness of Pike's much celebrated bosom to hearken properly to decent conversation."

The Archduke colored just slightly. "There now!" He smacked his lips. "How clumsy of me to speak of such triflings with *you,* the great teratologist who has performed such services for my humble state and for which I am forever grateful."

"And your return to flattery, cousin, heralds the end of our conversation," she returned mildly. "I go to knave. Good day." Without curtsies or niceties, the heiress of Naimes turned on boot-heel and strode boldly down the nearest avenue and out from those oppressing trees.

Hastening after, Rossamünd did not dare a word, aware of the shadowy escort of the two wits keeping pace nearby. Collecting his digitals in the obverse, he exited that illustrious menacing court pregnant with malignant suspicions in mighty relief and clambered back into the day coach waiting faithfully for them out on the Florescende.

"A wanton waste of a day's travel . . . ," Europe said quietly as Latissimus took them home.

"Might he have had us arrested?" Rossamünd asked carefully.

The heiress of Naimes fixed him with hard eyes. "He has not the stomach to risk a brawl with me in his own courts, nor to upset the delicate humours of my mother and all the states in between should a bump even come upon my crown in his city." She settled in her seat and stared at the passing world with its simpler cares. "No, he will set a watch on us if he has not already; have all his earwigs and peter-peepholes ogle us . . ." She smiled thinly. "Watch as you will, cousin gapeseed," she suddenly spoke to the air, "there is little enough to see."

For a time there was tight, vibrating silence, Rossamünd's thoughts pivoting rapidly about the meeting with the Archduke. Soon his deliberations spiraled inward to one painful point. "Miss Europe?" he tried.

Her chin resting with light and practiced poise upon gracefully bent knuckles, the fulgar peered at him, her expression beckoning him to continue.

"Do . . . Do you truly believe that monsters are only good for sport or slaughter?" he managed.

The fulgar's eyes narrowed, and Rossamünd wondered for one astounded moment if he had achieved the improbable and confounded the impenetrable fulgar.

"Can you imagine me holding to a different thought, little man?"

Rossamünd blanched and looked to the floor of the landaulet.

"What might you have me say?" his mistress insisted. "You have seen for yourself the wickedness that a handful of nickers might bring."

He nodded, the violent end of Wormstool clear in his mind.

"Without me and all the teratologists, monsters would rule supreme." Europe's voice remained frighteningly steady. "I can hardly conduct my necessary labors fussing over whether one hairy brute chewing on a child might be in a better frame of mood on some other, sunnier day! Or if a ravening bugaboo ruining some rustic gent's life and future really might prefer to sip sillabub with demented old eeker ladies out in the swamps!" She took a breath. "You might meet some soft-headed teratologist who is prepared to ponder the motivations from one tribe of bogles to another— and I *know* such as they are about—but occurrence enough has taught me that such flimsy souls soon come to surprised and nasty ends." She stared hard at him. "Would you rather that I grow philosophical and let the next murderous monster we hunt rip me and you and the world about us asunder just for the sake of a few felicitous feelings?"

Rossamünd shook his head, but this time held her gaze. "No . . . Yes . . . I . . ." He paused to collect himself, then chose each word with care. "Where—where do *I* figure in your reckoning of things? Don't *I* change your mind in some part?"

Her stare hardened to a glare, anger flashing in her eyes.

"*You* figure very much in my thinking, Rossamünd! Of that you may be certain."

In deep confusion he said nothing more and watched the city passing.

They returned to Cloche Arde and the final preparations for departure, neither speaking again that day upon the meeting with Maupin or Swill or the Archduke.

In the deep hush of night Rossamünd stirred and lay for a moment in his downy bed tracing the whorls in the ceiling and wondering in frustration why he was awake when he so dearly wanted sleep before the early start. He could hear the careful rasp of cautious carriage wheels and muffled hooves came from the Harrow Road below.

They slowed . . .

. . . then stopped.

Instantly every fiber within him imploded with pain, the drawing, agonizing scathing of a wit doubling him over in its excruciating grip.

Through his anguish he heard a shocked cry come from somewhere within Cloche Arde, quickly followed by a woman's shrieking.

The whole house is under assault!

He clutched at the pain, trying to fight off the silent, pulsing torment that pinned him. For a moment he was master of himself, yet this served only to tumble him in a tangle of bedclothes onto the floor.

Immediately below was a racket of thumping footfalls on carpet and board and stone. The front door slammed open and boot steps ground speedily on gravel. The flat *pop!* of one—two—three firelocks sounded from the street, immediately followed by the deadened fizzing thump of a detonating potive. A shout. A sudden crack of a whip and the answering snorts of frightened horses set carriage wheels in more hasty motion. The scathing abruptly ceased, leaving ears ringing and a muffled clamor of distress elsewhere in the house.

With but a breath to right himself, Rossamünd snatched up his digitals on their thin belt, clumsily slid on soft slippers as he left his room and fairly leaped the flights down to the front door. Out in the chill yard he found Europe wrapped in a thin seclude but heavy-booted, standing at the locked gate and speaking with hushed agitation to someone beyond on the street, her unbound hair fine fluttering gossamer on the nocturnal currents. Rossamünd could make little of the dim figure standing in the shadow of the wall except that he was rather thin. Another similarly reluctant companion stood across the other side of the Harrow Road. He wore a device of pewter and enamel and lenses strapped to his head—a sthenicon, Rossamünd supposed, though of a kind he had never seen—and bore heavy pistols in hand.

"She departed in haste once we fired on her cart," Europe's interlocutor was saying as Rossamünd hurried to see who it was. "They were not expecting a repulse from the flank." His voice held a subtle note of amusement. "Just a common takeny, nothing especial to pick it out . . ."

"Of course," Europe replied. "They do not want to spell out their deeds too simply . . . Your assistance and the aim of your shooting irons were as timely as they were unsought, Mister Slitt."

The fellow moved a little into the gate's light to reveal himself as the man who, with the Baron Finance, had intercepted them that very morning. "I—and Mister Camillo with me," he said, gesturing to the pistol-wielder behind, "are in your service, ma'am . . . and yours too, Mister Bookchild," the rather unassuming fellow said to Rossamünd in turn as he drew close.

"Was that Anaesthesia Myrrh?" Rossamünd asked in reply.

Turning suddenly at her factotum's approach, Europe replied rather curtly, "I am *reckoning* it was, yes . . . Unless Maupin has an entire hand of wits at his beck."

The two obscure guardians chuckled.

"Apart from the one he lost so recent," Elecrobus Slitt elaborated, "I know of no others in his service, good lady . . . Else Pitter-Patter has himself 'come a wigbold."

The Branden Rose smiled darkly. "There is scant we can do about it tonight, and I have a knave to begin tomorrow," she declared with the tone of conclusion. "So I thank you again, Mister Slitt. Be sure to thank your master for his *motherly* care."

With humble nods the two men returned to the shadows, and Europe and Rossamünd to the violated safety of Cloche Arde.

13

THE KNAVING BEGINS

pipistrelle light onshore winds that make for good sailing of small-sailed vessels such as sloops or brigantines. Their presence is seen as a sign of favor by all seafaring folk, but they are known to be fickle benefactors, turning all too quickly into mortal tempests.

DESPITE the attack in the night and the buffeting winds coming up from the gulf of the Grume the next morning, they departed very early and one day later than planned.

No serious hurt had come from the carriage-borne witting. One of the maids had become hysterical, needing a soporific—brewed by Rossamünd himself. Nectarius the nightlocksman took a tumble under the frission and upset some valuable and precariously perched item, smashing it. Beyond aching heads, Craumpalin and Fransitart were unharmed, the old dispenser griping about "blighted three-bell scoundrels" ruining his "sounded sleep."

Fitful for the remainder of the night, Rossamünd began the new day keen to be away from this troublesome city. Rising before the sun, he went forth wayfarer-ready in full harness, baldric and knife, satchel and salt-bag, stoups and digitals, completed by black thrice-high. About his throat he had knotted a white silken vent, loose enough, he hoped, to be easily pulled over mouth and nose. Bought at Pauper Chïves', it was guaranteed by the salt-seller as being the best potive-resisting neckerchief he owned. He had arranged all scripts and parts—checked and rechecked—in their proper containers ready handy in order of importance and frequency of use.

"Catch an eye of ye, fitted with all yer saltoons!" Fransitart said as they collected out in the yard. "Ye look ready to repel a whole maraude, like Harold hisself."

Rossamünd grinned gratefully.

Wrapped in a thick pallmain and a gray woolen scarf, the ex–dormitory master bore a modest satchel filled with wayfoods and useful things, and the same stocky musketoon he had leveled on Pater Maupin two days ago. "Borrowed it from a mate o' Casimir Fauchs," Fransitart declared, lifting the firelock confidently. Its metal coated in stickbrown, this was obviously a naval weapon. "He has a chest full o' them from our time a-sea together, fine fellow." A bent and stained tricorn sat jauntily on his hoary head, and a heavy naval hanger was strapped to his hip.

Pink-faced and puffing, Craumpalin wore the frock coat and longshanks he always did, a drab woolen wrap wound warm around his shoulders, and an old capuche—or cap of wool—of the same covering his crown. He bore a cudgel in hand, and his own stoup of potives hung at his side.

Against the cold Europe set out in a sumptuous scarlet

272

fur-hide coat—a flugalcoat—and fur-trimmed boots. Once more her hair was knotted and held in a pointed comb and crow's-claw hair tine. Streaming out from about her throat into the bluster was a silken scarf of dark olive broidered with trails of wind-dancing birds. Ledger under arm and peering confidently up at the cold dome of morning, she seemed greatly improved in mood from the angry impatience of yesternight. She even offered a smile at the dim day.

Darter Brown too turned out, perching upon the head of a dog statue, ruffling himself impatiently and clearly aware that travel was afoot.

With the household staff arranging themselves in neat quasi-military order on Cloche Arde's front steps for the farewell, Latissimus brought a pair of sturdy young horses stretched now and ready for harness. Rufous and Candle, Rossamünd heard a stableryhand call them, the first dull russet, the other soap-white. Both were partially shabraqued in petrailles of black lour thoroughly doused in sisterfoot, a nullodour that Rossamünd had himself made in the restlessness of the previous afternoon from the pages of the compleat.

"Fine-stepping horses for town, cobs fo' the country," the gentleman-of-the-stables had explained. "Though you are going out into caballine lands where horses ought to be safe," he explained, patting the beast's proofing, "there's still wisdom in keeping them from harm's chances."

The young factotum grinned at the beasts and fancied they grinned at him too.

"Back to simpler lives now, Mister Kitchen," Europe said

in goodbye as Rossamünd handed her aboard. "You may drop the flag; I leave you to peace and routine."

"Farewell, my gracious lady," the steward returned. "Return to us hale." He bowed, a long stoop, and the household did the same, openly displeased to see the fulgar depart.

"Drive on, Master Vinegar," the fulgar called to Fransitart's back.

"Aye, aye, ma'am. Drivin' on!" With a flick of reins and a click of the tongue, the old vinegaroon started the horses.

The knaving was begun.

Obedient to Europe's laconic directions, Fransitart proved—to Rossamünd's enduring satisfaction—that handling a two-horse team was within his grasp; he humored the reins with surprising subtlety.

Out beyond the substantial suburbs they went, through mighty curtain gates, by row on row of cheap half-houses that coagulated about the stacks of tall isolated mills or long work halls, through markets already teeming with dawn-risen custom.

Looping along beside the landaulet in that hurried, dipping way such birds do, Darter Brown shot from fence-spike to red lamp-crown. Rossamünd looked kindly at his little escort.

Progress became spasmodic as eager early traffic—farmers' wagons, firewood drays, stinking night-soil carts—crammed the highroads.

A smartly clad figure stepped out of the disorder and made directly for the landaulet. Before a warning was properly forming on Rossamünd's lips, this impertinent fellow sprang up and, grasping the sash of the door, stood upon the side step to pinch a ride.

"Good morning, Lord Finance," Europe said in quiet greeting.

"A hale morning to you, Lady of Naimes," the importunate side-step coaster returned between heavy breaths, miming a bow with his free hand. "Not as spry as I once was."

"Have you taken up cadging as your latest sport, good baron?" the heiress of Naimes asked mildly. "Is my mother not giving you enough to do . . ."

"No fear, gracious lady." Finance took a breath. "Could I by some trick of habilistic conjury live three times over, I should still be hard pressed to complete all the labors you and your most estimable and Magentine mother provide."

The fulgar smiled slightly. "I thank you for the service of your Mister Slitt last night—he is a very *useful* fellow."

"He is indeed, m'lady, a genuine jewel in our already glittering staff." The Chief Emissary dipped his head gratefully. "And it is about his usefulness to you that I come once again. The Archduke was none too pleased after his interview with you yesterday . . ."

"That makes us twin," Europe murmured astringently.

"Yesternight was but the first bout with Pater Maupin, Secretary Sicus and his surgeon pet—an unhallowed alliance if ever there was one. They grow bold with the Lord of Brandenbrass' support. Your absence may not be enough this time, duchess-daughter."

"Yet I go nonetheless, dear baron." Europe remained unfazed.

Finance regarded his mistress long, a passion of esteem gleaming from his eyes. "Have a care, fine lady," he said, "and an eye for followers . . ." and with the nod of a bow leaped from the landaulet and disappeared into the press of people and carriages.

"And you, sir," Europe murmured once he was gone.

Craumpalin revolved in his seat and with a polite cough asked, "Are all thy commerces in this city so . . . *botherous,* m'lady?"

The fulgar peered at him thoughtfully. "I find my time in Brandenbrass either sappingly dull or intrusively trouble-some. If it were not so conveniently placed to my common work, I doubt I would ever come here at all. However, I find it best to leave boredom and trouble to themselves."

"A storm avoided is a wrecking saved," Fransitart concurred.

"Aye," Craumpalin said into his beard, "but a difficulty shirked is adversity delayed."

"Are you always so dreary, Master Salt?" Europe retorted.

The old dispenser's shoulders lifted briefly. "'Tis usually Frans' part," he said with a grin.

Smiling, Rossamünd could see his onetime dormitory master hunch and mutter unintelligibly, flicking Rufous and Candle to quicken their step.

At last, after inspection by a platoon of black-and-white-mottled gate wards, the landaulet passed into the left of a twin of tunnels that ran beneath an immense bastion, the last port in the outermost curtain of Brandenbrass. The Two Sisters—or so Europe called it. Above the massive fortress with its steep roof of iron and spiny watchtowers flew enor-

276

mous spandarions—one half leuc, the other sable—cracking proudly like thunder in the rising winds from flagpoles as thick as ram masts.

Out again, Rossamünd saw a brazen statue set proudly on the projecting keystone of the arch and standing guard above the entrance of the tunnel. As tall as three tall men, dressed in flowing robes, lower legs metal-armored, the figure clutched a mighty sword to her bosom; this was the southern sister, green-streaked with rainwashed corrosion. The likeness of a windswept veil was fashioned with great cunning as if blowing across her face, yet her fixed expression of wild defiance was unmistakeable. With a shiver, Rossamünd realized this was the image of one of those very ouranin sisters upon which the Lapinduce spoke, ancient rossamünderling defenders of Brandenbrass. Twisting in his seat, he stared at the effigy like some long-gone kin and smiled grimly at how quickly this majestic protector would be torn down should the citizens of this city discover her true monstrous nature.

Beyond the twin gates the city yet lingered, the last of the high-houses and dormitories clinging like children to the outward hem of Brandenbrass' pristine wall. Then, all too quickly, it gave way to a more bucolic scene. One moment they were in a Brandenard street, the next running by wicket-fenced fields where stupidly dignified goats with great, flopping ears and fat, overlong noses stared at them solemnly. A wide fertile plain spread out before them—the Milchfold, lively with cows and goats and laborers. Reached by long tree-lined lanes that crossed and recrossed the whole plain, the homes of dairy herds and landholders stood like martial towers. A handful of miles to the west the land rose to a blunt escarpment, becoming the feet of dark crouching hills, the Brandenfells.

The red lamps and paved stone of the Hardwick gave over to the lightless, packed clay of the Athy Road, going northwest by lush flat fields of peas, cow pastures, goat-breaks and barren saltpeter farms where moilers masked in vented scarves tilled in the brimstone stink.

In a blur, Darter Brown joined them, fluttering up to land on Rossamünd's knuckle as it rested on the sash.

"Good morning, my shadow," the young factotum murmured genially to his feathered friend.

It twittered at him urgently, as if trying to communicate something more complex, but Rossamünd could not decipher its meaning.

"My, my! He doth speak with the animals!" Europe declared. "Perhaps you could call in a bird each for us, little man; then we could start a menagerie, charge a subscription for people to come and see, and cease this violent life for good."

Rossamünd knew the fulgar was jesting, but he blushed anyway.

The fulgar cocked her head to scrutinize the sparrow with a raised brow. "I cannot say that when I first submitted myself to the hands of Sinster's sectifers I anticipated taking on the services of a bird to hunt the monster—and a rather scrawny one at that."

To this the watchful sparrow gave an irritable *tweet!*

"And saucy too," the fulgar continued with an amused

sniff. "My, what a collective I have gathered about me. I doubt any other teratologist could boast such peculiar staff."

The ground rose gradually to the bluffs reaching around from the northeast, bending gradually southwest to disappear from sight behind themselves. Farther south Rossamünd could see mounts of black tumbling east to the coast: the Siltmounds, great dunes of swarthy sand hemming the city's southern walls. At a crossing of minor drives with the main way stood several lofty poles, thick like trees, buried deep in the compacted soil and topped with overlarge cartwheels. Daws, magpies and crows hovered, squabbling over several of these mucky and blackened platforms, yet leaving one to the mastery of a single bald-headed assvogel. Startled, Darter Brown took wing and vanished among the stalks of wide hilly pastures.

A dread chill flushed from Rossamünd's innards to his crown.

Catharine wheels . . . These were the infamous mechanisms of torture and execution for murderers, traitors and . . . sedorners. Thick-growing briars were twined and pinned about the lower portions of the mast to prevent rescue. From one roses were blooming, declaring to all the world— so tradition held—that the judged soul rotting on high was a sedorner through and through.

Pulling his sight free, Rossamünd refused to gaze any closer as they passed beneath this grisly stand.

"Pay no mind to these wicked coldbeams, Rossamünd," Fransitart called doggedly over his shoulder.

There, bizarrely, standing under them, was a reddleman

with his many dyes in a square handcart, smock *and* skin stained by his products. As they rattled by, Rossamünd could hear the fellow singing, as happy as you like, cawing along with the carrion birds:

Hey, ho, what's the time?
Hang my smallclothes on the line.
If they tear,
I don't care,
I'll just dye another pair.

His head down, the young factotum watched Europe fixedly from the corner of his vision. The fulgar stared ahead, glancing occasionally at the foul devices, undaunted. Catching her factotum's unease, she laid her hand lightly on Rossamünd's clenched fist until they were past, her simple-seeming yet uncommon kindness touching him so profoundly it banished his alarm.

The sun was shining as the landaulet climbed, yet mile upon mile away south a dark churning horizon sparked elegant lightning straight to the ground—kinked electrical charges miles long, arcing against the black. An arrowed formation of silent ibis winged high above, driven over the hills by the freshening winds that brought delayed levin grumbles.

"The pipistrelle turns dirty," Fransitart said of the distant thunder, Rossamünd recognizing the vinegaroon name for the light winds of the Grume. "The spring glooms have come. Ye'll be needin' a bolt-hole to keep yer pretty pate dry, m'lady, afore the day is out."

280

"For you such turns of weather might be dirty, Master Vinegar," Europe replied, "but a levining sky is a happy roof for a thermistor."

Climbing beside a rocky winding stream made rapid by the slope, the Athy Road took them steadily higher into the drab hills of the Brandenfells. Even from this distant vantage, Brandenbrass looked enormous, her many rings of fortification clear, her long pale harbor with its countless berths and piers squashed with vessels, a poisonous haze hanging low over the seaside milling districts. The lofty towers of the countinghouses and the great many fortified gates thrust high above the great spreading mass. Highest and sturdiest of all in its midst stood the Brandendirk, seat of the ducal line, and a little north in the city's very center brooded the dark smudge of the Moldwood, unguessed, untroubled and unchallenged; two powers opposed, with Brandentown pinched between.

Ahead, myrtles and bent pines sprouted in ones and twos like thinning hair on the near-bald crowns of the Brandenfells, thickening into woods down in the convoluted valleys twisting steeply back through many spurs and folds.

While the four travelers supped on prunes, cold beef clumsy smeared with soft Pondsley cheese and claret, the sky grew louring dark and heavy with water.

With a suppressed rumble, rain arrived, large dollops that had an uncomfortable knack of landing on exposed skin: the back of the neck, the wrist at the cuff . . . Sorry for his old masters left out in the wet, Rossamünd extended the bonnet-like canopy as Craumpalin struggled on his oiled pallmain.

Some miles ahead, upon the summit of a distant spur,

Rossamünd spied a single orange glimmer, lit perhaps against the growing gloom, the only evidence of a dwelling.

"Wood Hole," Europe explained. "Pleasant enough for a hill town, though it is not our goal. There is a wayhouse in a dell about a mile from here. We shall shelter there."

The road veered behind the lee side of the hills, descending to loop about the folds of land, the mossy stones of its foundation reaching down to the bubbling creek only a few yards below. A tenuous threwd dwelt here, as if the stream brought the watchfulness from more haunted heights. But for the dripping trickle of rain-wash and runnel, and the uneven viscous clops of hoofs, the world was reverentially silent. Trees grew densely along the verge: dark olive, age-twisted pine and pale laurel. Between their trunks Rossamünd thought he could see a light ahead, the corona of cool clean seltzer light, a welcome pilot in the sodden obscurity. The shadows slowly parted to reveal a great-lamp on the right of the way, lifted on a black post above a solid gate in a high stone wall. Nestled in a cleft beyond this gate was a house half excavated into the hillside beside a brimming, chattering weir.

There was no sign, just this single signal flare.

"Welcome to the Guiding Star," said Europe. "We shall abide here for now."

With no small relief they entered the foreyard and got out of the rain.

The foul weather had blown itself out overnight and now, in the still cool, a lustrous blond sky joyfully declared the new day. Cooing encouragements to the horses and sipping one of Craumpalin's restorative draughts from a biggin, Fransitart guided the landaulet away from the wayhouse. No one spoke as they wended through woodland din, the gray bosky half-light whispering with the lingering riddles of the long night.

Bending around several tight spurs, the valley road climbed the grassy flank of a low hill, bringing them to a new and welcome prospect. Soft-lit by the porcelain radiance of heaven's dome, wide downs of ripening pastures folded away before them, fresh with soaking dew, scattered with trees, tall garners and low farmsteads and oddly regular woodlands as far as vision could grasp.

From an ancient myrtle on the crown of the next hillock, a magpie gave throat to its happy quavering music full of primeval wisdom, and morning's joy. Inwardly, Rossamünd soared with the birdsong.

"The Page," Europe proclaimed, interrupting his flight. "Here, Rossamünd, is *parish* land, a pleasant change from the ditches where you last served." She pointed with open hand to the vista.

To Rossamünd the scene seemed tilted to the left, descending to the far-off basin, a dark line at the edge of sight where the entire southern sky was brooding again upon another squall. To the north, the hill they stood upon reached for miles to join with its sisters, rising yet farther to meet a distant hedge of grimmer higher mounts.

"Take us on, Master Vinegar, if you please."

Moilers and faradays were out early in the fields, scything

and wrenching at weeds that grew thick at this part of the season and threatened to overwhelm whole crops.

"They could come and clear the verges while they're about it," Fransitart grumbled, veering the landaulet into the sprays of mustard weed and fennel thick on the brink of the road as he attempted to find a path through a herd of dairy cows.

The beasts' hay ward—a fellow in the meager proofing of a long smock—gave the four travelers a bold *"halloo!"* and a cheerful wink from beneath the wide brim of his catillium as he lazily goaded his charges with a spearlike mandricard.

"*Halloo* to ye too, ye mischievous grass-combing kine-kisser," the ex–dormitory master muttered under his breath as Craumpalin adopted a cheerier face.

The day-orb rose and spring's early bees hummed about them inquisitively before winging away to pollinate the feral plants. Butterflies, bright azure or patched orange and black, tumbled their crazy courses. Droning wasps and emperor-flies hovered, hunted, joined by curious predatory bugs unusual in bright colors. Somewhere near, just beyond sight, a cow bellowed.

"Cowherds and honeybees; what an enchanting place," Europe uttered sardonically.

"Aye, this is a pleasant way to serve," Fransitart offered with gruff cheer. "Sittin' high aboard a wheel-ed barque upon a sea o' weeds is a fine way to see out yer days."

"Very poetical, Master Vinegar," said the fulgar, affecting just the right pitch between interest and indifference.

The ex–dormitory master half turned to catch Rossa-

284

münd's eye. "Can't say I've e'er wanted to perish mopin' in some damp hut complainin' of the rheum."

"No, indeed," Europe returned with a smile. "That is not an end I intend for myself either, chair-bound and sciatical. 'To die in harness' is the phrase, I believe."

"Aye, madam, that's th' one." Fransitart nodded philosophically. "To perish with yer hand to the plow, to bow out still swinging—"

"To push on to th' end . . . ," Craumpalin added glibly.

"We are of one accord then, sirs," Europe declared with a flourish of a graceful hand. "A life of adventure for us it is, until the very end."

The two ex-vinegaroons chuckled together.

Rossamünd joined them with a sad smile of his own.

With increasing frequency they found baited animals hung, dead, on fence posts: foxes, hares, possums, mink— left to be taken by peltrymen or soapers. Though the land was long cicurated and barely threwdish, Rossamünd expected to spy some small bogle murdered and stiff, strung up on some fence-post hook.

Though a well-used, well-founded thoroughfare bending through the domed pasturelands, the Athy Road was not broad and straight like the Wormway that ran east from Winstermill. Several times was Fransitart forced to slow and pull aside or stop for oncoming traffic: local folk commuting carefree between towns; post-lentums or hired canty-coaches carelessly hustling to the great city; lumber wagons from the plantations or ore-carters from the local coal mine, driven by hardy wagoners and under the escort

285

of saturnine harnessguarde in the employ of some mining cartel. With these obstacles and the usual privacy stops taken at conveniently luxuriant bushes, when sundown came they were still short of Spelter Innings, a proper wash and a cozy bunk.

"The town is really only a skip over those hills," Europe advised, pointing away northwest. "Yet the twist of the road makes it much farther. Let us stop at the nearest nook; this part of the map is easy for sleep."

Muttering of a softer seat for his aging tailbones, Fransitart willingly complied, urging the horses to pick up their trot.

In the cool, clear luster of a just-set sun, they halted in a deep crease on the right-hand side of the road, a bay in the downs that sheltered a stand of young, self-sown white oaks. To the soft chorus of sparse crickets they settled themselves for food and sleep.

"Ahh, lad, look at thee test like a wise old rhubezhal," Craumpalin observed proudly as Rossamünd made treacle.

The young factotum stood a little taller as he brewed, nearly forgetting the foul sensation as he poured the Sugar of Nnun. "Give me elbow-way, Master Pin. I don't want to topple this nasty stuff on you!"

It was a cold camp—no fire at least. However, the laborium made for an excellent pot, and once Rossamünd was done with his brewing, Craumpalin assumed the role of cook and soon had a savory medley sizzling out its friendly aromas.

"This is a decidedly pleasant shift from my usual encampments," Europe announced. "Hearty food and plaudamentum fit for the dinner table. If I could have, gentlemen, I would have employed all three of you years ago."

Despite the general reputation this land had for being friendly and peaceful, the night was divided into three watches—Europe neither offering nor expected to take part and Rossamünd taking the middle watch. Curled on the landaulet seat and well asleep under ample blankets, he reluctantly woke at Craumpalin's firm shaking and softly rasping voice.

"Rouse out, me hearty, all is well! Tumble up and shake thyself. Time to watch the midnight world!" The dispenser pointed to the proverbial green star rising with a bulging moon in the eastern firmament. "When Maudlin's at her height, be waking ol' Frans for last lookout; don't let his limping or his groaning drive thee to too much sympathy."

Rubbing eyes and yawning wide, Rossamünd climbed as easy as he could from the carriage. With a yawn, he hooked his baldric with its attached stoup over his shoulder, adjusted the digitals at his waist and made ready for all surprises.

The night was prickling cold, the air sharp with the tang of frost and damp grasses as his breath made steam in Phoebë's rising gleam. Cheeks stinging, Rossamünd wrapped a blanket of silken wool about him and listened, blinking, holding his breath to better hear any furtive hints. In this cleft the air was still, rare puffs setting the knuckled branches of the oaks to an arid rattling. Up on high in the spangled firmament where Gethsemenë sparkled brightest, flat fragments of clouds raced, thin luminous veils that left the world of men and monster untroubled in their chase.

287

Rossamünd drew deeply of the frosted night.

Somewhere away to the left a boobook gave voice to a husky, cautious *hu-hoo,* speaking twice then lapsing to quiet.

His bladder griping for his attention, the young factotum awoke more fully. "Give me a moment, Master Pin," he said as the old dispenser was settling himself for sleep. "I need the jakes."

Grumbling to himself, the old dispenser kept hold of the musketoon and consented to watch the sleepers a little longer.

With a quick look about, the young factotum sought the privacy of a flowering hawthorn up on the brow of the left-hand hill. This was deceptively steep, and he was well awake and near bursting as he reached the blossoming tree. Finding relief just in the nick, Rossamünd was gifted with an enchanting, almost endless panorama of the vales and swards beyond, a silver-lit sea of flattened downs bounded only on the east by the low and distant umbra of the Brandenfells. Most obvious in this midnight charm were the twinkling lights of a settlement in a shallow combe west-by-north-west, not much more than two miles away.

Spelter Innings.

Rearranging himself and about to descend, Rossamünd caught movement in the field across the way. Before him the earth dipped abruptly to a plant-choked runnel, the other bank rising to a larger, almost perfectly round hillock. In Phoebë's stark light, bright enough to obliterate the sight of many stars, the young factotum could see this hillock was sprouted all over with slender square-sided markers of stone tapering to pyramid points or blank orbs. *Crown-stones! A whole mass of them!* This was a boneyard, perhaps the very one identified in the first singular for the corpse-eating Swarty Hobnag—the one already filled by some other tera-tologist.

Something shifted in the necropolis, a careful, contained action in the shadows of the stones. At the base of an unre-markable crownstone, some stooped figure was pawing at the soil. In full sight from Rossamünd's vantage, it clearly thought itself hidden from view of the middling distant town. Even in the three-quarter lunar light the young facto-tum had the awful dawning it was not an everyman.

Was this *the Swarty Hobnag?* Surely not . . . Surely it was just a corser or an ashmonger. *Which is worse?*

Drawing cautiously down the hill in the hide of the long grass, moon shadows as his ally, Rossamünd could feel a faint, unpleasant threwdishness tingling in his backbone and shivering along both arms. The furtive digger pivoted unex-pectedly and stared suspiciously at the slope, its attention fixing disconcertingly close to where the young factotum huddled. Distorted blunt-jawed face plain in the moon-glow, it let out a very un-humanlike hiss, then returned to its gruesome excavation.

Surely it was *the Swarty Hobnag!*

Clearly the teratologist who had taken the singular for its annihilation was in no hurry to complete the labor . . . or had met his end at the creature's hands.

He thought to go for Craumpalin's help, but feared the creature might leave in the time it would take to climb down and come back. Rossamünd sneaked closer, determined to confront the creature before Europe did and drive it away. As carefully as he could, he scampered down to the trickling runnel and pushed through the thick fennel, releasing its pungent licorice perfume into the night. Catching hold of the rough top of the boneyard's drystone wall, Rossamünd heaved himself over, to land in the stubbly rabbit-mown lawn of the necropolis.

A caste of beedlebane was in Rossamünd's grip in a trice as he toiled up the incline. Rounding the memorial obstacles, he was startled to find the creature so close, so stocky, so real and apparently awaiting his approach.

"UHH!" He gave voice to wordless dismay.

The Swarty Hobnag unbent to its full height. Even on stout legs it was a foot taller than Rossamünd, its gangling forelimbs thick and prodigiously muscled, all fingers ending in obtuse claws. Its face was bluff and chinless, its skin parched black. Thin nostrils in a small, sharply pointed nose flexed and narrowed as the monster sniffed and snorted. Its lips parted obscenely, rolled back over blenched gums and protruding carnivorous teeth as once more the creature hissed.

"Go back to the wilds!" Rossamünd demanded. He had traded words with an urchin-king; he could banter with a lesser nicker. "The lands of everymen are not for you!"

The creature stared at him with jet-dark eyes made luminous by Phoebë's unsympathetic luster. Tainted threwd seethed from the bogle, a broken, confused malice as clear now to the young factotum as the rising reek of the opened grave.

THE
SWARTY HOBNAG

"The long-gone have not been put here just for you to eat," Rossamünd pressed, self-doubt beginning to gnaw.

"What are thee to prat at me about mine own doings!" the Hobnag coughed, its voice somewhere between a belch and a wheeze. "What are thee with thy rosy cheeks, thy puffy lips and thy dandy naughtbringerling drapes? Thee clearly lives false among the menly ones. Dost they love thee like thee was their own?" it heckled, then spat.

"I am Rossamünd, known to the Lapinduce, whose realm you are spoiling, watched over by the sparrow-duke, and servant to the Branden Rose," Rossamünd retorted, the words just spilling out. "Nought but bad can come from your worthless digging. My mistress will not be so kind."

"Hark thee, the little blithely hinderling, quothing thy poxy masters!" it spat. "I fully ken whose borders I invade, Pinky! What might the Largoman do to me so far from his hiding hole? Has he sent thee to chasten me?" it continued in a mockingly saccharin voice. "Or hast thy sparrow-prince doomed thee to bring us all to harmony?"

"There is a writ taken against you . . ."

"Bah! Thou blithely ones always wheedle and nag at me!"

"You *will* be found and killed," Rossamünd pressed, regretting already entering into parley with this wretched thing. "You must go—"

"Humbuggler!" it barked. "Why don't *thee!*"

At this the foul thing sprang from the hole it had fashioned. Without hesitation, Rossamünd threw the beedle-bane. Yet the nicker leaped higher, narrowly clearing the glaring sickly orange burst of the potive as it struck the globe of an intervening crownstone with a *whoomp!* In that single bound, the Hobnag covered the five-yard gap between them and more still, landing adroitly behind Rossamünd. Before the young factotum could turn, it struck him hard in the side with a mighty backhanded swat, lifting him clear off his feet and sending him smacking, back and shoulders, into a crownstone ten feet uphill. The carven rock cracked with the blow of Rossamünd's fall, and the heavy top slipped and tottered. Rossamünd sagged back against the memorial. Weird lights crowded his vision's edges, and an iron taste rose in the back of his throat.

Head craning to see the fall of its victim, the blunt-faced monster shambled up and past the bubbling remains of the burst beedlebane, thinking perhaps its diminutive foe done in.

Dragging himself out of the blankness that sought to submerge him, Rossamünd pulled up his legs to stand, pains flashing all about his battered body. With a dry, stony *pop!* the top of the crownstone came loose and toppled directly over the young factotum. Rossamünd's senses were a sudden clarity as he reached into his strength and caught the heavy thing in both arms, holding it before it could squash him. He heaved to his feet, the stone still in his grasp, as the cunning Hobnag rushed him with loping leggy strides. Head craning back and jaws stretched impossibly wide with teeth fully exposed, it charged like some jutting jagged saw, seeking to carve Rossamünd to mince and jelly. Yet, with strangely indifferent lucidity, Rossamünd stepped aside, swinging the crown-piece like some battering post, striking the nicker on throat and jaw to send it colliding with the broken base. The

293

foul creature reeled and stumbled, lurching back down the boneyard hill. Tripping on another crownstone, it came to a stop, parched black skin on its left temple torn to reveal lurid flesh seeping in the moonlight.

"So thee has found thy strength . . . ," the Hobnag muttered, facing him cautiously now.

Chest heaving, hurting sharply with every gasp, Rossamünd caught his breath. Though the shadowy hint of its face was a dismal blank, the young factotum somehow perceived a kind of bafflement in the wretched thing.

"I want food, not fighting," it seethed, and with that it sprang nimbly away and hared across the flank of the hill, attempting escape between the stones.

Mindlessly, Rossamünd dared his strength and with an almighty heave flung the crown-piece at the retreating creature, throwing it astonishingly far to catch the Hobnag a glancing cuff upon its hip. An audible *crack!* broke the night quiet and the wretch tumbled to the mold, pitching head over end to disappear among the grave-markers. Seizing a caste of Frazzard's powder, Rossamünd hurried as fast as his own bashed body would allow through the tall slender crownstones like some avenging heldin glorified so often in his old pamphlets. Not far on, where he thought he saw the nicker fall, he found the crownstone piece, but the Hobnag was gone. He spied a glimpse of it, staggering through the stones toward the iron-bound entrance on the opposite side of the hill.

"What good does it do to make everymen your prey?" the young factotum cried futilely after it.

"Humbuggler!" he heard it hiss at him in turn. Struggling

294

over the iron-arched gate, the thing was gone into the night.

Rossamünd thought to follow it, but he did not have a single notion what he would do if he caught up with the creature. To kill in the passion and mayhem of a fight was one thing, to destroy by cold choice another, and that he did not think he could do.

His perception swam and oblivion crowded.

Something sharp and deep hurt in his right side.

His back pained.

He knelt for a moment in the graveyard soil and took as deep a breath as his aches would allow.

A terrifying, reedy wailing, an alto voice of sorrow and rage rose and fell on the shifting airs.

Then silence.

No other sound punctuated the quiet, that complete and buzzing silence that seemed to follow every fight; even the crickets were still.

Anxious to get back to Craumpalin waiting so stoutly, Rossamünd clambered to his feet, gathered up the fallen crown-piece in one arm as if it were a light thing and went to the partly exhumed grave. Hastily kicking the new-turned soil back into the hole, Rossamünd refused to look too closely at the ashen dome of the putrefying head poking through where the Hobnag had been digging. Evidently, the dear departed were humed here feet-first too, just as in Winstermill, but that was already more than he wanted to know. Returning the crownstone piece to its original stump, he gingerly scaled the wall and returned up the hill and back to his watch.

All twinges and stabbing aches, he looked to the slow-spinning heavens; the Signals had barely moved. From when he left till his return and the great struggle for life and limb in between had taken little more than one quarter of an hour.

At the camp, he found Craumpalin sitting in a sagging huddle propped against the musketoon and nodding in sleep, unmolested and serene. With a wry sniff, he thought to wake the old salt, tell of his exploits and receive some skillful care. Yet what was there to say? Smiling ruefully to himself, he left the old fellow to his slumber.

Probing his flanks and chest, he sought the manner of his injuries for himself. No cuts or gashes, no blood, just a very sore trunk. Fossicking a gray vial of levenseep from his stoup, he took a swig. His mouth was filled with a taste like fallen leaves that spread an inward cheer, dulling pain, lifting weary thoughts. Invigorated, the young factotum sat cross-legged by the landaulet's rear ladeboard wheel with the musketoon across his lap. To the soft sounds of Europe's regular slumbering breaths and Craumpalin's restless grumbles, he settled himself and—almost as if nothing untoward had ever happened—waited for his stint to end.

THE PATREDIKE

gregorine(s) common name for gater and parish border warden in the rural parts of the central Soutland states; also gregoryman, and so called because they serve as protectors. In the Grumid lands they are sometimes named bindlestiffs—a term usually retained for more vagrant types in other parts of the world—for the time they will spend patrolling their parish boundaries, living rough. Traditionally employed as protectors against the nickers and bogles, in safer parishes gregorymen often become more concerned with the small disputes of parochial parish pride as small regions vie and squabble with their neighbors like full-grown states.

P HOEBË's thoughts were on setting and Maudlin was glimmering verdantly in heaven's acme when, in the small of the night, Rossamünd and Fransitart finally changed watches.

The old salt readily accepted Rossamünd's story of his confrontation with the Swarty Hobnag. "Methinks, lad," he said, gently examining Rossamünd's torso for the nature of his hurts, "that on the next occasion, ye come rouse me out whene'er there be an enemy in sight. I would rather ye stayed hale an' let yer enemy go free on the breeze than have us towin' ye home with yer stern-lights stove in an' yer rudder shot through."

Rossamünd had no response to this. He peered at Fransitart's haggard, sea-scarred dial and wrestled inwardly if *this* was the moment to tell him of the Lapinduce. The longer left, the harder to do. *Is this how his master carried the secret of his own origin for all that time?*

Doting just a little, the aging vinegaroon poured him a tot of claret. "It does me old wind good, though, to see ye win the day," Fransitart said with a chuckle, ending the awkwardly extending pause. "At but half their ages ye're already accomplishin' the feats of them heldin-swells ye always love to read on."

"Well . . . I . . . ," Rossamünd mumbled, sipping his claret awkwardly. Using his satchel as a pillow he stretched out, wrapped once more in the blanket. Part of him wanted sleep, but his heart still hurried and his thoughts still jumped with the lingering, passion of the fight. "Master Frans, what is a humbuggler?"

Huddled cross-legged nearby, musketoon now in hand, the ex–dormitory master seemed to start and took a moment to answer. "Not a very pleasant word, is what it is, lad. It's the foul name given to a blaggardly cove who acts the opposite of what he says."

"A hypocrite?"

"Aye, that's the one; a hypocritactical cur . . ." Fransitart regarded his young companion closely. "Don't ye be frettin' for what ye are, Rossamünd; ye're exactly what ye're s'posed to be, just as Providence determines for each o' us. The sleep of the victor is for ye now, lad. Turn to your hammock else ye'll be shot through and sinking tomorrow."

Content to accept the simple honest refuge of Fransitart's wisdom, Rossamünd let his head sag under the sway of the claret. What was left of the night was of jabs and tweaks and swirling dreams of monsters rushing at him: horn-ed things, slavering corpse-things, great ettin-beasts coming at him over and over.

To the lowing of distant cattle, the four adventurers got under way early. Before going on, Craumpalin had bound Rossamünd's still aching chest in a bitter-smelling brew. "This will seep into bone and gristle and give thee ease," the dispenser insisted, wrapping him so firmly the young factotum had difficulty bending. Aboard the landaulet he was unable to slouch or slump or sag but was forced to sit as straight as the Branden Rose herself; he felt sorely used and most definitely shot through.

Upon hearing of yesternight's stouche, Europe's first response was open displeasure. "You were content then, Rossamünd," she had said with forcibly leveled tone, "to let this beast be free to spoil these good people's graves and eat their long-loved dead like nothing more than scringings from a licensed victualer."

"Of course not, Miss Europe!" the young factotum protested, stung more than all by the realization that he had not properly considered this last night. "I—I had to stay to my watch!"

"Aye, better a safe camp than personal glory," Fransitart added stoutly, frowning in support.

The fulgar regarded the old marine society master as if

looks alone might flatten him. "The next time you go to play the teratologist, Rossamünd, know your place and seek *me* for the work!" she reproached him, pressing fingertips to forehead in exasperation. "My capacity to protect you will be greatly diminished if you warn off every prize and make me the poorer for it!"

"Aye . . ." Rossamünd had kept his voice firm.

On the move again, and with treacle in her humours, Europe had found calm. "It occurs to me a touch peculiar, Rossamünd," she declared almost absently, sucking daintily on some common rock salt, "that you were not aware of your bogle-slaying strength earlier in your life."

Rossamünd had no answer for this. "I——," he tried, but did not know how to put into words that only under great threat had he discovered more vigor in him than expectation led him to reasonably employ; that this *bogle-slaying strength* was more like a well within him than a constant state of being; it was something, he was learning, that he could draw from by choice rather than just continuously and thoughtlessly available thew.

The fulgar's eyes glittered with mild mischief. "What of your *younger* days playing at slaps or parleys with the other bookchildren? Did you terrorize your fellows with great feats of might, little man?"

"I did not know I had such strength to use," the young factotum replied with a shrug. Freckle had once said a long time gone some obscure clue about Rossamünd having to yet learn this strength. He grimaced. *I guess I am learning it now.*

"Aye," Craumpalin said in support. "Thou cannot spend money thee doesn't know thee has."

"Perhaps," Europe replied musingly.

Although from the view atop the hawthorn hill it seemed only a few mounded fields over from their night camp, Spelter Innings proved to be well more than an hour distant by the circuitous wendings of the Athy Road. The day-orb peeped above the folded greening and warmed the travelers as they traversed a small arch over a reedy creek. At its end, they were confronted by a stone wall spiked with what appeared to be newly cut thorn-withies. In this was a heavy, cast-iron gate as tall as three tall men, the portal into the town at last.

"Who comes hence!" the heavy-harnessed gaters challenged peevishly, appearing from small sallies hidden by the dense runners. For simple gate wardens they were as impressively dressed as their courtly counterparts back in the halls of the Archduke. Looking terribly harassed, they showed themselves willing, with muskets cocked and fends lowered, to vent their troubles on any awkward foreigner.

"You recognize me full well, you uppity gregorine!" Europe bit in turn, causing every single gate ward to blanch. "Next you will be asking me for patents of my degree and proofs of my station! Know your place! Open up and let us through!"

In contrast to the sour welcome, Spelter Innings was a gorgeous town, nestled in the shallow folds between the meadows. Bustling with morning activity, every street and lane was a flourishing avenue of spring blossoming almond, lime, cherry and plum, filling the morning with perfumed glory, sweetening the fragrant wood-smoke. Local geriatrics sat on the small balustraded porticoes of their simple high-houses built right up against the main way, watching the passing of all below, with a friendly "halloo" to their neighbors and a mistrustful stare for strangers.

Curiously, as they passed from the town by its farther gates, Rossamünd spied a reddleman among the traffic, the dye-seller walking in the same direction. *Is that the same fellow we found under the Catharine wheels?* Yet this was not possible; how could a foot-going vendor overtake them?

Catching his shrewd inspection, the bedraggled hawker called, "One sparkle gets a fine bit of madder for the rich gent!" and held up a pot in hands tainted bright scarlet. There was something slightly off-beam in the fellow's eyes, something frantic and overexercised.

The young factotum ducked his head and pretended not to hear.

Leaving the red-stained dye-seller far behind, they continued deeper into the wide, fertile peace of the Page, traveling under a dome of near infinite blue, clean white clouds plumping on the horizon ahead. Trees here were far and few, lonely, wind-bent pines and myrtles pruned by hungry herds into elegant parasol shapes. It was only when they were well into the day that Rossamünd realized that Darter Brown had not shown himself. The young factotum began to half consciously search the skies for his miniature friend, scrutinizing every bush or spray of weeds, but not a glimpse could he find.

They went through several hams not properly marked on Craumpalin's map, homey sheltered nooks built in shallow dingles fenced with guarding pines and turpentines and the rubble of ancient stones, each settlement bearing a peculiar name like Windle Comb, Plummet Fulster or the Larch. The folks of these places reckoned themselves so unfailingly safe they went about in only day-clothes, with at best a single garment of proofing. It was a stark contrast to the vigilant rural settings Rossamünd had encountered in the Idlewild. The night was spent in the major civil center of Spokane, a bustling place of high slate houses approaching the gravity of a small city.

In the cheerful clarity of a fresh day, Rufous and Candle took them faithfully north out from Spokane along a busy road called Iron Street that cut high muddy-sided channels through steep wood-fenced meadows of fallow loam or rippling green. Stunted self-sown blossom trees prettied the verges of their path with their pink plum blossoms or sprouted from the lee crest of a hill. Here and there were prominences clearly artificially enlarged into broad oblong mounds of ancient stone, some topped by stocky tumble-down towers, the relics of another people's departed glory decaying beneath teeming weeds.

Rossamünd spent much of his time distractedly looking out for Darter Brown, but could find no hint of him, and of the many little birds he saw, none flew up to greet him.

In twinkling twilight they found a village called the Broom Holm, a timber and mutton town built near the northwestern tip of what Craumpalin's chart named the great forest of thornwood and protected with the more usual high stone curtain. The most remarkable feature of this modest settlement was the grand copper-domed tower of a tocsin that rose well above its other humbly proportioned structures, a self-important display of the success and circumstance of this parish.

Tail-sore and bleary, the four found their rest at the White Hare, a three-story wayhouse established to service the vigil jaunts of wealthy city folk, providing all the luxuries they expected.

"I could grow right partial to such traveling comforts," Craumpalin observed, smiling a little dreamily as he surveyed the plush room, all creams and whites and subtle greens. "Never in me life have I known such a run of cozying beds."

"Aye," said Fransitart, clearly at ease. "It ne'er stops amazin' me to think souls live all their days like this."

"The reverse never stops amazing me," Europe returned.

The fourth day of the knave was gray and threatening, spring yearning for winter's return. Europe's mood—already mildly amiable—lifted that little more. Out the other side of the Broom Holm, the pastured meadows gave over to wide spreading vineyards, roll upon roll of land striped with dark parallel lines of grapevines. Sighted briefly between cedar hedgerows and the folding land stood the ancestral homes of the landed peers. Some were blocky, fortified greathouses standing watch over anciently righted holdings;

others were grandly modern palaces of the new rich whose only concession to the rumored assault of monsters was to have their lowest windows set higher than a tall man could reach.

The Duchess-in-waiting of Naimes inhaled deeply and looked about complacently. "How I much prefer this open-seat travel to going cooped in a stuffy cabin, to feel the wind's breath on my brow and the taste of the land on my lips."

"Can't say I smell more than dirt," Fransitart offered, scowling over his shoulder at the dark billows that were blowing up from the southwest and bringing with them a sweet sea tang. "We salts bain't much use for snufflin' things—the sea encourages us ter forget that sense as soon as is naturally possible."

Europe arched a brow and sniffed.

Fixing his sabine scarf about his throat a little more warmly, Rossamünd grinned. Come weather fair or foul, he too could travel all his days like this, floating somewhere between destinations, the cares of before left behind, the cares ahead yet to come. Smiling at the flattening vales of ordered green, one eye still out for a glimpse of Darter Brown, he became steadily alive to a hidden and unfamiliar disquiet. "The land is not as restful as the rich builders with their low windows reckon on," he said, gaining only puzzled glances from both his old masters and new mistress.

The Branden Rose peered at her diminutive employee with shrewd calculation. "You speak evidently of the subtleties of the threwd, little man."

"Aye, Miss Europe." He looked at her earnestly. "It is only slight, but it is not kindly."

"Hence our need to come here, yes?"

"Aye," he returned inaudibly.

Attending to the directions given by Craumpalin from the written pilot provided to Rossamünd when he accepted the singular, Fransitart turned them off Iron Street and took a tributary drive marked by a thin white stone. In excellent repair—probably through private funds—this path made for good speed, and the landaulet fairly clipped by flat pastures interspersed with vines and orchard groves in full and glorious flower. Watching their flocks in sheep-mown fields, heavily armed and harnessed shepherds peered at the rapidly passing newcomers and did not return Craumpalin's curt wave.

As the gray day dimmed toward its conclusion, they came into view of a large handmade hill, its broad, level summit ringed thickly with cedars, from behind which rose the chimneys, ridge-caps and gables of an enormous manor.

"Our destination, I am thinking," Europe observed.

Finding a somewhat precipitous ramp rising along the northern flank of the hill, Fransitart encouraged the weary horses to climb this last obstacle. Through open gates at its summit they entered unchallenged into a broad, partially paved square with service buildings on every side and a neat garden copse of large ornamental pear trees and a spreading cedar in the middle. Veering left and scattering chickens, Fransitart brought them to a halt before the outspread steps of a stately façade of pink stone and a great many windows.

Striding down to them from the doubly high front doors, the anonymous pastoralist of the second singular, splendidly attired in a wide frock coat of expensive indigo, met them. "Welcome! Welcome well to the Dike!" he cried, his arms gratifyingly wide. Introducing himself with a long bow as Monsiere Decius Trottinott, Companion Imperial of the Gate and heir of the Patredike, their host handed Europe from the landaulet as his yardsmen took Rufous and Candle, the carriage and the luggage too into their charge. Without even a glance at any documentation, Monsiere Trottinott welcomed the Duchess-in-waiting and her faithful staff openly to his bastionlike home and holdings.

"You can well imagine how hopeful I was when the communication arrived from the coursing house that it was the great Branden Rose who consented to effect my solution," he declared with gusto. "How gratified I was when I received communication from your own gracious hand confirming the same!"

Europe received his enthusiasm with queenly equanimity, neither falling into aloof superiority nor letting herself be caught up in the tide of his candid delight.

Despite his southern name, Monsiere Trottinott spoke with a refined and common Grumid accent, spontaneously showing away his wide barns sheltering all manner of rural equipages, his buried cellars smelling of musty grapes and full to their low groin-vaulted ceilings with innumerable wine presses and pipes of properly aging vin, and the gala hall with its family crypt beneath, entombing generations of his line back to the founding of Patredike in HIR 1401.

"Ahh, but pity us, your graciousness," Monsiere Trottinott went on as he showed them at last through the domed entry hall of the main manor to a grand hiatus, "that in our two hundredth year we are beset by some secreted evil that steals my sheep, tears up my precious vines and— foulest of all—wounds and attempts to carry off my loyal sheepmen!"

"The pity, Monsiere, is that I could not come to you sooner," Europe replied with practiced grace.

Trottinott nodded and gave a gratified bow, offering Europe a plush seat and simpler benches for her three fellows. "Your graciousness is most gracious."

The day's early threatening gray finally brewed into a storm, rattling windows, gusting down chimneys, setting sumptuously liveried servants in silken blues to hurry closing shutters and drawing drapes.

A jut-jawed steward entered bringing a tray of fine Heil glasses of delicate powdery blue and a refreshment the Monsiere called agrapine.

"You must try," he insisted. "It is from the *gleanings* of my own pressings, would you believe! It tastes full, though it is not at all strong—perfect for just before a meal."

Taking his portion, Rossamünd surreptitiously eyed the wonderful luxurious clutter of the many-windowed hiatus. Between bookshelves swollen with books and red marble columns, every panel and wall was hung with paintings, large and small, mostly of people in portrait or action, and making the room seem filled with a veritable crowd of souls. Even the lofty coffered ceiling was alive with many prospects, in-

308

MONSIERE TROTTINOTT

cluding—directly above him—a glorious campaign scene of a man in the mottle of the Empire standing prominent in a mass of wrestling warriors in Imperial and Turkic harness.

"That is the moment when my grandsire earned his honor and his title, and his ever-grateful heirs their elevation," the Monsiere offered smilingly, breaking into Rossamünd's craning fixation.

"Aye, sir, at the Battle of the Gates, just when—late in the day—the Turkoman flank was collapsing," Rossamünd returned in uninhibited enthusiasm, "just before Haroldus met and slew the Slothog!"

"One and the same!" Trottinott clapped once in delight. "Hark, here is a proper student of matter to show my boys how it is done! I must praise you, Duchess Rose, for your young servant's fine address; how excellent it must be to be served by such learned fellows."

Europe gave a single, slow blink. "Indeed it is, Monsiere . . . *very* excellent."

The young factotum blushed as Craumpalin gave him a subtle nudge. Vaguely conscious of his mistress' gaze upon him, Rossamünd fixed his attention on his delicate glass of sweet yet sour agrapine.

Settled, they were joined by a handsome woman in a flaring dress of rich satin, grass-hued with thin peach pink stripes, her entrance marked with the comforting *swish-swish* of her skirts. Trotting dutifully beside this gracious woman came two children, both boys, turned out in neat suits of deep warm blue like their father: one little, the other nearer to Rossamünd's own age.

"Allow me to name my wife—Lillette, the Madamine Trottinott . . ."

The auburn-haired beauty curtsied low with well-practiced ease and a slight creak of stays, her elaborate curls falling about her face and neck. "Gracious lady," she said with great gravity, the doubt in her eyes at this martial peeress discreetly contained.

"And two of my triple joys, Autos . . ."

The older boy bowed, saying with already breaking voice, "I am delighted, graciousness."

". . . and Pathos."

The younger boy grinned. "Hullo, my lady!" he said with a slight rustic burr.

"And *hullo* to you, small fellow," Europe returned with the perfect model of an amiable smile.

"He loves to spend his days with my moilers," the father offered by way of explanation. "Their older sister, Muse, is boarded at the aplombery in Lo, applying herself to finishing her womanly graces."

Europe sniffed bitterly as if to say exactly what she thought of aplomberies, yet when she spoke, she was civil and smooth. "So tell me more, Monsiere, of this creature that besets you. Have you seen it?"

Trottinott's face fell. "Ah. That I have not, gracious lady, though several of my tenants and servants have. All that is sure is the evidence of their ravages: my kennels empty." He looked nervously to his sons, clearly uneasy about saying too much in front of them. "Vines in ruins, flocks . . . *decimated,* their herdsmen hurt and demanding exorbitant

311

incentive to stay to the watch of their folds. It would be best to speak with them. I shall call them out tomorrow. They have had closest dealings with the . . . troublers . . . Apart, that is, from the fugelman we sought from Dough Hill to hunt it—but alas, he never returned, precipitating the very writ you have so fitly answered . . . Ah! But listen to me! It is a long road from the bright city to here." The Monsiere spread his hands before them. "You should take a day to re-cover yourselves."

"Idle hands find mischief, good sir, and idle minds even more," Europe proclaimed, to the gentleman's clear relief. "We shall begin tomorrow. Now, if you please, direct my factotum to the place most appropriate where he might make my plaudamentum."

OF BLOOD AND BASINS

parmister essentially a foreman in charge of the various workings and facets of a franchise. Whether it is the shepherds and their flocks, the hay wards and their herds, the swains and their farrows, the moilers and their fields, the pruners and their trees, the pickers and their vines, the garnerers and their stores, there is a parmister in charge of each, and a master-parmister in charge of all and answering only to the owning lord or his seniormost agent.

INN the half-light of a fresh, still day, gentle servants roused Rossamünd early. With careful quiet they stoked the hearth and set more wash-water on the nightstand, then left him be. In the serene luxury he bathed away the stains of travel in the balmy comfort of the copper basin. After a dinner the night before of a full five removes and glacés, he had been too fatigued to do more than collapse on the opulent bed and sleep, despite the gale pounding at the shutters and howling desolately down the chimney flue.

A hesitating knock stirred him and had him leaping from the water to hurry on smalls and longshanks. Fransitart and Craumpalin had come, faces kindly, eyes shining with a strange agitation.

"Slept the slumber o' the innocent, 'ey, lad?" Fransitart smiled earnestly.

Rossamünd could not conjure the words to fit his confusion. He stared hopefully at his old masters and realized that Fransitart was just in shirt and weskit, that he was carrying his heavy frock coat and the long shirtsleeve on his left arm—his puncted arm—was loose. "Master Frans . . ."

With a look to the door, the dormitory master drew back the cloth of his sleeve and bared the pallid flesh on the underside of his forearm. "It's showed itself, lad . . ."

There, marked by the butcher Grotius Swill during the inquest at Winstermill, and clean of any scab, was a small, scarce-begun cruorpunxis of faint red-brown lines—a monster-blood tattoo made from Rossamünd's very own blood.

For a moment the young factotum simply stared at the incomplete figure. In the short time he had been afforded to work before Europe's intervention, Swill had still managed to mark what was recognizably a curling brow, a whorled eye and a nose. He was barely surprised to see it revealed, yet something within Rossamünd still knotted, bringing with it a peculiar sense of dislocation, of observing himself as if from without.

"Ahh . . . I'm sorry, Rossamünd," Fransitart murmured,

shaking his venerable head as if *he* were at fault, quickly concealing the pristine cruorpunxis again under his sleeve.

Rossamünd drew in deeply of the delicately scented air
of the room. "I already know . . . ," he breathed, a disconcerting ringing setting in his ears.

Craumpalin nodded sagely. "I can't say I am in any stretch
flabbergasted meself, lad."

"No," the young factotum persisted. *Time to be out with
it all, time to trust these faithful men as good as fathers* . . . "A
monster-lord told me so."

"A monster-lord?"

"Where, lad? Out in the Paucitine?"

"No." Rossamünd closed his eyes. "In the Moldwood in
Brandenbrass . . . The Duke of Rabbits . . ."

"In the middle of a city!" Fransitart bridled. "Surely the
line of dukes would've had a battalion of pugilists in there
quick as levin to winkle it out?"

"It is too mighty for that, Master Frans. Most of the
whole city doesn't fathom it's there. They never have, and I
reckon they never will . . ."

"Sparrows! Rabbits!" Fransitart exclaimed softly. "Brace
me to a mizzenmast tree, what else be out there?"

"More'n common folk would reckon upon," Craumpalin
replied knowingly, tapping his vinegar-scarred temple.

Rossamünd let out a long and shuddering sigh.

The ex–dormitory master gripped him firmly by the
arms and held him in his narrow, wondering gaze.

As unlikely and bizarre as it was, Rossamünd was not just
some causeless aberration; real though occult processes had

315

brought him to be. He had been formed by ancient unsullied forces, a child of the threwd, of the very earth.

Suddenly, the young factotum flung himself into the old salt's grasp, Fransitart gathering him in to clasp him close and hard, somehow managing to smother him with his thin, still-strong arms. With a great gust of tears muffled in the rough stale proofing of the old salt's weskit, Rossamünd poured out the weight and agony of it all.

"If ye were knit of me own stuff, boy, I could not love ye better!" Fransitart whispered.

"Aye, lad . . . ," Craumpalin's emotion-cracking murmur confirmed.

Fransitart released him from his paternal embrace and he looked at his masters squarely. In return the two vinega-roons regarded him in wonder.

"Well, let's have a squint at thy trunk," said Craump-alin matter-of-factly, finally breaking the tender quiet. He held up his own satchel with its brews and bandages. "All gone," he marveled as Rossamünd submitted to the scrutiny. "Nought left but slight bruemes."

Indeed, where livid bruises had covered half his ribs only two days ago there were but faint shades of the old contusions.

"Tend thy pumps and tell me if it hurts . . ."

Obediently, Rossamünd took a deep breath . . . Barely a twinge.

"Thee always was a prodigious quick healer," Craumpalin said knowingly, patting him in fatherly fashion on the crown.

"Wish I could say the same," Fransitart muttered sardoni-cally, bending with a wince at the hips. He fixed Rossamünd with a determined eye. "We'll 'ave to be showin' me mark to yer mistress, lad," he said with old masterly firmness.

Rossamünd returned his gaze reluctantly. What he was afraid of he did not know . . . Europe's rejection? Her fury?

"She surely fathoms it's comin'," Fransitart pressed. "Prob'ly been countin' th' days . . ."

"Aye," Craumpalin added. "A spoiled tooth is best pulled quick."

Fransitart nodded, *hmm*ing in solidarity.

The young factotum smiled for but a moment; then, innards knitting, he finished dressing and firmed his courage to face his mistress with this final and unavoidable proof.

By the guidance of the Patredike's amiable servants Rossamünd went to the kitchen in the main house to test the morning's plaudamentum. He brewed with a distant and instinctive care while his old masters waited unobtrusively in an adjacent parlor, sipping sillabub made straight from the cow. When the draught was done, they were shown upstairs down a golden hall carpeted with blue and lined with tall alabaster urns fashioned after some ancient style. Rossamünd's footfalls were a grim echo to the apprehensive pounding in his ears as they approached the eggshell-blue door of the temporary boudoir of the heiress of Naimes.

Gritting his teeth, Rossamünd knocked—faintly first, firmer second—and entered.

In a suite of white ceiling and walls striped deep rose and pale geranium Europe was breakfasting alone. Already fully harnessed, she sat in a high chair by a thin-legged table, star-

317

ing out the enormous windows to the panorama of half-lit vineyards and a sky scoured clean by the night's tempest. Appearing at ease in the friendly light of the full-fledged dawn, she barely acknowledged Rossamünd or the two old men as she took her morning dose in its flute glass, shifting slightly in her seat, not turning her head.

"Miss Europe, Master Frans' mark has shown . . . It is a . . . cruorpunxis." Frowning, Rossamünd held his breath.

In verification, Fransitart stepped forward and turned his sleeve to show the underside of his forearm.

Uttering a quiet unamazed "hmph," the fulgar barely cast a glance at the proffered limb. "It turns that our foe the dastard surgeon has correctly surmised your origin after all, little man," she said evenly as she sipped her plaudamentum, keeping her attention fixed on the vista.

Fransitart and Craumpalin retreated from the room.

"So rossamünderlings are truly real . . . ," Europe murmured, as if to herself. "Your strength is not just some happy aberration . . . An ünterman in service to a teratologist . . ." Finally she turned to behold him fully, her expression tight yet eyes inquiring.

He held her searching stare unflinchingly, hoping—aching—for her to take him just as he was.

She blinked slowly, bitter perceptions roiling in the depths of her gaze. "You worry I might fly into a rage? Slay you where you stand?" Her voice was low and dangerous. "And after this collect my prize at the closest knavery so to be held a savior for defending goodly folks from a most insidious trickery?"

Shrinking from her, Rossamünd was not at all certain what he thought. "I . . ."

The fulgar's mien clouded. Draining the dregs of her draught, she stared again out the window. Steepling her fingers, she pressed the foremost to her lips. "I am not entirely the thoughtless invidist you might suppose me, Rossamünd. I slay the monster out of need, out of right, out of . . ." She hesitated.

Rossamünd stared in awe at her unfamiliar confusion.

"I slay the monster because long ago a silly hoyden, too well used to good living and in flight from her mother, sought to make much money where much money was to be made. Dazzled by the great prizes offered to teratologists, she mindlessly chose the knaving life and, being slight and terribly silly, thought a fulgar would be the best and simplest kind. No need for aptitude or muscle, just point and *zzick!* It has served her well, protecting her from *monsters* without the city and those within . . ." She closed her hazel eyes as if against some dark memory. When she opened them again, they were clear, determined. Reaching out, she touched his arm with surprising tenderness. "Nothing changes, Rossamünd. You are my factotum, I am your mistress; the plot thickens, that is all."

A small warmth of hope unfolded within him, infusing its tender solace through every fiber of his being until he near sang with the relief of it. Of a sudden, he clasped her from the side as she sat, an awkward honest embrace filled with the smell of her, feeling just how wastedly thin the mighty Branden Rose was made by her lahzarine organs.

Startled by his action, Europe held her hands up in surprise, relented and held him in return with those same graceful hands. Releasing him quickly, she made a wry face. "A delicious irony, do you not think, little man, that it is *you* who has won my affections . . . A pretty paradox to figure through."

Rossamünd smiled happily. "Aye."

The fulgar nodded briefly, *yes, yes.* "Mind on the knave now," she declared more firmly. "We have lesser creatures to find today."

To aid the course for the secreted evil, Monsiere Trottinott had sent for his squires and parmisters, parcel-holders and various tenant farmers who worked his historied franchise. By midmorning, when Rossamünd emerged on the heels of the Branden Rose, most of these various heads and local men of import were gathered in the square before the enormous manor, with others yet arriving by horse, cart or carriage. Most were dressed in frock coat and longshanks—the usual country-gentry attire. Yet a few were decked in more peculiar garb of voluminous white sleeves under proofed vests of red or black, deep brown or gray, and thick high-waisted skirts striped vertically and across with bands of brown and black or brown and blue, wearing their own hair long and pulled back with broad black ribbons. Piltmen chiefs, the Monsiere quietly called them, "the descendants of the original folk that once prospered in the lands about before my sires came." Keeping apart, these chiefs spoke to each other with the same strange lilting song in their words that many of the Trottinotts' servants shared and stared at Europe with guarded wonder. "Our Bright Lady Schurmer," they dubbed her, and honored her with many solemn bows.

A table had been brought out and placed with plush chairs amid the graceful trees of the wooded park in the middle of the grounds. Here Europe sat, proofed in her usual scarlet harness, sucking on rock salt and sipping agrapine as the warming sun eased over the high roof of the main manor. She looked like a queen holding court as showy country gents and shy taciturn laborers took their turn to tell her what they knew.

For his part, Rossamünd was given the role of amanuensis, writing with a stylus all pertinent evidence into the Branden Rose's ubiquitous ledger. The details he accumulated were little different from the particulars related by the Monsiere himself last night: nocturnal commotions; vines ruined; sheep sucked dry of their humours; nightwatching men attacked, bruised and half strangled. There was confusion about the number of their foe: some said a great swarming many; others told of a lone giant. Together they were unable to give a more substantial description than *black*, *slimy* and *prodigious great thew*.

"They . . . it . . . is gettin' bolder, miss!" a ruddy laboring parmister attested. "Waylaid us in our homes in the storm last night; hammerin' and hissin' and tryin' to tear out the bars of our winders. We already toil hard on the common diems, wi'out being made to risk on our rightful vigil . . ."

"Monsters seldom observe the scales of rest," Europe answered grandly, "and—good fortune for you—neither do I."

"They seem to have a taste fer soured milk, ma'am . . . ," one bashful fellow with sad eyes and a fluttering, nervous smile volunteered, telling rapidly of night after night where pails holding milk on the turn were upset or drunk dry.

"Then that shall be our lure!" The fulgar clapped her hands just once. "Monsiere Trottinott, I shall need dishes of the stuff before the day is out . . . And perhaps—if you will allow it—some drops of sheep's blood with it as a further incentive."

"Surely, my lady."

The parmisters and landholders murmured in approbation as the meeting was concluded and dispersed.

Trottinott beamed in pleasure at them, Europe and the world in general. *Ahh, my problem is solved!* was writ clear across his genial dial.

A pair of Trottinott's servants as their guides, Fransitart and Craumpalin went by one of the Monsiere's dozen carriages to Angas Welcome to retain any pathprys or other lurking fellows they could discover. Remaining at the manor to prepare, Europe and Rossamünd took an early lunch with the family, supping in a modest but excellently appointed room attached to an enormous golden dining hall.

With the glow of good food in belly, Rossamünd rode with Europe and Trottinott in the landaulet, driven—with the fulgar's permission—by one of the Monsiere's own men, the Monsiere himself well proofed and armed with a long-rifle richly ornamented with curling pearlescent devices. After much boyish persistence Autos had been allowed to come too, to the howling dismay of his little brother and

ROSSAMÜND

clinging apprehension of his mother. Solemn-faced and harnessed like his father, the heir of Patredike now sat across from Rossamünd, staring at him owlishly as they were taken down to a place called Scantling Aire. A small settlement of shepherds, vineyardists and hurtlemen, it was a bare few miles to the north and the site of the previous night's theroscade.

"Have you slayed many nickers?" Autos finally spoke, his voice stiff with contained intensity. He looked straight at the young factotum with serious, gray-blue eyes.

"I—ah—aye, some few . . . ," Rossamünd admitted after a small, sad breath. A memory of Threnody attempting to wit snarling, slavering nickers on the road before flashed unpleasantly in his thoughts.

The other boy's expression went wide, *How can a boy my own age have already killed a nicker!* obvious on his face.

For a moment Rossamünd had an inkling of how peculiar he might look clad in his heavy proofing and laden with stoups and digitals like a proper skold.

"Where was this, young sir?" the Monsiere interjected, betraying no little amazement himself in his quizzically frowning mien.

"Ah . . . Out Bleak Lynche way, sir . . . on the Conduit Vermis," he added.

"Ahh, yes. I have heard some fluttering rumor that speaks of disquiet among the therian over that way," Trottinott observed. "I wonder if it bears any connection with our own distress."

"Perhaps," came Europe's soft reply.

Scantling Aire consisted of four round towers arranged in a square, the spaces between closed with a tall fence of stone and iron. Smilingly self-sufficient, the local parmister in plain gray soutaine greeted them in the iron-girded yard between these four tall cottages. They were quickly joined by many tired, solemn-eyed women dressed in white bagged sleeves and long-hemmed bibs of gray or brown, and ruddy barefoot children clad in sacklike smocks regardless of gender. These were the sheepwives and their bantlings—amiable enough, yet their hospitality was diminished by a deep fatigue.

There were, however, no other men.

Introduced as Master Parfait, the parmister was a windy, posturing, rooster of a man. He showed Europe about his tiny constituency with all the self-satisfaction of the sole male among a throng of frightened women.

"The men are all out in field or sleeping," Parfait explained to his lofty lady guest. "Some brave fellow has to keep eyes out for these lonesome ladies."

Rossamünd looked away to hide his sour face.

"I am sure their menfolk have much to say about your *bravery,*" Europe returned coldly.

The smug fellow's countenance fell. "Well . . . They . . . I—uh . . ." He spluttered and blundered to silence and was ignored forevermore.

In a flurry of curtsies and breathless "M'lady's!" the sheepwives were nevertheless reluctant to sacrifice a sheep to the demands of a fulgar. Yet, with some quiet encouragement from Trottinott, they singled out a young beast from the domestic pen. To their relief, Europe required only a little of its ichor let run into a bucket from a small hole pricked in its neck, and the life of the bewildered hogget was spared.

At the fulgar's instruction, this bucket of gore, two pails of soured sheep's milk and an armful of pudding basins were hefted by a quarto of doughty wives, carried outside of Scantling Aire's wall and about it to the meadow behind. This procession—Europe, Rossamünd, the Monsiere and his son, and the senior-most wives of the village—was joined by children crowding and shouting and running after them as if it were a summerscale vigil.

Europe put Rossamünd to work under the giggling gaze of the fascinated children peeking from the shade of the village wall.

The natural mound on which the community had been founded was knobbled with ancient, lichen-blotched boulders. Standing down on the meadow proper, elbow in hand, knuckle pressed to lip, the Branden Rose instructed Rossamünd to set six pudding basins on the rocks, calling left, calling right until she was satisfied the bowls were spaced the correct number of yards apart along the whole eastern slant. His next task was to ladle soured sheep's milk from pail to basin, followed by a little sheep's blood.

"Make it twenty parts milk to one part red!" Europe instructed him as if it were some regular script.

The gore stained the curdlings the color of a person's skin; this sight and the accompanying smell made Rossamünd's digesting stomach queasy. When all the pudding basins were full, he followed Europe out into the gray, broadly undulating land, dribbling a trail of blood-curdle from a gory bucket onto the teeth-mown turf. At a hundred yards he was instructed to place an earthen bowl down and fill it. He then trickled the bait for a similar distance and placed another blood-curdled bowl. This was repeated until the bucket was empty. To Rossamünd's astonishment they had come near on a quarter of a mile.

"This should make an excellent slot for our hob-possum to follow to the bait proper," Europe observed, peering out into the pastures and up at the great hemisphere of patchy sky. "How sits the threwd?"

Found dumb for a moment by the directness of her question, Rossamünd squinted into the east, to where they were told the threat usually arose. "It is unsettled," he replied carefully. "Not unfriendly, more . . . *uncomfortable*." It was the best word he could reckon.

The fulgar pursed her lips, her sharp gaze shifting from tussock to tussock as if monsters skulked behind every one.

"Miss Europe, what if this nicker is blithely?"

"I think you will find, Rossamünd, that these humble people care little how *blithely* a nicker might be" was her quick reply, hazel eyes still intently scrutinizing their surroundings. "A beast of any stripe is a bane to a farmer if stealing his flocks."

Rossamünd sighed. "Aye."

Europe arched a brow. "This nicker has begun to assail people's houses—hardly the evidence of a kindly nature, I would have thought . . ." Her expression abruptly hardened, and her attention fixed on something behind them, something toward Scantling Aire. "We are followed."

Rossamünd spun about.

Maybe fifty yards behind stood Autos, hesitating, expression shifting manifestly between unease and keen inquisitiveness. "What are you doing?" he called as he dared to approach. Behind him, back by Scantling Aire, his father was standing among the boulders, watching apprehensively, hands cupped to mouth to shout his son back.

"I am making a slot for the unkindly nicker to follow," Europe explained bluntly. "Go back to your papa . . ."

"But *he* is no older than me!" Autos pointed stubbornly to Rossamünd, his cracking voice an honest plea. "*He* helps you! *I* have an excellent fowling piece and can course with a whole kennel of talbots—"

"*He* is my factotum for a reason, child," Europe replied, her tone a warning, "holding vastly greater parts and practice than you! *Go!* I do not want to be forced to souse you with this bloody milk and leave you out here as part of the bait!"

Autos paled, blushed, then scowled—torn between horrified belief in her words and the desire to remain and appear very brave.

"She is jesting, young master," Rossamünd finally said when it became clear his mistress was going to leave the poor fellow in his distress, frowning to hide his own satisfaction at her compliments.

"Just barely," the fulgar breathed.

Autos pulled himself up and puffed out his chest, his brow

deep-furrowed, his eyes holding insult and hurt. Snorting through his nose like some panting horse, the boy looked on the brink of a petulant retort. Yet the anxious calls of the Monsiere finally gained the attention of the young heir of the Patredike with their uncommon rancor, provoking him to pivot quickly and hurry a retreat.

Europe clucked her tongue and addressed Rossamünd as if nothing had occurred. "Now, throw the bucket out farther; it shall be the first incentive of our little trick . . . Mind your pitch!" she added quickly as Rossamünd wound back for the toss. ". . . Not too far."

In his keenness to oblige, he fumbled his toss so that the empty bucket so that it fell a paltry distance.

"Perhaps a mite farther than that . . . ," Europe offered, touching her lip with her long forefinger to hide a grin.

Rossamünd gritted his teeth on an embarrassed retort.

The second attempt a better length, they walked back to Scantling Aire.

As they climbed the settlement's mound to where the Monsiere and his party waited, Europe's manner was all innocence and serene expertise. "At night's fall my factotum and I shall sit ourselves up there and watch," she declared to the Monsiere as she stepped up to him, pointing to the roof of the southeastern cottage, partly obscured by the thick growth of a pine. "Have a scale set upon the southern wall that I might climb and descend again quickly at need."

Though Trottinott and his embarrassed son were to remain with them through the night, Europe would not allow them to join her on the roof, insisting they sit and watch from the small windows of the round houses' upper stories. "I do not want to be accountable for your hurts should you stumble into my way," she warned. "And please do not shoot at anything until I have endorsed such activity." She arched a brow at the Monsiere's long-rifle. "I will not like a musket ball in my back, and whoever delivers it will like it even less."

Smiling uneasily, Trottinott nodded.

Autos stayed behind his father.

At day's end, with the clear sky a glorious dusty pink, the husbands, sons and fathers of Scantling Aire returned home to a mood of increasing hope: the Branden Rose had come to deliver them all from their terrors. Sending the large roof-dwelling skinks scuttering to hide, Rossamünd and Europe climbed the triangular scale to sit on the slightly shifting tiles. Screened by resin-scented needles, they had an excellent sight of the six baited pudding bowls below. From such a height the spreading pastures, broad and flat to the north, appeared to sink to the east down to a far-off patch of murky ground and the smudge of low hills well beyond. At middle distance, shepherds bearing long, faintly glimmering limn-thorns could just be made out goading white fluffy lumps by the hundred before them, driving them north. To the right, away to the south, Rossamünd spied the twinkling window lights of Patredike.

Breathing deeply of the tepid evening, the young factotum checked the priming of the flammagon supplied from the Monsiere's own modest armory. He wondered absently if his old masters were even now returning with a cunning lurksman or other patefract in tow.

A hamper had been packed by the Monsiere's kitchen— under instruction from his wife—and as evening came, he shared this with all the cottagers and the two roof-borne watchers too.

"The long night begins," Europe murmured, sitting cross-legged on the tiles and nibbling deftly on cold quail's wing and taking sips of fresh-brewed plaudamentum in between. "Let us hope our prey is an early riser . . ." After a moment she added with hushed words, "When we come to the fight, I think it best—if you are resolved to action—that you stay to using potives, little man; we do not want to startle these simple people with uncommon feats of thew." She lapsed to silence.

Similarly mute, Rossamünd shifted the flammagon over his shoulder, ate and watched.

16

THE HUNT FOR
THE SECRETED EVIL

peltrymen though once used to mean trappers, this term is more and more coming to include venators—that is, hunters; indeed, it is becoming the catchall word for any woodsman. One of the notable historical details of peltrymen is that the ambuscadiers of armies of the Half-Continent model their own harness on the accoutrements of peltryfolk, a practice originating from the recruiting of skirmishing volunteers from the people best suited to skulking and ambushing: woodsmen and peltrymen.

TAIL-SORE Rossamünd had been sitting stoutly for a goodly long time on the roof peak, right hand stiff from clutching the high chimney, legs twitching from holding his weight against the incline of the tiles. Attention drum-skin taut, his hearing pricked to every sound that disturbed the night's hush: the snuffles and hoof-stamps of animals tethered in the Scantling yard; the muffled conversation of folks watching from the attic just below them; the merest creak of pine bough; and beside him, Europe's near-imperceptible breathing. Indefatigable in her concentration, the heiress of Naimes had barely stirred for the entire watch. The priming in the pan of his broad-barreled flammagon already checked many times, Rossamünd refused the compulsion to do so again and kept his drowsy eyes moving from shadow to shadow out on the meadow.

The color of rich cheesecake in the thin olive sky, rising Phoebë was a full hand span above the horizon and Maudlin green, already hoisting herself up heaven's darkling dome when something barely distinguishable shifted out in the gloomy fields. It came first as an unusual threwdish twitching, still far off, arresting Rossamünd's tiring attention before he saw a subtle yet rapid motion.

"They come," Europe exhaled, so softly it might have been the night breezes.

Shapes amorphous and shifting were approaching along the line of the blood-curdle trail, writhing shadows that refused to solidify into anything recognizable despite the creamy lunar light. At first Rossamünd thought they might be a pack of little blightlings rushing in a horde. But when they reached the foot of the settlement, the shapes resolved into five large ambiguous silhouettes, each bending over its own pudding basin. At this the young factotum next thought them a tribe of brodchin-beasts like the horn-ed nickers that had attacked in the Briarywood near Winstermill.

As the creatures settled themselves to feed, Europe slid silently to the scale and, with infinite care, eased onto it, sucking an impatient breath as it softly creaked. Her right eye clear in a dapple of moonlight, she gave Rossamünd a brief but pointed look, then descended with deft alacrity.

Near as fast as the lightning she held, the Branden Rose was out from the shadows of the south side of the cottage foundation. Springing between wall and pine trunk, fuse in hand, she was on the first shadow before it was aware of the danger. Rossamünd watched her spin about the rock that held the basin to strike the shadow high on its back. *Zzick!* The briefest green-blue glare and everything went strange. Rather than bellow or collapse, the obscure figure burst into many parts. At first Rossamünd thought the fulgar had simply hit it with such potency that it had been blown to splinters, yet he quickly realized, as the various parts sought to flee or fight individually, that their foe was something else entirely.

Bracing himself on the tiles, he fired the flammagon high, giving his mistress better sight as she swung at one of the *pieces,* striking it with another glaucous flash.

In the brilliant pink light of the flammagon flare swarmed slithering black saps, more like worms than serpents, working in disconcerting union, their slick, pulsating hides ridged and bulging, far stranger than any terrestrial nicker or bogle Rossamünd had known before. Exclamations of disgust and wonder came from the watching cottagers witnessing from the windows below.

In defense of their fellows, the other forms fell apart into a mass of saps, how many hundreds Rossamünd could not count. A score tried to surge Europe, to engulf her with their coils and their spiny sucking mouths. With a hurtling sweep of her sizzling fuse she kept them bayed, leaping lightly onto the boulder and sending the half-full basin tumbling. Gaining the higher vantage, she seemed for a moment on an island awash in a seething inky sea, swatting down every slick, black, lashing fluke with flash after flash of violent light. Yet a fight did not prove to be the wriggling things' primary desire. Protected by the aggression of a few, the great bulk of the foul worms slid away with astonishing speed into the benighted meadow.

A musket shot coughed, and another. An eruption of gun-smoke fouled the air before Rossamünd.

"STOP!" he hollered, sliding upon his stomach down the incline of the roof, barely catching himself on the lip of the tiles, his thrice-high tumbling to the ground far below, the flammagon spared such treatment by the tangle of its strap about Rossamünd's shoulders. Craning his neck to look beneath the eaves, he was confronted by the startled upside-down face of a determined Master Parfait, still with smoking long-rifle in hand. "YOU'LL *HIT* HER!"

The admonition did nought to halt the disgruntled par-mister, who, already in the throes of reloading, primed his pan and thrust his musket out of the upper window to take aim. Rossamünd would have none of this, and stretching precariously, humours swelling in his head, he snatched the barrel of the firelock and wrested it from the uppity fellow's misguided grasp with a smart tug.

A muffled girlish shriek from a lady-watcher at another window and Rossamünd looked up to see in the sinking glow of the flammagon that the remaining saps harrying Europe had wound themselves together into a single form. The bulging, oversized creature bent up, whipping its single worm head at the fulgar and forcing her to spring in elegant retreat off the rock.

Rossamünd scrambled, almost toppling, to the scale and

335

blundered down, leaping the last third in anxious hurry as he saw the secondhand flash and heard another arcing *zz-zock!* Pouncing around the corner, stolen musket still in hand, he saw Europe standing higher up the slope, her back to the settlement wall. Brandishing the fuse like some ancient heldin's spear, she drove it right into the heart of the collective triple-sized worm. With a satisfying *zzzzack!* the foul things flailed apart, their grip on each other loosening in their demise. They fell twitching dead to the grass, until only one remained upright, skewered through its mouth by the fulgaris, its slimy hide hissing and bubbling where it had split apart under Europe's eclatics. With a grimace, she withdrew the fuse from the charry mess and scowled out to the moonlit pastures.

Rossamünd could not find any others near; nor, as he clambered atop the very rock from which Europe had first fought, did he spy any hint of motion on the meadow. "They've escaped," he declared redundantly, unsure what to feel, touching his nose against the musty metallic stink hanging in the air.

"Exactly why I have already sought a pathpry," said the fulgar tetchily, stepping beside him and handing him his hat. "Tomorrow, first peep of dawn—if your masters have proved successful—we shall track them to their lair." Stalking the mound, she set to finishing those saps that yet twitched with the weak ebbing of their previous animation, until all were dead. "Oh," she said placidly, standing over one lifeless worm lying by the foot of the mound, a neat bullet wound in its flank, "they actually managed to hit one."

"I tried to stop them." Rossamünd grimaced, holding up the purloined firelock.

"Hmm" was all the fulgar answered.

Monsiere Trottinott was thoroughly impressed, and all the citizens of Scantling Aire were amazed at the feats performed by the Branden Rose.

"The job is but part done, sir," she replied to the Monsiere's breathless enthusiasm as they entered the safety of Scantling Aire's yard. "There is one dead out there, pierced by a musket hole that one of your wayward franklocks ought to claim"—the Monsiere looked ashamedly to the floor—"though I do not think the ichor of such unnaturally foul things would be any use for puncting—nor would I risk it if I were you."

The defense declared a great victory; it was universally agreed that the sloe saps—as folks began to call them—were unlikely to return.

As a precaution, Rossamünd set small purple cones of repellent—compounded ash of Mehette—atop the rocks where the pudding basins of blood-curdle had previously rested. Found by the box in the saumery, the repellent had a familiar noxious reek that summoned a powerful memory of Licurius doing much the same about the night camp long ago.

With admirable persistence, Autos insisted upon helping, bearing candle and taper to light each cone and following so zealously close that the young factotum was grateful for the darkness to disguise his discomfort in handling it. The faint grassy breeze coming off the meadows shifted and sent the merest whiff of Mehette-fume up Rossamünd's nose, stunning him, his vision flashing, intellectuals reeling, sending him staggering away from the vile stuff in a fit of coughing.

"It must be very strong," Autos marveled, thumping Rossamünd on the back as if food were choking him.

"It—is—," Rossamünd squeezed out between gags, sight blurred with tears, bent double and rocking under the well-intentioned blows. "K-keep . . . b-back!"

Granted sleep for the remains of the night, he was shown by a plump-faced dame in earth-brown shirts up to one of the cottages' higher rooms. Its crude walls were white and lumpy, its shallow wood-beam ceiling angling down to a dormer window that looked west onto a field of vibrant stars and black land. Rossamünd found that a simple wool-stuffed pallet had been laid for him on the floor at the foot of a remarkably downy boxed bed where Europe reclined still fully harnessed, already sighing in the depth of easy sleep.

In the fresh of the morning, Fransitart and Craumpalin arrived by the Monsiere's coach midway through breakfast and treacle testing, their relief at Rossamünd's well-being evident in their gruff greetings. Accompanying them were three hard-looking fellows in woodland-hued proofing of leather and buff, animal pelts draped over their shoulders. They bore barbed boar-spears and elegant fusils with muzzles fashioned in the form of snarling bestial mouths. These were peltrymen from Lambingstone—or so they said of

338

themselves—working the folds of Broad Trim and happy to accept the lucrative terms offered by Europe through her two crusty mediums. The eldest of them spoke for all with a thick accent Rossamünd at first found hard to follow. Introducing himself as Quietis Furrow, he first presented his brother, Agitis Furrow, and then their young prentice, Bodkin Ease, who wore an olfactologue upon his face much like the box of a sthenicon except that it covered only his mouth and nose. Buff-brown faces clenched in permanent squint beneath greasy, battered tricorns, they greeted the Branden Rose and the Monsiere with deep, frowning nods that did for a bow and listened silently, expressions sharp, shadowed eyes bright to the recounting of the night.

"Thee can keep thy dollars and scruples, missus, till job's did done," Quietis Furrow said when part of their fee was offered. "That'n way thee'll know we 'tend to see this all right through to satisfaction."

Europe happily accepted this, saying, "Your integrity is laudable, sir."

"Hark!" Trottinott declared warmly. "Happy the day spent dealing with straight country lads. A boon on those who found you!"

Fransitart and Craumpalin limited their display of satisfaction at this approbation to a slight puffing of the chest.

The three peltrymen were provoked to the slightest surprise when shown a single sap, spiked now to the inside gate post. Stretched as it was from the spike, it still kept much of its structure: fat in its middle, tapering to either end, its spiny sucking mouth sagging viscously from the lower termination, the disturbingly fleshy pallor of the gums a stark contrast to the glistening black hide. No eyes were evident, just a series of holes open to the air and running down every quarter of the creature. Orange ooze leaked from the bullet wound and the spike hole, and the whole thing smelled oddly flat, almost odorless but for a fetid hint like rotting kelp washed on a shore.

"Looks like a smaller kind of them siphunculus beasties we fought off Langoland, 'ey, Pin?" Fransitart observed quietly.

The old dispenser nodded sagely.

"A right squirmerly bull-beggar," the younger Furrow brother muttered dourly.

"I reckon I made out a reddleman cove yesterday, while Pin an' me were on th' look for these 'ere fellows," Fransitart went on to report. "'E was much like th' one ye exchanged a word with back at Spelter Innings, Rosey me lad. But it can't 'ave been, for 'ow could the ruddy fellow 'ave got ahead o' us already on only feet, an' pushin' a cart?"

Rossamünd frowned. Surely this was more than coincidence or mistaken identities.

"Hmm, most perplexing, Master Vinegar," Europe said airily, but, preoccupied with the saps and the course ahead, she offered nothing more.

Advised by the still-sulking Parfait—now restored to his weapon—that the meadows were unfit for carriages, the landaulet was left and Craumpalin and Fransitart with it. The ex–dormitory master was well displeased with this arrangement, but his old friend was resolute.

"Thy joints will not suffer such wearing, Frans," Craumpalin scolded. "Thee daren't want to be laid up and useless by unneedful confustication to thy joints."

To this Fransitart only growled.

A billy-pot, faggots, kindling and a tinderbox were provided in a burlap sack for boiling Europe's treacle. After a quiet word of encouragement from his old masters, Rossamünd fixed his vent better about his throat, ordered his stoups, reloaded the flammagon, stowed food in his satchel, shouldered waterskins, and stood ready to go.

The creased foreheads of the peltrymen creased only slightly more at Rossamünd's inclusion in the course.

Taken out back to the scene of the adventure, Quietis Furrow and his colleagues quickly picked the faintly slimed slot, a metallic gossamer shimmer scarcely detectable among the spring-fresh grass.

"Thy worms are cunning baskets," Quietis informed the half circle of watchers. "They squirm out in line wit' each other to keep their count a secret, yet e'en wit' so many they barely trouble a blade or weed."

Like a pack of slothounds eager for the chase, the peltrymen set off. With a strange lift of excitement in his belly, Rossamünd paced after, Europe close behind.

Quick and sure, the Furrow brothers kept well ahead, peering at the ground, sometimes bent almost double in their search, Bodkin Ease turning his boxy snout left and right to catch every scent, but seldom slackening stride. The path of the worms was unerring, almost directly east to the sunken land Rossamünd had spied from the ridge-caps last night. The peltrymen spoke of older or lesser trails meandering off north and south into the green folds, of running shepherds, of lame sheep among a flock of a hundred, but the freshest drag was ever east.

Europe gave a grim smile at this intelligence. "How happy for us that they are so single-minded."

When the sun was at its highest, they lunched in the warm day on cold helpings provided by the cottagers, sitting by a stile over a drystone wall beneath a lone apple tree, young and straight with a thick white coat of full-blooming blossom. About them, all manner of bugs hummed and bumbled, curious of the food. The peltrymen exchanged muttered tidings and kept to themselves but for a brief report that the trail passed over the wall.

Much to Europe's increasing disgust, the day remained gloriously blue and clear except for a high mist of ice. The vermid trail took them far out into uncultivable eastern fields until the land began to lean downward by slight degrees, granting a low vista of the dark expanse of brown bog ahead, the sunken region Rossamünd had seen the previous evening from the roof of Scantling Aire. A rank vegetable stink increased with its proximity, until Bodkin Ease was forced to remove his olfactologue for fear of fainting dead away under the amplified fetor.

Continuing on, the party arrived at the salt-crusted brink of a sodden stretch where the green of spring refused to take. A gray heron sprang to wing at their approach, interrupted in its hunt for slimy wriggling morsels and giving a soft remonstrating croak as it circled over them and away.

"This here be the Pout, missus," Quietis somberly informed them, pushing his tricorn back on his pate. "It is the sink for the Foist stream yonder north." He pointed vaguely after the retreating heron. "Folks di'n' come here a-much on the count of it being too unwelcoming, though we've had good trapping on its edges up by Angas Welcome."

"And the slot takes us in?" Europe inquired.

"That it does, missus."

"Then let us keep to it."

"Even in this lately-ing part o' day?"

"Even then . . . Lead on, man."

The gluey track of the saps paid little heed to the miry obstacles and sludgy pits that hindered the way of their human-framed pursuers. Where young Bodkin Ease had been allowed to lead the lurk on easy pastures, the elder Furrow now took over. With admirable patience the peltryman directed them around every boggy impediment, always keeping to firmer ground until he found the trail again, holding to the course until the next puddle diverted them. Several times Rossamünd managed to slip on swampier soil, griming hands and stockinged knees, once sinking to the hem of his longshanks in flesh-colored murk, yanking his leg out violently when he felt an all-too-lively slithering about his shin.

Back to the mud from where I did come . . .

"Do try, dear Rossamünd, not to soil your harness," Europe chided almost smirkingly. Somehow, she always managed to pick a surer path and never once looked even slightly troubled by the difficult route.

As the westering sun drooped below gray strips of low

cloud, they neared a gloomy hollow, and Rossamünd spotted figures in long robes well away to their left, crouched and furtive, running north with many a backward glance out of the depression. Although it was impossible to be sure, Rossamünd had the impression they were wearing white masks.

"They surely di'n' want to be met with," Quietis observed.

Europe watched the receding runners narrowly.

"No," she said slowly. "They surely do not."

"Commercial gents, perhaps," Agitis offered, Rossamünd understanding him to mean smugglers.

"Or coursers like us," Rossamünd added.

"Perhaps . . ." was all the fulgar said, little convinced.

Making directly for a sunken bowl of some sickly brown discharge, the mucous drag came to an end. A grotesque threwd brooded in this hollow, forbidding enough to make nervous even the hardened hearts of the peltrymen and troubling Rossamünd with its unwontedness. The pool of black muck in the midst was mirror-still, dead, its edge a fringe of wilted lilies and sparse brown rushes. Wind hissed in reeds but barely stirred the surface. Anything could be lurking in there. At the farther end were three posts of rotting wood daubed with white lime and looking like some marker or hasty memorial. Cords of some unidentifiable substance had been strung over and over between the posts and the soft southwesterly blew on them a doleful two-pitch tune.

Europe eyed the scene wearily. "A feculent place, if ever there was."

Staying many yards back, Rossamünd stared at the water: it looked the perfect home for the sloe saps, and the threwd spoke clearly to him of the fact. "This is where they hide . . . ," he murmured to her.

"Not for much longer," she returned matter-of-factly.

The Furrow brothers sought about the entire rim of the sump, but the trail did not pick up again on any side. "It'll be a'lurking in yonder welk," Quietis muttered, bobbing his head at the pond as they gathered by its southern bank. "O' that I would stake me certainty." He held up a white porcelain cup he had found, decorated about its rim in delicate blue. But for its missing handle and a disturbing brown crust inside, it was a strangely civilized item out here in the mire. With it the elder peltryman produced a strange blob of black wax wound with greasy string, formed like some fat man with a peculiarly skinny head. "There's a chest o'er by them song-poles, holdin' some lime and a daub-brush and a wicked-curved knife too. I reckon thy prize has jack-ornerers encouraging its hucilluctions . . . Those very lads we saw darting away."

His younger brother spat. "Prostematin', muck-moundin' fictlers!" he cursed.

Europe gave a sour look to the thrumming poles. "I thought such cross-eyed folks liked to stay in those hills," she observed, looking to the dark, distant eastern downs. "I wonder if our Monsiere realizes he has fantaisists on his threshold."

Fantaisists! Rossamünd's heart missed beats in his dread. *False-god worshippers! What have we found for ourselves?* Surely

345

the worms were not a false-god, not out here so far from the vinegar sea. False-gods were meant to be uncontainably massive, invincible, able to turn men to their idiot wills.

With a long-suffering glance at the still, clear evening, Europe bowed her head and stood in thought.

Knowing better than to disturb his mistress, Rossamünd laid down the burlap bag and set about building a fire upon a low brown stone nearby. Filling the small billy-pot with water to boil, he stared about uneasily at the unsettling mire. *Did I truly come from such a place?* he wondered, studying the pool and its slimy banks. It seemed to him too distinctly dreary, too outlandishly hostile to be a font of life.

A single lonely cricket sent out a desultory rasp.

Some distant *hoom*ing beast uttered three short, unhappy calls.

Drawn by the barely adequate fire, the peltrymen huddled together, peering uncomfortably at the dour surrounds. Nodding to yellow Ormond as the ever-early star rose into the russet haze above the hills, they muttered uneasily of their desire to depart. About them all the pregnant quiet expanded, trickling with many tiny waters humming faintly with the gloomy monotone of the corded poles.

The treacle made, Rossamünd dared to approach his mistress, offering her levinfuse and saltegrade with it, grateful these alembants did not require further preparation; he did not relish remaining here until night in the creatures' dominion.

Nor, evidently, did the fulgar.

Quaffing levinfuse and downing the plaudamentum with

her usual inelegant promptness, she strode into the mire, pouncing from tussock to tussock to keep out of the filth, chewing on the purple lump of saltegrade as she went. At the rim of the pool she drove her fuse directly into the water.

Rossamünd peered in bafflement at her.

The water about the fuse started to hiss. Little waddling things were soon hastily exiting the pool while a colorless fish bobbed to float dead on its surface.

She arcs the water!

Soon enough the black element began to ripple and trouble. With a sudden great splashing, the sloe saps emerged, writhing, almost leaping out onto the bank opposite the arcing fulgar.

A caste of beedlebane was instantly in Rossamünd's hand; he thought to try his strength but hesitated, uncertain both of his accuracy with such a throw and the deservingness of these things to die.

Three near-unison pops of musketry cracked the air off to the left as the peltrymen tried their aim.

Rapidly the sloe saps rushed together from all reaches of the farther shore. Coiling, writhing over each other, unhindered by three frank musket shots, the wrigglers began to knot together, tightening steadily into a larger and larger ball-like mass. Building higher and higher, the bulk of worms rolled about the western bank of the inky pool, fashioning themselves into some fore-determined shape as they moved.

Collecting herself, Europe sprang from sure footing to sure footing, making straight for the mass as she cried angrily to the peltrymen to cease their shooting.

347

"I shall do this, thank you!"

Meeting it halfway about the pool, Europe struck at the swarming host as it formed, jabbing her fuse with a ringing *zzzack!* into the coagulating worms, seeking to arc it to pieces just as she had done to the lesser collection last night. Instantly a sinuous cord of worms lashed out like an arm and swatted the fulgar, hitting her as she twisted to avoid the blow. Flung back several yards, she landed heavily in the mire between Rossamünd and the reloading peltrymen, her fuse still caught like a twig in the belly of the beast now grown too big to end in a single blast.

The young factotum ran to his mistress' aid.

Before them an obese figure rose as tall as five tall men, a tapering collection of worms ending in a single sap for the head, its bloated torso seething with a wriggling legion of inky skins. A powerful hostility surrounded it, unlike anything Rossamünd had felt before, an oppressive *un*-threwd, a dread of abysmal airless depths where wicked mindless behemoths crawled and fed. Rossamünd gagged and smacked his mouth against a bitter aftertaste stinging the back of his throat.

With a shudder of effort the sapperling lifted its now ponderous bulk, rising upon three stiltlike legs made entirely of worms wrapping tightly about each other, stiffening to bear the weight of their brethren.

"What by the hide of me chin be *that*?" one of the peltryman hissed in awe as the three moved aside in sluggish amazement to get a better shot.

Hair askew, Europe looked dangerously unamused as,

winded, she leaned on Rossamünd to stand. "If it is all right with you, little man," she added with a sardonic murmur, "I won't be chatting with this one."

While the struggling fulgar achieved her feet, the Furrow brothers fired again at the lumbering, squirming collection toiling toward them about the western edge of the pond. Their united shot hit the heaving vermiculate flesh of its belly with livid orange splats.

"Stay your shots, gentlemen!" she snarled. "You will have your fee; this is mine to kill, and I do not intend to share the prize."

Faster than whips, quicker than shouted warnings, a massive tentacle of worms spat out from its middle straight at the reloading peltrymen, the sapperling getting thinner as the arm flew farther. Three gaping wormy fingers grasped Agitis Furrow about neck and chest and hoisted him off his feet. With astounding reflexes the peltryman snatched up his boar-spear stuck ready into the soggy loam and began to jab wildly at the great arm as it raveled, pulling him back into the main mass of the sapperling. Flourishing his mighty spear, Agitis skewered the thing right in the fat of its belly as it sought to swallow him whole. The great, heaving mass of wormy flesh received the long spear with a quiver of shock, sliding unflinchingly up it to engulf the entire blade, unhindered by the wide tangs.

"AGITIS! AGITIS!" his brother shrieked, taciturn composure unraveling, as beside him Bodkin hurriedly primed his weapon. Throwing down his musket, Quietis dashed forward and grabbed one of his brother's flailing legs, heaving, managing to halt Agitis' vile fate for a breath.

With a snarl of "Thew-brained fools!" Europe steadied on her feet and began to tip one hand over the other in small back-and-forth motion, sending arcs strobing brightly from palm to palm, thin strands of her hair bristling with static as she strode toward the seething behemoth.

Two arms—if such they could be called—flashed out from different points upon the sapperling's body, one grasping the younger Furrow more firmly about the head, the other seeking the older man. His brother's leg snatched irresistibly from his futile grip, Quietis drew forth a heavy hanger and a tomahawk and, dodging the smaller limb, lashed at the main arm, severing it with three rapid hacks. The massive thing shuddered at the wound as it sucked Agitis into its squirming bulk, the peltryman's horrified screams stifled by a wormy gag wrapping about his face.

Unable to simply let the fellow be engulfed, Rossamünd dashed forward, almost upending himself in a puddle, and flung the caste of beedlebane at the creature, whipping out another from his digital and throwing that too as the first burst with an orange flare against its thick neck. The sapperling reeled at the small eruptions. Though its gathering of slick hides was too slippery to take to flame, it staggered back yet, two dead worms slithering loose from the mass and falling to the earth. Scuttling in to try his strength extracting Agitis from the sapperling's inexorable consuming belly, Rossamünd was struck by a smaller *arm,* even as he reached for the peltryman's twisting leg. The confounding clout sent him spinning like a toy to land seat-first in the icy shallows of the vile inky pond.

Retching on the greasy waters, Rossamünd flailed for the shore, vaguely aware that Quietis had ducked low and was now under the sagging beast's pendulous abdomen. Pulling himself to slightly firmer sludge, he could see the older pelt-trapper chop at the nearest worm-formed leg, hewing at it over and over. Yet with each blow new worms descended from the belly to cover over and support their wounded fellows.

Face smeared with phlegm and tears, Bodkin let fly another musket shot, striking the sapperling's coiling neck, giving it such a smart it collapsed forward on its weakened leg, Quietis barely tumbling clear. Yet as the creature fell, Rossamünd could see Agitis' now motionless body still being consumed, drawn in by abrupt stages through belly-folds of worms until only a single gaitered leg protruded— then that too was gone.

Still tossing arcs from one palm to the next, Europe stood before the sapperling. As it toppled, it fell toward her and she grabbed at the head, letting all her collected charge out with a mighty *ZIZzzZACK!*—a blinding glare, blasting the members of the head and neck apart in gouts of hissing orange mess and flapping worm bits.

She's done it!

Carried away by the rush of the fight, Rossamünd yelled wordlessly in victory as the sapperling floundered, single worms losing grip and rearing individually from the deforming bulk to hiss at her silently.

But Quietis was not finished. Desperate for his brother,

he began to slash and gouge blindly at the beast's pulsating belly, seeking to hack his way in.

"AWAY WITH YOU, SIR!" Europe roared with a volume Rossamünd had never known her use before. "Had you left it in the first, your brother would not have been taken!"

The peltryman just snarled at her and kept at his chopping. He lifted his orange-gored hanger for yet another cut and a new pair of reforming worm-limbs suddenly sprang out from the sapperling's shoulders. The first took the ferocious peltryman midswing by his sword arm, lifting him, though Quietis would not be so easily subdued and flailed wildly, striking the limb repeatedly with his tomahawk as he was hoisted high.

Exhausted of a more potent charge, it was all Europe could do to keep the second limb from coiling about her as she drew quickly back, slapping *zick! zick! zick!* at the wriggling fingers that clutched and writhed and tried to end her as they had poor Agitis.

Rossamünd hurled his last handy caste of beedlebane, the sharp burst of falsefire scoring the base of the arm that harried the fulgar. It recoiled, leaving the Branden Rose free to withdraw.

Quivering, the worms pulled tightly back together and the sapperling heaved itself to stand once more, keeping its grip on the struggling elder Furrow.

Europe did not give ground too far. Mounting a half-submerged log only a handful of yards away, she put some rock salt in her mouth and began once more to swap an arc from palm to palm. "Your intervention would be timely, lit-

THE SLOE SAPPERLING

tle man," she called across to him with preternatural poise.

Quick as he could, Rossamünd snatched a caste of asper—the strongest potive he possessed—from its digital niche and shied it at the raging monster. The repellent hit the sapperling low on its side with a singular black gust, forcing it to stumble once more as it tried to escape the radiating sphere of acrid oily stuff. That same instant Quietis, shouting in a fury of success, amputated the arm that still held him, falling free, a single worm still gripped to his waist. Yet, as the asper boiled into a blistering inky froth that sent a veritable rain of stricken worms tumbling to the sludge, still another limb formed on the sapperling's opposite flank. Snatching the peltryman about his legs before he hit ground, it jerked him high over its lofty bulk and before anything could be done to stop it threw the madly bawling fellow down to the sod with deadly might.

"NO!" Rossamünd and Bodkin Ease cried together, the young factotum despairing as to what it would take to best this crawling-fleshed horror.

This at last was too much for the lone surviving peltryman; wailing, Bodkin Ease ran into the mire without pause or a backward look, fleeing in mad terror and misery.

Reduced in size now, yet still thrice a tall man's height, the sapperling shrank from the seething residue of the asper. Oozing back, it seemed to pause, swaying, Europe's fuse still protruding from high on its left flank. All about it, single fallen worms hurt but not slain began to wriggle back to the main mass. The long-necked head slowly reformed.

Fury growing in his gorge, rising as a growl, the young

factotum took a caste of loomblaze in one hand and Frazzard's powder in the other and stumbled toward the creature, ready to use all the might he possessed.

"Wait, Rossamünd," the fulgar said calmly as he stepped past her, strands of fine hair standing out crazily.

Certain he could hear the crackle of static in her words and smell it in the air about her, he obeyed, all too alive to the consequences of the reverse.

"Stay," she commanded. "I *shall* be back."

Stepping lightly off the half log, the Branden Rose advanced through tufts and stumps toward the sapperling once again. At her approach, the worm-thing bent its head as if to regard her properly. After all the desperate mayhem, the scene seemed oddly tranquil in the failing light.

Europe raised her arms, holding them up and out to her sides.

What is she doing? Rossamünd paced as far as he dared to the right, seeking a better view.

Without any alerting reflex or countermotion, the vermid thing shot out a grasping limb, snatching the unresisting fulgar about her waist and yanking her in to engulf her just as it had poor Agitis.

"NO!" Rossamünd shrieked a second time. Instantly he was to action, hurling both potives to detonate yellow-green and blue about its shoulders.

The sapperling tried to reach out and grasp him too but shuddered, the half-fashioned arm twitching, hesitating, retracting. Its sides appeared to flex and bloat.

Rossamünd finally stood still.

The tapered head began to whip about violently. The saps that formed it wilted and fell. The legs collapsed, and the bulk dropped into the filth with a loud squelch. Flickers of static forced their way through the mutual grip of the remaining worms, lighting the bog with a dazzling, strobing brilliance. Of a sudden, the distending mass of worms sucked inward. An almighty deafening bang, like the cracking of the back of the world, a stupefying flash and the entire creature was flung apart, its bits thrown wide, Europe's fuse flying to strike the ground shudderingly not one yard from Rossamünd. A subtle growl like the echo of distant thunder rolled about the sink as a drizzle of orange muck and particles of black hide fell all around.

The sapperling beast was no more.

In its place, amid a mess of worm-parts, stood the Branden Rose, arms akimbo, fist clenched, head down, hair loose and hair tine missing, ruffled but unharmed. She looked up to Rossamünd, his cheeks smeared with unabashed tears of relief, then down with vague irritation at the messes that smeared and tearings that dulled her once-sumptuous coat.

"My best Number 3 ruined," she said.

OF FÊTES AND FICTLERS

fictler(s) worshippers and followers of false-gods, the name coming from the notion that these folk honor fictions, that is, false notions of the false-gods. They are typically regarded as a type of sedorner, yet they hold themselves as entirely distinct from sedorners and outramorines—opposites in fact, seeking the false-gods to rise up to rid the world of the landed monsters, the true foes of everymen. They prefer to call themselves gnosists, that is, "the knowers," for the higher knowledge they believe they possess, yet are not above the use of human sacrifice in their fervor to summon forth their chosen false-god.

THE celebration at Europe's success and defeat of the worm-formed sapperling was great. At first those left to wait at Scantling Aire had dreaded the worst. This fear was distressingly amplified when Bodkin Ease emerged from the deep of night, bruised and delirious with grief, yammering death and violence and a great black ettin built of worms and muck descending to destroy them whole. In this light Europe and Rossamünd's dawn return was hailed with an effusion of joy, and none was more delighted than Fransitart, who had not slept a nod, lying fully dressed upon his borrowed cot and "fretting like a fussy old panderer"—as Craumpalin reported it.

"Well done, lad" was all the dormitory master would say

as he gripped Rossamünd firmly by both shoulders.

Told the very hour of their return, Europe's account of the victory—spoken as she drank an entire pail of water straight from the well—had been brief, the merest details and a single dead worm the testament to her success. Taking it as his own, the Monsiere elaborated her tale most handsomely to all who would listen. Through his audience it spread, greatly enlarged and with astonishing speed, to other knowing souls who, in their turn, transmitted the story of the slaying with all the confidence and gory clarity of actual eyewitness.

Soon the whole region buzzed with it; on their return to the manorburg the landaulet was laden with gifts of sheep-cheese and woolen skin warmers as they were farewelled by cheers from the cottagers. Their whole journey back was attended by *huzzahs!* from joyful vine dressers and herders standing upon the rough verges.

Craumpalin declared himself mystified and Rossamünd with him; Europe raised her brows briefly but said nothing.

Safe again in the Patredike, Rossamünd was allowed to sleep for the remainder of the day, waking in time for supper to learn, firstly, that Craumpalin had tried at Europe's treacle with only modest success; and secondly, that Monsiere Trottinott, his fellow landed lords and the parish burghers had met that afternoon to decree the very next day a vigil for all staff and workers, calling it *Sappis Deflectere*.

"The worm has been turned!" the Monsiere cried in happy explanation. "It shall be marked on our calendars hereafter and your names writ in the parish transactions and on the Register of Distinction! I was just telling your mistress that tomorrow night we shall hold a fête in your joint honor, young sir!" He raised his fine glass to Rossamünd.

To his great satisfaction, Europe tipped him a nod of her own goblet, her eyes knowingly bright.

Glad as he was that they had survived, Rossamünd spared some grief for the poor worthy peltrymen he barely knew, courageous fellows who had paid so dear a price for their honest exertions.

"Hucilluctors and woodsmen know the harshness of their trade, little man, and peltrymen's lives are consequentially short," Europe said when he spoke quietly to her of them later that evening, sitting easy in the Dike's billiard room. "Such a shame their youngest member had to run off so. He could, at least, have received the triple fee due him as recompense, scant as it might be.

Trottinott barely mentioned the missing Furrow brothers, and the local masters uttered not a word of suspicion or even bland inquiry on them. No one, it seemed, wanted to spoil their delight by mourning for a pair of greasy, anonymous pelt-trappers. These same masters, when they met again that morning in the Monsiere's large green-walled observatory, were more animated with concern for the evidence of fantaisists in their parish.

"They can keep to their puzzled ideas up in the rises," one bluff-browed worthy decried, pausing in his scrutiny of a wide scenograph of the Trottinotts' entire property that hung among a collection of many delicate water-tints of the local varieties of flora beside the Monsiere's great desk.

"Hear, hear, Mayor!" another old fellow in an uncomplimentary black wig enthused. "We have little need for them down here and even less for what they bring with them."

"Our constables will ferret them out," the Monsiere added, "and drive them back to the fells in the east."

The corners of Europe's mouth twitched, the barest tic articulating perfectly what she thought of the stern claim to the efficacy of the local constables.

Rossamünd harbored a small lament, scarcely admitted to himself, for the passing of the sapperling beast: foul, violent yet bafflingly constructed, somehow wondrous and dire at once. With its end the world to him felt smaller, reduced—such as at the ending of the Herdebog Trought or the Misbegotten Schrewd. He was happy to sink these bitter sentiments in the joyful promise of the fête.

By servant and ambler, word of the event was sent to all around, yet with his usual harness so badly soiled by the fight and being cleansed by the fuller, Rossamünd had only his old coat as replacement. This was such unfitting garb for an assembly that he feared he might not be able to go. How utterly grateful he was when, upon observing this, Madamine Trottinott insisted he be furnished for the fête with his choice of beautiful coats and suits summoned from Autos' own wardrobe. In his borrowed room, suit after suit was tried for fit and look, the Madamine fussing over him as if Rossamünd were one of the family. What Autos made of this as he stood watching with large intense eyes from the door, the young factotum could not discern.

"Such a foolishly brave young man," she cooed. "It is utterly scandalous to send one so young to contend with such dangers. How you have come back so little changed in countenance I can barely comprehend!" She scrutinized him keenly. "I would never let Autos out on such a risky foray," she added, to the audible agreement of the panderer waiting nearby. "Not until he is at least fifteen, and maybe not even then!"

With a scowl, her elder son ducked his head and quickly left.

Held in the high vaulted glass and stone of the Trottinotts' pageant-room, the fête that night was as much a spectacle as Rossamünd hoped. Conveyances, drivers and footmen near filled the great yard as everyone in the parish of even slightly worthy station gathered, invited or otherwise, to rejoice in the salvation of their pastures. It was more folk than Rossamünd thought possible in such a broad and seemingly empty land. And here he was, in a silvery satin frock coat over a suit of weskit and longshanks cut from the same cloth, and—for the first time in his existence—stockings with buckled slippers, an honored guest among them all.

Seated beside him on a curling gilt highback at one end of the hall, the Branden Rose was marvelously conspicuous among all the wide skirts and bustles and stays. Dressed in finery brought against such an eventuality, she wore a sleeveless frock coat of royal carmine velvet, its broad frock splitting apart at the waist to show the tunic of supple milk-colored linen she wore underneath. The exposed sleeves of the tunic bagged just above her elbows and spilled out wide and loose, falling back to reveal her bare arms and the sets

361

of tiny X's puncted in rows upon them. Her chestnut hair was gathered in a basket plait out of which radiated several hair tines like the sticks of a fan.

Dressed in full courtly attire including his grandsire's colorfully embroidered caudial honor hanging from his waist, Monsiere Trottinott stood upon the other side and introduced the Duchess-in-waiting of Naimes to a long line of leading families. There was the Marchess-dowager of the Midden: "Ah, my dear, please send my felicitations to your mother!"; the Reive and Reivine of the Trim: "Our most humble admirations . . ."; the Reive and Reivine of Pedester: "Well-a-day to you, gracious lady, are you acquainted with the Duke-Originaire of Haquetaine?"; the Armige of Uffing Lee and the Lady Grey: "Delighted"; the Mayor of Angas Welcome and his large family: "Welcome biddings again, oh Gracious Saving Lady!" . . . And on it went for much of the night.

Every invitation to dance, whether from senior lord or young master, Europe declined with, "I am a little battered from my victory."

Yet many of the most elevated, however happy they were of their release from their distress, seemed to evince veiled yet supercilious disapproval of their deliveress. Rossamünd was sure he caught several disdainful gazes sent Europe's way by the congregations of gloriously refined women that collected between each dance. With such creatures the Branden Rose, duchess heir or not, would never fit. The young factotum wondered wryly how many of them might have gossiping aunts or sisters or daughters writing them from Brandenbrass.

Such grim turns of mind did not last long against the compelling melodies of the half orchestrato on loan from the Earl of Holly. Turned out in pristine white wigs and gorgeous golden livery, the musicians played almost ceaselessly from an elevated gallery. Beneath them sat a great covered trestle spread with food, its centerpiece a disturbing replica of the sap fashioned in blackberry flummery. Peering at this remote feast hungrily—though keeping his gaze from the flummery—Rossamünd became aware of a giggle of young girls assembled among the tall white and blue urns that stood between the windows of the left-hand wall. They were staring at him and bending toward each other to whisper behind pretty hands. He did not know what to do with such attention but redden about the ears and try to keep his show of solemn concentration resolutely on the dizzying sway of merry dancers strutting a saraband so finely across the wide space before him, or on the many glimmeralls bright overhead.

At a lull in the music, a tall girl in a gown of shimmering silvery white, with wood-dark eyes and hair the hue of rare honeycomb, detached herself from her corner of friends and approached, quiet defiance in her mien. Cheeks aflame, Rossamünd made to be suddenly and very seriously fixated on somewhere else. Yet his play was foiled, for she stood right beside him and, to his mortal embarrassment, said with many blushes of her own, "I-I would like it very much, s-sir, if-if you would ask me to-to dance . . ."

Had it been Threnody before him, she would have made the whole operation simpler by demanding, but *he* was being asked to *ask*. In a panic as terrible as one caused by a ravening nicker, Rossamünd looked to Europe for help, but she was occupied with the fuss being made of her by some septuagenarian dame in an enormous silver-pink wig. Swallowing hard, Rossamünd fumbled and, heart skipping uncomfortably, managed, "W-would y-you care to dance, miss?"

The girl in shimmering silvery white agreed, of course—though for a moment he madly feared she would not—and they danced a pavane, just once and not very well, treading on each other in equal measure. Near dumb with awe, he thought her the most splendid being he had ever encountered and kept blinking at her rosy face and sparkling auburn eyes. All through their turn they spoke little beyond soft apologies, and at the conclusion separated with only awkward thank-yous, Rossamünd never discovering her name.

Harnesses laundered and properly dried, prizes paid—including treasures of gratitude for Fransitart and Craumpalin from the Monsiere's much-vaunted cellars, and for Rossamünd the silvery suit he had worn the night before—the four left the Patredike the next morning.

Just south of Broom Holm, Fransitart was directed to take a lesser yet straighter way to Luthian Glee, "The quicker to Pour Clair and our next prize," Europe explained.

Too soon the quality of road failed, the ruts made by overladen wagons and drays often so deep that the landaulet's axles near scraped the ground. In the rain-shadow of the low ranges, the land was stony and dry, covered more and more by olive groves and apple orchards tended by cheerful, singing bough dressers as it rolled up gradually to the gloomy hills ahead.

"Folks are said to disappear all too often in them there mounds," Craumpalin said, low and serious.

"We shall have to make certain we are not among them, sha'n't we?" the fulgar returned lightly, chewing on a whortleberry. "We have actually crossed into the merry parishes of Fayelillian," she explained. "I believe, Rossamünd, your once marshal-lighter comes from this land."

Rossamünd took in the scene with greater curiosity, wondering bitterly if the Lamplighter-Marshal, the Earl of Fayelillian, might win free of the damning political games played in the Considine and return to this, his home.

At day's closing the four travelers found the walled town of Luthian Glee, built over a stream among spires of lichen-scabbed stone and a thin woodland of young myrtles. In the loom of the hills, the town looked very old, the stones of its walls worn and black with mildew, the whole settlement possessing an air of dogged persistence. Yet the heavy-proofed gaters standing warden at a minor gate conducted themselves graciously enough when reviewing nativity patents, and the townsfolk were equally affable, tipping hats to Fransitart and Craumpalin, the old salts doing so in return.

The proprietor of the crowded hostelry, the Alabaster Brow, proved friendliest of all when shown the tint *and* weight of Europe's coin.

"Our senior suite is reserved particularly for such eminence as your own, good madam." The boniface smiled with only the merest hesitation at the small diamond spoor above her left brow. Leading them up the many-flighted stairs, the fellow made much of the hostelry's upper room vistas, boasting that it was one of the tallest structures in their humble municipality.

Standing alone upon the modest balcony while the proprietor continued to show away the room's few comforts, Rossamünd could not but agree that it did afford an excellent view of the entire eastern sweep of dirty lichened roofs and puffing chimneys and the darksome bluffs rising beyond. The threwd about was all but absent, the place being long settled by everymen. Yet as he continued to watch in the evening hush, Rossamünd had the tenuous sensation of the stony hills brooding with watchful unwelcome, an oppressiveness not entirely threwdish. Looking back inside as the proprietor bid them good eve, Rossamünd was certain the fellow had given the rise a melancholy look as he left.

"The Witherfells," Europe declared, joining Rossamünd on the undersized perch. "Our road will take us into them tomorrow. Our next prize, the Gathephär, lairs itself somewhere in their folds. We may need more than peltrymen to pry it out."

"It might find us," Rossamünd answered, eyeing the hills uncertainly.

"That would certainly make our task simpler."

Marked the Pendlewick on Craumpalin's chart, the way into the Witherfells was empty of even the usual infrequent country traffic as it cut a serpentine path up the blunt heights of corroded stone, their dark flanks streaked with rust, their summits crowned with anciently gaunt myrtle and pine. A feat of historied engineering, the road entered the hills through a great channel carved by hands long dead and disappeared from human record. Flattening as it wound about spurs and gullies, their way crossed the troughs between crags upon narrow stone dykes, the yawning dells thick with trees where unseen birds belled mournfully, their slow cries reverberating in the closeness. A heaviness dwelt in these heights, a nameless dread souring the soul and turning thoughts unhappily inward.

On a lofty pinnacle obscured by rock and tree, Rossamünd glimpsed the evidence of a fortification. It seemed to him that there was a remnant path leading to it from the road, and he was possessed with a strong desire to go up and explore.

"It is likely a Burgundian fastness." Europe answered his inquiry with a mildly didactic tone, chewing on a cold spatchcock greme clumsy supplied from the Monsiere's own larder. "Built during the subjugation of the monster-worshipping Piltdowners who were said to crowd these hills. This is how my schooldames taught it to me . . . though it has been some time now since my instruction at Fontrevault."

"Fontrevault?"

"The sequestury and aplombery of the Right of the Open Hand. My mother boarded me there, little doubt believing that training in the five graces would calm me. She did not, however, account for the bastinado and sagaris also taught there, nor my facility in them . . . Happy times." Europe's smile was ironic.

"Ye were lettered with calendars?" Fransitart asked over his shoulder.

"Indeed . . . and was expelled by them too." Europe sipped at her wine with an arch and sardonic air. "It was not much later that I left Naimes for good."

They moved up into the next crag and the sight of the ruin was lost.

As sour winds blew up from the distant Grume and the day grew gloomy and gray, they came to a ravine crossed by a viaduct known as the Cold Beam Bridge. Two likely fellows in heavy linen smocks were sitting on a large gray rock by the stony post of the bridge, fishing with long poles and even longer twine into the gorge below. There seemed to Rossamünd something slightly repellent about them, though he could not say what it was, and neither Europe nor his old masters seemed to heed it.

"Ahoy, mates!" Fransitart slowed the landaulet and hailed them. "Don't ye know there is a fierce-some bugaboo about?"

"Ahoy ye back, ye salty scoundrel! Ye are far from the treacherous sea!" the older one returned, squinting skeptically at them all from under his wide floppy hat, one eye going only a little wide when he caught a sight of Europe. "Ye speak of the Gutterfear, little doubt."

Fransitart glanced quizzically back to Europe, who nodded.

The old fisher blinked at her. "I hear-ed this flaysome *bugaboo* were a nightly beast and no threat to daytime strollers . . . Besiden which," he added pointedly to Fransitart in forced whisper, "I figure with yer pugnacious lady arrived there, that the beastie will soon cease to be a problem at

368

all." He nodded sagely and tapped his nose with the switch of grass he had been chewing.

"Aye," his younger compatriot agreed, patting a simple digital hanging from his sable and leuc baldric. On the back of the man's left hand Rossamünd discerned an odd smudge over the second knuckle: a small spoor made in a variation on a lesser-case "e."

He had never seen such a thing.

"Besiden which," the young man was continuing, "we has our stinks *and* fitter trinkets to see it off with, so we'll fish till then, unbothered."

The other fellow nodded resolutely and, bowing to Europe, said, "In point of fact, m'lady, I have heard it that the Gutterfear is scunnered—"

"*Scunnered,* sir?" Europe leaned forward in her seat, causing the landaulet to rock slightly.

"Aye." The old fisher blanched, and bobbed another bow. "Left us, miss, gone north or east or somesuch, spotted with a batch of other seltlings all a-traveling in the same direction, leaving man and beast a'be, such was their determination."

"Well, I thank you for your intelligence." Europe sat back. "We shall continue on our course until I know this for myself. Go on, if you please, Master Vinegar."

"By the looks, the weather'll turn dirty afore the day

is out, me hearties," Fransitart warned them as he set the horses to walk and the landaulet began to go on. "Best make yer way under roofs afore long."

They waved but did not show themselves the least inclined to heed him.

The blustering night was spent in a collection of squalid high-houses called Scough Fell, gray hovels made of gray wood and gray thatch built into the gray stony banks either side of the road, guarded by thick gates hung with great conical thurifers—brass censers of night-burnt repellents. Louse-bitten and sleep deprived at the outset of the new day, Craumpalin and Rossamünd sought to freshen the sisterfoot on Rufous and Candle's shabraques, but Europe stopped them.

"This is not a pleasant vigil amble," she insisted tartly. "Our objective is to attract a nicker, not hide from it, and horse meat is a compelling enticement."

The four went on their way out soon after, watched keenly by the cheerless, ill-humored denizens peering suspiciously from shuttered gaps or muttering together in hostile assemblies. Muffling themselves against the surprising cold, they broke their fast on the road. An hour on and the Pendlewick forked; the wider divergence to the right quickly became a channel cut into the rusted stone, its sides stained by black dribbles. The left way ascended steeply through knotted pines and cracking boulders, climbing a hill to a stoutly walled town of tall fortified high-houses rising out of the trees. A heavy sorrow seemed to emanate from this hilltop fastness. The forbidding hush in this empty land vibrated silently with unwelcoming vigilant malice, stifling conversation.

A moldering wooden post had been fixed on the prow of rock that split the two roads. Near its top was nailed a flayed skin, blackened with parch and rot, its origin obscure, yet most certainly not human. Rossamünd thought he could make out a wide grinning mouth and pointed ears. Scrawled in white and some other dark substance upon the rock about it were the very same "e" signs they had seen on the young fisher's knuckle the day before.

"Pendle Hill," Europe declared grimly, her gaze narrowed on the far-off glimpse of shingles and chimneys. "The very hub of all the fantaisists and the cross-eyed folk."

"What are all those marks?" Rossamünd asked. "That fisher had one such as this."

"Allegories," Craumpalin offered. "Find them often enough on vinegars . . ."

Fransitart ruttled disapprovingly. "They think it'll protect 'em against kraulswimmers."

Rossamünd was none the wiser. "Allegories?"

"Cult signs," Europe finally said, pouring herself some claret. "The little signals the fantaisists in their various septs like to leave each other to say which false-god they fancy."

"Those fishers were for Sucoth," Craumpalin added soberly. "Who is spoke of as the worst of 'em all . . ."

Ashen-faced, the young factotum scrutinized every threatening vacancy between tree and rock.

"Take us right, Master Vinegar, if you please."

Past the mile-long channel and deeper into the Witherfells the hilltops grew rounder, the valleys less steep. Turpentine and pine grew thickly on the slopes, their roots tangled with spreading thorny blackberry, the ceaseless rushing of the wind in their upper stories drowning the clop of hoof and jink of horse harness. With the day's decline, Rossamünd's inkling of hostile scrutiny grew until Fransitart warned of someone ahead, a single watcher standing at a major divergence of ways on the right-hand margin of the road. It was an arrogant figure wrapped in a heavy coachman's cloak of the deepest purple, face masked with a white oval striped with four level bars, head crowned with a high-fronted hevenhull stuck with five large white feathers tipped with red.

"Blighted fictler!" the ex–dormitory master hissed.

Craumpalin cocked the hammer of the musketoon resting in all appearance of ease in his lap.

"Just keep us steady ahead, Master Vinegar," Europe instructed, sitting erect in queenly composure. "Not too swift, not too leisurely either."

Head down, Rossamünd kept his eyes on the bizarrely dressed fictler. An abysmal foulness issued from the figure, filling the young factotum with an appalling terror of black and suffocating deeps. Pulling a thennelever of glister dust from his right-hand stoup, Rossamünd wrestled against the near-whelming urgency to hurry the landaulet along.

The disquietingly blank face regarded them boldly as they passed, the clatter and hiss of the wind-tossed treetops, the clop of hoof and the squeak of axle and harness the only

FEATHERHEAD

sounds. Fransitart tipped his hat saucily to the figure, but it did not speak, or gesture, or shift its feet; it simply watched.

Rossamünd peered into the shadowy pine wood fully expecting an ambuscade, yet it seemed empty, untenanted but for the single doleful caw of a crow.

The four wayfarers went by unmolested.

"Hmm, very peculiar," Europe said once they were past.

Looking behind as they rounded a bend and the road cut again into rock, Rossamünd found the feather-headed figure still there, still looking after them, unmoved.

Not far on they came to a fortified bridgehead and a high gray tower, gated and well guarded. Its Branden-mottled gate wards proved unfriendly and taciturn, allowing Europe and her staff to pass only after punctilious inspection of the appropriate documents. Through the arching tunnel of the fortalice they came to a deep ravine and on the other side, upon a massive wedge of rock, stood a small grim city. Behind its high wall rank upon rank of tall white buildings rose up from the sheer rock, their roofs lead-gray or grimy clay-red. Many lofty stacks fumed from amid the usual bristle of slender chimneys, guttering dirty smokes into the wind. Great murders of crows and pied daws circled among them or gathered on rooftops to call to each other with strangely melodious songs.

"Pour Clair," Europe said matter-of-factly.

They traversed the gap upon a thin curving bridge of stone spiked with a line of great-lamps that terminated at a whitewashed double-turreted gatehouse. The steady rumble of a rushing, spouting torrent rose from the giddying rift beneath, its growling an ever-present undertone in all the township's bustle.

By Europe's direction Fransitart took them along precipitous ramps and awkward lanes to the civic hall. Named the Fallenthaw, it was tall and narrow like every other structure in this cramped, perilously situated place; its foundations were bare stones, its upper walls whitewashed, its dark roof lead shingles. It began to rain as they were admitted by stern wardens to proceed easily into the tight courtyard of white daub and dark wood pillars. Here, under a long portico drumming with the downpour, a trio of silk-wigged and silk-suited representatives of the district lords promptly met with the Branden Rose. After anxious, becking greetings, they confirmed the suppositions of the bumpkin fishermen: the dread oppressor, Gathephär, had vanished, not seen nor heard for nigh on a fortnight, where once it was troubling people twice or thrice a week.

"I am sorry, m'lady, but the job is no more and its prizes withdrawn," the senior envoy explained with clerical immovability. "We *did* send to Brandenbrass knavery to cancel the singular as soon as it was apparent a knave was not needed," he continued more nervously, passing to the highly unamused fulgar the proper reply from the coursing house.

The fulgar regarded the chief of the uncomfortable representatives narrowly. "Your civic masters are a mite premature in their cancellation, sir. Have their best eyes confirmed its evaporation?"

"They have, m'lady," the fellow replied with a half bow, passing her the lurksman's account.

Europe read this account then gave it to Rossamünd. Written five days earlier, it was simple enough:

> The creature known by most as the Gutterfear or by the books as the Gathephaar is as big as houses and wrapped in dread so thick you could pickle it. I could never get close to the nucker. The snares and poisons I laid did nought to hinder it. Six nights gone I heard a loud hallooing of many throats in Timbrelle Vale where it likes to den. Upon a search at first dawn I found slot and drag that told of other nickers come in from the north to meet with our own—for I do not know how else to describe it. These same traces followed back out again—the treads of the Gutterfear with them—all scunnered to the north, the whole brood quitting the hills together. I have lurked the hills ever since, but there is nought of the beast to be found.
>
> This be an honest and true statement made of one with sound mind, marking in his own hand.

Grammaticus, lurksman and pathpry.

12th Unxis 1601 Horn. Imp. Reg.

"We can have done no more, good lady," the representative pleaded, scampering in the rain after Europe, who was now striding back to the landaulet. "Our masters are sincerely sorry for your inconvenience and can offer you residence and resupply without rate as you need. It is the least we can perform for you, come so far . . ."

"Your masters may keep their guilty offerings," she answered stiffly, Rossamünd handing her into the now-covered carriage. "I shall make do for myself."

They took lodging at the Spout & Hearth on a precipitous street not far from the Fallenthaw. Despite its comforts, Europe's soured mood remained all through the short end of the afternoon. It had not lightened by the time Rossamünd and the old vinegaroons returned from a brief visit to the mighty cataract that poured from the far end of the fortress town as if from the very foundations. The best treacle Rossamünd knew how to testtelate did not cheer her that evening, nor did the broken night full of watery mutterings do much to improve her temper, and the next morning, they promptly pursued their way out from that disappointing, precarious city.

They were going home, the knave barely mitigated by the success at Patredike.

Their adventure was nearly over.

So soon . . .

"Well, this used to be more . . . *fun,*" the fulgar muttered darkly. "The only felicity is the weather," she added, rolling her hazel eyes to the new diem's lowering cloud as the landaulet rolled back along the bridge they had arrived upon the day before.

No masked fictler awaited them at the intersection as Fransitart took them now left to continue on down a road named the Holt Street, riding between promontories of native stone thrusting from the heights, pouring with thin cataracts from their summits or fissures in their flanks. Eventually these gave over to low fells dark with haphazard woodlands of native myrtle, turpentine and beech. Frequently they passed great lines of neatly planted teak and oak, ringing with the *cough cough cough* of distant chopping or the sighing rasp of a saw. Tiny tan-and-white birds chased even tinier bugs among it all, tetching minutely at the travelers for daring to trespass.

At the next major divergence they found a large stone-and-wood wayhouse signed THE SAWYERS' SLAKE and built right under the reach of towering ancient pines. Marked by a milestone, the main way went almost directly south to Coddlingtine Dell, hidden miles away in its leafy vale, whereas the lesser road—Holt Street—continued in a gentle curve slightly south of east. Drawing carefully through a herd of crotchety pigs let to graze the verges by their surly floppy-hatted swain, Fransitart eased the landaulet to a halt before the wayhouse to let Rufous and Candle water themselves from the common trough. On again, about a mile down the Coddling Road they found the route blocked by a handful of stationary conveyances, themselves stopped by a pair of enormous trees fallen directly across the road. Folks from the held-up carriages of either side were clambering over the mighty trunks, hacking at them with whatever tools were handy—hangers, hatchets, heavy knives—one fellow even bashing at lesser branches with the butt of his musket.

"Some gent's gone to fetch a woodsman or sawyer or some such to cut us proper clear," a genial lenterman called over his shoulder to Fransitart—and by association his mistress—from his high seat on a glossy yellow lentum-and-four just before them. "Might be a while till they come though . . ."

"Aye," interjected a grumpy wagoner from his long tarpaulin-covered dray next to the lentum. "But it will still be a blighted sight quicker'n going the Holtway," he said, swinging his arm in an exaggerated arc, "all the way about to the Dell."

"I tire of rural main streets anyway," Europe declared. "We shall take the long way to Brandenbrass and sleep rough for our last nights out."

Fransitart backed the landaulet, turned them about and returned through the swain and his hogs to take the old Holt Street. They ate a luncheon of crocidole and Scantling Aire cheese as they went, and the farther they traveled, the surer Rossamünd became of human scrutiny. Yet, if it were so, no impertinent, blank-faced observer materialized this time to prove his suspicions.

The terrain became increasingly downhill, the way bending steadily south about the flank of a high round rise until it emerged from the woods between two house-sized boulders. On the right now between hill and road ran an open culvert fashioned of ancient concrete, its sluggish effluent congealed with algae of a deep and vibrant green. Hidden

379

frogs buzzed with truculent grating voices, and humming emerald emperorflies hovered low, prowling ever-hungry over the sludge. Beyond this the side of the hill climbed, dense with pine and myrtle. Upon the left along the verge grew an unbroken line of elegant pines, and past their rough trunks the wooded land fell quickly to a panorama of a near-treeless wold, purple gray with flowering mercy jane, rolling down and away to the distant milk green sea. The pungence of the ocean blew gently on them, mellowed by the strawlike perfume of the downs.

Back prickling apprehensively, Rossamünd thought he heard travelers approaching from behind, but every time he turned, the bend of road stayed empty.

"Something bain't right," Fransitart muttered.

Europe pursed her lips, eyes flicking alertly from the height on their right to the drop on their left.

Taking the gentle unerringly right-handed crook of the culvert road slowly, Fransitart slowed yet further as the way ahead contracted to pass between two large olives growing from the base of the low wall that bisected the road. Where the wall cut the culvert like a gate, rusted bars stood vertically across the drain, a sieve collecting all manner of debris. Several yards beyond this obstacle, the unfolding bend of the road revealed a curricle leaning sharply on its side, one wheel off and sitting conspicuously across the road. Beside it stood a singularly white-skinned woman in a white summer dress, all embarrassed smiles and fluttering lashes. Waving to them, her attention flicked to an angry twittering commotion in the olive trees.

Something small dashed in on the wing from the great bush, chattering angrily, diving at the ears of Rufous and Candle, flying almost into their faces, desperately seeking their attention otherwise blocked by winkers.

Darter Brown!

Fransitart cursed loudly as the two horses tossed their heads and jerked violently to the left and back, shying wildly to avoid the fierce sparrow's diminutive assault.

Standing in his seat to call Darter Brown to stop and knowing full well he had no such command over the perplexing bird, Rossamünd saw hurried movement in the tree to the right, people hefting something large and round and then running with all haste. The horses reared, tossing him back into the seat. In an abrupt, shattering flash the ex–dormitory master's imprecations were cut short as the world burst, an eruption of soil and stones and sharp fragments that engulfed the poor horses with a detonation so loud it was like silence. The almighty gust of smashing air and dust lifted Rossamünd from his seat, throwing him high and long to land with numbing impact, skidding and rolling on grass and needles to halt with a *crack!* in a cleft of spreading pine roots. Pummeled and confounded, for untellable moments he just lay there, cap-a-pie, ears deaf with a thousand stentorian ringings, unable and unwilling to move. Yet one thought shimmered clear. *We have been ambushed!*

18

THE AID OF FRIENDS UNBIDDEN

testudoe(s) heavy-ended bludgeon, five to seven feet long, knobbled with metal studs or wooden knots and giving a powerful and nasty blow. A very old pattern of weapon finding its way into Soutland culture from the Lauslands—who took it from the passionate folk of Ing—testudoes are traditionally made of wood and as such provide some protection from the arcs of a fulgar if you should ever choose to take on such a foe.

THE first sensation to puncture Rossamünd's numbness was the shouting of many voices from every cardinal; angry cries surrounded them, accompanied by the dire pops of several firelocks.

NO! Fransitart! Craumpalin! Europe!

Sight still reeling, he felt rough hands grip him hard about each arm, lifting him well off his feet. At once he reckoned Fransitart and Craumpalin had endured the blast to come gather him, but there was something unkind in the handling, and the sweaty pungence that accompanied the two heavy figures hefting him was frighteningly foreign. Senses clarifying in his alarm, Rossamünd saw his captors as strangers man-shaped and man-sized, robed in black and wearing white oval masks striped with two blood-dark bars. Rossamünd's innards froze.

Fictlers . . .

With a coughing growl he exerted his strength, and, to a duet of startled yelps, pulled his arms together, throwing both masklings into each other with a fatty slap. Skulls collided, masks cracked. Rossamünd wrested himself free as the two would-be captors toppled to the ground. Dropped onto his knees, he spluttered and blinked at the fume of dust and powder smoke rolling about him and drifting down the incline. Thick as it was, the roil was quickly settling, revealing the landaulet between the trunks well above and to the left, the carriage broken and tipped back, its thills now splinders. Some large pallid bulk half hung over the road-edge between two pines. With a choke of grief Rossamünd realized it was Candle, ripped and fatefully still. Sobbing in a rising rage, he clawed desperately at the slope, slipping on the mat of needles as he tried to climb, pulling on thistles and barely sprouted treelings. In confused and frantic fear, he cast about the trees for his masters.

No Fransitart.

No Craumpalin.

No Europe.

There was a great furor on the unseen side of the smashed carriage, a desperate struggle of life and limb. Three penetrating *zzacks!* rang clear, eliciting muffled cries of agony. With this came a splash as a heavy thing slid into the mucky drain and two fellows in white masks scurried back down the road, hands over heads and wearing the scorching of a fulgar's defense.

The Branden Rose emerged swiftly from behind the

383

landaulet, shockingly bloodied and sporting a limp, yet very much alive and alert. Her eyes deadly slits, her fuse already in hand, she did not heed her young factotum struggling through the saplings and berry runners below.

In the intensity of his relief, Rossamünd let out a bubbling, choking laugh, yet the sound of it was blanked by the staccato popping of musket fire bursting with white puffs from among the dark conifers high upon the farther bank of the culvert where hidden musketeers plied fire down upon his mistress. Rossamünd threw himself to the hillside by the roots of a tree, glimpsing Europe stagger and drop out of sight beyond the matted brink.

NO!

Smitten dumb in horror, he flicked a caste from his right-hand digital and threw it at the musketeers, a prodigious lob flying clear over the landaulet and the drain. The orange glare of beedlebane flashed among the trunks where the marksmen hid. Another he tossed, and another after that, the blue gust of Frazzard's powder and the yellow-green glare of loomblaze flickering a yard left and right of the orange fire.

"You little muckhill!" someone shockingly close cursed.

Rossamünd spun about to catch the butt-end of a firelock in his right shoulder, the hit driving him to earth. In the flaring of pain he saw a person clad in leathers of bosky drab, face concealed behind a sthenicon, looming over him, flourishing a long-rifle high and clearly intent on staving his face with the stock.

Addled, Rossamünd did the best thing that occurred to him in the moment and simply caught the swinging rifle butt with both hands, stopping its savage momentum dead.

In shock the lurksman tugged ferociously to get his weapon back, but the young factotum held fast. Thwarted, the lurksman let go and went to draw a blade.

Still gripping the firelock by its stock, Rossamünd did not afford him the chance but drove the barrel hard into the man's abdomen. Thrust bodily backward, the lurksman buckled in a whimper of agony about the blow, collapsing in on himself as he toppled and half slid, half tumbled down the steep hillside until he was halted by a tree. With a box-deadened gag, the fellow sagged and did not move again.

Struggling, slipping, dragging himself up the sharp slope, Rossamünd could hear the increasing shouts of the hurried advance of a multitude rattling and tramping among the trees. Pivoting his gaze urgently one way and the other, he searched for sign of Europe, of Fransitart, of Craumpalin, of anything . . .

On his right, about the northern curve from where they had first arrived, he could see the heads of perhaps a dozen violent fellows coming with all haste. Half were masked fictlers wielding gabelüngs, war-rakes and long spittendes—every one a wooden weapon that did not easily transmit a fulgar's arcs. With them came savage-looking fellows carrying large round shields and long thorny clubs, braces of pistols and wickedly barbed blades of black. Wildmen they were, their shaggy hair bound in all manner of knots and spikes, wearing thick Piltmen skirts belted high over their bare chests, running barefoot, their lower legs bound in bands of hide. Most sinister yet among all these were heavier figures swathed about their shoulders in matted furs, their heads casqued in round helmets perforated with many holes sprouting horns or antlers. In thickly armored grips they bore immense wooden testudoes, wickedly barbed and knobbled, each as long as a man is tall. Conspicuous among this motley horde was the feather-hatted stranger with the four-barred mask, the silent watcher from the day before clearly commanding those about with emphatic gesticulations.

His line of sight impeded by the camber of the road and trees sprouting all along its edge, Rossamünd could hear yet another gang rushing from the left. Closer and closer the stouching parties drew, two jaws of a trap, coming headlong from north and south, caterwauling to steel their nerve. At the same moment the clatter of a small but violent turmoil sounded down past a screen of olives upon a lower slope.

Fransitart? Craumpalin!

Ready to dash to this new commotion, he was stopped as Europe's head and shoulders thrust into view above the matted verge of the roadside. The fulgar hunkered by the rear wheel of the landaulet, leaning on her fuse. Saved by the excellence of her proofing, her expression bleak yet unflinchingly resolute, she glared back and forth rapidly between the all-too-quickly encroaching gangs.

Hollering obscenities at their lonely foe as they drew in sight of her, the wild southern horde swarmed along the road on either side of the broken landaulet. Impassioned by more than common battle fervor and howling like crazed hounds, they pushed the carriage in their rage. It tottered on the brink, and with a great creak and a corporate shout of success tipped between the line of pines and off the road. In a clash of splinters it hurtled rearward down the slope, flattening myrtle saplings as it bore toward Rossamünd. Its rear right wheel struck some unseen obstruction in the weeds and needle. The whole vehicle leaped, spraying chests and prizes and lesser effects as it flipped onto its side. Sliding, it smashed to a halt a few feet to Rossamünd's left against a row of lower trees.

Driven into the open, Europe leaped away and back along the road, limp forgotten, spinning in a martial dance, frock and petticoats twirling. Fuse twisting faster than eye could follow, she made headlong for the northern party, now charging her too.

Overeager to grapple with their vaunted adversary, some wildmen sprang ahead to point and fire their pistols, their shots joined by those of the surviving musketeers skulking in the trees of the higher bank across the culvert. Once more the Branden Rose was felled, toppling to the bellowing glee of her antagonists and a cry of anguish from Rossamünd.

Snatching the single caste of asper from its digital, the young factotum let it fly through the line of pine trees at the attackers. The caste struck an antlered foe. Boiling black falsefire expanded rapidly to completely engulf the fellow, spreading farther yet to swallow those about. Horrified, Rossamünd watched as those caught in the oily vapor were blistered black, screeching their pain. Three fellows stumbled off the road and tumbled down the bank, to land steaming and lifeless.

However, the general press was not thwarted, and almost as a single creature the reckless mass of bravoes rushed to where the fulgar must have lain vulnerable on the road.

With an almost joyful "HA!" Europe abruptly appeared, springing to her feet and thrusting her fuse into the sky. A mighty lightning bolt spat down from the murk and struck the fulgaris, coruscating down the fulgar's upraised arm. Passing right through her, it stabbed out blindingly from her outstretched hand. The writhing bolt struck the massed company, leaping from one man to the next, calling more lightning from the roiling heavens independent of the fulgar's summoning, smashing all about her. Rossamünd cowered at the roar, stumbling against the bole of a pine, hands over ears, sure that they and the whole world with them would rupture. Bolt after bolt stabbed with bursting, crushing thunderings—five—six—seven—eight, slaying most fellows instantly, leaving others shattered while the remaining few recoiled, some already scampering away.

Even as reverberations of thunder rolled about the wold, Rossamünd was struck hard from the left, a potent blow skewering him in his kidneys, sending him sprawling to the mold. Seeing stars, he felt a rough-clothed arm pinch him about his neck in a malicious embrace, pressing his face into the leaf litter and dust. An all-too-familiar threwdless dread constricted in his soul. *Rever-man!* A second great strength pinned him in the small of his back, holding him to the ground while a cruel, cold grip took hold of his arms. He flailed his legs, bucking with all his might, near dislodging his captors' callous clutches. He got one brief and terrifying hint of an expressionless, empty-eyed face before a coarse sack was jerked forcibly over his own head and then cords wrapped about his throat to be pulled choking tight.

Swallowing hard against the pressure on his gourmand's cork, Rossamünd refused to let this be his end. Somehow he managed to get a toe-hold in the slippery needles and with every mite of his thew pushed, wrenching sideways, breaking the hold on his wrists. Kicking out savagely, his left foot connected with something yielding. Instantly realizing he was free of constraint, he flung himself down the slope, tumbling, hitting the ground hard over and over with shoulders and back. His career stopped with a neuralgic jolt, leaving him winded and sitting on flatter land. Tearing the cord from his throat and the bag from his head he saw that he had landed in the very midst of the tumbledown foundations of some roofless dwelling. Built on a small cobbled shelf, it was clearly long abandoned, its crumbling sandstone stained and moldering.

The stuttered cough of firelocks resounded flatly from the trees above, followed by a shout diminishing in volume and a powerful *zzack!*

Europe!

Crashes in the nearby underbrush descended swiftly toward him. Scrabbling to stand and drawing a caste of Frazzard's powder, Rossamünd spied a misshapen figure plunging down the hill. Pulling his clammy vent about his mouth and nose, the young factotum recoiled as the assailant burst through a stand of juvenile pines at the edge of this level shelf. But for the threwdless emptiness of this being, he

389

might have thought by its filthy frock coat and jauntily tilted tricorn that he was beset by a drunkard. Formed from cloth and wood and metal springs as much as of fleshly parts, this thing was not the headlong, bloodthirsty bits of meat the revermen he had met before had been. It seemed careful, almost calculating, as it regarded him from the black holes in its sack-cloth head, its eyes perpetually open in an exaggerated expression of horror. This was a jackstraw, the acme of a black habilist's arts.

Regardless, the swift familiar hatred expanded within Rossamünd's bosom. Drawing away, he had the strangest impression of a subtle *almost*-witting, not the stark frission of a neuroticrith, rather something communicative fluttering on the boundaries of sensation.

Gurgling, the jackstraw sprang at him, reaching with arms ending in long fiendish blades scissoring where palm and fingers should have been, their filthy corroded edges glinting dully.

Reeling, Rossamünd pitched the Frazzard's at the thing's head with a deft flick, the repellent bursting with blue-flashing detonations right upon its sack-draped face. The jackstraw stumbled briefly yet righted itself, dribbling fizzing mucus from a rent scorched in the cloth. The young factotum retreated through the remnants of a door, reaching into his stoup for a lepsis of greenflash, putting a broken stub of a wall between him and his hunter.

In a glimpse of something incongruously pale above, he spied the white woman in the summer dress who had first hailed them on the road, now standing several yards farther

A JACKSTRAW

up the incline, her eyes knotted closed in an expression of severe—almost ravenous—concentration. Arms bent out at the elbows, both her hands were stretched and grasping at the blank air with jerky and ferocious passion.

The thin witting sensation fluctuated. Surely she and the cloth-man were connected. She witted, it moved.

Was such a thing possible?

Attention fixed on the jackstraw stalking before him, Rossamünd found and clasped the caste of greenflash. As he drew it forth, a crushing blow slapped him upon the side of his head, sending him sprawling, skidding across the moss and paving to crumple into the roofless remains of a small room. Intellectuals swimming, he shook his head to right himself, a sharp iron tang in mouth and nose. Sight blurred and swimming, he forced himself to his feet even as he realized that there was a second cloth-made reverman coming at him, leaping over the wall, the newcomer possessing a wooden box for a head. They were on him just as he understood his peril. With no time to think, Rossamünd clapped the egg-caste of greenflash still in his grasp on the chest of the nearest jackstraw.

In a white flash, a thousand writhing agonies tore at him within and without. All notion was obliterated in a vast, ringing nothing . . . Something heavy in his hearing reverberated with a damp gonging. His skin crawled; his innards writhed. With a nauseating heave the cosmos reformed again, leaving Rossamünd anguished and beaten, gagging for air against a sucking wetness about his mouth and nose. He clawed clumsily at his face with limbs sluggish and unhelpful, half tearing the vent away in suffocating distress to let blood flow unhindered from his nose. He looked in amazement at his hand, discovering the palm of his glove scorched completely away, the flesh beneath blistered and bloodied, and marveled dumbly at how little it hurt.

Burnt and torn, the two jackstraws had been thrown back too, sprawled akimbo against the farther wall. The rever with the wooden head was missing an arm, but far from undone, it staggered to stand, trying to reach for him with its remaining hand, mummified and black.

Suddenly, over the near wall of the ruin, only a few yards from Rossamünd's shoulder, a third cloth-man reared. With cruel deliberation, it pulled itself over the stonework to crouch upon the crumbling masonry on what appeared to be the legs of a donkey. Giving voice to a hissing ruttle through sagital teeth of befouled iron set in gums swollen and diseased, it reached for him.

Rossamünd shrank from the vile grasp, pushing wildly with wounded hands and aching legs to win clear, the tenuous, clutching witting all about.

His two original corpse-made assailants righted themselves and the three cloth-men pounced at him. Pitiless claws seized him. Iron bit at his proofing. But the costly gaulding proved its worth and held. He kicked and felt something squish and yield, yet the more Rossamünd struggled, the more he seemed to be ensnared. A loathsomely cold hand clamped across his throat but did not squeeze. Without the vent to shield his nose, he inhaled the purulent fetor of his half-rotted foes and screamed a loud, long wordless terror.

A distant chirruping fury grew rapidly louder, a strange and angry *chatter-chatter-chatter* in the boughs above clear in the nearly silent struggle below it.

Darter Brown!

Impossibly, his tiny friend had not perished in the great blast on the road.

Right in the madness of the struggle, pressed down in the corner of a broken building, Rossamünd could hear the vehement chattering, swooping and harrying just above. There was a sudden ferocious whirling and much of the overpowering assault was abruptly released.

Jerking free from the confusion and heaving himself upright on the foundation wall, Rossamünd perceived a small, oddly proportioned figure in what would have once been the very next room, grappling viciously with the much larger donkey-legged jackstraw. Dressed in a frock coat of peacock blue, it had the greatly enlarged head of a sparrow. In an astonished inkling, Rossamünd knew that he had seen this creature once before and *heard* of it many times more.

Cinnamon!

Here, surely, was the very creature who had deposited him, pink and wailing, into Fransitart's reluctant arms, now bartering mighty buffets with a jackstraw, terrible hits of hoof and beak and claw that sent the other reeling.

Thrown to the weedy cobbles only a few feet away, the other two clothmen righted themselves. Dribbling maddened spittle, Sackhead scuttered forward on bladed hands and toes to pinch the young factotum about his ankle with cruel iron fingers. Tripping back, Rossamünd was saved from a fall by the stub of wall behind him. Levering against it, he kicked and lashed with his unhindered leg, pounding the jackstraw's arm and wrist, feeling bone and desiccated tendons crack and crush under heel. Above, Darter Brown flapped, cursing in the abominable creature's face and soiling on its already filthy clothes.

With a *spang!* of metallic joints, the wood-headed jackstraw rose sluggishly from the remains of the doorway where Cinnamon must have thrown it down. Its box staved in at one side, and seeping black, it fixed the appallingly vacant hole of its single eye upon Rossamünd.

Rossamünd heaved on the wall to flip himself over and was seized by the foot once more. Twisting away from the rotten merciless grasp, he tripped and slid jarringly down the wall onto his side.

Abruptly, a sizeable stone smote Woodenhead on its already damaged cranium panels. Another struck it an instant later and the jackstraw faltered in midstep. At this a veritable rain of rocks, branches, pinecones and dried dung began to hail on the cloth-man rever. Beyond the tumbledown wall Rossamünd spied a tiny figure on the other side of the level, its yellow eyes angry-wide.

"FRECKLE!" he cried involuntarily, kicking with fresh vigor at the sack-faced fiend trying again to stand and lift him by his leg. *Dear Freckle!*

Flinging whatever came handy at the pestilent creature, the glamgorn blinked at him in recognition. Many of the lighter missiles bounced off harmlessly, almost comically. Some showered around Rossamünd, but with the muffled clunk of rock on metal and wood, many stones flew true and the rever's body began to buckle under the mucky, stony sleet.

The flat staccato cough of a volley of firelocks sounded from the heights, accompanied by shouts and a single dull pop. Just as dread for Europe and his old masters rose, a blitz of lightning struck again, three swift strikes hitting the hill above, silencing all else as it shattered the very air.

With a mighty wrench of his fettered leg Rossamünd pulled free of Sackhead, clawing and pulling at the cobbles to get himself away. Woodenhead collapsed to its knees but still crawled on. In that instant the young factotum glimpsed Cinnamon through the door gap of the other room, skipping under the third jackstraw's wicked grasp. The nuglung seized the abomination by hip and chest, and in a twinkling tore it completely in two. Without a pause the bogle-princeling tossed the top half of the rever far into the precipitous woods and, swinging the bestial legs, rushed to Rossamünd's aid. Leaping lightly over boy and wall, he bore down on the limping jackstraw clutching relentlessly for its prey with a *click-clack* of its metal talons—battering the vile thing with the riven legs, hitting again and again with such savagery that bits of jackstraw quickly began to flick and spatter.

Arms full of old debris, Freckle sprang onto the top of the adjacent wall, pummeling Woodenhead with stone after stone. When his armload was spent, he jumped down to bounce upon the cloth-man, yipping loudly and with relish as he pounded the thing to bits.

In awe, Rossamünd strove to stand, his whole body thudding with hurts, blasted hand slick with gore slithering off whatever they touched. Another pop of a firelock from the woods and he revived. At the left side of the level he saw a sheer flight of crumbling stone stairs that climbed the hill from the edge of the foundation. Running out of the ruin's vestigial entrance, he mounted this stairway, Darter Brown winging to join him. Sucking at the air in rasping gulps, Rossamünd clawed up the sheer path. Many yards to the right, half hidden in a grove of pine trees, he caught sight of the woman in the white dress, sagging where she stood—heedless of the world—braced with one gloved hand upon a trunk, her face a sickly gray under its pretty bonnet.

A close clash of weapons and Rossamünd had a brief sight of Fransitart higher up the bank, standing at the threshold of an enormous bush of olive that grew beside the steps. White hair flying, musketoon in one hand and his hanger in the other, the ex–dormitory master was sparring sword to gabelüng with a fictler who was flailing with a young man's impatience against Fransitart's watchful defense. Across the curve of the incline, a wild Piltdowner man, bloodied and angry-eyed, crouched in the concealment of the tipped and broken landaulet to level a firelock on the old vinegaroon. Snatching up the first projectile handy, Rossamünd pitched a pinecone, the seedy bullet humming smartly as it flew, hitting the Piltman on the cheek in a mighty spray of splintering cone at the very instant of firing. In the *CRACK!* of the shot, Fransitart struck his adversary a telling cut upon the neck and toppled with the dying foe to the ground.

The Piltman staggered off down the hill, tripping on weeds and roots. Rossamünd did not wait to know the man's fate but pivoted and dashed to the great olive where Fransitart had fallen, terrified of what he would find.

Between him and his purpose crawled a lone jackstraw, legs torn away, pawing at the weeds and dirt, scaling the hillside with arms alone, metal teeth gnashing, more the mindless unrelenting predator now.

"ENOUGH!" Fury boiling in a red instant, Rossamünd snatched at a broken piece of wall embedded in the hillside—a stone as big as his own chest—and heaved it from the soil with both hands. In a spray of worms and woodlice and soil, he hefted the stone high, and, dropping to his knees, brought it down with all his monstrous might right on the wretched laboring abomination's sack-cloth skull, burying the stone and putrid flesh with it a hand span deep into the mold.

About him silence settled on the woods: no crack of firelock, no clash of blows, just the anxious hush of an aftermath.

"Well done, dear lad . . . ," Fransitart's voice broke through his desolation.

Heart leaping, Rossamünd looked up.

The old vinegaroon was limping toward him, clutching at his stomach and using the musketoon as a crutch along the uneven ground. His face was dreadfully swollen about the eyes, his bottom lip split and gory, his hair congealing with red.

With a sob of relief, Rossamünd sprang the scant yards and clasped arms with the startled sea dog. "And Craumpalin. . ."

In the cool of the enormous olive, Fransitart revealed the dispenser, propped in the deep bole of the tree, partially concealed by the roots and a smooth stone about which the olive had matured, making it almost a part of itself. Craumpalin was disconcertingly still, his eyes closed, his beard bedraggled with blood, his breath shallow huffs. A soaking bloodied scarf lay near, and another was bound about his throat.

"Master Pin . . ." Rossamünd dropped to his knees beside the fallen fellow.

"He's been poorly handled, lad. That bang let off by them filthy scupperers gave 'm a prodigious bad gash in th' neck 'ere—" Fransitart drew a line on the left side of his neck with his finger as he spoke out of the side of his wounded mouth. "I reckon 'is legs are broke . . . but 'e's holdin' together, though 'e'll need a seam-stitcher an' two good splints afore too long."

"I have thrombis and strupleskin." Rossamünd reached for his left stoup. "We can stop the holes at least." Only now, in the numb astonishment after hand strokes, did he become properly alive to the sharp hurt of his own hand, finding too a vigorous ache in his shoulders, as if someone had tried to unattach his arm at its socket. He gingerly hooked the parts-container—baldric and all—from his shoulder. "Could you please find them?" he asked his old master sheepishly.

"What have ye done to yer paw, lad?" The ex–dormitory master scowled at the burnt flesh as he took the stoup.

"I—I broke a potive." The young factotum made a wry face at his old master's sharp astonishment. "Where are your hurts?" he inquired evasively.

"I've got a prodigious crack on me crown an' a smart thump to me chest beams," Fransitart explained as he fossicked for th' right items. "We were pitched cap o'er end down the hill. After clearin' me intellectuals, findin' an' a-haulin' dear Pin into th' bush, I found this 'ere musketoon still fit to fire an' took one of them baskets aimin' on yer miss with it, then swapped a swing o' blows with another. Did th' same again shortly after, then ye showed yerself . . ."

Underbrush rustled and a small form pushed into the haven of the dense olive boughs.

Fransitart almost dropped the stoup as he reached in fright for his hanger.

"You can keep your blows to be kept to themselves, master seaswimmer!" came a bleeble-blabble voice, its merry speaking at odds with the stern warning.

"Freckle!" Rossamünd whispered.

Sheepishly, the glamgorn revealed itself, alone.

Where Cinnamon was the young factotum could not see.

In unabashed wonder, the ex-vinegaroon regarded the little barky-skinned bogle wearing a child's longshanks pulled high about its chest rather than the usual swaddle of rags. "So 'ere's th' little fellow . . ."

"It is we who win this day, yes we do, and the day is won!" Freckle smiled, his huge eyes disappearing in the wrinkles of its grinning. "Oh . . ." Its gaze alighted on Craumpalin and he became instantly solemn. "Keep your powders in their pots, Rossamünd who is Rossamünd even more than before; we shall tend all hurts . . ."

A heavy boom of thunder rumbled some distance to the north, exciting a discord of startled crows high in the trees. From somewhere far off came a faint cry of anger.

"Miss Europe!"

"Bind yer hand first, lad," Fransitart advised, holding out some bandages to him, "and then go find 'er—she probably reckons us all dead . . ."

"Yes, yes!" Freckle enjoined, squatting at Craumpalin's side. "Find your angry mistress and flutter not for your seaward fathers; they will have their bashings mended."

"My hand can wait," Rossamünd insisted, and dashed away. Tugging his torn and bloodied vent from his neck, and his stock with it, he clumsily wrapped his stinging palm as he went. Halting momentarily to listen and to tie off his bindings, he climbed watchfully to the road. Drawing near the epicenter of the ambush, he peered over the brink of the way, gaping saucer-eyed at the wreckage the fulgar had brought. Bodies lay shattered, some flung down into the pines or foul culvert slime, some still quick, sniveling, trying to claw themselves away.

A sullen hint of asper hung yet over the road, lingering threateningly above the steaming remains of those it had slain—that *he* had slain—as if to make certain they stayed dead. Yet no other threat seemed obvious in the dreary silence of the woods. The higher bank across the drain was unnaturally still. A white mask lay in the shadows and some yards to the right the splintered, smoldering stumps of several lithe pines spoke of the gap-leaping success of the fulgar's deadly lightnings.

In the hush of whispering needle leaves and squeaking, softly clacking boughs, no new contestant stepped upon the path or took a shy at him from cover. Darter Brown alighted on the chest of a fallen fictler splayed upon the path. Hopping forth and back on its grisly perch, the sparrow flicked his wings, perhaps to show that all was safe.

Satisfied, Rossamünd ran beside the road, skirting the sooty fizz of asper, returning along their original route, finding more ruined fictlers and wildmen thrown down in the dust and needles. Among the fallen, he found an uncanny figure stained red, spent pistols still in scarlet hands, lifeless face aghast.

The reddleman! This frowsty discolored dye-seller had been lurking them after all.

A glaring blue flicker lit up the darkening trees ahead about the bend. Scrambling onto the road itself, he hurried stoutly to it, half in hope, half in fear.

The Branden Rose hove into view, grimed with gore, hair askew, proofing starkly bruised, boots scuffed, the weep of dark green tears lining each cheek like ghastly spoors. The fulgar was bent over a slouched figure, Featherhead, the chief of the fictlers, feathered hat discarded on the road. Four-bar mask plucked away from his very normal, very human face, now clenched in pain, his eyes were rolling with blank fear. One arm was raised feebly to keep the fulgar bayed.

Yet even in defeat, the abysmal foulness Rossamünd had first felt when they had passed the fictler-lord standing on the side of the road the day before still issued from the fallen fellow.

Rossamünd's stride quickly slackened still several yards from Europe and her captive and, taking a few cautious steps more, he halted.

With a small *cheep!* Darter Brown settled on his shoulder.

Laying the fuse beside her, Europe squatted to grip the stricken fellow by both sides of his battered head, her knuckles white. Through gritted teeth she seethed a single vehement word. *"Who!"*

Shuddering involuntarily, the fellow fought the fulgar's coercion, his eyes revolving convulsively. His arms jerked, his legs kicked and bent.

She arcs him! Rossamünd realized in horror.

"WHO!" the Branden Rose spat with venomous volume.

The fellow's nodding, shuddering head was almost contracting into his body as his eyes rolled back into their sockets. "M—M—Maupin . . . ," he gurgled, and, with a strange crick of the neck, expired.

Rossamünd felt his innards contract into a sickly chill.

The reach of their foes was long indeed.

I have caused all this, he groaned inwardly, barely able to comprehend so powerful an appetite for revenge that could summon such an ambush and put it into action.

Finally Europe looked up. The whites of her eyes were entirely bloodshot—solid red like a falseman's orbs—as she fixed weary attention on Rossamünd. "There you are, little man." Though she breathed fitfully as she spoke, her voice was as hard as iron. "You have lost your hat, I see."

19

TRAVELING LIGHT

belch pot also known as a kluge pot—for no known reason remembered in history, in the Gottskylds, where it is reputed to have been devised, it is known variously as a kaput-tenkessel (breaking kettle) or furzentopf ("farting pot"). Infamous devices used by bandits, rough wild folk, and some armies too, belch pots are makeshift artillery made of great clay pots or iron cauldrons filled with black powder and jagged, thorny flotsam, half sunk in the soil and set off by a burning fuse. Any soul caught direct in its burst is sure to be flayed to splinters. Used to shape and channel the direction of a charge of fulminant, they are typically destroyed in the blast; a favorite of irregular fighters all through the Sundergird, the clay version being particularly inexpensive and simple to fashion.

I N the gaping, harrowed aftermath, Rossamünd and the Branden Rose returned along the culvert way, the fulgar gripping the Featherhead's mask like a rare proof. "Such are the benefits of good fighting weather" was all she said of the butcher's bill of bodies. Beyond brief inquiry after Rossamünd's health and the well-being of the two old vinega-roons, Europe remained disconcertingly silent, her expression taut with unsympathetic vigilance. She stepped callously over one hefty fellow still shuddering for breath, horned helmet wrenched loose to reveal within the nimbus of a fur collar his thick-jawed face, skin near white like that of the woman in the summer dress. *A Heilgolundian.* Hailing from far south beyond the Pontus Canis and across the Gurgis Main, where people fade for lack of sun, this dying man had come a long way to perish so uselessly.

Reaching for his stoup of tending scripts, Rossamünd realized they were left with Fransitart and Freckle.

"Leave the hurt, little man!" The fulgar glowered at Rossamünd fleetingly. "Others of their own will come back to retrieve them soon enough . . . or the crows to peck—it is of little concern to me which." Whether she swooned from unseen hurts or turned an ankle on some detritus on the road as she pivoted back to rebuke him, Europe abruptly buckled at her knees and staggered. She tottered backward, twisting partly as if to catch herself, her fuse clattering on the ground.

Rossamünd sprang to her, his arms wide, catching the fulgar before she went down, bearing her weight, surprised at her lightness.

Gripped in his impromptu embrace, Europe regarded him silently, her scowl tempered by surprise.

So close to her, Rossamünd could plainly see wounds through smears and tears: a bullet graze on the left side of her pate, clotted cuts on scalp, forehead, ears, down her neck.

"We have done well today, you and I," she said at last, a softer thought in her appallingly red-shot eyes as she found her own balance and stood to her feet once more. "Better than we ought . . ."

"I thought we were done for." Rossamünd kept his voice steady against the unexpected dizzying rush of relief. Somehow, when all was set against them, they had won . . .

405

Brushing her hems and unruffling the sit of her collars, Europe said bluntly, "What have you done to your hands?"

Rossamünd told her of his own fight, and at the mention of jackstraws the fulgar's eyes narrowed; at the mention of Cinnamon and Freckle they became ill-humored slits.

"How fortunate to be helped by bogles against the agents of those who accuse us as sedorners," she muttered darkly, gathering up her fuse and the fallen fictler's mask. "A splendid irony."

The young factotum gave a grim smile. "If the jackstraws had been more intent on ending me than carrying me away I reckon I'd be ashes by now."

"It seems our many *friends* think themselves in possession of a long reach, to send such a menagerie against us to pluck you away." She fixed him with a look partly satirical, partly in deadly earnest. "As for your paws, Rossamünd, I recommend that before you next opt to play with sparks, you visit Sinster as I have done to get the necessary additions first." Her expression grew wry and she added, "Though I would recommend you kept your true nature a secret from all those fossicking transmogrifers while you were there . . ."

They came about the bend and his dismay deepened as he saw again the shattered bodies of Rufous and Candle lying before the low walls that had hid the ambuscade. Debris of the original blast was thrown wide, a great elliptical fissure in the road. On the right, the once-thick olive was rent and bedraggled, the wall before it charred, the corners broken and missing.

To the left, amid the lower pines, the landaulet was

little more than a suite of beautifully upholstered seats, three wheels and a mess of lacquered firewood, its contents strewn about.

The sparrow gave a bright *cheep!* then leaped away, winging ahead and down the hill.

"We will be walking out, it seems," Europe observed, then hesitated.

From behind the low left-hand wall Craumpalin appeared to be floating unconscious and lolling up the side of the hill and toward the road. Fransitart was there too, toiling up behind, the wounds and scabbed blood on his face shocking in the yellowing of the late day. To Rossamünd's delight, Cinnamon stepped out from the blind of the low wall, the nuglung humbly carrying the ailing old dispenser pig-a-back, hauling him like some overburdened porter.

"Oh, what fun . . . ," Europe purred. Her sanguine gaze, fixed upon Cinnamon, barely shifted when Freckle emerged behind, leading Fransitart by the hand.

Twittering merrily, Darter Brown circled about the head of the nuglung-prince, settling finally on the wall to sing.

Reaching only to Rossamünd's shoulder in height, Cinnamon regarded the fulgar with its great black, knowing eyes, turning its head to look with one eye then the next. It was clad like a gentleman, complete with white-and-black-striped weskit under its frock coat, with stiff shirt-collar, black stock, and buttons made of polished bone. Though the beauty of the coat was marred with many dark bruises, Rossamünd could see that it was in truth made of the living petals of some dazzling blue flower fashioned together so closely as to look like woven cloth. A nebulous threwd surrounded the blithely creature, less potent than that which wreathed the Lapinduce, but clearer, kinder, more hopeful, stirring in Rossamünd faint notions of ease and security and bringing too a sweet, clinging rind-and-honey scent mixed with the piquant stink of feathers.

Gently depositing Craumpalin on the road, it—or *he* perhaps, for it bore the facial colorations of a male sparrow and, moreover, there was a distinct *he*-ness about it . . . about *him*—*he* bowed to the fulgar, one arm bent at his middle, the other outstretched, clawed hand gracefully posed. "Hail, lady astrapeline," it called, its voice rising and falling like the melancholy music of the Duke of Rabbits, "protectress of our foundling child. Your enemies are many and far-traveled: I am glad to have arrived to help thee."

In her turn, Europe remained unmoved, chin raised, terrible thermistor-red eyes fixed upon this bogle-prince. Rossamünd was sure he smelled the metal tang of building levin on her. "So here is Rossamünd's deliverer," she said with menacing care. "I commend you on your *fortunate* timing, sir. I understand that ultimately it is to *you* that I owe my far-traveled enemies."

Cinnamon straightened, expression impenetrable. "Providence works as Providence wills, Lady of Roses," he warbled, "even through the littlest of us." He crooked a claw and Darter Brown flew to perch upon it. "And it was not *I* who had you take Rossamünd the mighty gudgeon-slayer into your staff."

CINNAMON

The Branden Rose arched a brow. "It is not usual for me to treat with those of your *tribe,* bogle."

"Nor mine with yours, fulgar," the bogle-prince returned evenly. "Too long has it been since two princes of our two kinds have spoken even a few fairer words as we do now."

"Ours is not the blame for that, sparrow-man," Europe answered, her expression remaining cold.

To this Cinnamon said nothing, but simply looked at the Branden Rose, his eyes unblinking. Glowering beside him, Freckle gnashed his teeth at her.

As true as he tried to be to his mistress, even Rossamünd was rankled at the injustice of Europe's remark and, not knowing what else to do, he dared to step between the nuglung and the fulgar. "Thank you, Lord Cinnamon," he said with his own bow to the bogle-prince, "for defending me. I was done in for certain otherwise."

The nuglung turned his piercing, glittering eyes upon Rossamünd. "Well-a-day, Master Gudgeon-slayer! Thee tussles admirably with the utterworsts. It is well to see thee growing strong and true."

"Th-thank you . . ." was all the young factotum could get out as he bowed once more.

"Yes, yes!" Freckle suddenly cried, stepping toward him but halting with many suspicious looks to Europe. "You have learned your true strength true and your strength is well learnt at last, as it was not in the bottom of that Hogglehead boat."

"Better rest for you is near," Cinnamon continued abruptly, the chirrup in his words almost mesmerizing.

410

"Hoarebeard"—he gestured with his small clawed hand to Craumpalin—"needs proper succor, and, if you will grant me this, oh Lady Europe, I shall lead thee all to a softer place for harms to heal away from common notice."

For just a flash, Rossamünd thought he spied his mistress taken aback, but if it were so, she quickly schooled her expression to its usual wry watchfulness.

"What polite speeches you make, little sparrow-man," she replied softly, her gaze shifting briefly to the poor senseless Craumpalin.

Propped against the broken wall, the old dispenser was looking much improved, his breathing less fitful, his throat bound with dense plaits of what looked to be just ordinary grasses and common weeds. Splints of thick branches were fastened about his legs with the same.

"I grant it," Europe conceded. "Though do not suppose for a moment I shall stay my hand should you turn on us and show yourself the monster after all."

Cinnamon bowed low and courtly. "Nor I if it proves true of you, Lady Europe."

"Rossamünd, come," the fulgar commanded frostily, and, revolving on her boot, she stepped lightly off the edge of the road and went down the hill toward the wrecked landaulet.

The young factotum gave an awkward beck to Cinnamon and hurried to follow his mistress, Darter Brown fluttering after.

A fume was billowing within the trees down where Rossamünd had slain the last jackstraw. With a sigh of irritation Europe approached it, fuse held ready, her young factotum

411

one step behind. The fulgar quickly relaxed her guard as she beheld the broken half of the cloth-made rever. Its head was driven into the soil, sinews beginning to fizzle and bubble, releasing a muddy steam that stank of bitter caustic and the vilest drouthy corpse-flesh.

"Your handiwork, I am thinking, little man," the fulgar uttered with a mite of satisfaction.

Entranced by the dramatic chemistry, Rossamünd shuddered but did not answer.

Before his very eyes the slain jackstraw was dissolving, effervescing like Frazzard's powder, breaking down to nought more than a puddle of corpse-liquor, metal frame and some mummified remains all wrapped in a threadbare suit of soiled clothes.

Little wonder Mister Sebastipole found no evidence of the gudgeon I bested under the manse. It must have frothed clear away before he could.

Europe blinked slowly. "Degenerate thantocriths!" she sneered with surprising vitriol. "They dare to call themselves *lahzar* . . ."

As if to some cosmic prompt, they caught sight of the woman in the summer dress, a white glimpse wandering aimless among the woods and across the slope below, her hems stained and torn, her bonnet gone. She stared about with a deranged and disconcerting fervor, her head lolling then flopping back, squinting at the dull afternoon light, face wrenched with anguish and bewilderment.

"So there is our canker-headed sciomane," Europe pronounced, a cold murmur matched by her soured mien.

412

Tangling in her skirts, the woman fell out of sight, uttering a thin shriek that set small birds belling in alarm. Darter Brown, perched on Rossamünd's shoulder, ruffled and trilled nervously.

Despite himself, the young factotum began to descend to help.

"Leave her to her grief, Rossamünd," Europe said with hushed contempt. "It is a fair prize for her service." The fulgar strode to the landaulet and began fossicking about the various chests thrown from the wreck.

Doggedly, Rossamünd continued down a little farther, watched a beat longer, craned his head to listen . . . but no peep of the white woman showed again between the trunks, nor any sound of her stumbling in the underbrush.

Time was wasting, light was failing, and Craumpalin needed a better bed.

Now for the quickest making that ever was made . . .

Fixed as it was to the landaulet's trunk-rail, the laborium was now wedged against the trunk of the pine that had halted the vehicle's career. Tipped on its side, its cover was twisted partly away, the off-smelling gastric contents dribbled out and soaking into the needles and dirt.

When he informed the fulgar of this impediment, she drew in a breath ready to vent her ire, yet scowled in pain and forestalled pungent words with a bitter sigh. "We have not the time for a fire . . . Syntony and sangfaire will have to make do for the present!" She pushed a trunk over with her boot to draw from it a clean, gaulded frock coat of sleek inky hide.

As quick as hurts would allow, they collected the necessary articles and handy luggage. Bending to take up the small assortment of sacks and satchels he had accumulated and with them a pair of unscuffed equiteer boots, Rossamünd grimaced at a dark jab in his belly as he straightened.

On the road, Freckle drew away at the fulgar's approach to sit on his haunches in the middle of the road, wide sun-hued eyes winking and blinking at the Branden Rose with dismay.

Dosed on balancing draughts, the fulgar chewed upon a whortleberry and paid the little fellow no mind at all.

Cinnamon left off his ministrations on Craumpalin to insist he tend to Rossamünd's hand before they went on.

Obediently, the young factotum unwound his ersatz dressings to reveal the raw weeping mess of his palm and fingers.

"Ahh, me lad!" Fransitart commiserated.

"That is why most skolds *throw* their potives," Europe remarked drolly, standing near, her scrutiny never leaving the ministering nuglung.

The ex–dormitory master snorted a slight laugh.

Rossamünd looked bemusedly at them both.

Taking a choice of bonny weeds and luridly blotched bulbs from his pockets, Cinnamon began to masticate them together with pronounced clampings of his bill. Gently, the nuglung took Rossamünd's hand in his own, the ashen skin cool and strangely calloused, its touch a comfort, and spat a gray-green mass directly onto the blistered flesh. Wherever the salivary poultice touched, the pain was immediately balmed.

414

"This is how you mended Numps," Rossamünd observed frankly, refusing to be disgusted as he watched the bogle-prince's careful tending.

"Such and more, yes," Cinnamon agreed. "The utter-worsts might have slain him else. Those vile festermen have brought as much misery to everymen as e'er they have to us."

The young factotum watched the ancient nuglung in patent wonder, struck by Cinnamon's incongruous pro-portions and queer alien beauty and the fragrance of feather and blossom mingled with that of fresh-turned loam that surrounded him. The nuglung bound Rossa-münd's hand, palm now covered with the physicking spit, in thick weeds—weevil lily, he called it—all fixed with a final binding of more usual bandage from the stoup. Cin-namon did not offer such aid to Europe, and the fulgar did not seek it.

"That's what caused yer blast," Fransitart called over the din of frogs that had begun to croak and trill all along the drain. Musketoon in hand, the old salt was hobbling beside the large elliptical crater. Abruptly, he kicked at an oddly bent plate of metal half buried in the upheaved soil, the iron piece torn and jagged as if mere paper. "A belch pot!" He spat and muttered something foul. "Breech-full o' cannon char . . ."

Rossamünd's eyes went round.

"If it weren't for them poor daft horses halting short an' liftin' their heads when they did," the old dormitory master went on in wonderment, "I doubt we would be about this world any more . . . A miss is as good as a mile, 'ey, lad!" He smiled ruefully, forgetful of his wound and stretching the gash in his lip. "Oh . . ." The ex-vinegaroon hastily stanched the flowing wound with a wad of weeds he had in his hand. "They were a right parsthel of blackheartsth!" he declared bitterly through the leafy muffle.

"Blackhearts, indeed, Master Vinegar," the fulgar returned flatly.

"Are you hale for the walk, Master Frans?" Rossamünd inquired of the old salt, who looked a little heartier with levenseep fortifying his humours.

"I have some wind left in me yet, lad, afore ye send me off to the tumblehome." The old fellow grinned wanly. "Lead on, Master Sparrow, sir. I'd rather a hard stroll to a better harbor than an easy sit here out o'doors vulnerable to any wild body."

As a final provision for their departure, Europe produced her small black-lacquered whortleberry box and offered one to Fransitart, then to Rossamünd.

"For Cinnamon and Freckle too," the young factotum said bluffly as the cheerful vigor of the dried berry swelled within.

Even in the dimming day he could feel his mistress' incredulity. "Do nickers and bogles gain benefit from them?"

A little offended, Rossamünd answered softly, "Well, I do . . ."

To this, the fulgar smiled the thinnest curl of a smile.

"Chortlingberries!" Freckle called them with equal delight, not even pretending to chew.

Despite his expressionless beak, a kind of grin seemed to

light Cinnamon's face when the morsel was offered. "Peri-acharës!" He gave a very bright birdlike chirp as he eagerly snapped down the withered thing, Darter Brown joining him in happy mimicry. With a *tweet!* Cinnamon gathered Craumpalin in his arms like a baby, the little nuglung's great strength clear as he shouldered a man twice his size on his back. His large bird's head bobbling as his regard twitched from one sight to the next, the bogle-prince set off, a slouching, tiny-legged lump with the dispensurist sagging on his back, looming over the little bogle and looking ready to tip to the road at any breath.

To the clamor of raucous frog song, the six of them made their way out from this terrible place, the most bizarre caravan surely to ever have wended the world.

Well ahead, Freckle and Darter Brown took turns to look farther, the sparrow streaking off and winging back to mutter in Cinnamon's hidden ears. At times the bogle-princeling would reply, uttering inexplicable phrases in sparrowlike song. Mists of minuscule bugs surged across the road, spinning about them in celebration of the arbustral evening, flying into eyes, up nostrils, into mouths opened to breathe.

A little way about the ever-bending path they found the curricle used as part of the trap set against them, its wheel still off, dragged no small distance in fright by the stolid gray pony still in its harness and gnawing ruminatively at the roadside herbage.

Putting Craumpalin ever so carefully down upon the weedy verge, Cinnamon stepped to the pony, reaching out for it to nuzzle his small black palm. "Meadows now thy stall shall be," the nuglung crooned, a strange flutter of authority stirring about him as, surprisingly familiar with carriage quipage, he unharnessed the poor beast. "And cloud and star thy stable. Make wild grass and unplucked weeds your fodder. Be wary now of men and blighted things and dwell untrammeled by thy former burdens."

At this the pony started, nostrils flaring, eyes rolling nervously. With a whinny and a kick, it galloped off down the road and away.

"No more heave and haul for her!" Freckle gurgled. "No more switches switching or bindings binding."

"A clever trick, Master Bogle," Europe offered wearily. "Might it not have been wiser to keep it for our own use?"

"We have limbs enough to hold our loads, oh Lady Lightning, and need not burden a beast," said Cinnamon, hoisting the senseless dispensurist once more onto his shoulders and walking on without a backward look.

As the leaden western sky transmuted to sullen crimson, and the east waxed brooding dark out over the pallid waters of the distant Grume, the nuglung took them deeper into the jagged shadows of the wood hill.

Patently untroubled by the dark, Freckle kept well ahead.

Yet stumbling over roots and rocks, Rossamünd, by all evidence, did not share such a sense. For his more *human* eyes—and for Europe and Fransitart too—he fetched his limulight from pocket and gave it to the ex–dormitory master to let the soft blue yellow effulgence guide their questing feet.

418

"Now, that's a handy article," the old salt whispered.

"Mister Numps gave it to me." Rossamünd spared a thought for the poor seltzerman hidden in the slypes and undercrofts of Winstermill's ancient foundations away from the conspiracies and schemes of Podious Whympre.

"The one named Numps does well enough in his hiding holes," Cinnamon declared, startling Rossamünd with his sudden proximity. "The clerking-master thinks him beneath his thinking, but I *and* my lord keep our watch on him. Many are the sparrows of Winstreslewe . . ." The saucers of his black eyes glittering in the gloaming with occult primordial thoughts, the nuglung raised his heavy beak to sniff at the air.

Rossamünd opened his mouth to speak, to dare to ask what he feared was the unaskable. "Lord Cinnamon, why did you have me live with everymen? Would I not be safer with the sparrow-king?"

Head now turning to him, those eyes regarded the young factotum blinkingly for several breaths. "*Safer?* Why, yes, thee would certainly have been *safer* . . . and more so should you choose to retreat to him now that men hunt thee." Cinnamon paused as if this was actually a question that needed answering.

Here once again Rossamünd had a *choice* amid all the *go* and the *do* to pick his own path, to live with the Duke of Sparrows, removed and untouchable.

"We have wanted thee to learn of love for everymen," the bogle-prince continued candidly. "'Twas a *gamble,* 'tis true, yet the lessons of the blightlings—if they were to find thee and keep themselves from eating thee—would have been

419

for nought but malice, for cruel destruction and all frames of sly-born misery. With my lord, the Sparrowlengis, thee might neither find love nor hate, but learn only of the everymen from afar as thoughtless and brutal and best to be avoided." Cinnamon stopped and turned to face him fully. "There is much mischief and violence in everymen—as you know right well," the nuglung said solemnly, with the merest flicker of a glance to Europe not far behind.

Rossamünd heard the fulgar sniff in objection.

"Yet they are loved and there is hope, so we defend them . . ." Though there was little change in his face, Cinnammon seemed to brighten. "And now too do thee, little Rossamünd. You see! Our gamble has been worthy. The everymen need all the *friends* they can against the sunderhallows and falsely gods." He gave a sharp *chirrup!* that ended conversation and set Darter Brown to expectant twitching. "Walk on, walk on," he declared, setting off again to lead them up an avenue of old conifers. "Thee and thine are close to succor now."

Wending about every fold and spur of the steepening combe into the round hills, they kept course beside a murmuring waterway, invisible in the dark to their left. Gully breezes stirred fitfully about them, rousing soft creakings and rattlings on either hand, bringing with them a profoundly earthy smell that hung heavier and heavier in the shifting valley air. By dim limulight Rossamünd found that the meager cart trail became a channel through thickly knotted thorns, a soughing briar grove tingling with a subtle threwdish caution—not unfriendly, just waiting. Beyond the spiny writhen boughs and thickset trunks he glimpsed lights. It seemed to him that one glow was brighter and swung more freely than the rest. It was a lantern. Someone was coming out to them.

"Ahoo! Ahoo! Prince Cannelle?" a man's voice called, husky with caution.

Cinnamon halted, giving a birdlike *chirrup!* as reply.

The lantern light approached, resolving into a bright-limn lifted now in the hands of a slight young fellow with dark, intelligent eyes, a broad round nose and curly black hair tied back. Dressed in a heavy coat with a white stock about his neck, the fellow had a stylus secured behind his ear. Beside him was a heavier gent in a properly proofed jackcoat, wearing an anxious face with a nigh absent chin beneath white scratch wig and broad-brimmed catillium. He bore a brace of unfriendly two-barrel hauncets.

With them came Freckle, looking powerfully pleased with himself.

Both men were goggling saucer-eyed from Cinnamon to Craumpalin hunched upon his shoulders.

"My dear Prince Cannelle," the slender young man said with a gracious bow to Cinnamon, his words having the tone of formula. "May the earth heal beneath your feet, and peace guard you—and ah . . . your companions wholly." He straightened.

The bogle-prince, still bearing the insensible dispensurist, bobbed his own curtsy and replied with a formula of his own. "May your days be long and you ever tell blight from blithe."

421

"Yon Lentigo near gave us all a chordic failure with his hammering at our door!" the older, bulkier fellow grumped, the slightest northern accent in his words. He added under his breath, "If it weren't a-troubling enough ter have hobthrushes come by at all hours unannounced, our fellow brings comp'ny . . . and hurt comp'ny at that."

Freckle grinned ever more broadly.

"Yes, thank you, Spedillo." The young man cleared his throat and returned his attention to Cinnamon. "You well know that you and little Lord Lentigo are welcome to Orchard Harriet at any juncture. I see tonight you have again brought us guests . . . ," he continued with polite understatement, bowing to the strangers. His astonishment broadened in realization at precisely who stood before him.

Europe stepped forward and introduced herself bluntly, bundling Rossamünd and Fransitart and Craumpalin together as her "staff." Waving aside the two fellows' evident bafflement—*Just what is Lord Cannelle doing with a fulgar!*—she continued with rare urgency. "I am in need of your hearth or stove, sir, so please, lead us on."

"Ah, yes, certainly." The young man floundered for a moment, half turning, then turning back. "Yes, certainly, indeed, our stove . . . and mayhap a bath too . . . I shall present your need to Fäbia, our housekeeper. Come along, please, good Lady Rose." He bowed again, handing the bright-limn to his hefty companion, who huffed grumpily as he took it and led them.

Soon the thorn grove gave over to honey-perfumed blossoming thickets of low ornamental trees. The party breathed its corporate relief as the dark ramshackle bulk of a fortified house hove into view, only three of its myriad window-lights lit and the front door open in welcome.

"Orchard Harriet," the young man proclaimed of the spreading structure with clear pride. "And if I may, I am Amonias Silence, poet and amanuensis, and my surly compatriot is Mister Spedillo, gardener, provenderer, nightlocksman."

The other fellow went on without acknowledgment toward the house of Orchard Harriet. Unclear in the darkness, it appeared an inky conglomeration of oddly placed turrets, high-pitched roofs and craggy battlements. A short projecting wing stood out from the building's upper story, making a porch over the foremost entrance, the arched space overlit with a friendly lamp, its seltzer clean and clear. Taken to this door, they were ushered into a narrow hall, long and doorless, walls souring white, smelling of the slate that made its floor. It was a kind of obverse, a coat stand and boot-scraper its only furniture.

Still bearing Craumpalin slumped insensible on his back, Cinnamon looked odd in such a domestic frame, yet past the sparrow-headed bogle another more disconcerting sight arrested Rossamünd's attention and stopped him smartly. At the far end of the hall stood an enormous looking glass, fixed to the wall, showing a ghastly reflection. Spreading out from his nose, his lower face, neck and a good portion of his quabard were dark with old blood; his left eye was already blackened and his fringe partly singed away; much of the thread-of-silver embroidery on the arms of his coat was charred. Turning his head left, then right, he found a clotted trail of blood from his ears. With such an appearance it seemed astonishing he was walking at all!

Europe caught a view of herself too, and even she betrayed shock seeing her dangerously pale, bloody, green-streaked face so starkly.

Mister Silence went hastily down the hall ahead of them, calling with all the gusto of a faraday as he went, and obstructing the shocking reflection.

Merry loud replies and heavy footfalls on rug and stone resounded from around some corner down the passage, and a middle-aged man with a shock of prematurely graying hair wearing a brocaded silk dressing gown of red and orange strode into view.

"Hulloo, hulloo, Master Sparrow!" the man cried to Cinnamon without the least shock at such an unlikely creature in his house. "Master Pococo!" he heartily welcomed Freckle in his turn.

Rossamünd looked quizzically at the little bogle jostling beside him. *Pococo? How many names can one creature have!*

Freckle just squinted a grin at him and shrugged. "Many names from many namings of many peoples past . . ."

The man drew close, a cloud of consternation fleeting across his merry visage as he saw his more human, bedraggled and bloodied guests. "The embattled party arrives, beset but unthwarted and bearing the crimson trophies of victory!" He peered at Europe with cautious recognition. "You keep strange company these days, Master Sparrow!"

"Hello to thee, Master Mattern," the nuglung chirruped as Fransitart gave an almost self-conscious bow. "Wounded souls need needful rest and a hearth for heating."

"Rest and hearth they shall have, sir!" the fellow responded heartily, inviting them in further with a sweep of his arms.

Cinnamon carried Craumpalin down the passage, Fransitart hobbling after. Freckle helped him in his weariness, the glamgorn's bare feet going *slap-slap* on the cold slate.

"Good-eve-of-night to thee, Branden Rose!" The fellow addressed the fulgar cheerfully despite their intrusion. "You are the last manner of soul I would expect to find gracing our threshold. Needs press as the nicker drives, hmm?" He touched his nose knowingly. "City whispers of your change of heart bear out, I see."

"Should I know you?" Europe's eyes narrowed.

"Ah—not directly perhaps, gracious lady, but you may have chanced to read my works; Gaspard Plume, gentleman, historian and metrician, at your convenience." He bowed.

Even in his exhaustion, Rossamünd realized he had knowledge of this fellow, had read articles attributed to him in the better quality of his pamphlets.

"Indeed. Your *kitchen,* sir," Europe said, a hard edge to her voice.

"Ah. Absolutely . . . Fäbia!" he suddenly hollered, a shrill edge in his voice. "FÄBIA!" he called again as he took them down the right-hand junction at the end of the obverse hall.

With the attendant rustle of skirts, a woman joined in step, her small brown face and dark and intense eyes star-

425

tling among the general white of her high bonnet.

All the way Gentleman Plume called directions to staff somewhere in the house about them—and to anyone else who might be listening—for linen, blankets, tubs, hot water and towels. ". . . And some nice saloop and spiced toast to warm their gizzards and console their wind!"

Suddenly, through a short, pale green passage and up stone steps, they were in a long and rather antiquated kitchen. Surrounded by sturdy timber beams and immemorial stone, on a chest-stove stoked and hot for dinner, Rossamünd tested the much-desired plaudamentum in a great pot ready for some other task.

Rossamünd was only dimly aware of Europe leaning in fatigue on a highback chair behind him. When the treacle was done and poured into a side-handle soup bowl, his mistress barely waited for the thick black draught to cool before consuming it in one single unending swallow.

"My, my, *that* good, is it?" their gentleman host marveled. He took them now up some narrow backroom stairs to a broad landing of dark-paneled walls, the flapping of Freckle's wide feet sounding somewhere near.

Bearing a steaming pitcher together, the maid, the night-locksman and several other serving souls hurried past.

In the simple comfort of the large room granted him, Rossamünd found Fäbia about to pour him a bath. Too tired for proper washing, he asked instead for just a basin.

His leaden eyelids becoming irresistibly heavy, he managed only a perfunctory scrub of his face, quickly turning the water brown, before he could resist fatigue no longer.

Curling himself, proofing and all, on the spongy rug beside the bed, he fell fast asleep. In his slumber he had a dreamy notion of Freckle coming into the room to coo peaceful words as the glamgorn covered him with a blanket . . .

20

ORCHARD HARRIET

fistduke(s) common corruption of the Heil word "viskiekduzär"—pronounced "viss-KYK-doud-saar" and meaning "vicious souls"—troubardierlike soldiery who will happily turn sell-sword and often serve the darkest causes. Braving the crossing of the Gurgis Main, they are hardened fellows and a favorite among the black habilists of the Soutlands, serving as spurns and bravoes or in whatever capacity money's hand might prompt them. Though they are not regarded as true lesquins, neither are they of the mercenary foedermen rabble, but have their own ghastly and well-earned reputation.

ROSSAMÜND did not return to the waking world—he learned soon enough—until the middle of the morning two days later. Vision swimming and rebellious, his first focus was the wide, somber red canopy of a bed. The last he had known was the rough comfort of the floor. *Someone must have put me here.* Tipping his head back, his sight quickly resolved on Darter Brown settled on the post of the headboard above him, the faithful sparrow's eyes half closed.

"Hello . . . ," Rossamünd composed with sluggish tongue. "How did you get in?"

The sparrow's eyes went swiftly wide. He gave a joyful *chirrrup!* and circled twice under the ruby-hued canopy before alighting on covers spread over Rossamünd's chest, fluttering and blinking happily.

Smiling, the young factotum dozed for a moment, unmindful of where he was or why he was there, staring absently at the slot of sky and thickly lichened tiles glimpsed through broad wooden window frames. Large clean clouds scudded across the gap of blue. Cooing dove-song soothed his soul fraught with adventure, and for a time he just wallowed in the forgetfulness, sliding his limbs under the cozying touch of the crisp bed linen and breathing in deeply on the peculiarly tangy yet musky woody aroma that permeated the room . . . Only when he went to rub the tip of his itchy nose did he rediscover the odd leafy bandages that bound his hand and remember all the whys and wherefores of his current comfort.

Europe's treacle!

He sat up quickly, giving his side a sharp tweak and launching Darter Brown from his chest, fluttering just below the canopy and chirping in fright. It was then that he became aware of someone sitting in the corner of his vision by his bed: Europe, arms folded and legs crossed, reclined on a tandem. She was dressed not in her telltale red or magenta, but in a peculiar long-hemmed gown of deep green, collared with thick black feathers and figured with vines of lighter hue. With deft applications of rouges and creams from her fiasco, she seemed fresh and well. Faint amusement played across her mien as she regarded him serenely.

"Yes, I *did* make it myself, if that is what troubles you . . ."—Rossamünd knowing full well she meant her treacle—"Many times . . . ," she added archly as she pulled a bell rope that hung between her and the bed, her eyes glittering with more than she said.

Rossamünd eased himself back down. "How is Master Pin?" he asked as Fäbia entered with a rattle of crockery, bearing a late breakfast tray: steaming dollops of porridge, brooded new season rhubarb and a pitcher of fresh juice-of-orange—a drink he would forever associate with Europe and convalescence.

"He will mend," the fulgar sighed as she smoothed the unfamiliar folds on her lap. "And despite catching a cold—what he calls a *blighted catarrh*—Master Vinegar fraternizes with the residents when he's not watching over you or Master Salt or blowing his ever-running nose . . ."

"And . . . and Cinnamon?" Rossamünd asked carefully.

Darter Brown gave a *cheep!*

Europe waited, watching Fäbia until the housekeeper left. "As pleased as I am for the sparrow-bogle's help, I do not care to be its keeper. I am more concerned about the puncture in your flank."

Rossamünd looked up from his rhubarb brood. *Puncture?* He immediately felt his side and found a thick bandage there, bound about front and back. His first inclination was to take it off and see what manner of wound was beneath, yet Europe and spilling brood stopped him.

"It is a neat hole right through from front to back," his mistress explained. "One of those jackstraws must have found a gap in your proofing. I have witnessed lesser cuts kill a man . . ." She looked at him long, her eyes glinting strangely. "It is a convenient thing to suffer such a hurt and not be overly . . . *discomfited*."

Rossamünd made a motion somewhere between a shrug and a nod.

"You have native thew that I have had to pay a duke's fortune to gain, little man," the fulgar pressed. "I would value it if I were you."

For a beat, Rossamünd was sure he saw a twinkle of envy in her gaze. "I do" was his only reply.

"Good." Europe chuckled as if to change the subject. She folded her hands across her knees. "Knowing all that the butcher Swill could tell him, Maupin has himself seen, I would think, a handsome profit in your capture."

"Aye." Rossamünd suppressed a shiver, revulsion alloyed with a frank and primal anger. "And to get to me they sought to *kill* you."

"Hmm . . ." The fulgar's gaze turned inward. "Just another casualty to the vagaries of travel on the Empire's harried roads . . . I am sure that is how my cousin Brandenate would word it in his condoling missive to my mother."

"We ought to go to the Duke of Sparrows, Miss Europe!" he offered with little hope. "Cinnamon as good as gave an invitation—"

"I do not think the sparrow-duke will let such as I in his home, little man . . . Not even on your say-so."

Rossamünd looked unhappily to his rhubarb.

Europe continued to regard him closely. "You are in danger wherever you might hide, and bring the same on those who harbor you. Nevertheless, I do not hold you to my service," she remarked softly and a little coldly. "If you *wish* it, I shall release you and you may leave for such shelter as the sparrow-man and his lord might grant you—I have learned well enough to make my own treacle since you first entered my employ . . ."

Blinking at her, the young factotum smarted at the subtle bitterness in her words.

"For mine, however," the Duchess-in-waiting added, "I would say that you are safest with me."

He could not agree with her here; surely the Duke of Sparrows—like the Lapinduce—could keep whole nations at bay. Yet Rossamünd did not remonstrate. He did not truly think Europe would be granted sanctuary in the Sparrow Downs either. "I am your factotum, Miss Europe; my lot is with you, wherever you go."

"Bravo!" Europe smiled, warmly at first, then becoming hawkish. "There will be much *going,* Rossamünd, for it is my intent for us to rest here for a time, gather ourselves and then return to Brandenbrass, where I shall make you safer still. What a dark shock they will have when they find that I am yet alive," she observed almost happily, then blinked. "Now, I have questions for our gracious and wide-read host, Master Plume, beyond imposing upon him further—if you are up to it, you may join me."

Twisting his middle, Rossamünd declared he felt taut enough to move about.

"I shall await you in my room." Europe rose carefully against her own cracked frame and shut the door quietly behind her.

Perfumed by ancient timber paneling and cold slate, the interior of Orchard Harriet felt cavernous, empty but for the murmur of amused conversation sounding from somewhere deeper. The passage to their host's file high in the northeastern wing of the manor was direct enough, though it kinked strangely as its walls went from wood panels to tinted plaster to bare stone in the space of a few strides. Though Europe held good posture, her manifold hurts kept her to a commendably sturdy hobble, for which Rossamünd—stiff and sore all over—was supremely grateful, feeling very ungainly with his sharply pinching side and his borrowed wardrobe of light day-clothes a size too small.

Coming right about a corner and stepping down then up an odd double flight of steps—one wood, the other stone—Rossamünd froze . . . For there, lying serenely in the passage and snoring lightly before a solid door of mahogany, was the largest Derehund he had ever encountered. It was bigger even than the monstrous beasts that guarded the lamplighter keep of Wellnigh House on the Wormway.

Unperturbed, Europe stepped about the giant dog without another thought.

Sitting on Rossamünd's shoulder, Darter Brown did not fly off in boisterous alarm but remained, eyes squinting again in a partial doze.

Rossamünd, however, took a backward step.

The dog stirred and almost immediately became aware of him. Giving a start, it sprang to its feet and turned to face the young factotum, its shrewdly pallid eyes level to his own eye, its damp twitching nose to his nose, pinning him to the wall with its proximity. The beast did not bark or even growl; it just stared.

Rossamünd swallowed and tried to slide sideways, toward Europe.

"Come, Rossamünd," his mistress called curtly. "You can play with the creature after . . ."

"Ah-hah!" He heard Gaspard Plume's voice as the heavy door at the end of the passage sprang open. "Don't be minding Baltissär! He's everyone's friend ever since Master Sparrow mended him."

Though this sounded perfectly wondrous and excellent, Rossamünd's frequent bitter experience with dogs of this ilk was not so simply assuaged. He inched forward past the beast, expecting at any minute to find his head inside the massive, drooling jaws not three inches from his face. It was the profoundest relief to finally cross the threshold into their host's room.

"Shoo, sir!" Gaspard commanded the Derehund, blocking the dog's curiosity with his body. "You know you are not allowed in here, Baltissär. Go! Keep the mousers honest," he added, and shut the door on the creature's mournful face.

Rossamünd relaxed as his mistress and their host traded greetings.

"I must say I was diverted by your works on the Didodumese, Master Plume," Europe observed, smiling shrewdly. "I can understand why you might choose to live so remotely after that particular endeavor. I heard that certain families have put a price upon your learn-ed pate."

"Yes, well . . ." The historian blanched a trifle. "Truth has few friends, madam, but those who love her do so dearly and will pay with everything to keep her at liberty."

A large space made of two long rooms, Gentleman Plume's file was cramped with the clutter of a curious mind. At various corners were globes and ambit rings, stuffed animals under bell jars, a skull in the middle of a large drum table surrounded by rolls of charts—one held open by a vase containing a single enormous turnsole. There were plush elbow chairs, a turkoman for reading, and shelf upon shelf of more books than Rossamünd knew had been made. Any spare glimpses of the paneled wall were padded with rich red cloth, hung with ephemerides or daubed with loose yet exquisite paintings of animals of the common sorts, the style of the artist familiar to Rossamünd.

Flanked by a massive chest of map drawers on one side and a tall bench with an equally tall stool on the other, Gentleman Plume's enormous desk dominated the second room. Behind it, draping the wall above a crackling hearth, was a large painted web of reds and golds, umbers and whites. Covering the chimney breast, it showed circles within squares within circles written over with the names of the eight winds, the old Phlegmish months, the skold's formula AOWM, and the obsolete appellations for the three original continents. A cunctus orbis, Mister Plume complacently called it—an ancient chart of the known world at the time of the Phlegms.

Painted and stitched with staggering precision, it had, as Rossamünd could see, the great city *Phlegmis* marked with a red star in its midst, the center of the world.

435

By the open southern window a glossy pied daw sat upon a wooden perch above a pan of grit, ogling the arrivals with shrewd yellow eyes. Giving a feisty twitter, Darter Brown shot up to Rossamünd's crown to stare and ruffle his feathers, little claws prickling at the young factotum's scalp.

"That is a fine wee bird on your skull, young sir," Plume suddenly said to him, nodding to Darter Brown. "Is it properly . . . *trained*?" he asked frankly. "Guano about the house and down one's back is not a good show, I would think."

Rossamünd blinked. He had never given the notion any thought. "I do not know, sir. He came to me out of the wilds just as he is."

"It is a rare thing for a fellow to have such a spontaneously loyal creature," Plume observed shrewdly. "You are fortunate to be held in this regard . . . He may share a perch with Pig if he wishes"—Plume indicated the daw—"should he need."

Pig, the pied daw, blinked at hearing its name.

"Uh . . . Aye, sir . . ."

"Mister Plume, you are vaunted as a man of many parts," Europe interjected after further brief pleasantries, taking a high-backed seat before the man's spreading desk. "Do you recognize this?" She produced the four-barred mask of the Featherhead chieftain, its fastening ribbons trailing from it. "Its owner was among our attackers." She gave a brief account of the ambush, shifting a little painfully in her seat as she made mention of blows delivered and received.

"Mmm, mighty deeds done at our very door." Plume chuckled gravely, tilting his head knowledgeably, turning the mask over and over. "Still, a good neighbor is better than a distant relative, and any soul in sore need sorely needs a neighbor! You are healing, m'lady?"

"As well as pith allows," she replied with an impatient twirl of her fingers. "What of the mask, sir?"

The genial fellow blinked tolerantly at her. "*This,* good lady, is the dial of a Grammaticar of a sept of the Seven Seven cult." He paused as if the gravity of his statement was obvious. "The Seven Seven are of the worst false-god adorants; worshippers of Sucathës, ruthless and bloodthirsty and all that . . . Fond of entering into a fight drunk on sanguinary draughts . . ."

Little wonder then they were so heedless! Rossamünd's thoughts must have shown on his face, for Plume beamed at him gratefully, glad to have affected at least one of his listeners.

"They are bad company to have at your tail, I am afraid, m'dear," Plume continued, "and here you have gone and done in one of their most senior members." He paused. "It ought be hoped you have annihilated this local sept, else they will come, hunt and find you . . ."

"I am not agitated by some local fictlers, sir," Europe replied, unmoved.

"Ah, yes, of course . . . Your confidence does you credit, madam; you are an ornament to your profession!" The historian cleared his throat. "As for the wildmen you describe, they are most likely to be the Widden—or so they call themselves, after their forebears. They are eastern Piltdowners, still embittered a thousand years on at the conquests of the Burgundians, of the Tutelarchs, of their western and southern Pilt brethren, using long history as an excuse for all kinds of brigandry . . ."

"I hope we have not brought undue threat to your house, Mister Plume," Rossamünd said in increasing concern.

The historian smiled. "Master Cannelle will have brought you unobserved and unfollowed. If it comes to it, we have seen such as them off before."

"You fought bandits from this house, sir?" Rossamünd gaped.

Gentleman Plume gave him a knowing wink. "I believe Mister Gutter, our resident playwright and sometime composer, is attempting to work a variety of the salient event into his second operetta."

Europe smiled patiently. "And the heavy warriors in the horn-ed casques?"

GASPARD PLUME

"Tüngid viskiekduzär," the historian said without hesitation. "From Dzïk on the southernmost edges of Heilgolund!" He sniffed and shook his head. "The Widden! The Seven Seven! Fistdukes!" He let the import of this list linger, a grim and learned grimace twitching on his lips.

"And that reddleman," Rossamünd inserted.

"Reddleman?" Plume's eyes sparkled bemusedly.

"Yes," Europe answered with a heavy sigh. "An agent of my foes, I would expect, disguised as a madder dye-seller."

"While we went by carriage," the young factotum expanded, "he was on foot pushing a cart, yet he kept watch on us the whole way from Brandenbrass to the ambush."

"Ahh, likely a brinksman," Plume said knowingly, adding at Rossamünd's obvious bafflement, "a person who uses sanguinary draughts to an extreme so they might do such feats as chase a horse and carriage all across a parish and back." He returned his sagacious attention to the Duchess-in-waiting. "You have certainly locked horns with someone possessing substantial grasp, Lady Rose!"

"Indeed, sir," the fulgar returned.

Plume drew in a noisy breath. "Still, in it all, it is a most fortunate thing to have the friendship of so blithely and potent a fellow as Cannelle."

Europe crooked her spoored brow and regarded Plume with narrow calculation.

The historian gave a gentle cough. "Dare I ask how *you* of all the people in the world, gracious Lady Rose, came to gain it? Or," he said hastily before Europe—her eyes flashing dangerously—could catch a breath to answer, "if I may say, it

440

comes as only small surprise, if the peculiar rumors of you that have made it even to us are to be countenanced . . ."

Europe bridled. "The set of my heart is mine alone to know, sir." She looked long at Plume. "It is clear you yourself are not to be troubled by such *rumors*."

"Indeed not, ma'am," the gentleman replied with a long, affirming nod. "And, if I might, m'lady, neither, it appears, are you . . ."

A bitter smile fluttered on Europe's lips. "Events of recent months have allowed me to consider anew the possible finer distinctions of monster-kind . . ."

"Ahh, yes." The historian nodded musingly. "The teratological complot—teratologists who seek to serve man and monster both."

The fulgar's gaze narrowed. "It would be a . . . *mistake,* sir, to state my position so blankly."

"Oh . . ." Gentleman Plume quickly schooled his mien to something a little less knowing. Repose quickly returning, the fellow leaned back in this chair. "How-be-it, if Master Cannelle associates with you so readily, then so shall we . . . Please continue as our most honored guests in this our modest haven of learning and enlightenment for as long as you have need."

In the bright cool of a clear afternoon, Amonias Silence and Spedillo returned from a morning excursion in their small sturdy carriage to the scene of the ambuscade, there to retrieve what they might of the four adventurers' chattels.

"We call the place Step Dribble," Mister Silence explained,

giving his account to the Duchess-in-waiting as she reclined with Rossamünd and Fransitart before the fire in her vasty guest room. "It is an obvious site for a trap, m'lady—by all evidence it was a mighty fight," he said with a pointed look of admiration to his listeners as Spedillo hauled in a trunk.

The fulgar nodded graciously.

"I am sorry to report that there were scant pickings," Silence went on. "Just the heaviest trunks and a farrago of matchwood that may once have been a fine cart of expensive fit. All of it has been picked over, horses and tackle taken, the fallen gone . . . We were desirous to remain and investigate but were encouraged to egress at the advent of several sullen, thick-browed gents, most probably associates of your original assailants," he concluded ominously. "I am sorry I could not be more illuminating."

With an uncurling of her fingers, Europe dismissed the fellow with a soft, "I thank you, sir."

That evening Europe and Fransitart and Rossamünd were invited to join Gentleman Plume and the rest of the household in a "grand supper," or so he named it. Going by back stairs, Rossamünd squeezed among the steaming and savory bustle of the kitchen—on the cusp of serving the first remove—to test. It was slow going, his hands stiff and unresponsive, but he got the treacle made. He returned via those same servants' steps to find his mistress already gone down to dine, and Fransitart with her. Craumpalin was left to sleep, chin to bosom, hoary beard lying out along his chest.

442

A biggin of plaudamentum in hand and changed into a glossy suit recovered from the wreck, Rossamünd descended the broad sweep of staircase that went down from the landing to a wide hall of old dark wood and white marble below. Following ears and nose, he easily navigated the narrow passages, passing closed doors and silent rooms to find his destination: an enormous dining hall of stone and tall, narrow windows to rival the banqueting palace of some fabled heathen king. Its walls were lined with many grand paintings, the grandest of all a vast fantastico of an ancient political scene strung above the mighty stone fireplace at the right end of the long space. On the hearth rug lay Baltissär, staring with hungry restraint at a whole gaggle of unknown souls who sat about a long oval dining table in the very midst of the hall. Their hubble-bubble filled the space as they chatted with happy animation among the candlesticks, glass and silverware.

Every attention turned expectantly to Rossamünd's arrival. The young factotum fumbled for a moment as he tried to take the entire scene in at once, until he spotted Fransitart, red-nosed, turning in his chair to see him come in, and beyond the old salt, Europe peering at him impassively. Sitting regally at the seat of honor, she was dressed in her more usual coat of brilliant scarlet hide rescued that very day from the wreck of the landaulet.

"Welcome to our Great Refectory, sir!" Gentleman Gaspard Plume greeted him from the other end of the board. "The timing of your stomach is impeccable! Late lunch—or epicibals, as we delight to call it," he added with a perceptive wink to his other guests, "is upon the very brink of being laid. Join us, fine fellow, join us!"

Rossamünd bowed confusedly, and a seat was found for him between Europe on the left and Amonias Silence on the right, the amanuensis looking fine in a soutaine of glossy gray and high starched collar and neckerchief of pristine white.

Taking her plaudamentum from him, the fulgar arched a reassuring brow.

As the first remove was served—pottage fancy, fresh rye cobs and pitchers of new spring water—Rossamünd was graciously introduced to the other sitters spaced widely about the enormous oval table. First among them, to Gentleman Plume's right, was a broad fellow with a famous name: Warder All, metrician and wilder, a man seeking "to preserve nature in *all* its pristine splendor against the unceasing, uglifying cicurations of everyman"—or so their host proclaimed. Clad in a sturdy proofed frock coat of a surprisingly delicate pink and a white-powdered bag-wig, he had arrived from Brandenbrass that very afternoon. "He spends far too much of his time petitioning the Archduke to treat the wild spaces kindly, but today has finally seen reason and come to hide here before he takes up a survey expedition to Thisterland. What is more, my fine fellow!"— Gentleman Plume turned to properly address the subject of his introduction with undiluted pleasure. "You have brought us krebin from the darksome east and oyster too—not pickled in Patriarch's Pond, mind, but fresh plucked from their native beds at the bottom of the Branden Roads, dulcified and put in ice from the floes of Heilgolund!"

Regarding Rossamünd with serene countenance, Warder All dipped his head in cool greeting.

Next to the wilder metrician was a cultivated woman in a high-collared jacket of deep viridian who wore her ginger hair up in a simple braided club as a man might. Pluto Six was her name—a name as recognizable to Rossamünd as Warder All. One of the permanent lodgers at Orchard Harriet, she was a frequent illustrator of the very pamphlets and gazettes Rossamünd preferred.

She welcomed him with a soft, precisely pronounced, "Well-a-day."

Rossamünd was ashamed to admit he had previously thought her a man, and inclined his head part in courtesy, part to hide the flush in his cheeks.

Next—and looking vaguely uncomfortable among so many people of higher station—came Fransitart. "Whom I am certain you know right well already," said Plume with a wink. Abruptly the ex–dormitory master sneezed into a cloth. "Beggin' ye pardon, me masters . . . ," he muttered, dabbing his nose.

Beside him and directly across from Rossamünd sat a man with a delicate face and resplendent in a broad-lapeled coat of dark silver blue, his rich black hair curled and long like a wig.

"Hesiod Gutter!" he said in introduction. "Playwright—though not of those awful populist pantos, mind." He reached across the table to vigorously shake Rossamünd's hand. "Manly grip!" he declared approvingly. "Excellent. Well met, sir."

"Our H. Gutter also dabbles in opera," Gaspard continued, smirking ever so slightly, "though don't let that dissuade you from further association with him."

Unfathoming at what must have been some private jape, Rossamünd smiled anyway, not in the least dissuaded.

"And here is your mistress, favoring us so with her company." Their host beamed to Europe, who smiled mildly in return.

Beyond Mister Silence, on Rossamünd's right, sat a solemn fellow. Though he was clothed in simpler workman's buffs and bore a gloomy aspect, his eyes were very much the mirror of Gentleman Plume's own.

"This is my elder brother, Philemon, Lord Plume, twenty-fifth Count of Windspect Folia, Master of Temburly Hall," Gaspard said finally.

Swaying a little, the Count of Windspect Folia blinked at Rossamünd languidly. There was something unhinged yet percipient in his look, and the young factotum thought for just a moment he was beholding Numps.

"Always a delight to have one of your tribe to dine," the Count said bluntly, blurring his words. "However, you will have to excuse Cannelle and little Pococo; they have had to go . . ." He leaned in a little, and with stage whisper added, "Urgent business." The Count then returned his attention to the crystal tumbler of thick dark red liquid he revolved slowly in his hand.

Their host, his younger brother, peered at him sadly for an inkling. Pointing open-handed to Rossamünd, he went on, undeterred. "And this is Rossamünd Bookchild, factotum to our other honored guest, the Branden Rose, and friend to our *ancient* friends . . . Rossamünd is correct, is it not?" Gaspard inquired, putting a little too much emphasis on the final vowel.

Rossamünd nodded. "Aye, sir."

"Not a name you want to get wrong, ey . . ."

"Ah, no, sir."

Introductions done, Plume asked Warder All to approve the meal.

"Let us give ponder to the unmerited bounty of nature . . . ," the metrician began with an impressively deep voice. He lowered his gaze and the other guests went silent.

Decidedly uncomfortable, Europe peered at Mister All with narrow scrutiny.

The memorial was brief, the eating long and conversation longer, ranging from the merits of one composer against another, one pen against another, one fabulist against another—each interlocutor clearly possessing his or her favorite.

For all their animation and easy familiarity, the dining talkers seemed wary of Europe—Warder All most of all. He appeared perplexed, and kept staring at her, his perceptive gray eyes clouded with bemused calculations.

In her turn, the Duchess-in-waiting spoke freely enough with those closest to her. As they waited for the second remove to be laid—spinach egg pie and grass-wine, maybe one of Monsiere Trottinott's own vintages—their host suddenly called her attention to the gigantic painting hung above the fire behind her.

447

"A recent purchase of mine," Gaspard said happily.

The whole party turned to look.

Framed in ponderous gilt, it showed an indomitable woman clad in peacock green and a splaying aura of feathers, proudly extending her hand to a wild yet magnificent-looking fellow knelt before her. Armored in buff and hide and fur, he bore an equally princely manner despite his genuflection. Standing amid the flotsam of just-won battle, the two were surrounded by a crowd of souls in ancient clothes, each showing a different face to the moment: grief, reverence, wonder. A well-dressed group of sages among the queen's own retinue had heads together in sly deliberation. A brazen plaque beneath read "Idaho the Great Receives Tribute from the King of Lethe."

"The Neo-Athic school, I believe," Hesiod Gutter observed.

"Completely correct, sir!" Gaspard concurred then continued, perhaps a little too chattily, to his illustrious guest. "Do you mark that rather martial-looking woman, madam, standing so alertly just behind the immortal empress?"

Slowly twisting in her seat to gaze more fully upon the image, Europe nodded.

Rossamünd nodded as he examined the impressive figure standing between the historied empress and her now infamous band of scheming advisers. Wielding a long-bladed spear, the woman was clad in a thick hackle of leonguile hide over a white laminated lorica and beneath this a wide skirt of red. On her head was a high bronze helm crested with black-and-white-striped horsehair, and red-and-white checks covering the crown. This casque was pushed back to reveal a sweet-faced woman, her ruby cheeks at odds with her warlike attire and soldierly stance.

I believe that is your ancient beldame," their host explained, unable to hide a tinge of pride at this revelation. "Eurodice, Speardame to Idaho, progenitrix—so the records have it—of Naimes' governing family line."

"Indeed it is, sir," Europe returned evenly, but offered nothing more; so started, the conversation promptly returned to its usual topics.

It may have been a trick of the eye, but Rossamünd reckoned a filial resemblance between the daubed, long-dead heldin dame and the living one who sat so close to him now.

"I am sorry to hear, Madam Rose, that you were attacked," declared the composer, Hesiod Gutter, upon the arrival of the third remove—spatched partridge in oyster jusine and blanched asparagus. "For all its grim reputation, ours is typically a pleasant spot in this wicked world."

"Wicked indeed, sir," the Branden Rose returned, inclining her head.

"Aye," Fransitart spoke up. "Especially when fictlers are sent out into it."

"Them fictlers is nowt but trouble . . ." Spedillo—who happened to be serving the ex–dormitory master at that very moment—interjected with compulsive severity, his masters not seeming to mind his exclamation one bit.

"Hear, hear!" Hesiod Gutter banged the table in passionate approbation.

"They seek to rid the world of nickers through the rising of the false-gods," Pluto Six declaimed, "yet even the most simply read in matter knows of the universal devastation a risen false-god will bring to all creatures: monsters, beasts *and* men!"

"What does it matter if some people choose to worship Lobe or Sucathës or Ninelap or *any* of the other however many score there are meant to be?" Gentleman Plume insisted, playing the part of contradictor. "They and their kind are far more powerful than those subject to them; as great as a man is to an ant. One so clearly superior might be said to deserve obeisance."

"Perhaps . . . ," Warder All countered, "but Lobe and all the false-gods are creatures just as we and no more able to determine our ultimate future than the ant over whom *we* have such apparent mastery. Indeed, we would do well to follow the ant's example, who does not give gigantic man glory or service, but maintains busy industry in the path set by Providence."

"Ah, spare us talk of Providence!" Gutter protested. "Arrant befuddling dribble . . . Leave it to the eekers, sir!" He grinned to soften the genuine intent of his words.

"What of you, Mister Fransitart?" Gaspard called. "You are a creature of the vinegar; how say you on the false-gods?"

Fransitart cleared his throat, as if he were about to address a room of marine society children. "Some lads scrawl themselves with their signs thinkin' it makes 'em safe against the nadderers, but those who reckon they've seen such false ones out in th' gurgis speak like they ne'er would want to again. That's enough for me, sir."

"Hear, hear!" was the general accord, much to the old dormitory master's satisfaction.

At the laying of the fourth remove—char-seared spit lamb and honey-roasted taters—Warder All stunned them all with the revelation that the Emperor was soon to arrive in the Soutlands upon a rare summer pageant. "He brings his youngest heir to show to we simple southern folk. And to commemorate this infrequent coming forth, the dear fellow has gone and changed the order of the arbustral months, citing his heir's name—Iudus Haacobin Manangës, or *Jude*—as a more fitting name for the month in which they intend to travel." To the general disbelief he presented a pristine bill properly authenticated with a madder note of Ol' Barny, the Imperial Owl.

"What month does that put us in now?" asked Gaspard, puzzled.

"We are in Unxis still, and Orio stays where it should," Hesiod Gutter explained, currently holding the offending bill. "Three days from now though, watch your hats! We will be in Narcis as if it is the end of the year, but no! One month still to come, poor once-forgotten Jude."

Rossamünd shook his head. He knew of the change made four centuries ago by Moribund Sceptic III for the sake of his truculent daughter—certain folks still spoke in consternation on it—but to actually witness such power to change even the very months was bafflingly impressive. One word from the Emperor and the whole world shifted. Surely he had better, more important tasks than making

451

alterations to the calendar that served no useful purpose at all.

Orio, Unxis, Narcis, Jude.

This new order, however, did have a more lyrical ring.

"Pettifogging poppicockery!" their host branded it hotly.

"An astonishing waste of paper and attention," agreed Warder All. "The Archduke spoke none too kindly of it in my seminar with him . . ."

"Them ink-drinking quill-lickers got nought better to do up in Clementine than burden us with needless change," Fransitart observed, to table-thumping approval.

"What other useless novelties do you bring from the city, sir?" asked Gentleman Plume.

"The usual wind of idle tongues," the metrician said with a quick and peculiar look to Europe, "which I will not bore you with here. However, among the oddities, Gyve's was only last week hosting lectures by an unknown yet patently well-connected habilist by the name of Swill or Swillings or the like. His obscurity matched only by his enthusiasm, the fellow was insisting that he has discovered a new *omilia* of teratoid."

Though master of his outer self, Rossamünd's innards twisted sharply. He became still, the better to listen carefully. *How would this be received?*

"Truly?" Plume breathed. "Has he identified a friend or a foe, I wonder?"

"Friend, I would hope," Warder All answered, then continued. "This fellow insisted on calling them *manikins*— monsters in an everyman's form, come from the muds just as some have posited üntermen do."

452

"What is novel about that?" Amonias Silence spoke. "Hasn't he heard of old Biargë?"

"Ah, yes, but this Swillings fellow seemed to think they are more than just some vinegar's cant; he held that they were living with us now."

"Well, that would certainly put the fox among the pullets." Gentleman Plume smirked.

"Or a pullet among foxes," Pluto said quietly.

Rossamünd peered through his brows at her gratefully.

"Swill, you say?" Hesiod tapped his chin ruminatively with a fork. "I was reading only yesterday in a *Mordant Mercer* of very recent publication that connects a fellow with such a name very unfavorably to the dark trades . . ."

Warder All made a noncommittal gesture. "Unsavory connections or no, the man went so far as to wave about some sanguine mark on his arm, saying that it was a cruorpunxis made with the blood of such a creature."

Rossamünd's ears began to ring and his vision vibrate.

Swill had done more than punct Fransitart. *He has marked himself!*

At last the young factotum shot a look to his mistress. To everyone else her face would have been nothing but attentive and serene. Yet to Rossamünd it was clear in the deeps of her eyes that her mind turned upon darker thoughts, and he knew then that their return to Brandenbrass would indeed be a violent one.

21

LIVING BY ANOTHER'S LEAVE

capstan songs lively tunes—what we would call "shanties"—a product of the harshness of sea-board life, at times bawdy but always very sing-able, sung by vinegaroons in any group labor such as hauling up the anchor or winding the capstan of a ram or other vessel. A new tune might make its way into common society and flourish there for a brief moment in pantos and tavern rounds, eventually returning to the obscurity of naval culture.

ETERMINED as she was to return to Brandenbrass and have at her antagonists, Europe was not fit enough for such a confrontation, nor was Craumpalin well enough for the journey. Though in truth it vexed her, the Branden Rose submitted to the scholarly security and unending comfort of Orchard Harriet until the four travelers had sufficiently recuperated. "A hasty step is ever a misstep," she said the next morning after the Grand Supper, sharing breakfast with Rossamünd in her room. "I can wait . . ."

Unaware of Rossamünd's injured flank, Gentleman Plume invited him for a stroll about "O' Harriet"—as the historian was fond of calling it. In the midst of the wooded hills, the manor itself was a peculiar conglomeration of found stone, dressed slabs, fired brick, aged timber. The main portion at the northern end was clearly the remains of an old fortress, with turrets, loophole windows and crenellated wall, a section at the back actually collapsed and unused, crawling with creeping vines and spangled with brilliant orange pumpkin flowers. Additions were built in stages over many centuries, completed with different processes and materials and scant regard for the manner of construction of the previous parts.

"Not the most attractive of structures, I'll grant you," Gentleman Plume admitted as they walked. "Its story is long and rather obscure, but it makes a perfectly excellent hiding hole and, properly fitted, is as snug as any fine city hall."

Nestled in the forested valley between great bald hills, this confused homey mass of stones sat among a field of turnsoles, surrounded by thick groves of blossoming fruiting trees. At the north end flowed a swift stream, its made banks dense with a narrow wood of beech and plane.

Despite Philemon Plume's vague hints about their departure, Rossamünd peered about in hope of Freckle or Cinnamon yet emerging. Upon the young factotum's inquiry the younger Plume declared himself at a loss.

"Neither of them has shown himself since two days gone," he mused. "That is ever their way, my boy—to come unbidden and leave inexplicably. Where they have got to, you can be sure it is needful."

Every morning Rossamünd would fright awake from rushing visions of masked perils and snarling, sermonizing jackstraws. Only after long moments would he feel with relief the warm and downy softness and fathom that his tarrying alarm was but the work of dreams' unruly vapors. With every new day he would inspect his wounds, observing in wonder the rapidity of their healing until he kept his flank and hand bandaged only to avoid intelligent questions. As friendly to monsters as these goodly folk might have been, they did not need to know that it was *him* about whom Swill was conducting controversial lectures.

Steadily—slowly—Craumpalin's legs knitted and he became more lucid; Fransitart's cold cleared, his bruises diminished. The bloom returned to Europe's cheeks, and a grim resolve set itself in her eye.

Most evenings Gentleman Plume would gather everyone in a large drawing room to share the fruits of their toils. Gaspard himself might read his day's theorizing. Pluto would show a particularly excellent drawing from her daily observations. Hesiod Gutter typically had them all take parts in the back-and-forth of his latest scene, or play upon the pianoforte a passage of a movement from his long-awaited second operetta. Amonias Silence usually graced them with doggerel or a sonnet penned in moments between pages of the Gentleman Plume's dictations:

> There was a young lady from Flint,
> Accused as a cold-hearted bint.
> She took a hot coal,
> And swallowed it whole;
> From then on she spoke with a glint.

Even Fäbia performed once, playing a cheerful tune with

456

marvelous dexterity upon a guittern, the lively unusual music at odds with the fixedly somber expression of the player.

Encouraged to the brink of discourtesy, the guests were prevailed upon to participate; Fransitart dared something Rossamünd had never known him do and sang a brief selection of mildly bawdy capstan songs, each one popular enough to have the whole room chanting, thumping tables and clapping along. Beetroot-red and feeling very bland, Rossamünd did the only thing he could think of, and shared definitions from a five-year-old peregrinat he had found in Gentleman Plume's well-stocked library.

"An excellent fact, sir!" Gaspard would utter, which he or Silence or Gutter would then enlarge on or correct.

To Rossamünd's profound amazement, Europe consented just once to take her turn on the pianoforte. Brow slightly creased in concentration, head erect, frame upright, she proceeded to play a strong and sweetly flowing piece.

"Ahh, *Phoebus Sonora in D minor*." Hesiod Gutter smiled warmly, tipping his glass of viscous, dark purple sirope in approbation. "What evening would be complete without a bit of Quillion?"

Europe played on, her eyes almost closing as she dared let the passion of the music have her, the melody transforming into a peculiarly melancholy second movement, then shifting pleasingly to a strident yet fitting finale. When she was finished, amid applause and commendations she returned to her tandem seat with a dignified air as if nothing had happened.

457

Philemon Plume would contribute only his presence to a night's diversions, sitting on an easy chair by the hearth, clutching an ever-present tumbler, a melancholy half smile rarely leaving his lips. Frequently, he would stare fixedly at a painting above the mantelshelf, an image of an unknown woman with bright face, lively eyes and raven-dark hair. Sometimes he would even raise his glass to it in sad salute to this mysterious absent lady.

At the start of their second week of secluded convalescence—early in the month now named Narcis—Rossamünd stood one morning in the main sitting room admiring a painting. A true original by Student, it depicted martial men handing other martial men a wad of wax-and-ribbon-endorsed paper, all looking out at the viewer with lofty expressions.

He sighed long-sufferingly.

Behind him, Europe sat by the broad sitting-room windows, wrapped in a coverlet and brooding over her ledger and a slowly accumulating collection of missives. Through the help of the ever-cheerful Amonias Silence or the ever-grumpy Spedillo trotting between Orchard Harriet and Coddlingtine Dell, the fulgar had managed to get several cryptically addressed messages out to various agents in the city and had that very day received replies.

"I am making designs for our return" was all she said on the matter.

She would not allow Rossamünd to see what she wrote, yet kept him close should she need an errand run. These were not frequent, and so he spent much of his day looking at the great variety of paintings hung here and throughout the grand manor.

Passing through on a task of her own, Pluto hesitated, and, approaching Rossamünd, politely remarked on his fascination with the image. "Would you care to join me out in the woods and vales to wander and draw?" she suddenly asked.

Rossamünd declared that he very much would, and, careful to take his leave of Europe, he left her to her secretive plans.

Going forth in a heavy proofed long-coat of sage green and glossy copstain stuck with the feather of some mighty hunting bird, Pluto also took a two-barreled hauncet in holster at her hip. She advised Rossamünd to do the same, and he proceeded in frock coat and weskit, and brought his digitals too. Giving him a small card-covered drafting folio and a stylus of his own, the fabulist took him roaming through combes tangled with only partly tamed pine woods and myrtle copses, to see, to draw, and climb the high bald hills to look east out over the pallid waters of the distant Grume. Tiniest oblong shapes, barely discernible, seemed to bob and twinkle distantly out on the waves, squadrons of rams and convoy of cargoes on their way to or from Fayelillian.

Immersed in the joy of leaf and branch and singing birds, Rossamünd near forgot his cares as Pluto shared her delight for all the humble things, pointing out the names of everything she knew the names for—weeds and bugs and fallen feathers from the great variety of woodland birds that twittered and dived and scooted above, welcoming Darter Brown among them with song.

Following her lead, Rossamünd pressed flowers medicinal and ornamental within the pages of his compleat or applied himself to her patient instructions to draw with a frustrating lack of success in his drafting book. Oftentimes they would lie staring down at tadpoles dancing in a pond or insect larvae playing for life in a tiny runnel chattering down the stony shoulder of some hill. On other occasions they would watch transfixed at safe distance azure-crowned asps or great dun snakes belly across one of the many obscure paths Pluto knew, or stand among a flurry of tiny lavender moths feeding on the pollens of the little white flowers that festooned the wild turf of the wooded hills. Many times they would sit on a highland meadow to gaze up at the wondrous shapes made in the vapors above by the large white springtime clouds and just breathe the curative, untrammeled aromas. Every day they ate lunch together in a small glade of tiny white flowers that grew at the base of a cliff higher up the valley.

"Oh, Rossamünd! If only people could behold the native wonder of humble things!" Pluto would cry in her precise, kindly voice that Rossamünd could have listened to for hours. "See how perfectly the seeds hang from the brome stalk! See the exquisite construction of the legs on that emperorfly! Or that pillboy working with such patient industry on his rotten log!"

If she could, the fabulist would hold up the honored item to him until she was satisfied Rossamünd could see what she saw, and then set about drawing it with rapid yet remarkable accuracy from as many poses as the thing would allow before it crawled away.

PLUTO SIX

This was the stripe of adventure he preferred, out among the earth and sap, in quiet, wondering awe. Many times Rossamünd wished he might stay for good, away from strife and vengeance, half hoping that Cinnamon would return so that he could go with him into the uncomplicated wilds.

"Pluto?" he asked as they sat one morning upon a gray lichen-grown rock protruding from the naked northern slopes above the Harriet. "Have you ever killed a soul?"

Staring out at windy hills and wooded vales, the fabulist thought long before answering. "I may have . . . Yes." Her eyes narrowed in contemplation. "Twice have we been put upon here at the Harriet, as its denizens called it. By desperate brigand bands of Widden-folk, and twice have I joined the defense, shooting from windows, but I never was certain of the fall of my shot." She sighed heavily. "If it is a choice between keeping my friends in peace or letting them suffer malice and violation, then I will always choose the former. My foe would surely have to accept fair portion of culpability if in bringing murder and violence to my door they find themselves hurt or killed in their turn. The moment a foe attacks you, whether they acknowledge it or no, they implicitly accept that you might best them and they instead might well die. In such event you—or *I*—surely hold no blame." She beheld him with a sad and thoughtful look. "Have *you*, Rossamünd?"

Bitter memories of those men he had felled only a few days before repeated like a series of flashes in his mind's eye. Bowing his head, Rossamünd nodded. "Aye."

Pluto clucked her tongue. "So young to learn the bitter truth of adventure's cost," she said with a rueful sigh.

To this the young factotum did not know what to say. "A foundling has no fancy," he offered finally.

The fabulist smiled at him sympathetically. "A soul does what a soul must," she concurred, and returned her attention to her drawing.

Eventually Rossamünd did the same.

Pluto took him out on most clear days, going greater distances with each new excursion. Yet on sudden rainy, miserable days that would sweep in from the Grume—driven north by the spring storms out in the wider gulf of the Pontus Canis—and make excursions out in the natural wonders impossible, Pluto insisted that the young factotum sit for his portrait.

"You shall take the finished canvas with you," she said, "or I shall have it sent to you if it is not completed in time . . ."

Rossamünd found himself sat, boots dangling, on a tall stool in the fabulist's high, stony painting room—her aletry. Found at the back of Orchard Harriet, its walls were perforated with a great many windows, its thick roof beams hung with all manner of mirrors on cables and guys that could be tilted to give the fabulist the right kind of light. Every corner or gap was stacked with canvasses already stretched and waiting to hold pictures; the very air was saturated with strong waxy odors of pigments and the volatile pungence of thinning oils.

Dressed in his fine yet clearly bruised harness cleaned

as best as possible, Rossamünd was told gently but firmly to remain still and quiet as Pluto stood before him, palette in arm and gripping a posy of brushes, to work intently behind a great easel bearing a modest canvas. Rossamünd did his utmost to fulfil this request, using his experience from standing long in pageants-of-arms to keep hand and arm, rump and foot from cramping or falling asleep.

At times the fabulist would draw her arm in wide expressive arcs or lean in and dab assiduously for what seemed an interminable time, constantly standing back to squint fixedly and tilt her head in critical regard of her labor.

Roosting high in the rafters, Pig the pied daw watched on, startling them both by swooping down upon the lizards that crawled the walls and the rodents that scurried in dark corners. Pluto would scold the bird, shouting at it, "You rat with wings!" as it upset pots and tools in its quest for food. Each time it would retreat to its lofty roost to peer at them smugly, some fat rodent or plump reptile in its stocky bill. Darter Brown joined them too, a quieter observer, restlessly swapping perches from Rossamünd's head to the top of the easel to up beside Pig.

Especially attentive, Baltissär—as friendly and as placid as he might be—was *not* allowed in. Whimpering, the beast peered mournfully at Rossamünd through the speedily diminishing gap of the closing aletry door.

"He normally reserves such silliness for Pococo or Master Sparrow," the fabulist said. "*What use is a tykehound who is fond of tykes?* as Mister Gutter likes to jest."

"How is it possible?" Rossamünd asked.

"Master Cinnamon civilized him . . . and saved his life too." Pluto became suddenly sad and inward. "It was when . . . when poor Philemon's dear wife, the . . . the Countess was . . . was taken, snatched by some wretchling nicker from the very steps of their home at Temburly Hall near on a decade ago. Baltissär fought in her defense but could not save her. By chance or Providence or the turnings of Droid—or whatever you might care to name such functions by—Cinnamon came along, too late to deliver the countess Plume, but in time to preserve this cheeky fellow here." The fabulist patted the unhappy dog on the crown before finally shutting the door. "He—like his master—has never been the same since . . . How I wish you might have known the Count and Countess before . . . before; *she* was like a clear day in winter and the truest of friends, *he* was a man of information and letters, taught in many obscure things and able to teach in turn." She looked at the brushes clustered in her hand.

"How is it you can call any monster friend after that, Miss Six?" Rossamünd dared quietly.

"Do you hate your friends because you were attacked by other men?" the fabulist returned.

Rossamünd opened his mouth, hesitated, shook his head.

Pluto regarded him gravely, then quickly brightened. "A cheerier face, please, Master Bookchild—I'll not paint you with such a pensive mien, sir."

At the end of each occasion he sat, Rossamünd would ask to see his portrait, and each time Pluto refused.

"Only when it is done," she insisted, and remained po-

465

litely obdurate over the subsequent painting days, covering the image with a strapped-down sheet of leather and locking the door to her aletry when the day's daubing was complete.

As time went on, Fransitart occasionally joined them out on their walks. It was clear the simple life did well for him, and he often set Pluto to bright laughter with the more agreeable of his salty stories.

Europe, however, kept her slow needful constitutionals close to the manor and absorbed herself in the scheme for their return. Impatient to recover, the Duchess-in-waiting had Rossamünd test for her—and Craumpalin too—all manner of little-used mending draughts, or sent to the kitchens for whatever hearty and balancing broths they could conjure. So ambitious was she to heal that she consented even to ingesting the rare weeds left for their curing by Cinnamon. By the middle of the month, her complexion restored, her cheeks almost rosy, Europe decided that the time for the return to Brandenbrass and all its troubles had come.

As the glowing pink of sunrise spread a brilliant rose patch over the deep purple clouds, showing darkly against the brightening golden green and blue of the western sky, Rossamünd, his mistress and his former masters departed.

"I will send you the painting as soon as I am able," Pluto called, risen rosy-cheeked and early to wave them farewell.

In the early cool, they were taken from Orchard Harriet's happy seclusion aboard the Plume brothers' sturdy lentum. Spedillo at the reins and Silence as his side-armsman, they wended the green miles through seldom-seen glades and wooded vales. Rossamünd smiled at fresh memories of their last Grand Supper of eight gizzard-splitting removes the night before, where Gentleman Plume refused to let his guests be glum and made fun for them all. Yet as they bent left at a junction that went down a long stony gully road to the purple gray wolds of mercy jane, Rossamünd's cheer began to falter. Other conveyances began to join them, heralding their return to common life. They skirted by the high palisade of a martial encampment teeming with companies of musketeers readying for summer campaigning. The sight, like a slap, reminded Rossamünd of the Archduke, of Pater Maupin and the coming strife.

A bare mile beyond, they arrived at Flodden Fild, a drab, treeless yet prosperous town behind strong walls, its walks thronged with many clean, contented people—high-bonneted ladies and ruddy-cheeked country gents in ill-fitting wigs. With them strutted an uncommonly high count of pediteers in Branden mottle, their officers in fussy harness making great show of themselves, greeting the many stiff-backed quality fellows in sleek coats and high hats riding by on sleek, leggy horses.

On their passage through the town, Rossamünd thought he spied a bill on a wall, the paper blazoned with a heading line that included the name *Winstermill!* yet lost sight of it before he could read it fully. With final farewells they were deposited at the bustle and din of the Thrust and Flurry, hostelry and local coach host on Broadstairs Lane, to charter the next carriage bound for Brandenbrass. Folk waiting with them in the plainly adorned parenthis seemed agitated, speaking together in fervently murmuring groups.

The depth of Europe's purse promptly secured them a lentum-and-six for Brandenbrass, and they did not remain long in that unsettling coach host. Out the opposite side of Flodden Fild they hurried, every stride of the horses taking them farther from peace and closer to strife.

In the rocking, increasingly dusty cabin, neither Rossamünd nor his companions were disposed to conversation, and spoke seldom beyond the necessities. Her hazel eyes obscured behind pink spectacles, Europe watched the rapidly passing view. Fransitart did much the same, frequently fondling the sleeve of his left arm—his puncted arm—as they bumped along. His still-splinted leg cushioned on the seat opposite and the crutch made especially by Spedillo resting by his side, Craumpalin nodded in slumber, his snores daring to interrupt the brooding, rattling silence of the cabin.

"We were reckonin' ye'd think it better to leave the lad behind or some such." The old dormitory master breached the impasse. "Them cunning poltroons may 'ave other surprises in wait to get at him . . . Have ye thought he might be better off living in some wild place than the shoaly dangers of *that there* city?"

"Yes, I have." The fulgar closed her eyes and touched fingertips to the bridge of her nose. "Many times . . ."

"Better to forgo the bait than struggle in the snare." Fransitart peered at Rossamünd, a haunted expression deep in the ex–dormitory master's weary eyes.

Europe bridled even as Rossamünd opened his mouth to

468 ·

speak. "This is not open to the ballot of some vulgar Hamlin parliament, sir. If my service is unpleasant to you, you may quit it. Perhaps living by Maupin's leave is more to your liking?"

Fransitart scowled but kept his counsel.

"I would have thought, Master Vinegar," the fulgar said mordantly, "that a vinegaroon of your length and quality of service would be better used to following commands."

"Aye," the old vinegar growled. "Well, per'aps this old vinegar is getting weary of living by another's leave!"

Staring glumly at the bland sunny scene of dashing hovels, high-houses and ancient manors, Rossamünd felt as miserable as he ever had, the cheerful light to him dismal and ominous. He watched a vast flock of starlings surging distantly over the elevated pastures, a harmoniously writhing mass so dense it looked like some roiling fast-moving mist, skimming the hilltops—a whole city of birds dancing in the sky.

Oh, that I could swoop with them.

As the day drew on, they crested the escarpment above the Milchfold and beheld Brandenbrass the Great, a many-spired crown sprawled along the coast and bejeweled with a hundred thousand lights—the glittering den of their foes. Rossamünd smiled wryly. He had once, in a straightforward and carefree time not too far gone, thought cities a place of simplicity and safety. Yet as they drew down to the plain of the Milchfold, he regarded this great seat of civilization much as he was sure all monsters did, as a dark fastness of bloodthirstiness and brutality, the brink of all woes.

On the flat of the Fold they went rapidly, and in the encroaching gloom of early evening passed into the brutal city, entering under the Moon Gate into the elevated northern suburbs about the fortress of Grimbasalt. Come away so quickly from the freedom of Orchard Harriet to these narrow beetling streets, Rossamünd was daunted by the sad, crowding business, the relentless pursuit of . . . of . . . whatever this ceaseless chasing served. Every face seemed turned to them, every eye watching for their return, every mouth ready to bring report of them to Swill and Maupin and their coterie of bloodthirsting allies. Muffling his nose with his still-torn vent against the stink of sluggish drains and close lanes and all ambition's decay, he glimpsed again a bill blazoned "Winstermill!" but now was too tired and too downhearted to care.

The lentum-and-six took them slowly into the yard of Cloche Arde, the high-house's solid grandeur bringing him some measure of comfort. There they discovered another coach arrived ahead of them. Rossamünd was certain he could see an oddly familiar figure stepping from it—a tall, skinny man wearing his own snow-white hair slicked and jutting like a plume from the back of his head and small bottle-brown spectacles.

"Doctor Crispus!" he cried, leaning dangerously over the sash.

The physician's face was drawn, his expression deeply anxious and not a little bewildered. Under his smudged, yet still sartorially splendid pinstripe gray coat, his arm was wrapped against his trunk, bandaged against a break. "Well

470

betide you, Lampsman Bookchild! Well betide you all!" he called. "Happy advents! This is your dwelling; my reconnaissance is proven true!" His face grew suddenly grave. "I have just come today from Vesting High . . ."

"And we from the hills," Europe answered a little more cautiously as he handed her out from the coach cabin. "You are an unlooked-for arrival, sir . . . Has the clerk-master given you some long-deserved leave?"

A strange, unreadable expression clouded the physician's face. "No, madam, no." He bowed low. "I bring the most pressing and astonishing news . . . Winstermill has fallen. The lighters of the manse are no more."

22

JUSTICE DELIVERED, VENGEANCE DELAYED

speculator private most commonly called sleuths, also speculators, sneaksmen, snugs-men or deductors; fellows offering their cunning, contacts and guile for a fee, to be employed in the discovery or repression of whatever or whomever is desired. Existing almost exclusively in cities, they operate under official license and are often engaged by the more proper authorities as thieftakers. A good sleuth will employ several undersleuths and have a wide association of informants and seeds, even possessing connections in other cities.

S TILL in their frowsty travel clothes, the five sat in the hiatus while Clossette and her various maids bustled about them to turn bright-limns and bring a hasty supper. So settled, Europe, Rossamünd and his two masters listened to Doctor Crispus' remarkable tale of panic and collapse in attentive silence.

The assault on Winstermill had come in the night. By devious means the nickers had foiled the portcullis guarding the roads that passed under the fortress and found their way in through the very clandestine passages and furtigrades where Rossamünd once vanquished the pig-eared gudgeon and Swill and the Master-of-Clerks conducted their wretched business.

"Such cruel speed, such mortal efficiency!" Crispus pressed his eyes with thumb and forefinger. "They seemed to pounce from every subterranean orifice, every door and closet."

Though the defenders roused quickly, they could do little to halt the inward attack.

"I could hear the frightful clamor of conflict through the walls of the infirmary," The Doctor recalled sadly. "The bells of the Specular ringing ceaselessly, cannon on the wall tops booming, muskets loosed by quarto in the very halls of the manse joined by the ranting cacophony of a bestial host. I am ashamed to admit that my first thoughts were to flight. This would not do, of course; what of the hurt in my own care? Who would seek out poor Mister Numps?"

Rossamünd wrestled the urge to interrupt and demand of Numps' fate.

"With only a lone epimelain to do the work with me—a dear girl who had stayed faithful through all the Master-of-Clerks' depredations—I sorted those who could walk out and those who needed carrying. Swill, the dog, would not help. Absent for the whole of last month, he had returned only a day or so before, come back from some dark errand, little doubt . . ."

Europe stirred on her tandem. "Little doubt, indeed . . . ," she said.

"Coming from some hidden nook, he was clutching a wad of books and documentation. 'They're in the kitchen!' he was crying. 'In the slypes!' and kept uttering like a man in fever, '*He* sent them! I do not know how, but that blighted

473

child is having his revenge!' Who this *child* might be, I can only conjecture . . ."

Rossamünd could not be sure, but he thought he saw the physician's harried regard flick to him ever so quickly.

"Swill useless, I sent the poor epimelain to get some other, sturdier help, but, alas!" The anguish on Crispus' face was distressingly candid. "She did not return . . ." He closed his eyes against foul memory. "If I had waited but a minute more, she would still be with us, for somehow in all the woe, our most wondrous Lady Dolours appeared, to pluck us all from the very clutches of doom. She and her columbines and that young Threnody lass you were chums with, Rossamünd, had lurked a veritable army of nickers only days before: a great hoard come out from the east and north, bent on Winstermill, plundering cot and field as they drew closer." He took a deep breath and his aspect grew tight. "With the very advent of these doughty damsels a great frenzy of bogles spilled from the Kitchen Ends into the infirmary; swarthy, hirsute toadlike things right in the heart of impregnable Winstermill. Hard were the calendars pressed to keep us safe and lead us out, trying to bring that rascal Swill with them. But afraid of the calendars as much as he was of the bogles, he ran from the infirmary, raving like a mad man, 'I'm not the one you want! I'm not the one you want!'"

A knock and Kitchen arrived with glasses of refreshingly dilute claret complete with pulped pear for them all.

"The brave calendars defended the sick even as they carried them from the manse proper," Crispus continued after a lengthy sip. "Out in the Broad Hall by the infirmary I caught my last glimpse of the clerk-master. Sans wig, he was among his troubardiers—and Laudibus Pile with him—all defending a stack of furniture and books set across the doors from the Broad Hall to the Ad Lineam, shooting pistols and fusils and jabbing their spittendes at the squabbling rabble of hobnickers beyond. Where the black-eyed witting fellow that Podius brought in was at, I do not know; I felt his work twice or thrice but never caught sight of him." He took another drink. "Winning out onto the Grand Mead, we found the Feuterers' Cottage and the gatehouse blazing torches. By this wicked light I saw the once-impassable gates thrown open and stormed by obscure beslimed things surging from the dense grasses of the Harrowmath. A great battle was unfolding on the grounds where we had paraded so often and boasted of our impregnability. Yet in the violence I could plainly see that it was no simple massacre; I witnessed monster at fight with monster!"

"Frogs and toads!" Craumpalin exclaimed quietly.

"Indeed, sir. As some sought to destroy men, so others strove to defend us. I have never known the like—I always thought the nicker universally black-hearted—as I know you shall agree, Madam Fulgar."

Rossamünd looked to the floor to hide a frown.

The Duchess-in-waiting simply nodded.

"Fighting a path through the hoots and howls and caterwauling harassments," Crispus pressed on, "the calendars seemed well learned in the distinction between friend and foe. The Lady Dolours was a wild thing, dashing here and there and laying all blighted beasts flat before her with equal measure of smokes and striving. Young Threnody too did her part, supporting the hurt, throwing back nickers when she had need—she seemed better at her witting than her poor reputation led me to believe." He gave a quick, sad look to Rossamünd. "All about I could feel what I believe some call *threwd,* a great swaying contest of it. If I did not know any better, I might have said it was as if two wills of clear and contrary intent were contending against each other: malice coming from north and east, benevolence from the south.

"I watched a vasty brute—born of logs and barks and sticks and wider than it was tall—flail against a band of grinning things. On the Forming Square an umbergog with the head of some malformed ram stood in a deadly bout against an absurdly enormous, bloated pillboy, all hunched and heavy in its swollen insect shell; who fought for whom I could not discern. The lighters who could united with us in our exodus, picking up the infirm that dying calendars dropped. Ahh, what unhappiness, Rossamünd, to run *from* calls of pain, not *to* them. Before us scourge Josclin fell beneath an ettin's stomp even as his chemistry burned the thing to its death. Brave Josclin—he performed marvels that night . . . Songs should be made of him . . . We found Swill too . . . Or, rather, what remained of him." The physician drew a hand across his brow. "Though his head remained whole, his members were torn asunder with such careless savagery that I believe not even the most skilled massacar could put him back together again."

Uncertain of what he felt, Rossamünd closed his eyes. The end of a foe—especially such a terrible and pitiless end—was not necessarily the great victory he had supposed it might be. It was instead a melancholy kind of relief; a threat was lifted but its consequences remained.

"The overweaning massacar missteps at last," Europe murmured with evident satisfaction.

"It's a pity the nickers di'n't get to 'im before 'e got to spreadin' 'is conjecturings over 'ere," Fransitart added darkly.

"They tried, Master Frans," said Rossamünd quietly, thinking bitterly of the poor doomed Herdebog Trought trying to rend its way into Winstermill, and the destruction of Wormstool. "They tried . . ."

A dull thump of luggage fumbled by Wenzel the footman out in the vestibule hall gave the physician a cruel start.

"I reckon thee might do well to unbrace thyself with a nice calmer," Craumpalin offered quietly, leg raised on a tandem. "I could test thee bestill liquor if thee likes."

"Indeed, sir; or perhaps Dew of Imnot might do me better, if you know how it goes—kinder upon my stomach," Crispus concurred solemnly. "I'll have out with my recounting, then take a draught after."

Rossamünd could stand it no longer. "But what of Numps?"

"Yes, yes, my boy." The physician adjusted his spectacles. "I was just coming to that. He is well, that I will say." He took a breath. "Where was I? Ah! Such a wild hooting and bellowing was pressing at every hand, and the very air assaulted us with dark and dreadful thoughts. As mighty as the Lady Dolours undoubtedly is, she and Threnody and their surviving sister columbines appeared to falter. A dark and awful form stood at the gate, head ducked under the arch, a horned and thorny beast of wicked antiquity. *Gathephär,* one of the calendars called it in her dread."

477

Those other monsters that Grammaticus fellow in Pour Clair wrote of must have called it away to join the assault! Doubly glad they had not found this dread monster themselves, Rossamünd glanced to Europe, who remained attentive to the doctor's telling.

"Slavering, it reached for us, swatting Dolours aside. Smaller wretchers dashed among us. I was thrown to the ground—which is where I suspect *this*"—the doctor wagged his bandaged arm, his voice rising in the passion of his recounting—"occurred. We were in danger of being eliminated where we stood! Quite suddenly, all oppressions and griefs were lifted as if by some mighty though kindly hand. Something small burst through us from behind, clad in fine coat, processing greatly distended sparrow's head upon his shoulders. I thought us finally undone."

"Cinnamon!" Rossamünd breathed excitedly. How fast and far must the nuglung prince have traveled to be present for the assault? *How did he ever know it was going to happen?*

"Indeed it was, my friend!" Crispus exclaimed in his very own amazement. "As I later learned. Such a diminutive creature, yet it sprang readily at this Gathephär, leaping so very high to strike at the monstrous thing with a long spittende, driving the Gathephär back after many fierce blows, to send it howling through the gate and away. For a moment the tide of baskets fell away. Delivered, we hurried out from that perishing fortress, this Cinnamon aiding Dolours, who still lived despite her buffeting. To our enduring delight we were joined by an assembly of survivors, women and children and various staff fleeing from the Low Gutter—and who do

THE GATHEPHÄR

you think should be at their lead?" He paused as if seeking an answer.

His listeners just blinked at him expectantly.

"Mister Numps! Unhurt, coming willingly through the butchery. Hand in hand with a wee wizened thing by the name of Freckle, our glimner friend was wearing the most rapt expression I have ever known him to show; he could have been on a summerscale picnic for all he cared of the desperate melee about. Defended by many wizened bogles—*glamgorns* is their designation, I believe—this second party had won through to us, and together we fled down the Approach and on to the Harrowmath. Even with these kindly creatures' aid, it was only a sorry remnant of calendars, clerks and lighters that got free."

"Master Sparrow and his tiny friend are busy fellows," Europe observed.

Doctor Crispus went on. "By the stars I could see that we were being taken southeast across the Harrowmath, reaching the marshes of Old Man's Itch at dawn. Past this Cinnamon took us, even to the wooded foothills of the northern extents of the Sparrowdowns, where only commerce men and fools will go." Crispus wagged his head, clearly still astonished at the journey. "Our way was necessarily slow, four days carrying hurt souls by boggy paths. Threnody, through all her sharp looks and squalls of temper, proved herself an august's daughter, seeking all our welfare, making sure stragglers did not fall too far behind. We fed on bulbs pulled from the ground and washed with trickling marsh water, and the bogles tended all hurts with skill—I say to my shame—

beyond my learning. As for Numps, I have never seen him appear in such ecstasy, such transports of delight; while we sagged in our weariness, he capered with glee, hugging and holding hands with Cinnamon and the one called Freckle."

Rossamünd grinned broadly, easily conceiving the happy babble that the simple glimner would have chortled: *My old old friends! Come to get me at last!*

"Some folk were not so easy with such ünterly company." Crispus let out a puff of air. "The calendars were perfectly at ease with monsters about them, yet several refugees lagged deliberately or slipped away at night to find their own way, ungrateful souls. Cinnamon did not prevent them, and I suppose I do not blame them—it is an altogether peculiar experience to be at a bogle's mercy. I certainly do not know what became of any of them." He paused a little ominously. "Finally, amid a great joyful flocking of sparrows and other small woodland birds swarming about us, we were met by the Duke of Sparrows—or so Dolours named him with surprising reverence—a lord of monsters, no less, direct from some spurious tome of legendry, as if monsters fighting monsters for the cause of men was not bamboozling enough!"

"You *saw* the sparrow-king!" Rossamünd was astounded.

Fransitart and Craumpalin murmured in wonder.

Europe arched her diamond-spoored brow.

"Only from afar, my boy, only from afar," the physician answered. "He is, it seems, loath to be plainly viewed, but I could *feel* him, Rossamünd, a profound and all-encompassing peace such as I have never known." A faint smile hovering on his lips, he closed his eyes. "Dolours was admitted to

481

go farther but soon returned in much better weal than when she went in. Only Numps was let right up to the strange creature, and it soon became patent that he was to remain within its realm." Crispus looked to Rossamünd. "Ahh, Rossamünd, I do believe we can finally count him at peace. Our dear Mister Numps wished for me to tell you *in coram*— face-to-face—that he is as well as he could ever wish to be, safe now with his *old, old friends,* as he seemed inclined to name the Duke of Sparrows and Cinnamon. Safe now and forevermore, he made sure to have me tell you as his *new old friend* that he is home at last!"

Rossamünd blinked rapidly. "Aye, Doctor . . . He is surely in the best hands now."

"It was a sore trial to leave that embracing calm, but more a human realm was best for us. With the glamgorn Freckle to help, the Lady Dolours and Threnody and their sisters saw the remaining hurt—now healing well—*and* myself safe to High Vesting. After this they departed again for their own clave-hall. Having set up the wounded at the local sanguinarium, *I* proceeded to charter the promptest packet out from that harbor and proceeded to you as quickly as I could."

"A remarkable tale, Doctor," said Europe. "It seems the season for adventure. Since you are now without a home, you may stay here for as long as is convenient."

Stretched thin and jaded, the physician looked for a moment as if he were about to burst into tears of gratitude. "Well, gracious madam, I must get to Mister Sebastipole now—bring him report of Numps as well."

"Nonsense, man," the fulgar retorted. "You are in no

humor for further travel. Write him a letter as you need, but for now, remain. Think of it as recompense for the diligent care you took of Rossamünd while he served with the lighters," she ended a little more kindly.

Protesting his wish not to be a burden, the physician finally accepted. "Well—well, I thank you . . . Oh," he went on, "and Threnody sends you word, Rossamünd. If she had had pen and paper, she would have writ something, but she asked me to convey . . . Now, what was it . . ." He pressed a knuckle to his lips. "Ah! That she hopes her words have not caused you too much harm and that she is glad you have got away clean with the Branden Rose."

"Got away clean indeed," Europe snorted quietly.

Rossamünd frowned at his mistress, grateful nevertheless to have news of the fractious girl lighter.

"What became of the Master-of-Clerks, do you think, Doctor?" he asked.

"The manse was wreathed in flame when last I saw it from across the sodden meadow. Few others fled after us—mostly the larger of our nicker allies fighting what appeared to be a rear-guard action. I cannot think he survived, nor Pile with him."

So the Master-of-Clerks had been served justice at last. The monsters had acted where men could or would not. "No more gudgeon-making there," Rossamünd murmured.

Doctor Crispus smiled mirthlessly as he sagged in his seat. "No, not in the manse's cellars, at least . . ."

"What will 'appen now, d'ye reckon?" came Fransitart's query.

The good doctor put a weary hand to his face. "I heard that the landsaire encampment near Silvernook moved themselves in the small of the morning of the assault and sought to retake the manse. Repulsed bloodily at the gates, they were unable to win inside and fell back in disarray." He sighed heavily and pressed a finger against his lips. "I little expect that the empire of man will allow monsters to remain in its precincts unchallenged. An army will be mustered and sent, of that you can be sure."

"Indeed," Europe inserted. "The Archduke might find a different use for his conquering regiments this summer."

After treacle and breakfast and letting Darter Brown outside to do those tasks it is a sparrow's part to do, the duties of the first day back in Brandenbrass began in Europe's file. Letters were waiting for them, a veritable bale of missives and communications collected over the time of their absence.

Only two were for Rossamünd, one thick, one thin.

Sitting on a tandem by the unlit hearth, Europe taking up a seat opposite, he broke the letter's red sealing ribbon. Clearly from Verline, it was dated the 17th of Unxis—the very day he and Europe and his old masters had been ambushed—and it read as follows:

> My beloved stout-hearted Rossamünd,
>
> What fright I had to read Master Fransitart's telling of your speedy exit from Winstermill Manse. What salve to know you are all well, though I do not know what to make of your succor at the care of that frightful Europa lady. She is a peer, however, so

it cannot all be bad. Master F declares he feels you shall remain safe with her for the time, and I hope he may finally have some chance to rest his trickety leg.

I too have some news for you. From the time darling Masters Fransitart and Craumpalin left to come to you, Old Carp and Master Barthomaeus employed the services of a snugman. This fellow, whom I greeted but once—a rather alarming meeting—proved his large fee and found Gosling down in Proud Sulking. Horribly wounded, the lost soul was laid in a subscription infirmary, and would not say how he came by such hurts. Either hand, under right of bounty, Gosling was brought straight back to Boschenberg and has only just now stood before the judges' bench. Their honors pronounced him guilty of (I think I am penning it rightly) *interitus causim incension,* which Master Barthomaeus informs me is "arsony occasioning death." He says that Gosling was fortunate not to suffer *caedes ad incendium* (or "murder by fire"—why they do not speak plain, I do not know). Because Gosling is so young, he is to be spared the noose, and is sentenced a convict to serve in the colonial quarries in Euclasia.

I went to him three times in the Lock, bringing food with me. The first he screamed and flailed at the door and tried to reach at me through the small holes in it. I was quite safe; the coston would never allow him near me. The second visit Gosling was quiet. I went in to him, but he simply stared at the wall with those uncommon black eyes. On the third he would not see me, though the goodly sergeant-coston let me take a look at him through the peep. I know all the wickedness he has done, yet still I cannot but feel sorry for him. Oh, if only you could have seen him as I did, Rossamünd, you might well share the same tenderness.

At this point Rossamünd stopped reading, eyes burning and milt colliding with a thousand unnameable emotions. Collecting himself and wiping his nose angrily on his sleeve, he pressed on:

> For now you can be at ease that after the terrible
> fire at the old foundlingery the children are all as
> best as can be done for. Most we have founded in
> better homes, some went to prentice early, and all's
> that's left of the littlest my most admirable sister
> and I have taken in for good under our own arm.

"My, my, rumor has spread to my mother at last," the fulgar said, interrupting Rossamünd's reading as she pored over a letter of her own. "She deplores my use of QGU in so squanderous a manner, of course . . ." She studied the missive some more. "The dear has never approved of my path—my *violent irresponsible cavortings*—and now she has heard of my taking up with sedorners . . . *Shall I bring the whole history of fair names to infamy?* she asks. A half truth is better than a whole lie." She put the communication aside with a long-suffering sigh and took up another.

Rossamünd went back to his letter.

> Far happier news is that now all legals have been
> settled, it turns that Madam Opera did leave the
> sum of her small wealth and worldly consequence
> to both Old Carp and me. Can you believe it! With
> it comes the marine society contract, which makes
> it now my right to set up the foundlingery again.
> My dear, dear brother-in-law has so taken to the
> littlest that Praeline and I still care for in our home

that he has agreed to buy an enormous old manor-burg on the Tuinwig, in Primvild—of all the best places!—and Praeline will assist me as mistress into the bargain. Can you believe this either, heart of my heart? I shall be a marine society proprietress! Carp and Barthomæus will be our starting masters, and I have sent to the Navy Board, who have willingly consented to continue with us and sponsor more salty old darlings like the two dears with you now to serve out better days here. Dear Masters Fransitart and Crowmpalin will always have a place here should ever they want an end to their adventuring days—I have written them so. I almost dare to believe that, with the money Praeline's husband is granting, the foundlingery might be better than before.

Providence ever turns bad to the good, if you have eyes to see it.

My blessings to you. Write to me so that I might know how you fare. Your previous letter was so short it troubles me so.

Forever and
always your

P.S. I have written of the same things to Masters F and C, so you do not need to pass this on to them.

It was signed with the flourish of a soul very much in a transport of happiness.

Blinking back bitter tears, Rossamünd read a second time, hastening over the tale of Gosling's downfall, relishing the prospect of a new and certainly *better* foundlingery.

There was also a short communication from Sebastipole. It was dated more than two weeks gone—well before the fall of Winstermill—and it read as follows:

> Rossamünd,
>
> I do not have time to write more than the briefest missive to convey to you my satisfaction upon the report that you have won free from the misuses of the Master-of-Clerks and are under the much vaunted care of so eminent a teratologist. With her you are most certainly safe.
>
> Here in the Considine the marshal continues his fight against false testimony, baseless accusation and the sluggish obstinacy of Imperial bureaucracy. Strange accounts come to us of the Surgeon Swill, that he makes a show of himself in Brandenbrass with a list of outrageous claims. I hope he has not caused you any discomfort. He might be dazzling the Branden court with his wild proclamations, but here in the sub-capital, report of such a carry on has only harmed his reputation—*and* those associated with him, and does our cause good. Thus encouraged, we go on until we prevail.
>
> I must cease, for we have just now been summoned to *yet another* review of informal inquiry.
>
> Of Discipline
> and Limb,
>
> Lamplighter's
> Agent &c
>
> The Considine

"Ah, excellent . . . ," Europe said eventually with feline satisfaction, rousing her factotum from his concentration once more. She lifted a wad of papers that had been a part of the mail—a large stack of pamphlets. "These should interest you," she said, reading one briefly before laying them with a flop on the seat beside him. Most obvious was an edition of the *Defamière*, and with it *Quack!, The Mordant Mercer, The Viper, Wasp* and several more—every one a scandal or low-toned pamphlet, and all the latest issue. Topmost was a list in Mister Carp's hand showing the name of each publication and beside each, page numbers.

"Miss Europe?" Rossamünd marveled, folding both missives neatly to put them safe in his inside weskit pocket where their words might be close to his soul.

"I have not lowered my tastes, if that is what you are thinking," she said flatly, fixing him with a pointed look. "Turn to each of those pages and read . . . A most excellent retort," she concluded with a contented half smile.

Doing as he was bidden, Rossamünd discovered in every pamphlet an article without title, featured near the front of the paper—usually the fifth page.

> The Duchess-in-waiting of Naimes wishes to refute previous claims held in other papers of low repute that she improperly exercised her born right of QGU in the defense of one of lower station against the designs of greater men bent on infamy. Her accusers have since sought to denounce her publicly for such an honest service

with implications of the basest sort, which can only be seen as regrettable and a symptom of their own villainy. Their intention base and self-interested gain, they embroil themselves most wholly and most treacherously with the darkest of all trades. Through the artifice of their own cunning they have eluded the just reach of Imperial Notice. We are now honor-bound to expose these dastards as base traitors. We properly await a swift righting of this great wrong.

"It seems I am not without my defenders," Europe said archly. "A rigorous counter-offend to their radix," she added, Rossamünd well recognizing terms of the Hundred Rules. "Thank you, Mister Finance . . ." Laying a bundle of papers down, she gave her young factotum an astute look. "Rossamünd . . . Monsiere Trottinott has inspired me," she said suddenly. "I am going to hold a grand gala, and not a simple silk rout, but a *sortire l'travesty*—a come-as-you-fancy ball."

Come-as-you-fancy? The young factotum regarded her in blinking bafflement. *Where folks dress up as kings or heldins or fabulous creatures or any other fancy notion?* "I thought you held galas and fêtes and routs and all to be interminably dreary," he said.

The Branden Rose blinked at him. "They are, exceedingly so . . . unless someone of genuine refinement holds them. *Ours* shall be especially grand, in honor of my successful coursing venture."

"But the knave *wasn't* a success," Rossamünd thought-lessly returned.

Europe became rather still, fixing him with a withering expression. "Was it not . . . ," she said in wintry tones. "My guests will not know that, will they?"

Bobbing his head, her factotum conceded. "No, they would not . . . What of Pater Maupin?" he dared, speaking with slow caution.

Europe's eyes twinkled with occult thoughts. "He may wait" was all she said.

Rossamünd frowned.

"You, my sour factotum, I charge with the task of pre-paring its food and decoration. Do not goggle, Rossamünd! Kitchen and Clossette will be your aides, of course, and I am sure Doctor Crispus and even your old masters could lend their capabilities in help." She smiled a sly smile. "As for myself, *I* shall take charge over the night's entertainments."

Taking a deep breath, he asked, "When will it be?"

"Midwich, the 20th of this month" was the quick reply.

Rossamünd did a hasty calculation of the time he had to accomplish impossibility.

A week from today!

23

OF OSSATOMY AND
OBFUSCATIONS

lesquins also called landsaire, the "high end" of mercenary soldiering, with equally high fees, the best proofing and weapons, and long lists of honors. Some companies are given to taking sanguinary draughts in order that they might ignore pain, fear and, even for a time, resist the frission or scathing of a wit.

INSTALLED in downstairs apartments of their own at the back of Cloche Arde, Fransitart and Craumpalin received the news of the grand gala with profound excitement.

"There's a kindly change o' wind I weren't expectin'," the ex–dormitory master exclaimed. "Here's me thinking it would be all clubs an' bruises an' hidden threats. What fancy will ye be dressing as, Rossamünd?"

Knuckle to chin, Rossamünd pondered a moment. "I don't rightly know . . . Myself? That is *fancy* enough, isn't it?" he concluded with a wry twist to his mouth.

"What of that More-pins looby?" Craumpalin asked, puckering his brow, his inquiring grimace making his face disconcertingly gaunt. "Thy mistress made to be prodi-

492

giously fixed on his just desserts. Seems a mite uncharacterly for her ladyship to let this More-pins off the hook so simply."

Rossamünd made a bemused face. "I do not reckon she has," he said.

Taking their rest from the rigors of the journey in a parlor overlooking the sluggish flow of the Midwetter, the old salts—as yet to receive their own communication from her—were greatly impressed by Verline's letter.

Craumpalin raised his glass tankard of soothing saloop. "Will be nice to have a place to settle to, once Rossamünd finds his feet and we lose the use of ours."

"Aye," Fransitart pondered solemnly. "I tell ye, I regret not bein' able to reform that Gosling."

Leg elevated on a turkoman, the old dispenser shifted awkwardly in his seat and snorted. "It'd take one hundred of you and one hundred of Verline one hundred years to even begin to set one twisted part of Gosling's inward places aright."

"Mayhap," the ex–dormitory master returned. "The mines of Euclasia will do naught to soothe his mucky soul, neither."

"Thee wants to light him away to some sweeter hole, Frans?" Craumpalin chided. "Take him under thy scrawny white oar and make good the rotten heart? Some folks just won't be learned under a softer hand."

"Aye," replied Fransitart sadly. "Aye . . ." He gave Rossamünd an unhappy and uncommonly confounded look.

The young factotum smiled sadly in return.

"Well, we won't be let off th' hook simple," Fransitart finally said. "It's going to be fetch an' carry unceasin' from now till next Midwich."

"Aye," Rossamünd concurred. "More than enough practicable to do even for you, Master Pin."

"Aye," Fransitart growled. "If I can get some vittles into 'im first!"

The old dispenser threw him a wink.

At the guidance of Kitchen and Clossette, Rossamünd quickly learned that a grand gala was no simple dance, though certainly dancing was a central part; it was rather a great unfolding of entertainments, to be held on almost every floor of Cloche Arde.

The hiatus was to serve as a coat room and milling space. The billiard room by Rossamünd's set was to be opened, but the other end of that level was to be occluded by a bom e'do screen guarded by Nectarius. The parlors and drawing rooms of the third story were set aside to host an oratory for rigorous debates directed by a set of orators; a glossary for thrilling gossip at the lead of a pair of talented glossicutes; and a leviate where souls could be refreshed while a quintet of fiddlers played to sooth overexercised nerves. There was to be a pantomime in the second drawing room and even a benign mesmerist to play tricks with people's senses. The ludion was set to be the main dance hall, the expanse of mirrors of the back wall folding aside and the partitions of chambers beyond—which to Rossamünd's astonishment turned out to be quite portable—removed, opening up the entire top story of Cloche Arde into an ample floor. Here, behind the stairs, a stand was laid for a pair of orchestras to play upon in rotating shifts of an hour each.

Europe's file was to be prohibited to all comers on the night, her staff included.

There was a boggling list of tasks, and the young factotum was at his utmost to keep it all properly ordered in his thoughts. Along with the marshaling and sending of invites—which Europe had written by a professional pen on silken, rose-colored paper—was the arrival of provender and with it the hiring of extra cooking and serving staff. With this was the springtime cleaning of the entire house, ready to then be festooned with fathom upon fathom of red or magenta taffeta and hanging lanterns. Every runner and rug, drape and coverlet was hung from windows sprung wide to be beaten within an inch; floors were swabbed till they gleamed . . . then swabbed again; windows washed inside and out, poor Wenzel and Nectarius hung out on rickety ladders to get at the upper stories. In apprehension of his little "parcels" left about the house, Housekeeper Clossette shooed Darter Brown outside, declaring tartly that he was "not allowed back in until he can school his bowels the better!"

Sickly indigent chimney sweeps were summoned from the workers' fair in Steepling Oak to scramble precariously up flues. *I thought teratology was dangerous,* Rossamünd pondered, watching in vague horror one gaunt boy half his own age clamber up the chimney of the file fire, *encouraged* by an older lad with a jointed pole. The thump and bang of the

495

labors sounded about Cloche Arde the entire day, and all the while the maids were polishing, polishing, polishing.

Charged with control of the Duchess-in-waiting's purse, Mister Carp was summoned into the madness. Yet the man's parsimonious reluctance was little needed, for Rossamünd was admirably troubled over the outflowing of his mistress' wealth.

"Miss Europe missed most of her prize-money on the knave," he said in a low voice, making careful inquiry of Mister Carp as the fellow looked over a bill of expense for the decoration of the lower floors. "I do not think she can afford all *this* after such losses."

"Ahh, what a happy fellow!" The man-of-business smiled with sudden and uncommonly genuine kindness. "May your credits always be greater than your debts! Calm your care, Master Bookchild; our mistress can compass the cost—she is worth ten thousand a year if she is worth a scruple!" His chest inflated a little.

"Ten *thousand?*" Rossamünd goggled. *Ten* thousand *sous!*

"Indeed! Each year."

Rossamünd almost choked.

Mister Carp veritably glowed with satisfaction. "Unlike many silk-purse peers, she is a shrewd patron and financier: holds interest in many prosperous endeavors. She shall make a formidable duchess should she ever consent to it."

After this, Rossamünd ceased fretting.

As for the Branden Rose, she spent much of her time in her file in close counsel with a continuous flow of kapelmasters and stepmasters, orators and amphigorers, psaltists and panto troupes. Interspersed among them were drabber souls who seemed unduly stern for such a festal occasion. First that Rossamünd saw among *these* was the colonel of a lesquin company dressed in a dark clerical suit. Arms laden with various folios, the colonel was accompanied by a strikingly harnessed captain, complete with caudial honor at waist, whose haunted eyes seemed to hold something occult and severe. Arrived early Domesday morning, they did not leave until Rossamünd delivered his mistress' treacle that evening, the colonel departing with the earnest pledge, "We are ready to put our hand to whatever the lady directs."

Europe said nothing on it and Rossamünd knew better than to ask.

The next morning, as he was again dispensing the fulgar's plaudamentum, a gentleman in drab proofing and blue-tinted spectacles obscuring laggard-colored eyes was shown into the file. Introducing himself in clipped tones as a Mister Rakestraw, speculator privite, he went immediately into a report. "We are near to weaseling out that dastard's bolt-hole."

At this point the fulgar stopped the fellow and bid her young factotum to depart to his needful gala preparations. Lingering at the file door as he closed it, he still managed to catch, "The fall of that lighters' fortress spooked him greatly and has driven him more deeply into cover. Yet I believe by tomorrow morn I shall be able to inform you of his exact locale."

Swill? Rossamünd pondered. Not for the first time he

wondered upon his mistress' real intent. Whatever it might be, her determination to leave him out of the scheme was abundantly clear.

In the afternoon, he sat in the file with Europe and her hired pen—a certain Mister Chudleigh. Together they were sorting the next dispensing of seemingly endless invitations to be handed to the platoon of scopps waiting in the vestibule, when Wenzel, red-faced and panting, bustled in to announce, "Lady Madigan, Marchess of the Pike!"

In a gray dress of flashing satin with sash of black tied in a great bow at the small of her back, the Lady Madigan's most striking feature was her sky blue eyes. Sad and penetrating, they lingered intelligently wherever she fixed her attention. Of similar generation to Europe, she bore a small, solid diamond etched under her lower lip like a deep blue dimple in her chin. She too was an aristocratic fulgar. A man perhaps in his thirties, dark-eyed and dark-haired with a long almost horselike face, followed her closely. Introduced as Mister Threedice, he was her factotum, a laggard of taciturn manners and blunt address. He stared at Rossamünd with a callous yet melancholy intensity. Rossamünd returned this untoward attention with a polite incline of his head, to which the other factotum simply looked away.

"Here is an innovation," said Lady Madigan coolly, speaking with a peculiar familiarity. "The Branden Rose turned hostess!"

Europe regarded her evenly but said nothing.

"You wish it be known to the world that all is fit and fine with you, sister," the Marchess of the Pike said as she sat on

THE **LADY MADIGAN**
MARCHESS OF THE PIKE

the edge of a turkoman and folded her daintily gloved hands in her lap.

"I do."

"I hear, dear one," Lady Madigan continued, "that you returned to Brandentown after an especially *rugged* outing."

"It is about the street, then?" Europe replied.

"Assuredly so, sister; certain *streets,* at least," Lady Madigan added wryly. "Is there a responsible party for this *especial ruggedness?*"

"Yes."

"Are you to do anything about them?"

Europe's eye gleamed as she quickly glanced to Rossamünd. "I may yet, my dear," she said.

"Am I invited?"

"Perhaps I shall tell you more at my little rout," the Duchess-in-waiting returned.

"Until then, sister."

"Indeed."

The Marchess of Pike stood, bowed and left.

Absorbed in his penmanship, Mister Chudleigh seemed not at all exercised by this odd conversation of lofty women, nor did he notice the Lady Madigan's departure, and Rossamünd kept his increasingly bemused ponderings to himself.

Into this contemplative silence there came a muted yet clear stentorian clatter and with it a loud "Whoop!" sounding very much as if it originated in the floors above. Sent upstairs to investigate, Rossamünd soon discovered Fransitart laid out on the ludion floor, cradling his arm, a scale toppled beside him and with it the embellishment he had clearly been attempting to fix to the wall.

"Broke it, lad," the ex–dormitory master, lying on the boards as the young factotum skidded to stop beside him, explained with wry grimace. "Tumbled like some self-for-gettin' Old Gate pensioner an' put out me wings to catch meself an' *SNAP!* . . . twice."

Rossamünd went round-eyed at the mangle of oddly shaped sleeve his old master gripped.

Crispus arrived in a puff, physic's bag in hand, calling orders for hot water, towels and directing immediately for a tandem to be brought up.

"My, my, my." The physician clucked his tongue as he prodded the limb in initial inquiry. He tried lifting it a little and Fransitart roared with pain. "Well, well, my etiolated friend, not that way then . . . ," he murmured. "We will have to cut the sleeve."

Giving the old vinegaroon the briefest swig of some stu-pefacting draught—obtorpës, the physician called it—and cord of leather to clamp between his teeth, Crispus began to cut at the cloth of the frock a coat sleeve.

Under the influence of the draught Fransitart bore his discomfort with greater calm, sweating profusely, teeth clenched on the leather bit.

Putting on his complex spectacles, Crispus looked up at the watchers—a veritable audience of staff—with an exag-gerated tilt of his head. "I would depart now if I were of sensitive constitution," he advised.

Coming to himself, Kitchen shooed the water-bringing

maids out of the room and the curious footmen with them. He, however, lingered to watch from the relatively less gruesome vantage of the door.

Uncertain as to whether he wanted to see the doctor at his work, Rossamünd nevertheless remained.

With the obstruction of the sleeve removed, Crispus began his investigation in earnest, palpating the swollen flesh . . . but Rossamünd could look no longer, his old master's restrained cries enough to go on.

"My, my," Crispus breathed, his tone of wonder catching Rossamünd's attention. The physician was bending over some obviously fascinating item on the mess of the old salt's forearm. The bandage that Fransitart had retained was gone.

The cruorpunxis!

The mark was there as before.

Rossamünd glanced anxiously to Kitchen, who was peering at it with waxing interest.

"Astonishing! Astonishing!" Crispus marveled. "Simply astonishing! Lah! To think that butchering novice got it correct!"

With the words *You know!* on his lips, Rossamünd checked himself and instead ordered Kitchen from the room.

Looking fit to disregard the young factotum's command, the steward reluctantly departed, closing the double doors behind him with a pointed thump.

Silence hung in the room like an admission.

"Oh, I have heard all about the inquiry," Crispus said with light factuality, blinking through his apparatus in wonder at the surprise of his listeners. "I could but not; the bruit of it went all through the manse. Swill marked *his own* arm with a complete cruorpunxis, then went about with it conspicuously bandaged almost the moment you departed. Add this to his attempt to bully me with the menace of charges of sedornition for supporting you, my friend, and I had clues enough. What he did not divulge through his threats and allusions about the inquiry's progress, Lady Dolours clarified later." The physician peered now at Rossamünd, his wondering eye enlarged and discolored by the apparatus lens. "To think that quackeen surgeon was correct . . ." He regarded Rossamünd with awe.

"So we keep saying . . . ," Fransitart muttered darkly through the leather cord. He spat out the gag. "Well, will ye have to chop my wing, phiz?" he gruffed.

"No, no, not a bit of it!" Crispus almost laughed, quickly restoring his focus to his patient. "It is a complex break, certainly, but never fear, sir! They might lop off limbs like a storm-cracked mast out at sea, but this is nothing my experienced ministrations will not heal. Breaks are a common hurt in my line of physicking."

"Oh . . ." Fransitart looked almost disappointed.

"Being a follower of obligantic ossatomy I shall trice your bones what you might call 'prodigious firm'—even with a wounded wing of my own." He wagged his own slung arm. "After that I am sure your old vinegar chum can make for you some of my most excellent draughts to help the whole process along."

Aided by Rossamünd, the physician helped Fransitart to a more comfortable seat and set about washing his battered limb, setting to the task with silent concentration.

"I must say, Rossamünd," Crispus eventually said, "it is uncommon irony that you now work for a teratologist; almost humorous if its consequence were not so serious."

"Aye." The young factotum smiled wryly.

"Ye seem well reconciled to th' revelation, Doctor C," Fransitart observed, under the calm of the obtorpës, "but about 'ere per'aps th' less said th' better, aye?" he suggested a little tartly.

"Oh, well, yes, as you say . . . Very wise . . . Very wise."

In the dim of the evening a peculiar figure came calling: a woman with a face striped like an animal, her head crowned with a dandicomb of elegantly curved and knobbled horns. She was a wandering caladine, clad in a bossock of prüs and sable. In a peculiarly husky voice, she introduced herself as Saphine of the Maids of Malady.

Rossamünd recognized her immediately as a caladine Threnody had named while they had sat with Europe months ago in the saloon of the Brisking Cat on the Wormway.

"I wish to speak with the Branden Rose upon the matter of a mutual adversary," the caladine Saphine explained to him, dipping her head with unselfconscious ease to navigate her horns through first the front and then the hiatus door.

"My, my, the plot swells thick indeed," Europe observed, recalling the woman too as—receiving Rossamünd's explanation of this new guest—she proceeded from an easy seat by the fire in her file to the hiatus. "Hello, Lady Saphine," she said evenly to the caladine waiting patiently, poised upon

504

the edge of a tandem. "It is an extraordinary cause to move a calendar to seek my door. Do you come for your sisters of Malady or for the Soratchë?"

"Both, Lady Rose," the caladine returned hollowly, standing to nod a bow. "The two claves are joined in this enterprise, and now it appears to us that your aims and ours have junctioned."

"By a merger of *aims* . . . " Europe's brow lifted subtly.

"Grotius Swill?"

"That I do, Lady Rose."

"That will be all, thank you, Rossamünd," his mistress said, excusing him. "Please summon Condamine to bring refreshments, and then you may return to the file to finish compiling the newest of our guests' replies and the receipts that must be sent tomorrow."

And closing the door after him, Europe remained to talk with this caladine while Rossamünd was once again left with only his suspicions and a pile of unsorted gala correspondence. Long into the night he worked, brooding upon his exclusion and the violence he was certain was coming, and when his mistress finally returned to the file, he was still at his desk.

"To bed with you now, Rossamünd," she murmured tiredly. "All this may wait for a new day. I need you fresh."

For long moments her factotum did not move, but sat staring at the profusion of replies and letters sorted and unsorted, mind turning, courage building, then failing. Finally an exasperated sigh from Europe as she removed her coat in preparation for retiring broke into his indecision. "I know

505

you are preparing to make at Maupin," he dared, looking at his mistress squarely.

A shrewd smile flickered briefly across Europe's dial. "Do you now?" she purred.

"Why won't you tell me what is happening?" he demanded with all the heat of a long-needed but unexpected release. "How can I serve you best as your factotum if you will not let me in on your plan?"

Her mien becoming quickly severe, the fulgar regarded him narrowly. "You serve me best, sir, by doing as I say."

Rossamünd glowered back at her. He had sacrificed the promised security of the Sparrowdowns to remain at her side and *this* was all she would give in return! Yet how he could say this so starkly?

"I think you have worked overlong, little man," Europe finally said, her tone wintry. "Bed is the best place for you now. Good night."

He remained, gaze locked with hers, yet his expression softened just a little, a constellation of conflicting notions dashing hither and yon in his thoughts. In the end, the silence unbroken, he relented, retreating dismissed to his set and an angry, restless sleep.

PLANS WITHIN PLANS

percursor also pnictor or sicarian; a part of the patefact set; professional murderer
working for states and kings, possessing a near-legendary facility in delivering death at
distance and by stealth. Almost every state, kingdom or realm employs them, the more
civilized places simultaneously denying their existence.

GROWN used to daily walks in green and lively hills,
Rossamünd found his confinement in this bland
urban setting hard to bear. After breakfast, four
days out from the grand gala, he took a turn about the foreyard. Keeping clear of vintners' wagons and their hauling
drudges laboring to enlarge Cloche Arde's already well-
stocked wine cellar, Rossamünd walked a circle about the
pencil pine, watching Darter Brown hop and hunt amid the
thin garden beds.

In the crystalline morning Rossamünd could just make
the faint tolling of far-off millhouse bells, telling of an approaching change of shift with knells loud enough to carry
well across the city. He imagined the lines of stoop-shoul-
dered swinks—mill workers—filing in and out of the darksome mills in their sad queues. He peered up at the thin

blue sky striated with icy white—unhappy fighting weather.

She will not attack Maupin today at least . . .

The sensation of Winstermill's fall had proliferated throughout the city, giving rise to a great unanswered fear that transformed into an impotent kind of anger. Unsatisfied, this anger was growing, becoming so palpable that even Rossamünd—stuck at Cloche Arde—could near taste indignation in the very air.

On Rossamünd's second turn about the yard, Doctor Crispus walked in from the Harrow Road and joined him in his stroll. "I have been designated to be one of the orators for the gala night," he declared after a cheerful greeting. "I had the briefest thought to posit the existence of goodly nickers. Unwise at the best of times, I know, and in light of the current temper"—he produced a creased and doubled broadsheet from under his arm, *The Assessor* scripted boldly at its head—"thorough folly. Consequently, I shall be hypothesizing upon the existence of Providence over the theory of Deeper Forces, especially as a benign corrective, *and,* if it does exist," he continued cryptically, "whether it is a personal cosmic *action* or an impersonal and reflexive cosmic rebalancing."

Rossamünd just blinked and nodded.

"Have you read the newest papers, m'boy?" the physician asked abruptly. "Things have certainly taken a remarkable turn," he added, pressing the paper open at a bold heading among other bold headings on the foremost page.

Expedition Relates of a Marshal 'Mongst the Fallen in the Sack of Sulk End Fastness; Survivor Gives Graphic Account of Terrible Atrocities Committed by Ravening Nickers

The *survivor* was named as one Laudibus Pile.

"*That* rascal made it out somehow," Crispus growled. "Probably by the cunning of his heightened senses . . ."

There was no mention of goodly monsters, nor of any of the dark deeds done that precipitated such *atrocities*.

"The sloppy erroneous scoundrel who penned the piece places Podius' rank incorrectly. He was Marshal-*Subrogate*, as you know, yet they have him as Marshal-Lighter. How-be-it, it is unquestionably Podius Whympre by description," Crispus explained, pointing to the finer print. "It is a form of due comeuppance, I suppose, though it does not make me smile . . ."

Such was the sum of the Master-of-Clerks' schemes.

On the next page Rossamünd found a line of lesser type, yet no less stunning.

Fabercadavery Uncovered in Emperor's Own Fortress!

Related by some other fellow, possibly a member of the expedition mentioned in the first report, it actually named Honorius Ludius Grotius Swill as the fabercadaverist implicated in the heading line, going so far as to make mention of his lectures held in Brandenbrass itself.

"Have you seen this, Doctor?" Rossamünd asked, passing the paper back.

"So that is what you were at, Grotius!" the physician declared with grim satisfaction as if Swill were there with them. "Lah! Who could possibly prognosticate such a twist of path, my friend?" he said to Rossamünd. "And in a mere two months?" Glancing up to a housemaid banging at a long Dhaghi carpet hung from Rossamünd's set, he lowered his voice. "It certainly puts any *accusations* they have brought against you or the dear Lady Rose in new light, does it not?" The physician stared with disconcerting intensity at the young factotum. "To think he was correct . . . ," he said after a moment's reflection.

"You mean Swill, Doctor?" Exposed or not, saying the surgeon's name set a subtle twist in Rossamünd's innards.

"Indeed." The physician stroked his chin. "However unwillingly, my respect for that quackeen's research is materially increased. Ah, mistake me not, Master Bookchild! Swill was an unalloyed monster; but truth is truth, whomever alights upon it . . . If that butchering novice was correct about your nature, then he might well have been correct about how . . . well, how you came to be, my friend. The power of fecund muds and turgid earths as the source of monstrous life—indeed of all life—was once widely held, especially by the Cathars and the Phlegms, that brilliant foolhardy race without whose learning I would not have a trade . . . And if he is correct about how they connect to you, well . . ."

"What, Doctor?"

510

"If they have it right, then surely it can only mean that in your members dwell the secrets to perpetual life!"

"Perpetual life?" Rossamünd almost did not want to know the answer—though in truth, he guessed at it well enough. The Lapinduce had said something of living on while the current generation passed.

"Perpetual life! Perpetuity, continual existence, vita semper, to live on and on unaffected by time or aging . . . This is a subject the dark trades find powerfully fascinating. Should more massacars and fabercadaverists discover your proper tribe, my boy, I do not think there will be any obstacle that would detain such determinedly contrary from trying to get at you."

"Such as ambushing us on some faraway road," Rossamünd returned grimly.

"Such as that, yes . . ." Crispus took off his brown-glass spectacles and wiped them with a brightly striped handkerchief, observing the young factotum from the corner of his eye. "If you do not mind my saying it, that despite all this you are a most remarkably favored fellow, Rossamünd, to be able to go on observing the course of history with your own eyes long after all today's scholars and matterns are slotted feet-first into the ground."

"And watch my friends and everyone I care for leave this world while I go on and on . . ."

"Ah . . . yes." The physician's crest fell. "There is that . . . The price of perpetuity . . . Something perhaps the massacars have not considered." He cleared his throat pointedly. "Stimulating as talking with you inevitably is, I must prepare

511

further for my oratory . . . I shall see you at middens, perhaps." He bid Rossamünd good morning and went inside.

Left to continue his constitutional alone, Rossamünd found his attention caught by furtive motion at the gate. Sneaking between the very bars, a rabbit slipped into the yard to briskly hide itself among the roots and trunks of the glory vines along the wall. Its fur dagged and dirty gray, the creature was made for creeping unremarked along dull city slate and stone.

As Rossamünd watched, another mangy coney passed nonchalantly across the mouth of the gate, disappearing farther up the Harrow Road.

Darter Brown hopped across the gravel to the glory vine to twitter at the first rabbit.

One ear tall and alert, nose twitching attentively, the rabbit-spy remained in its place, even when the young factotum sidled over to finally stand before it and cautiously look it in the eyes. One orb was glittering black, but the other was a filmy, sightless blue; the ear above it drooped unmoving down its neck—this creature had lived hard in this pugnacious city.

On a peculiar flash of intuition Rossamünd gave it the merest nictation. Speaking low, almost under his breath, he addressed it. "Hail, servant of the ancient and rightful duke of Brandenbrass. You would do me great service if you should keep watch of my mistress wherever she might go in this city." He was no monster-lord, but it was worthy of a try.

The rabbit, however, did not move but simply peered at him, nose a-twitch twitch.

Rossamünd gave a sad shrug and turned away. Yet, returning to the house, he chanced to see the little watcher wriggle back out through the bars of the gate and disappear down the Harrow Road with all the purpose of a scopp.

Taking an audition in the hiatus of an armoniam player hoping to sweeten the mordant tattle of the glossary, Europe received the latest report of Swill and the Master-of-Clerks with typical composure.

"Choked upon their own rope at last" was all she said, a slight *I-told-you-so* look passing across her face.

Lost in the bliss of his art, the armoniam player played on.

Shivering, Rossamünd clenched his teeth against the high notes. He wanted to say something to her—sorry for the tussle of words two nights gone, for the bad feeling it had brought between them. Yet he did not see that his was the fault, and fixing on this thought, said nothing.

"THANK YOU, SIR!" Europe called over the barely melodic shriek, interrupting the slightly put-out musical gent in the very midst of his transports. "That shall make a perfect accompaniment, thank you," she said, and bid the self-important fellow good day.

Even as the man left, the Baron Finance was shown into them, his rouged cheeks more rosy than usual with a natural glow of exertion. The Chief Emissary smiled warmly and gave Rossamünd a brief, curiously knowing look as he bowed low in greeting.

"Gracious duchess-daughter! I was hearing such rumors of your misfortune. You went out to knave fully provisioned in your best fit, yet returned—to the great dismay of Pater Maupin and his associates—much lighter in luggage, by a red-doored canty-coach. Yet here you are now planning a great celebration. You have us all more perplexed, m'lady, than the swapping of springtime months!"

"Truly, Mister Finance?" the fulgar chided mildly, her face a placid blank. "I would have thought you'd have plumbed such mysteries already."

The Chief Emissary dipped his head. "I have found it is far simpler to ask directly where one can, gracious lady . . ." He waited expectantly.

Europe took her time to answer. "Master Maupin and his surgeon pet set a nice trap for us to spring on the Holt Street in the eastern Brandenfells," she said matter-of-factly. "By the attendance of the Seven-Seven sept and a base-born sciomane with her pack of jackstraws, I would say that he did not intend me to survive."

Finance allowed frank indignation to play across his handsome features. "And you *know* it was purposely set by Maupin, m'lady?"

"Surely with your long experience, Mister Emissary, you ought to have learned that an astrapecrith's full arts are subtler than just blasting life and limb. *We,* sir, are the great undiscovered falsemen!"

"Indeed" was all the Chief Emissary said at first, then added cautiously, "One might hold that after such an affront you might have chosen to return with more furtive care."

"I do not do *furtive,* sir," Europe instantly corrected him. "You of all souls ought know this."

LESQUIN CAPTAIN
AND **COLONEL**

The Baron inclined his fastidiously powdered head in capitulation.

"Hiding my return, dear Finance, is not possible," she continued. "Hiding my intent now that I am here, however, *is*."

The Baron smiled. "As is penetrating Maupin's own schemes," he returned.

Europe looked at him steadily, *Go on* writ clear in her expression.

· Finance obliged her. "After his clandestine assault on this house, Pater must have mistaken your prompt departure from Brandenbrass for knaving as weakness."

"Silly fellow," Europe put in.

"As you have figured it yourself, gracious heir, Maupin gained the interest and the backing of a dark commerce principal and a massacars' league. He holds this interest still, despite Swill's ruin at the fall of the fortalice out Sulk End way and with it the removal of ducal approval. Now that you are returned to us, Maupin has grown rather anxious to fortify his dens and is hiring as many sturdies and mercenary fellows as will place themselves under his banner. And with all this, he remains determined to have at Mister Bookchild here, blinking so perplexedly beside me."

Rossamünd schooled his lids to a facsimile of unruffled stillness.

"Pater has run himself out so far on the credit of the Archduke's favor in his desire to get at me," Europe posited, "I would think he had scant option but to burrow himself in so deep. Especially now that he knows his attempt at my elimination failed."

"If I may, gracious daughter . . ." The Baron Sainte smiled as he went on. "Whatever you intend, Maupin is nicely perplexed at your gala."

The fulgar gave a cryptic smile. "Nothing like a festivity to lift the common spirits distressed at distant Winstermill's fall," she said.

"Of course . . ." The Baron Finance's expression took on the dogged cast of someone fully expecting that which he did not at all desire. "To that end I can offer you intelligence of perhaps a deeper and better sort than your Mister Rakestraw has garnered. Though I am certain Mister Rakestraw's scarlets are competent enough, you ought to take the services of one or even two of my percusors. Messrs. Slitt and Camillo are most excellent for the purpose."

Percusors! They always made it into pamphlets as the worst of all scoundrels: murderers for sport, money and state.

"What might your duchess say of such a common use of her political apparatus?" Europe inquired, arching a brow.

"I have always had the understanding, gracious lady, that your most excellent mother approves of whichever course I choose to travel, to maintain or increase the prospects of our sovereign state." He leaned forward a little. "And if I may, ma'am, I myself most heartily wish to see you preserved in so fraught an adventure."

"*Fraught,* is it?" A wry grimace flickered at the edges of the fulgar's mouth.

Finance tapped his nose again. "Your graciousness knows full well that to vie with the dark trades or one that they patronize is to clutch at great girth with small hands."

517

"And *you* know well, oh Baron, that my hands are thew enough to grasp anything onto which they lay themselves. There shall be no safety for me or mine unless I put out the eyes of this froward gentleman. Your intelligence I gratefully receive, but yet again I must decline the use of your staff."

Finance conceded with an elegant nod.

After the perplexing agent departed with many gracious words, Europe added to Rossamünd, "He will help regardless of my wish."

Rossamünd nodded. *Help in what?*

Three days before the gala, with Rossamünd deep in ever-quickening preparations, Mister Oberon performed an examination of his mistress. At its conclusion he sought Rossamünd out and advised him to make emunic reborate, a treacle found in Europe's expurgatory and good for fulgars given to overexerting themselves in the stouche.

"Unlike plaudamentum, it keeps for a small while," the transmogrifer explained, "and is to be drunk a few hours before a fight. Please make sufficient doses to be taken over the next four days."

And with that Oberon left.

In the afternoon, with the sky remaining blue and unrepentantly clear, Mister Brugel the armouriere presented to Europe a most exquisite set of proofing. It was, he assured her in the most grandiloquent terms, the best protection money could gain while still holding easy movement. With

Claudine and Brugel's female assistant to help with points, frogs and buckles, it took the fulgar more than an hour to fit.

Once all was in place, the Branden Rose immediately went up to the ludion, drawing a line of spectators after her. With dancelike spins and vaults over the glossy dark boards of the broad hall, she tested the freedom of the harness. Watching on in bliss, Brugel sat with his assistant on a row of leather campaign stools beside the large fireplace of green stone at the far end of the ludion as the Branden Rose proved the suppleness and robustness of his creation. In joy he would frequently spring from his seat and hurry over to the fulgar to point out the virtues of his design or clap and cry compliments to the lady's grace.

"Brava! M'lady! Brava! You are a jewel amid jewels! How well you set off my cuts!"

Over the usual layers of white petticoats was a black soe coat of flaring frock and high fan-shaped collar that protected the nape and base of Europe's head. Bound in at the elbow and forearm by sturdy vambrins of stiffened black soe, its sleeves were loose and puffed. Unusually, they were made of a different cloth: a glossy delicate grass green that shifted hues as it moved to a warm pale yellow, and patterned with daisylike flowers of fiery red. Over the hem of the coat was fitted a second skirt split into four panels: the sides and back were black, finished in a band of cloth-of-silver with silver brocade; its front panel was an apron of the same patterned mercurial material as the sleeves. This was held to Europe's body by a broad sash of glossy black wrapped about her whole torso, binding her chest firmly,

519

fastened at the back with frogging and finished in a large bow. Atop this she finally donned what Brugel called an eighth, a short pollern-coat of buff that barely covered her bosom, fastening down the left and under her arm, its collar and frogging brocaded in deep red.

Eyes alive with a joy Rossamünd rarely saw, the fulgar watched herself—or rather, the new harness—in the long mirrors, bending and flexing, stretching seams as far as she could, extending cloth as far as it might, seeking small adjustments. Standing with Claudine and Kitchen by the tall windows, Rossamünd watched his mistress' dance with breath held.

When she was finished, it was to a small clatter of wondering applause.

"This will do nicely as my new Number 3, Mister Brugel," she said matter-of-factly, a patina glowing on her wan brow. "You have excelled as always."

The armouriere beamed.

With that she departed the ludion to change into more domestic attire.

In the gray hours Rossamünd felt himself shaken awake.

"Mister Rossamünd, sir." It was Pallette, anxious, fretting at Rossamünd's hand.

"Miss Europe is in trouble?" he asked, rubbing at the blear clouding his senses, squinting into the steadily brightening bright-limn the alice-'bout-house gripped so shakily.

"No, sir, no! She is well," she returned, puzzled. "It's Mister Vinegar—that is to say, Master Fransitart, sir—"

"What about Master Fransitart?" Rossamünd sat up quickly, suspicions coming home to roost.

"Nectarius here says he let him out after we had all turned in last night, opened the gate again under promise that Master Fransitart be back by now, but he has not shown as agreed!"

Standing at the foot of the stairs in the vestibule hall, the nightlocksman, bearing his own bright-limn and looking sheepish with battered tricorn wrung in fist, told the same story.

"Did he say where he was going?" Rossamünd demanded.

"Na—"

"*He's* in here, me hearties!" came Fransitart's own faltering voice, trying to sound strong as he called from the hiatus. There they found him, old and wan, grotesquely lit by the swinging limnulight. Head lolling, eyes red-rimmed and watery, the ex–dormitory master peered up at him groggily. Instead of a broken limb there was no limb at all, just a neatly capelined stump just below the shoulder.

"Master Frans!" Rossamünd cried.

"He must've just turned in," Nectarius grumbled querulously, "while I was gettin' Miss Pallette 'ere."

"Pallette, get Crispus!" the young factotum ordered. "Nectarius, hold the doors for me!" Careless of the spectacle, the young factotum lifted the old vinegaroon from his couch and carried him bodily from the hiatus to his room, ignoring Fransitart's grizzling complaints that he could walk on his own!

The nightlocksman was so stunned at this small show of

Rossamünd's strength that he forgot to prop open the servants' port.

"The *door,* Nectarius!" Rossamünd barked, not caring about the puzzled and uneasy looks the nightlocksman gave him as he struggled by and on to Fransitart's cot.

"Blood and bruises, man! Are you always the source of such dramas?" Crispus demanded of the old dormitory master as, clad in dressing gown, his hair a feral spray of white, the physician hurried into the pallet. "Where is your arm at now, sir!" All mildness gone, he rebuked Fransitart with a martial rigor Rossamünd had seen him use only against the Master-of-Clerks. "The erreption of a limb is no simple occasion; implements must be thoroughly thatigated, vital vessels duly cautered! What backlot shambleman did this *favor* for you?"

Plainly addled by some kind of soporating spirit, Fransitart ducked his head and muttered a sullen obscenity.

"It'd be Master Meech," Craumpalin interjected in a guiltily quiet voice, struggling with crutches to rise from his own cot.

"And pray who is he?" the physician demanded hotly.

"He served as a loblolly on the *Venerable* with us, got a dischargement back in seventy-one on account of his sick mother and his game leg; settled in this here city on Change Lane to take up taxidermy."

"A *taxidermist!*" Crispus almost spat the word.

"Always loved stuffin' his animals." Fransitart chuckled woozily. "Had a whole cabin squashed with 'em by the end, an' 'is shop is to the top with 'em . . . I reckon he must give service to a great lot of folks, 'cause 'e 'as some right sharp bone knives handy . . ."

"Master Frans!" Rossamünd added some chiding of his own.

With a snort of reproach, Crispus bent to examine the stump closely. "Well, you can thank the course of the Lots and the will of Providence too that this *Meech* fellow seems to be handy with his business. You fellows!" he commanded Nectarius and Wenzel, standing as humbly as they could by the door as Kitchen appeared yawning. "Fetch me extra pillows. Mister Craumpalin! Master Bookchild! I am sure you know the script for birchet and vauqueline—"

"Aye, that we do . . ."

"Then go and test them. Let us hope this Meech is as good as the knot and fit of his bandaging suggest!"

At this, the young factotum and the old dispenser meekly obeyed, brewing as fast as sensitive processes of chemistry and Craumpalin's crutch-slow gait would allow. In his haste, Rossamünd left the old dispenser to come at his own pace from the saumery and hurried ahead with the vauqueline to find Europe just arrived at the old salts' humble quarters. She looked unruffled at such an unseemly hour yet was clearly unhappy at the fuss.

"Well betide you, madam." The physician greeted Europe in his stiffest physicking manner. "Our friend is as well as can be expected, though perhaps feeling a little foolish . . ."

Despite the meek slump in his shoulders, an obstinate gleam in the vinegaroon's eye spoke most eloquently that he was yet determined in the set of his course.

The fulgar took in the entire scene in an inkling. "The break not enough for you, Master Vinegar?" she asked coolly.

"Why did you do it, Master Frans?" Rossamünd breathed.

The ex–dormitory master regarded his onetime charge somberly, eyes full of a thousand thoughts.

Folding her arms, Europe leaned against the doorjamb. "Indeed, Master Vinegar!" she said huskily. "Simply removing the offending patch of flesh would have sufficed, sir. What use are you to me with one limb?"

Grumbling incoherently, Fransitart became genuinely sheepish. "Vinegars get their wings off for bone breaks all th' time and still go on a-servin' . . ." was about all that Rossamünd could make out, and maybe, "Ye need not fear—I'll not be a make-weight to ye."

Realizing the moment, Crispus excused himself quietly, softly calling Pallette out with him.

There was a bump at the door and Craumpalin bumbled back into the room, toiling in on his crutch, his brow glistening with sweat as he bore a pot of foul-smelling birchet. "Here, thee daft basket!" he gruffed. "Drink and get healing." He nodded to the bandaged stump. "So it's gone at last. Are thee any happier?"

"Ye know full well, Pin, I took th' mark back at that fortress 'cause o' the two of us, I can afford to lose a wing easiest," Fransitart gruffed in return. Rubbing his eyes irritably, he drank the foul-smelling draught.

"You always meant to get it cut?" Rossamünd gasped incredulously.

"I have to own that it's so, lad, aye." The old salt's dogged expression fell. "I might 'ave got it off sooner but that I was put upon by my own girlish curiousness to see for sure if th' punct would prove."

"But Swill had one anyway!" Rossamünd insisted, with as much hope as conviction.

"Aye . . . There is that," the ex–dormitory master conceded. "But 'e's gone now. . ." He looked hard at Rossamünd, pain and confusion suddenly clear. "Don't ye see, lad!" he returned bitterly. "One ill-got mark is enough in a lifetime, but two o' them—*an'* one made from yer own ever-livin' claret, lad—is more'n I can bear!"

Rossamünd had no answer to this. He grasped Fransitart's free hand—his *only* hand—and as the old salt drifted off, just held it.

25

THE GRAND GALA

flitterwills small winged bogles, their form often a crude simulacrum of everymen yet with more distorted proportions. One of the few flying bogles—since the exodus of the naeroë—who make use of the winds and air, they are found only in the remotest, often terribly threwdish places, though there are meant to be many lurking in the Schmetterlingerwald north of Wörms and ruled by the Duchess of Butterflies. This is all conjecture, of course; ancient texts hold them to be among the tribe of monster known as nissë, but in common culture flitterwills are pure myth.

THE day of the grand gala finally arrived with a growl of far-off thunder.

"Perfect!" Europe declared, sipping the morning's plaudamentum and staring from her file window at the frowning southern sky. "Perfect . . . ," she repeated softly.

Cloche Arde was properly "tricked out"—as Fransitart called it, recovering well from his lost limb in one of the less prettified parts of the house—looking now like some Occidental pavilion. Europe's entire set of bom e'do screens were placed to direct where to and where *not* to go, and the ceiling was virtually hidden behind a veritable constellation of lanterns—great *skies* of red, orange, yellow-green and white. Staging refectories were established on each floor so that the footmen could fetch and deliver drinks and the simpler vittles without the need to descend constantly to the kitchen.

Feeling by middens that he had run a half mile making certain all was truly set, Rossamünd knocked at Europe's door to inquire of his mistress to come out and give her own endorsement of the arrangements.

"I am sure it is all excellent, Rossamünd," she said with distracted impatience, strolling quickly about the ludion where the first orchestra—fully costumed in magenta frock suits and magenta bag-wigs—was already at its tuning on the elevated stage behind the stairs. "You and Kitchen and Mistress Clossette will have done a fine job," she added, and returned to her file.

In the afternoon the dance masters and entertainers arrived, all shown to their respective habitats to begin their own preparations, swelling the numbers already crammed into Cloche Arde until Rossamünd wondered where the guests themselves might fit. Chief among these was a Master Papelott, the paraductor—the master of the unfolding of the entire night—recommended by the Lady Madigan. Exchanging greetings in the hiatus, Rossamünd peered a little dubiously at the slight, almost sickly, man. Despite the gorgeousness of Master Papelott's golden silk frock coat, it did little to give mass to his scrawny frame, yet when he spoke with what he called his "assembly tone," he straightened admirably and the most articulate and astonishingly powerful voice boomed from his undernourished bosom and wiry throat. With such volume he easily marshaled the entire company of additional staff—mostly footmen dressed in full red and magenta livery—in the vestibule for inspection and instruction.

Among the planned diversions, Rossamünd was gratified to discover that Europe had hired the lank-haired concometrist who had approached her for work when they had first come to Brandenbrass. "I'm to draw spedigraphs of as many guests as want them," he explained, looking much less dismayed and introducing himself as Economous Musgrove.

Yet the most unusual of the performing set was Madam Lux, the benign mesmerist, her head utterly bald—surely as naked as the day she entered this world—and the corners of her eyes spoored with upward bent arrows. Above the gathered neckline of her draping cloak of soft silver peeped the dark red curlicues of many, many cruorpunxis, scrawled about the entire circumference of her throat. Here was the rarest of all rare creatures—an old lahzar. Walking with the help of a young woman—her own factotum, no doubt—and speaking so softly Rossamünd was forced to lean in to hear, Madam Lux presented a spectacle of harmlessness. Even so, the young factotum thought it very peculiar of the Branden Rose to allow a wit, no matter how aged, into her house.

Everything about Europe is peculiar at the moment, he reflected with an inward shrug, showing the madam mesmerist to her place at a small black side table in the easily reached hiatus.

When all was as ready as it could be, Rossamünd left the chaos in Master Papelott's and Kitchen's care, brewed treacle and deposited it at his mistress' door, then finally retired to get ready. In his set the young factotum dutifully scrubbed himself twice, and after this submitted to a thorough primping. Teeth polished, nails pared, hair trimmed and waxed, he emerged from behind the screen in his finest shirt and longshanks to find a box left for him on the coverlet of his bed. It was wrapped in expensive red paper, and a simple card was slotted in its black ribbons.

> To My Fine Factotum,
>
> In anticipation that you have forgotten your own costume fancies, I provide this for you, *and* for our own and private jest.
>
> EU

Prising the wrappings apart with shaking hands, Rossamünd let out a short barking laugh, for inside he found a maschencarde mask exquisitely fashioned in the form of a sparrow's face. Beside it was laid a peacock blue coat made of shimmering cloth much in the hue of Cinnamon's own flower-petal jacket and a white-and-black-striped weskit. To the bemusement of Pallette, he laughed again when he put it all on and reviewed himself in the mirror through the mask's ample-looking holes. Perched on the sill of the open windows, Darter Brown flew in, and, twittering joyously, made circling loops about the young factotum's sparrow-masked head.

As Pallette left, Rossamünd held out his finger for the little fellow to alight upon. "Keep an eye out for Miss Europe, Darter," he said.

Peering at Rossamünd with almost human pondering, the he-sparrow voiced a single clear and positive *chirrup!* and launched himself outside once more.

"Well-a-day, Master Sparrow!" Crispus chortled, recognizing Rossamünd's fancies instantly as the young factotum entered Fransitart and Craumpalin's pallet. "Your mistress plays a handsome joke!"

Rossamünd gave half a beck in gratitude.

Fransitart frowned. "A mite too *handsome,* I reckon . . . ," he growled. Dressed in a lustrous black suit, the ex–dormitory master had the role for the evening—and Craumpalin too—of helping to keep the various drivers and lesser staff who would inevitably attend fed and occupied. Looking pale but well—his empty left sleeve pinned up to his shoulder like a naval hero's—Fransitart pulled at the especially high collar and stock and tilted his head to and fro against the constriction. "Someone might guess at who he is."

"Aye," said Craumpalin, clad very much like his friend. "Thee'd think there was enough dark conjecturing boiling away without throwing powder on the fire."

Crispus smiled. "I doubt *anyone* coming here tonight would know near enough of the true nature of the great world out *there*"—he waved his hand vaguely—"to deduce the truth of the origin of Rossamünd's fancies."

As for the physician, he was dressed as a lamplighter. "In honor of our fallen manse and worthy brothers," he elaborated. For Imperial quabard he had a simple soft vest half red, half yellow; for fodicar a broom shaft painted black with some sticks adhered to the top to simulate the crank-hook and sleeve-catcher. His stiff hair was pointing per-pendicularly from the back of his head, gathered as best it could be in a gray bow. He was very nervous and kept rocking on his heels and shuffling through the cards he had prepared of his salient points for the oratory. "The big event has almost come."

As they talked, Wenzel appeared at the pallet door, red-faced and frustrated. "I 'ave been trying to find you all af-ternoon, sir," he began. He then informed Rossamünd that an odd manner of parcel had arrived for him earlier that day and was even now sitting in the obverse. "It was the least troublesome resting place for it, sir," he concluded, almost apologetically.

Rossamünd asked who had delivered it, but Wenzel de-clared himself mystified.

"I weren't the one who took the delivery," he explained. "But the general word is that it is most certainly yours."

Negotiating a way through the madness of final gala preparations, Rossamünd, and the three curious older men with him, found a broad yet shallow wooden box as Wenzel had said—no missive with it, not even an addressing bill or return directions, just blank dark wood bound tight in hemp strapping. Impatient, Rossamünd hurried it back to Fransitart and Craumpalin's pallet and broke the bands with his hands alone, to find thick canvas wrappings within pro-tecting . . . a painting.

"It's of you, Rosey me lad!" Fransitart exclaimed.

Indeed it was, for there in rich, deftly applied paint was

531

Rossamünd, staring out at himself. "Miss Pluto has finished it!" he cried in amazement, unable to help staring right back at himself in his delight.

The portrait was astoundingly lively, showing him sitting at the three-quarter yet looking squarely out from the picture with an expression of such frank and earnest searching that Rossamünd was forced to ask of the older men, "Do I truly look like this?"

"I reckon Miss Pluto's got yer fixed just right," Fransitart chuckled.

Grinning, Craumpalin nodded emphatically. "She's shown thee true, me lad."

"What will ye do with it?" Fransitart asked, a hint perhaps of his own desire to possess the piece in his tone.

"I—I do not know . . . "

"A fine, fine likeness," Crispus proclaimed, holding the portrait at arm's length to squint at it as if this might improve his view. "You ought to show it to your mistress."

Rossamünd shook his head. "I do not reckon she will appreciate it at this moment," he said. Yet, returning to his duties with the image wrapped once more and under his arm, he thought again on his original determination. Approaching Europe's file, he placed his portrait carefully against the carven door and there he left it.

The sun's sanguine glow finally faded in the west, flushing the sky a deep evening rose. The rain that had spent the day growling at the edge of the world blew up from the Grume. With its arrival came the gala's first guests, dashing under parasols from their glossy carriages to the melodious and courtly welcome of Cloche Arde. *Fighting weather,* Rossamünd observed gravely at the grumble of thunder as he stood in the vestibule to welcome the invitees.

As proper night enfolded them all, Master Papelott stood at the top of the first flight of the stairs, and, with an august cry, declared, "Hale night and merry! The Duchess-in-waiting of Naimes welcomes all comers!" The grand gala was set under way.

Unlike the joyous sweaty simplicity of a country fête, the grand gala was a noble gathering of graceful souls. In the ludion there was little laughter, scant clapping and certainly no appreciative stomping of feet. Instead it was a-buzz with restrained genteel conversation and the audible shuffling of august folk promenading with exquisite swaying unison to the playing of either of the thirty-piece orchestras that took turns to give them music. With much bowing and curtsying and subtle playing up to each other, these lofty people danced a turn or two, spoke and ate in exclusive huddles and strolled every floor taking in the entertainments, settling longest in the room most suited to their temperament or returning to dance again.

At every turn on every floor Rossamünd was met with grave faces and serious conversation, the precise studied manners of the gala-goers at odds with the garish and often quite ludicrous costumery draping them. The quality of the fancies varied greatly, from simple paper and card facsimiles to real teratological equipment undoubtedly gained at great expense. There was many a goggle-eyed nicker and buck-toothed bogle as well as beasts from distant lands—

533

crocidoles, lyons, even an orange-furred aurang; a set of women in clear cahoots were festooned in diaphanous wings like mythic flitterwills. Pretty—and not so pretty—young ladies in quest of advantageous marriages costumed themselves with clinching, flattering dresses and maschencarde masks to set off their fluttering lashes. Wrapped in flowing robes, many elder guests came as kings or queens of ancient days, though none dared dress as Idaho or Dido—such claims of costume would be gauche and overreaching in the extreme. Yet by far the most popular theme of costume for the night was teratologist, and of these, antique monster-slaying heldins were commonest.

Grand and poised though this night might be, it certainly was noisy; not a general boisterousness, but rather a universal medley of conversation that swelled as certain *personalities* made exhibitions of themselves in mirth or passion. Moving between floors—from the methodical madness of the kitchens to the stately motion of the ludion—Rossamünd was constantly met with a cacophony of music and ceaseless conversation. Soon his night settled into rounds about the house, bumping through the tide of gentry seeing, strutting and being seen, to identify problems and offer to all who asked the formula he had been given earlier that day, "The Duchess-in-waiting makes especial preparations for the night and will attend as soon as she is able." Met with many strange looks and interrupted conversations reduced to furtive whispering, Rossamünd never remained stationary long enough to hear more than snippets of talk, yet after only a short while his thoughts revolved unceasingly about sentences only partly heard.

"I have it that her coursing party was not near as successful as this little gathering suggests."

"What was she doing on a private hunt, I ask you, when our very colonial bastions were being assaulted? Why was she not there to avert disaster? . . ."

"How surprised I was to receive *her* invitation; she *never* responds to mine . . ."

"I heard our thorn-ed miss sent the Archduke packing at her most recent visit to the 'Dirk, the creature! Left him all in blushes and stutters."

"Hush, dear! The *creature's* servant listens."

"Isn't there meant to be something peculiar about her newest factotum? Something *untoward* . . ."

On the steps between the ludion and billiards and oratory, the young factotum passed the Lady Madigan. Though distinguishable in telltale gray, the fulgarine peer had come in oddly modest attire: a robe of flowing gray, its sleeves baggy to the elbow, ballooning over the sturdy vambrins of gray soe about her forearms and over her hands. Clinched about her chest and middle she wore a stomacher of spangled gray soe stiffened with buff lining fastened with a small bow at her diaphragm. But for the quality of the cloth, the obvious shimmer of gauld on harder proofing, she looked a poor moiler scratching a life out in the Paucitine. Even in such dowdy attire, whenever Rossamünd spotted her, she was encircled by a host of admiring men, each making loud and flowing praise of her clever variation on the theme. She smirked and smiled and gave clever answers and kept each fellow hanging on every word. Threedice, her factotum, seemed to have come as himself, though in slightly heavier proofing than such an evening required. Staying a respectable but constant pace behind, he glowered unremittingly with more than professional intent at his mistress' gallants.

Rossamünd spotted Mister Carp in the ludion, the man-of-business dressed as an elephantine, his oversized coat stuffed with great paddings of pillows and cloth, conspicuous as the only one of such fellows at the gala, real or contrived. He had come with his wife—a wife Rossamünd did not know he had. Introduced as Madam Germinë Carp, she was a small slender woman almost lost inside a great pile of gauzy cloth. What she was meant to be Rossamünd could not tell, yet he did not think it polite to ask. Of few words and wide wet eyes, Madam Carp looked uncomfortable to be squeezed with so many of the lofty and grand. Rather strangely, Carp himself did not possess his usual swagger, and the two sat on their own at the edge of the gaieties exchanging looks and brief remarks with each other. Rossamünd tried to swap a friendly word with them as often as he could and was happy when he finally saw them in close conversation with Crispus down in the billiard room.

Several times Rossamünd thought he spied the brightly armored colonel of the lesquin company Europe had met with several times over the week talking closely with Mister Rakestraw, the sleuth in drab and heavy proofing.

"Well now, Mister Bookchild! A sparrow seems a rather dowdy creature for such a fine rout," a jolly voice declared with breezy pointedness, picking Rossamünd in the crowd of the hiatus despite his sparrow mask.

Turning, the young factotum found Baron Finance, come as the most *fluffy*, dandidawdling fluff it was possible to be, his silvered wig so high and his cheeks so rouged as to be almost feminine. "Where is your mistress at, sir?" the Chief Emissary pressed with affable persistence as Rossamünd lifted the mask up over his crown to greet him properly. "Still at her evening toilet despite the festivities?"

"I am sorry, Baron, sir," Rossamünd offered, reiterating the formula he had repeated many, many times already that night.

"I am sure she will," Finance replied knowingly, then said more seriously, "Though I cannot say her guests will make much good from such excuses . . . Ah, but what can we do, Mister Bookchild?" He smiled suddenly. "We are merely satellites trapped in her inexorable gravity."

For a moment they watched a trio of smirking flitterwills sit themselves before Madam Lux and submit to the benign mesmerist's outré expertise. Clearly skeptical as they watched the old wit close her eyes and touch lightly at her left temple with shaking hand, the three young women were soon exclaiming and drawing attention to themselves at the imagined sensations stirring in their thoughts.

"I hear trumpets!" one girl declared in frank wonderment, looking up as if the room were full of heralding cornets and flugels.

Whatever misery Madam Lux might have brought to monster-kind in her prime, reduced by time and infirmity to such trickery—however skillfully achieved—seemed an

537

ignoble end for a once-mighty neuroticrith.

"If I might say, sir . . . ," Baron Finance interposed on Rossamünd's thoughts, his tone lowered discreetly. "Whatever predicaments your *irregularities* might have brought her"—*and me,* his eyes said—"the home of our duchess-daughter is a most cheery place since your replacement of the *previous fellow*"—Rossamünd knowing full well he spoke of Licurius—"and, quite confoundingly, *she* is of much better countenance too. At my report, our benevolent mistress, the Duchess herself—ever concerned after her daughter, however much the scion of the house of Naimes persists in a life of her own—desires me to welcome you as an appendant to the Court of Naimes."

"Uh . . ." Rossamünd bowed to this lofty acknowledgment. "Tell her graciousness thank you, sir," he said, straightening, and, with a sick thrill of dismay, discovered Scrupulus Sicus, Imperial Secretary, emerging from the endless flow of people leaving coats and making first meetings in the hiatus.

What is he doing here! Europe cannot have invited him?

Complete with olive wreath and voluminous wrappings of white robes, Sicus had come as a gilded glaucologue of the Empire's first formation. Yet, far from the authoritative hauteur of the inquiry at Winstermill, the Imperial Secretary looked patently nervous to find Rossamünd in the press. Bending humbly at the middle, he held out his invitation like a patent of nativity demanded by gate wardens and inquired after the "rightful and most gracious lady of the house." His flattery was a long way from the strident terms he used at the lamplighters' once-great fortress.

Flagitious shrew was one such strident term that rose in Rossamünd's mind. He beheld the man stoutly, seeing full well that this fellow knew exactly who *he* was and in what circumstances they had last met.

The Imperial Secretary squirmed for just a moment and then, with several clearings of his thickly wrapped throat, said, "Well, young master, at the Duchess-Heir's most *gracious* invitation I can only offer her my unqualified support against such a scoundrel as Honorius Swill. He fooled us all, I would say"—the fellow's face paled slightly—"with his apparently learn-ed convictions. The authority of the well-read, ha ha . . ."

Rossamünd did not smile.

"Your benevolent mistress, however," the man pressed on awkwardly, glancing to Finance only a few feet away, "has showed her abounding and much-praised quality in seeing through him in the first. I can only regret any . . . *misunderstanding* that may have arisen betwixt your mistress and the Emperor through myself over this affair, and can only assert in the most earnest terms that the Lady of Naimes has once more—indeed, never lost—the Emperor's full and complete confidence. *This* elaborates most fully on the matter." He held up a red-wrapped buff wallet. "I am sure the Duchess-Heir will find it most satisfactory." Upon discovering Europe had yet to display herself, the Imperial Secretary showed open relief and gave the red-buff wallet to Rossamünd.

The young factotum smiled inwardly at the irony as he took the Imperial parcel. Would the Emperor be so quick with this *confidence* if he knew the nature of the soul to whom his agent was speaking? "I shall give her your *apology*, sir." He bowed, alert to this Imperial bureaucrat's clear discomfort at the emphasis of this word. "I am sure she will give it the proper merit."

"Ah, most excellent, young fellow," Sicus returned, brows creasing slightly as he tried to fathom whether his interlocutor was being genuine or pointed. "I—uh—thank you."

"May you have a good night, sir," Rossamünd returned, trying to achieve the same unequivocal poise of his mistress.

"Ah, yes . . ." Bending a final unfinished bow and giving a last uncomfortable look to Finance, the Imperial Secretary left them.

"Swill's allies forsake him utterly now he is dead," said the Chief Emissary in low voice, his expression grim indeed as he watched Sicus retreat into the ceaseless motion of fancied guests to find more comfortable company.

"Secretary Sicus seemed a mite happy to *not* properly meet with Miss Europe," Rossamünd observed, savoring this rare moment of vindication.

The Baron Sainte could not help a grin. "*That,* Mister Bookchild," he said happily, observing Madam Lux convince a dashing young fellow swatting and ducking at empty air that he was bothered by a host of buzzing flies, "is the nearest a person might come to an endorsed and proper *sorry* in this Empire of ours."

A little past eight-of-the-clock the Archduke himself—and his large retinue with him—arrived, gracing Europe's soirée costumed in a long black tourette upon his crown and dressed in an antiquated harness hung with many bright-black stoups. Rossamünd instantly recognized him as Harold, champion of the Battle of the Gates, perceiving the Archduke's intent to style himself in the same heroic line as a staunch defender of the people against all foes. Of his retinue came a veritable quarto of men of the highest stature with such titles as Prime Minister, Captain-Marshal of the Lifeguard, Chief Draw of the Purse—people Rossamünd recognized by face if not by name from his brief visit to the Brandendirk. With them too was a woman of dark and foreign beauty whose presumably natural dress of gold scales and diaphanous cloth of mauve and gold was sufficiently exotic to class as fancies. "The Princess Awahb, Fatemah of Pander Tar! Heiress to the Peacock Throne!" the doormen on every floor announced as she ascended, to the general wonder of all.

Receiving the heiress of Naimes' formula for nonattendance with smiling grace, the Archduke nevertheless appeared slightly provoked not to be personally greeted by Europe.

He hopes to show off his princess and trump Europe with her, Rossamünd could not help but think.

Indeed, the ruler of the mighty city of Brandenbrass, with his Princess—quickly becoming the darling of the gala—had to wait for nigh on an hour to play his trump, for it was not until nine-of-the-clock precisely that the Branden Rose made her appearance. Loudly announced by Master Papelott, she stepped gracefully into the now hushed ludion, astonishing everyone with her costume.

541

Assuming she was to be wearing the gorgeous harness she had tried three days earlier, Rossamünd was himself taken aback.

Clad in a wide skirt of deep red and a lorica of burnished bronze scales draped in a thick hackle of leonguile hide, she wore a high bronze helm pushed back upon her head, its crown crested with horsehair of black-and-white stripes.

Recovering, Rossamünd understood immediately who she intended herself to be.

Euodice, the historied speardame to Idaho.

To those in the company of revelers who knew their matter, the import of Europe's fancy dress was bold and clear. *I am of the Old Blood,* it said; *my line is more ancient than the Empire.* It was an incontestable claim and it was also a challenge.

People began crowding into the ludion, all eager to hear what the Branden Rose might have to say at such an uncharacteristic social display.

His mistress finally debouched from her boudoir, Rossamünd felt the release of some inward knot he did not know he had. *At last!* A part of him could not help but wonder if she had marked the painting waiting by her door.

Handed by the Archduke himself onto the orchestra's rostrum, the Duchess-in-waiting of Naimes looked like an Attic empress staring complacently out at the great company in their fancies. To Rossamünd it seemed by the glimmer in her cool hazel gaze that she was laughing inwardly at the ludicrous spectacle of costume before her.

"I thank you all for condescending to my little event," she said with bold clarity, "to help me rejoice in the success

EUROPE
IN SPEARDAME FANCY

of another course and to bring a correction to the current of recent *ill* wind." She glanced ever so briefly—the merest nigh-undetectable flicker of her eyes—to the Archduke. "Many of you might marvel at such a turn of character; yet I seek only—with this little affair of mine—to offer to you that which so many of you have so unflaggingly offered to me over the long years." Europe smiled with such winsome warmth that it left little room for any offense. "I place no limit on this night. Remain in my hospitality for as long as you will. So now, continue as I presently attempt a feat greater than the slaying of any prowling bogle and speak with you *all* before the night is through. I thank you."

While the Branden Rose descended, nodding and smiling piously to general applause, an immense white molded dessert was brought up to the ludion. Carried in a broad tray upon the shoulders of four footmen, it was made in the shape of the trefoiled heart of Naimes and swam in a bath of deep pink raspberry glatin. "Victory Flummery" Papelott called it, "in honor of our gracious hostess' success!" Served in fine Heil glassware of the most rarefied rosy tint, it was flavored with what was proudly declared as vanilla. People *ooh*ed at so rare and fashionable a novelty. Dressed in a maschencarde mask of a horse, a learned fellow near where Rossamünd stood at the summit of the steps loudly enlightened all in earshot—listening or otherwise—that it was gained from the pod of some singular orchid growing in the febrile islands of the Sinus Tintinabuline. Opposed to the flummery model of the Sloe Sapperling at the Patredike, this dessert looked positively delectable, and the young factotum eyed it hungrily on his way to his mistress' side.

Proudly he followed behind her as she proved herself true to her determination to exchange a word or two with all, her manner as bland and accommodating as he had ever known it to be. It was wearying to watch and to hear; he was amazed at the duchess-daughter's fortitude.

One aged dame in virginal white, whose gelid expression told far more clearly her true sentiments toward Europe than her silken words, dared a remark on Rossamünd, declaring with saccharine notes, "So young in his trade, my dear, and we've heard such *things* about him . . ."

"Only good *things,* I am sure," the Duchess-in-waiting returned wintrily, her smile thin.

"Oh, ah, yes yes." The woman blanched, realizing she had miscalculated. ". . . Certainly."

As for the Princess of Pander Tar, sat at one end of the hall among a throng of admirers both adoring and purely inquisitive, Europe did not—of course—prove at all trumped. Paying no more respect than she received, the Duchess-in-waiting was perfectly measured at their meeting, her greeting as cool as the Princess'.

"I know you will not mind my bringing such an august guest uninvited to your night, dear cousin Naimes," the Archduke purred smugly in aside to his hostess. "As especial guest in my courts I could not very well leave the Fatemah behind . . ."

"A new bosom to distract you, sir," Europe returned discreetly. "Be careful, Lady Madigan might grow jealous."

"Hmm." The Archduke smiled through his teeth. "Indeed . . ."

Though many looked at her with unaffected awe and respect, there were a few with whom the heiress of Naimes exchanged genuine felicitations. Much of the way about the ludion—and with the other floors still to visit—Europe abruptly insisted Rossamünd take his leave of her. "It shall be easier for me to make my path among the rest if I am unattended," she said.

Both relieved and a little perplexed to be so released, Rossamünd descended to the floor below, moving through the billiard room with its swaggering young players to look in on the oratory happening in the parlor beyond. His own oration done, Doctor Crispus was arguing robustly with those guests who reckoned themselves erudite or scholarly, who had perhaps sat a foundation at an athenaeum or abacus. It was a *rigorous* conversation that Rossamünd little understood, perpetually on the brink of devolving into more physical arguments. As for Mister and Madam Carp, they had apparently departed almost immediately after Europe had presented herself.

In the rear quarters the young factotum made another inquiry on his old masters' weal. Finding them both pale and flagging, he sent Fransitart and Craumpalin both—despite their grumbling about missing out—to their pallet to rest, ensuring healthy portions of the night's fare were sent promptly for them to sup on.

Under the sway of the latening hour and many a jovial glass, the solemnity of the gala began to unravel, and its graceful grandeur descended to something more akin to a country fête. As one of-the-clock was announced by Master

Papelott, the more sensible people began to have thoughts for home. As was only proper, these prudent souls sought to say good night to their hostess. Disgruntled murmurs began to ripple through the collected gentry that the Duchess-in-waiting could not be found. Calls for a search came from bolder throats, and though Papelott and Rossamünd, the footmen and most of the house staff sought high and low for her, it was to no avail.

The heiress of Naimes was gone.

Greatly affronted—all the work of Europe's bland affability undone in a moment—the sensible departed anyway, sniffing at apologies and claiming this as typical of such a fractious and unmanageable creature as the Branden Rose.

"She has invited us only to toy with us!" one grand dame declared severely on her exit.

"What do you expect from one who *has her own money?*" her equally elderly companion concurred, to the murmured agreement of all who heard.

At two—striking on Cloche Arde's long-case clocks, mantel timepieces and from the many repeaters in gentlemen's pockets—the orchestras finally submitted to exhaustion and, stowing their hundredweight of instruments aboard a large dray, left.

The fashionably or truly nocturnal remained, however, determined to avail themselves of the other entertainments while they were still to be had. Leaving these to the grace of Papelott and the footmen, Rossamünd continued to seek his mistress from highest loft to lowest buttery, from the most rearward pantry to the very gates of Cloche Arde, finding the Lady Madigan was missing too, with her Mister Rakestraw *and* the lesquin colonel. Even Baron Finance had departed, gone without a word. What was more, Darter Brown was nowhere to be found.

Standing finally in the foreyard, Rossamünd stared into the gloomy night and fathomed full well what was up.

From almost their first day at Orchard Harriet, Europe must have been developing her scheme, sending letters, drawing in her influence even from that remote haven, plotting the entire undertaking down to a device sure to keep Rossamünd out of her way. Even as *he* was occupied with the plans and arrangements for the grand gala, *she* had set deeper strategies in motion, and while *he* busied himself so self-importantly with the immediacy of his duties, *she* had brought her scheme to fruition . . . And now the Branden Rose was gone out into the perilous city to bring vengeance upon Pater Maupin while Rossamünd, her own factotum, had been left deliberately and uselessly behind.

26

UNINVITED CALLERS

Lampedusa deep-dwelling kraulschwimmen serpent and mighty sea-wretchin who terrorized the waters of the Grume for a thousand years before it was called by that name. Finally, bearing the mythic spiegel-blade, *Paschendralle*, the legendary Piltdown heldin-king, Tascifarnias, stood upon the shore where Brandenbrass now has its harbor and challenged Lampedusa to a contest to see who should rule land and sea. There upon the sand they fought, Tascifarnias slaying Lampedusa even as he was slain, the flowing of their combined blood purported to have changed the white sand black.

ROSSAMÜND stood alone by an open window in his set. Behind him the house of the Branden Rose ticked, empty now of its revelry, starkly silent but for the sporadic thump or clink of clearing and cleaning after such a magnificent event. Though the desire was strong with those desperate for fun to remain into the small hours, the departure of the orchestra, for all intents, spelled the end of the gala. In various fine conveyances—a number including the Archduke, his lofty friends and sycophants— they left with a profound rattling of hoof and wheel to find a suitable small-hour club to pursue delight.

Outside it had become cold and still like a breath held, the low clouds fluorescing with Phoebë's radiance as she climbed to her acme beyond them.

She was out there somewhere amid the increasingly shadowy city and its inscrutable buildings, perhaps even now coming to hand strokes with Maupin and his agents, wrestling on public greens, in lanes, in cellars, room to room in those high ubiquitous half-houses.

Rossamünd drew in a frustrated breath, smelling fresh-fallen rain.

Crickets made sweet sparse song down in the yard.

He stood and he watched . . .

Of all the staff, only Kitchen was unsurprised at the extraordinary and unseen departure of the Duchess-in-waiting of Naimes. "I have given my word to her, sir," the steward said bluntly when pressed, and would not be prevailed upon to speak more.

Crispus declared himself utterly flummoxed at her disappearance. "It is a plum ruse," he observed when Rossamünd quietly divulged his suspicion of her whereabouts. "But a rather excellent one too, don't you think."

The young factotum had to agree.

Well to the southeast, out in the sea of roofs and chimneys and trees a tiny orange glimmer shot on a steep and shuddering arc up into the heavens, then another of pinker hue sped into the inky firmament a little to the north. *Flares!* A third farther south joined them, a glittering delicate green. A thin wailing blew to him on the gusting, rising wind.

Rossamünd knew with a certainty that these were the heralds of Europe's assault.

The flares, their light quickly extinguishing on their

downward path, gave only the most general sense of direction, far too vague for a successful navigation. By such scant evidence he might spend all night till the assault was done, lost uselessly in unfamiliar streets trying to find her. *I could go to the Broken Doll . . .* Yet it was supremely unlikely Maupin would have his true den in so obvious a location.

The hall clock tocked ponderously.

The house breathed.

Peeping through a torrid gap in the heavenly fume, the moon lit the glistening, dripping turnabout beneath for a merest breath, long enough for Rossamünd to see sly activity: little lumps nosing about at the base of the cypress, one venturing toward the front door of the house itself.

A rabbit!

The tramp of Nectarius on his periodic round and the nimbus of his bright-limn coming about the corner of the lane running the side of Cloche Arde sent the furtive movement scattering. Holding his breath, Rossamünd watched the nightlocksman, lantern up, peer skeptically at the yard. Something fluttered obviously in the cypress. Nectarius gave a start and shook a fist at the little fellow, growling calumnies about "that unwholesome bird and its unwholesome master!" as he turned inside.

A flurry of air passed over his head, and a little thing swooped about him around and around.

"Darter!" he whispered. "Where is Miss Europe? Is she well?"

Darter Brown, faithful bird, chirruped loudly as he hovered agitatedly in front of him, giving a series of sporadic tweets as he alighted for a beat on the windowsill to catch a breath before dashing back into the night.

Rossamünd's heart missed a beat.

The little sparrow knew where she was!

Listening for the three telltale lots of thumps and clunks of the nightlocksman's retreat through the front, obverse doors and servants' port, Rossamünd hurried on his best proofed coat over the fanices he still wore. Taking up his digitals and stoups, his rod of keys and moss-light from the bedside dresser, he eased discreetly out onto the landing. Pallette was there, looking shot through, a pail of steaming water in one hand and a scrubbing brush in the other.

"I must be going out a moment," Rossamünd said quickly.

The alice-'bout-house blinked muzzily at him and his harness and said with a clumsy half curtsy, "As you like, sir."

"And go to bed, all of you," he added. "I reckon cleaning will be done just as properly in the morning. Tell Mister Kitchen I said so."

"Yes, sir . . ."

Stepping down to the rain-washed yard, Rossamünd was immediately met by Darter, who fluttered in agitation a few paces ahead, looping steadily toward the gate. Alert to the faintest tingle of threwd and moss-light thrust before him, Rossamünd trod lightly in the huskily grinding gravel, peering about with straining, searching eyes. There among the glory vine runners in the wan effulgence of limulight and gate-post lamp, tiny black pearls glinted beadily back at him from a dark soft-furred face. Long ears folded back over a downy rump. This was not just some ordinary rabbit, Rossamünd realized suddenly—certainly not the dreary one-eyed creature he had seen on his walk the other day; it was Ogh, one of the Lapinduce's own servants!

There was a soft press at his calves. It was Urgh, the twin of Ogh, urging him on.

Ogh took a long step toward the gate.

Darter Brown hopped about the ground between them in twittering agitation, patently keen to be on his way. *Chirrup!* cried the sparrow emphatically. *Chirrup! Chirrup!*

Humours beating loudly in his ears, Rossamünd unfastened the lock of the gate and stepped out onto the Harrow Road to find three more rabbits, meaner, mangier-looking beasts surviving in the city itself, noses patiently twitching. *Have they actually done as I have asked?* he marveled. Securing the lock, he properly belted his digitals and stoups about his waist as Darter Brown took a perch upon his shoulder.

At the lead, this little drove of rabbits immediately set off, taking him south over the Footling Inch Bridge and toward Brandentown proper. On puddled moon-shone streets, Rossamünd followed the pallid flash of the rabbits' cotton-tails as the blithely beasts bounded steadily from shadow to shadow. Often they would spring well ahead to wait on the edge of lantern light. When Rossamünd drew near, on they would hop to the next bend or corner to wait once more. Whenever some night-active person crossed their path— a night-soil-man with stinking cart or a desperate takeny seeking a late fare—the rabbits would scurry into the murk and obstacles of the street, to emerge once more when the way was clear.

Going left off the Harrow Road it was a long jog before they finally approached the circuit before the Moldwood. Rossamünd wondered for a moment as they passed its iron-bound entrance what the Lapinduce might think of his little charges heeding Rossamünd's bidding. *He must surely know . . .* Here they were met by another rabbit, as large as Ogh and Urgh yet with velvet fur of distinguished and near-invisible black, who took the lead and without hesitation continued onward down the Dove.

The blockhouse of the Cripplegate loomed, guarded even at this waning hour by a trio of flagging gate wards drooping on their muskets by a burning brazier in the shadow of the gate's great arch. Senses taut, Rossamünd watched as first Ogh and Urgh passed through unremarked in the shadows of the deep slate gutters between road and walk, barely daring to breathe as he went along himself.

"A *little* late for the *little* lord, ain't it? Yer mistress got ye baiting lovers, 'ey, boy-o?" was the sole comment, which set the three gate wards to lewd chuckling. Mercifully, however, they did not press further with awkward questions.

Just beyond the Cripplegate the rabbits halted.

Grateful for the pause and wishing he had thought to bring a skin or biggin of water, Rossamünd cautiously drew closer and saw them in silent communion with another of their tribe, a small and shabby beast. Their conference complete, the growing trace of coneys sprang off as one, made an abrupt left off the Dove and went down a street, running in the shadow of the curtain wall and its hem of half-houses. Rossamünd glimpsed a sign calling it Cannon Street,

OGH AND DARTER BROWN

and it proved a long curving way, the rabbits keeping to it as Phoebë reached her acme and began her descent of the murky, partly spangled sky. Finally at a fork they were met with another shabby city-living lapin-beast who assumed the role of pilot and took them right. On a lesser perpendicular junction yet another coney met them and took charge, keeping to the way they were on.

Abruptly a bedraggled hungry-eyed dog sprang bawling from some narrow alley and bore down on the coneys, intent on making one its late supper. The mangy rabbits disappeared in a trice, haring back past Rossamünd, while Ogh and Urgh and their larger brother remained frozen in lantern light. Rossamünd leaped forward to intervene, his sudden action flinging a sleepy Darter Brown from his shoulder roost. He need not have worried, for as soon as the cur closed, all three rabbits jumped high about it and kicked the dog savagely in its snout and neck, avoiding snapping jaws and kicking again and again.

The dog howled and stumbled. Utterly confounded, it scrabbled back.

Ogh and Urgh chased it down, still trying to kick it, sending the dog yowling to vanish down the lane whence it had sprung.

From a window high above, some surly soul half hollered for quiet.

Grown to a crowd of well over a dozen, the rough-rabbits reappeared and the weird band continued, new coneys materializing from obscure nooks at each significant change in course to take the lead. On streets empty and strangely still,

Rossamünd jogged stumblingly on, the rabbit-drove ever before and about him. Spotting a grand fountain bubbling on his left, set at the end of a very short alley in a tall alcove made into the side of some windowless wall, he called quietly for his guides to halt. Slaking his thirst with rapid slurping handfuls of the musty waters and joined by many of the rabbits too, he stared at the sculpted faucet. Made of black marble, its eyes a glaring gleaming white, it was a full-proportioned figure of the heldin Tascifarnias wrastling the great sea-wretchin Lampedusa, gripping the nadderer in a mortal stranglehold even as the beast pierced him through with its spines. Though he was certain the sculptor had not intended it, the image seemed to him apt: that the more everymen fought the monsters, the more they did themselves in . . .

Wetting a handkerchief broidered elaborately at the corners with red and magenta, he went to dab at his forehead and found that the sparrow mask was still there, pushed up on his crown and forgotten.

A boom like the detonation of a cannon seemed to roll up from the harbor.

Europe's assault was proceeding more violently than he had imagined.

With one last noisy mouthful of water, Rossamünd was quickly on the way again, a whole herd of rabbits stretched before him across the ancient paving. Though he could not be certain, their number seemed to have increased to near three dozen even as they had paused, becoming a tide of downy fur flowing through the streets and the small-hour hush of the city. Yet, such a crowd as they were, loping before or beside or behind him and even through his legs, Rossamünd neither trod on one nor was tripped.

On the other side of an elegant four-arched bridge crossing a broad, hissing stream, Rossamünd realized he was being escorted into the seedy side of the city: the dockland suburbs, where shadows were long, streets crooked and terrible affairs easily hidden. They moved in a patter of paws like muted rain down ancient stinking laneways whose cloacal reek even the approaching pungence of the Grume could not cover, passing rickety tenements whose foundations were laid before the Tutelarchs first arrived.

Somewhere near in this brooding den a fiddle and fife trilled a merry jig and voices called and jeered in desperate, almost angry pleasure.

Fastening his frock coat higher as if to ward himself, Rossamünd pulled his sparrow mask over his face, hoping his own bizarre appearance might give folks given to violence cause to think again.

Grown to more than two score and ten, the drove of rabbits proved strangely and surprisingly certain in this menacing place, keeping confidently to their path despite the many blind lanes and bad-ending ambulatories. They surged by the few folk milling in self-absorbed groups or stumbling, soused, along the threatening row. Amazingly, the rabbits went largely ignored, and if acknowledged, they were greeted with either flabbergasted stupefaction or a kind of fumbling, familiar horror, even sending some poor soul blubbering and hastening some other way.

"Away with thee, Rabbit-o'-Blighty! Ex munster vackery!"

The sweetly acrid stink of the vinegar sea was doubled by an undeniably fishy odor as the streets gained a clutter of lobster pots and smudgy upside-down jolly boats.

Another powerful boom ahead set windows rattling.

Heads poked from windows and doors, all looking in the same direction.

"Been goin' on fer an hour now," he heard called above him by a crotchety onlooker.

"Full-blowed war right in the Alcoves," complained another. "Good gracious, what's that below us?"

"Blight me white, it's the Sparrownucker-man!"

Hurrying, panting, shuffling on, Rossamünd thought he smelled powder smoke as he left the distressed natives to their alarm. Some way ahead came the echoing clatter of musketry, far off yet unmistakable. Gasping in air, he pushed against the waxing pangs in limb and lung.

The drove swollen surely beyond count, Rossamünd was led on to broader streets, empty again, lined with sheers and loading stages: the stowage roads between storehouses, weighhalls and shipping clericies that went down to the harbor proper and the muffled tolling of buoys. At first lost, he still had a sense of heading south and east as he was guided far into this dockland, until as they came to a road of identically commonplace half-houses, he had notion he had seen such streets before . . .

On the way to the Broken Doll with Rookwood . . .

Brazen plaques fixed to the twin ranks of their front steps spoke universally of tolling offices, shipping clerks and maritime lawyers. Yet here on this dull street the great horde of coneys finally stopped. As a single creature they gathered on road and pavement to stare at one particular building some way down on the left and as unremarkable as every other grubby edifice on the entire row: same false arched windows, engaged columns and mass-produced entablatures, same rearing stone grindewhals projecting from curling pediments and clutching meaningless street numbers, same gray slate steps going up to glossy black doors.

Perplexed, Rossamünd stood before the place, lifting his mask clear to suck in great lungfuls of sweet, healing air. There was no fight here, no battling roughs or debris of fallen bodies, just an empty street and these indistinguishable buildings.

Upon the homogenous post at the foot of the steps, a stained and corroded plaque read:

The structure did not look any different from the half-houses either side but for a lone rabbit sitting at its threshold at the summit of the steps.

With a chill of astonishment, Rossamünd beheld that it was the very half-blind, broken-eared creature he had greeted in the yard of Cloche Arde.

"Oh, faithful beast!" Rossamünd breathed. "All of you!" he wheezed to the mass of rabbits and Darter Brown too.

The coneys simply stared at him, snouts ever twitching.

Behind the sole-eyed rabbit the door to the house stood ajar.

Rossamünd took it to mean only one thing: it was here that Europe had begun her assault on Pater Maupin and all those with him, and that somewhere within, his mistress was to be found.

There came another muted concussion, somewhere ahead and to the left.

The sole-eyed rabbit turned and pushed through the mere gap between door and jamb to disappear within.

With Phoebë well descended from her apex and Darter Brown flapping ahead, Rossamünd flicked a caste of Frazzard's powder into hand, took out his moss-light, climbed the stone steps and went inside.

CONTESTS DARK AND VENOMOUS

peltisade hiding place of significant size, large enough for a person to live in permanently, with space for staff and entertainments, often functioning as the dens of the ne'er-do-well set of folk with enough money and influence to create such havens. Such structures are more common in cities than authorities would care to ponder upon, yet as universal as they might be, they are little reckoned to exist by most folk, which is precisely the point.

ILLUMINATED feebly by a single yellowing bright-limn, the small front hall of the office of Messrs. Gabritas & Thring was dominated by a narrow stair. Europe was not here; nor, it seemed, was anyone else. Pausing, ear cocked, Rossamünd listened. The building's emptiness was almost a presence in itself, an oppressive absence of activity, yet a memory of violence hovered in the untenanted space.

Sole-eye was nowhere to be seen.

To the left of the stairwell, light was faintly showing, as from a door ajar to a lit room. Boldly, Darter Brown disappeared into the dimness of the hall beside the stair, the sparrow's thin tweeting coming back to Rossamünd as if to say, "All is well!"

Moss-light in one hand, caste of Frazzard's in other, the

young factotum crept forward, regretting every groan or thump of the boards amplified in the surrounding silence. At the far end of the passage he could see a narrow lozenge-shaped bar of light—a door ajar indeed—and in its glow sat the sole-eyed rabbit waiting for him, Darter Brown standing between its ears.

Drawing toward them, Rossamünd perceived a whiff of arcing in the sterile atmosphere. He felt a thrill of fear as he spied through the gap into the room beyond, the body of a well-armored fellow lying face to the ceiling, body bent in the telltale rictus contortion of an arcing demise. Not far into the room another sturdy rough was stretched, his countenance frozen in surprise, a neat bullet hole in the unfortunate man's brow.

To wing again, Darter flitted over these new-made corpses and in through the lit doorway, his peremptory chirp ringing from within, calling Rossamünd on.

Sole-eye, however, remained in the hall.

Rossamünd gave the dogged, scrawny creature a brief parting beck. "Thank you," he said, stepping cautiously over the dead warden into the room.

Here in the wan illumination of a single light he found some manner of clerical file. Its walls, of a particularly sickly hue of green, were hung with certificates of charter and lists of fares and tolls, its space cluttered with chairs, desks and cabinets arranged about a shoddy imitation Dhaghi carpet. Thrown down on this rug was a man in dark and innocuously ordinary clothes, laid upon his side, his face shockingly marred by some recipe of mordant script, tumblerpicks splayed from his lifeless hands on the bare boards.

A lockscarfe! A professional break-and-enter man.

By the body stood a posticum—a secret door made to look part of the wall—released and exposed. Disguised as a bracket for a dependent bright-limn, its lock was freshly scarred, partly melted too by the very trap that surprised and ended the days of the scarfe, partly scorched by some small but powerful blast.

Beyond the forced posticum—into what was most likely the building next to Messrs. Gabritas & Thring—the young factotum found a strong room. Still secured, metal-barred cabinets along the walls held a selection of firelocks and other implements devised for harm. At the far end a desk of hard and heavy wood had been hastily thrown over and now squatted like a bastion, straight-back chairs tipped and scattered about it; Darter Brown perched upon its uppermost edge. From behind this barricade protruded a pair of black-booted legs.

Europe!

Yet hurrying up he quickly discovered that—too large and too blunt-toed—the boots belonged instead to a flourishingly harnessed pistoleer slain by implacable eclatics, his many pistolas useless in their many holsters. With the shootist was another pair of fallen sturdies, their final stand overcome.

The levin-scent of a fulgar's labors lingered in the close space.

Beyond the table another innocuous slab of wall was slid aside to reveal a doorway—Pater Maupin was nothing if not determined to hide this back door into his realm. Through this was a thin passage, a slype running into darkness. Here Darter Brown did not go on alone, but with a small *tweet!* took his place on his master's shoulder. Edging forward, Rossamünd shone his limulight into the chute and, determined to find his mistress come what may, entered. Mercifully short, the slype deposited him in a space that appeared limitlessly dark in the weak glow of his effulgent moss, thick beams above hardly high enough for a man to walk fully straightened. Rossamünd listened. Nothing shifted in this sepulchral hush but the rush of his own inward parts in his ears. Some several yards ahead he gradually perceived an insipid light, picking out a veritable forest of thick supporting posts all about him, as if the floor above was expected to bear immense weight. The bright stink of eclatics was stronger in here, sharp against the flat damp of dust and old sacks.

Darter twittered softly in unease.

Frazzard's held tense and ready, Rossamünd crept deeper into the cavity, progressing obliquely through the posts toward the weak glow, passing down one of the passages made among the countless square posts. In the stagnant twilight, he tripped over something fleshy-soft. Stumbling, he swung the moss-light, ready to hurl chemistry. Yet there was no lunging attacker. Rather he discovered an inert lump tepid with ebbing life lying at his feet, some unguessable breed of dog, large and lean with a blunt black snout and great rounded ears, vile and frightful even in death. The smoking burn of arcing unmistakable in its flank, it stank repulsively of an almost monsterlike musk. The dog's breathless mouth

565

was jellied with gore, as if it had savaged another before its demise. Progressing cautiously, yet desperate to find his mistress, Rossamünd passed a feeble seltzer-light, accounting for two more of the blunt-snouted beasts in the paltry illumination, both slain by a fulgar's power.

A cough wheezed out of the dusty gloom, setting his heart leaping, freezing him in mid-creep.

It had almost sounded like a call.

Easing his foot flat and pressing his limulight against his belly to douse its glow, Rossamünd harkened wide-eyed to every nuance and shift of air. There ahead, someone—or some*thing*—was breathing heavily . . . Frazzard's ready, the young factotum slid toward the sibilant clue, keeping a row of posts between him and where he imagined the wheezer to be.

"H-hello, young sir . . . ," a voice called feebly from the dark.

Rossamünd near dropped his caste in shock.

Peering about a thick post, he spotted a man dangerously drawn and pale, spread-eagled on the gritty floor, head leaning against a wooden pillar. Rossamünd took a moment to recognize the fellow in the diffuse, almost powdery glimmer of his moss-light.

"Mister Rakestraw!" he hissed, shuffling hastily to him.

"One and . . . and same." Clutching a sthenicon to his chest, the sleuth smiled fitfully, his weird laggard's eyes rolling, focusing for a moment, rolling again. "I am of the . . . of the thinking that y-your mistress would be unhappy you . . . you are here . . ."

"Is she well?"

566

"Aye, aye, last I saw of her . . . better'n me in the least." Rakestraw looked down at his broken body. Bound inadequately in neckcloths and handkerchiefs, his hand and wrist were mangled, and his right thigh torn by jaws powerful enough to break flesh even beneath the good proofing of his longshanks. "I . . . I told your mistress to leave me . . . No time to lose . . . I'll be right enough . . . been worse . . . ," he said with obvious braggadocio. "Just getting my . . . my wind back . . ."

Rossamünd frowned over the horrid and hastily tended wounds.

"H-how'd you find us . . ." Rakestraw roused a little. "It took my best . . . sneaks and many dabs o' precious . . . precious anavoid to . . . to crack this place and—" He winced. "And here you stroll in . . . like it's . . . it's a common shop."

Dipping his head as if peering with necessary concentration at the man's wounds and making much of his investigations of his stoops, Rossamünd let the question by without a word. Applying the flesh-brown strupleskin paste to any tear of skin or tissue, he bound the fellow's thigh tightly with bandages from his stoup. Twice he paused, thinking he heard portentous bumping in the murk of this hall of shadow.

"They got me with their foreign dogs . . . ," Rakestraw murmured, shaking his head in chagrin.

"I saw three of them." The young factotum cocked his head to indicate the fallen beasts lying like a trail behind.

Rakestraw grimaced. "Aye . . . I'd say they were left . . . left in here to prowl about these garners . . . unhindered . . . A permanent guard. I smelled them easy enough . . . great

567

blighted tykehounds . . . Saw 'em too, pacing in the dark . . . c-coming for us. But the one that got me was a . . . surprise . . ." He tried to chuckle, to make light of the terrible. "Striking from the side while our . . . our attention was taken by those in front of us, it was snapping and shaking at me before I . . . before I knew better. Your Lady Naimes did it in before it had too much of me, though not soon enough to prevent my dis . . . disqualification from . . . from the rest of the venture." He smiled wanly.

As many cuts and gashes as he could find with the scanty limulight daubed and bound, Rossamünd gave the man a dose of levenseep. He was gratified to see it promptly restore some of the flush of vigor to Rakestraw's cheeks and a glimmer of clarity to his gaze.

"Give the siccustrumn time to firm, Mister Rakestraw," Rossamünd warned, "and then you may hobble as best you can anywhere you like—though I reckon right out the way you came in will be the best path for you."

"Th-that'll be enough for me, lad—I shall win out on my own handsomely now." The sleuth gritted his teeth, forcing himself to sit straighter. "Our ladyship planned this expedition down to the dot," he wheezed. "Even as we sit here, you and I, having our nice little chat, she has an armed party at the beck of that antlered Maids of Malady lass raiding a meeting of necromancers gathered unawares in their coven's cellar down south, while not too far from here Lady Madigan and that surly Threedice chap are leading a company of lesquin troubards to make strike at Maupin's seaside chancery."

Shaking his head to himself, Rossamünd marveled at the full scale of Europe's plan. "Where is she now?" he asked, standing and resettling his stoups.

Rakestraw gestured ambiguously to the left of Rossamünd's original path. "I sent her down that way, with a dozen stout lesquin sell-swords and my remaining two scarfes to sniff out the proper path. As I warned her ladyship, have a care, young fellow . . . I might give you this to guide your way by"—he patted the sthenicon, still grasped at his bosom—"but it would only confuse your unperspicuous senses . . ."

"I reckon a trail of the fallen will lead me near as well, Mister Rakestraw," Rossamünd replied.

Darter Brown ruffled himself and made a peculiar burring noise as if to be included in the tally of guides.

The sleuth snorted a weak laugh. "Well they might . . . There's always a path for the patient eye. But they have sunk pits in here to catch ignorant intruders and . . . as fortunate as you have been to come so far without tumbling in one, you had better step careful . . ."

Giving Rakestraw a parting draught of lordia for humours dangerously unbalanced by blood's free flow, Rossamünd thanked him and pressed onward into this dark forest of beams. Alert now to the threat of pitfalls, he crept among the seemingly ceaseless rows of posts, the greening light of poorly maintained bright-limns haphazardly piercing the murk, the faintest eddy in the lifeless air drawing him on.

Hopping before him, Darter Brown tested the boards for abrupt voids. Suddenly the little sparrow disappeared, only to flutter into view with a surly *cheep!* from the cavity of a pitfall.

Circumspectly, Rossamünd toed the boards to left and right, feeling his way about the trap and pressing on, Darter resuming his reconnaissance in front. Several times they found their path steered by high stacks of blocking crates and hemmed by pits. Growing quickly tired of the obstacles, Rossamünd drew on his strength and simply heaved the crates opposing him until in a great clattering crash they toppled and the way was cleared.

Ahead the gloomy light was becoming a little more general, its source more than the infrequent and ill-kept limns, until Rossamünd found himself standing at the edge of the forest of pillars before a most astonishing sight. Like a glade in a wood, a great oblong space had been made through every level of this vast storehouse, the vacancy rising above him for four whole floors to open out to the wide night-gray sky. At the far end of this clearing stood the façade of a grand terrace house, not some small abscondary but a full-blown peltisade ascending for all four stories.

Here at last was the hidden home of Pater Maupin.

Greened by artfully clipped shrubs growing from large hogshead casques, the "yard" of wooden boards before this indoor house was laid with many dead. Most of the slain were sturdy roughs in mixed proofing, but among them lay a single gaudily harnessed lesquin. Lorica and metal helm savagely dented and flesh pierced with a score of wounds, the fellow had sold his own life dearly. Bruised by inaccurate potive work, the yard's walls and boards were smeared in bursts of deep spraying green or gaunt mauve, their surfaces scored and pitted with the scorching of many arcs.

Europe's work . . .

From somewhere came a sullen booming.

Fixing his vent over nose and mouth against the faint and lingering fug of vapors and returning the sparrow mask over his face as further protection to hide it, Rossamünd approached the entrance of the peltisade, a thick ironbound door more like the port to a vault than a dwelling, forced open now and hanging by one bent hinge.

To wing at last, Darter Brown shot into the house.

Quick to follow, the young factotum progressed into a broad and well-furnished hall, the once-dank setting entirely refurbished: carpets and cornice-work and all, complete with plinths bearing alabaster busts and wall-hung daubs of august yet forgotten figures.

Circling for a moment below the low warehouse beams dark with wax, Darter Brown alighted upon a broken side table, flicking his wings agitatedly as he waited.

Shoes clicking on polished boards, Rossamünd stepped into this comfortably furnished and bizarrely urbane field of battle illuminated by a row of colorful glass carbuncles hung from the coffers between the ceiling beams. A score of bodies were flung to all points about spontaneous barricades built of tandems and bookshelves, overturned and thrown down vainly to halt the relentless fulgar and her supporters. Loopholes in the yellow-plastered walls stood open between the paintings, each a gaping black oblong scorched about its framed mouth, one seeping unctuous smoke that smelled distinctly of recently ruptured asper. The splintered punctures of musket and pistol ball perforated every surface, and with these, greater dents as large as Rossamünd's hand. Horsehair puckered from rents in fine furnishings, statues lay fallen and shattered, threadbare carpets were blemished with darkly wet stains. A bright-clad pistoleer lay dead amid the defenders, and by her a stoup-bearing skold burned by the interrupted action of his own scripts. Three more lesquins lay dead here too, one laid back bent unnaturally over a toppled seclude, his casque struck off his head. Some of the fallen were still quick with life, wide-eyed with pain, flinching in alarm at Rossamünd as he threaded his way among them.

The clash of arms rang from beyond white double doors agape at the other end of the hall.

With Darter Brown dashing ahead, Rossamünd hastened through and immediately stepped onto a landing before a short drop. He had come to a gallery that looked down through wooden arches upon a sunken basement quadrangle ringed by several stories of finely molded balconies and narrow, mullioned windows. Below in the quadrangle square, the clamor of the fight swelled; an exclamation of angry insults, shouts of fright and rage, labored gasps and the clout of landing blows, the infrequent report of pistol-shot joined by the repeated crackle of a fulgar's arcs.

How the fight had come to be down in this lower court, Rossamünd could not tell.

The uneven flicker of deadly levin and the flash of muzzle revealed figures in many fashions of lurid harness striving, spinning and swinging in the dance of death over colored flagstones laid in a spiral of red and white and strewn with human wreckage. For now the lesquins faced more than hired roughs and common door wards: sabrine adepts had joined the defense of Maupin's hidden house, and their grace and cunning were an obvious match for their opponents' brute power and thick skins.

In it all spun a figure in wide-swinging hems of black and red embroidered green, flourishing a short stave that arced with a revealing glaucous glare—*zzack!*—driving back two finely dressed sabrine adepts. Rossamünd had seen such a harness before just once, many days ago, prancing about the ludion before admiring staff.

EUROPE!

Eyes staring terribly, her head high and poised, the Branden Rose skipped and stepped masterfully between the adepts' feints and ruses. Her fuse nowhere to be seen, she held only her shorter stage, brandishing it like a cudgel, the tip fizzing and hissing with deadly arcing potential.

Among the enemy, the most implacable was a swaggering swordist crowned in a soft tarbane hat and wielding a long pallid blade, the very fellow who had cut the Handsome Grackle in the rousing-pit and come with Maupin to Cloche Arde. In dismay, Rossamünd beheld his therimoir sword, exotic and venomous, made eons ago to slay monsters and swung now with such expertise. He had already witnessed it cut deep into monster flesh and watched now as it tore through the steel of a lesquin's lorica with little hindrance; what it could do to a lahzar in fine proofing he did not want to behold.

Flash went this blade in the lamplight.

The lesquins were alert to its power too, and strove to keep well clear of the swordist and his deadly swipes.

About to leap down to his mistress' defense, Rossamünd was baulked by at a sudden shiver of frission. The sabrine adepts and the few drab roughs left with them attempted to draw away, pulling back to the farther side of the quadrangle. Barely released from hand strokes, the reduced quarto of lesquins reeled under an invisible assault. Rossamünd could feel the edge of scathing frission centered on the quadrangle below, the vaguest fluttering in the very midst of his head that brought a twinge of pain.

Yet under such inward violence only one troubardier collapsed, snarling so volubly through the constrictions of his casque that the young factotum heard it from his balcony perch just above. Remarkably, the other bravoes remained on their feet, shaking their armored heads dazedly but very much unconquered.

How is it possible?

Europe stood, eyelids fluttering with almost manic rapidity under the impulse of her own puissance, keeping the scathing at bay.

Presuming their foes unbalanced, the swordists rushed to attack.

A wordless shout and Europe leaped at them, her lesquins eagerly with her.

In pure reflex, Rossamünd threw the caste of Frazzard's powder and another, true and fast, catching several sturdy roughs who hung back from the fight in a shower of popping blue sparks. Startled, the swordists writhed clear of the spray, glaring up at the floors above, trying to find the origin of the chemistry; their assault turned to defense as, with a brute cry, the lesquins pressed the sudden switch of advantage.

Despite this, from his perch, Rossamünd could see that Europe was being cornered. A swordist in garish vermilion and white and a black arming-cap was pounding at the fulgar with an incessant gust of blows of his heavy wide-bladed sword, bravely endeavoring to dominate the fulgar's attention while lesser roughs sought to pull her down.

Eyelids still flickering, Europe turned the swordist's blade and pounced away to catch one rough with a vigorous revolving kick to the abdomen, then spun aside, to crack him ringing blows to head and arms with her stage. Yet there was no zap, no retaliating arcing flash—the very skill that saved her from the affliction of the scathing prevented the Branden Rose from afflicting others with her own puissance. With all her grace and deadly aptitude, under assault from within and without, Europe could surely not prevail long.

Rossamünd clenched empty hands and knew that sturdier tools were needed. Dashing back into the hall behind, he snatched up a pair of pistols from the fallen pistoleer, thinking that their heavy barbed handles would make perfect cudgels once they were fired. Darting back to the balcony, he found that in this briefest divagation Europe and a mere pair of her lesquin allies were now left to contend against only two of Maupin's swordists—the one in garish vermilion brandishing the heavy sword, the other the turbane-hatted wielder of the therimoir, his dread spathidril blade held curving up behind his back as it had been before cutting the Grackle. The three against the two, they circled each about the other among the litter of hurt and dead with wary concentration until now the swordists stood between Rossamünd and his mistress.

That very moment, Europe looked up and she saw him, knowing him full well in his fancy mask. A distinctly protective fury convulsed for a beat in her face, making her thoughts plain——*What are you* doing *here!*——and setting a guilty gripe in Rossamünd's milt.

Suddenly, beyond her, a fresh commotion thrust into the quadrangle, bursting from an oblong tunnel set between heavy beams well back in the deep shadows beneath the balcony at the far end. Proofed in deep green, these arrivals were clearly door wards from the Broken Doll, fighting desperately against unseen assailants in the passage beyond, and collected protectively about a singular figure. In the quick glare of a gunshot Rossamünd saw clear that it was Pater Maupin, limping as he came, shouting directions and warnings, stout hanger in one hand, pistol in the other, marvelous wig askew.

With their appearance the frission ceased, its dread and unseen wielder perhaps overset in the confusion.

Attention swiveling quickly between the sabrine adepts before her and this new scrimmage behind, Europe must have discovered Maupin too, for she became sudden action, pressing with her last two lesquins to finally get at him.

Realizing he was beset from in front and behind, the proprietor of the Broken Doll called warning, and the rearmost of his lifeguard faced about to meet this new assault.

Yet even as Europe went for her prize, the swordists went for her.

Eyes fixed in horror on the gore-smeared white of the therimoir blade, Rossamünd leaped the railing to drop down to the quadrangle floor, springing forward the very moment his feet slapped on the flagstones and sprinting at the adepts. He gave a shout to draw their attention away from his mistress, which for a moment appeared to succeed. Thinking themselves properly ambushed, the pair of swordists looked to him in surprise, expressions quickly composing in realization of their error. The therimoir swordist gave a disdainful scowl and, showing his back to Rossamünd, set himself against the Branden Rose, leaving a mere *boy* to his vermilion-clad brother-in-arms. The vermilion swordist came at Rossamünd directly, swatting at him with many mighty swings of his broad, heavy blade. Tripping back, the young factotum fired a pistol at the adept, the shot striking the man square in the bosom. Yet the bullet was foiled by stout proofing. Pointing the second firelock directly into the swordist's scowling face, he fired, his aim knocked aside in the very moment of detonation by a deft sweep of the vermilion adept's arm. Driven into the shadows beneath the balcony from which he had just sprung, Rossamünd was nearly ended by several strokes, contorting himself left and right, scarcely fending each artful blow with his borrowed pistols. Desperate to get to Europe's side, he could see her, alone in a press of green door wards, twisting, skipping, striking left and right, the therimoir swordist trying to close, her arcs free again and keeping all at bay.

Beyond, a confused swelling melee began to once again fill the quadrangle: fistdukes in their bizarre pot helmets and yet more green-clad door wards striving against the fury of a company of staunch lesquins, their gloriously harnessed captain—the very fellow who had visited Cloche Arde—at their lead. A leap of hope in his innards, Rossamünd barely glimpsed Lady Madigan, Marchess of the Pike, in the fray. Her face a bloody mask, the lahzar was locked elbow in elbow with Threedice, her factotum, the two pivoting on each other in splendid unison amid their enemies, Madigan's arcs flashing, Threedice's own pistols popping.

Tall among Maupin's foul defenders was a woman in a wide lustrous black dress, the pastiness of her bald head framed exquisitely against her gauzy fanlike collar of black, the flesh about the left eye dark with great diamond and arrow spoor—a dexter's marking.

Anaesthesia Myrrh!

All this Rossamünd saw in a twinkling even as he defended himself, dodging and thwarting the swordist's blows, one block leaving a spent pistola hacked clean in two. Darter Brown swooped down to pester and curse in the swordist's face, checking the relentless fellow for the merest beat. That was all Rossamünd needed. Throwing the intact pistol at the swordist, with a bark of fury he launched himself at the startled man. Calling all the strength he could muster, he drove his fist into the vermilion swordist's middle, amazed at

ANAESTHESIA MYRRH

the heave and turmoil of sinews beneath his knuckles. With a wheeze of wind and crack of bone the wretched foe was lifted clear off his feet, tumbling back several feet to collapse.

Rossamünd did not wait for more but, attention fixed upon his mistress, took up the hefty blade of his fallen opponent as easily as if it were but a butter knife, and with it sought to win to her through the stouche. Even as he did, he saw Europe, pressed on all sides, artfully dodge yet another thrust of the swordist's white blade, only to be struck from behind by a cudgel-wielding door ward. A viper-quick contortion of her body and the Branden Rose ended the fellow with a flash of levin. In that very instant, the soft-hat swordist sprang to the fulgar's left, and, dancing somehow under her guard, swung about behind the Branden Rose to cut at her. In complete horror Rossamünd witnessed the white spathidril incise through the fulgar's superior proofing and bite deeply into her side. Crying out—and Rossamünd with her—Europe recoiled from the aggrieving hit, instantly swinging her stage to whip the swordist viciously about the head once, twice, thrice, until the weapon bent and broke. Snarling, the Branden Rose gripped the fellow, stunned and bleeding about the throat, stiffening the swordist dead with her sparks. Letting the lifeless man drop, she swooned herself, tottered . . .

Heedless of anything but Europe, Rossamünd shoved some obstructing figure aside—friend or foe he did not know or care. He could see Pater Maupin realize his chance and pounce with two door wards, intent on finishing Europe where she faltered.

Her stage now two useless ungainly parts connected by unraveling copper wire, the fulgar flung it at Maupin, rapping him smartly on the cheek.

"Am I a dog, oh thorn-ed Rose, that you come at me with sticks!" Europe's adversary spat, making light of the stunning hit as he blundered in reverse.

Winning through the mayhem, Rossamünd stood over the lifeless therimoir adept and spied the malignant blade lying discarded upon the flags. Ignoring the offensive taint of its touch, he seized the ancient monster-destroying weapon in his other hand and, Darter Brown chattering passionately just above him, threw himself at his mistress' foes. Cutting down one door ward with shocking ease, he drove Maupin back with great sweeps of heavy sword and poisonous white blade, flourishing them like a mad thing. Here now he could himself end the proprietor cowering before him and bring this terrible night to a close.

In the very moment of a final upswing, a crushing frission smote Rossamünd, a driving agony that bore searingly into the very crux of his soul. Dropping the swords, the young factotum was forced to his knees. Yet as quickly as the tempest arrived, it cleared, replaced by a strangely effervescent sensation in his brain and belly that set his eyelids flickering. Blessed with this buzzing clarity he first saw, then felt, the Branden Rose's grip on his wrist.

She is vacillating me too! he realized.

Half prone, Europe pushed herself up where she lay by her other hand, a grimly ephemeral smile dancing like a small triumph upon her worryingly pale lips. Yet her attention was not on Rossamünd. Rather it was in Maupin's direction, fixed with murderous intent upon Anaesthesia Myrrh standing protectively in all her silken swart-clad glory before the proprietor of the Broken Doll. Her hand lifted to her sallow temple, she regarded Europe with narrow scorn, a contemptuous smirk visible through the gossamer vent the dexter wore over nose and mouth.

Pressing hard upon Rossamünd to stand, the fulgar remained clasped with the dexter in their invisible wrestle.

Suddenly the lesquin captain stepped into the gap, flourishing a heavy war hammer in his steel-armored grip. A snort and a flick of her hand, and the black-hearted dexter struck the lesquin with a peculiar glaucous flash, the same combined witting-arcs Rossamünd had seen her use at the rousing-pit long weeks ago. Stoutly the captain stood his ground, ducking as if walking into a headwind, seeking to swat the woman down. A second time the dexter struck and the sell-sword staggered.

Still acting as a crutch for his mistress, Rossamünd reached into his rightmost pocket to find a thennelever of glister. Grasping the flute, he tossed a measured dose of mild repellent at the dexter, the glister scattering in an effervescent crackle about her. In a beat, Rossamünd shook the thennelever and strewed yet more of it, a veritable fog of tiny detonations that balked their foe despite her vent.

In the brief reprieve the lesquin captain came at the dexter anew, but, twisting away from the glister-fume, Anaesthesia struck the fellow a third time with her disembodied arcs and sent him toppling lifelessly away.

Barely on her feet, the Branden Rose let Rossamünd go and lunged, leaping at the dexter through the glister. Leading now with her left, the Duchess-in-waiting of Naimes began pounding upon Anaesthesia, sending out arcs at every clout, yet the dexter, unharmed, seemed to *catch* each hit and return it with arcing knocks of her own. Blow after crackling, coruscating blow they pummeled at each other, boxing and blocking punches with deft pivots of arm and torso, catching hits with a flash and throwing them off again, neither able to do real harm to the other.

Abruptly, shockingly, Europe shouted in pain.

Anaesthesia had found the fulgar's worst wound and was striking at her opponent's flank again and again.

Rossamünd pounced to his mistress' defense, Darter Brown with him.

"Rossamünd!" Europe cried, her voice thin. "No!"

The dexter flung her arm at him, and he was instantly smitten with the bizarre and fiendish amalgam of witting and arcing. He was hurled away, thrown clear across the quadrangle yard, the thennelever he yet held flying from his grasp as he skated along his rump to collide with a shock into a heavy supporting post in the gloom well under the floor above. The world convulsing, Rossamünd shook his head and squeezed his eyes to try to bring clarity.

Emerging from behind the protection of his deadly dexter spurn, Maupin approached as quickly as his injured gait would allow.

Rossamünd tried to rise on legs rebelliously unstable.

"Hello, little bird," the proprietor of the Broken Doll

purred. "You are a *very small* little bird to have a place in this fight."

Limbs needling painfully, the young factotum labored to his feet only to be instantly witted; a stifling trammeling frission drove the young factotum back to his knees. *WHERE IS EUROPE?* his galloping thoughts screamed, they alone free of the dexter's wicked work. He was suddenly aware of the dark form of Anaesthesia looming over him, bleeding and bruised.

She snatched Rossamünd by his hair and tore his sparrow mask and vent away.

"Our prize has come to us, it seems!" Maupin declared, his voice exhausted yet triumphant. "'Tis a *brave* little mouse who dares trespass into the mouser's den . . ."

Tormented, the young factotum writhed and swatted at the dexter spasmodically as she scratched and clutched to keep a hold on him. A wicked jolt zapped through him, driving down into his very core. His vision narrowed to a dazed circular slot filled with oddly writhing checkers.

"Try not to kill him, dear," came Maupin's cool voice. "His living bones will fetch good price; I might yet salvage *something* from this shambles."

This will not be! With a vigor called from the very depths of his milt, Rossamünd forced out a cry. Hoarse at first, it rose to a bellow that sounded like the roar of some wounded ettin in his own ears, banishing for a glimpse the worst of the writhing frission. He planted his feet and refused his abduction, gripping the hands that gripped him, tearing them free of his hair, feeling follicles go with them. Instantly he was an agony of sparks.

At a clap of pistol shot the arcing abruptly ceased.

Rossamünd was released.

With another roar, the young factotum twisted his whole frame, and with another roar joined by the tiny ferocity of Darter Brown threw the dexter bodily in a blur of black gauze and satin into a near post, the vile woman colliding with such force that wood cracked as she sagged lifelessly.

Liberated, stumbling, Rossamünd was instantly dealt a mouthful of some foul repellent, burning down his windpipe before he could react and shut breath away. Lurching backward, he grasped at the air, retching powerfully as his vision swayed. There came a strangely loud *slap!* right in his face. Rossamünd felt something clout him powerfully in the throat through his stock and collars, and could make out Maupin pointing a smoking pistol directly at him. *I'm shot!* flashed through Rossamünd's mind like panic. Grasping his neck, the young factotum swooned and sat with an inelegant flop on the cold stone. Convulsing, he struggled for breath—even a single gasp of cleansing air. His sight narrowed to a pivoting, pulsating slot, and in it loomed Maupin, the venomous therimoir now in his grasp, its tip hovering mere inches from Rossamünd's face.

"If you will not come easily living, I will have you dead!" Maupin seethed, all scruples for the sake of salvage clearly abandoned.

In a rush of deep, desperate fortitude, Rossamünd sucked in a rattling gasp of wind. Forcing himself to move, he scrambled away from the proprietor and his dread weapon, trying to put a balcony post between him and a ghastly end.

"You truly are a monster . . . ," Maupin breathed with all the passion of a damning accusation as he rounded the pillar in pursuit.

Glowering in utter fury, Europe emerged from the thinning fight, gripping her abdomen, the tingle of growing power already about her as her disheveled hair stood on end. Snarling, she bore down on the chancery proprietor.

"No, you filthy blaggard," she spat, "*we* are the monsters . . ."

Lurching away, Maupin tried to hack her with the therimoir but tripped on a wounded lesquin's legs, his wig tumbling from his crown to reveal his clothbound head.

Catching the once-relentless fellow by his coattails, Europe hauled Maupin to her. Seizing his head in both hands, she cried out—somewhere between triumph and despair—and poured all the power she possessed into the wretched man. Eyes forced wide by the currents arcing through him, unable to voice his agony, Pater Maupin, owner of the Broken Doll and patron of the roust, suddenly blackened, and with a look of exquisite dismay burst into a flurry of ashen atoms and flying empty clothes.

28

A LIFE OF ADVENTURE,
A LIFE OF VIOLENCE

occludile of lazarin one of the rare scripts employed by transmogrifers immediately upon inserting memetic organs into a person to make them a lahzar. Its rarity is in part attributable to the illicit and very difficult-to-obtain parts in its constitution, and also the limits of its use. As any transmogrifer worth his or her fee will tell you, it also can serve as an aid for fortifying the memes (foreign organs) already within a lahzar's body.

IN the ringing hollow that followed Maupin's final end, silence and stillness ruled.

Rossamünd's senses swam, and he collapsed at last against a post.

Have we won?

On the edge of his awareness, he was aware of movement about him, of forms deliberate and slow in the aftermath of battle. Nearby he could make out a slender figure stumbling toward him. It took a moment to realize it was Europe, sooty with the ashes of her blasted enemy, her face frightfully pale, her eyes fixed on Rossamünd. The fulgar's expression was hard, as if expecting to discover the worst. She faltered for a few steps more, and then Europe sagged to her knees. She tried to stand, but dropped fully to the flagstones, to lie with her unraveled fringe across her face.

Despite the acute pounding within his skull and the acrid burning in his throat, Rossamünd sucked a great gulp of wind to clear the miasma in his lungs and sat up. Grinding his teeth against the agony in his neck, he went on hands and knees to her side, fumbling bandages from his stoup as he came. He could easily see the dark wet slash in the right panels of her proofing. "You are cut, M-miss Europe . . . ," he said rapidly, fumbling in his stoup for the pot of sealing paste. Using bindings torn from Europe's own petticoats, he tried to stanch the laceration in her side, smearing struple-skin among all the red, wrapping the rudimentary bindings as fast as he could. Yet, for all this, the wound refused to be stanched.

His mistress laid a shaking hand on his arm. "S-save some for your own," she hushed, fingers vaguely gesturing to his neck where it hurt so powerfully.

"It is nothing!" Rossamünd insisted, impatient while his mistress lay so damaged.

"It is a hole right through the . . . the side of y-your throttle, little m-man," the fulgar insisted. "Y-you ought to be dead."

Rossamünd felt at his neck and, in a thrill of fright, found on the left side a long and terrible gash where the ball had scored his flesh. "I feel well enough . . ." Quickly, he bound the wound up with his stock, as much to hide it as to stanch it.

Stepping from the gloom beneath the balcony of the

quadrangle the slender figure of Elecrobus Slitt approached, smoking pistols in hand and death in his eyes. "You set us a fine chase to find you, m'lady . . . ," he said quietly, concern clear in his otherwise flat voice. "You have a fine victory here for me to report to my Baron Finance . . ."

"Yes, yes, man." Europe's voice sounded far away. "We may sing the . . . the glory of my success to y-your master later . . ."

"*You* may tell him sooner, fairest duchess-daughter," the percusor returned. "My *master* awaits you in his drag down on the street you first came in by. I suggest we be quick to go to him. You look sore and in need of a physic's help."

Rossamünd's thoughts hurtled madly upon how he could make treacle in this blighted place. "There ought to be a kitchen here!" he commanded desperately, looking up into the balconies rising on every side like the sides of a grave to a pallid rectangle of early morning gray. "A pot! A fire! I can make plaudamentum! Vauquelin too!"

"Ahh . . . I think it will take more than vauquelin, little man."

Fumbling levenseep to her mouth, Rossamünd would not give in. "I saved you in the Brindleshaws. I can again." Sobbing, staggering to his feet, he took the fulgar under her arms and began to haul her just as he had on the sandy forest road so long ago.

From the dim fume of firelock smoke and settling potive fume, Madigan emerged, bloodied and disheveled, her man, Threedice, limping close behind and clutching his arm as if it were broken.

"I have o-overreached myself . . . ," Europe declared to her approaching friend.

"Nonsense, dear one," Madigan asserted softly, grim concern darkening the tender light in her eyes as she crouched to clutch her fellow fulgar's hand. "That wretched blade has poisoned my organs . . . M-my natural humours take their revenge . . ." Europe's smile was alarmingly wan.

"Indeed, sister," Madigan agreed. "We shall make a dash ahead of you to the house of your man, Oberon; he shall set you to rights. Meanwhile, this lovely boy"—she smiled briefly at Rossamünd—"and these hefty fellows bear you to your waiting Baron." With that, she and Threedice departed, going with all haste out by the tunnel through which they had first forced their way in.

Smattered with gore, the handful of remaining lesquins promptly fashioned a litter of two poleaxes and the proofing cursorily stripped from fallen door wards. Upon this they—and Rossamünd with them—lifted his mistress as gently as haste would allow. Europe gave a terrible cry, an animal sound born as much of frustration and the anger of fear as it was of pain. In shock, Rossamünd clamped his teeth upon a sob.

The lesquins went to put her down again, but she insisted they go on.

Elecrobus Slitt at the lead and bearing the terrible therimoir, they took the Branden Rose from that hidden den, retracing the original path through the dark of the hall of posts, the secreted chute and the blasted posticum.

Looking often to the rudimentary bandaging about Eu-

ELECROBUS SLIT

rope's side—slowly reddening despite the strupleskin—Rossamünd refused to heed the threatening crushing hopelessness that hovered in the darkness about the edge of his soul. Head ringing with a terror far greater than any felt in the midst of battle or facing a foe, he repeated, *I saved her before, I can save her again* under his breath until the words lost all meaning.

They progressed at times with necessary yet frustrating deliberation, lest they bump or twist Europe and harm her further, finally descending the stairs of the file of Messrs. Gabritas & Thring to shuffle out onto the peaceful street, gray in the primal gleam of dawn. Baron Finance was indeed there, standing anxiously by a large and proper carriage.

"Ahh, duchess-daughter!" he exclaimed in undisguised consternation as he beheld the Duchess-in-waiting on her makeshift cradle. "If only you had included *me* in your machinations, dear hope of our state, I would have sent Mister Slitt with you. He might have kept you from such a disorder as I find you in now!"

Lifting her head, Europe made a show of strength she did not truly have. "But, Baron, y-*you* were my yardstick," she said. "If I was able to keep my . . . my plan from you, then . . . then there was s-scant chance Maupin could . . . could discover it."

"All plans be dashed and secrets revealed!" Finance cried, taking her hand. "I have failed you, and your mother too!"

"Dear Baron . . ." Europe's voice was profoundly tender. "Y-you did not fail, s-sir, I b-bested you . . . that is all . . ."

592

The anguish on the Chief Emissary's face was more than Rossamünd could bear to behold, and he looked to his own feet.

As hasty arrangement was made for Mister Slitt to remain with the lesquins and ensure that Europe's task of annihilation was complete, the fulgar was lifted with profound tenderness into the cabin and laid endwise across the soft seats.

Fighting to master himself among all these valiant men, Rossamünd climbed in after, heedful not to rock the fit too much.

With scarce enough room for him in the cabin, Finance mounted up beside the driver of the park drag and shouted the fellow on. "Quick, man!" Rossamünd heard his command clear and urgent. "To Bankers Lane, Risen Mole! Fast as you can and spare our lady your jolts."

A shrill keening high in the southern sky above dark roof-ridges and thorny chimneys drew their attention to a bright, upward-hurtling flare of pallid green.

The Duchess-in-waiting strained to see the sailing light through the cab window. "Ahh," she sighed, her head dropping heavily back down. "B-bravo . . . Lady Saphine of the Maids of Malady w-wins her fight in the coven cellar . . . Maupin and his allies are done in; y-you are safe, little man . . . for now."

Aye, Rossamünd cried within, *but at what cost!* "I—I . . ." was all his mouth for a moment could say. "I have not kept *you* safe!"

Europe smiled feebly, cupping his cheek and chin in her

soft hand—the very hand that had arced him so long ago in the Brindleshaws, the very hand that had spent itself to vie and defeat *his* foes, now so clammy and cold. "A life of adventure, a life of violence . . . A t-teratologist is not . . . not m-*meant* to be safe . . ."

"B-but *you* are!" he returned in an overpowering swell of grief and confusion, and insisted she swallow another dose of emunic reborate followed by a second vial of lordia.

"M . . . my organs are souring within me, Rossamünd," Europe murmured, head lolling to the steady rock of the Baron's carriage, face afflicted with a gray pallor.

Rossamünd wanted to shriek his pain, to scream at the blighted world and its blighted senselessness. He clutched her hand to his chest.

Perched on the sill of the door, Darter Brown began to chitter loudly, a tiny avian wail.

"I am the cause of all this . . . ," Rossamünd breathed.

"*This* was m-*my* choosing, little man . . . ," Europe retorted with a cough, "the m-moment I cried QGU."

Perhaps this was so, but what next? His staunch loyalty to his mistress was not as virtuous as it might appear. Surely it could only bring more strife. Rossamünd's thoughts revolved with premonitions of an unceasing and ever-escalating series of trials ahead.

At Oberon's house—a tidy three-story dwelling in the fine middling suburb of Risen Mole—Europe was taken with careful haste to the lone bed of the transmogrifer's private ground-floor infirmary. Here, treacle brewed but moments before by Threedice—arrived ahead of them and already testing some subtler draughts—was given to her.

"She is cut," Rossamünd said in report. "by a blighted spathidril sword. I have used all my strupleskin, but she still bleeds!"

"The wound must be abluered—cleansed—before siccustrumns will take," the examining transmogrifer replied, peering intently at the hurt beneath Europe's lacerated proofing. "Thus is the dread efficacy of such a blade." Taking a stylus and slip of paper, he wrote out the script for a substance he named munditi corpum, penning it without reference to any compleat or other book. "To clear the wound and make a siccustrumn stick," he elaborated as he returned to scrutinize the cut. "Even so, I shall have to stitch you, madam," he continued with clear distaste, "to be certain to stop any sanguinary flow."

Europe's expression soured. "Ugh . . . ," she muttered, perplexingly flippant as her faculties failed. "A s-scar . . ."

In waxing urgency, Oberon shooed all comers but for one maid from the room that he might examine the Branden Rose with the necessary quiet and privacy.

His dread for his mistress in some small part quieted by the examining transmogrifer's steady and confident manner, Rossamünd let himself be shown across the vestibule to a small but well-stocked saumery. Here he found Threedice hard at brewing, despite his wounded arm. With little room for the labor of two over the single stove, Rossamünd collected the parts the script for munditi corpum required from their various, clearly marked receptacles and set to testing in the hearth, already lit against the morning's chill.

Bearing the final, nacrescent gray draught to his mistress, the young factotum was refused entry even as the potive was taken from his grasp. Impatient, Rossamünd returned and, despite the other factotum's obvious reluctance at sharing the task, assisted Threedice in his making of what the older factotum brewed what he named occludile of lazarin.

Two more times he delivered necessary scripts from Threedice's testing, and each time he was disallowed entry. Thwarted, Rossamünd paced in the vestibule before the infirmary, refusing the little triangles of buttered bread and warmed saloop served so politely by Oberon's prim steward. He was certain that Cinnamon could fix his mistress' hurts with ease and not need Rossamünd to be absent in the process.

Nearby, the Lady Madigan, her face now washed of its battle-grime, sat upon a chair brought especially by servants. Her pose was straight and alert despite a whole night spent fighting, yet her eyes were closed as if she slept and the piece of buttered bread in her delicate grasp remained uneaten. Beside her stood Finance, rocking restlessly on his heels, his expression tight, his eyes rarely leaving the infirmary door and then only to look hard—almost reproachfully— at Rossamünd. For a beat the Chief Emissary appeared on the point of saying something to him, yet, perhaps to check himself, took a bite of his bread-and-butter slice instead.

Patently sensing the man's scarce-restrained agitation, Madigan stirred. "She pays a terrible price for her hardheadedness," she said, without opening her eyes.

"She always has," Finance returned tautly. "Though perhaps not as *high* as she does now . . . ," he added, looking reprovingly to Rossamünd once more. *Your fault!* was writ clear on his dial.

Finally, the port sprang open and the examining transmogrifer emerged.

"Please," he offered somberly, bowing to Madigan, then beholding Finance and Rossamünd in turn. "Return."

Upon the sole infirmary bed, Europe lay, pale and drawn, her breaths coming in shallow gasps, staring at the ceiling as if consumed by her struggle. Hands and face cleansed in part of stains and Maupin-dust, and her proofing folded upon a chair beside the bed, she looked much as he remembered her lying so terribly wounded in the downy cot at the Harefoot Dig so long ago.

"M-miss Europe . . . ?" Rossamünd said as he approached.

The dread fulgar turned her head and blessed him with an ailing smile. "Oberon s-says I m-may yet live to . . . to fight on . . . ," she said, her tone bemusingly sardonic in one so hurt.

Scarce reckoning it possible, Rossamünd felt his soul give an ecstatic leap.

"Ah-hah!" Finance uttered in relieved delight. "Well done, sir!"

Oberon coughed with ever-so-subtle annoyance. "Well, yes, you *ought* to, good madam," he said first to Europe, then regarding his other guests continued matter-of-factly. "Yet, before we run away with our gladness, as good as my ministrations have been, time is in the pinch and our continued alacrity essential. For, as I was just concluding to our lady,

597

she—only so *soon* come back from Sinster—will need to return there with all haste if she is to survive such a *mis*-use of her memetic tissues."

Rossamünd's innards dropped at the mention of this infamous city where lahzars are made, full to its ridge-caps with massacars and bloodthirstily curious investigators. Hopes so quickly restored were complicated once again.

"T-twice to Sinster in one year is not an . . . i-*ideal* record, I suppose," Europe added mildly.

"Indeed it is not, m'lady," Oberon returned with all the gravity of a schooling master.

We barely survived Brandenbrass, Rossamünd marveled inwardly. *How could we prevail in a place crammed with massacars and monster-fossicking transmogrifers? One rumor of me and we will be done for!* Yet, with all these caring folk bustling and hovering about Europe's sickbed, this was no place to say so.

A long case clock in the vestibule struck six times.

"The first of the day's quick boats will be setting out soon," Finance declared with revived hope in his voice. "I shall go immediately and secure you your own vessel, dear duchess-daughter."

"And, if you will, sister, Threedice and I shall join you on your quick boat as you hurry off to Sinster," proclaimed the Lady Madigan.

Proving his intent, the Baron Finance dashed off in his park drag for the commutation docks of Middle Ground. While a message was dispatched to Kitchen to send luggage—a day-bag and linen package for the immediate journey—forthwith to the docks, with a trunk to follow on the next available passage—Oberon's simple carriage was brought to the front of the house.

Before Rossamünd could catch a settled thought, he was working with the house staff to carry his mistress out to the plain black fit and they were on their way once more. The Lady Madigan and Threedice in their own carriage ahead, the young factotum and the Branden Rose rode alone, the fulgar propped on many cushions, half sitting, half lying along the whole backseat. For several suburbs neither looked at the other, but both stared at the steady passing of gray, shadowy streets, Rossamünd scarcely remarking the fleeting sights or the growing activity of the city's early risers or late finishers in his turmoil. From the corner of sight he became aware that Europe was staring at him, could *feel* her observation like burning in his conscience. Still he would not look at her, for to look at her would be to admit a conclusion he did not want to admit.

"H-how fares your neck?" she asked, her tone mild.

Humours thumping down his neck, across his scalp, in his ears, he finally looked.

There she was, propped on the makeshift comfort of cushions, her face gray—ghastly, even—yet somehow queenly despite it all in this carriage taking them to Sinster; Sinster of hope, Sinster of dangers multiplied until all Rossamünd could foresee was that he would be nabbed the very instant he touched foot to its docks.

He touched the thick bandage about his throat hiding the gash made by the bullet's path. "It . . . I staunched it with a sicustrumn from Mister Oberon's saumery . . . between treacles," he said, then added quickly, "No one saw it."

His mistress nodded slowly, eyes glittering with that same part-born envy she had beheld him with at Orchard Harriet. "W-would that I might be so . . . *robust* . . . ," she returned.

Rossamünd half grinned; he thought her very *robust* already. Thrice now he had seen her smashed and each time recover from the brink. The silence broken, he went to open his mouth and speak his mind at last, but balked at the very moment of revelation. *It must be this way,* he schooled himself, and took a breath. "Miss Europe," he began, a great tightening in his chest, "I . . . I would sail with you across the Gurgis Main and back . . . but . . . but I cannot go with you to Sinster . . ."

The Branden Rose beheld him with serious and ponderous understanding. "Nor," she added carefully, "c-can I keep you safe *here* while I am *there* . . ."

Rossamünd held her bleared yet clearly searching gaze. The realm of everymen had nothing but danger to offer; the world of monsters could surely be no worse.

Without words, Europe knew his mind. "I r-release you from my service, little m-man . . . ," she said, so softly he barely heard her. "I release y-your masters, too—you may tell them for me."

Rossamünd blinked in amazement. *Has the end come so quickly?* "I . . . I will," he said.

She closed her eyes. "You sh-should go . . . now . . . I w-will not stand long-drawn and m-maudlin goodbyes . . ."

A goodbye—most likely long-drawn *and* maudlin—was on his lips, yet, regardless of his mistress'—his *former* mistress'—distaste for it, he could not bring himself to say it. "I will visit with you when I can," he said instead, more in hope than certainty.

The Branden Rose chuckled grimly, then coughed over again with the strain of her mirth. "Th-that, I think, w-would not be wise."

"Aye . . ." Caught between a sob and a wry smile, Rossamünd ducked his head.

"I-I have your portrait—that will be . . . enough."

He looked up. She *had* found Pluto's portrait after all.

"Dear, per . . . perplexing Rossamünd . . ." Europe touched him gently on the cheek and fixed him with a look of finally unveiled affection. "Wh-who will you make s-such fine treacle for now . . ."

Careful of her wounds, he threw his arms about the mighty fulgar's neck and buried his face in her fine brown hair. "Thank you!" he began, but his whole frame was rocked as tears burst their dams at last, tears of gratitude, tears of regret, tears of farewell.

The fulgar held him firmly in her slight arms. "T-tish tosh . . . ," she whispered by his ear, her voice strangely thick.

The carriage slowed and Rossamünd—factotum no longer, nor foundling, nor lamplighter—leaned to look out at the dawn spreading out like the proof of a promise behind the ponderous buildings of Brandenbrass. Looking down the way from which they had come, he was sure he could see a small mob of rabbits scurrying in shadows and keeping pace behind. Giving voice to an urgent *tweet!* Darter Brown sprang from the carriage to fly back toward these chasing beasts. As the carriage went carefully about a right-angle bend, he opened the door of the moving fit. "Not all monsters are monsters," Rossamünd said in parting, surprised at his own resolve.

Europe beheld him keenly, as one wishing to fix a face in their memory. "Yes," she said. "I know."

Rossamünd held her gaze for what was surely the last time, his eyes stinging as he tried to express through these agents alone all that he felt and admired and . . . dare he own, *loved* in this most terrible of women.

"And be sure to find yourself another hat, little man," she added, the edge of her mouth twitching with mirth, nodding to Rossamünd's crown, hatless and naked yet again.

"I shall," Rossamünd returned, and with that, leaped from the drag and landed squarely on his feet, startling red-coated limn-men dousing a line of red-posted curb lamps in the lessening gloom of the fresh day.

29

LAST WORDS

To: Mistress Verline

Versierdholte

Halt-by-Wall

Boschenberg City

Hergoatenbosch

Newwich 1st Jude-was-Narcis, HIR 1601

Dearest, most precious Verline,

So much has happened since my last, too-short
letter. Yet, all that I have to tell you now that matters
is that my service as the factotum to Europe,
Duchess-in-waiting of Naimes, has come to an end.
Miss Europe has done all to keep me safe, but even
she cannot defeat the whole world, and now she
is gone to Sinster where I cannot go, and it is too
dangerous for me to stay in Brandenbrass—or in any
city at all. Frans and Pin are set on returning to you
to take up their foundlingery mastering again, yet,

as much as they urged me otherwise, I will not be coming with them.

I do not wish to startle you, but I am about to write something of such strangeness I would not blame you for disbelieving every word. It is the reason for the danger and for the hurts that drive Miss Europe to take her journey to the surgeons and has all to do with what troubled our dear cryptical Master Frans before he left you. For, when Master Frans first got to Madam Opera's, he did not find just a babbie on the doorstep—like the story usually goes—but a sparrow bogle with the babbie in his arms. It was this bogle who gave Master Frans the babbie, saying that it was not normally born but had come from the living mud far out in threwdish places. With his usual wisdom, Master Frans took the baby at once and gave it to Madam Opera. That babbie was me.

I am a rossamünderling, Miss Verline, a manikin, just like Biargë the Beautiful, who you might know from Master Frans' or Master Pin's sea stories. I am sorry if this is hard to read; it is not at all my intention to worry you or burden you with things too big to fathom or bear. It has been said to me that I am as much a man as a monster, neither more one nor less the other. I do not know what to reckon; I am just me. I have always been me. Not all monsters are monsters, just like Master Frans always rightly said.

Hard as this is to write and harder yet to act on, it is time for me to leave. Where I go I will not say, but I have tried the path of an everyman and now I go to find my proper place. I am sorry to write this, dearest Verline. Please do not take it too hard, nor fret, for those I go to have proved true friends.

Rossamünd

Farewell.

Forever your

604

P.S. It would be best to destroy this letter as soon as you have done reading it.

If I can, I will write you again.

I love you.

In the cool gloom of a late spring evening—while the heiress of Naimes, bound by fast-sailing sloop for Sinster, rounded the stony headlands of Needle Greening—a boy, a sparrow and a wizened little bogle left Brandenbrass. By hidden unfrequented paths and the covering shadows of night, these three traveled about the northern shores of the Grume to cross the mouths of the Marrow, finally passing on to the Sparrow Downs and out of the accounts of men.

FINIS TRIOLIBRIS
[END BOOK THREE]

EXPLICARIUM
BEING A GLOSSARY OF TERMS
& EXPLANATIONS INCLUDING
APPENDICES

NOTES ON THE EXPLICARIUM

A word set in *italics* indicates that you will find an explanation of that word also in the Explicarium; the only exceptions to this are the names of *rams* and other vessels, and the titles of books, where it is simply a convention to put these names in italics.

"See (entry) Book One" or "Book Two" refers the reader to the Explicarium in *Foundling*, The Foundling's Tale Book One or *Lamplighter*, The Foundling's Tale Book Two, by D.M. Cornish.

PRONUNCIATION

ä is said as the "ar" sound in "**a**sk" or "c**a**r"

æ is said as the "ay" sound in "h**ay**" or "**ei**ght"

ë is said as the "ee" sound in "scr**ea**m" or "b**ee**p"

é is said as the "eh" sound in "sh**e**d" or "**e**veryone"

ö is said as the "er" sound in "l**ear**n" or "b**ur**n"

ü is said as the "oo" sound in "w**oo**d" or "sh**ou**ld"

~ine at the end of pronouns is said as the "een" sound in "b**ean**" or "s**een**"; the exception to this is "Clementine," which is said as the "eyn" sound in "f**ine**" or "m**ine**."

Words ending in *e*, such as "Verline" or "Florescende": the *e* is not sounded.

SOURCES

In researching this document the scholars are indebted to many sources. Of them all the following proved the most consistently sourced:

The Pseudopædia

Master Matthius' Wandering Almanac: A Wordialogue of Matter, Generalisms & Habilistics

The Incomplete Book of Bogles

Weltchronic

The Book of Skolds

& extracts from the *Vadè Chemica*

A

abacus a place where mathematicians are trained, living what we would call a monastic life as they learn the numerical systems by which the cosmos are knit together. Abaci produce all the Empire's calculators, indexers and bench- and counting clerks, indeed any person devoted to what might essentially be called the "worship" of numbers and their manipulation. The masters of abaci hold themselves the true inheritors of the ancient geometry of the Phlegms and sneer at the modern learnings of the rival *athenaeums*. See *mathematician(s)* in Book Two.

abscondary small hidden dwelling where one might live unseen and safe. Typically this will be in the form of a secret room found between walls or cellar bolt-hole in some abandoned building.

Alabaster Brow, the ~ hostelry in Luthian Glee named in honor of the famously beautiful wife of a previous duke of *Fayelillian*.

Alcoves, the ~ collective noun for some of the "slummier" harborside suburbs, not only in *Brandenbrass* but in many cities in the Soutlands, so named for the dangerous nooks and blind alleys that are always found in such districts. The common term for what we would call a slum is a "nudge."

aletry artist's studio.

all-a'glory all or nothing.

allegories marks or cult signs made with rue in conspicuous placee by *fictlers* to show which *false-god* they revere and as a ward against monsters, the great foes of the *false-gods*. By extension, vinegars often take up such marks in the belief they will keep the all-too-common sea-nickers off.

alosudnë ancient and original name of the sea-lords who, later, through their treacherous desire for power over the land and the air too, became the *false-gods*. It is the name given to them still by their adherents.

amphigorers writers of nonsense and spreaders of gossip making their living through writing articles of dubious veracity for pamphlets, taking their part calling out their nonsense in a panto or as a *glossicute* in a *glossary*. Such is the taste in the greater cities for constant diversion that amphigorers are rarely without work.

Anaesthesia Myrrh see *Myrrh, Anaesthesia*.

anavoid rare and expensive script, a paste that to a normal nose is odorless yet possesses a hidden scent only a sthenicon- or *olfactologue*-wearing leer or lurksman can detect. Drying clear and without stain, it allows a box-wearer, when it is dabbed upon a target, to follow the distinctive odor anywhere without the target knowing that he or she is marked. Each anavoid will have such a distinct smell known only to its applier that even other leers and lurksmen will generally be unable to detect its presence.

aplombery sometimes referred to as mulierbriums ("women-makers"); what we might consider "finishing schools" for young well-to-do or aspiring women. The original aplomberies closely instructed their charges upon the *five graces*—along with other goodly and socially correct conduct—and over time have included varying degrees of instruction in such things as rimitry (simple mathematics), generalisms (geography and current affairs), *matter* (history) and the like, with the five original necessary graces. Those few hosted by a calendar clave at a calanserie or *sequestury* concentrate less on the graces and more on practical learnings of mind and also body, and here a girl might learn a whole lot more than might be thought ladylike, especially how to fight.

Arborlustra, the ~ great series of tree-grown halls in the main palace of the *Low Brassard*. The first trees were once original woodland simply built about as a show of accord between the first masters of *Brandenbrass* and the *Lapinduce* (the Concordis Cuniculum, it was called, not that any of the current inner sanctum of the city's masters care to recall it). Many of those great plants have since died, as has the memory of the old accord between men and monster-lord, the Rabbit-duke now never acknowledged and the dead trees replaced with more even rows of sycamore and turpentine—the light and dark hue of their trunks standing for the mottle of the Branden princes (now dukes). In one rarely visited corner of the Arborlustra a section of virgin wood remains, ancient trees living on through the centuries and tended with great care and gentleness by their keepers.

arbustra mundi Tutin phrase literally meaning "spring world" and what we would call a spring cleaning.

archduke or sometimes grand duke; the highest rank one can ascend to without provoking the ire of the other duchies of the Soutland states and declaring yourself king or queen.

Archduke of Brandenbrass see *Brandenbrass, Archduke of ~*.

archivist properly the name for someone in charge of a set of texts in a library, but also given to someone well versed in the contents of old and/or near-forgotten books.

arming cap small close-fitting cap, usually of proof-steel covered with gaulded cloth, and typically worn under more elaborate headwear that may not provide much protection.

armoniam unusual instrument made of glass discs—properly called phlanospheres—laid in sequence upon a central axis within a wooden box. The entire axis—and the glass discs with it—is turned using a treadle beneath the main box, and sound is achieved by gently touching the required glass disc for the required note. Simple armoniams have a single octave; the best—about the size of a small harpsichord—possess three full octaves. Its sound is hollow, bright and warbling, considered by some as eerie and modern and musical, but by others as unbearably shrill.

arx maria Tutin word meaning quite simply "sea fort"; heavy fortifications—castles really—set in the roads or at the mouth of harbors to guard against foes, nickerly and human. In *Brandenbrass* five major fortifications lie in a squashed semicircle about its harbors. Playing a significant part in several desperate seaward defenses of the great city, each has been given a suitably grand name: the northernmost Cauda Caputum ("head of the tail"), then Fidelis Fidës ("constant ally"), Saxum Cor ("stone heart"), Scorpis Aculeum ("scorpion sting") and finally Ocula Austerima ("southernmost eyes").

asper also known as malfais and not to be confused with the venificant *aspis* containing a lot of wormwood and ladapütch, it is the strongest sort of repellent employed by no-scourges. Partly an *urticant* and a fulminant of expanding oily black bubbles, it can give your typical nicker such a smarting, searing pain that the creature will leave you be for a goodly long time, and concentrated exposure has been known to scald a man dead. As such it must be handled with the utmost care.

aspis powerful contact toxin; when unable to procure a *spathidril*, swordists will almost always coat their weapons in aspis to gain some small measure of the deadly effect of those other ancient and terrible *therimoir* blades. See Book Two.

assvogel southern species of vulture.

athenaeum learning houses of the *metricians,* where they are first trained and then may continue to have as their home, venturing out to measure and record the world and bringing their observations back to the place of their first training. Not as closed as the *abacus* of the mathematicians, these will take in any soul who seeks to serve there, though they are strict upon the genuinely lazy. A soul is more likely to be able to take a *foundation*—a basic higher-level education—at an *athy* than an *abacus*. See also *concometrist* in Book One.

athy short for *athenaeum*.

austerating farting; wind that comes from the "south"—that is, the lower end of a person, the word coming from Auster, the wild southern wind that blows up over the Gurgis Main from Heilgoland. The other three cardinal winds are Auila = north, Eurus = east an, Favonis = west. Their names are actually taken from lords of the long-gone *naeroë,* though there are now no everymen who know this.

autumn more properly "autumnland"; the domains and seats of power of the monster-lords, *urchins, wretchins* and *petchinins*.

B

bastler ironclad gastrine fishing vessel with high wooden gunwales to protect the piscators aboard—deep-water fishermen and hunters of seanickers who wear proofing at sea and are expert shots with the large number of lambasts that line a bastler's deck.

Battle of Maundersea see *Maundersea, Battle of ~*.

baum fur from smaller carnivores like stoats or martens or gales (small, meat-eating, mouse-like creatures) of good quality, though each critter provides only scant pickings.

belch pot also known as a kluge pot—for no known reason remembered in history; in the Gottskylds, where it is reputed to have been devised, it is known variously as a *kaputtenkessel* ("breaking kettle") or *furzentopf* ("farting pot"). Infamous devices used by bandits, rough wild folk and some armies too, belch pots are makeshift artillery made of great clay pots or iron cauldrons filled with black powder and jagged, thorny flotsam, half-sunk in the soil and set off by a burning fuse. Any soul caught directly in its burst is sure to be flayed to splinters. Used to shape and channel the direction of a charge of fulminant, they are typically destroyed in the blast and are a favorite of irregular fighters all through the Sundergird, the clay version being particularly inexpensive and simple to fashion. ❧

benign mesmerists old wits serving in a kind of semi-retirement using their powerful skills reduced by ailing faculties to still somehow pay their way. Most wits will consider it fortunate that because of the violence of their lives and the precarious nature of the foreign organs inside them they are unlikely to see such decrepit days. "Mesmerist" is from the old Attic word *"mesmera,"* meaning "to addle or stupefy, to soothe into false comfort."

"bent like a Hamlin bow" contorted or crooked of frame, usually in reference to pains in the limbs or back. The term comes from the mighty bows used by the mercenary thoxothetes of Cloudeslee and their more mighty neighbors, Hamlin.

bestill liquor basic draught from a set of restoratives called lenitives or slakes, made for calming nerves and settling overwrought humours. The crudeness of its parts, although making it easy and inexpensive to brew, causes some folk with delicate innards to feel a little nauseated.

bettel what we would call red capsicum or bell pepper.

billiard room the "tabled game" is steadily becoming so popular that fine houses set aside rooms for them and organize evenings about sets of games played on them.

birchet foul-tasting draught useful for fortifying the constitution after an injury and helping to reduce any bruising or swellings of injured flesh. See Book One.

black habilist(s) researchers in forbidden learnings who, despite their bad reputation, insist that the drive of their blasphemous and dangerous researches are in the service of humankind, especially in the search for perpetual life and a final solution for the problem of the monsters. See Book Two, and *habilistics* in Book One.

Black Straps, the ~ a regiment of *lesquins* with noble bearing and a fearful reputation. They gain their name from the black cingulum all their number wear, a powerful show of loyalty, declaring in this way that their membership is of greater moment than any is to home or the land of an individual's nativity.

bom e'do *Sipponese* term meaning "spring silk-house"; the name given to one style of tall folding screen made in the *Occidental* lands of *Nenin* and *Sippon,* with frames of lacquered wood covered in artfully painted silk. They are collectables in the Haacobin Empire, eagerly sought yet hard to get from across the vast and dangerous *gurgis* that must be crossed to reach the Occident. Cheaper versions can be got from Ing, but these are considered inferior. There are also sum e'do or "winter silk-house" and do i'sen or "house of air," each type varying in style of image, attachment of silk to frame, the number of frames and manner of hinges and other minute details so loved by collectors.

Brandenbrass one of the largest cities of the Soutlands, situated at the top of the Pontus Canis on the northwestern shore of the Grume. It was established in the early eighth century HIR by *Burgundian* princes foiled by the might of the Skylds and their Gottish descendants to the east and expanding westward. Putting to flight the wild, monster-worshipping *Pilts*, the Burgund adventurers chose an advantageous harborage on the coast in the midst of wide fertile land and well-wooded forests to found the twin fortresses of the *Low Brassard* and Grimbasalt—which the locals called Branden Grim—about which settlements were established and spread, eventually joining into one, the city of Brandenbrass. During this time it was an independent princedom, until the arrival of the Tutins in the second Tutelarch invasion, when the old *Burgundian* lords of Brandenbrass managed to strike a bargain with the conquerors and so preserve their city from sacking. One of the leaders in Soutland commerce and politics, Brandenbrass is famous for its ram-building yards, arms mills and *athenaeums,* and is home to *the Black Straps* and to two of the known world's leading banks.

Brandenbrass, Archduke of ~ hereditary title of the ruler of that vaunted city, once the rank of prince when the great city was still a *Burgundian* province. Being unwed and childless, the Archduke of this tale is causing his ministers no end of distress; afraid that the Emperor will install his own man in the powerful seat should the current succession fail, they nag the Archduke endlessly about producing an heir. For his part, the Archduke is more interested in galas, the intrigues of court and summer campaigning against whoever presents the best target (at the time of this tale, this would be the sedorner-kings of the Lausid states).

Brandentown local name given to the regions of *Brandenbrass* within the first two curtain walls—the Inner Ward and the Prim Ward—and most especially to the older sections about the *Low Brassard*. Beyond this region are the Second Ward, the Out Ward, and the Lists—being the outermost suburbs between the first and second curtain walls.

brey murky or seething water, a name often given to the vinegar seas.

bridleminders low-class folk who make their scant living holding the reins of the carriages of other folk for one every quarter-hour or part thereof.

brinksmen properly called pathicords, these are *sanguines* who take the imbibing of various draughts to professional extremes, allowing them to run fast, ignore the need for sleep, think quickly and all the rest, then counter the effect of immunity over time by taking yet other draughts to still their overwrought humours and members and bring them promptly back to normal. Along with possible addiction, they risk the complete failure of their bodies' usual function.

brodchin most bestial-looking of the monsters, often moving in packs, perpetuating themselves by bizarre and unknown methods.

bruemes bruises and swellings of the flesh.

bruinins glamgorns, the mythic *flitterwills,* hollyhops and such related creatures of the woodland deeps and remote prairies.

Burgundian(s) of the race of princely historied Burgundy, who, between the arrival then inevitable lapse of the Tutelarchs (Dido's descendants) and the return of the Tutins, expanded west (for east were the implacable Gotts and the wild originine races), becoming settlers and founders of *Fayelillian, Brandenbrass,* Doggenbrass and many towns between, slowly conquering the *Pilts* in a protracted campaign of subjugation and integration whose hurts still linger today.

C

cabinet pictures among those of disposable means and dark tastes there is a fashion for depictions of the foulest violence and horror, showing the spoiling of monsters by despicable acts. There is a vigorous clandestine trade in such images, and those who produce them are greatly esteemed by *graphnolagnian* connoisseurs and make good money from the trade. Many struggling fabulists have been forced by poverty to try their hand at such depravity, and though never signing such pieces, some who have gone on to more legitimate fame have an anonymous catague of cabinet pictures ready to bring them to ruin.

cacoglumbs ancient collective name for what everymen know as ettins and umbergogs.

cadging, to cadge to hitch or sneak a ride upon a carriage or other conveyance; to be carried along by the endeavors of another; from the frame, or cadge, for carrying the hunting birds—hawks and kites and the like—once popular among the lofty set.

caffene what we would call coffee. Some varietides are N'gobi, Cassim, Engabine, Kasongo nd, Mong.

calipace bony plates of "armor" that cover many kraulschwimmen and watery beasts.

calling games games in which chancers shout their guess for the fall of a lot, the turn of a card or the toss of a coin, wagering on the outcome and putting their path in the trust of the *Signal of Lots*.

callow-jack sleek fish of moderate size and fair taste that do not need to be *dulcified* to be eaten, which means they can be caught, cooked and consumed straight from the main.

cankour-headed cankours or cankers are tumorous growths or malformations, and the term "cankour-headed" is used against *sciomanes* as a derogatory reference to the louthy gudgeon flesh they have inserted into their heads to gain control of that gudgeon.

Cannelle old and traditional name for *Cinnamon,* who was known to the ancient Tutelarchs, to the Attics before them, to the Phlegms, even to the near-forgotten Oghs and Urghs. As such he has been known and named by nearly all the races of the Altgird, the continental mass of which the Half-Continent is a part.

cap-a-pie • "from head to toe," as in completely. • to have your hind end higher than your head; to be upside down, to have everything contrary to how it should be.

capstan songs lively tunes—what we would call "shanties"—a product of the harshness of sea-board life, at times bawdy but always very sing-able, sung by vinegaroons in any grouped labor such as hauling up the anchor or winding the capstan of a ram or other vessel. A new

616

tune might make its way into common society and flourish there for a brief moment in pantos and tavern rounds, eventually returning to the obscurity of naval culture.

carboy(s) large cylindrical glass receptacles housed inside wooden cases for durability, the top of the cylinder sharply tapering to a narrow spout that protrudes from the top of the case for pouring. Mostly used to store acids and bases and other dangerous fluid.

Carp, Pragmathës *man-of-business* with the usual grand design to be a magnate. A true calculator trained at the Trigonon—the rhombus of *Brandenbrass* named after the great seat of mathematical learning in Clementine—he is correctly parsimonious, thorough, bureaucratic and honest in appropriate ways without possessing an overly weak con-science, and holds excellent standing with the bankers and brokers of *Brandenbrass*. Such a perfect combination of traits has secured him the patronage of both the Branden Rose and the Marchess of the Pike, and in not too many more years he will surely find himself achieving the wealth and consequence he desires.

casque • square boards of hardwood that are clamped about neck and wrist, functioning in much the same way as handcuffs do in our society. • another name for the proof-steel helms worn by *troubardiers*.

Casque Rogine, the ~ also known as the *Rotkappchen*—both names meaning "red cap" or "red hood," a *fulgar* from Gottingenin, so named for the scarlet cowl she wears wrapped about her head. She is one of the more (in)famous beldames—or "fighting women" and sometimes mispronounced "bedlams"—of current times, those that you will find most frequently in the *scandals* and *obsequine* pamphlets. Some others include Julliette Season, Rupunzelle, Serenissimë, Catharine Bonniface and, of course, the Branden Rose; indeed, there are a whole lot more.

catarrh what we would call a common cold.

caudial, caudial hem, caudial honor also just caude, caudia, lim-bus or caudilimb; attachable piece of cloth typically worn tied about the waist and hanging to the knees (sometimes possessing tails and tas-sels and ribbons that drape even lower). Generally distinctly patterned, embroidered with the figure of a heldin of old and edged with thread-of-silver and/or gold, a caudial is one of the manner of distinctions or credentials known as a garland, that is, an award of merit and honor, usually given for courage and sacrifice in the stouche or for some great deed of benefit to a peer, the ministers or plenipotentiary of a state, or the Emperor himself. In battle or on duty, caudials are worn over harness, but in civilian dress they are fixed under your coat, protruding from your weskit.

chancery gambling house. By law they are illegal in the Haacobin Empire, yet in practice they are found in almost every major city of the Soutlands.

chaste scripts that are still potent and usable, which have not *sophisticated,* that is, soured and lost their usefulness or become dangerously unstable.

Chïves, Pauper ~ obscure script-grinder of great and subtle skill and old friend to Craumpalin. His famillinom (see *family name* in Book One) is said "Cheevs."

choke kind of *vent* made of a high collar covering both neck and shoulders, loosely gathered about the throat, to be easily pulled up over the lower face to ward against choking gases and toxic fumes. Favored mostly by *sabrine adepts,* being a part of their professional costume.

Cinnamon mighty nuglung servant of *the Duke of Sparrows,* almost as old as the land itself. An expression of the sparrow-duke's will and character, he ranges wide and far to do good for the needy of all Providence's creatures: üntermen, everymen and simple beasts. Master of the tongues of birds, he sends out many wing-ed messengers to watch, to protect, to return and report, as do many lords of monsters and other mighty nickers. See Cannelle.

circuit meeting of many ways (not necessarily circular), especially in a city, and as convergences of city life often the busiest places there.

cleat(s), cleate slits in the skirt of a frock coat or other kind of coat to allow scabbards, holsters, stoups and other such accoutrements to protrude from under the coat.

clericy (ies) what we would call an office space.

cleveland land for common uses typically protected as such by some law or local ban.

Cloche Arde said "KLOASH Ard," being *Etaine* for "tower of flint." Built more than a hundred years before the time of this tale, it was located, inspected and bought near a dozen years ago by *Pragmathës Carp* on behalf of Europe, one of his first assignments as her *man-of-business*.

clumsy what we would call a sandwich, so called because it is an easy way to eat for the busy or the moving ("clumsy" once meaning "fast moving, running").

cob(s) • dull-coated horses preferred for transport out beyond the safety of a city, so employed because losing a lesser-quality beast to the hunger of a monster is far better than the slaughter of your best high-stepping trotter with its glossy coat and proud, pleasing form. • two-guise piece—one 240th of a sou.

cofferdam chamber or channel used for repairing vessels below the waterline.

cognizance facility of a wit to be able to "see" by witting.

cold beef clumsy sandwich of "yesterday's" beef.

coldbeam collective vernacular for a Catharine wheel, gibbet or gallows, coming from an old *Pilt* word meaning "death wood."

colonel civilian "contractor" for a *lesquin* regiment, organizing the provision of supplies (weapons, harness, provender), billeting and work to his regiment. They do not fight or serve on the field of war; rather they do battle with the various suppliers ever looking to diddle a customer and with the secretaries and lawyers of the various states and realms ever seeking to gain the most for the least.

colonial quarries mines and quarries of the Verid Litus sponsored under Imperial license by the states of the Soutlands and worked largely by those convicted by law or, paradoxically, fleeing such conviction.

come-as-you-fancy fancy dress; elaborate fantastical costume.

compleat skold's "recipe book" full of lists of draughts and potives. These are either compiled and bound by the skold or purchased printed, with blank sections allowing for the reader's own additions. The lost or hidden compleats of the greatest skolds of yore are rumored to hold some forgotten and mighty scripts, and are sought by collectors, ambitious individuals and ruthless governments alike.

compounded ash of Mehette slow-burning repellent, excellent to place about a camp at night and burn to keep monsters at bay while you sleep.

"Coneys in their covets . . ." little pap-nanny rhyme; among the

silly songs of unknown origin sung to children to set them at ease—
usually . . .

> Coneys in their covets,
>
> Bunnies in their holes,
>
> But who shall ferret my meal?
>
> A fig and a date,
>
> A fig and a date,
>
> Quince paste and orange peel.

congress • (verb) to meet or have dealings with another. • (noun) a "weekender," an extended "vacation," usually only the privilege of the monied and high stationed. Increasingly, however, the merchant classes are gaining enough affluence to partake in such a custom. Currently a popular congress is a *summerscale* outing to fortified, naturally sweet-watered beaches or a tour of the often empty country manors of the city landowners and title holders.

consumptive palsies of '85, the ~ in 1585 HIR, much of the northern Soutlands and spreading as far east as Flint were afflicted with a plague of consumptive palsy, a wasting and crippling disease said to be spread by small infiltrating monsters and any of their outramorine adherents (in truth spread by lice and rats). Lasting three years, it weakened the resources of the states enough to make their enemies bold, leading to such things as the Gotts' suppression of the Flints, the increase in piracy of the Lombards and a relaxing of colonizing pressure upon the monsters dwelling at the fringes of human settlement. Although cases of the consumptive palsies are now few, the recovery from the thinning is steady but slow.

copstain(s) tall cylindrical hat with a thin brim, what we would call a top hat.

coston(s) gaol guard; typically pensioned and often maimed pediteers, who can make income on top of their meager pay through bribes and extorting money from the supporters of the imprisoned, giving promises in exchange to deliver messages, letters, food and even clothes to the incarcerated.

court-plaster what we might call masking tape, a tough paper strip clean on one side and smeared with a firmly adhesive glue upon the other.

crawdod(s) what we would call crayfish or lobster.

cresset(s) iron bowl fixed to a post or directly to a wall and used to burn oil as a torch.

crimp(s) privately operating impress contractor, that is, a group or individual licensed to press people into naval or military service. They are usually given a quota by a ram's captain or a regimental *colonel* and with this authority trawl the streets of less well-heeled districts, seizing anyone appearing at that moment not to be engaged in gainful activity, regardless of the poor soul's true employment status. Drunkards are a common target, as are those living rough or without proper documentation (such as someone who has just been thoroughly turned over by a *grabcleat* or the like); if a gang of crimps is desperate, they may well have an arrangement with a local gaoler to fill their quota with a number of criminal sorts. The contractor is paid head money for each person he brings back and a bonus for making quota. A current work docket or a *Presage Exemption* is the best defense against such artless thuggery.

crocidole what we would call a crocodile. In the Half-Continent such creatures are little known except as the Figure 5 Brutes card in the traditional deck or as a delicacy among the rich.

crossing sweeps people who use besoms (brooms rough-made from twigs bundled about a long branch for a handle) to sweep away the ubiquitous animal dung that smears a city's streets. A very necessary though largely unrecognized role performed for a half-goose piece per crossing by old folks, children of destitute families, released prisoners of war with no possible way to get home or rural refugees of battle or theroscades—any of those one step away from vagrancy.

crownstones also known as mourndials; tall hand-carved blocks set in memorial above the head of a person, dead and buried.

cunctus orbis Tutin term meaning "the entire sphere," that is, the whole world; being the old Attic and Phlegmish maps of the known world at the time of the Phlegms, cherished by the Tutins and their descendants as a connection to that great, annihilated race.

D

demijohn bottle with a thin, fluted neck, its base enclosed in a wickerwork basket.

Dere Reader, the ~ translation of an ancient book full of horrors and foul and recondite learning, said to be the major source book for transmogrifers, massacars and *graphnolagnians* alike.

Dew of Imnot a slake or calming draft of fine parts suitable for even the most sensitive of stomach.

dexter *fulgar* and wit in one, typically either wits who want some measure of protection from their foes—the *fulgars*—by taking on their power too and thereby nullifying it, or *fulgars* who desire to be able to find their prey without reliance upon other staff or hirelings to help them. Aside from possessing the puissance of both an astrapecrith and a neuroticrith, a once quite unforeseen combination of these has brought about a new "power," petrusion, whereby a dexter can smite someone with a barely seen static blast without the need of touching them, though a foe still needs to be near at hand (say half a dozen yards at most away). Of course, a dexter's "range" with petrusion will increase with practice. As they become more proficient, they can begin to choose to hit something farther away, or hit them hard when close.

Didodumese part of the Antique Sanguines, the direct and widespread heirs and descendants of Dido, the original Empress of the Tutins. Their claim to heritage gives them a powerful stake in the Empire, often courted by the Haacobin Emperors (whose great sire Menangës wrested Imperial power from the Sceptic dynasty, the legitimate heirs of Dido's legacy) seeking still to secure their own dynasty's legitimacy. See *Dido* in Book One.

digitals sets of small, cylindrical, felt- or velvet-padded chambers typically made of enameled pewter and hung from a belt, baldric, pocket or sash and in which potive castes are kept safe yet ready for use. A caste is slotted into the top of each cylinder, which is then secured shut by a fastening lid. Each potive is released by a quick flick of an independently clasped cover at the base of each cylinder, allowing the caste to slip out easily into the user's hand.

Dogget & Block, the ~ one of the more interesting but little known histories surrounding this very old hostelry is that its name is derived from an incident in *Brandenbrass'* early history. "Dogget" is an obsolete term for a monster, especially one of the more bestial form, and the forgotten incident was quite simply the execution by beheading of a monster near the hostel in the square now known as Tight Penny Circle.

dolly-mops daughters of the lower *lectry* and commonality, who walk in safety in crowds to mills and workhouses and low-end files; dressed as mere maids despite their higher situation, they are hardened and prematurely aged by the harsh rigors of their labor.

dote(s) scripts used on *vents* and fascins to make them retardant to other draughts and fumes.

Droid second-brightest star in the *Signal of Lots*, the constellation presiding over choices and chances; it is the superlative (Signal Star) most sought when testing fate and taking knowing risks, its position in the heavens relative to other lights telling on your future, should you care to heed such stuff—though such scrying is said to be the province of scoundrels, mendicants and the weak-headed.

duffers constabulary, thief takers and carriage-pointers of *Brandenbrass*. Faithful employees of the Duke and his *metropolitans*, they also enforce such civic laws as the one ensuring that the pistols men carry about as fashion, and that teratologists bear as tools, are loaded with sack rather than deadly lead shot.

Duke of Rabbits, the see *the Lapinduce*.

Duke of Sparrows, the ~ lord of sparrows, finches and all such small wing-ed critters who has watch over Rossamünd and all the small, weak or and misunderstood who wander in the reaches of his realm. As with all nimuines—all monster-lords, the most mighty of the *urchins, wretchins* or *petchinins*—the Duke of Sparrows tends to remain at the heart of his domain, venturing out seldom but sending agents and "spies" instead to keep watch and perform necessary deeds. Only such terrible events as the rising of a *false-god* from the deeps would induce a *monster-lord* to shift itself from its seat of power and rise up with all the might that is its own. Otherwise they remain sedentary, lost in melancholic contemplations or bitter plottings or blissful reverie, their sway—their "influence"—over the land seeping out from them and deepening with the passing of the centuries.

dulcifer concoction of chemicals in which sea-caught fish and the like are soaked (usually for a day), leeching out dangerous salts to make them edible. Without such treatment, an unsweetened fish (if a person could endure the foul taste) would make a person sick, and persisting over many meals might eventually kill the eater. There are many naturally occurring dulcifers in the wild: plants and barks and roots, often forming the basis for more refined recipes. These usually include some kind of seasoning, without which the soaked seafood would be bland.

dulcify to soak in a *dulcifer*.

Dzïk wild land on the southernmost edges of Heilgoland of partly subjugated people with a long proud history (and now current secret practice) of servitude to the *wretchin* ice-lords Lod and Panebog (or just Pan) of ice-bound Magog (the very bottom of the world where, as you pass through, down on the map becomes up again). Such service has been the only way they have been able to endure against the wild, wide-faring Tung and the empire-desiring Heil. Nevertheless, their northern tribes live under the auspices of the Heil Empress, serving her, and in such service they have discovered the rest of the world, venturing far to advance many dark causes in the name of their secret monstrous masters.

E

earwig listener for gossip, rumor and damning hints to then spread with expert subtlety.

eclatics skill-set or puissance of a *fulgar*. See also *fulgar(s)* in Book One.

elephantine(s) named for their great corpulence, these folk are the highest rank of magnate in central Soutland society. Much of the Half-Continent pivots on the idea that certain folk are better than others, that some are worthy and most of all should lead and succeed, whereas others are not worthy and ought to suffer at their betters' expense. This is very much the stated position of the peers, lords and princes—an inherited notion fundamental to their understanding of themselves and their place in relation to other lesser folk, the wellspring of their callousness and arrogance abetted by all levels of society and the source of their social power. Magnates also aspire to such a position, the assumption of status and natural superiority sought through great material consequence and generous sponsorship of often far poorer betters. Born of inferior station, they are resented by the peers (often deeply), yet are granted a kind of borrowed rank in return for their support and investment. Elephantine is the highest position such a monied "upstart" can reach. Though dukes, marches, counts and barons may in their heart of hearts look down upon the elephantines, *vulgarines* and other magnates, the raw power that money affords induces the former to concede and treat them as equal.

emperorflies what we would call dragonflies.

emunic reborate strengthening draught taken particularly by *fulgars* and especially thermistors, to fortify their health and strength and allow them to dare great exertions of puissance. Unlike Cathar's Treacle it keeps for many days before spoiling.

enginry collection of mechanical devices, especially the various gastrine- or water-driven machines used in mills.

ephemerides tables showing seasonal planetary positions.

erreption correct *physical* name for an amputation, including the proper sealing of the gory stump and its major vessels.

Etaine language spoken by most of the peoples of the Patricine states and very much like French in our own world.

etiolated sickly and pale.

Euclasia mining colony in the resource-rich lands of the Verid Litus governed by Boschenberg.

eurinië, eurinin(s) original name given to patrons of all things moving on and in the earth. In the time after the treachery of the *alosudnë* and then of the everymen, they fractured in their purposes to become the *urchins,* the *petchinins* or the *wretchins*.

euriphim all monsters together; derived from *eurinië,* it is a name they give themselves as of old.

"Ex munster vackery!" vulgar corruption of the warding phrase "Ex monstrum vacarè," that is, "of monsters be free!" Such warding phrases are part of a dialect known properly as grammar or cantrics most commonly spoken among the *fictlers*.

expurgatory or lahzar's list; handmade books containing excerpts of the *Vadè Chemica* and the *Dere Reader* and consequently a forbidden thing within the Empire. Of course it is well known that lahzars possess them, but such folk are needed too much for such a proscription to be enforced.

F

fabercadavery also known as necrology or necromancy, the making of revers and other gudgeons, including *jackstraws*. The practitioners of such vile research swear that their main intent is not to make something worse than monsters but to discover the very functions of life and seek to bring the boon of such discovery to everymen. Regardless, excesses in such endeavors are said to have been part of the downfall of the Phlegms. Therefore, in nearly every realm of the Half-Continent, fabercadavery is illegal (even the liberal surgeons of Sinster regard it with caution), and its practitioners are often hunted down and gaoled or even slain.

false-god(s) or pseudobaths; also known as amathabrins ("foolish-arrogants"), basbathonids ("deep-lords"), catabrathins ("great deep ones," a name used for any big sea-monster, including kraulschwimmen), demiurges, falacitines, fichtärs, pseudomaurins ("false-fools"), pseustis ("liars") and nausithoë (though this is a more general term for any sea-monster). False-gods were once the equals of the *eurinines,* back in the Aforetime when all things that are were being made and known first as the *alosudnë* ("the sea-born"). The antiquated, fragmentary catalogs say many things, but most hold that they were the lords and agents of life in the seas, as the secretive *eurinines* were of the lands, and the gossamer *naeroë* were of the air. Yet as rulers over the most fiercesome creatures in all the realms the *alosudnë* grew proud; as caretakers of the middle portion—the portion air being greatest (in size) and land least—they grew jealous and rose up against the *naeroë.* Surprised, the "sky-lords" and their servants were defeated and the survivors fled the deuter (the world), leaving the skies empty of all but clouds and wind (the birds actually belonging to the land, for they need to perch). It is said that Providence, seeing this arrogance, roused the *eurinines,* who threw the *alosudnë* back into the deeps; then Providence caused the deep-lords to become idiot and, renaming them the amathabrins, set the kraulschwimmen as watch over them. It is held that false-gods are sources of prognosis (the original, secret knowledge of the world's founding) and those that are known are actually worshipped by some everymen (as stated in Book One). These worshippers are known to other right-thinking folk simply as *fantaisists* ("dream-believers") or *fictlers* (also thralls, dullards) and consider them the most blighted outramorines—to be rooted out and obliterated. This is often a great consternation to the *fantaisists,* who typically reckon the *eurinines* to be foul usurpers, and are as much haters of bogles and nickers as the most inveterate invidist. Among themselves *fantaisists* are variously called helots or gnosists ("knowers of special knowledge"; also achätastars [said "ak-KAR-tast-tarz" = "the fickle ones"]—often shortened to tastards; goests, goestës or goestins—basically "user of powerful [harmful] knowledge"; or therapards, "god-servers"). *Fantaisists* refuse to use such terms as "fichtär" or "false-god," calling them instead the basbathonids, bathonions or "our bathic lords." Gathering themselves into groups called *septs,* each will revere a single fichtär above all others, the most terrible *sept* being the Saccour or Sucärines—the bloodthirsty, cannibalistic worshippers of *Sucoth* the Decayed, the Swallower of Men. Each *sept* holds to strange and erroneous doctrines they collectively name mutebaths—Tellings of the Deep Things—and right-thinking folk call falsagoes or falsities. The mutos or mutes (dogma) of a particular sept's mutebath will declare their own fichtär as ultimate lord, and will contain fragmentary prescriptions of the manner in which one might raise a chosen false-god for an unending period of glory. *Fantaisists* tend to be vague on what it actually *is* they are seeking (except the servants of *Sucoth,* who seek annihilation and oblivion). Antiquarians and learned habilists are much clearer on what the advent of a false-god will mean: much suffering and ruination—at least in the region in which one is called up. Regardless, each *sept* will argue even violently with the others that their own basbathonid is the greatest, producing their mutebaths and the apparently original ancient texts and relics to reinforce their claims, though many of these items are fakes—even old, obscure fakes, believed real by their *sept.* Despite the discrepancies, vagaries and disagreements, most *septs* agree that *Lobe,* a famuli—or lesser fichtär—is the chief medium by which one gains the "ears" of the others, and you will find him occurring frequently in *fantaisist* litanies and mutes. None of recent times can confirm whether their false-god responds at all to summons and commands. Worshippers take dogged encouragement from the rumors of Phlegm's destruction and more recently an apparently successful raising of Inchyitutyll, the Shrunken, by an unknown people once living in what is now called the Slough of Despond near the Flintmeer. This unknown people (probably one of the wild tribes of the Erzgebirge) left no evidence of their success but were instead wiped out by Inchyitutyll, who in turn was roundly beaten back into the waters by the *Duke of Sparrows* and two other urchin-lords, never to rise again. As terrible as all this fichtär-worship might appear, *fantaisists* are very much seen as an idiot fringe whose own infighting does as much to weaken and suppress as any subversive work by the Emperor's special, dedicated agents. More disturbing, and little

627

known, is that *massacars* go to the *septs* to inquire of their chosen lord in the hope of gaining insight into the spark of life and its manipulation. The advent of gudgeons is said to be the result of one such successful "conversation" many centuries ago between an unknown *black habilist* and Ode, the Sweet Death, Sister of *Lobe*. The surgical and mimetic knowledge required to transmogrify lahzars is said to have come from a similar source: a historied communion of Cathartic scholars and the servants of the bathic lords—though lahzars themselves utterly refute such an assertion and transmogrifers remain silent. Over the centuries many false-gods have gained names, though it is unclear whether all those named truly exist, slumbering and drooling undiscoverable at the very bottom of the crushing mares.

fancies fancy-dress, elaborate "party costume."

fantaisist(s) also phantastes, *fictlers,* helots ("the bound" or "owned"), legiters or categists—an uncommon name gained from their practice of cater legite or cantrics, the superstitious practice of concentrating the will by calling or singing as a group into the deep places—whether land or sea—trying to rouse and summon the *false-gods* and/or their beastly servants.

fantastico painting of an imagined scene, either a real event of old, or some figment of imagination or ancient myth.

faraday vulgar corruption of "fare-a-day," meaning laborers who work for daily hire, possessing many varied skills and traveling the lands to find employment in right season.

farced pounding similar to meat loaf; though prepared in a more fancy manner and strongly seasoned, it is still humble fare. It is a current fashion among rural peers to eat it, signifying simplicity and self-conscious connection with the lowly folk upon whose labor the landed gentry depend.

Fayelillian northern neighbor of *Brandenbrass* and ancestral home of the disgraced Lamplighter-Marshal contending for his honor in the Considine. See Book Two.

fête night of eating and dancing, a term used especially out in the parishes but losing fashion in the city.

fictler(s) worshippers and followers of *false-gods,* the name coming from the notion that these folk honor fictions, that is, false notions of the *false-gods*. They are typically regarded as a type of sedorner, yet they hold themselves as entirely distinct from sedorners and outramorines—opposites in fact, seeking the *false-gods* to rise up to rid the world of the landed monsters, the true foes of everymen. They prefer to call themselves gnosists, that is, "the knowers," for the higher knowledge they believe they possess, yet are not above the use of human sacrifice in their fervor to summon forth their chosen false-god. See *fantaisists*.

Finance, Baron Idias ~ the Baron of Sainte (a wealthy region in Naimes proper), Captain-Secretary (the seniormost clerk) and Chief Emissary of Naimes' diplomatic mission to *Brandenbrass*, is under permanent charge from the Duchess of Naimes to keep an eye on that state's wayward daughter, Europe, the Branden Rose. He discharges this duty happily, as much for his deep regard for the Duchess-in-waiting as from obedience to his proper mistress. As much as Europe might deny her connection to her mother, she still holds a level of authority over the Baron.

fistduke(s) common corruption of the Heil word *viskiekduzär*—pronounced "viss-KYK-doud-saar" and meaning "vicious souls"—troubardierlike soldiery who will happily turn sell-sword and often serve the darkest causes. Braving the crossing of the Gurgis Main, they are hardened fellows and a favorite among the *black habilists* of the Soutlands, serving as *spurns* and bravoes or in whatever capacity money's hand might prompt them. Though they are not regarded as true *lesquins*, neither are they of the mercenary federmen rabble, but have their own ghastly and well-earned reputation.

fitch usually referring to a proofed-feathered collar, it is also a broad term for any gaulded neck-and-shoulder wrapping.

fits carriages, coaches and carts collectively.

five graces, the ~ also called the Pendecora, the ancient time-honored accomplishments thought worthy of a lady of good blood or fine beginning: conversation, elegance, femininity, meekness and posture.

flammagon stubby, large-bore firelock used to fire flares high into the air. In a pinch it can double as a weapon, but it is best suited as a launcher of bright signals.

flitterwills small winged bogles, their form often a crude simulacrum of everymen yet with more distorted proportions. One of the few bogles—since the exodus of the *naeroë*—who make use of the winds and air, they are found only in the remotest, often terribly threwdish places, though there are meant to be many lurking in the Schmetter-lingerwald north of Wörms and ruled by the Duchess of Butterflies. This is all conjecture, of course; ancient texts hold them to be among the tribe of monster known as *nissë,* but in common culture flitterwills are pure myth.

Florescende, the ~ named after a great meadow of wildflowers out in the western wilds beyond the Path, the Florescende is a great tessel-lated square in the very midst of the Brandendirk, so called for the great floral tessellations of its paving. Originally it was the forming ground for soldiery, but as the buildings of government expanded out from *the Low Brassard* and the city grew and became safer, it has taken on a more civic role. On special vigils and memorials, pediteers are still marshaled upon it for the Archduke to inspect and his people to be impressed by.

Fontrevault *sequestury* and calanserie of the *Right of the Open Hand,* found on the border between Naimes and Maine in the rolling lands of the Cassalis Hills. It is here that Europe began her turbulent public career free of the stuffy courts of the Naimes duchy.

foundation course of instruction in *matter* and generalisms; what we would consider basic tertiary education, and leading to all manner of bureaucratic work and the possibility of further advancement.

fowling piece flintlock rifle of extra-long barrel, typically elaborately formed and decorated, with robust mechanism and excellent aim used to hunt birds and small game.

frair name monsters give to each other as a collective, meaning "brother" or "family member."

franchise parcels of land granted by a landed lord to his *moilers* and pastoralists to farm and make profit for themselves and more especially their lord in varying measure, depending on the magnanimity (or its lack) of the lord. The fairest known division of income in current Sout-land pastoral practice is a 60/40 split twixt laird and laborers, seen by most as astoundingly fair though the fact that the pastoralist will have to pay wages for seed and equipment from this 40 percent spoils the figure some.

Frazzard's powder named after its long-dead inventor, Immoli-ens Frazzardas, and popular for its simplicity: 1 part clubmoss, 1 part ladapütch, ½ part escalat. Being so simple, however, it lacks the power of some more complex *urticants* (fizzing, bursting scripts), and its wide-spreading fumes are less contained and therefore less precise than others.

fugelman locally elected or appointed teratologist, sponsored by subscription of the local folk and/or by the patronage of a parish's peers and magnates. This is not a popular occupation for any monster-hunter worth his prize-money; consequently, only the more infamous or inept stripe of teratologist will generally fill such a position on the principle that anything is better than nothing. If a hireling from without the community is not available, the people might very well nominate—even force—one of their own to fill the role, even paying (in part at least) for his training in whatever manner of teratology they want or the community decides the person should have, as with Sallow Meermoon in Book One.

fulgar(s) though much about these lightning-wielding lahzars is covered in Book One, there is yet more in a fulgar's arsenal:

• vendette—make someone confess something—to tell the truth, usually only one item before the sheer agony and destructive shock kill them.

• defeasance—also called scinderation, the rare and risky capacity to run such a quantity of charge through living matter that any liquid within becomes "super-heated" and it will literally burst.

See *fulgar(s)* in Book One for more.

fulgars' doses beyond Cathar's Treacle, an astrapecrith will need, at various times, fulgura sagrada, rock salt, levenseep, and the ready-made balancing draughts syntony and sangfaire.

Fyfe, Rear-Admiral Patchword captain and civic leader of the late sixteenth century HIR; born 1539 HIR in Brandenbrass, he began his glittering naval adventure as a midshipman aboard the twenty-four-gun-broad frigate NB *Spritely*. Rising over one of the briefest periods in Imperial naval history, he added to his martial glory by marrying Thalistia Saakrahenemus, therefore joining himself into one of the Empire's ancient family lines. His stellar career was cut short by his death in 1588 at *the Battle of Maundersea* while he led a campaign against the Lombardy picaroons and their state sponsors. In all his escapades he fathered only one child, *Rookwood*.

Fyfe, Rookwood Saakrahenemus son of *Rear Admiral Fyfe*; properly orphaned at age eight, he has been a wayward charge for his aunt Saakrahenemus ever since, living off the stipend paid from his closely controlled fortune (the hereditary wealth of his mother and the residue of prizes won by his glorious father) and doing little but roaming about town with his *obsequine* friends, practicing his aim and getting into some form of strife or other.

G

gabelüng meaning "fork in the road"; club made from a forked branch from a hardwood tree, the stunted forks forming the head, the handle usually wrapped in doeskin or sergreen for greater grip, some also fitted with a roundel to protect the hand from deflected blows. With the rise of *fulgars* the use of wooden weapons has continued in the Sundergird and beyond, for astrapecriths are quite happy to send arcs back along any weapon that might hit them, and metal devices aid them in this much better than wood.

garland •also known as a pattern book or cicerone (after the city whence they were first reputed to be invented), often very large, heavy-bound periodicals released by collectives of dressmakers, tailors, gaulders, armourieres, haberdashers, furriers and any other sort involved in the provision of high fashion. • award of merit and honor, usually given for courage and sacrifice in the stouche or for some great deed of benefit to a peer, the ministers or plenipotentiary of a state, or the Emperor himself. See *caudial, caudial hem, caudial honor.*

garner grain store; a granary.

Gaspard Plume see *Plume, Gaspard.*

Geiterwand lit. "goat-wall"; large fortified gate not far north of Poéme and the burned-out ruin that was once Madam Opera's Marine Society. It is most notable for the fine kennel of selthounds it keeps, animals of such high breeding that feuterers from all the lands about—even as far as Turkmantine and the N'go—come to breed their bitches with them.

genis main grouping of like creatures such as glamgorn, nuglung, feline, canine, and so on.

gleedupes sellers of song words and bad fruit at pantos and other entertainments. They might also offer simple food to eat (nestled alongside the molding fruit, of course).

glimmerall also glimmeramo; what we might call a chandelier; a collection of bright-limns in a large, often intricately decorated frame suspended from a chain or gilt ropes and lowered for servants to turn each light on its pivot as required. Some are so large they require special framing to be added to a ceiling and a whole staff to lower, light and clean them.

glossary frivolous counterpart to an *oratory* at a high-class society event, where gossip and controversial nonsense are the rule, proceeding under direction of a *glossicute* who keeps conversation light and topics saucy or fatuous and rolling along in a continuous flow of gasps and scandalized laughter.

glossicute(s) "referee" of a *glossary*; the most skillful possess great wit and know all manner of rumor and scandal with which they can spin a seemingly endless fribble of chatter and gossip. Glossicutes are known for the acidity of their words and the level of vitriol they allow among the participant guests, and are hired accordingly.

goat weed, extract of ~ additive meant to make the imbiber feel good about himself and the world in general; of ill reputation among upstanding folk, as it makes addicts of frequent users, numbing them to other people's suffering or concerns.

gosling half-guise (or half-goose) piece.

grabcleat(s) muggers, grabbers of the hems and folds of one's frock coat.

Grammaticar seniormost leader of a group—or *sept*—of *fictlers,* derived from the notion of grammar, that is, the right formulas of words spoken into the deeps to attempt to rouse the slumbering *false-gods* to rise and deliver everymen from the scourge of nickers and all their vile kind.

graphnolagnian(s) one given over to an obsession with obscene pictures; the self-named connoisseurs of *cabinet pictures*.

grass-wine what we would call champagne or sparkling white.

Greenleaf Whit see *Whit, Greenleaf.*

gregorine(s) common name for gater and parish border warden in the rural parts of the central Soutland states; also gregoryman, and so called because they serve as protectors. In the Grumid lands they are sometimes named bindlestiffs—a term usually retained for more vagrant types in other parts of the world—for the time they will spend patrolling their parish boundaries, living rough. Traditionally employed as protectors against the nickers and bogles, in safer parishes gregory-men often become more concerned with the small disputes of parochial parish pride as small regions vie and squabble with their neighbors like full-grown states.

grindewhal also grindewail or grindywill; known as the "rats of the sea" (or, farther north, the "jackals of the sea"), the Gotts naming them *fifflecrawe* ("sea-crows"). A monstrous type of fish, they come in many variations of shape and size, all of them ugly: hunched, humped backs, long slender snaggle-toothed snouts, tiny piggy eyes. They are considered merelings, that is, neither inoffensive sea-animal nor true sea-nicker, rather something in between. One of their main vices (as reckoned by vinegars) is not that they attack vessels and their crews, but that as prey they attract yet larger and nastier critters hunting them. Despite this, they are reckoned especially good eating (if you can catch one) and so, on the balance, are considered a necessary evil. They are plentiful despite constant predation and can be found in every sea and ocean the world over.

Guiding Star, the ~ the only wayhouse on the Athy Road between *Brandenbrass* and the pastoral lands of the *Page,* its rear quarters actually delved some way into the hills behind it.

gurgis(es) deep oceans between continents filled with storms and sea-monsters.

H

Hamlin parliament rare populist regime where representatives of the people (wealthy middle class and peers at least) in a parliament actually elect their ruler, who is known as a high-elector. Such a system of seem-ingly arbitrary government is horrifying to the hereditary sovereigns of the Imperial states that are Hamlin's northern neighbors, but what else can be expected from such a realm of likehandlers sharing all the needs of life with each other and paying subscriptions to help the poor?

Handsome Grackle, the bizarre creature of the *genis* sea-hag, identi-cal in form at either end, its landward name derisively given it by the piscators who snared it. Small as sea-beasts go yet nigh indestructible, the Handsome Grackle is routinely swallowed by the great kraulschwimmen and other vasty beasts of the depths, only to travel the entire length of their alimentary canal and emerge at the other end, unharmed and setting off on its own obscure business once again.

hard-waters spirits; drinks with high alcohol content.

harnessguarde the armed escort of a merchant train or other such caravan of beasts and goods and/or goodly personages. Usually such work is taken by less notable *spurns* or those with pretensions to an adventurous life but without the skill to properly live it.

Heilgolundian of or from Heilgoland (also referred to as Heilgolund by the more pretentious or learned), that is, the vast kingdom beyond the great southern oceans, whose warriors have ever fought both the snow-dwelling nickers of their land and their wild everymen neighbors, and dare the dangerous waters to serve in the armies of Half-Continent realms.

hinderling(s) rossamünderlings, so called for the fact that they are reborn from the remains—the "hind-pieces"—of everyman.

hookpole used by takenymen and other carriage drivers to open the doors of their *fits* without having to get down from their seat; also to pull unwanted custom from within once the door is opened, and even to reach and snag items from the wayside.

horologue an innovation on the clock that does not have to be perfectly still or vertical to work, therefore allowing it to be carried on board rams and other vessels, greatly aiding navigation. What in our world would be called a chronometer.

Hullghast Articled Ordnance Company built off the main thoroughfare of the Mill Strand, the complex of Hull AO Company slipways protrude well out into the milky *brey*. Great moats reach back from them, cutting across the very street to disappear into mysteriously dark tunnels made in the main mill's thick wall, deep enough that an unmasted ram can slide unobtrusively and largely unobserved from mill to slipway. Each moat is traversed by a series of enormous braice-iron bridges allowing hoof and wheel and foot to cross unhindered and largely unaware. Arm-thick iron fences and equally hefty gates run right along this part of the harbor, preventing any access to the moats, the slipways or the half-done rams they hold.

humbuggler hypocrite; a speaker of humbug, that is, of deceptive nonsense.

I

intent complex document formally stating all the particulars relating to a teratologist's ability and availability to knave.

J

jack-ornerers collective colloquial name for monsters.

jackstraw(s) also called *flayderhauf*, and sometimes scours, wanderoo, haimians, spargamen and thanantës. Distinct from *rever-men*, they are considered a superior form of gudgeon, their bodies made from meldings and bindings of muscle and flesh and bone with metal and wood and clothes all motivated by the stuff of a human brain. They usually look like nothing more than what we would call scarecrows, zombielike scarecrows. The name *"flayderhauf"* comes from the use of the exceedingly rare and powerful *flayderia exia* in their making, a near-mythic substance that is reputed to force flesh to meld with other biological matter (wood, cloth, bone, plant stuff), the latter taking on some of the quicker character of the meat. They are said to be the best autonecraughts (revers that can be controlled by a *thanatocrith*) because the lesser amounts of human matter in them make them less innately rebellious.

junk chopped portions of old rope used in many different processes, as wadding or sponges or padding.

K

Kitchen steward to Europe and clerk-of-the-closet, having charge and responsibility over the fulgar's household while she is gone, and making sure the pantry is stocked and restocked. He was once of the staff of Europe's mother, Europe's childhood secretary and friend to Licurius, and when the Branden Rose was revealed in *Brandenbrass,* he was sent to seek out the wayward daughter of Naimes. His affection for the Duchess' daughter has meant that he largely and long ago abandoned his role as clandestine observer, and Europe's own regard for him is such that as she became aware of his double role, she kept him on anyway.

kraulswimmers vernacular for kraulschwimmen, the mighty seamonsters of the deeps guarding over the idiot *false-gods*.

krebin giant land crabs, viscous and tasty, dwelling principally in the Erzgebirge in the Gottlands.

L

laborium also called a gastric stove or a calimere ("warm ocean"); fairly recent rediscovery of an ancient technique of producing heat through chemistry rather than fire. It comprises a small braiced-copper cauldron with a lid under which is an aegurogastre—or silver-stomach—a chamber made of silver in which the heating chemistry occurs. These two are held in a double wooden box with air spaces, making it possible to hold the laborium in one's hands even as it boils. Through both boxes and into the aegurogastre is a stoppered silver tube called a tibium, by which the necessary reactive script known as gastra regia is introduced. When food and an accelerant are then added to the gastra regia through the fistula, the reactive quickly begins to digest the additives, making heat intense enough to boil water and almost any part. The heat goes once all the food is consumed or by the intervention of a script known as a delay. Laboriums are a great innovation that should improve the practices of skolds and habilists the world over.

lagi oil greasy discharge secreted on the skin of *lagimopes,* protecting their skin from the caustic waters of the sea and possessing a foul taste that makes *lagimopes* unpleasant to eat by larger sea-beasts.

lagimopes commonly shortened to "lagis"; small opportunistic sea-nickers who gain safety by swimming in great swarms following feeding kraulschwimmen and other sea-nickers to scavenge upon the scraps and leavings. Loathed by vinegaroons and all other seafarers, they often shadow vessels, waiting for an unobserved moment to snatch some soul alone or otherwise vulnerable on deck. In the excitement of a thalasmaché they can become much bolder still.

lahzarine ravage "wasting," or absence of any fat, caused by a lahzar's metabolism made overactive by the foreign organs put within.

Lampedusa deep-dwelling kraulschwimmen serpent and mighty sea-*wretchin* who terrorized the waters of the Grume for a thousand years before it was called by that name. Finally, bearing the mythic spiegel-blade, *Paschendralle,* the legendary Piltdown heldin-king, Tascifarnias, stood upon the shore where *Brandenbrass* now has its harbor and challenged Lampedusa to a contest to see who should rule land and sea. There upon the sand they fought, Tascifarnias slaying Lampedusa even as he was slain, the flowing of their combined blood purported to have changed the white sand black.

landsgarde vessels detailed to protect a harbor and its related shipping, and to patrol the coastlines of the harboring state in search of *nadderer* nests or dens of pirates, *fictlers,* smugglers, or any dark trader.

Langoland more sailorly rendering of Langeland, a far-off snowbound region southeast beyond the Hagensere.

Lapinduce, the ~ tlephethine or *petchinin*-lord of rabbits, hares and all other such creatures, eoned ruler of the region once known as Cacolagia, who in younger eons once roamed his land in youthful delight. Heavy have the long bitter centuries now become to him, and he stays in his parkland warren recalling the times of youth and vigor and watching the brief puff of each person's life spin in their multitudes about him. Driven neither by hatred for everymen nor the desire to aid them, he now remains in the heart of *Brandenbrass,* undetected and unguessed, that city's great and terrible secret, keeping watch over the city that once bore his name through the agency of his rabbit horde. See also *Duke of Sparrows, the.*

lard-barrow also called pinguiflecterns, fattrusses or strollers. It is the fashion in Burgundis, *Brandenbrass* and some of its closer southern neighbors for those of wealth who want to show it to allow themselves to grow fat, proving the abundance of their success—and with it their larders. For the highest order of magnates—the *elephantines* and *vulgarines*—this fashion is taken to absurd excess, their prosperity and worldly circumstance proved with grotesque obesity. This can become so extreme that they require devices to help them move around. These are the lard-barrows, contraptions of stiffened bone framing with broad belts and strapping of leather lifting up the fat about the magnate's middle and putting the weight onto wood-and-metal struts reaching to the floor, their bases attached to small wheels. The most effective version of such machines allows the wearer to coast along with small kicks of the toe, barely having to walk unaided. Such stoutness cannot, of course, be good for thew or soul, so these adipose magnates take treacles distantly related to those imbibed by *fulgars* to keep themselves in the realms of the living for as long as possible.

Indeed, many are eager to find the vaunted life-extending properties said to be sought by the *black habilists* and are frequent secret supporters of the same. As for lard-barrows, the states of the lower Soutlands know of them as *mettre gras* or *gros etalage,* and Gotts call them *speckenstands,* both names containing the idea of fatty meat laid out for sale at a market and expressing the mutual disgust at such a fashion and its related practice.

lard of Nmis tallowlike jelly; one of the parts usually employed in *sanguinary draughts,* its inclusion in Cathar's Treacle produces some of the performance-enhancing euphoria it does in its more typical use.

Laughing Spectioneer, the ~ alehouse in *Brandenbrass,* getting its name from an eel inspector of the State File of Comestible Reference.

lectry folk fifth and sixth tiers of society, the middle class. See *social status* in Book One.

leonguile meaning "cunning lion"; what we would call a cheetah, living and thriving in faraway N'go, its skins inevitably furnishing a robust fur trade for almost every land in the Harthe Alle.

lepsis egg-caste, also called oodis or quasspots; castes made from the emptied eggs of various birds, an old technique of the first skolds still employed in these modern times, especially by those *saumieres* who hold that certain scripts remain more stable inside a lepsis, and those who simply like the style of such castes.

lesquin(s) also called landsaire, the "high end" of mercenary soldiering, with equally high fees, the best proofing and weapons, and long lists of honors. Some companies are given to taking *sanguine draughts* in order that they might ignore pain, fear, and even for a time resist the frission or scathing of a wit. See Book Two.

leviate room set aside at rowdy or lively society events to allow guests to withdraw without disgrace from the otherwise often incessant activity. A good leviate will have gentle music playing to aid the calm.

Lillian of the Faye simply an old designation of *Fayelillian,* the home of the Lamplighter-Marshal. See *Fayelillian* in Book Two.

limner makers of bright-limns, including the mixing of seltzer and the growing and tending of bloom.

limnlass, limnlad young girl or boy who makes a meager living carrying a light to guide lightless customers at night; limnlads are young boys who do the same. It is a highly dangerous occupation, lighting the path for unknown people to wherever they wish to go throughout the entire city for a flat fee of one guise. After an especially long journey, a limnlass or lad can demand another half-goose to go farther but will as likely as not get satisfaction. Such vulnerable souls are among the most commonly disappeared, abstracted for the nefarious demands of benighted laboratories and dark habilistics.

Lobe more fully, Lobe the Lord of Listening, the Great-eared One, the Ear of All; a well-known famuli (lesser servants to the *false-gods,* also known as autonids, pseudotherpës, pseudotheons, theärpids) who are said to be in communion with many great fichtärs (*false-gods*). There are many stories about all kinds of fichtärs, and Lobe is a major player or minor participant in most of them. The Saccour hold Lobe as the "lover" of Bathst, (the Grieving One, Consort of *Sucoth,* Lips to the Ear), communing with "her" while the Swallower of Men sleeps. They say that if you can rouse Lobe to continue to make advances to Bathst that either "she" will rouse her slumbering lord, *Sucoth,* to tell him or *Sucoth* himself will rise up in jealousy. The trick is actually getting Lobe to do such a thing, what with him being so busy running errands for all the other *septs*.

loblolly assistant to a ram's surgeon or—if they are fortunate enough—physician.

lockscarfe break-and-enter thief skilled in foiling locks and other barriers, in sniffing out traps and hazards placed about hidden things.

lorgnette pronounced "lorn-YET"; a somewhat basic version of what we would call opera glasses.

lots what we might call dice, though their construction is different from that of our six-sided cubes, being blunt hexagonal cylinders with one end marked 7 and the other usually red or marked with a death's head or other significant sign and the six faces etched with signs of ascending value. Originally a Nenese invention, lots are used widely about the whole civilized world.

Low Brassard, the ~ original stronghold built by the *Burgundians* when they arrived to subdue the lands of the northwest Grume, and sister to the fortress of Grimbasalt in the north of the city. Over the years it has been enlarged and beautified, but in all this the first fortress remains, dominating the Brandendirk with its sinister spires.

ludion room in a house or attached to it dedicated to physical activities: sports, jousting, fencing—usually windowless but for a ring of small ventlike windows all about the tops of the walls. In *Cloche Arde* the ludion occupies the entire third floor with a great fireplace at one end, and its walls are entirely of glass.

M

madamielle *Etaine* for "miss"; used for a young, usually unwed woman.

Madigan, the Lady ~ the Marchess of the Pike (a collection of suburbs in the western part of Brandenbrass' Second Ward [see *Brandentown*] known as the Pikemarch), she is responsible for the civic needs of the people living there. As a *fulgar* of no mean skill, she is also one of the few women in the Empire with whom Europe, the Duchess-in-waiting of Naimes, can happily keep company.

Maids of Malady calendar clave seeking to curb the activities of the dark trades and the excesses of *black habilists,* working toward this end in partnership with an even more aggressive clave, the *Soratchë*. See Book Two.

make-weight fifth wheel; an unnecessary appendage, a useless item.

mandricard exceptionally long and sharp goad that can be used as a weapon too.

manikin common name for a rare and little-known aberration in the natural order, a monster in human form. Many insist that it is impossible for such a creature to exist.

man-of-business one who acts partly as lawyer, computer, counterman, broker, manager, representative, secretary and clerk. They are either hired in their hundreds by the great mercantile firms or work individually for select, well-paying clientele, those with kinder souls representing the less shrewd in the maddening world of bureaucracy. In practice these fellows can range from the most sedentary quill-licks to the keenest, most ruthless minds of the day. Men-of-business are a veritable plague in the cities, the gears of private bureaucracy unable to shift without them, many with open or secret ambitions to themselves rule the organs they slave within. This is no idle fancy either, for some of the most powerful magnates were once lowly men-of-business; more so, this is how many of them still refer to themselves.

Most of the middling classes are utterly dependent on the patronage of the higher stations (commonly very erratic), and it is a known but seldom acknowledged practice that men-of-business ride the successes of their patrons—and line their own pockets on the way—to achieve heights of their own.

maschencarde papier-mâché; apologies to some for the seemingly gratuitous reinvention of a perfectly usable word. In my defense, sometimes a word will just look too rooted in our own reality, and so I change it to maintain verisimilitude.

matter(s) events of history.

mattern as *matter* is history, so a mattern is a historian.

Maundersea, Battle of ~ naval battle fought in 1588 HIR between an allied fleet of Grumid and Sangmaund rams (the *Brandenbrass* squadron at the command of *Rear-Admiral Patchword Fyfe*) against the might of picaroons from the Pontus Canis—known together as the Sea Dogs or Sea Beggars and grown so much more active immediately after the general weakening of naval strength in 1585—and their sponsors the Lombards. It was fought in the Maundering Sea east off the Sangmaund coast and began with a long chase started by Fyfe aboard the drag-mauler NB *Rebuke*. Leading a wide-flung coursing squadron of drag-maulers and fast frigates on the prowl along the usual trade routes northeast of Start Point for piratical activity, the *Rebuke* was alone when she surprised the piratical freebooter (a type of fast overgunned frigate), *Vinegar Strumpet,* in the very act of waylaying a Boschenberg *packet ram*. One sight of the larger ram and—in the usual pattern of picaroons—the *Vinegar Strumpet* fled south. The *Rebuke* gave chase, setting flares and running out her mile-line (a large kite by which to send signals high into the air) to summon the assistance from her scattered fellows, the drag-mauler NB *Redoubtable* and the frigate NB *Likely*. Three hours into the chase a Brandenard privateer frigate, *Fox*, out on a mission of its own, joined them. Matched speed for speed, they gained little headway. The *Strumpet* sent up a kite, gaining the aid of two more freebooters, the *Black Joke* and the *Red Dart* (its hull painted a brilliant and bloody red). After a brief stouche the freebooters took flight once more, rounding the northern tip of Lombardy and drawing the four Branden rams on. Whether by chance or some prefigured scheme, the chase was now met by a small but proper fleet of Lombardy cruisers—five drag-maulers and an equal number of frigates (too many to name here). Fortunes were reversed and it came for *Rebuke* and the other Brandenard vessels to take flight, going directly west into the setting sun, heading for the distant shores of the Soutlands well over the horizon. Lanterns were doused and silence kept all through the night—but for the necessary communication from vessel to vessel— yet morning revealed the Lombard picaroons still in sight, stretched from north to south across the glorious arc of the world's morning rim. Harried by the shot of the picaroons' chasers, all limbers to the screw and hands to the treadle, the Brandenard rams kept just ahead in the "blightedly empty sea!" Finally, on the morning of the third day, with the coasts of the Sangmaund barely in view and the overworked gastrines near collapse, Fyfe and his faithful followers found fortune of their own, coming within hailing distance of a squadron of five main-rams of Maubergonne. After much frantic, terse and rather politically loaded signaling, these heavy rams turned rescuer and entered the fray on the Brandenard side. Odds evened and the picaroons' wind welled up; a great melee ensued, where the *Rebuke* rammed and sank three vessels, including the lone Lombardy capital, the seventy-four-gun-broad *Serieux*. Even as she pulled back and away from the savagely holed main-ram, the *Rebuke* herself was struck by the *Black Joke,* and she and the *Serieux* sank side by side with all hands, including the dashing Rear-Admiral Fyfe. Soon after, the remaining picaroons, including the *Vinegar Strumpet,* fled. The Battle of Maundersea is also notable as a fleet action fought more by cruisers than by rams-of-the-line.

Maupin, Pater Pontiflex originally of a poor yet well-to-do dog-breeding family of Languedock on the Sangmaund, he fled to *Brandenbrass* as a young man to avoid embarrassing connections to the operation of a syndicate of *grabcleats* and profit from the same. Immediately after he arrived in the vaunted city, he continued where he had left off, wheedling his way into many schemes both legitimate and criminal, finding greatest success with Fench Tinger, the former owner of the Broken Doll gambling house. After Tinger's "mysterious" demise, Maupin presented himself up as the old proprietor's heir, taking control of the *chancery* and gathering about him a crowd of similarly ambitious souls to do his bidding. He has continued his own twist on the family interest in dogs through his investment in the hidden rousing-pit below the *chancery.*

mercy jane also jenmerry, a hardy, prickly weed with small violet flowers that, when in great numbers, can make a field a spectacle of spreading purple.

metrician common truncation of the name "concometrist," those learned and purposely equipped souls trained at one or several *athenaeums* about the Soutlands. Great rivals of the more contemplative and introverted mathematicians, the metricians pursue the great quest of measuring and documenting the entire known and—better yet—the unknown world.

metropolitan(s) original lords and now senior ministers of the *Archduke of Brandenbrass*.

Middle Ground one of the main harborages of *Brandenbrass*, occupying—as its name suggests—the central part of the eternally busy waters before the famous city. Other parts of the harbor (though not all) include Gatlin Pond (also known as Admiralty Sink), where only naval vessels might anchor or move; Ives Steps; Mill Pond, the waters before the milling districts of the city; Sour End, the quieter weedy waters at the farthest reach of the harbor proper; the Branden Roads—calm sheltered waters northwest off Exodus Island where vessels wait to be piloted into a proper harborage; and the Chops—rip waters out beyond the Branden Roads not safe for sailers or smaller gastriners.

moilers farm laborers, especially those employed in turning the soil.

Moldwood Park, the ~ remnant of a once-great woodland stretching untamed upon the coastal plain that became *Brandenbrass* and its immediate pastureland of the Milchfold. Felled and steadily shrunk over the years, its borders were established by legal compact between the *Lapinduce* and one enlightened *Burgundian* prince. If the current lords of the city know of the power that dwells at its heart, they do not let on. Yet despite all the pressure of progress and a city pressed at times for room, the boundaries of the park remain. Greensmen keep its fringes somewhat manicured now, but in its heart the Moldwood is as untamed as it ever was.

moll potny women (usually girls) on street corners and *circuits* who sell dubious-looking stews from steaming cauldrons, doing trade with only the famished or the ironclad of stomach. If you know which moll potny to go to, however, these rough-made victuals can be highly tasty and not too distempering to your inner workings.

much exercised worried, anxious and fretful, given to sleepless and troubled nights.

Munkler's Court, the ~ collective of *panto plays* whose central story revolves around a woodsman in search of love; one of the more outrageously invidical stage shows written by Pendrift.

murmurs lesser players on a stage who, in certain forms of play, give clues to the audience about whether the moments in it are happy, sad, frightening or relieving, and whose ultimate ends in the tale are determined by the deeds of the main players, perishing or thriving as the protagonist perishes or thrives.

Myrrh, Anaesthesia a native of Flint, she began her career in teratology as a pure *fulgar*. Witnessing and indeed suffering the wrong end of the potency of a wit, she became jealous of their puissance and returned to Sinster to go again under the transmogrifer's catlin. Originally plying her trade about the Gott protectorates of the Enne, she was compelled by troubles with a highly stationed woman over the latter's husband to seek a less complex situation. Taking passage over the Pontus Canis, and after many adventures, she found herself in *Brandenbrass*. Here she learned that the money was better and the "targets" less troublesome doing the dark work of the well connected, and committed herself to spurning work.

N

nadderer(s) common name for sea-nickers of all kinds, but specifically any of those that are not kraulschwimmen or *false-gods*.

naeroë said in the most ancient of myths to be the original patrons of the air, of sky and cloud and rain and storm, driven away by the malice and violence of the rebelling *alosudnë*. None now know where they have fled to; the rare ancient texts that speak of them insist on their eventual return and mark the occasion as the end of all things.

naivine person who has never ventured far beyond a city or safe town, who has never seen a monster or is sensible of them beyond story, tradition and rumor. Some of the more "knowing," self-approving naivines with a voice and an audience declare monsters to be a fiction, to be nothing more than large and rampant animals or other natural forces talked up into terrible beasts to keep society meek and pliable.

naval college some cities have naval colleges (or nautical academies) where if you are independently well off, have married guardians or are sponsored by a patron (e.g., a captain or the state), you can get a much more fulsome lesson in the skills of running a vessel: rimitry and orthitry (mathematics), weltergraphie (wind and waves), tungolitry (astronomy), naval architecture, and instrument construction. Much more thorough, and producing more learned captains and lieutenants than those trained twixt cockpit and quarterdeck, though what these lesser fellows lack in formal education they amend for with experience and levelheadedness in battle.

Nenin major realm of the *Occidental* kingdoms to the far, almost mythic west of the Half-Continent across the great western *gurgis*. Though for most "Sundergirdians" the name is a catchall for the whole Occident, it is indeed just one of many realms therein, and certainly among the most dominant.

Neo-Athic more recent artistic style and movement reviving the acute attention to detail so revered in the ancient fabulists of long-gone Attica.

night steppers people out for fun at night.

nissë name not even known among everymen but in the most abstruse texts; the ancient designation for the nuglungs, second born after the *eurinië*, sent to aid them against the *alosudnë*.

nuncheon any meal not had at the usual times of breakfast, middens/lunch or mains/supper.

nuntio(s) official messengers of the Emperor and his regents, and, when required, bearing the authority of the one who sent them. Their private counterparts—used by magnates and peers—are the sillards (sing. silas). Both are distinct from *scopps* and mercers in that they are especially engaged by individuals for their exclusive service, rather than being available for general hire.

O

obligantic ossatomy school of bone-setting practice advocating the use of tight bindings to "oblige" or immobilize and support a break. Its disadvantage—so its rival practice ferile ossatomy (which touts the use of splints and other supportive casings) holds—is that if the break is in a limb, it is not free to be used.

obsequine also known as tweenies, flamboyaunts or fancyblands; lahzar "groupies," true devotees of teratologists; what we would think of as "rabid fans," writing letters to, finding and following, seeking the mark or discarded items of their chosen monster-slayer, finding and buying every skerrick of printed information on them. The more reasonable and mature will be allowed to be in the company of their favorite, and most obsequines—who, not appreciating the demeaning sound of the word, prefer to call themselves cathabrians or cathadulators—aspire to such an honor. Their greatest aspiration is indeed to be made into a factotum or other such body in service to their mighty hero.

obtorpës powerful stupefactant; that is, a draught that sedates the recipient.

obverse also known sometimes as a front room, comprising a main entry hall with a solid front door at one end and an equally solid inner door at the other, flanked by narrow passages on either hand perforated with thin, heavily gated loopholes from which defenders can fire upon who- or whatever is in the entry hall. A place of defense should a monster or other undesirable manage to make it through the front door, these are (and have always been) very necessary in dwellings out in rougher regions. With this universal approval and long-standing use, obverses are to be found in almost any building throughout the lands, even when these structures have ceased to need such defenses.

Occidental the empire of *Nenin* and the kingdom of *Sippon,* among other realms of the great landmass across the western *gurgis,* whose cultures are what we would consider Oriental or Asian in character.

occludile of lazarin one of the rare scripts employed by transmogrifers immediately upon inserting mimetic organs into a person to make them a lahzar. Its rarity is in part attributable to the illicit and very difficult-to-obtain parts in its constitution, and also the limits of its use. As any transmogrifer worth his fee will tell you that it also can serve as an aid for fortifying the memes (foreign organs) already within a lahzar's body.

olfactologue of similar basic construction to a sthenicon, an olfactologue does not have the sight-enhancing organs and mechanisms of the latter, but only augments the user's sense of smell. Full sthenicon wearers hold that olfactologues are what we would call a "baby step" into the world of fully heightened senses, and lurksmen-in-training will often start with it before progressing to the full sensoria. True olfactologue wearers will claim that they are at far less risk of having the organs within trying to grow up into their faces with prolonged wear. Quite rightly too, for on its own the scent tissue of an olfactologue is far less aggressive than it is when combined with sight-enhancing organs inside a sthenicon.

ol' touchy also the touch, torch, ol' torch or the gripes; a fiery beverage made from cacti juice, first drunk by the pirates of the Sin Tin. The drink is known among most vinegaroons even though almost all would have no idea what a cacti was, looked like or even that they existed, growing as they do almost exclusively in the northern parts of Parthia, that terrible land far beyond the Brigandine states. Torch (as it is most commonly called) is made almost exclusively by the pirate-kings of the Brigandine and exported to seaside drinkeries the world over.

omilia habilistic and also natural philosophy term meaning the particular type of monster within a greater *genis*—or grouping of like types; what less learned folk might term a tribe.

oppilative another word for a siccustrumn, that is, the group of potives involved in stopping blood flow and hastening the healing of open wounds.

orator(s) "referee" of an *oratory,* who governs the course of arguments and makes sure certain passions do not rise to the point of ruining the debate.

oratory debate or formally organized argument upon a set topic; properly meaning the lecturing and debating hall of an *athenaeum,* it has come to be an entertainment at higher-class fêtes, galas and other social events.

Orchard Harriet meaning "home of the fruit grove," a name given it by *Gaspard Plume* when he bought it twenty years ago from a local lord and leaseholder pressed by gambling debts who had—with certain additions—employed it as a barn. The core structure is an old fortalice, part of the defenses built to guard the ancient, now abandoned mines that riddle the hills about. Used variously since as a bogle haunt, a den of brigands, a family home, a storehouse and a barn, its accretion of space and rooms serves it well in its current role as the hideaway for disaffected, thoughtful and creative souls.

orchestrato what we might call a chamber orchestra, that is, a small collection of players of orchestral instruments used in more intimate situations or where room and/or money are constrictions.

ouranin ancient term monsters have for a rossamünderling.

P

packet ram any class of ram that has been radicaled, that is, had part of its lower decks cleared of guns and at least one of its masts unstepped (lowered or removed, making the vessel "short-masted") to allow for the taking on of cargo and/or passengers. Such vessels are usually privately owned, the tariffs for loading and unloading and the fares being their owners' income. Neither fighting vessel nor true cargo, nevertheless what a packet ram loses in carrying capacity it makes up for in firepower and—in the case of a converted frigate—speed.

Page, the ~ amiable part of the world farmed for longer than Imperial charters record, with every little parish holding itself distinct from its neighbors as if each were a state to itself. The ancient locals are very proud of their ideal life, yet it is falling prey to the grasping greed of peers seeking seats in the state parliament. These city swells send cease-less chains of lawyers and *men-of-business* to dispute the ancient uses of folkland and haggle the expansion of their *franchises*.

pallet sleeping quarters for staff and servants, usually situated at the rear of a house closest to the working places; the domestic version of a billet.

Pander Tar vulgar Soutland rendering of Pandataar—capital of the Principalitine far to the north beyond the Sinus Tintinabuline—a col-lective of princes ruled by *the Peacock Throne* found in Serringpahttam.

Pantomime Lane found in many cities of the Soutlands and beyond; a Pantomime Lane—or Street or Walk, or its linguistic equivalent—is the district designated as the center of frivolous distractions, though only sometimes connected with the districts of high theater.

panto-play(s) medley of many small shows, constituting interme-dio that have become more popular than the full dramas (comedie a'manners or heldic tragedy); they originally supported and now col-lect into a single act, farces and mimes—short comic routines making sport of whoever it is currently fashionable to tease and made especially for the panto, interludes performed by normal folk seeking a moment of fame or fun, and even morality cycles done by well-meaning calendar claves or brave collectives of apostrophizers. Most popular of all are the arbitrarios—or doubles—romance comedies with set roles but ad lib scripts performed by concoctors, with simple, compact yet still gorgeous production so that doubles might be done as easily on small platforms as grand stages.

paphron skirtlike apron usually of proofed leather, wrapping high about the stomach and flaring from the hips to just below the knees. Part of its manufacture is what we might call a "utility belt" plus pockets and slots for holding tools.

paraductor master of the progress of a high-society event, with the production and timing of all the entertainments under his command, keeping with great tact and sensitivity all things in their right place and proceeding smoothly.

parmister essentially a foreman in charge of the various workings and facets of a *franchise*. Whether it is the shepherds and their flocks, the hay wards and their herds, the swains and their farrows, the *moilers* and their fields, the pruners and their trees, the pickers and their vines or the garnerers and their stores, there is a parmister in charge of each, and a master-parmister in charge of all and answering only to the owning lord or his seniormost agent.

Parvis Main main structures and public buildings built around the *Florescende* and a major part of the whole Brandendirk. It is here that common folk may come to deal and treat with the Archduke's officials and various governing boards.

patefract "revealer"; also sometimes called an index; courtly spies sometimes hiring themselves out to more vulgar folk to supplement income and better employ any downtime. In this capacity they become one of a class collectively known as "splints" or *"sleuths,"* and behave in the manner of a "private eye" in our own world, treading into the realms of the sleuths of the local constabulary and the freelancing, common street detinctives (detectives).

Pater Maupin see *Maupin, Pater Pontiflex*.

Patredike, the ~ corruption of an *Etaine* word meaning "shepherd's mound"; the ancestral home of the Trottinotts, built by Grimspan Trottinott, who served with great distinction and almost unto death at the Battle of the Gates (see Book One) in HIR1397. Called the Trottinseat or Trotthall by the locals, the original dike (the high mound upon which

650

the buildings are established) and the manor proper took seven years to complete, with additions being added by almost every generation ever since.

Paucitine, the ~ eastern, least fertile region of the Idlewild, the seat of the now destroyed cothouse, Wormstool, where Rossamünd served for a bare few months. See Book Two.

pauldrons proof-steel protection for the shoulders, upper arm and partly the chest, typically possessing ridges or flutes of steel near the neck to protect from inward-turning deflecting blows.

Pauper Chïves see *Chïves, Pauper*.

pavane slow dance of many couples in a kind of choreographed procession, unfashionable now in the cities but still stepped in rustic places.

PDetC "Pro Dux et Civitas," the motto of *Brandenbrass*; a Tutin phrase meaning "For duke and state."

Peacock Throne, the ~ oddly impersonal name for the actual person of the overlord of the Principalitine states far, far to the north.

peltisade hiding place of significant size, large enough for a person to live in permanently, with space for staff and entertainments, often functioning as the dens of the ne'er-do-well set of folk with enough money and influence to create such havens. Such structures are more common in cities than authorities would care to ponder upon, yet as universal as they might be, they are little reckoned to exist by most folk, which is precisely the point.

peltrymen though once used to mean trappers, this term is more and more coming to include venators—that is, hunters; indeed, it is becoming the catchall word for any woodsman. One of the notable historical details of peltrymen is that the ambuscadiers of armies of the Half-Continent model their own harness on the accoutrements of peltryfolk, a practice originating from the recruiting of skirmishing volunteers from the people best suited to skulking and ambushing: woodsmen and peltrymen.

People of the Dogs "classical" designation for the folk of the city-state of Doggenbrass.

percusor(s) also pnictor or sicarian; a part of the patefact set; professional murderer working for states and kings, possessing a near-legendary facility in delivering death at distance and by stealth. Almost every state, kingdom or realm employs them, the more civilized places simultaneously denying their existence.

perfervid(s) antiquated term for vigorants. Despite its antiquity it is still used by many script-grinders, one of those strangely persistent linguistic relics.

permanare per proscripta perpetually binding ruling, usually made in the sectioning of land by a regime intent on preserving its uses into the next generations, for example the sequestering of great stretches of land by Emperor Haacobin Conflans II in the early sixteenth century HIR with the infamous Survey Act for the growing of timber for the making of rams and cargoes. To break a proscription requires an act of Imperial will ratified by the necessary state(s) concerned.

perruquier makers of wigs, often called skull-thatchers by less well-spoken folk, though such a term is used to refer more particularly to your less competent wig-stitcher.

perto adversus meaning essentially "to face openly"; an innovation on the usually fixed positions—or first stances—that tradition dictates a fighter begins. Involving simply standing fully facing your adversary, it provides the practitioner flexibility in reaction by not restricting the hand and/or leg that can be first employed.

petchinin(s) monster-lords most concerned with their own immediate needs and their own schemes, neither attacking nor defending everymen except as circumstances might dictate or if said everymen are encroaching upon a petchinin's patch or plans. As such they are scorned—or at the very least, mistrusted—by both *urchins* and *wretchins*.

petrailles part of a set of horse-proofing or shabraque, covering the main part of the body. See *shabraques* in Book Two.

Philemon Plume see *Plume, Philemon*.

physical of or pertaining to a physician and physics, their field of expertise; medicinal.

pied daw large, heavy-billed relative of the crow, called a currawong in this real world of ours.

pignone knitted cap of wool, ungaulded, most commonly worn by sailors and children. Its name is a corruption of a southern word for mushroom.

pilot • person who knows well the lay and threats of a harbor or other

652

body of water, who goes out to vessels, navigating their way through this water to show them the best path through, either by taking the wheel, standing beside the master or captain and instructing them or leading a vessel from the front in some smaller, more nimble craft—usually called pilot boats. • written description of the directions and landmarks to a desired location, often including salient notes on points of interest or danger.

Piltdowners the *Pilts,* the people of the *Piltdowns.*

Piltdowns, the ~ both the general region of the once-great nation of the *Pilts* and also the spreading range of hills along the northwestern coast of the Grume of which the Brandenfells (Wood Hole, the Dells, the Milchfold Leens, Twifold Rise, the Janeswolds—or Underdowns) and Witherfells are a part.

Piltmen collective name of the once-tribal people of the northwest Grumid region. See *Pilts, the.*

Pilts, the ~ proud, dignified yet rough-living people, the original people of the Grumid regions, driven into the hills by the Tutelarchs, partly conquered by the *Burgundians* and then the Tutins. They have a strong sense of the wider family, of the inviolate connections of extended kinship, and gathered in large familial groups, which collected into assemblies for protection (mostly against other assemblies). These eventually coagulated into three loose confederacies—or venes—that held (and still hold to this day) themselves distinct from each other yet were governed by a single king (or queen). This king was at first the strongest warlord among them all, but over time became a kind of detached judge and father figure. Their greatest and most tragic king was Oddvicar, who unified the fractious Pilts in their struggle against the *Burgundian* usurpers, only to finally lose to the princes of Burgundy at the Battle of Assembled Mile (the consequence of which was the resettling of his people in the Piltlaw, a region beyond *the Page* granted to the defeated foe). Unrecognized by the Haacobin emperors—or the Sceptics before them—the rank of Piltic king remains in Pilt society, obscure, often wretched fellows whose role for their people in current times has become much more one of cultural focus and wishful remembrance. Indeed, in the centuries of occupation, especially since the Tutins, it is common to find somewhat idealized, even maudlin images—usually a cheap etching copy of some proper painting—of their current exiled or reduced king hanging somewhere in a

Pilt home. Now an obscure group, the pilts once roamed the whole land from the Grumid shores to Thisterland, from Hergoatenbosch to Haquetaine, and though their king is reduced to mere citizen of the Empire, they still hope one day to rise untrammeled again as their own people. They are reputed to have been monster-worshippers in times of yore, and this grim reputation clings to them still as a vague distrust in the conquering folk about them.

Piltdowners the *Pilts,* the people of the *Piltdowns.*

pipistrelle light onshore winds that make for good sailing of small-sailed vessels such as sloops or brigantines. Their presence is seen as a sign of favor by all seafaring folk, but they are known to be fickle benefactors, turning all too quickly into mortal tempests.

pistoleroes dramatic name for pistoleers, originating from Seville.

planquin-chair or just planquin; an open box set upon long poles to be carried by people or beasts, typically containing a plush seat screened from view by solid doors of wood or elegant drapes. The larger "model" has two seats facing each other and is carried by a larger complement of bearers.

Plume, Gaspard *mattern* (historian), amateur philosopher and the owner of *Orchard Harriet,* he is responsible for *a* revealing and controversial book *A Proper Reading of the Great Didic Descendancy,* tracing the true lines of the heirs of Dido and Idaho, an exposition that cost several eminent families countenance and brought their standing into general and unwanted scrutiny. As such it caused Gaspard profound and unforeseen social exclusion, and after much distress he was forced to retreat from his high city life to his obscure hinterland abode, becoming in the process an unwitting beacon for other disaffected intellectuals.

Plume, Philemon once energetic count of *Windspect Folia* and elder brother of Gaspard, who, after the death of his beloved wife at the hands of some pernicious nicker, declined shockingly. Though lord still of *Temburly Hall* and the countenancy about it, he dwells now in dissipated seclusion in his brother's much humbler crumbling abode, touched— some more sensitive souls might say—after his terrible contact with monster-kind by some special insight into the monstrous.

Pluto Six see *Six, Pluto.*

Pondsley cheese smooth, soft cheese from the Pondsley region, possessing a pleasantly sharp aftertaste; spreads well upon toast or slices of meat.

pottage fancy exceptionally thick soup made with swollen water-soaked barley or other grain and healthy portions of vegetables in a fish or poultry broth, the best also including chunked meats of various kinds, often marinated in ale or wine.

Pour Clair Brandenard city serving the woodsmen and mines of the northern Brandenfells, built on a wedge of rock at the meeting of two river gorges atop a waterfall; whether the cataract gave the town its name or the town gave it to the cataract none can recall.

Pragmathës Carp see *Carp, Pragmathës.*

Presage Exemption a document normally granted by a peer, proper employer or agent of government that allows its bearer to avoid being pressed into naval service by a press gang or the *crimps.*

primmling first monsters to tread the earth, breathe the air and drink the water, coming even before everymen and—as legend would have it—playing a role in the forming of all animals that walk, crawl, fly, swim or slither.

proporium or *salt-store,* the stockroom of a parts-seller, usually furbished with shrewdly compact storage to make the most of typically limited space. In them are usually columns of square drawers as deep as a grown man's arm, diminishing in size as they rise—large, medium, small—with an eye-befuddling array of tiny drawers all along the very top; broad, flat trays arranged with whole dried plants; wood-housed *carboy*s holding toxic and corrosive waters that—with a cunning push—tilt out to be lifted and poured; and retractable racks housing stoppered porcelain beakers of unstable or fragile stuffs.

prosternatin(g), prosternation monster-worship; from the Tutin word for debasing oneself, and used to refer as much to *fictlers* and out-ramorines.

pullet and ramsin broth garlic (ramsin) chicken (pullet) soup, and normally rather heavy on the garlic.

pyet ponce strangely crunchy stew made from magpie cooked slow and long until the bones are chewable.

Q

quarter five-guise piece, or one quarter of a sequin.

Quillion eminent composer of the first half of the last century, who composed for the Imperial court in the Considine. He is best known for his flowing, intimate pieces for a lone or small collection of players, and though he is long dead, his music has continued in popularity through all manner of fashions.

quisquillian trifling, small.

R

Ratio a clown of ancient days reputed to have performed heroic deeds in the defense of his people—soothing a rampaging umbergog—and turning aside a forgotten barbarian king bent on pillage—with his antics.

red hag and both crocidoles very low hand in most Half-Continent card games, though not the lowest. There are four Houses of cards (in descending value): Lairds, Dames, Jacks and Brutes. In each House are two Casts (or sets), red and black, of seven Figures, Figure 1 being the highest, Figure 7 the lowest in value (depending on the game, of course). The Figures, red and black, are as follows:

Figure ~	House ~ Lairds	Dames	Jacks	Brutes
1	King	Queen	Fool	Lyon
2	Duke	Duchess	Chancer	Ass
3	Minster	Damsel	Flimsy	Daw
4	Master	Pander	Braggart	Aurang
5	Hedge	Fraught	Butcher	Crocidole
6	Vinegar	Sculler	Souse	Selt
7	Churl	Crone	Dorner	Hag

Because playing cards are often hand drawn, their figures can sometimes be of topical events or notable folk of the moment rather than the traditional images. Players generally do not mind what the figures are on the cards, as long as their House and values are clearly marked.

refectry highbrow corruption of "refectory," that is, a place for eating.

rever-man handmade reanimate creature fashioned from bits of corpses of any living creature; the most simple-minded of the walking-dead gudgeons. See Book One and *gudgeon(s)* in Book Two.

ribauld very heavy firelock musket firing a half-pound ball. The wielder of a ribauld, who requires great strength, is known as a ribauldaquin. The ribauld's advantage is the heavy blow of its shot, which can knock down a foe even armored in the heaviest proofing.

Right of the Open Hand, the ~ also known as the Main Ouvere; calendar clave found on the border between Naimes, Maine and Aufricaine, enduring in its fortress hold of *Fontrevault*. The calendars' main labors are acts of generosity, and their *aplombery* is sought as the destination of many of the high-station daughters of the surrounding lands.

roast hart's tongue a most tender cut of meat, individual hart's (female deer) tongues being so small they are often pressed together into a more meaty "loaf." It is a happy day for anyone when hart's tongue is on the board.

Rookwood Saakrahenemus Fyfe see *Fyfe, Rookwood Saakrahenemus*.

rumspice(s) strong-smelling perfume used by men to ward off the foul airs and bad smells of the street and harbor; what we would call a cologne or aftershave.

S

sabrine adept(s) also called percerdieres, lehrechtlers or *spathidrils*; said to be the cousins of the sagaars, originating long ago in some foreign northern land. Revering swordplay as the sagaars revere the dance, some go so far as to almost worship their swords, ancient *therimoirs* of forgotten make, though they have no time for devotion to constant motion as the sagaars do. The best of them, those warranted to teach, are known as sabrine magists or master swordplayers, and will gather about them a loose association of adepts, serving together for a common ideal. Almost every sabrine adept is enamored with myths of the supreme vitales—the "ultimate" swords—such as the Gloomsword, whose wounds afflict men with great anguish and darkening of soul; the Spade of Finicule and Hildebrandt, both said to cut through armor and move of their own accord; Erbrechenbrand, reputed to burn constantly with falsefire; and Miserichord, a spiegelsword possessing its own will and held to be fashioned by the blasphemous Cathars out of an entire hollyhop—a rare, near-mythical monster formed of twigs and branches and leaves come alive by the power of the fecund muds—distorted by arts now lost into a weapon. But the most revered is the Alethspadis or Lethspatha or Letsbadis—the Sword of Providence—and though very little is known of it at all, it is said to be able to cleave all, even a being's soul from their marrow.

sagital needlelike; a somewhat technical word used particularly in the discipline of *fabercadavery* (rever-making) for describing teeth or claws.

salamander(s) catchall name for the more monstrous creatures of the oceans and waterways.

salt-store room of a *saumiere* where parts and many complete scripts are stored. Poorly made or rundown salt-stores will reek of the items they hold, the absence of any bad odor evidence of a salt-store of shrewd and excellent make kept in admirable repair.

sang egregia one of the set of *sanguinary draughts,* and said to make a person ignore pain sustained in the stouche.

sanguine user of *sanguinary draughts,* the most extreme users known as pathicords.

sanguine or sanguinary draughts various alembant concoctions properly called anima furia or cardifuriants that bring upon the imbiber what is commonly called a war-spasm, making them brave, numb to pain, swollen with passion and even lusting for the fight, the best even rendering a person momentarily immune to the grim talents of a wit. Of those who dare such altering chemistry, there are those few who take it to extremes and make a living from such practice; see *brinksmen.*

saraband lively, widely known and currently fashionable dance based on a simpler rustic jig of the Patricine hinterlands.

saumiere fancy name for a parts-grinder or salt-seller.

scale ladder whose two posts lean slightly in to each other with inner and outer rungs, the latter being pegs arranged farther apart to allow a person to rapidly descend with controlled drops from one peg to the next.

scandals gossip and rumor pamphlets publishing lies, exaggerations, hyperbole and just plain unseemly truth. More notable and continental issues include *The Wasp* and *The Scorpion.* Made in *Brandenbrass, Defam-*

iere is more local, its fame confined to Grumid states. As much as folk might scoff and sniff at such rot, ceaseless demand provides a continuing market.

scarlet(s) lockpick or break-and-enter thief, a contraction of the name *lockscarfe*.

scarper rat-catcher. Their telltale sweet smell comes from the sickly concoction of sugared fruit juices they smear over their hands and arms to entice a rodent into their grasp. Consequently, scarpers have many nasty infected wounds on their hands.

sciomane(s) more common name for what are technically known as *thanatocriths*; the name once meant—back in the ancient Phlegmish times—a person who attempted to commune with the dead.

scopp(s) children employed as mercers, waiting at important and useful places ready to take a message anywhere required within the city walls (and even rare adventures beyond—for the right money). Obvious in their frockless suit jackets of white flannel and red *pignone* cap, they can be seen running all over most major cities of the Grume. Exempted of the restrictions that keep common folk out of governmental edifices, scopps are aided in their essential task by having their very own set of clerks who mark their coming or going and grant them more rapid access into the deeper sanctuaries of power.

scringings also griddled scringings or scringed seethings; fried collection of various edible or partly edible items—the less edible items often including sawdust and boiled bone—most typically ground poor cuts and the dag end of seasonal greens. Heavily seasoned (and spiced, depending on the city or region) and cooked so long it is all very tasty and toothsome.

scruple(s) any smallest denomination of coin of any region.

scupperer ambusher, bandit.

sea-marks buoys.

seclude a nightgown or dressing gown, fashioned especially for women.

seethe to fry; "seethed" means "fried in oil or fat."

seltling increasingly obsolete term for a monster, especially of the landed kind, hags being its equivalent for monsters of the seas and waterways. In these times folk will use the word more in reference to a hand of cards than an example of the real creature.

se'night, sennight seven-night, a week; therefore a sennight pair is a fortnight.

sept(s) collection of *fantaisists* or *false-god* worshippers who revere a specific *false-god*.

sequestury private and protected places run by calendars for the lodging and care of women in threat of ruin or even death. See Book Two.

seven-night paired fortnight; two weeks.

Seven Seven, the ~ one of the more prominent *septs* in worship and service of *Sucoth,* given to human sacrifice and bizarre rituals in the quest to wake and call their chosen *false-god* from the deeps. Their full and proper title is the Seven Brothers of the Seven-mouthed Lord.

shambleman butcher, and by extension, a surgeon, especially one with scant training or of wicked reputation.

shard-born made or emerged from the muck, the soil; made from poo; a rather offensive term when used by an everyman in reference to an ünterman. Fortunately it is a largely forgotten word, known now only by the very old and backward and the bookish.

sheer(s) winching crane.

sibaline flare a signal flare attached to a flighted reed—or piece of cut cane—so that when the flare descends, the reed whistles, ensuring attention is drawn to the flare. The shrill whistling also means a sibaline can be fired even in the broadest day and still be marked.

Signal of Lots, the ~ or simply, the Lots, the Signal Stars said to have determination of the course of chances and mishaps. See the *Signal Stars* in Book One.

Singular Contract, a ~ also known as a personal assignment or simply a singular; an offer of employment made by a private citizen or organization seeking a teratologist to hunt and claim the prize-money for killing a troublesome nicker. In providing such an offer, the private concern undertakes to pay all monies promised, often securing this with a portion paid up front—known as attainment money or, in the vernacular, ballast. Once a singular has been accepted by a teratologist or teratologist's representative, its acceptance is written up in an ongoing ledger called a count and a description of the job (including as much information on the prize—the monster—as is available) known as a Representation is filled. With this is given a Bill of Attainment (a certificate of acceptance), holding the knave to completing the task or risk paying a fine known as a Fee of Refusal or balker's toll. Provided along with the attainment is a franked Certificate of Recompense or a capital (so called because it is compensatory head-money given in place of a proper prize)—a guarantee by the knavery to reimburse a hireling pugnator should the job prove to be false or lapsed or flitched/jobbed (the monster slain by another teratologist—the first term meaning "by accident," the second "by *intent*"). Singulars are the private counterpart of the bureaucratic Writs of the Course, that is, official, governmental commissions to slay teratoids. Both can be obtained at a knavery, though singulars, often offering less prize-money, are surprisingly preferred, as typically they are more promptly paid.

siphunculus giant terrible sea-worms that dwell with the kraulschwimmen and *false-gods* in the crushing deeps.

Sippon, Sipponese realm of the *Occident,* smaller than *Nenin* yet probably equal in power, a refined culture that has endured and matured over millennia, producing many, many pieces of furniture and fabulary (art) eagerly sought by Haufarine (Half-Continent) collectors. *Bom e'do* are among the best known of their artifacts in the east.

Six, Pluto the middle daughter of a middle-class family who have high hopes for elevation of all their children, sending each to Foursdike Athenaeum to gain a *foundation.* However, Pluto's use of this excellent start to pursue the life of a fabulist is a great bemusement for her family. She lives at *Orchard Harriet* as much to avoid their disapproval as she does to escape the unwanted advances of a minister in the Archduke's court, gaining work from the city through an agent there while enjoying the peace and beauty of the hills. It is also a place where she might entertain less-than-acceptable musings of the true nature of monsters without fear of reprisal.

Skarfithin Greater Derehund employed as a fighting tykehound and named (though misspelled) after one of the more famous heldins of the historied Hagenards (see *Biargë the Beautiful* in Book Two).

slaps or parleys common children's games, slaps being a challenge of reflex and tolerance of pain, parleys a kind of "chasey" or "tag"—as we might call it—that involves wrestling too.

slype(s) any hidden passage, especially those between walls.

snugman also snugsman; privately hired obstaculars, zealous thieftakers, "bounty hunters," the rougher sort of speculator willing to do any manner of work. See *obstacular(s)* in Book Two.

song-and-fruit seller street-walking vendors who offer popular tunes and love songs, usually cheap-pressed or hand-copied from stolen scores pinched by sly fingers from rehearsing players. The fruit, as is said, is for throwing during a performance—or eating, if the need takes you, though the quality of the produce normally encourages its use as a projectile rather than sustenance. Some song-and-fruit sellers also carry about a besom and double as *crossing sweeps* for the tip of extra *scruples*.

sophisticated term used to describe a script that has soured—gone bad—or lost its virtue—that is, its desired effect.

Soratchë clave of calendars seeking to end the blasphemies of massacars and other *black habilists*. See Book Two.

soulettes shoe-proofing, strapped over the arch and ankle to provide extra protection to this vulnerable area, especially by equiteers and other horse-riding folk. Also sometimes called boot-roses, though those of high fashion will hold that these items are distinct from each other.

spandarion the main flag of an empire, realm or state.

spatchcock greme spatchcock in an olive marinade; this is more common on Patricine or Sedian tables.

spathidril(s) name for both a toxic blade of ancient make and also its wielder, more commonly named a *swordist*.

speculator private most commonly called sleuths, also speculators, sneaksmen, snugsmen or deductors; fellows offering their cunning, contacts and guile for a fee, to be employed in the discovery or repression of whatever or whomever is desired. Existing almost exclusively in cities, they operate under official license and are often engaged by the more proper authorities as thieftakers. A good sleuth will employ several undersleuths and have a wide association of informants and seeds, even possessing connections in other cities.

spedigraphs what we would call sketches, quick portraits done in chalk or ink, a more recent development on the fashion for silhouettes.

spice aura expensive scented powder—or sweet-puff—used by the well-to-do to block the smell of the street or harbor or other noisome odor.

spittende(s) long pike with barbed tip and a crosspiece to prevent a skewered beast from shoving gorily down the shaft. See Book Two.

sprosslings "second-born," coming after the *primmlings* in the order of creation. Their numbers include the nuglungs, the ningauns and the most ancient glamgorns, *cacoglumbs, brodchin,* famuli and all such creatures.

spurn(s) what we would call bodyguards, a "fashion accessory" for any man or woman of station and circumstance who believes their person is in need of bodily protection.

"Stays of bone!" exclamation of surprise or exasperation, and sometimes of delight.

stickbrown coating applied to iron and steel items that reacts slightly with the surface, making it brown and sealing it against the corrosive action of the vinegar seas. Though it is good for protection against all weathers and conditions, it is used most at sea.

Stillicho ancient actress said to have played to save the slaughter of her city at the hands of the vile Lechemen, dying in her deed but delivering her people from a cruel end. She is now honored as the patroness of all tragedic players.

"A stitch is as good as a strum" ~ used in the way we might say "six of one or half a dozen of another" and meaning quite literally that a wound closed with needle and twine is as good as one sealed with a siccustrumn. Most physicians would probably disagree.

strupleskin pronounced "STROO-pull-skin," the word is a corruption of the Lausland term *"struplescin"* (said "stroop-LESS-chin"), meaning "a woven scab." It is given to one of the most superior siccustrumn known to skolds, one that will do its healing work without the need for bandages, forming a porous plug over a wound that allows for fittest healing. High quantities of silver in the script—which exists in small traces in even moderately efficacious *oppilatives*—greatly improves its healing properties but raises the price.

Stumphelhose eminent composer of the previous century whose lively melodies are still very popular among the lower stations.

Sucoth said "SOO-koth," known also as Sucathës, Sucoth the Decayed, the Seven-mouthed Lord, the Swallower of Men, the Great and Terrible Maw, Pseustës ("Liar" or "Slanderer"), the Koprocatës (the "Dung-lord"), said to be the most terrible of all the *false-gods*, reputed to slumber in the deepest depths of the Gurgis Mange (or Gurgis Magna) and whose rising is held to spell the end of civilization. It was the summoning of Sucoth by the goestes of Phlegm that is said to have brought that once near-almighty race to its ruin. Sucoth is also the least sapient or active of all the *false-gods*; indeed, it is comatose, and could be roused only by greater learning than any person currently possesses. The Saccour (the Servants of the Most Low Sucoth) and the *Seven Seven,* both feared and opposed even by the other *septs,* relentlessly seek this obscure knowledge, desirous to bring an end to all things and the sweet oblivion of Sucoth's reign.

summerscale, summerscale vigil what we would call summer vacation. See *congress.*

sunderhallow any monster—either *wretchin* or lesser beast—that has set itself most earnestly against everymen and any other monster that supports or defends them.

Sunt Veil, the ~ low sea wall that runs before Fishguarde, Little Beachey and Hard Mile. It continues for miles south and north, following every promontory and inlet, gaining different names at different parts, yet is all the same long wall.

Swarty Hobnag, the ~ very old bogle warped by his loathing of everymen to desire to eat their rotting flesh.

sweeten to soak in a *dulcifer,* to *dulcify.*

swink(s) city laborer, one who works the mills and foundries of the city magnates.

swordist more common name for a *sabrine adept* or sabrine magist.

T

taffies and glairs what we might call lollies or candy or sweets, taffies being the harder sort and glairs the softer. Some of the more common include sugar-purses, triple boilers, syrup-marrows, rose-marrows, clementine glairs and honeyed persimmons—even boschenbread (see Book Two) is considered a taffie.

talbot breed of seekhound, a dog bred to track all manner of living thing but not to fight with them. Similar to our beagles, though perhaps a little sleeker and a little taller.

tandem comfortable seat made to fit two or more bottoms, hence the name, for a tandem is intended to give ease to more than one person.

Imported at first from exotic northern lands such as Turkemantium and Dhaghestahn, such original items of furniture are not common even among the middling classes, yet more local artisans have made themselves very rich indeed imitating the style. It is fashionable among the fluffs to sleep sitting upon one of these. Exitious or broken-faced leers (those with sthenicons grown into their faces) also prefer such sleeping arrangements, as the permanently attached sthenicon does not allow for lying down comfortably without the requirement of a specially fashioned pillow to keep the head from lolling during the night.

telltale's gaze, beneath a ~ to be subject to the scrutiny of a falseman so as to determine if you are lying or speaking the truth.

Temburly Hall hereditary manor house of the Counts Plume and their ancestors, a grand spreading structure now maintained by a mere skeleton of staff in the grieving absence of their grieving lord, *Philemon Plume,* elder brother to *Gaspard Plume.*

testudoe(s) heavy-ended bludgeon, five to seven feet long, knobbled with metal studs or wooden knots and giving a powerful and nasty blow. A very old pattern of weapon finding its way into Soutland culture from the Lauslands—who took it from the passionate folk of Ing—testudoes are traditionally made of wood and as such provide some protection from the arcs of a *fulgar* if you should ever choose to take on such a foe.

tetter-faced covered with tetters, that is, acne.

thanatocrith technical name for a *sciomane,* a controller of gudgeons and *rever-men,* though *jackstraws* are held to be the most pliant of all the tribe. Using a variety of puissance called striction—and somewhat similar to a wit's frission—they can achieve control or obligation over a single gudgeon, or two or three or four or even more gudgeons as they increase in skill and experience. Through this control they can obligate the gudgeons, dictating to some extent their actions, their intent, though if left without an obligation a rever will do as it determines according to its nature. This capacity to obligate *rever-men* is gained through transmogrifying surgery that takes some tiny fraction of the head-matter of the person and swaps it for some of the head-matter of the gudgeon. Combining this with select memes (mimetic organs) from the patibilic system (the pinguis patibila) more typically found in a wit gives the desired control through the employment of the frissionlike striction. The more gudgeons in your fold the more head-matter required, and the farther they get from you, the weaker your obligation. The term "thanatocrith" comes from the Attic root *"thanatis"* for the moment of transition from life to death, from Phenomena to Tharma. They are rare in the Half-Continent and will usually be found only at rousing-pits or in the hidden employ of some *black habilist* or dark trading magnate. In places with lesser moral nicety (such as Heilgoland), however, they are common enough and perform with particular distinction as *percursors*.

thatigated sterilized. Brought in by the transmogrifying surgeons of Sinster nearly two hundred years ago, thatigation is a relative newcomer to more common *physical* learning; such cleaning of all surgical implements has markedly reduced deaths on the table and, even more so, after surgery.

thaumacra technical term for script "recipes."

thennelever tube, usually of wood, used for safely containing the more dangerous kind of powdered potive. As thick as two fingers and as long as a hand, it has a wax-leather cap fastened to one end and fixed down by a metal ring. Within the tube is an upper segment in which a dose resides, shaken in from the main receptis beneath. You remove the top, fling the opening away from you into the air, releasing the potive several yards in the desired direction, return the top, tip it up, shake in another portion and repeat.

therimoir(s) terrible toxic weapons, mostly of historied manufacture. See Book Two.

thorn-withies species of box-thorn called the sentis magna, lance-leaf or leuce thorn (leuce prickle), which provides thorns of a foot or more in length with a basal diameter of three inches or even more. These thorns are "harvested" and used along the tops of walls and the upper margins of their face as a scaling deterrent; those on the upper wall-face pointing down at an acute angle to needle a climbing foe make the placing of scaling ladders difficult.

three-bell scoundrels late-night, closing-time troublemakers.

Three Brothers Hob, the ~ nonsense poetica—or performed poem—about three hungry nickers. In its entirety it goes something like this:

Frair Clog, Log and Nog
Three hobs in a bog;
One turns to the others to say,
"Brother Clog! Brother Log!
We wallow like hog
While yon tasty morsels do play!"
So these hobs from bog
Step out of the sog
To snatch neighbor eekers away.
These eekers did cog
This maraude from fog
And bent o'er in prim fancies to pray.
Yet Clog, Log and Nog
Still came from the sog
And took off those daft eekers as prey.
Three hobs from the bog
Heft meals still agog,
To return on their swamperling way.
Yet back in the bog
Nog turned to hob Clog,
Said, "Already I've eaten today!"
Then frowning to cog
Clog figured for Nog
An answer to his brother's dismay.
Spake he, "Brother Nog,
You'll do like the hog
And sink your food down in the brey."
"Why, my brother Clog,
You're clever to flog
such nouse from a head full of clay!"
So hob Clog and hob Log

Ate quick at the jog,

While Nog and his meal strayed to play.

The eeker of Nog

Sunk squealing in sog

was forgot and remains so this day.

A less commonly known variation also includes these two additional didactic verses:

Avoid hobs from bog

Keep clear of the sog

Daren't follow the eekerly way.

Walk safe with a dog

Take spurns on a slog,

Though behind walls 'tis best you should stay.

threwd watchful memory of the vitality and purity of the first days, dwelling in both untamed lands and—in varying degrees—in monsters themselves. Though it is rarely, if ever, officially acknowledged, land can return to threwd if left alone, this being known to happen even in neglected parkland copses right in the middle of some little-used city green or garden. See Book One and Book Two.

thrisdina also called tree-hair, an edible moss that grows happily from the very bark of trees, preferring threwdish environments. If water is available, thrisdina alone is able to sustain a person for a fair time, though you might get fed up with the dirty taste rather quickly.

thurifers large conical brass censers with a many-holed base and open at the top to allow the flow of air, stoked with coals and various burning repellents, typically hung above gates to add olfactory protection to the more physical barrier of the gates themselves.

ticket-of-leave men vinegaroons granted shore leave with a chit that states precisely the period of freedom granted to them and the vessel from which they come. This chit also gives permission to appropriate authorities to return said bearer to his vessel should he still be at liberty beyond the stipulated time.

tidal millwheels once a major source of *enginry* motivation for the mills using the action of wave and tide, although now their motions are a mere assistance to the labors of the gastrine works. Half obscured in their wooden housings and tall sea-paddle towers and jutting like great pegs from the water, each is connected to the land by an umbilicus of wooden chutes held aloft on trestled beams.

tocsin watchtower hung with warning bell common to many rural townships, the lookouts on watch for enemies both monstrous and human.

tortue among some dandidawdlers is the southern fashion of wearing neckerchiefs of excessive volume and "height," reaching up even under the jaw and ears.

transmogrificate to transmogrify, that is, to make a person into a lahzar.

trefoiled heart heart-shape with a reversed lobed leaf within it and meaning "stoutness" or "courage"; most commonly seen in the sigil of Naimes.

trestle stepladder made of two beams fixed in an A-frame with horizontal rungs set at intervals up it.

troubardiers most heavily proofed of all the pediteers, troubardiers don proof-steel armor and wield heavy, bludgeoning weapons to crack open their foe. In battle they walk at a measured pace, weathering all shots and blows until they close with the enemy ranks and wreak great harm. See Book One and Book Two.

tumblehome billet and infirmary for old, fully retired or infirm vinegaroons; paid for by annual subscription from every sailor's pocket, his pay and prize-money docked automatically. Such a fund is actually rather large, and you can be sure that the more dishonorable bureaucrats frequently siphon sums of the funds for their own ends.

Tüngid viskiekduzär proper *Heilgolundian* name for *fistdukes*.

twenty sous just for the record, 20 sous is worth 320 sequins or 6,400 guise. This is all pure arithmetic, however, for in practice having 320 sequins is not quite the same as having 20 sous—though technically these are an identical amount. Folks consider the higher-denomination currencies as having greater value in themselves, so having sous is better than having sequins and far better than having guise, even by the bagful.

Should you turn up, say, at your favorite wayhouse, perhaps the Frantic Mile on the way to Proud Sulking, where best board for a week is 1, 2, 0 (1 sou, 2 sequins, 0 guise), it might end up costing 400 guise or more if that is all you had, though the arithmetically proper amount is only 360 guise. Such practice is disallowed by law but is not strictly policed and, as it is founded in such old concepts of money in its various parts, some lofty modern edict is unlikely to alter it.

Two Sisters, the ~ • also the Twin Sisters, and among the more learned known as the Beladice; Radica and Dudica, twin girls and ancient citizens of a younger *Brandenbrass*, they are famed for defending a stile of the city's outer defenses from a theroscading horde come to steal and eat the goats and cows and herders in pasture there. The name given to gates reputedly built on the very spot where they conducted their glorious defense, their statues above the gates of *Brandenbrass* are sometimes referred to as the Beladice or the Sorori. This latter name comes from twin girls, Io and Ix, who are reputed to have helped the Attics mightily in an occasion of need, their names now given to the twin planets that circle closest to Eudops, the sun. • the western gate in the Broadwall, Brandenbrass' outer curtain wall, possessing two lancet-arched tunnels each a hundred feet long that burrow right through the foundations of the fortress, with ironbound draws at both ends and a system of four portcullis to block and trap unwanteds within.

U

undercrofts secret cellars and hidden buried places.

unperspicuous not possessing the heightened senses of a leer, or not being able to interpret the sensations that come through a sthenicon or *olfactologue*.

unsweetened refers to the fact that an edible sea-caught creature has not been previously *dulcified*; seafood brought straight from the water.

urchin(s) historied sources cite that urchins are specifically the more benevolent of the monster-lords, seeking to protect and aid everymen, with the *wretchins* being the more malevolent and the *petchinins* seeking to be left in peace to achieve their own ends. See Book One.

urticant(s) technical name for any stinging script such as the vast collection of repellents.

V

vaingloria also called a fanfaronade or boasting-book; a collection of documents stating a teratologist's merit. Much of the most glowing documentation is written by panegyrists, pens skilled at turning, with a few clever twists of phrase, small courage into great feats and a little action into conquest. As an added glory, more successful teratologists will have illustrations of themselves in action, or a study of the beast they slew, or both, drawn either from their own description or by an eager imagineer hired to sketch the drama after the event. Written papers commonly included in a vaingloria are as follows:

• vaunts—private letters of satisfaction made out by pleased individuals seeking, in their enthusiasm, to enhance a teratologist's worthiness. If necessary these can act as proxy for a teratoid's head, when getting such an object back to the knavery is not possible or practicable;

• panegyrics—boasts of feats commissioned by the teratologists themselves upon the slaughter of a particular beast and written by professional panegyrists. These are trained in penning the best-sounding boasts: not too much blustering, yet enough showing away to impress. Panegyrists are often asked to accompany a teratologist to see the victory for themselves so that they might write of it fully. If this is not possible, a panegyrist will want to see the head of the slain beast as proof at least and then pen a description of the chase from the teratologist's own account;

• advocations—official certificates of merit, usually given upon the happy completion of a *writ* or singular.

vauqueline restorative draught for righting an imbalance of sanguine humours, given to those who have suffered the loss of much blood.

vent(s) in its most basic form, a cloth soaked in neutralizing potives typically called *dotes* and fastened about the neck to be pulled over the face as needed as protection against the poisonous gases of a skold, scourge, fume-exhaling monster or even the reek of the sea. Thin-worked leathers and other hides are also used in such a way and are called loup mielles; they make for better protection yet are more restrictive of breathing.

vin cheap, readily available wine.

vinaigrette tin, pewter or silver case often elaborately decorated or inlaid with precious items and used for carrying scented powders or ground perfumes to be sniffed or otherwise inhaled whenever any mephitic odor is encountered. Although in part such a practice is a missish distaste of bad smells, it has a genuine purpose, for ever since the advent of lahzars and the processes of surgery that make them, a common awareness of bad and contagious airs has proliferated. Therefore the sweetening of any foul stink is held to protect you from the contraction of many ailments frequent in squalid places.

vin-compte wine list and bill-of-fare combined, offered only at the best eateries and listing only the most expensive dishes.

vinegar pie pie made from the less useful bits of fish and eels and other edible sea animals, seasoned and spiced and cooked down into a stew and placed in pastry.

vinothe *hard-water*—strong drink—made of raisins fermented in a honey spirit, smooth in the mouth, sweet yet clear, like a breath of raisin-perfumed air. Originally from Turkmantine or some other Foulside region up north, it was brought back to the Soutlands by widefaring vinegaroons and happily accepted into their culture.

Violette Lune scourge teratologist of wide and violent notoriety, coming once from Tunes and given to wearing purple fascins and spectacles of the same hue.

vizer's hoard vizers are semi-independent lords of Turkmantine border provinces. They are famous for possessing great hoards of jewels and wealth by which they fund the armies that help maintain their semi-independence.

W

weed-bunts small flat-bowed, sharp-prowed wooden sailers used by kelpmen to cut through and gather kelp, matted algaes and other sea weeds for either disposal or use, keeping common lanes clear of screwfouling growths. A ubiquitous sight in any harbor, their operators labor in the hope that they might find some chance treasure churned up from the deeps by storms or the titanic struggles between the great beasts that dwell in the crushing dark.

whip-stock long tail of hair completely bound in ribbon but for a small tuft at the end.

Whit, Greenleaf modern composer of *Brandenbrass* continuing in the lively modes of *Stumphelhose* (which is why Rookwood confuses the two) despite a growing taste for more regal and somber music among the gentry.

Widden, the ~ originally one of the minor yet feared tribes of the *Piltmen,* they are now a violent and perpetually disgruntled group impatient for the return of *Pilt* greatness and independence. More a self-justifying rabble of brigands, their ideas far outstrip their actual achievements, and many who call themselves so are scarcely the heirs of Pilt glory at all.

wigbold(s) wit who prefers complete anonymity, refusing to make any signifying spoors or other marks and covering his or her telltale hair loss with all manner of wig—hence the name. Some wear pieces so outlandish they are a signifier in themselves; yet other wigbolds dress as normally as is fashionable, deadly *lahzars* walking about unheeded by the unsuspecting.

Windspect Folia small countenancy (the hereditary holding of a count) northeast of Coddlingtine Dell.

wine euphemistic name for the vinegar seas, from the notion of real vinegar coming from wine.

Wood Hole home to a multitude of out-of-the-way hamlets of hillvale goatherds, beekeepers, reticent *peltrymen,* parts-gatherers and other furtive souls that reputedly populated these ranges.

worm a wooden shaft about seven to nine feet long, ending in an iron "corkscrew" and used every half-a-dozen shots to pull out any debris left in the breech of a cannon that might otherwise foul the vent hole and prevent firing.

wretchin(s) the darkest of the monster-lords, actively seeking the destruction of everymen, often gathering about themselves hordes of lesser üntermen like an army to harass and harry people. At certain times in history a single wretchin or—more often, a congress of wretchins—has managed to coerce enough of their brother monsters to pose a genuine threat to more than the pastoral fringes of man's domains. Often then, it is only the intervention of the *urchins* that has prevented utter ruin to some city or region.

writ public or bureaucratical version of a *Singular Contract,* posted by governmental agencies seeking assistance with a monster.

written pilot "map" made of written descriptions rather than diagrams or chartings and often a part of the paperwork of a *writ* or *Singular Contract*.

X

Nothing for "X" now? Surely this is not possible!

Y

yearnling someone who wants to and is preparing to become a lahzar. In their eagerness they can sometimes dress and mark themselves as if they already were, running the risk consequently of being accused as fakehands, false lahzars—everymen pretending to be ubelmen. Lahzars take very grimly to this, and some even go so far as to rough the offending soul—others even kill them!

Z

zin cool, sharp white wine from the vineyards of the Basket of northeastern Wörms.

(What do you know, finally an entry for "Z"!)

APPENDIX 1(A)

THE 16-MONTH CALENDAR OF THE HALF-CONTINENT

~WITH CHANGES TO MONTHLY ORDERS AS DECREED BY ORDER OF IMPERIAL BULL EW7~1601

THE NEW YEAR ALWAYS STARTS ON NEWWICH

Season	Month	1	2	3	4	5	6	7	8	9	10	11	12	13	14	15	16	17	18	19	20	21	22	23	NUMBER OF DAYS
SUMMER ~A~ (THERISTRUM) (JUVINAL) (SANG – BLOOD)	(S) CALOR (CALORIS)	N	L	M	M	D	C	S	N	L	M	M	D	C	S	N	L	M	M	D	C	(S) S	(S) N		22
	ESTOR (ESTORIS)	L	M	M	D	C	S	N	L	M	M	D	C	S	N	L	M	M	D	C	S	N	L	M	23
	PRIOR (PRIORIS)	M	D	C	S	N	L	M	M	D	C[1]	S	N	L	M	M	D	C	S	N	L	M	M	D	23
	LUX% (LEUC)	C[2]	S	N	L	M	M	D	C	S	N	L	M	M	D	C	S	N	L	M	M	D	C	S[3]	23
AUTUMN ~O~ (PETILIUM) (SENTIMUR) (MELANCHOLE – BLACK BILE)	◐ PILIUM (LIDE)	N	L	M	M	D	C	S	N	L	M	M	D	C	S	N	L	M	M	D	C	S	◐ N	◐ L	23
	CACHRYS+	M	M	D	C	S	N	L	M	M	D	C	S	N	L	M	M	D	C	S	N	L	M	M	23
	LIRIUM‡ (LIRIO)	D[4]	C	S	N	L	M	M	D	C	S	N	L	M	M	D	C	S	N	L	M	M	D	C	23
	PULCHRYS*	S	N	L	M	M	D	C	S	N	L	M	M	D	C	S	N	L	M	M	D[5]	C	S	N[6]	23
WINTER ~W~ (DIVORTIUM) (BLINDUR) (PHLEGMIS – PHLEGM)	(S) BRUMIS* (THE BRUME) (MIDDLEMONTH)	L[7]	M	M	D	C	S	N	L	M	M	D	C	S	N	L	M	M	D	C	S	(S) N	(S) L[8]		22
	PULVIS*	M	M	D	C	S	N	L	M	M	D	C	S	N	L	M	M	D	C	S	N	L	M	M	23
	HEIMIO*	D	C	S	N	L	M	M	D	C	S	N	L	M	M	D	C	S	N	L	M	M	D	C	23
	HERSE	S	N[9]	L	M	M	D	C	S	N	L	M	M	D	C	S	N	L	M	M	D	C	S	N[10]	23
SPRING ~M~ (ARBUSTRUM) (CALIBUR) (CHOLER – YELLOW BILE)	◐ ORIO (ORIS)	L	M	M	D[11]	C	S	N	L[12]	M	M	D	C	S	N	L	M	M	D	C	S	N	L	◐ M	23
	UNXIS (JUDE)	◐ M	D	C	S	N	L	M	M	D	C	S	N	L	M	M	D	C	S	N	L	M	M	D	23
	NARCIS	C	S	N	L	M	M	D	C	S	N	L	M	M	D	C	S	N	L	M	M	D	C	S	23
	JUDE (LESTMONTH)	N	L	M	M	D	C	S	N	L	M	M	D	C	S	N	L	M	M	D	C	S	I		22
		I																							(1)

MIDDLE-MONTH EVE

FOUR-YEAR'S EVE (ONCE EVERY 4 YEARS)

LESTWICH (YEAR'S END)

APPENDIX 1(B)

DAYS OF THE WEEK (7)

N - NEWWICH first day of the week
L - LOONDAY
M - MEERDAY
M - MIDWICH
D - DOMESDAY a day of rest
C - CALUMNDAY
S - SOLEMNDAY

- DAYS OF OBSERVANCE
(THESE NUMBERS CAN BE FOUND IN THE CALENDAR)

1 - MALBELLTIDE
2 - HALFMERRY DAY
3 - MELLOWTIDE
4 - MANNER
5 - VERTUMNUS
6 - EIGHT-MONTH'S EVE
   (CLERK'S VIGIL)

7 - MIDTIDE
8 - NYCHTHOLD
9 - GALLOWS NIGHT
10 - DIRGETIDE
11 - THISGIVINGDAY
12 - PLOUGHMONDAY

(S) = SOLSTICE
(E) = EQUINOX

THE DATE UPON WHICH
THE SOLSTICE & EQUINOX
OCCUR IS VARIABLE, HENCE
THE TWO POSSIBLE TIMES
SHOWN FOR EACH EVENT.

* SAID TO BE THE COLDEST MONTHS,
UNFRIENDLY TO TRAVELERS.

% IN THE OLD CALENDARS THIS WAS
ONCE THE FIRST MONTH OF THE YEAR.

+ THESE TWO MONTHS WERE ONCE IN
THE REVERSE ORDER. THEY CAME TO
BE SWAPPED WHEN THE EXCEEDINGLY
TALL AND EXCESSIVELY SPOILED
DAUGHTER OF MORIBUND SCEPTIC III
COMPLAINED SO BITTERLY THAT SHE
SHOULD HAVE BEEN BORN IN THE
BEAUTIFUL-SOUNDING MONTH OF
LIRIUM RATHER THAN THE UGLY-
SOUNDING (AS SHE THOUGHT IT)
MONTH OF CACHRYS. SHE MADE
COURT LIFE IMPOSSIBLE UNTIL HER
MUCH-HARASSED FATHER DECREED
THE SWAP BY IMPERIAL EDICT. THE
CHANGE HAS REMAINED EVER SINCE,
EVEN AFTER A WAR WAS FOUGHT
OVER IT.

APPENDIX 2

A troubardier in court harness
based on one of the Archduke of
Brandenbrass' own lifeguards—the
Grognards—wearing a combination
of functional protection and high
courtly fashion.

evenly weighted
hammerheads
make for well-
balanced swinging

martel

tourette

collar of white shirt
worn beneath coat
and lorica

hair tied back
with black riband

cuffs of white
shirt hang
over the hand

buff leather
at elbows

heavy boot-
cuffs on sleeves
provide extra
protection for
the forearms

proof-steel lorica
blacked with
chequer-form
in the mottle of
Brandenbrass

roundel

digital holding
potives for use
against everymen as
against nickers; this
fellow possibly even
carries some kind of
smarting-salts to aid
against a wit

The lower lames of
the back plates are
left clear because
the manner in
which the lames
overlap would cause
unsightly scuffing on
the blacking.

bright-black satchel
with full hide facing,
attached to belt worn
under the lorica

pistol holster,
pistola might be
loaded with skold-
shot, depending
upon the fellow's
place of service

tassards
(proof-steel)

long pleated frock of
frock coat, the inner
facings a showy white
to contrast with the
black soe

*All proof-steel armor
is worn over thickly
padded wrappings
known as pulvinards;
if such pliant under-
garments are not worn,
the blow, especially of
a firelock shot, on the
unpadded metal plate
would transmit such
shocks through the
metal as to seriously
bruise or even kill
the wearer.

longshanks

stockings of azure blue,
the color denoting the
service of a duke

soulette

mules

APPENDIX 3

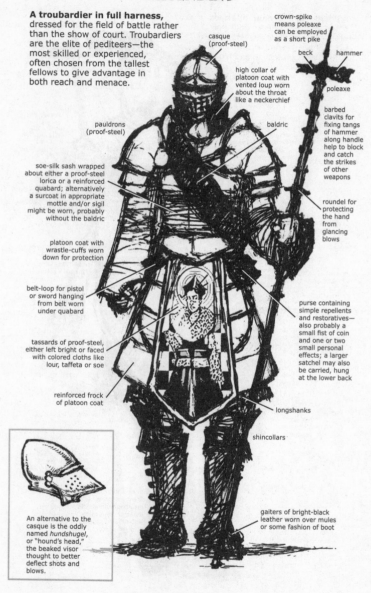

A troubardier in full harness, dressed for the field of battle rather than the show of court. Troubardiers are the elite of pediteers—the most skilled or experienced, often chosen from the tallest fellows to give advantage in both reach and menace.

casque (proof-steel)

crown-spike means poleaxe can be employed as a short pike

beck   hammer

poleaxe

high collar of platoon coat with vented loup worn about the throat like a neckerchief

pauldrons (proof-steel)

baldric

barbed clavits for fixing tangs of hammer along handle help to block and catch the strikes of other weapons

soe-silk sash wrapped about either a proof-steel lorica or a reinforced quabard; alternatively a surcoat in appropriate mottle and/or sigil might be worn, probably without the baldric

roundel for protecting the hand from glancing blows

platoon coat with wrastle-cuffs worn down for protection

belt-loop for pistol or sword hanging from belt worn under quabard

purse containing simple repellents and restoratives— also probably a small fist of coin and one or two small personal effects; a larger satchel may also be carried, hung at the lower back

tassards of proof-steel, either left bright or faced with colored cloths like lour, taffeta or soe

reinforced frock of platoon coat

longshanks

shincollars

An alternative to the casque is the oddly named *hundshugel*, or "hound's head," the beaked visor thought to better deflect shots and blows.

gaiters of bright-black leather worn over mules or some fashion of boot

678

APPENDIX 4

A sabrine adept in complete harness, the style coming from the non-Imperial origins of this rare class of teratologist.

tarbane (folium)

the tarbane has so many folds of cloth in it that it offers excellent protection for the crown

white-bladed laminargis or spathidril, an ancient therimoir forged from a flexible yet hard material called ossa ferra ("bone-steel"— a bizarre alloy of antimony and other traces, its making now lost—the blade imbued—as are all the therimoirs—with monster-slaying toxins; blade may also be bluish, pale or even translucent

choke or haute soaked with venting potives to protect against a skold's trickeries

proofed sash

pleated sleeves of undershirt, puffed and gathered

baute or laminarca (sword-box), usually not worn in a stouche

vambrard; a tighter variation on vambrins

stoup

the unusual grip this adept has of his sword is typical of adepts' fighting forms, more about fluidity of motion and single killing blows than hack, thrust, slash and parry

lap breve or brevis, being a high-waisted frock coat with short sleeves and usually without a high collar

hose are often two different colors and/or patterns, the right leg usually bearing the distinct mark of the adept's troupe

hem of long tunic worn beneath; tunics are regarded as rather odd by most folks of the Haacobin Empire, yet adepts believe them fundamental to their freedom of movement

hose—either having their own soles incorporated into the make or worn with soft-proofed slippers or quiet-shoes

A Soutland variation on the traditional wear of an adept is a flattened wide-brimmed tricorn known as a *cham-de-jeu* (meaning "field of play").

679

APPENDIX 5

A caladine spendonette—that is, a wandering calendar pistoleer—in full mottle-and-harness, geared up with a plethora of pistols and wearing proofed-leather boots and leg attachments known collectively as hauncin-busks or buskins.

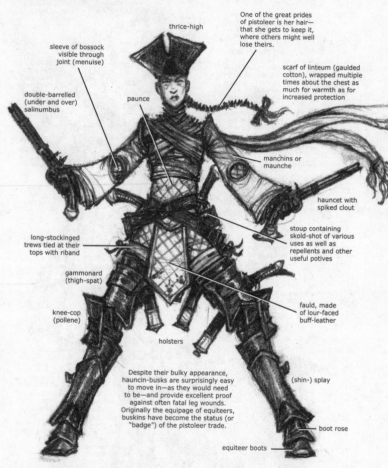

thrice-high

One of the great prides of pistoleer is her hair—that she gets to keep it, where others might well lose theirs.

sleeve of bossock visible through joint (menuise)

scarf of linteum (gaulded cotton), wrapped multiple times about the chest as much for warmth as for increased protection

double-barrelled (under and over) salinumbus

paunce

manchins or maunche

hauncet with spiked clout

long-stockinged trews tied at their tops with riband

stoup containing skold-shot of various uses as well as repellents and other useful potives

gammonard (thigh-spat)

knee-cop (pollene)

fauld, made of lour-faced buff-leather

holsters

Despite their bulky appearance, hauncin-busks are surprisingly easy to move in—as they would need to be—and provide excellent proof against often fatal leg wounds. Originally the equipage of equiteers, buskins have become the status (or "badge") of the pistoleer trade.

(shin-) splay

boot rose

equiteer boots

The handles of her various pistolas are all capped with some manner of spiked or club-like clout, designed to make the firelock double as a melee weapon once shots have been fired. With the rise of the lahzars it is becoming increasingly the mode for pistoleers of any stripe to either train in the use of a sthenicon or soak their eyes in Bile of Vatës to give them greater accuracy, and equalize the disparity of power.

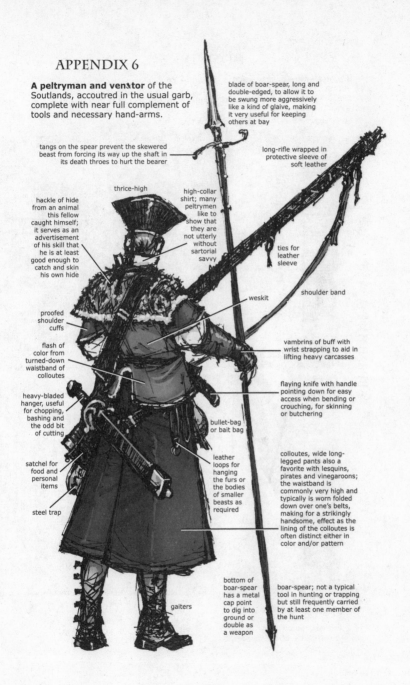

APPENDIX 6

A peltryman and venator of the Soutlands, accoutred in the usual garb, complete with near full complement of tools and necessary hand-arms.

blade of boar-spear, long and double-edged, to allow it to be swung more aggressively like a kind of glaive, making it very useful for keeping others at bay

tangs on the spear prevent the skewered beast from forcing its way up the shaft in its death throes to hurt the bearer

long-rifle wrapped in protective sleeve of soft leather

thrice-high

hackle of hide from an animal this fellow caught himself; it serves as an advertisement of his skill that he is at least good enough to catch and skin his own hide

high-collar shirt; many peltrymen like to show that they are not utterly without sartorial savvy

ties for leather sleeve

weskit

shoulder band

proofed shoulder cuffs

vambrins of buff with wrist strapping to aid in lifting heavy carcasses

flash of color from turned-down waistband of colloutes

flaying knife with handle pointing down for easy access when bending or crouching, for skinning or butchering

heavy-bladed hanger, useful for chopping, bashing and the odd bit of cutting

bullet-bag or bait bag

colloutes, wide long-legged pants also a favorite with lesquins, pirates and vinegaroons; the waistband is commonly very high and typically is worn folded down over one's belts, making for a strikingly handsome, effect as the lining of the colloutes is often distinct either in color and/or pattern

satchel for food and personal items

leather loops for hanging the furs or the bodies of smaller beasts as required

steel trap

bottom of boar-spear has a metal cap point to dig into ground or double as a weapon

boar-spear; not a typical tool in hunting or trapping but still frequently carried by at least one member of the hunt

gaiters

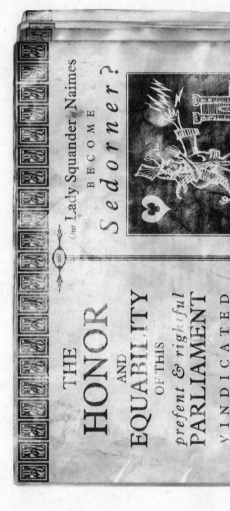

Our Lady Squander *of* Naimes

BECOME

Sedorner?

Winstermill

as related by one Commendatus Sinque —

The "bee's buzz" — as the vulgar cant goes, and come to me this very day from the bumpkin lands of ... *Silk End* — is that the B..dden Rose... ...umored to have wielded OGU in the defence and release ...

THE

HONOR

AND

EQUABILITY

OF THIS

prefent & rightful

PARLIAMENT

VINDICATED

as related by an Estimable Gentleman of Court

Against such calumnous accusations as particular ill-reputed agitators have stirred ag'st our own tireless D..re & Ministers of the Ducal Court ... ...nd by a... ...*dent Inquiry* of th... ...s Secretarial & Other Rightful Notables, ...c that both ins.. gable and tally are most just and rightful taxatio... to be placed upon the Fair Peo... ple of this Fair City.

This statement exists against the Misrepresent- at..ns contained in other Tracts & Writings ...f lesser import and consequence who that have sought by their Hyperbol... Bombast to *Materially Harm* our Great City's prospects and place as the Pre-eminent P..ninotenti-

APPENDIX 8
A CHART OF COMPARATIVE SIZES

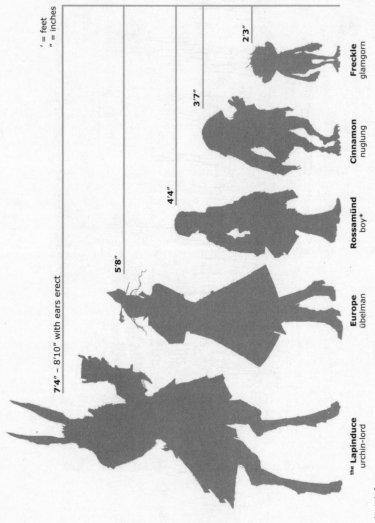

' = feet
" = inches

7'4" – 8'10" with ears erect

5'8"

4'4"

3'7"

2'3"

the Lapinduce urchin-lord

Europe übelman

Rossamünd boy*

Cinnamon nuglung

Freckle glamgorn

*or is he?

ENTER THE WORLD YOU'LL NEVER WANT TO LEAVE....

THE
FOUNDLING'S TALE
by D. M. Cornish